KU-631-448

THE
VAMPIRE
LESTAT

THIS BOOK MAY BE PART EXCHANGED
IF IN GOOD CONDITION, AT

**BOBBIES
BOOKSHOP**
£3-99

75 EASTER ROAD
181, DALRY ROAD
EDINBURGH

Also by Anne Rice

INTERVIEW WITH THE VAMPIRE
THE QUEEN OF THE DAMNED

THE VAMPIRE LESTAT

THE SECOND BOOK
IN THE
CHRONICLES
OF THE VAMPIRES

by

ANNE RICE

Futura

A *Futura* Book

Copyright © 1985 by Anne O'Brien Rice

The moral right of the author has been asserted.

First published in the USA by Alfred A. Knopf, Inc
This edition published in 1986 by Futura books,
a Division of Macdonald & Co (Publishers) Ltd
London & Sydney
Reprinted 1990, 1991, 1992 (twice), 1993 (three times)

*All characters in this publication are fictitious
and any resemblance to real persons, living or dead,
is purely concidental.*

All rights reserved.
No part of this publication may be reproduced,
stored in a retrieval system, or transmitted, in any
form or by any means without the prior
permission in writing of the publisher, nor be
otherwise circulated in any form of binding or
cover other than that in which it is published and
without a similar condition including this
condition being imposed on the subsequent purchaser.

ISBN 0 7088 3153 2

Printed in England by Clays Ltd, St Ives plc

Futura Publications
A Division of
Macdonald & Co (Publishers)
Brettenham House
Lancaster Place
London WC2E 7EN

This book is dedicated
with love
to
Stan Rice, Karen O'Brien,
and Allen Daviau

Downtown
Saturday Night
in the
Twentieth Century

1984

I AM the vampire Lestat. I'm immortal. More or less. The light of the sun, the sustained heat of an intense fire — these things might destroy me. But then again, they might not.

I'm six feet tall, which was fairly impressive in the 1780s when I was a young mortal man. It's not bad now. I have thick blond hair, not quite shoulder length, and rather curly, which appears white under fluorescent light. My eyes are grey, but they absorb the colours blue or violet easily from surfaces around them. And I have a fairly short narrow nose, and a mouth that is well shaped but just a little too big for my face. It can look very mean, or extremely generous, my mouth. It always looks sensual. But emotions and attitudes are always reflected in my entire expression. I have a continuously animated face.

My vampire nature reveals itself in extremely white and highly reflective skin that has to be powdered for cameras of any kind.

And if I'm starved for blood I look like a perfect horror — skin shrunken, veins like ropes over the contours of my bones. But I don't let that happen now. And the only consistent indication that I am not human is my fingernails. It's the same with all vampires. Our fingernails look like glass. And some people notice that when they don't notice anything else.

Right now I am what America calls a Rock Superstar. My first album has sold 4 million copies. I'm going to San Francisco for the first spot on a nationwide concert tour that will take my band from coast to coast. MTV, the rock music cable channel, has been playing my video clips night and day for two weeks. They're also being shown in England on 'Top of the Pops' and on the Continent, probably in some parts of Asia, and in Japan. Video cassettes of the whole series of clips are selling worldwide.

I am also the author of an autobiography which was published last week.

Regarding my English — the language I use in my auto-biography — I first learned it from the flatboatmen who came down the Mississippi to New Orleans about two hundred years ago. I learned more after that from the English language writers — everybody from Shakespeare through Mark Twain to H. Rider Haggard, whom I read as the decades passed. The final infusion I received from the detective stories of the early twentieth century in the *Black Mask* magazine. The adventures of Sam Spade by Dashiell Hammett in *Black Mask* were the last stories I read before I went literally and figuratively under-ground.

That was in New Orleans in 1929.

When I write I drift into a vocabulary that would have been natural to me in the eighteenth century, into phrases shaped by the authors I've read. But in spite of my French accent, I talk like a cross between a flatboatman and detective Sam Spade, actually. So I hope you'll bear with me when my style is inconsistent. When I blow the atmosphere of an eighteenth-century scene to smithereens now and then.

I came out into the twentieth century last year.

What brought me up were two things.

First — the information I was receiving from amplified voices that had begun their cacophony in the air around the time I lay down to sleep.

I'm referring here to the voices of radios, of course, and phonographs and later television machines. I heard the radios in the cars that passed in the streets of the old Garden District near the place where I lay. I heard the phonographs and TVs from the houses that surrounded mine.

Now, when a vampire goes underground as we call it — when he ceases to drink blood and he just lies in the earth —

he soon becomes too weak to resurrect himself, and what follows is a dream state.

In that state, I absorbed the voices sluggishly, surrounding them with my own responsive images as a mortal does in sleep. But at some point during the past fifty-five years I began to 'remember' what I was hearing, to follow the entertainment programmes, to listen to the news broadcasts, the lyrics and rhythms of the popular songs.

And very gradually, I began to understand the calibre of the changes that the world had undergone. I began listening for specific pieces of information about wars or interventions, certain new patterns of speech.

Then a self-consciousness developed in me. I realized I was no longer dreaming. I was thinking about what I heard. I was wide awake. I was lying in the ground and I was starved for living blood. I started to believe that maybe all the old wounds I'd sustained had been healed by now. Maybe my strength had come back. Maybe my strength had actually increased as it would have done with time if I'd never been hurt. I wanted to find out.

I started to think incessantly of drinking human blood.

The second thing that brought me back — the decisive thing really — was the sudden presence near me of a band of young rock singers who called themselves Satan's Night Out.

They moved into a house on Sixth Street — less than a block away from where I slumbered under my own house on Prytania near the Lafáyette Cemetery — and they started to rehearse their rock music in the attic some time in 1984.

I could hear their whining electric guitars, their frantic singing. It was as good as the radio and stereo songs I heard, and it was more melodic than most. There was a romance to it in spite of its pounding drums. The electric piano sounded like a harpsichord.

I caught images from the thoughts of the musicians that told me what they looked like, what they saw when they looked at each other and into mirrors. They were slender, sinewy, and altogether lovely young mortals — beguilingly androgynous and even a little savage in their dress and move-

11

ments — two male and one female.

They drowned out most of the other amplified voices around me when they were playing. But that was perfectly all right.

I wanted to rise and join the rock band called Satan's Night Out. I wanted to sing and to dance.

But I can't say that in the very beginning there was great thought behind my wish. It was rather a ruling impulse, strong enough to bring me up from the earth.

I was enchanted by the world of rock music — the way the singers could scream of good and evil, proclaim themselves angels or devils, and mortals would stand up and cheer. Sometimes they seemed the pure embodiment of madness. And yet it was technologically dazzling, the intricacy of their performance. It was barbaric and cerebral in a way that I don't think the world of ages past had ever seen.

Of course it was metaphor, the raving. None of them believed in angels or devils, no matter how well they assumed their parts. And the players of the old Italian commedia had been as shocking, as inventive, as lewd.

Yet it was entirely new, the extremes to which they took it, the brutality and the defiance — and the way that they were embraced by the world from the very rich to the very poor.

Also there was something vampiric about rock music. It must have sounded supernatural even to those who don't believe in the supernatural. I mean the way the electricity could stretch a single note forever; the way harmony could be layered upon harmony until you felt yourself dissolving in the sound. So eloquent of dread it was, this music. The world just didn't have it in any form before.

Yes, I wanted to get closer to it. I wanted to *do* it. Maybe make the little unknown band of Satan's Night Out famous. I was ready to come up.

It took a week to rise, more or less. I fed on the fresh blood of the little animals who live under the earth when I could catch them. Then I started clawing for the surface, where I could summon the rats. From there it wasn't too difficult to take felines and finally the inevitable human victim, though I

12

had to wait a long time for the particular kind I wanted — a man who had killed other mortals and showed no remorse.

One came along eventually, walking right by the fence, a young male with a grizzled beard who had murdered another in some far-off place on the other side of the world. True killer, this one. And oh, that first taste of human struggle and human blood!

Stealing clothes from nearby houses, getting some of the gold and jewels I'd hidden in the Lafayette Cemetery, that was no problem.

Of course I was scared from time to time. The stench of chemicals and petrol sickened me. The drone of air conditioners and the whine of the jet planes overhead hurt my ears.

But after the third night up, I was roaring around New Orleans on a big black Harley-Davidson motorcycle making plenty of noise myself. I was looking for more killers to feed on. I wore gorgeous black leather clothes that I'd taken from my victims, and I had a little Sony Walkman stereo in my pocket that fed Bach's Art of the Fugue through tiny earphones right into my head as I blazed along.

I was the vampire Lestat again. I was back in action. New Orleans was once again my hunting ground.

As for my strength, well, it was three times what it had once been. I could leap from the street to the top of a four-storey building. I could pull iron gratings off windows. I could bend a copper penny double. I could hear human voices and thoughts, when I wanted to, for blocks around.

By the end of the first week I had a pretty female lawyer in a downtown glass and steel skyscraper who helped me procure a legal birth certificate, Social Security card, and a driver's licence. A good portion of my old wealth was on its way to New Orleans from coded accounts in the immortal Bank of London and the Rothschild Bank.

But more important, I was swimming in realizations. I knew that everything the amplified voices had told me about the twentieth century was true.

As I roamed the streets of New Orleans in 1984 this is what I beheld:

The dark dreary industrial world that I'd gone to sleep in had burnt itself out finally, and the old bourgeois prudery and conformity had lost their hold on the American mind.

People were adventurous and erotic again the way they'd been in the old days, before the great middle-class revolutions of the late 1700s. They even *looked* the way they had in those times.

The men didn't wear the Sam Spade uniform of shirt, tie, grey suit, and grey hat any longer. Once again, they costumed themselves in velvet and silk and brilliant colours if they felt like it. They did not have to clip their hair like Roman soldiers anymore; they wore it any length they desired.

And the women — ah, the women were glorious, naked in the spring warmth as they'd been under the Egyptian pharaohs, in skimpy short skirts and tunic-like dresses, or wearing men's trousers and shirts skintight over their curvaceous bodies if they pleased. They painted, and decked themselves out in gold and silver, even to walk to the grocery store. Or they went fresh scrubbed and without ornament — it didn't matter. They curled their hair like Marie Antoinette or cut it off or let it blow free.

For the first time in history, perhaps, they were as strong and as interesting as men.

And these were the common people of America. Not just the rich who've always achieved a certain androgyny, a certain joie de vivre that the middle-class revolutionaries called decadence in the past.

The old aristocratic sensuality now belonged to everybody. It was wed to the promises of the middle-class revolution, and all people had a right to love and to luxury and to graceful things.

Department stores had become places of near Oriental loveliness — merchandise displayed amid soft tinted carpeting, eerie music, amber light. In the all-night drugstores, bottles of violet and green shampoo gleamed like gems on the sparkling glass shelves. Waitresses drove sleek leather-lined automobiles to work. Dock labourers went home at night to swim in their heated backyard pools. Charwomen and plumbers changed at the end of the day into exquisitely cut manufactured clothes.

In fact the poverty and filth that had been common in the big cities of the earth since time immemorial were almost completely washed away.

You just didn't see immigrants dropping dead of starvation in the alleyways. There weren't slums where people slept eight and ten to a room. Nobody threw the slops in the gutters. The beggars, the cripples, the orphans, the hopelessly diseased were so diminished as to constitute no presence in the immaculate streets at all.

Even the drunkards and lunatics who slept on the park benches and in the bus stations had meat to eat regularly, and even radios to listen to, and clothes that were washed.

But this was just the surface. I found myself astounded by the more profound changes that moved this awesome current along.

For example, something altogether magical had happened to time.

The old was not being routinely replaced by the new anymore. On the contrary, the English spoken around me was the same as it had been in the 1800s. Even the old slang ('the coast is clear' or 'bad luck' or 'that's the thing') was still 'current'. Yet fascinating new phrases like 'they brainwashed you' and 'it's so Freudian' and 'I can't relate to it' were on everyone's lips.

In the art and entertainment worlds all prior centuries were being 'recycled'. Musicians performed Mozart as well as jazz and rock music; people went to see Shakespeare one night and a new French film the next.

In giant fluorescent-lighted emporiums you could buy tapes of medieval madrigals and play them on your car stereo as you drove ninety miles an hour down the freeway. In the bookstores Renaissance poetry sold side by side with the novels of Dickens or Ernest Hemingway. Sex manuals lay on the same tables with the Egyptian *Book of the Dead*.

Sometimes the wealth and the cleanliness everywhere around me became like an hallucination. I thought I was going out of my head.

Through shop windows I gazed stupefied at computers and

telephones as pure in form and colour as nature's most exotic shells. Gargantuan silver limousines navigated the narrow French Quarter streets like indestructible sea beasts. Glittering office towers pierced the night sky like Egyptian obelisks above the sagging brick buildings of old Canal Street. Countless television programmes poured their ceaseless flow of images into every air-cooled hotel room.

But it was no series of hallucinations. This century had inherited the earth in every sense.

And no small part of this unpredicted miracle was *the curious innocence* of these people in the very midst of their freedom and their wealth. The Christian god was as dead as he had been in the 1700s. *And no new mythological religion had arisen to take the place of the old.*

On the contrary, the simplest people of this age were driven by a vigorous secular morality as strong as any religious morality I had ever known. The intellectuals carried the standards. But quite ordinary individuals all over America cared passionately about 'peace' and 'the poor' and 'the planet' as if driven by a mystical zeal.

Famine they intended to wipe out in this century. Disease they would destroy no matter what the cost. They argued ferociously about the execution of condemned criminals, the abortion of unborn babies. And the threats of 'environmental pollution' and 'holocaustal war' they battled as fiercely as men have battled witchcraft and heresy in ages past.

As for sexuality, it was no longer a matter of superstition and fear. The last religious overtones were being stripped from it. That was why the people were around half naked. That was why they kissed and hugged each other in the streets. They talked ethics now and responsibility and the beauty of the body. Procreation and venereal disease they had under control.

AH, THE twentieth century. Ah, the turn of the great wheel. It had outdistanced by wildest dreams of it, this future. It had made fools of grim prophets of ages past.

I did a lot of thinking about the sinless secular morality, this optimism. This brilliantly lighted world where the value of human life was greater than it had ever been before.

IN THE amber electric twilight of a vast hotel room I watched on the screen before me the stunningly crafted film of war called *Apocalypse Now*. Such a symphony of sound and colour it was, and it sang of the age-old battle of the Western world against evil. 'You must make a friend of horror and moral terror,' says the mad commander in the savage garden of Cambodia, to which the Western man answers as he has always answered: No.

No. Horror and moral terror can never be exonerated. They have no real value. Pure evil has no real place.

And that means, doesn't it, that *I* have no place.

Except, perhaps, in the art that repudiates evil — the vampire comics, the horror novels, the old gothic tales — or in the roaring chants of the rock stars who dramatize the battles against evil that each mortal fights within himself.

IT WAS enough to make an Old World monster go back into the earth, this stunning irrelevance to the mighty scheme of things, enough to make him lie down and weep. Or enough to make him become a rock singer, when you think about it. ...

BUT where were the other Old World monsters? I wondered. How did other vampires exist in a world in which each death was recorded in giant electronic computers, and bodies were carried away to refrigerated crypts? Probably concealing themselves like loathsome insects in the shadows, as they have always done, no matter how much philosophy they talked or how many covens they formed.

Well, when I raised my voice with the little band called Satan's Night Out, I would bring them all into the light soon enough.

I CONTINUED my education. I talked to mortals at bus stops and at gas stations and in elegant drinking places. I read books. I decked myself out in the shimmering dream skins of the fashionable shops. I wore white turtleneck shirts and crisp khaki safari jackets, or lush grey velvet blazers with cashmere

17

scarves. I powdered down my face so that I could 'pass' beneath the chemical lights of the all-night supermarkets, the hamburger joints, the carnival thoroughfares called nightclub strips.

I was learning. I was in love.

And the only problem I had was that murderers to feed upon were scarce. In this shiny world of innocence and plenty, of kindness and gaiety and full stomachs, the common cut-throat thieves of the past and their dangerous waterfront hangouts were almost gone.

And so I had to work for a living. But I'd always been a hunter. I liked the dim smoky poolrooms with the single light shining on the green felt as the tattooed ex-convicts gathered around it as much as I liked the shiny satin-lined nightclubs of the big concrete hotels. And I was learning more all the time about my killers — the drug dealers, the pimps, the murderers who fell in with the motorcycle gangs.

And more than ever, I was resolute that I would not drink innocent blood.

FINALLY it was time to call upon my old neighbours, the rock band called Satan's Night Out.

AT SIX thirty on a hot sticky Saturday night I rang the doorbell of the attic music studio. The beautiful young mortals were all lying about in their rainbow-coloured silk shirts and skintight dungarees smoking hashish cigarettes and complaining about their rotten luck getting 'gigs' in the South.

They looked like biblical angels, with their long clean shaggy hair and feline movements; their jewellery was Egyptian. Even to rehearse they painted their faces and their eyes.

I was overcome with excitement and love just looking at them, Alex and Larry and the succulent little Tough Cookie.

And in an eerie moment in which the world seemed to stand still beneath me, I told them what I was. Nothing new to them, the word 'vampire'. In the galaxy in which they shone, a thousand other singers had worn the theatrical fangs and the black cape.

18

And yet it felt so strange to speak it aloud to mortals, the forbidden truth. Never in two hundred years had I spoken it to anyone who had not been marked to become one of us. Not even to my victims did I confide it before their eyes closed.

And now I said it clearly and distinctly to these handsome young creatures. I told them that I wanted to sing with them, that if they were to trust to me, we would all be rich and famous. That on a wave of preternatural and remorseless ambition, I should carry them out of these rooms and into the great world.

Their eyes misted as they looked at me. And the little twentieth-century chamber of stucco and pasteboard rang with their laughter and delight.

I was patient. Why shouldn't I be? I knew I was a demon who could mimic almost any human sound or movement. But how could they be expected to understand? I went to the electric piano and began to play and to sing.

I imitated the rock songs as I started, and then old melodies and lyrics came back to me — French songs buried deep in my soul yet never abandoned — and I wound these into brutal rhythms, seeing before me a tiny crowded little Paris theatre of centuries ago. A dangerous passion welled in me. It threatened my equilibrium. Dangerous that this should come so soon. Yet I sang on, pounding the slick white keys of the electric piano, and something in my soul was broken open. Never mind that these tender mortal creatures gathered around me should never know.

It was sufficient that they were jubilant, that they loved the eerie and disjointed music, that they were screaming, that they saw prosperity in the future, the impetus that they had lacked before. They turned on the tape machines and we began singing and playing together, jamming as they called it. The studio swam with the scent of their blood and our thunderous songs.

But then came a shock I had never in my strangest dreams anticipated — something that was as extraordinary as my little revelation to these creatures had been. In fact, it was so overwhelming that it might have driven me out of their world and back underground.

I don't mean I would have gone into the deep slumber again. But I might have backed off from Satan's Night Out and roamed around for a few years, stunned and trying to gather my wits.

The men — Alex, the sleek delicate young drummer, and his taller blond-haired brother, Larry — recognized my name when I told them it was Lestat.

Not only did they recognize it, but they connected it with a body of information about me that they had read in a book.

In fact, they thought it was delightful that I wasn't just pretending to be any vampire. Or Count Dracula. Everybody was sick of Count Dracula. They thought it was marvellous that I was pretending to be the vampire Lestat.

'*Pretending* to be the vampire Lestat?' I asked.

I looked at all of them for a long moment, trying to scan their thoughts. Of course I hadn't expected them to believe I was a real vampire. But to have read of a fictional vampire with a name as unusual as mine? How could this be explained?

But I was losing my confidence. And when I lose my confidence, my powers drain. The little room seemed to be getting smaller. And there was something insectile and menacing about the instruments, the antennae, the wires.

'Show me the book,' I said.

From the other room they brought it, a small pulp paper 'novel' that was falling to pieces. The binding was gone, the cover ripped, the whole held together by a rubber band.

I got a preternatural chill of sorts at the sight of the cover. *Interview with the Vampire.* Something to do with a mortal boy getting one of the undead to tell the tale.

With their permission, I went into the other room, stretched out on their bed, and began to read. When I was half finished, I took the book with me and left the house. I stood stock-still beneath a street lamp with the book until I finished it. Then I placed it carefully in my breast pocket.

I didn't return to the band for several nights.

DURING much of that time, I was roaming again, crashing through the night on my Harley-Davidson motorcycle with the Bach Goldberg Variations turned up to full volume. And I was asking myself, Lestat, what do you want to do now?

And the rest of the time I studied with a renewed purpose. I read the fat paperback histories and lexicons of rock music, the chronicles of its stars. I listened to the albums and pondered in silence the concert video tapes.

And when the night was empty and still, I heard the voices of *Interview with the Vampire* singing to me, as if they sang from the grave. I read the book over and over. And then in a moment of contemptible anger, I shredded it to bits.

FINALLY, I came to my decision.

I met my young lawyer, Christine, in her darkened sky-scraper office with only the downtown city to give us light. Lovely she looked against the glass walls behind her, the dim buildings beyond forming a harsh and primitive terrain in which a thousand torches burned.

'It is not enough any longer that my little rock band be successful,' I told her. 'We must create a fame that will carry my name and my voice to the remotest part of the world.'

Quietly, intelligently, as lawyers are wont to do, she advised me against risking my fortune. Yet as I continued with mania-cal confidence, I could feel her seduction, the slow dissolution of her common sense.

'The best French directors for the rock video films,' I said. 'You must lure them from New York and Los Angeles. There is ample money for that. And here you can find the studios, surely, in which we will do our work. The young record producers who mix the sound after — again, you must hire the best. It does not matter what we spend on this venture. What is important is that it be orchestrated, that we do our work in secret until the moment of revelation when our albums and our films are released with the book that I propose to write.'

Finally her head was swimming with dreams of wealth and power. Her pen raced as she made her notes.

And what did I dream of as I spoke to her? Of an unprece-dented rebellion, a great and horrific challenge to my kind all over the world.

'These rock videos,' I said. 'You must find directors who'll realize my visions. The films are to be sequential. They must tell the story that is in the book I want to create. And the songs, many of them I've already written. You must obtain superior instruments — synthesizers, the finest sound systems, electric guitars, violins. Other details we can attend to later. The designing of vampire costumes, the method of presentation to the rock television stations, the management of our first public appearance in San Francisco — all that in good time. What is important now is that you make the phone calls, get the information you need to begin.'

I DIDN'T go back to Satan's Night Out until the first agreements were struck and signatures had been obtained. Dates were fixed, studios rented, letters of agreement exchanged.

Then Christine came with me, and we had a great leviathan of a limousine for my darling young rock players, Larry and Alex and Tough Cookie. We had breathtaking sums of money, we had papers to be signed.

Under the drowsy oaks of the quiet Garden District street, I poured the champagne into the glistening crystal glasses for them:

'To The Vampire Lestat,' we all sang in the moonlight. It was to be the new name of the band, of the book I'd write. Tough Cookie threw her succulent little arms around me. We kissed tenderly amid the laughter and the reek of wine. Ah, the smell of innocent blood!

AND when they had gone off in the velvet-lined motor coach, I moved alone through the balmy night towards St. Charles Avenue, and thought about the danger facing them, my little mortal friends.

It didn't come from me, of course. But when the long period of secrecy was ended, they would stand innocently and ignorantly in the international limelight with their sinister and reckless star. Well, I would surround them with bodyguards and hangers-on for every conceivable purpose. I would protect them from other immortals as best I could. And if the immor-

22

tals were anything like they used to be in the old days, they'd never risk a vulgar struggle with a human force like that.

AS I walked up to the busy avenue, I covered my eyes with mirrored sunglasses. I rode the rickety old St. Charles street car downtown.

And through the early evening crowd I wandered into the elegant double-decker bookstore called de Ville Books, and there stared at the small paperbook of *Interview with the Vampire* on the shelf.

I wondered how many of our kind had 'noticed' the book. Never mind for the moment the mortals who thought it was fiction. What about other vampires? Because if there is one law that all vampires hold sacred it is that *you do not tell mortals about us.*

You never pass on our 'secrets' to humans unless you mean to bequeath the Dark Gift of our powers to them. You never name other immortals. You never tell where their lairs might be.

My beloved Louis, the narrator of *Interview with the Vampire,* had done all this. He had gone far beyond my secret little disclosure to my rock singers. He had told hundreds of thousands of readers. He had all but drawn them a map and placed an **X** on the very spot in New Orleans where I slumbered, though what he really knew about that, and what his intentions were, was not clear.

Regardless, for what he'd done, others would surely hunt him down. And there are very simple ways to destroy vampires, especially now. If he was still in existence, he was an outcast and lived in a danger from our kind that no mortal could ever pose.

All the more reason for me to bring the book and the band called The Vampire Lestat to fame as quickly as possible. I had to find Louis. I had to talk to him. In fact, after reading his account of things, I ached for him, ached for his romantic illusions, and even his dishonesty. I ached even for his gentlemanly malice and his physical presence, the deceptively soft sound of his voice.

Of course I hated him for the lies he told about me. But the love was far greater than the hate. He had shared the dark and romantic years of the nineteenth century with me, he was my companion as no other immortal had ever been.

And I ached to write my story for him, not an answer to his malice in *Interview with the Vampire*, but the tale of all the things I'd seen and learned before I came to him, the story I could not tell him before.

Old rules didn't matter to me now, either.

I wanted to break every one of them. And I wanted my band and my book to draw out not only Louis but all the other demons that I had ever known and loved. I wanted to find my lost ones, awaken those who slept as I had slept.

Fledglings and ancient ones, beautiful and evil and mad and heartless — they'd all come after me when they saw those video clips and heard those records, when they saw the book in the windows of the bookstores, and they'd know exactly where to find me. I'd be Lestat, the rock superstar. Just come to San Francisco for my first live performance. I'll be there.

But there was another reason for the whole adventure — a reason even more dangerous and delicious and mad.

And I knew Louis would understand. It must have been behind his interview, his confessions. I wanted mortals *to know* about us. I wanted to proclaim it to the world the way I'd told it to Alex and Larry and Tough Cookie, and my sweet lawyer, Christine.

And it didn't matter that they didn't believe it. It didn't matter that they thought it was art. The fact was that, after two centuries of concealment, I was visible to mortals! I spoke my name aloud. I told my nature. I was there!

But again, I was going farther than Louis. His story, for all its peculiarities, had passed for fiction. In the mortal world, it was as safe as the tableaux of the old Theatre of the Vampires in the Paris where the fiends had pretended to be actors pretending to be fiends on a remote and gaslighted stage.

I'd step into the solar lights before the cameras, I'd reach out and touch with my icy fingers a thousand warm and grasping hands. I'd scare the hell out of them if it was possible, and charm them and lead them into the truth of it if I could.

24

And suppose — just suppose — that when the corpses began to turn up in ever greater numbers, that when those closest to me began to hearken to their inevitable suspicions — just suppose that the art ceased to be art and became real!

I mean what if they really believed it, really understood that this world still harboured the Old World demon thing, the vampire — oh, what a great and glorious war we might have then!

We would be known, and we would be hunted, and we would be fought in this glittering urban wilderness as no mythic monster has ever been fought by man before.

How could I not love it, the mere idea of it? How could it not be worth the greatest danger, the greatest and most ghastly defeat? Even at the moment of destruction, I would be alive as I have never been.

But to tell the truth, I didn't think it would ever come to that — I mean, mortals believing in us. Mortals have never made me afraid.

It was the other war that was going to happen, the one in which we'd all come together, or they would all come to fight me.

That was the real reason for The Vampire Lestat. That was the kind of game I was playing.

But that other lovely possibility of real revelation and disaster ... Well, that added a hell of a lot of spice!

OUT of the gloomy waste of Canal Street, I went back up the stairs to my rooms in the old-fashioned French Quarter hotel. Quiet it was, and suited to me, with the Vieux Carré spread out beneath its windows, the narrow little streets of Spanish town houses I'd known for so long.

On the giant television set I played the cassette of the beautiful Visconti film *Death in Venice*. An actor said at one point that evil was a necessity. It was food for genius.

I didn't believe that. But I wish it were true. Then I could just be Lestat, the monster, couldn't I? And I was always so good at being a monster! Ah, well ...

I put a fresh disk into the portable computer word processor and I started to write the story of my life.

25

THE EARLY EDUCATION
AND
ADVENTURES
OF
THE VAMPIRE LESTAT

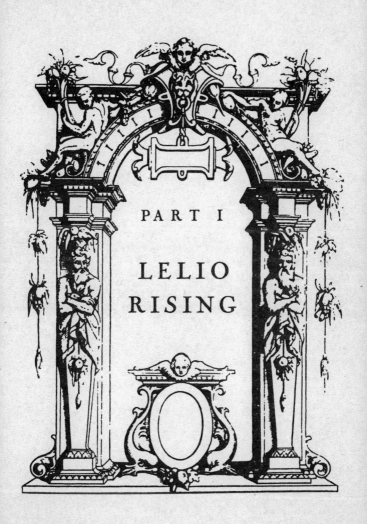

PART I

LELIO
RISING

1

N THE winter of my twenty-first year, I went out alone on horseback to kill a pack of wolves.

This was on my father's land in the Auvergne in France, and these were the last decades before the French Revolution.

It was the worst winter that I could remember, and the wolves were stealing the sheep from our peasants and even running at night through the streets of the village.

These were bitter years for me. My father was the Marquis, and I was the seventh son and the youngest of three who had lived to manhood. I had no claim to the title or the land, and no prospects. Even in a rich family, it might have been that way for a younger boy, but our wealth had been used up long ago. My eldest brother, Augustin, who was the rightful heir to all we possessed, had spent his wife's small dowry as soon as he married her.

My father's castle, his estate, and the village nearby were my entire universe. And I'd been born restless — the dreamer, the angry one, the complainer. I wouldn't sit by the fire and talk of old wars and the days of the Sun King. History had no meaning for me.

But in this dim and old-fashioned world, I had become the hunter. I brought in the pheasant, the venison and the trout from the mountain streams — whatever was needed and could be got — to feed the family. It had become my life by this time — and one I shared with no one else — and it was a very good thing that I'd taken it up, because there were years when we might have actually starved to death.

Of course this was a noble occupation, hunting one's ancestral lands, and we alone had the right to do it. The richest of the bourgeois couldn't lift his gun in my forests. But then again he didn't have to lift his gun. He had money.

Two times in my life I'd tried to escape this life, only to be brought back with my wings broken. But I'll tell more on that later.

Right now I'm thinking about the snow all over those mountains and the wolves that were frightening the villagers and stealing my sheep. And I'm thinking of the old saying in France in those days, that if you lived in the province of Auvergne you could get no farther from Paris.

Understand that since I was the lord and the only lord anymore who could sit on a horse and fire a gun, it was natural that the villagers should come to me, complaining about the wolves and expecting me to hunt them. It was my duty.

I wasn't the least afraid of the wolves either. Never in my life had I seen or heard of a wolf attacking a man. And I would have poisoned them if I could, but meat was simply too scarce to lace with poison.

So early on a very cold morning in January, I armed myself to kill the wolves one by one. I had three flintlock guns and an excellent flintlock rifle, and these I took with me as well as my muskets and my father's sword. But just before leaving the castle, I added to this little arsenal one or two ancient weapons that I'd never bothered with before.

Our castle was full of old armour. My ancestors had fought in countless noble wars since the times of the Crusades with St. Louis. And hung on the walls above all this clattering junk were a good many lances, battleaxes, flails, and maces.

It was a very large mace — that is, a spiked club — that I took with me that morning, and also a good-sized flail: an iron ball attached to a chain that could be swung with immense force at an attacker.

Now remember this was the eighteenth-century, the time when white-wigged Parisians tiptoed around in high-heeled satin slippers, pinched snuff, and dabbed at their noses with embroidered handkerchiefs.

And here I was going out to hunt in rawhide boots and buckskin coat, with these ancient weapons tied to the saddle, and my two biggest mastiffs beside me in their spiked collars.

That was my life. And it might as well have been lived in the Middle Ages. And I knew enough of the fancy-dressed travellers on the post road to feel it rather keenly. The nobles in the capital called us country lords 'harecatchers'. Of course we could sneer at them and call them lackeys to the king and queen. Our castle had stood for a thousand years, and not even the great Cardinal Richelieu in his war on our kind had managed to pull down our ancient towers. But as I said before, I didn't pay much attention to history.

I was unhappy and ferocious as I rode up the mountain.

I wanted a good battle with the wolves. There were five in the pack according to the villagers, and I had my guns and two dogs with jaws so strong they could snap a wolf's spine in an instant.

Well, I rode for an hour up the slopes. Then I came into a small valley I knew well enough that no snowfall could disguise it. And as I started across the broad empty field towards the barren wood, I heard the first howling.

Within seconds there had come another howling and then another, and now the chorus was in such harmony that I couldn't tell the number of the pack, only that they had seen me and were signalling to each other to come together, which was just what I had hoped they would do.

I don't think I felt the slightest fear then. But I felt something, and it caused the hair to rise on the backs of my arms. The countryside for all its vastness seemed empty. I readied my guns. I ordered my dogs to stop their growling and follow me, and some vague thought came to me that I had better get out of the open field and into the woods and hurry.

My dogs gave their deep baying alarm. I glanced over my shoulder and saw the wolves hundreds of yards behind me and streaking straight towards me over the snow. Three giant grey wolves they were, coming on in a line.

I broke into a run for the forest.

It seemed I would make it easily before the three reached me, but wolves are extremely clever animals, and as I rode hard for the trees I saw the rest of the pack, some five full-grown animals, coming out ahead of me to my left. It was an ambush, and I could never make the forest in time. And the pack was eight wolves, not five as the villagers had told me.

Even then I didn't have sense enough to be afraid. I didn't ponder the obvious fact that these animals were starving or they'd never come near the village. Their natural reticence with men was completely gone.

I got ready for battle. I stuck the flail in my belt, and with the rifle I took aim. I brought down a big male yards away from me and had time to reload as my dogs and the pack attacked each other.

They couldn't get my dogs by the neck on account of the spiked collars. And in this first skirmish my dogs brought down one of the wolves in their powerful jaws immediately. I fired and brought down a second.

But the pack had surrounded the dogs. As I fired again and again, reloading as quickly as I could and trying to aim clear of the dogs, I saw the smaller dog go down with its hind legs broken. Blood streamed over the snow; the second dog stood off the pack as it tried to devour the dying animal, but within two minutes, the pack had torn open the second dog's belly and killed it.

Now these were powerful beasts, as I said, these mastiffs. I'd bred them and trained them myself. And each weighed upwards of two hundred pounds. I always hunted with them, and though I speak of them as dogs now, they were known only by their names to me then, and when I saw them die, I knew for the first time what I had taken on and what might happen.

But all this had occurred in minutes.

Four wolves lay dead. Another was crippled fatally. But that left three, one of whom had stopped in the savage feasting upon the dogs to fix its slanted eyes on me.

I fired the rifle, missed, fired the musket, and my horse reared as the wolf shot towards me.

As if pulled on strings, the other wolves turned, leaving the fresh kill. And jerking the reins hard, I let my horse run as she wanted, straight for the cover of the forest.

I didn't look back even when I heard the growling and

snapping. But then I felt the teeth graze my ankle. I drew the other musket, turned to the left, and fired. It seemed the wolf went up on his hind legs, but it was too quickly out of sight and my mare reared again. I almost fell. I felt her back legs give out under me.

We were almost to the forest and I was off her before she went down. I had one more loaded gun. Turning and steadying it with both hands, I took dead aim at the wolf who bore down on me and blasted away the top of his skull.

It was now two animals. The horse was giving off a deep rattling whinny that rose to a trumpeting shriek, the worst sound I have ever heard from any living thing. The two wolves had her.

I bolted over the snow, feeling the hardness of the rocky land under me, and made it to the trees. If I could reload I could shoot them down from there. But there was not a single tree with limbs low enough for me to catch hold of.

I leapt up trying to catch hold, my feet slipping on the icy bark, and fell back down as the wolves closed in. There was no time to load the one gun I had left to me. It was the flail and the sword because the mace I had lost a long way back.

I think as I scrambled to my feet, I knew I was probably going to die. But it never even occurred to me to give up. I was maddened, wild. Almost snarling, I faced the animals and looked the closest of the two wolves straight in the eye.

I spread my legs to anchor myself. With the flail in my left hand, I drew the sword. The wolves stopped. The first, after staring back, bowed its head and trotted several paces to the side. The other waited as if for some invisible signal. The first looked at me again in that uncannily calm fashion and then plunged forward.

I started swinging the flail so that the spiked ball went round in a circle. I could hear my own growling breaths, and I know I was bending my knees as if I would spring forward, and I aimed the flail for the side of the animal's jaw, bashing it with all my strength and only grazing it.

The wolf darted off and the second ran round me in a circle, dancing towards me and then back again. They both lunged in close enough to make me swing the flail and slash with the sword, then they ran off again.

I don't know how long this went on, but I understood the strategy. They meant to wear me down and they had the strength to do it. It had become a game to them.

I was pivoting, thrusting, struggling back, and almost falling to my knees. Probably it was no more than half an hour that this went on. But there is no measuring time like that.

And with my legs giving out, I made one last desperate gamble. I stood stock-still, weapons at my sides. And they came in for the kill this time just as I hoped they would.

At the last second I swung the flail, felt the ball crack the bone, saw the head jerked upwards to the right, and with the broadsword I slashed the wolf's neck open.

The other wolf was at my side. I felt its teeth rip into my breeches. In one second it would have torn my leg out of the socket. But I slashed at the side of its face, gashing open its eye. The ball of the flail crashed down on it. The wolf let go. And springing back, I had enough room for the sword again and thrust it straight into the animal's chest to the hilt before I drew it out again.

That was the end of it.

The pack was dead. I was alive.

And the only sound in the empty snow-covered valley was my own breathing and the rattling shriek of my dying mare who lay yards away from me.

I'm not sure I had my reason. I'm not sure the things that went through my mind were thoughts. I wanted to drop down in the snow, and yet I was walking away from the dead wolves towards the dying horse.

As I came close to her, she lifted her neck, straining to rise up on her front legs, and gave one of those shrill trumpeting pleas again. The sound bounced off the mountains. It seemed to reach heaven. And I stood staring at her, staring at her dark broken body against the whiteness of the snow, the dead hindquarters and the struggling forelegs, the nose lifted skyward, ears pressed back, and the huge innocent eyes rolling up into her head as the rattling cry came out of her. She was like an insect half mashed into a floor, but she was no insect. She was my struggling, suffering mare. She tried to lift herself again.

I took my rifle from the saddle. I loaded it. And as she lay tossing her head, trying vainly to lift herself once more with that shrill trumpeting, I shot her through the heart.

Now she looked all right. She lay still and dead and the blood ran out of her and the valley was quiet. I was shuddering. I heard an ugly choking noise come from myself, and I saw the vomit spewing out onto the snow before I realized it was mine. The smell of wolf was all over me, and the smell of blood. And I almost fell over when I tried to walk.

But not even stopping for a moment, I went among the dead wolves, and back to the one who had almost killed me, the last one, and slung him up to carry over my shoulders, and started the trek homeward.

It took me probably two hours.

Again, I don't know. But whatever I had learned or felt when I was fighting those wolves went on in my mind even as I walked. Every time I stumbled and fell, something in me hardened, became worse.

By the time I reached the castle gates, I think I was not Lestat. I was someone else altogether, staggering into the great hall, with that wolf over my shoulders, the heat of the carcass very much diminished now and the sudden blaze of the fire an irritant in my eyes. I was beyond exhaustion.

And though I began to speak as I saw my brothers rising from the table and my mother patting my father, who was blind already then and wanted to know what was happening, I don't know what I said. I know my voice was very flat, and there was some sense in me of the simplicity of describing what had happened.

'And then ... and then ...' Sort of like that.

But my brother Augustin suddenly brought me to myself. He came towards me, with the light of the fire behind him, and quite distinctly broke the low monotone of my words with his own:

'You little bastard,' he said coldly. 'You didn't kill eight wolves!' His face had an ugly disgusted look to it.

But the remarkable thing was this: Almost as soon as he spoke these words, he realized for some reason that he had made a mistake.

Maybe it was the look on my face. Maybe it was my mother's murmured outrage or my other brother not speaking at all. It was probably my face. Whatever it was, it was almost instantaneous, and the most curious look of embarrassment came over him.

He started to babble something about how incredible, and I must have been almost killed, and would the servants heat some broth for me immediately, and all of that sort of thing, but it was no good. What had happened in that one single moment was irreparable, and the next thing I knew I was lying alone in my room. I didn't have the dogs in bed with me as always in winter because the dogs were dead, and though there was no fire lighted, I climbed, filthy and bloody, under the bed covers and went into deep sleep.

For days I stayed in my room.

I knew the villagers had gone up the mountain, found the wolves, and brought them back down to the castle, because Augustin came and told me these things, but I didn't answer.

Maybe a week passed. When I could stand having other dogs near me, I went down to my kennel and brought up two pups, already big animals, and they kept me company. At night I slept between them.

The servants came and went. But no one bothered me.

And then my mother came quietly and almost stealthily into the room.

2

T WAS evening. I was sitting on the bed, with one of the dogs stretched out beside me and the other stretched out under my knees. The fire was roaring.

And there was my mother coming at last, as I supposed I should have expected.

I knew her by her particular movement in the shadows, and whereas if anyone else had come near me I would have shouted 'Go away,' I said nothing at all to her.

I had a great and unshakeable love of her. I don't think anyone else did. And one thing that endeared her to me always was that she never said anything ordinary.

'Shut the door,' 'Eat your soup,' 'Sit still,' things like that never passed her lips. She read all the time; in fact, she was the only one in our family who had any education, and when she did speak it was really to speak. So I wasn't resentful of her now.

On the contrary she aroused my curiosity. What would she say, and would it conceivably make a difference to me? I had not wanted her to come, nor even thought of her, and I didn't turn away from the fire to look at her.

But there was a powerful understanding between us. When I had tried to escape this house and been brought back, it was she who had shown me the way out of the pain that followed. Miracles she'd worked for me, though no one around us had ever noticed.

Her first intervention had come when I was twelve, and the old parish priest, who had taught me some poetry by rote and to read an anthem or two in Latin, wanted to send me to school at the nearby monastery.

My father said no, that I could learn all I needed in my own house. But it was my mother who roused herself from her books to do loud and vociferous battle with him. I would go, she said, if I wanted to. And she sold one of her jewels to pay for my books and clothing. Her jewels had all come down to her from an Italian grandmother and each had its story, and this was a hard thing for her to do. But she did it immediately.

My father was angry and reminded her that if this had happened before he went blind, his will would have prevailed surely. My brothers assured him that his youngest son wouldn't be gone long. I'd come running home as soon as I was made to do something I didn't want to do.

Well, I didn't come running home. I loved the monastery school.

I loved the chapel and the hymns, the library with its

thousands of old books, the bells that divided the day, the ever repeated rituals. I loved the cleanliness of the place, the overwhelming fact that all things here were well kept and in good repair, that work never ceased throughout the great house and the gardens.

When I was corrected, which wasn't often, I knew an intense happiness because someone for the first time in my life was trying to make me into a good person, one who could learn things.

Within a month I declared my vocation. I wanted to enter the order. I wanted to spend my life in those immaculate cloisters, in the library writing on parchment and learning to read the ancient books. I wanted to be enclosed forever with people who believed I could be good if I wanted to be.

I was liked there. And that was a most unusual thing. I didn't make other people there unhappy or angry.

The Father Superior wrote immediately to ask my father's permission. And frankly I thought my father would be glad to be rid of me.

But three days later my brothers arrived to take me home with them. I cried and begged to stay, but there was nothing the Father Superior could do.

And as soon as we reached the castle, my brothers took away my books and locked me up. I didn't understand why they were so angry. There was the hint that I had behaved like a fool for some reason. I couldn't stop crying. I was walking round and round and smashing my fist into things and kicking the door.

Then my brother Augustin started coming in and talking to me. He'd circle the point at first, but what came clear finally was that no member of a great French family was going to be a poor teaching brother. How could I have misunderstood everything so completely? I was sent there to learn to read and write. Why did I always have to go to extremes? Why did I behave habitually like a wild creature?

As for becoming a priest with real prospects within the Church, well, I was the youngest son of this family, now, wasn't I? I ought to think of my duties to my nieces and nephews.

Translate all that to mean this: We have no money to launch a real ecclesiastical career for you, to make you a bishop or cardinal as befits our rank, so you have to live out your life here as an illiterate and a beggar. Come in the great hall and play chess with your father.

AFTER I got to understand it, I wept right at the supper table, and mumbled words no one understood about this house of ours being 'chaos', and was sent back to my room for it.

Then my mother came to me.

She said: 'You don't know what chaos is. Why do you use words like that?'

'I know,' I said. I started to describe to her the dirt and the decay that was everywhere here and to tell how the monastery had been, clean and orderly, a place where if you set your mind to it, you could accomplish something.

She didn't argue. And young as I was, I knew that she was warming to the unusual quality of what I was saying to her.

The next morning, she took me on a journey.

We rode for half a day before we reached the impressive château of a neighbouring lord, and there she and the gentleman took me out to the kennel, where she told me to choose my favourites from a new litter of mastiff puppies.

I had never seen anything as tender and endearing as these little mastiff pups. And the big dogs were like drowsy lions as they watched us. Simply magnificent.

I was too excited almost to make the choice. I brought back the male and female that the lord advised me to pick, carrying them all the way home on my lap in a basket.

And within a month, my mother also bought for me my first flintlock musket and my first good horse for riding.

She never did say why she'd done all this. But I understood in my own way what she had given me. I raised those dogs, trained them, and founded a great kennel upon them.

I became a true hunter with those dogs, and by the age of sixteen I lived in the field.

But at home, I was more than ever a nuisance. Nobody

really wanted to hear me talk of restoring the vineyards or replanting the neglected fields, or of making the tenants stop stealing from us.

I could affect nothing. The silent ebb and flow of life without change seemed deadly to me.

I went to church on all the feast days just to break the monotony of life. And when the village fairs came round, I was always there, greedy for the little spectacles I saw at no other time, anything really to break the routine.

It might be the same old jugglers, mimes, and acrobats of years past, but it didn't matter. It was something more than the change of the seasons and the idle talk of past glories.

But that year, the year I was sixteen, a troupe of Italian players came through, with a painted wagon in the back of which they set up the most elaborate stage I'd ever seen. They put on the old Italian comedy with Pantaloon and Pulcinella and the young lovers, Lelio and Isabella, and the old doctor and all the old tricks.

I was in raptures watching it. I'd never seen anything like it, the cleverness of it, the quickness, the vitality. I loved it even when the words went so fast I couldn't follow them.

When the troupe had finished and collected what they could from the crowd, I hung about with them at the inn and stood them all to wine I couldn't really afford, just so that I could talk to them.

I felt inexpressible love for these men and women. They explained to me how each actor had his role for life, and how they did not use memorized words, but improvised everything on the stage. You knew your name, your character, and you understood him and made him speak and act as you thought he should. That was the genius of it.

It was called the *commedia dell'arte*.

I was enchanted. I fell in love with the young girl who played Isabella. I went into the wagon with the players and examined all the costumes and the painted scenery, and when we were drinking again at the tavern, they let me act out Lelio, the young love to Isabella, and they clapped their hands and said I had the gift. I could make it up the way they did.

I thought this was all flattery at first, but in some very real way, it didn't matter whether or not it was flattery.

The next morning when their wagon pulled out of the village, I was in it. I was hidden in the back with a few coins I'd managed to save and all my clothes tied in a blanket. I was going to be an actor.

Now, Lelio in the old Italian comedy is supposed to be quite handsome; he's the lover, as I have explained, and he doesn't wear a mask. If he has manners, dignity, aristocratic bearing, so much the better because that's part of the role.

Well, the troupe thought that in all these things I was blessed. They trained me immediately for the next performance they would give. And the day before we put on the show, I went about the town — a much larger and more interesting place than our village, to be certain — advertising the play with the others.

I was in heaven. But neither the journey nor the preparations nor the camaraderie with my fellow players came near to the ecstasy I knew when I finally stood on that little wooden stage.

I went wildly into the pursuit of Isabella. I found a tongue for verses and wit I'd never had in life. I could hear my voice bouncing off the stone walls around me. I could hear the laughter rolling back at me from the crowd. They almost had to drag me off the stage to stop me, but everyone knew it had been a great success.

That night, the actress who played my inamorata gave me her own very special and intimate accolades. I went to sleep in her arms, and the last thing I remember her saying was that when we got to Paris we'd play the St.-Germain Fair, and then we'd leave the troupe and we'd stay in Paris working on the boulevard du Temple until we got into the Comédie-Française itself and performed for Marie Antoinette and King Louis.

When I woke up the next morning, she was gone and so were all the players, and my brothers were there.

I never knew if my friends had been bribed to give me over, or just frightened off. More likely the latter. Whatever the case, I was taken back home again.

Of course my family was perfectly horrified at what I'd done. Wanting to be a monk when you are twelve is excusable. But the theatre had the taint of the devil. Even the great Molière had not been given a Christian burial. And I'd run off with a troupe of ragged vagabond Italians, painted my face white, and acted with them in a town square for money.

I was beaten severely, and when I cursed everyone, I was beaten again.

The worst punishment, however, was seeing the look on my mother's face. I hadn't even told her I was going. And I had wounded her, a thing that had never really happened before.

But she never said anything about it.

When she came to me, she listened to me cry. I saw tears in her eyes. And she laid her hand on my shoulder, which for her was something a little remarkable.

I didn't tell her what it had been like, those few days. But I think she knew. Something magical had been lost utterly. And once again, she defied my father. She put an end to the condemnations, the beatings, the restrictions.

She had me sit beside her at the table. She deferred to me, actually talked to me in conversation that was perfectly unnatural to her, until she had subdued and dissolved the rancour of the family.

Finally, as she had in the past, she produced another of her jewels and she bought the fine hunting rifle that I had taken with me when I killed the wolves.

This was a superior and expensive weapon, and in spite of my misery, I was fairly eager to try it. And she added to that another gift, a sleek chestnut mare with strength and speed I'd never known in an animal before. But these things were small compared to the general consolation my mother had given me.

Yet the bitterness inside me did not subside.

I never forgot what it had been like when I was Lelio. I became a little crueller for what had happened, and I never, never went again to the village fair. I conceived of the notion that I should never get away from here, and oddly enough as my despair deepened, so my usefulness increased.

I alone put the fear of God into the servants or tenants by

the time I was eighteen. I alone provided the food for us. And for some strange reason this gave me satisfaction. I don't know why, but I liked to sit at the table and reflect that everyone there was eating what I had provided.

SO THESE moments had bound me to my mother. These moments had given us a love for each other unnoticed and probably unequalled in the lives of those around us.

And now she had come to me at this odd time, when for reasons I didn't understand myself, I could not endure the company of any other person.

WITH my eyes on the fire, I barely saw her climb up and sink down into the straw mattress beside me.

Silence. Just the crackling of the fire, and the deep respiration of the sleeping dogs beside me.

Then I glanced at her, and I was vaguely startled.

She'd been ill all winter with a cough, and now she looked truly sickly, and her beauty, which was always very important to me, seemed vulnerable for the first time.

Her face was angular and her cheekbones perfect, very high and broadly spaced but delicate. Her jawline was strong yet exquisitely feminine. And she had very clear cobalt blue eyes fringed with thick ashen lashes.

If there was any flaw in her it was perhaps that all her features were too small, too kittenish and made her look like a girl. Her eyes became even smaller when she was angry, and though her mouth was sweet, it often appeared hard. It did not turn down, it wasn't twisted in any way, it was like a little pink rose on her face. But her cheeks were very smooth and her face narrow, and when she looked very serious, her mouth, without changing at all, looked mean for some reason.

Now she was slightly sunken. But she still looked beautiful to me. She still was beautiful. I liked looking at her. Her hair was full and blonde, and that I had inherited from her.

In fact I resemble her at least superficially. But my features are larger, cruder, and my mouth is more mobile and can be very mean at times. And you can see my sense of humour in my expression, my capacity for mischievousness and near

45

hysterical laughing, which I've always had no matter how unhappy I was. She did not laugh often. She could look profoundly cold. Yet she had always a little girl sweetness.

Well, I looked at her as she sat on my bed — I even stared at her, I suppose — and immediately she started to talk to me.

'I know how it is,' she said to me. 'You hate them. Because of what you've endured and what they don't know. They haven't the imagination to know what happened to you out there on the mountain.'

I felt a cold delight in these words. I gave her the silent acknowledgement that she understood it perfectly.

'It was the same the first time I bore a child,' she said. 'I was in agony for twelve hours, and I felt trapped in the pain, knowing the only release was the birth or my own death. When it was over, I had your brother Augustin in my arms, but I didn't want anyone else near me. And it wasn't because I blamed them. It was only that I'd suffered like that, hour after hour, that I'd gone into the circle of hell and come back out. They hadn't been in the circle of hell. And I felt quiet all over. In this common occurrence, this vulgar act of giving birth, I understood the meaning of utter loneliness.'

'Yes, that's it,' I answered. I was a little shaken.

She didn't respond. I would have been surprised if she had. Having said what she'd come to say, she wasn't going to converse, actually. But she did lay her hand on my forehead — very unusual for her to do that — and when she observed that I was wearing the same bloody hunting clothes after all this time, I noticed it too, and realized the sickness of it.

She was silent for a while.

And as I sat there, looking past her at the fire, I wanted to tell her a lot of things, how much I loved her particularly.

But I was cautious. She had a way of cutting me off when I spoke to her, and mingled with my love was a powerful resentment of her.

All my life I'd watched her read her Italian books and scribble letters to people in Naples, where she had grown up, yet she had no patience even to teach me or my brothers the alphabet. And nothing had changed after I came back from the monastery. I was twenty and I couldn't read or write more than a few prayers and my name. I hated the sight of her books; I hated her absorption in them.

And in some vague way, I hated the fact that only extreme pain in me could ever wring from her the slightest warmth or interest.

Yet she'd been my saviour. And there was no one but her. And I was as tired of being alone, perhaps, as a young person can be.

She was here now, out of the confines of her library, and she was attentive to me.

Finally I was convinced that she wouldn't get up and go away, and I found myself speaking to her.

'Mother,' I said in a low voice, 'there is more to it. Before it happened, there were times when I felt terrible things.' There was no change in her expression. 'I mean I dream sometimes that I might kill all of them,' I said. 'I kill my brothers and my father in the dream. I go from room to room slaughtering them as I did the wolves. I feel in myself the desire to murder ...'

'So do I, my son,' she said. 'So do I.' And her face was lighted with the strangest smile as she looked at me.

I bent forward and looked at her more closely. I lowered my voice.

'I see myself screaming when it happens,' I went on. 'I see my face twisted into grimaces and I hear bellowing coming out of me. My mouth is a perfect O, and shrieks, cries, come out of me.'

She nodded with that same understanding look, as if a light were flaring behind her eyes.

'And on the mountain, Mother, when I was fighting the wolves ... it was a little like that.'

'Only a little?' she asked.

I nodded.

'I felt like someone different from myself when I killed the wolves. And now I don't know who is here with you — your son Lestat, or that other man, the killer.'

She was quiet for a long time.

'No,' she said finally. 'It was you who killed the wolves. You're the hunter, the warrior. You're stronger than anyone else here, that's your tragedy.'

I shook my head. That was true, but it didn't matter. It couldn't account for unhappiness such as this. But what was the use of saying it?

She looked away for a moment, then back to me.

'But you're many things,' she said. 'Not only one thing. You're the killer and the man. And don't give in to the killer in you just because you hate them. You don't have to take upon yourself the burden of murder or madness to be free of this place. Surely there must be other ways.'

Those last two sentences struck me hard. She had gone to the core. And the implications dazzled me.

Always I'd felt that I couldn't be a good human being and fight them. To be good meant to be defeated by them. Unless of course I found a more interesting idea of goodness.

We sat still for a few moments. And there seemed an uncommon intimacy even for us. She was looking at the fire, scratching at her thick hair which was wound into a circle on the back of her head.

'You know what I imagine,' she said, looking towards me again. 'Not so much the murdering of them as an abandon which disregards them completely. I imagine drinking wine until I'm so drunk I strip off my clothes and bathe in the mountain streams naked.'

I almost laughed. But it was a sublime amusement. I looked up at her, uncertain for a moment that I was hearing her correctly. But she had said these words and she wasn't finished.

'And then I imagine going into the village,' she said, 'and up into the inn and taking into my bed any men that come there — crude men, big men, old men, boys. Just lying there and taking them one after another, and feeling some magnificent triumph in it, some absolute release without a thought of what happens to your father or your brothers, whether they are alive or dead. In that moment I am purely myself. I belong to no one.'

I was too shocked and amazed to say anything. But again this was terribly terribly amusing. When I thought of my father and brothers and the pompous shopkeepers of the village and how they would respond to such a thing, I found it damn near hilarious.

If I didn't laugh aloud it was probably because the image of my mother naked made me think I shouldn't. But I couldn't keep altogether quiet. I laughed a little, and she nodded, half smiling. She raised her eyebrows, as if to say, We understand each other.

Finally I roared laughing. I pounded my knee with my fist and hit my head on the wood of the bed behind me. And she almost laughed herself. Maybe in her own quiet way she was laughing.

Curious moment. Some almost brutal sense of her as a human being quite removed from all that surrounded her. We did understand each other, and all my resentment of her didn't matter too much.

She pulled the pin out of her hair and let it tumble down to her shoulders.

We sat quiet for perhaps an hour after that. No more laughter or talk, just the fire blazing, and her near to me.

She had turned so she could see the fire. Her profile, the delicacy of her nose and lips, were beautiful to look at. Then she looked back at me and in the same steady voice without undue emotion she said:

'I'll never leave here. I am dying now.'

I was stunned. The little shock before was nothing to this.

'I'll live through this spring,' she continued, 'and possibly the summer as well. But I won't survive another winter. I know. The pain in my lungs is too bad.'

I made some little anguished sound. I think I leaned forward and said, 'Mother!'

'Don't say any more,' she answered.

I think she hated to be called mother, but I hadn't been able to help it.

'I just wanted to speak it to another soul,' she said. 'To hear it out loud. I'm perfectly horrified by it. I'm afraid of it.'

I wanted to take her hands, but I knew she'd never allow it. She disliked to be touched. She never put her arms around

49

anyone. And so it was in our glances that we held each other. My eyes filled with tears looking at her.

She patted my hand.

'Don't think on it much,' she said. 'I don't. Just only now and then. But you must be ready to live on without me when the time comes. That may be harder for you than you realize.'

I tried to say something; I couldn't make the words come.

She left me just as she'd come in, silently.

And though she'd never said anything about my clothes or my beard or how dreadful I looked, she sent the servants in with clean clothes for me, and the razor and warm water, and silently I let myself be taken care of by them.

3

BEGAN to feel a little stronger. I stopped thinking about what happened with the wolves and I thought about her.

I thought about the words 'perfectly horrified', and I didn't know what to make of them except they sounded exactly true. I'd feel that way if I were dying slowly. It would have been better on the mountain with the wolves.

But there was more to it than that. She had always been silently unhappy. She hated the inertia and the hopelessness of our life here as much as I did. And now, after eight children, three living, five dead, she was dying. This was the end for her.

I determined to get up if it would make her feel better, but when I tried I couldn't. The thought of her dying was unbearable. I paced the floor of my room a lot, ate the food brought to me, but still I wouldn't go to her.

But by the end of the month, visitors came to draw me out.

My mother came in and said I must receive the merchants from the village who wanted to honour me for killing the wolves.

'Oh, hell with it,' I answered.

'No, you must come down,' she said. 'They have gifts for

50

you. Now do your duty.'

I hated all this.

When I reached the hall, I found the rich shopkeepers there, all men I knew well, and all dressed for the occasion.

But there was one startling young man among them I didn't recognize immediately.

He was my age perhaps, and quite tall, and when our eyes met I remembered who he was. Nicolas de Lenfent, eldest son of the draper, who had been sent to school in Paris.

He was a vision now.

Dressed in a splendid brocade coat of rose and gold, he wore slippers with gold heels, and layers of Italian lace at his collar. Only his hair was what it used to be, dark and very curly, and boyish looking for some reason though it was tied back with a fine bit of silk ribbon.

Parisian fashion, all this — the sort that passed as fast as it could through the local post house.

And here I was to meet him in threadbare wool and scuffed leather boots and yellowed lace that had been seventeen times mended.

We bowed to each other, as he was apparently the spokesman for the town, and then he unwrapped from its modest covering of black serge a great red velvet cloak lined in fur. Gorgeous thing. His eyes were positively shining when he looked at me. You would have thought he was looking at a sovereign.

'Monsieur, we beg you to accept this,' he said very sincerely. 'The finest fur of the wolves has been used to line it, and we thought it would stand you well in the winter, this fur-lined cloak, when you ride out to hunt.'

'And these too, Monsieur,' said his father, producing a finely sewn pair of fur-lined boots in black suede. 'For the hunt, Monsieur,' he said.

I was a little overcome. They meant these gestures in the kindest way, these men who had the sort of wealth I only dreamed of, and they paid me respect as the aristocrat.

I took the cloak and the boots. I thanked them as effusively as I'd ever thanked anybody for anything.

And behind me, I heard my brother Augustin say:

'Now he will really be impossible!'

I felt my face colour. Outrageous that he should say this in the presence of these men, but when I glanced to Nicolas de Lenfent I saw the most affectionate expression on his face.

'I too am impossible, Monsieur,' he whispered as I gave him the parting kiss. 'Someday, will you let me come to talk to you and tell me how you killed them all? Only the impossible can do the impossible.'

None of the merchants ever spoke to me like that. We were boys again for a moment. And I laughed out loud. His father was disconcerted. My brother stopped whispering, but Nicolas de Lenfent kept smiling with a Parisian's composure.

AS SOON as they had left I took the red velvet cloak and the suede boots up into my mother's room.

She was reading as always while very lazily she brushed her hair. In the weak sunlight from the window, I saw grey in her hair for the first time. I told her what Nicolas de Lenfent had said.

'Why is he impossible?' I asked her. 'He said this with feeling, as if it meant something.'

She laughed.

'It means something all right,' she said. 'He's in disgrace.' She stopped looking at her book for a moment and looked at me. 'You know how he's been educated all his life to be a little imitation aristocrat. Well, during his first term studying law in Paris, he fell madly in love with the violin, of all things. Seems he heard an Italian virtuoso, one of those geniuses from Padua who is so great that men say he has sold his soul to the devil. Well, Nicolas dropped everything at once to take lessons from Wolfgang Mozart. He sold his books. He did nothing but play and play until he failed his examinations. He wants to be a musician. Can you imagine?'

'And his father is beside himself.'

'Exactly. He even smashed the instrument, and you know what a piece of expensive merchandise means to the good draper.'

I smiled.

'And so Nicolas has no violin now?'

'He has a violin. He promptly ran away to Clermont and sold his watch to buy another. He's impossible all right, and the worst part of it is that he plays rather well.'

'You've heard him?'

She knew good music. She grew up with it in Naples. All I'd ever heard were the church choir, the players at the fairs.

'I heard him Sunday when I went to mass,' she said. 'He was playing in the upstairs bedroom over the shop. Everyone could hear him, and his father was threatening to break his hands.'

I gave a little gasp at the cruelty of it. I was powerfully fascinated! I think I loved him already, doing what he wanted like that.

'Of course he'll never be anything,' she went on.

'Why not?'

'He's too old. You can't take up the violin when you're twenty. But what do I know? He plays magically in his own way. And maybe he can sell his soul to the devil.'

I laughed a little uneasily. It sounded tragic.

'But why don't you go down to the town and make a friend of him?' she asked.

'Why the hell should I do that?' I asked.

'Lestat, really. Your brothers will hate it. And the old merchant will be beside himself with joy. His son and the Marquis's son.'

'Those aren't good enough reasons.'

'He's been to Paris,' she said. She watched me for a long moment. Then she went back to her book, brushing her hair now and then lazily.

I watched her reading, hating it. I wanted to ask her how she was, if her cough was very bad that day. But I couldn't broach the subject to her.

'Go on down and talk to him, Lestat,' she said, without another glance at me.

4

T TOOK me a week to make up my mind that I would seek out Nicolas de Lenfent.

I put on the red velvet fur-lined cloak and the fur-lined suede boots, and I went down the winding main street of the village towards the inn.

The shop owned by Nicolas's father was right across from the inn, but I didn't see or hear Nicolas.

I had no more than enough for one glass of wine and I wasn't sure just how to proceed when the innkeeper came out, bowed to me, and set a bottle of his best vintage before me.

Of course these people had always treated me like the son of the lord. But I could see that things had changed on account of the wolves, and strangely enough, this made me feel even more alone than I usually felt.

But as soon as I poured the first glass, Nicolas appeared, a great blaze of colour in the open doorway.

He was not so finely dressed as before, thank heaven, yet everything about him exuded wealth. Silk and velvet and brand-new leather.

But he was flushed as if he'd been running and his hair was windblown and messy, and his eyes full of excitement. He bowed to me, waited for me to invite him to sit down, and then he asked me:

'What was it like, Monsieur, killing the wolves?' And folding his arms on the table, he stared at me.

'Why don't you tell me what's it like in Paris, Monsieur?' I said, and I realized right away that it sounded mocking and rude. 'I'm sorry,' I said immediately. 'I would really like to know. Did you go to the university? Did you really study with Mozart? What do people in Paris do? What do they talk about? What do they think?'

He laughed softly at the barrage of questions. I had to laugh myself. I signalled for another glass and pushed the bottle towards him.

'Tell me,' I said, 'did you go to the theatre in Paris? Did you see the Comédie-Française?'

'Many times,' he answered a little dismissively. 'But listen, the diligence will be coming in any minute. There'll be too much noise. Allow me the honour of providing your supper in a private room upstairs. I should so like to do it –'

And before I could make a gentlemanly protest, he was ordering everything. We were shown up to a crude but comfortable little chamber.

I was almost never in small wooden rooms, and I loved it immediately. The table was laid for the meal that would come later on, the fire was truly warming the place, unlike the roaring blazes in our castle, and the thick glass of the window was clean enough to see the blue winter sky over the snow-covered mountains.

'Now, I shall tell you everything you want to know about Paris,' he said agreeably, waiting for me to sit first. 'Yes, I did go to the university.' He made a little sneer as if it had all been contemptible. 'And I did study with Mozart, who would have told me I was hopeless if he hadn't needed pupils. Now where do you want me to begin? The stench of the city, or the infernal noise of it? The hungry crowds that surround you everywhere? The thieves in every alley ready to cut your throat?'

I waved all that away. His smile was very different from his tone, his manner open and appealing.

'A really big Paris theatre ...' I said. 'Describe it to me ... what is it like?'

I THINK we stayed in that room for four solid hours and all we did was drink and talk.

He drew plans of the theatres on the tabletop with a wet finger, described the plays he had seen, the famous actors, the little houses of the boulevards. Soon he was describing all of Paris, and he'd forgotten to be cynical, my curiosity firing him as he talked of the Ile de la Cité, and the Latin Quartre, the Sorbonne, the Louvre.

We went on to more abstract things, how the newspapers reported events, how his student cronies gathered in cafés to argue. He told me men were restless and out of love with the monarchy. That they wanted a change in government and wouldn't sit still for very long. He told me about the philosophers, Diderot, Voltaire, Rousseau.

I couldn't understand everything he said. But in rapid, sometimes sarcastic speech he gave me a marvelously complete picture of what was going on.

Of course, it didn't surprise me to hear that educated people didn't believe in God, that they were infinitely more interested in science, that the aristocracy was much in ill favour, and so was the Church. These were times of reason, not superstition, and the more he talked the more I understood.

Soon he was outlining the Encyclopédie, the great compilation of knowledge supervised by Diderot. And then it was the salons he'd gone to, the drinking bouts, his evenings with actresses. He described the public balls at the Palais Royal, where Marie Antoinette appeared right along with the common people.

'I'll tell you,' he said finally, 'it all sounds a hell of a lot better in this room than it really is.'

'I don't believe you,' I said gently. I didn't want him to stop talking. I wanted it to go on and on.

'It's a secular age, Monsieur,' he said, filling our glasses from the new bottle of wine. 'Very dangerous.'

'Why dangerous?' I whispered. 'An end to superstition? What could be better than that?'

'Spoken like a true eighteenth-century man, Monsieur,' he said with a faint melancholy to his smile. 'But no one values anything anymore. Fashion is everything. Even atheism is a fashion.'

I had always had a secular mind, but not for any philosophical reason. No one in my family much believed in God or ever had. Of course they said they did, and we went to mass. But this was duty. Real religion had long ago died out in our family, as it had perhaps in the families of thousands of aristocrats. Even at the monastery I had not believed in God. I had believed in the monks around me.

I tried to explain this in simple language that would not give offence to Nicolas, because for his family it was different.

56

Even his miserable money-grubbing father (whom I secretly admired) was fervently religious.

'But can men live without these beliefs?' Nicolas asked almost sadly. 'Can children face the world without them?'

I was beginning to understand why he was so sarcastic and cynical. He had only recently lost that old faith. He was bitter about it.

But no matter how deadening was this sarcasm of his, a great energy poured out of him, an irrepressible passion. And this drew me to him. I think I loved him. Another two glasses of wine and I might say something absolutely ridiculous like that.

'I've always lived without beliefs,' I said.

'Yes. I know,' he answered. 'Do you remember the story of the witches? The time you cried at the witches' place?'

'Cried over the witches?' I looked at him blankly for a moment. But it stirred something painful, something humiliating. Too many of my memories had that quality. And now I had to remember crying over witches. 'I don't remember,' I said.

'We were little boys. And the priest was teaching us our prayers. And the priest took us out to see the place where they burnt the witches in the old days, the old stakes and the blackened ground.'

'Ah, that place.' I shuddered. 'That horrid, horrid place.'

'You began to scream and cry. They sent someone for the Marquise herself because your nurse couldn't quiet you.'

'I was a dreadful child,' I said, trying to shrug it off. Of course I did remember now — screaming, being carried home, nightmares about the fires. Someone bathing my forehead and saying, 'Lestat, wake up.'

But I hadn't thought of that little scene in years. It was the place itself I thought about whenever I drew near it — the thicket of blackened stakes, the images of men and women and children burnt alive.

Nicolas was studying me. 'When your mother came to get you, she said it was all ignorance and cruelty. She was so angry with the priest for telling us the old tales.'

I nodded.

The final horror to hear they had all died for nothing, those long-forgotten people of our own village, that they had been innocent. 'Victims of superstition,' she had said. 'There were no real witches.' No wonder I had screamed and screamed.

'But my mother,' Nicolas said, 'told a different story, that the witches had been in league with the devil, that they'd blighted the crops, and in the guise of wolves killed the sheep and the children —'

'And won't the world be better if no one is ever again burnt in the name of God?' I asked. 'If there is no more faith in God to make men do that to each other? What is the danger in a secular world where horrors like that don't happen?'

He leaned forward with a mischievous little frown.

'The wolves didn't wound you on the mountain, did they?' he asked playfully. 'You haven't become a werewolf, have you, Monsieur, unbeknownst to the rest of us?' He stroked the furred edge of the velvet cloak I still had over my shoulders. 'Remember what the good father said, that they had burnt a good number of werewolves in those times. They were a regular menace.'

I laughed.

'If I turn into a wolf,' I answered, 'I can tell you this much. I won't hang around here to kill the children. I'll get away from this miserable little hellhole of a village where they still terrify little boys with tales of burning witches. I'll get on the road to Paris and never stop till I see her ramparts.'

'And you'll find Paris is a miserable hellhole,' he said. 'Where they break the bones of thieves on the wheel for the vulgar crowds in the place de Grève.'

'No,' I said. 'I'll see a splendid city where great ideas are born in the minds of the populace, ideas that go forth to illuminate the darkened corners of the world.'

'Ah, you are a dreamer!' he said, but he was delighted. He was beyond handsome when he smiled.

'And I'll know people like you,' I went on, 'people who have thoughts in their heads, and quick tongues with which to voice them, and we'll sit in cafés and we'll drink together and we'll clash with each other violently in words, and we'll talk for the rest of our lives in divine excitement.'

He reached out and put his arm around my neck and kissed me. We almost upset the table we were so blissfully drunk.

'My lord, the wolfkiller,' he whispered.

When the third bottle of wine came, I began to talk of my life, as I'd never done before — of what it was like each day to ride out into the mountains, to go so far I couldn't see the towers of my father's house anymore, to ride above the tilled land to the place where the forest seemed almost haunted.

The words began to pour out of me as they had out of him, and soon we were talking about a thousand things we had felt in our hearts, varieties of secret loneliness, and the words seemed to be essential words the way they did on those rare occasions with my mother. And as we came to describe our longings and dissatisfactions, we were saying things to each other with great exuberance, like 'Yes, yes,' and 'Exactly,' and 'I know completely what you mean,' and 'And yes, of course, you felt that you could not bear it,' etc.

Another bottle, and a new fire. And I begged Nicolas to play his violin for me. He rushed home immediately to get it.

It was now late afternoon. The sun was slanting through the window and the fire was very hot. We were very drunk. We had never ordered supper. And I think I was happier than I had ever been in my life. I lay on the lumpy straw mattress of the little bed with my hands under my head watching him as he took out the instrument.

He put the violin to his shoulder and began to pluck at it and twist the pegs.

Then he raised the bow and drew it down hard over the strings to bring out the first note.

I sat up and pushed myself back against the panelled wall and stared at him because I couldn't believe the sound I was hearing.

He ripped into the song. He tore the notes out of the violin and each note was translucent and throbbing. His eyes were closed, his mouth a little distorted, his lower lip sliding to the side, and what struck my heart almost as much as the song itself was the way that he seemed with his whole body to lean into the music, to press his soul like an ear to the instrument.

I had never known music like it, the rawness of it, the intensity, the rapid glittering torrents of notes that came out of the strings as he sawed away. It was Mozart that he was playing, and it had all the gaiety, the velocity, and the sheer loveliness of everything Mozart wrote.

When he'd finished, I was staring at him and I realized I was gripping the sides of my head.

'Monsieur, what's the matter!' he said, almost helplessly, and I stood up and threw my arms around him and kissed him on both cheeks and kissed the violin.

'Stop calling me Monsieur,' I said. 'Call me by my name.' I lay back down on the bed and buried my face on my arm and started to cry, and once I'd started I couldn't stop it.

He sat next to me, hugging me and asking me why I was crying, and though I couldn't tell him, I could see that he was overwhelmed that his music had produced this effect. There was no sarcasm or bitterness in him now.

I think he carried me home that night.

And the next morning I was standing in the crooked stone street in front of his father's shop, tossing pebbles up at his window.

When he stuck his head out, I said:

'Do you want to come down and go on with our conversation?'

5

FROM then on, when I was not hunting, my life was with Nicolas and 'our conversation'.

Spring was approaching, the mountains were dappled with green, the apple orchard starting back to life. And Nicolas and I were always together.

We took long walks up the rocky slopes, had our bread and wine in the sun on the grass, roamed south through the ruins of an old monastery. We hung about in my rooms or sometimes climbed to the battlements. And we went back to our room at the inn when we were too drunk and too loud to be tolerated by others.

And as the weeks passed we revealed more and more of ourselves to each other. Nicolas told me about his childhood at school, the little disappointments of his early years, those whom he had known and loved.

And I started to tell him the painful things — and finally the old disgrace of running off with the Italian players.

It came to that one night when we were in the inn again, and we were drunk as usual. In fact we were at that moment of drunkenness that the two of us had come to call the Golden Moment, when everything made sense. We always tried to stretch out that moment, and then inevitably one of us would confess, 'I can't follow anymore, I think the Golden Moment's passed.'

On this night, looking out the window at the moon over the mountains, I said that at the Golden Moment it was not so terrible that we weren't in Paris, that we weren't at the Opéra or the Comédie, waiting for the curtain to rise.

'You and the theatres of Paris,' he said to me. 'No matter what we're talking about you bring it back to the theatres and the actors — '

His brown eyes were very big and trusting. And even drunk as he was, he looked spruce in his red velvet Paris frock coat.

'Actors and actresses make magic,' I said. 'They make things happen on the stage; they invent; they create.'

'Wait until you see the sweat streaming down their painted faces in the glare of the footlights,' he answered.

'Ah, there you go again,' I said. 'And you, the one who gave up everything to play the violin.'

He got terribly serious suddenly, looking off as if he were weary of his own struggles.

'That I did,' he confessed.

Even now the whole village knew it was war between him and his father. Nicki wouldn't go back to school in Paris.

'You make life when you play,' I said. 'You create something from nothing. You make something good happen. And that is blessed to me.'

'I make music and it makes me happy,' he said. 'What is

61

blessed or good about that?'

I waved it away as I always did his cynicism now.

'I've lived all these years among those who create nothing and change nothing,' I said. 'Actors and musicians — they're saints to me.'

'Saints?' he asked. 'Blessedness? Goodness? Lestat, your language baffles me.'

I smiled and shook my head.

'You don't understand. I'm speaking of the character of human beings, not what they believe in. I'm speaking of those who won't accept a useless life, just because they were born to it. I mean those who would be something better. They work, they sacrifice, they do things ...'

He was moved by this, and I was a little surprised that I'd said it. Yet I felt I had hurt him somehow.

'There is blessedness in that,' I said. 'There's sanctity. And God or no God, there is goodness in it. I know this the way I know the mountains are out there, that the stars shine.'

He looked sad for me. And he looked hurt still. But for the moment I didn't think of him.

I was thinking of the conversation I had had with my mother and my perception that I couldn't be good and defy my family. But if I believed what I was saying ...

As if he could read my mind, he asked:

'But do you really believe those things?'

'Maybe yes. Maybe no,' I said. I couldn't bear to see him look so sad.

And I think more on account of that than anything else I told him the whole story of how I'd run off with the players. I told him what I'd never told anyone, not even my mother, about those few days and the happiness they'd given me.

'Now, how could it not have been good,' I asked, 'to give and receive such happiness? We brought to life that town when we put on our play. Magic, I tell you. It could heal the sick, it could.'

He shook his head. And I knew there were things he wanted to say, which out of respect for me he was leaving to silence.

'You don't understand, do you?' I asked.

'Lestat, sin always feels good,' he said gravely. 'Don't you see that? Why do you think the Church has always condemned the players? It was from Dionysus, the wine god, that the theatre came. You can read that in Aristotle. And Dionysus was a god that drove men to debauchery. It felt good to you to be on that stage because it was abandoned and lewd — the age-old service of the god of the grape — and you were having a high time of it defying your father —'

'No, Nicki. No, a thousand times no.'

'Lestat, we're partners in sin,' he said smiling finally. 'We've always been. We've both behaved badly, both been utterly disreputable. It's what binds us together.'

Now it was my turn to look sad and hurt. And the Golden Moment was gone beyond reprieve — unless something new was to happen.

'Come on,' I said suddenly. 'Get your violin, and we'll go off somewhere in the woods where the music won't wake up anybody. We'll see if there isn't some goodness in it.'

'You're a madman!' he said. But he grabbed the unopened bottle by the neck and headed for the door immediately.

I was right behind him.

When he came out of his house with the violin, he said:

'Let's go to the witches' place! Look, it's a half moon. Plenty of light. We'll do the devil's dance and play for the spirits of the witches.'

I laughed. I had to be drunk to go along with that. 'We'll reconsecrate the spot,' I insisted, 'with good and pure music.'

It had been years and years since I'd walked in the witches' place.

The moon was bright enough, as he'd said, to see the charred stakes in their grim circle and the ground in which nothing ever grew even one hundred years after the burnings. The new saplings of the forest kept their distance. And so the wind struck in the clearing, and above, clinging to the rocky slope, the village hovered in darkness.

A faint chill passed over me, but it was the mere shadow of the anguish I'd felt as a child when I'd heard those awful words 'roasted alive', when I had imagined the suffering.

Nicki's white lace shone in the pale light, and he struck up a gypsy song at once and danced round in a circle as he played it.

I sat on a broad burned stump of tree and drank from the bottle. And the heartbreaking feeling came as it always did with the music. What sin was there, I thought, except to live out my life in this awful place? And pretty soon I was silently and unobtrusively crying.

Though it seemed the music had never stopped, Nicki was comforting me. We sat side by side and he told me that the world was full of inequities and that we were prisoners, he and I, of this awful corner of France, and someday we would break out of it. And I thought of my mother in the castle high up in the mountain, and the sadness numbed me until I couldn't bear it, and Nicki started playing again, telling me to dance and to forget everything.

Yes, that's what it could make you do, I wanted to say. Is that sin? How can it be evil? I went after him as he danced in a circle. The notes seemed to be flying up and out of the violin as if they were made of gold. I could almost see them flashing. I danced round and round him now and he sawed away into a deeper and more frenzied music. I spread the wings of the fur-lined cape and threw back my head to look at the moon. The music rose all around me like smoke, and the witches' place was no more. There was only the sky above arching down to the mountains.

We were closer for all this in the days that followed.

BUT a few nights later, something altogether extraordinary happened.

It was late. We were at the inn again and Nicolas, who was walking about the room and gesturing dramatically, declared what had been on our minds all along.

That we should run away to Paris, even if we were penniless, that it was better than remaining here. Even if we lived as beggars in Paris! It had to be better.

Of course we had both been building up to this.

'Well, beggars in the streets it might be, Nicki,' I said.

'Because I'll be damned in hell before I'll play the penniless country cousin begging at the big houses.'

'Do you think I want you to do that?' he demanded. 'I mean run away, Lestat,' he said. 'Spite them, every one of them.'

Did I want to go on like this? So our fathers would curse us. After all, our life was *meaningless* here.

Of course, we both knew this running off together would be a thousand times more serious than what I had done before. We weren't boys anymore, we were men. Our fathers *would* curse us, and this was something neither of us could laugh off.

Also we were old enough to know what poverty meant.

'What am I going to do in Paris when we get hungry?' I asked. 'Shoot rats for supper?'

'I'll play my violin for coins on the boulevard du Temple if I have to, and you can go to the theatres!' Now he was really challenging me. He was saying, 'Is it all words with you, Lestat? With your looks, you know, you'd be on the stage in the boulevard du Temple in no time.'

I loved this change in 'our conversation'! I loved seeing him believe we could do it. All his cynicism had vanished, even though he did throw in the word 'spite' every ten words or so. It seemed possible suddenly to do all this.

And this notion of the meaninglessness of our lives here began to enflame us.

I took up the theme again that music and acting were good because they drove back chaos. Chaos was the meaninglessness of day-to-day life, and if we were to die now, our lives would have been nothing but meaninglessness. In fact, it came to me that my mother dying soon was meaningless and I confided in Nicolas what she had said. 'I'm perfectly *horrified*. I'm afraid.'

Well, if there had been a Golden Moment in the room it was gone now. And something different started to happen.

I should call it the Dark Moment, but it was still high-pitched and full of eerie light. We were talking rapidly, cursing this meaninglessness, and when Nicolas at last sat down and put his head in his hands, I took some glamorous and hearty swigs of wine and went to pacing and gesturing as he had done before.

I realized aloud in the midst of saying it that even when we die we probably don't find out the answer as to why we were ever alive. Even the avowed atheist probably thinks that in death he'll get some answer. I mean God will be there, or there won't be anything at all.

'But that's just it,' I said, 'we don't make any discovery at that moment! We merely stop! We pass into nonexistence without ever knowing a thing.' I saw the universe, a vision of the sun, the planets, the stars, black night going on forever. And I began to laugh.

'Do you realize that! We'll never know why the hell any of it happened, not even when it's over!' I shouted at Nicolas, who was sitting back on the bed, nodding and drinking his wine out of a flagon. 'We're going to die and not even know. We'll never know, and all this meaninglessness will just go on and on and on. And we won't any longer be witnesses to it. We won't have even that little bit of power to give meaning to it in our minds. We'll just be gone, dead, dead, dead, without ever knowing!'

But I had stopped laughing. I stood still and I understood perfectly what I was saying!

There was no judgment day, no final explanation, no luminous moment in which all terrible wrongs would be made right, all horrors redeemed.

The witches burnt at the stake would never be avenged.

No one was ever going to tell us anything!

No, I didn't understand it at this moment. I *saw* it! And I began to make the single sound: 'Oh!' I said it again 'Oh!' and then I said it louder and louder and louder, and I dropped the wine bottle on the floor. I put my hands to my head and I kept saying it, and I could see my mouth opened in that perfect circle that I had described to my mother and I kept saying, 'Oh, oh, oh!'

I said it like a great hiccuping that I couldn't stop. And Nicolas took hold of me and started shaking me, saying:

'Lestat, stop!'

I couldn't stop. I ran to the window, unlatched it and swung out the heavy little glass, and stared at the stars. I couldn't stand seeing them. I couldn't stand seeing the pure emptiness, the silence, the absolute absence of any answer, and I started roaring as Nicolas pulled me back from the window-sill and pulled shut the glass.

'You'll be all right,' he said over and over. Someone was beating on the door. It was the innkeeper, demanding why we had to carry on like this.

'You'll feel all right in the morning,' Nicolas kept insisting. 'You just have to sleep.'

We had awakened everyone. I couldn't be quiet. I kept making the same sound over again. And I ran out of the inn with Nicolas behind me, and down the street of the village and up towards the castle with Nicolas trying to catch up with me, and through the gates and up into my room.

'Sleep, that's what you need,' he kept saying to me desperately. I was lying against the wall with my hands over my ears, and that sound kept coming. 'Oh, oh, oh.'

'In the morning,' he said, 'it will be better.'

WELL, it was not better in the morning.

And it was no better by nightfall, and in fact it got worse with the coming of the darkness.

I walked and talked and gestured like a contented human being, but I was flayed. I was shuddering. My teeth were chattering. I couldn't stop it. I was staring at everything around me in horror. The darkness terrified me. The sight of the old suits of armour in the hall terrified me. I stared at the mace and the flail I'd taken out after the wolves. I stared at the faces of my brothers. I stared at everything, seeing behind every configuration of colour and light and shadow the same thing: death. Only it wasn't just death as I'd thought of it before, it was death the way I saw it now. Real death, total death, inevitable, irreversible, and resolving nothing!

And in this unbearable state of agitation I commenced to do something I'd never done before. I turned to those around me and questioned them relentlessly.

'But do you believe in God?' I asked my brother Augustin, 'How can you live if you don't!'

'But do you really believe in anything?' I demanded of my blind father. 'If you knew you were dying at this very minute, would you expect to see God or darkness! Tell me.'

'You're mad, you've always been mad!' he shouted. 'Get out of this house! You'll drive us all crazy.'

He stood up, which was hard for him, being crippled and blind, and he tried to throw his goblet at me and naturally he missed.

I couldn't look at my mother. I couldn't be near her. I didn't want to make her suffer with my questions. I went down to the inn. I couldn't bear to think of the witches' place. I would not have walked to that end of the village for anything! I put my hands over my ears and shut my eyes. 'Go away!' I said at the thought of those who'd died like that without ever, ever understanding anything.

The second day, it was no better.

And it wasn't any better by the end of the week either.

I ate, drank, slept, but every waking moment was pure panic and pure pain. I went to the village priest and demanded did he really believe the Body of Christ was present on the altar at the Consecration. And after hearing his stammered answers, and seeing the fear in his eyes, I went away more desperate than before.

'But how do you live, how do you go on breathing and moving and doing things when you know there is no explanation?' I was raving finally. And then Nicolas said maybe the music would make me feel better. He would play the violin.

I was afraid of the intensity of it. But we went to the orchard and in the sunshine Nicolas played every song he knew. I sat there with my arms folded and my knees drawn up, my teeth chattering though we were right in the hot sun, and the sun was glaring off the little polished violin, and I watched Nicolas swaying into the music as he stood before me, the raw pure sounds swelling magically to fill the orchard and the valley, though it wasn't magic, and Nicolas put his arms around me finally, and we just sat there silent, and then he said very softly, 'Lestat, believe me, this will pass.'

'Play again,' I said. 'The music is innocent.'

Nicolas smiled and nodded. Pamper the madman.

And I knew it wasn't going to pass, and nothing for the moment could make me forget, but what I felt was inexpressible gratitude for the music, that in this horror there could be something as beautiful as that.

You couldn't understand anything; and you couldn't change anything. But you could make music like that. And I felt the same gratitude when I saw the village children dancing, when I saw their arms raised and their knees bent, and their bodies turning to the rhythm of the songs they sang. I started to cry watching them.

I wandered into the church and on my knees I leaned against the wall and I looked at the ancient statues and I felt the same gratitude looking at the finely carved fingers and the noses and the ears and the expressions on their faces and the deep folds in their garments, and I couldn't stop myself from crying.

At least we had these beautiful things, I said. Such goodness.

But nothing natural seemed beautiful to me now! The very sight of a great tree standing alone in a field could make me tremble and cry out. Fill the orchard with music.

And let me tell you a little secret. It *never did pass, really.*

6

HAT caused it? Was it the late night drinking and talking, or did it have to do with my mother and her saying she was going to die? Did the wolves have something to do with it? Was it a spell cast upon the imagination by the witches' place?

I don't know. It had come like something visited upon me from outside. One minute it was an idea, and the next it was *real.* I think you can invite that sort of thing, but you can't make it come.

Of course it was to slacken. But the sky was never quite the same shade of blue again. I mean the world looked different forever after, and even in moments of exquisite happiness there was the darkness lurking, the sense of our frailty and our hopelessness.

Maybe it was a presentiment. But I don't think so. It was more important than that, and frankly I don't believe in presentiments.

BUT to return to the story, during all this misery I kept away from my mother. I wasn't going to say these monstrous things about death and chaos to her. But she heard from everyone else that I'd lost my reason.

And finally, on the first Sunday night in Lent, she came to me.

I was alone in my room and the whole household had gone down to the village at twilight for the big bonfire that was the custom every year on this evening.

I had always hated the celebration. It had a ghastly aspect to it — the roaring flames, the dancing and singing, the peasants going afterwards through the orchards with their torches to the tune of their strange chanting.

We had had a priest for a little while who called it pagan. But they got rid of him fast enough. The farmers of our mountains kept to their old rituals. It was to make the trees bear and the crops grow, all this. And on this occasion, more than any other, I felt I saw the kind of men and women who could burn witches.

In my present frame of mind, it struck terror. I sat by my own little fire, trying to resist the urge to go to the window and look down on the big fire that drew me as strongly as it scared me.

My mother came in, closed the door behind her, and told me that she must talk to me. Her whole manner was tenderness.

'Is it on account of my dying, what's come over you?' she asked. 'Tell me if it is. And put your hands in mine.'

She even kissed me. She was frail in her faded dressing gown, and her hair was undone. I couldn't stand to see the streaks of grey in it. She looked starved.

But I told her the truth. I didn't know, and then I explained some of what had happened in the inn. I tried not to convey

70

the horror of it, the strange logic of it. I tried not to make it so absolute.

She listened and then she said, 'You're such a fighter, my son. You never *accept*. Not even when it's the fate of all mankind, will you accept it.'

'I can't!' I said miserably.

'I love you for it,' she said. 'It's all too like you that you should see this in a tiny bedroom in the inn late at night when you're drinking wine. And it's entirely like you to rage against it the way you rage against everything else.'

I started to cry again though I knew she wasn't condemning me. And then she took out a handkerchief and opened it to reveal several gold coins.

'You'll get over this,' she said. 'For the moment, death is spoiling life for you, that's all. But life is more important than death. You'll realize it soon enough. Now listen to what I have to say. I've had the doctor here and the old woman in the village who knows more about healing than he knows. Both agree with me I won't live too long.'

'Stop, Mother,' I said, aware of how selfish I was being, but unable to hold back. 'And this time there'll be no gifts. Put the money away.'

'Sit down,' she said. She pointed to the bench near the hearth. Reluctantly I did as I was told. She sat beside me.

'I know,' she said, 'that you and Nicolas are talking of running away.'

'I won't go, Mother ...'

'What, until I'm dead?'

I didn't answer her. I can't convey to you my frame of mind. I was still raw, trembling, and we had to talk about the fact that this living, breathing woman was going to stop living and breathing and start to putrefy and rot away, that her soul would spin into an abyss, that everything she had suffered in life, including the end of it, would come to nothing at all. Her little face was like something painted on a veil.

And from the distant village came the thinnest sound of the singing villagers.

'I want you to go to Paris, Lestat,' she said. 'I want you to

71

take this money, which is all I have left from my family. I want to know you're in Paris, Lestat, when my time comes I want to die knowing you are in Paris.'

I was startled. I remembered her stricken expression years ago when they'd brought me back from the Italian troupe. I looked at her for a long moment. She sounded almost angry in her persuasiveness.

'I'm terrified of dying,' she said. Her voice went almost dry. 'And I swear I will go mad if I don't know you're in Paris and you're free when it finally comes.'

I questioned her with my eyes. I was asking her with my eyes, 'Do you really mean this?'

'I have kept you here as surely as your father has,' she said. 'Not on account of pride, but on account of selfishness. And now I'm going to atone for it. I'll see you go. And I don't care what you do when you reach Paris, whether you sing while Nicolas plays the violin, or turn somersaults on the stage at the St.-Germain Fair. But go, and do what you will do as best you can.'

I tried to take her in my arms. She stiffened at first but then I felt her weaken and she melted against me, and she gave herself over so completely to me in that moment that I think I understood why she had always been so restrained. She cried, which I'd never heard her do. And I loved this moment for all its pain. I was ashamed of loving it, but I wouldn't let her go. I held her tightly, and maybe kissed her for all the times she'd never let me do it. We seemed for the moment like two parts of the same thing.

And then she grew calm. She seemed to settle into herself, and slowly but very firmly she released me and pushed me away.

She talked for a long time. She said things I didn't understand then, about how when she would see me riding out to hunt, she felt some wondrous pleasure in it, and she felt that same pleasure when I angered everyone and thundered my questions at my father and brothers as to why we had to live the way we lived. She spoke in an almost eerie way of my being a secret part of her anatomy, of my being the organ for

72

her which women do not really have.

'You are the man in me,' she said. 'And so I've kept you here, afraid of living without you, and maybe now in sending you away, I am only doing what I have done before.'

She shocked me a little. I never thought a woman could feel or articulate anything quite like this.

'Nicolas's father knows about your plans,' she said. 'The innkeeper overheard you. It's important you leave right away. Take the diligence at dawn, and write to me as soon as you reach Paris. There are letter writers at the cemetery of les Innocents near the St.-Germain Market. Find one who can write Italian for you. And then no one will be able to read the letter but me.'

When she left the room, I didn't quite believe what had happened. For a long moment I stood staring before me. I stared at my bed with its mattress of straw, at the two coats I owned and the red cloak, and my one pair of leather shoes by the hearth. I stared out the narrow slit of a window at the black hulk of the mountains I'd known all my life. The darkness, the gloom, slid back from me for a precious moment.

And then I was rushing down the stairs and down the mountain to the village to find Nicolas and to tell him we were going to Paris! We were going to do it. Nothing could stop us this time.

He was with his family watching the bonfire. And as soon as he saw me, he threw his arm around my neck, and I hooked my arm around his waist and I dragged him away from the crowds and the blaze, and towards the end of a meadow.

The air smelled fresh and green as it does only in spring. Even the villagers' singing didn't sound so horrible. I started dancing around in a circle.

'Get your violin!' I said. 'Play a song about going to Paris, we're on our way. We're going in the morning!'

'And how are we going to feed ourselves in Paris?' he sang out as he made with his empty hands to play an invisible violin. 'Are you going to shoot rats for our supper?'

'Don't ask what we'll do when we get there!' I said. 'The important thing is just to get there.'

7

NOT even a fortnight passed before I stood in the midst of the noonday crowds in the vast public cemetery of les Innocents, with its old vaults and stinking open graves — the most fantastical marketplace I had ever beheld — and, amid the stench and the noise, bent over an Italian letter writer dictating my first letter to my mother.

Yes, we had arrived safely after travelling day and night, and we had rooms in the Ile de la Cité, and we were inexpressibly happy, and Paris was warm and beautiful and magnificent beyond all imagining.

I wished I could have taken the pen myself and written to her.

I wished I could have told her what it was like, seeing these towering mansions, ancient winding streets aswarm with beggars, pedlars, noblemen, houses of four and five storeys banking the crowded boulevards.

I wished I could have described the carriages to her, the rumbling confections of gilt and glass bullying their way over the Pont Neuf and the Pont Notre Dame, streaming past the Louvre, the Palais Royal.

I wished I could describe the people, the gentlemen with their clocked stockings and silver walking sticks, tripping through the mud in pastel slippers, the ladies with their pearl-encrusted wigs and swaying panniers of silk and muslin, my first certain glimpse of Queen Marie Antoinette herself walking boldly through the gardens of the Tuileries.

Of course she'd seen it all years and years before I was born. She'd lived in Naples and London and Rome with her father. But I wanted to tell her what she had given to me, how it was to hear the choir in Notre Dame, to push into the jam-packed cafés with Nicolas, talk with his old student cronies over English coffee, what it was like to get dressed up in Nicolas's fine clothes — he made me do it — and stand below the footlights at the Comédie-Française gazing up in adoration at the actors on the stage.

But all I wrote in this letter was perhaps the very best of it, the address of the garret rooms we called our home in the Ile de la Cité, and the news:

'I have been hired in a real theatre to study as an actor with a fine prospect of performing very soon.'

What I didn't tell her was that we had to walk up six flights of stairs to our rooms, that men and women brawled and screamed in the alleyways beneath our windows, that we had run out of money already, thanks to my dragging us to every opera, ballet, and drama in town. And that the establishment where I worked was a shabby little boulevard theatre, one step up from a platform at the fair, and my jobs were to help the players dress, sell tickets, sweep up, and throw out the trouble-makers.

But I was in paradise again. And so was Nicolas though no decent orchestra in the city would hire him, and he was now playing solos with the little bunch of musicians in the theatre where I worked, and when we were really pinched he did play right on the boulevard, with me beside him, holding out the hat. We were shameless!

We ran up the steps each night with our bottle of cheap wine and a loaf of fine sweet Parisian bread, which was ambrosia after what we'd eaten in the Auvergne. And in the light of our one tallow candle, the garret was the most glorious place I'd ever inhabited.

As I mentioned before, I'd seldom been in a little wooden room except in the inn. Well, this room had plaster walls and a plaster ceiling! It was really Paris! It had polished wood flooring, and even a tiny little fireplace with a new chimney which actually made a draught.

So what if we had to sleep on lumpy pallets, and the neighbours woke us up fighting. We were waking up in Paris, and could roam arm in arm for hours through streets and alleyways, peering into shops full of jewellery and plate, tapestries and statues, wealth such as I'd never seen. Even the reeking meat markets delighted me. The crash and clatter of the city, the tireless busyness of its thousands upon thousands of labourers, clerks, craftsmen, the comings and goings of an endless multitude.

By day I almost forgot the vision of the inn, and the darkness. Unless, of course, I glimpsed some uncollected corpse in a filthy alleyway, of which there were many, or I happened upon a public execution in the place de Grève.

And I was *always* happening upon a public execution in the place de Grève.

I'd wander out of the square shuddering, almost moaning. I could become obsessed with it if not distracted. But Nicolas was adamant.

'Lestat, no talk of the eternal, the immutable, the unknowable!' He threatened to hit me or shake me if I should start.

And when the twilight came on — the time I hated more than ever — whether I had seen an execution or not, whether the day had been glorious or vexing, the trembling would start in me. And only one thing saved me from it: the warmth and excitement of the brightly lighted theatre, and I made sure that before dusk I was safely inside.

Now, in the Paris of those times, the theatres of the boulevards weren't even legitimate houses at all. Only the Comédie-Française and the Théâtre des Italiens were government-sanctioned theatres, and to them all serious drama belonged. This included tragedy as well as comedy, the plays of Racine, Corneille, the brilliant Voltaire.

But the old Italian commedia that I loved — Pantaloon, Harlequin, Scaramouche, and the rest — lived on as they always had, with tightrope walkers, acrobats, jugglers, and puppeteers, in the platform spectacles at the St.-Germain and the St.-Laurent fairs.

And the boulevard theatres had grown out of these fairs. By my time, the last decades of the eighteenth century, they were permanent establishments along the boulevard du Temple, and though they played to the poor who couldn't afford the grand houses, they also collected a very well-to-do crowd. Plenty of the aristocracy and the rich bourgeoisie crowded into the loges to see the boulevard performances, because they were lively and full of good talent, and not so stiff as the plays of the great Racine or the great Voltaire.

We did the Italian comedy just as I'd learned it before, full of improvisation so that every night it was new and different yet always the same. And we also did singing and all kinds of nonsense, not just because the people loved it, but because we had to: we couldn't be accused of breaking the monopoly of the state theatres on straight plays.

The house itself was a rickety wooden rattrap, seating no more than three hundred, but its little stage and props were elegant, it had a luxurious blue velvet stage curtain, and its private boxes had screens. And its actors and actresses were seasoned and truly talented, or so it seemed to me.

Even if I hadn't had this newly acquired dread of the dark, this 'malady of mortality', as Nicolas persisted in calling it, it couldn't have been more exciting to go through that stage door.

For five to six hours every evening, I lived and breathed in a little universe of shouting and laughing and quarrelling men and women, struggling for this one and against that one, all of us comrades in the wings even if we weren't friends. Maybe it was like being in a little boat on the ocean, all of us pulling together, unable to escape each other. It was divine.

Nicolas was slightly less enthusiastic, but then that was to be expected. And he got even more ironical when his rich student friends came around to talk to him. They thought he was a lunatic to live as he did. And for me, a nobleman shovelling actresses into their costumes and emptying slop buckets, they had no words at all.

Of course all that these young bourgeois really wanted was to be aristocrats. They bought titles, married into aristocratic families whenever they could. And it's one of the little jokes of history that they got mixed up in the Revolution, and helped to abolish the class which in fact they really wanted to join.

I didn't care if we never saw Nicolas's friends again. The actors didn't know about my family, and in favour of the very simple Lestat de Valois, which meant nothing actually, I'd dropped my real name, de Lioncourt.

I was learning everything I could about the stage. I memorized, I mimicked. I asked endless questions. And only stopped my education long enough each night for that moment when Nicolas played his solo on the violin. He'd rise from his seat in

77

the tiny orchestra, the spotlight would pick him out from the others, and he would rip into a little sonata, sweet enough and just short enough to bring down the house.

And all the while I dreamed of my own moment, when the old actors, whom I studied and pestered and imitated and waited upon like a lackey, would finally say: 'All right, Lestat, tonight we need you as Lelio. Now you ought to know what to do.'

It came in late August at last.

Paris was at its warmest, and the nights were almost balmy and the house was full of a restless audience fanning itself with handkerchiefs and handbills. The thick white paint was melting on my face as I put it on.

I wore a pasteboard sword with Nicolas's best velvet coat, and I was trembling before I stepped on the stage thinking, this is like waiting to be executed or something.

But as soon as I stepped out there, I turned and looked directly into the jam-packed hall and the strangest thing happened. The fear evaporated.

I beamed at the audience and very slowly I bowed. I stared at the lovely Flaminia as if I were seeing her for the first time. I had to win her. The romp began.

The stage belonged to me as it had years and years ago in that far-off country town. And as we pranced madly together across the boards — quarrelling, embracing, clowning — laughter rocked the house.

I could feel the attention as if it were an embrace. Each gesture, each line brought a roar from the audience — it was too easy almost — and we could have worked it for another half hour if the other actors, eager to get into the next trick as they called it, hadn't forced us finally towards the wings.

The crowd was standing up to applaud us. And it wasn't that country audience under the open sky. These were *Parisians* shouting for Lelio and Flaminia to come back out.

In the shadows of the wings, I reeled. I almost collapsed. I could not see anything for the moment but the vision of the audience gazing up at me over the footlights. I wanted to go right back on stage. I grabbed Flaminia and kissed her and realized that she was kissing me back passionately.

Then Renaud, the old manager, pulled her away.

'All right, Lestat,' he said as if he were cross about something. 'All right, you've done tolerably well, I'm going to let you go on regularly from now on.'

But before I could start jumping up and down for joy, half the troupe materialized around us. And Luchina, one of the actresses, immediately spoke up.

'Oh no, you'll not *let* him go on regularly!' she said. 'He's the handsomest actor on the boulevard du Temple and you'll hire him outright for it, and pay him outright for it, and he doesn't touch another broom or mop.' I was terrified. My career had just started and it was about to be over, but to my amazement Renaud agreed to all her terms.

Of course I was very flattered to be called handsome, and I understood as I had years ago that Lelio, the lover, is supposed to have considerable style. An aristocrat with any breeding whatsoever was perfect for the part.

But if I was going to make the Paris audiences really notice me, if I was going to have them talking about me at the Comédie-Française, I had to be more than some yellow-haired angel fallen out of a marquis's family onto the stage. I had to be a great actor, and that is exactly what I determined to be.

THAT night Nicolas and I celebrated with a colossal drunk. We had all the troupe up to our rooms for it, and I climbed out on the slippery rooftops and opened my arms to Paris and Nicolas played his violin in the window until we'd awakened the whole neighbourhood.

The music was rapturous, yet people were snarling and screaming up the alleyways, and banging on pots and pans. We paid no attention. We were dancing and singing as we had in the witches' place. I almost fell off the window ledge.

The next day, bottle in hand, I dictated the whole story to the Italian letter writer in the stinking sunshine in les Innocents and saw that the letter went off to my mother at once. I wanted to embrace everybody I saw in the streets. I was Lelio. I was an actor.

By September I had my name on the handbills. And I sent

those to my mother, too.

And we weren't doing the old commedia. We were performing a farce by a famous writer who, on account of a general playwrights' strike, couldn't get it performed at the Comédie-Française.

Of course we couldn't say his name, but everyone knew it was his work, and half the court was packing Renaud's House of Thespians every night.

I wasn't the lead, but I was the young lover, a sort of Lelio again really, which was almost better than the lead, and I stole every scene in which I appeared. Nicolas had taught me the part, bawling me out constantly for not learning to read. And by the fourth performance, the playwright had written extra lines for me.

Nicki was having his own moment at the intermezzo, when his latest rendering of a frothy little Mozart sonata was keeping the house in its seats. Even his student friends were back. We were getting invitations to private balls. I went tearing off to les Innocents every few days to write to my mother, and finally I had a clipping from an English paper, *The Spectator*, to send her, which praised our little play and in particular the blond-haired rogue who steals the hearts of the ladies in the third and fourth acts. Of course I couldn't read this clipping. But the gentleman who'd brought it to me said it was complimentary, and Nicolas swore it was too.

When the first chill nights of autumn came on, I wore the fur-lined red cloak on the stage. You could have seen it in the back row of the gallery even if you were almost blind. I had more skill now with the white makeup, shading it here and there to heighten the contours of my face, and though my eyes were ringed in black and my lips reddened a little, I looked both startling and human at the same time. I got love notes from the women in the crowd.

Nicolas was studying music in the mornings with an Italian maestro. Yet we had money enough for good food, wood, and coal. My mother's letters came twice a week and said her health had taken a turn for the better. She wasn't coughing as badly as last winter. She wasn't in pain. But our fathers had disowned us and would not acknowledge any mention of our names.

We were too happy to worry about that. But the dark dread, the 'malady of mortality', was with me a lot when the cold weather came on.

THE cold seemed worse in Paris. It wasn't clean as it had been in the mountains. The poor hovered in doorways, shivering and hungry, the crooked unpaved streets were thick with filthy slush. I saw barefoot children suffering before my very eyes, and more neglected corpses lying about than ever before. I was never so glad of the fur-lined cape as I was then. I wrapped it around Nicolas and held him close to me when we went out together, and we walked in a tight embrace through the snow and the rain.

Cold or no cold, I can't exaggerate the happiness of these days. Life was exactly what I thought it could be. And I knew I wouldn't be long in Renaud's theatre. Everybody was saying so. I had visions of the big stages, of touring London and Italy and even America with a great troupe of actors. Yet there was no reason to hurry. My cup was full.

8

BUT in the month of October when Paris was already freezing, I commenced to see, quite regularly, a strange face in the audience that invariably distracted me. Sometimes it almost made me forget what I was doing, this face. And then it would be gone as if I'd imagined it. I must have seen it off and on for a fortnight before I finally mentioned it to Nicki.

I felt foolish and found it hard to put into words:

'There is someone out there watching me,' I said.

'Everyone's watching you,' Nicki said. 'That's what you want.'

He was feeling a little sad that evening, and his answer was slightly sharp.

Earlier when he was making the fire, he had said he would never amount to much with the violin. In spite of his ear and his skill, there was too much he didn't know. And I would be a great actor, he was sure. I had said this was nonsense, but it was a shadow falling over my soul. I remembered my mother telling me that it was too late for him.

He wasn't envious, he said. He was just unhappy a little, that's all.

I decided to drop the matter of the mysterious face. I tried to think of some way to encourage him. I reminded him that his playing produced profound emotions in people, that even the actors backstage stopped to listen when he played. He had an undeniable talent.

'But I want to be a great violinist,' he said. 'And I'm afraid it will never be. As long as we were at home, I could pretend that it was going to be.'

'You can't give up on it!' I said.

'Lestat, let me be frank with you,' he said. 'Things are easy for you. What you set your sights on you get for yourself. I know what you're thinking, about all the years you were miserable at home. But even then, what you really set your mind to, you accomplished. And we left for Paris the very day that you decided to do it.'

'You don't regret coming to Paris, do you?' I asked.

'Of course not. I simply mean that you think things are possible which aren't possible! At least not for the rest of us. Like killing the wolves ...'

A coldness passed over me when he said this. And for some reason I thought of that mysterious face again in the audience, the one watching. Something to do with the wolves. Something to do with the sentiments Nicki was expressing. Didn't make sense. I tried to shrug it off.

'If you'd set out to play the violin, you'd probably be playing for the Court by now,' he said.

'Nicki, this kind of talk is poison,' I said under my breath. 'You can't do anything but try to get what you want. You knew the odds were against you when you started. There isn't anything else ... except ...'

'I know.' He smiled. 'Except the meaninglessness. Death.'

'Yes,' I said. 'All you can do is make your life have meaning, make it good —'

'Oh, not goodness again,' he said. 'You and your malady of mortality, and your malady of goodness.' He had been looking at the fire and he turned to me with a deliberately scornful expression. 'We're a pack of actors and entertainers who can't even be buried in consecrated ground. We're outcasts.'

'God, if you could only believe in it,' I said, 'that we do good when we make others forget their sorrow, make them forget for a little while that ...'

'What? That they are going to die?' He smiled in a particularly vicious way. 'Lestat, I thought all this would change with you when you got to Paris.'

'That was foolish of you, Nick,' I answered. He was making me angry now. 'I do good in the boulevard du Temple. I feel it —'

I stopped because I saw the mysterious face again and a dark feeling had passed over me, something of foreboding. Yet even that startling face was usually smiling, that was the odd thing. Yes, smiling ... enjoying ...

'Lestat, I love you,' Nicki said gravely. 'I love you as I have loved few people in my life, but in a real way you're a fool with all your ideas about goodness.'

I laughed.

'Nicolas,' I said, 'I can live without God. I can even come to live with the idea there is no life after. But I do not think I could go on if I did not believe in the possibility of goodness. Instead of mocking me for once, why don't you tell me what you believe?'

'As I see it,' he said, 'there's weakness and there's strength. And there is good art and bad art. And that is what I believe in. At the moment we are engaged in making what is rather bad art and it has *nothing* to do with goodness!'

'Our conversation' could have turned into a full-scale fight here if I had said all that was on my mind about bourgeois pomposity. For I fully believed that our work at Renaud's was in many ways finer than what I saw at the grand theatres. Only the framework was less impressive. Why couldn't a bourgeois gentleman forget about the frame? How could he be made to look at something other than the surface?

I took a deep beath.

'If goodness does exist,' he said, 'then I'm the opposite of it. I'm evil and I revel in it. I thumb my nose at goodness. And if you must know, I don't play the violin for the idiots who come to Renaud's to make them happy. I play it for me, for Nicolas.'

I didn't want to hear any more. It was time to go to bed. But I was bruised by this little talk and he knew it, and as I started to pull off my boots, he got up from the chair and came and sat next to me.

'I'm sorry,' he said in the most broken voice. It was so changed from the posture of a minute ago that I looked up at him, and he was so young and so miserable that I couldn't help putting my arm around him and telling him that he must not worry about it anymore.

'You have a radiance in you, Lestat,' he said. 'And it draws everyone to you. It's there even when you're angry, or discouraged —'

'Poetry,' I said. 'We're both tired.'

'No, it's true,' he said. 'You have a light in you that's almost blinding. But in me there's only darkness. Sometimes I think it's like the darkness that infected you that night in the inn when you began to cry and to tremble. You were so helpless, so unprepared for it. I try to keep that darkness from you because I need your light. I need it desperately, but you don't need the darkness.'

'You're the mad one,' I said. 'If you could see yourself, hear your own voice, your music — which of course you play for yourself — you wouldn't see darkness, Nicki. You'd see an illumination that is all your own. Sombre, yes, but light and beauty come together in you in a thousand different patterns.'

THE next night the performance went especially well. The audience was a lively one, inspiring all of us to extra tricks. I did some new dance steps that for some reason never proved interesting in private rehearsal but worked miraculously on the stage. And Nicki was extraordinary with the violin, playing one of his own compositions.

But towards the end of the evening I glimpsed the mysterious face again. It jarred me worse than it ever had, and I almost lost the rhythm of my song. In fact it seemed my head for a moment was swimming.

When Nicki and I were alone I had to talk about it, about the peculiar sensation that I had fallen asleep on the stage and had been dreaming.

We sat by the hearth together with our wine on the top of a little barrel, and in the firelight Nicki looked as weary and dejected as he had the night before.

I didn't want to trouble him, but I couldn't forget about the face.

'Well, what does he look like?' Nicolas asked. He was warming his hands. And over his shoulder, I saw through the window a city of snowcovered rooftops that made me feel more cold. I didn't like this conversation.

'That's the worst part of it,' I said. 'All I see is a face. He must be wearing something black, a cloak and even a hood. But it looks like a mask to me, the face, very white and strangely clear. I mean the lines in his face are so deep they seemed to be etched with black greasepaint. I see it for a moment. It veritably glows. Then when I look again, there's no one there. Yet this is an exaggeration. It's more subtle than that, the way he looks and yet ...'

The description seemed to disturb Nicki as much as it disturbed me. He didn't say anything. But his face softened somewhat as if he were forgetting his sadness.

'Well, I don't want to get your hopes up,' he said. He was very kind and sincere now. 'But maybe it *is* a mask you're seeing. And maybe it's someone from the Comédie-Française come to see you perform.'

I shook my head. 'I wish it was, but no one would wear a mask like that. And I'll tell you something else, too.'

He waited, but I could see I was passing on to him some of

85

my own apprehension. He reached over and took the wine bottle by the neck and poured a little in my glass.

'Whoever he is,' I said, 'he knows about the wolves.'

'He what?'

'He knows about the wolves.' I was very unsure of myself. It was like recounting a dream I had all but forgotten. 'He knows I killed the wolves back home. He knows the cloak I wear is lined with their fur.'

'What are you talking about? You mean you've spoken to him?'

'No, that's just it,' I said. This was so confusing to me, so vague. I felt that swimming sensation again. 'That's what I'm trying to tell you. I've never spoken to him, never been near him. But he knows.'

'Ah, Lestat,' he said. He sat back on the bench. He was smiling at me in the most endearing way. 'Next you'll be seeing ghosts. You have the strongest imagination of anyone I've ever known.'

'There are no ghosts,' I answered softly. I scowled at our little fire. I laid a few more lumps of coal on it.

All the humour went out of Nicolas.

'How in the hell could he know about the wolves? And how could you ...'

'I told you already, I don't know!' I said. I sat thinking and not saying anything, disgusted, maybe, at how ridiculous it all seemed.

And then as we remained silent together, and the fire was the only sound or movement in the room, the name *Wolfkiller* came to me very distinctly as if someone had spoken it.

But nobody had.

I looked at Nicki, painfully aware that his lips had never moved, and I think all the blood drained from my face. I felt not the dread of death as I had on so many other nights, but an emotion that was really alien to me: fear.

I was still sitting there, too unsure of myself to say anything, when Nicolas kissed me.

'Let's go to bed,' he said softly.

PART II

THE LEGACY

OF

MAGNUS

1

I T MUST have been three o'clock in the morning; I'd heard the church bells in my sleep.

And like all sensible men in Paris, we had our door barred and our window locked. Not good for a room with a coal fire, but the roof was a path to our window. And we were locked in.

I was dreaming of the wolves. I was on the mountain and surrounded and I was swinging the old medieval flail. Then the wolves were dead again, and the dream was better, only I had all those miles to walk in the snow. The horse screamed in the snow. My mare turned into a loathsome insect half smashed on the stone floor.

A voice said 'Wolfkiller' long and low, a whisper that was like a summons and a tribute at the same time.

I opened my eyes. Or I thought I did. And there was someone standing in the room. A tall, bent figure with its back to the little hearth. Embers still glowed on the hearth. The light moved upwards, etching the edges of the figure clearly, then dying out before it reached the shoulders, the head. But I realized I was looking right at the white face I'd seen in the audience at the theatre, and my mind, opening, sharpening, realized the room was locked, that Nicolas lay beside me, that this figure stood over our bed.

I heard Nicolas's breathing. I looked into the white face.

'Wolfkiller,' came the voice again. But the lips hadn't moved, and the figure drew nearer and I saw that the face was no mask. Black eyes, quick and calculating black eyes, and white skin, and some appalling smell coming from it, like the smell of mouldering clothes in a damp room.

I think I rose up. Or perhaps I was lifted. Because in an instant I was standing on my feet. The sleep was slipping off me like garments. I was backing up into the wall.

The figure had my red cloak in its hand. Desperately I thought of my sword, my muskets. They were under the bed on the floor. And the thing thrust the red cloak towards me and then, through the fur-lined velvet, I felt its hand close on the lapel of my coat.

I was torn forward. I was drawn off my feet across the room. I shouted for Nicolas. I screamed, 'Nicki, Nicki!' as loud as I could. I saw the partially opened window, and then suddenly the glass burst into thousands of fragments and the wooden frame was broken out. I was flying over the alleyway, six storeys above the ground.

I screamed. I kicked at this thing that was carrying me. Caught up in the red cloak, I twisted, trying to get loose.

But we were flying over the rooftop, and now going up the straight surface of a brick wall! I was dangling in the arm of the creature, and then very suddenly on the surface of a high place, I was thrown down.

I lay for a moment seeing Paris spread out before me in a great circle — the white snow, and chimney pots and church belfries, and the lowering sky. And then I rose up, stumbling over the fur-lined cloak, and I started to run. I ran to the edge of the roof and looked down. Nothing but a sheer drop of hundreds of feet, and then to another edge and it was exactly the same. I almost fell!

I turned desperate, panting. We were on the top of some square tower, no more than fifty feet across! And I could see nothing higher in any direction. And the figure stood staring at me, and I heard come out of it a low rasping laughter just like the whisper before.

'Wolfkiller,' it said again.

'Damn you!' I shouted, 'Who the hell are you!' And in a rage I flew at it with my fists.

It didn't move. I struck it as if I were striking the brick wall.

I veritably bounced off it, losing my footing in the snow and scrambling up and attacking it again.

Its laughter grew louder and louder, and deliberately mocking, but with a strong undercurrent of pleasure that was even more maddening than the mockery. I ran to the edge of the tower and then turned on the creature again.

'What do you want with me!' I demanded. 'Who are you!' And when it gave nothing but this maddening laughing, I went for it again. But this time I went for the face and the neck, and I made my hands like claws to do it, and I pulled off the hood and saw the creature's black hair and the full shape of its human-looking head. Soft skin. Yet it was as immovable as before.

It backed up a little, raising its arms to play with me, to push me back and forth as a man would push a little child. Too fast for my eyes, it moved its face away from me, turning to one side and then the other, and all of these movements with seeming effortlessness, as I frantically tried to hurt it and could feel nothing but that soft white skin sliding under my fingers and maybe once or twice its fine black hair.

'Brave strong little Wolfkiller,' it said to me now in a rounder, deeper voice.

I stopped, panting and covered with sweat, staring at it and seeing the details of its face. The deep lines I had only glimpsed in the theatre, its mouth drawn up in a jester's smile.

'Oh, God help me, help me ...' I said as I backed away. It seemed impossible that such a face should move, show expression, and gaze with such affection on me as it did. 'God!'

'What god is that, Wolfkiller?' it asked.

I turned my back on it, and let out a terrible roar. I felt its hands close on my shoulders like things forged of metal, and as I went into a last frenzy of struggling, it whipped me around so that its eyes were right before me, wide and dark, and the lips were closed yet still smiling, and then it bent down and I felt the prick of its teeth on my neck.

Out of all the childhood tales, the old fables, the name came to me, like a drowned thing shooting to the surface of black water and breaking free in the light.

'Vampire!' I gave one last frantic cry, shoving at the creature with all I had.

Then there was silence. Stillness.

I knew that we were still on the roof. I knew that I was being held in the thing's arms. Yet it seemed we had risen, become weightless, were travelling through the darkness even more easily than we had travelled before.

'Yes, yes,' I wanted to say, 'exactly.'

And a great noise was echoing all around me, enveloping me, the sound of a deep gong perhaps, being struck very slowly in perfect rhythm, its sound washing through me so that I felt the most extraordinary pleasure through all my limbs.

My lips moved, but nothing came out of them; yet this didn't really matter. All the things I had ever wanted to say were clear to me and that is what mattered, not that they be expressed. And there was so much time, so much sweet time in which to say anything and do anything. There was no urgency at all.

Rapture. I said the word, and it seemed clear to me, that one word, though I couldn't speak or really move my lips. And I realized I was no longer breathing. Yet something was making me breathe. It was breathing for me and the breaths came with the rhythm of the gong which was nothing to do with my body, and I loved it, the rhythm, the way that it went on and on, and I no longer had to breathe or speak or know anything.

My mother smiled at me. And I said, 'I love you …' to her, and she said, 'Yes, always loved, always loved …' And I was sitting in the monastery library and I was twelve years old and the monk said to me, 'A great scholar,' and I opened all the books and could read everything, Latin, Greek, French. The illuminated letters were indescribably beautiful, and I turned around and faced the audience in Renaud's theatre and saw all of them on their feet, and a woman moved the painted fan from in front of her face, and it was Marie Antoinette. She said 'Wolfkiller', and Nicolas was running towards me, crying for me to come back. His face was full of anguish. His hair was loose and his eyes were rimmed with blood. He tried to catch me. I said, 'Nicki, get away from me!' and I realized in agony, positive agony, the sound of the gong was fading away.

I cried out, I begged. Don't stop it, please, please. I don't want to ... I don't ... please.

'Lelio, the Wolfkiller,' said the thing, and it was holding me in its arms and I was crying because the spell was breaking.

'Don't, don't.'

I was heavy all over, my body had come back to me with its aches and its pains and my own choking cries, and I was being lifted, thrown upwards, until I fell over the creature's shoulder and I felt its arm around my knees.

I wanted to say God protect me, I wanted to say it with every particle of me but I couldn't say it, and there was the alleyway below me again, that drop of hundreds of feet, and the whole of Paris tilted at an appalling angle, and there was the snow and the searing wind.

2

I WAS awake and I was very thirsty.

I wanted a great deal of very cold white wine, the way it is when you bring it up out of the cellar in autumn. I wanted something fresh and sweet to eat, like a ripe apple.

It did occur to me that I had lost my reason, though I couldn't have said why.

I opened my eyes and knew it was early evening. The light might have been morning light, but too much time had passed for that. It was evening.

And through a wide, heavily barred stone window I saw hills and woods, blanketed with snow, and the vast tiny collection of rooftops and towers that made up the city far away. I hadn't seen it like this since the day I came in the post carriage. I closed my eyes and the vision of it remained as if I'd never opened my eyes at all.

But it was no vision. It was there. And the room was warm in spite of the window. There had been a fire in the room, I could smell it, but the fire had gone out.

I tried to reason. But I couldn't stop thinking about cold white wine, and apples in the basket. I could see the apples. I felt myself drop down out of the branches of the tree, and I smelled all around me the freshly cut grass.

The sunlight was blinding on the green fields. It shone on Nicolas's brown hair, and on the deep lacquer of the violin. The music climbed up to the soft, rolling clouds. And against the sky I saw the battlements of my father's house.

Battlements.

I opened my eyes again.

And I knew I was lying in a high tower room several miles from Paris.

And just in front of me, on a crude little wooden table, was a bottle of cold white wine, precisely as I had dreamed it.

For a long time I looked at it, looked at the frost of droplets covering it, and I could not believe it possible to reach for it and drink.

Never had I known the thirst I was suffering now. My whole body thirsted. And I was so weak. And I was getting a little cold.

The room moved when I moved. The sky gleamed in the window.

And when at last I did reach for the bottle and pull the cork from it and smell the tart, delicious aroma, I drank and drank without stopping, not caring what would happen to me, or where I was, or why the bottle had been set here.

My head swung forward. The bottle was almost empty and the faraway city was vanishing in the black sky, leaving a little sea of lights behind it.

I put my hands to my head.

The bed on which I'd been sleeping was no more than stone with straw strewn upon it, and it was coming to me slowly that I might be in some sort of jail.

But the wine. It had been too good for a jail. Who would give a prisoner wine like that, unless of course the prisoner was

94

to be executed.

And another aroma came to me, rich and overpowering and so delicious that it made me moan. I looked about, or I should say, I tried to look about because I was almost too weak to move. But the source of this aroma was near to me, and it was a large bowl of beef broth. The broth was thick with bits of meat, and I could see the steam rising from it. It was still hot.

I grabbed it in both hands immediately and I drank it as thoughtlessly and greedily as I'd drunk the wine.

It was so satisfying it was as if I'd never known any food like it, that rich boiled-down essence of the meat, and when the bowl was empty I fell back, full, almost sick, on the straw.

It seemed something moved in the darkness near me. But I was not sure. I heard the chink of glass.

'More wine,' said a voice to me, and I knew the voice.

Gradually, I began remembering everything. Scaling the walls, the small square rooftop, that smiling white face.

For one moment, I thought, No, quite impossible, it must have been a nightmare. But this just wasn't so. It had happened, and I remembered the rapture suddenly, the sound of the gong, and I felt myself grow dizzy as though I were losing consciousness again.

I stopped it. I wouldn't let it happen. And fear crept over me so that I didn't dare to move.

'More wine,' said the voice again.

Turning my head slightly, I saw a new bottle, corked, but ready for me, outlined against the window's luminous glow.

I felt the thirst again, and this time it was heightened by the salt of the broth. I wiped my lips and then I reached for the bottle and again I drank.

I fell back against the stone wall, and I struggled to look clearly through the darkness, half afraid of what I knew I would see.

Of course I was very drunk now.

I saw the window, the city. I saw the little table. And as my eyes moved slowly over the dusky corners of the room, I saw *him* there.

He no longer wore his black hooded cape, and he didn't sit or stand as a man might.

Rather he leaned to rest, it seemed, upon the thick stone frame of the window, one knee bent a little towards it, the other long spindly leg sprawled out to the other side. His arms appeared to hang at his sides.

And the whole impression was of something limp and lifeless, and yet his face was as animated as it had been the night before. Huge black eyes seeming to stretch the white flesh in deep folds, the nose long and thin, and the mouth the jester's smile. There were the fang teeth, just touching the colourless lip, and the hair, a gleaming mass of black and silver growing up high from the white forehead, and flowing down over his shoulders and his arms.

I think that he laughed.

I was beyond terror. I could not even scream.

I had dropped the wine. The glass bottle was rolling on the floor. And as I tried to move forward, to gather my senses and make my body more than something drunken and sluggish, his thin, gangly limbs found animation all at once.

He advanced on me.

I didn't cry out. I gave a low roar of angry terror and scrambled up off the bed, tripping over the small table and running from him as fast as I could.

But he caught me in long white fingers that were as powerful and as cold as they had been the night before.

'Let me go, damn you, damn you, damn you!' I was stammering. My reason told me to plead, and I tried. 'I'll just go away, please. Let me out of here. You have to. Let me go.'

His gaunt face loomed over me, his lips drawn up sharply into his white cheeks, and he laughed a low riotous laugh that seemed endless. I struggled, pushing at him uselessly, pleading with him again, stammering nonsense and apologies, and then I cried, 'God help me!' He clapped one of those monstrous hands over my mouth.

'No more of that in my presence, Wolfkiller, or I'll feed you to the wolves of hell,' he said with a little sneer. 'Hmmmm? Answer me. Hmmmm?'

I nodded and he loosened his grip.

His voice had had a momentary calming effect. He sounded capable of reason when he spoke. He sounded almost sophisticated.

He lifted his hands and stroked my head as I cringed.

'Sunlight in the hair,' he whispered, 'and the blue sky fixed forever in your eyes.' He seemed almost meditative as he looked at me. His breath had no smell whatsoever, nor did his body, it seemed. The smell of mould was coming from his clothes.

I didn't dare to move, though he was not holding me. I stared at his garments.

A ruined silk shirt with bag sleeves and smocking at the neck of it. And worsted leggings and short ragged pantaloons.

In sum he was dressed as men had been centuries before. I had seen such clothes in tapestries in my home, in the paintings of Caravaggio and La Tour that hung in my mother's rooms.

'You're perfect, my Lelio, my Wolfkiller,' he said to me, his long mouth opening wide so that again I saw the small white fangs. They were the only teeth he possessed.

I shuddered. I felt myself dropping to the floor.

But he picked me up easily with one arm and laid me down gently on the bed.

In my mind I was praying fiercely, God help me, the Virgin Mary help me, help me, help me, as I peered up into his face.

What was it I was seeing? What had I seen the night before? The mask of old age, this grinning thing cut deeply with the marks of time and yet frozen, it seemed, and hard as his hands. He wasn't a living thing. He was a monster. A vampire was what he was, a blood-sucking corpse from the grave gifted with intellect!

And his limbs, why did they horrify me? He looked like a human, but he didn't move like a human. It didn't seem to matter to him whether he walked or crawled, bent over or knelt. It filled me with loathing. Yet he fascinated me. I had to admit it. He fascinated me. But I was in too much danger to allow such a strange state of mind.

He gave a deep laugh now, his knees wide apart, his fingers resting on my cheek as he made a great arc over me.

'Yeeeees, lovely one, I'm hard to look at!' he said. His voice was still a whisper and he spoke in long gasps. 'I was old when I was made. And you're perfect, my Lelio, my blue-eyed young one, more beautiful even without the lights of the stage.'

The long white hand played with my hair again, lifting up the strands and letting them drop as he sighed.

'Don't weep, Wolfkiller,' he said. 'You're chosen, and your tawdry little triumphs in the House of Thespians will be nothing once this night comes to its close.'

Again came that low riot of laughter.

There was no doubt in my mind, at least at this moment, that he was from the devil, that God and the devil existed, that beyond the isolation I'd known only hours ago lay this vast realm of dark beings and hideous meanings and I had been swallowed into it somehow.

It occurred to me quite clearly I was being punished for my life, and yet that seemed absurd. Millions believed as I believed the world over. Why the hell was this happening to me? And a grim possibility started irresistibly to take shape, that the world was no more meaningful than before, and this was but another horror...

'In God's name, get away!' I shouted. I *had* to believe in God now. I had to. That was absolutely the only hope. I went to make the Sign of the Cross.

For one moment he stared at me, his eyes wide with rage. And then he remained still.

He watched me make the Sign of the Cross. He listened to me call upon God again and again.

He only smiled, making his face a perfect mask of comedy from the proscenium arch.

And I went into a spasm of crying like a child. 'Then the devil reigns in heaven and heaven is hell,' I said to him. 'Oh, God, don't desert me...' I called on all the saints I had ever for a little while loved.

He struck me hard across the face. I fell to one side and almost slipped from the bed to the floor. The room went round. The sour taste of the wine rose in my mouth.

And I felt his fingers again on my neck.

'Yes, fight, Wolfkiller,' he said. 'Don't go into hell without a battle. Mock God.'

'I don't mock!' I protested.

Once again he pulled me to himself.

And I fought him harder than I had ever fought anyone or anything in my existence, even the wolves. I beat on him, kicked him, tore at his hair. But I might as well have fought the animated gargoyles from a cathedral, he was that powerful.

He only smiled.

Then all the expression went out of his face. It seemed to become very long. The cheeks were hollow, the eyes wide and almost wondering, and he opened his mouth. The lower lip contracted. I saw the fangs.

'Damn you, damn you, damn you!' I was roaring and bellowing. And he drew closer and the teeth went through my flesh.

Not this time, I was raging, not this time. I will not feel it. I will resist. I will fight for my soul *this* time.

But it was happening again.

The sweetness and the softness and the world far away, and even he in his ugliness was curiously outside of me, like an insect pressed against a glass who causes no loathing in us because he cannot touch us, and the sound of the gong, and the exquisite pleasure, and then I was altogether lost. I was incorporeal and the pleasure was incorporeal. I was nothing but pleasure. And I slipped into a web of radiant dreams.

A catacomb I saw, a rank place. And a white vampire creature waking in a shallow grave. Bound in heavy chains he was, the vampire; and over him bent this monster who had abducted me, and I knew that his name was Magnus, and that he was mortal still in this dream, a great and powerful alchemist. And he had unearthed and bound this slumbering vampire right before the crucial hour of dusk.

And now as the light died out of the heavens, Magnus drank from his helpless immortal prisoner the magical and accursed blood that would make him one of the living dead.

Treachery it was, the thief of immortality. A dark Prometheus stealing a luminescent fire. Laughter in the darkness. Laughter echoing in the catacomb. Echoing as if down the centuries. And the stench of the grave. And the ecstasy, absolutely fathomless, and irresistible, and then drawing to a finish.

I was crying. I lay on the straw and I said:

'Please, don't stop it ...'

Magnus was no longer holding me and my breathing was once again my own, and the dreams were dissolved. I fell down and down as the nightful of stars slid upwards, jewels affixed to a dark purple veil. 'Clever that. I had thought the sky was ... real.'

The cold winter air was moving just a little in this room. I felt the tears on my face. I was consumed with thirst!

And far, far away from me, Magnus stood looking down at me, his hands dangling low beside his thin legs.

I tried to move. I was craving. My whole body was thirsty.

'You're dying, Wolfkiller,' he said. 'The light's going out of your blue eyes as if all the summer days are gone ...'

'No, please ...' This thirst was unbearable. My mouth was open, gaping, my back arched. And it was here at last, the final horror, death itself, like this.

'Ask for it, child,' he said, his face no longer the grinning mask, but utterly transformed with compassion. He looked almost human, almost naturally old. 'Ask and you shall receive,' he said.

I saw water rushing down all the mountain streams of my childhood. 'Help me. Please.'

'I shall give you the water of all waters,' he said in my ear, and it seemed he wasn't white at all. He *was* just an old man, sitting there beside me. His face *was* human, and almost sad.

But as I watched his smile and his grey eyebrows rise in wonder, I knew it wasn't true. He wasn't human. He was that same ancient monster only he was filled with my blood!

'The wine of all wines,' he breathed. 'This is my Body, this is my Blood. And then his arms surrounded me. They drew me to him and I felt a great warmth emanating from him, and he seemed to be filled not with blood but with love for me.

'Ask for it, Wolfkiller, and you will live forever,' he said, but his voice sounded weary and spiritless, and there was something distant and tragic in his gaze.

I felt my head turn to the side, my body a heavy and damp thing that I couldn't control. I will not ask, I will die without asking, and then the great despair I feared so much lay before me, the emptiness that was death, and still I said No. In pure horror I said No. I will not bow down to it, the chaos and the horror. I said No.

'Life everlasting,' he whispered.

My head fell on his shoulder.

'Stubborn Wolfkiller.' His lips touched me, warm, odourless breath on my neck.

'Not stubborn,' I whispered. My voice was so weak I wondered if he could hear me. 'Brave. Not stubborn.' It seemed pointless not to say it. What was vanity now? What was anything at all? And such a trivial word was stubborn, so cruel ...

He lifted my face, and holding me with his right hand, he lifted his left hand and gashed his own throat with his nails.

My body bent double in a convulsion of terror, but he pressed my face to the wound, as he said: 'Drink.'

I heard my scream, deafening in my own ears. And the blood that was flowing out of the wound touched my parched and cracking lips.

The thirst seemed to hiss aloud. My tongue licked at the blood. And a great whiplash of sensation caught me. And my mouth opened and locked itself to the wound. I drew with all my power upon the great fount that I knew would satisfy my thirst as it had never been satisfied before.

Blood and blood and blood. And it was not merely the dry hissing coil of the thirst that was quenched and dissolved, it was all my craving, all the want and misery and hunger that I had ever known.

My mouth widened, pressed harder to him. I felt the blood coursing down the length of my throat. I felt his head against me. I felt the tight enclosure of his arms.

I was against him and I could feel his sinews, his bones, the very contour of his hands. I *knew* his body. And yet there was this numbness creeping through me and a rapturous tingling as each sensation penetrated the numbness, and was amplified in the penetration so that it became fuller, keener, and I could almost see what I felt.

But the supreme part of it remained the sweet, luscious blood filling me, as I drank and drank.

More of it, more, this was all I could think, if I thought at all, and for all its thick substance, it was like light passing into me, so brilliant did it seem to the mind, so blinding, that red stream, and all the desperate desires of my life were a thousandfold fed.

But his body, the scaffolding to which I clung, was weakening beneath me. I could hear his breath in feeble gasps. Yet he didn't make me stop.

Love you, I wanted to say, Magnus, my unearthly master, ghastly thing that you are, love you, love you, this was what I had always so wanted, wanted, and could never have, this, and you've given it to me!

I felt I would die if it went on, and on it did go, and I did not die.

But quite suddenly I felt his gentle loving hands caressing my shoulders and with his incalculable strength, he forced me backwards.

I let out a long mournful cry. Its misery alarmed me. But he was pulling me to my feet. He still held me in his arms.

He brought me to the window, and I stood looking out, with my hands out to the stone on either side. I was shaking and the blood in me pulsed in all my veins. I leaned my forehead against the iron bars.

Far far below lay the dark cusp of a hill, overgrown with trees that appeared to shimmer in the faint light of the stars.

And beyond, the city with its wilderness of little lights sunk not in darkness but in a soft violet mist. The snow everywhere was luminescent, melting. Rooftops, towers, walls, all were myriad facets of lavender, mauve, rose.

This was the sprawling metropolis.

And as I narrowed my eyes, I saw a million windows like so

many projections of beams of light, and then as if this were not enough, in the very depths I saw the unmistakable movement of the people. Tiny mortals on tiny streets, heads and hands touching in the shadows, a lone man, no more than a speck ascending a windblown belfry. A million souls on the tessellated surface of the night, and coming soft on the air a dim mingling of countless human voices. Cries, songs, the faintest wisps of music, the muted throb of bells.

I moaned. The breeze seemed to lift my hair and I heard my own voice as I had never heard it before crying.

The city dimmed. I let it go, its swarming millions lost again in the vast and wondrous play of lilac shadow and fading light.

'Oh, what have you done, what is this that you've given to me!' I whispered.

And it seemed my words did not stop one after another, rather they ran together until all of my crying was one immense and coherent sound that perfectly amplified my horror and my joy.

If there was a God, he did not matter now. He was part of some dull and dreary realm whose secrets had long ago been plundered, whose lights had long ago gone out. This was the pulsing centre of life itself round which all true complexity revolved. Ah, the allure of that complexity, the sense of being *there* ...

Behind me the scratch of the monster's feet came on the stones.

And when I turned I saw him white and bled dry and like a great husk of himself. His eyes were stained with blood-red tears and he reached out to me as if in pain.

I gathered him to my chest. I felt such love for him as I had never known before.

'Ah, don't you see?' came the ghastly voice with its long words, whispers without end, 'My heir chosen to take the Dark Gift from me with more fibre and courage than ten mortal men, what a Child of Darkness you are to be.'

I kissed his eyelids. I gathered his soft black hair in my hands. He was no ghastly thing to me now but merely that which was strange and white, and full of some deeper lesson perhaps than the sighing trees below or the shimmering cry calling me over the miles.

His sunken cheeks, his long throat, the thin legs ... these were but the natural parts of him.

'No, fledgling,' he sighed. 'Save your kisses for the world. My time has come and you owe me but one obeisance only. Follow me now.'

3

DOWN a winding stair he drew me. And everything I beheld absorbed me. The rough-cut stones seemed to give forth their own light, and even the rats shooting past in the dark had a curious beauty.

Then he unlocked a thick iron-studded wooden door and, giving over his heavy key ring to me, led me into a large and barren room.

'You are now my heir, as I told you,' he said. 'You'll take possession of this house and all my treasure. But you'll do as I say first.'

The barred windows give a limitless view of the moonlit clouds, and I saw the soft shimmering city again as if it were spreading its arms.

'Ah, later you may drink your fill of all you see,' he said. He turned me towards him as he stood before a huge heap of wood that lay in the centre of the floor.

'Listen carefully,' he said. 'For I'm about to leave you.' He gestured to the wood offhandedly. 'And there are things you must know. You're immortal now. And your nature shall lead you soon enough to your first human victim. Be swift and show no mercy. But stop your feasting, no matter how delicious, before the victim's heart ceases to beat.

'In years to come, you'll be strong enough to feel that great moment, but for the present pass the cup to time just before it's empty. Or you may pay heavily for your pride.'

'But why are you leaving me!' I asked desperately. I clung to him. Victims, mercy, feasting … I felt myself bombarded by these words as if I were being physically beaten.

He pulled away so easily that my hands were hurt by his movement, and I wound up staring at them, marvelling at the strange quality of the pain. It wasn't like mortal pain.

He stopped, however, and pointed to the stones of the wall opposite. I could see that one very large stone had been dislodged and lay a foot from the unbroken surface around it.

'Grasp that stone,' he said, 'and pull it out of the wall.'

'But I can't,' I said. 'It must weigh —'

'Pull it out!' He pointed with one of his long bony fingers and grimaced so that I tried to do it as he said.

To my pure astonishment I was able to move the stone easily, and I saw beyond it a dark opening just large enough for a man to enter if he crawled on his face.

He gave a dry cackling laugh and nodded his head.

'There, my son, is the passageway that leads to my treasure,' he said. 'Do with my treasure as you like, and with all my earthly property. But for now, I must have my vows.'

And again astonishing me, he snatched up two twigs from the wood and rubbed them together so fiercely they were soon burning with bright small flames.

This he tossed at the heap, and the pitch in it caused the fire to leap up at once, throwing an immense light over the curved ceiling and the stone walls.

I gasped and stepped back. The riot of yellow and orange colour enchanted and frightened me, and the heat, though I felt it, did not cause me a sensation. I understood. There was no natural alarm that I should be burned by it. Rather the warmth was exquisite and I realized for the first time how cold I had been. The cold was an icing on me and the fire melted it and I almost moaned.

He laughed again, that hollow, gasping laugh, and started to dance about in the light, his thin legs making him look like a skeleton dancing, with the white face of a man. He crooked his arms over his head, bent his torso and his knees, and turned round and round as he circled the fire.

'*Mon Dieu!*' I whispered. I was reeling. Horrifying it might have been only an hour ago to see him dancing like this, but now in the flickering glare he was a spectacle that drew me after it step by step. The light exploded on his satin rags, the pantaloons he wore, the tattered shirt.

'But you can't leave me!' I pleaded, trying to keep my thoughts clear, trying to realize what he had been saying. My voice was monstrous in my ears. I tried to make it lower, softer, more like it should have been. 'Where will you go!'

He gave his loudest laugh then, slapping his thigh and dancing faster and farther away from me, his hands out as if to embrace the fire.

The thickest logs were only now catching. The room for all it size was like a great clay oven, smoke pouring out its windows.

'Not the fire.' I flew backwards, flattening myself against the wall. 'You can't go into the fire!'

Fear was overwhelming me, as every sight and sound had overwhelmed me. It was like every sensation I had known so far. I couldn't resist it or deny it. I was half whimpering and half screaming.

'Oh, yes I can,' he laughed. 'Yes, I can!' He threw back his head and let his laughter stretch into howls. 'But from you, fledgling,' he said, stopping before me with his finger out again, 'promises now. Come, a little mortal honour, my brave Wolfkiller, or though it will cleave my heart in two, I shall throw you into the fire and claim for myself another offspring. Answer me!'

I tried to speak. I nodded my head.

In the raging light I could see my hands had become white. And I felt a stab of pain in my lower lip that almost made me cry out.

My eyeteeth had become fangs already! I felt them and looked to him in panic, but he was leering at me as if he enjoyed my terror.

'Now, after I am burned up,' he said, snatching my wrist, 'and the fire is out, you *must* scatter the ashes. Hear me, little one. Scatter the ashes. Or else I might return, and in what shape that would be, I dare not contemplate. But mark my words, if you allow me to come back, more hideous than I am now, I shall hunt you down and burn you till you are scarred the same as I, do you hear me?'

I still couldn't bring myself to answer. This was not fear. It was hell. I could feel my teeth growing and my body tingling all over. Frantically, I nodded my head.

'Ah, yes.' He smiled, nodding too, the fire licking the ceiling behind him, the light leaking all about the edges of his face. 'It's only mercy I ask, that I go now to find hell, if there is a hell, or sweet oblivion which surely I do not deserve. If there is a Prince of Darkness, then I shall set eyes upon him at last. I shall spit in his face.

'So scatter what is burned, as I command you, and when that is done, take yourself to my lair through that low passage, being most careful to replace the stone behind you as you enter there. Within you will find my coffin. And in that box or the like of it, you must seal yourself by day or the sun's light shall burn you to a cinder. Mark my words, nothing on earth can end your life save the sun, or a blaze such as you see before you, and even then, only, and I say, only if your ashes are scattered when it is done.'

I turned my face away from him and away from the flames. I had begun to cry and the only thing that kept me from sobbing was the hand I clapped to my mouth.

But he pulled me about the edge of the fire until we stood before the loose stone, his finger pointing at it again.

'Please stay with me, please,' I begged him. 'Only a little while, only one night, I beg you!' Again the volume of my voice terrified me. It wasn't my voice at all. I put my arms around him. I held tight to him. His gaunt white face was inexplicably beautiful to me, his black eyes filled with the strangest expression.

The light flickered on his hair, his eyes, and then again he made his mouth into a jester's smile.

'Ah, greedy son,' he said. 'Is it not enough to be immortal with all the world your repast? Good-bye, little one. Do as I say. Remember, the ashes! And beyond this stone the inner chamber. Therein lies all that you will need to prosper.'

I struggled to hold on to him. And he laughed low in my ear, marvelling at my strength. 'Excellent, excellent,' he whispered. 'Now, live forever, beautiful Wolfkiller, with the gifts nature gave you, and discover for yourself all those most unnatural gifts which I have added to the lot.'

He sent me stumbling away from him. And he leapt so high and so far into the very middle of the flames he appeared to be flying.

I saw him descend. I saw the fire catch his garments.

It seemed his mouth became a torch, and then all of a sudden his eyes grew wide, and his mouth became a great black cavern in the radiance of the flames and his laughter rose in such piercing volume, I covered my ears.

He appeared to jump up and down on all fours in the flames, and suddenly I realized that my cries had drowned out his laughter.

The spindly black arms and legs rose and fell, rose and fell and then suddenly appeared to wither. The fire shifted, roared. And in the heart of it I could see nothing now but the blaze itself.

Yet still I cried. I fell down upon my knees, my hands over my eyes. But against my closed lids I could still see it, one vast explosion of sparks after another until I pressed my forehead on the stones.

4

OR years it seemed I lay on the floor watching the fire burn itself out to charred timbers.

The room had cooled. The freezing air moved through the open window. And again and again I wept. My own sobs reverberated in my ears until I felt I couldn't endure the sound of them. And it was no comfort to know that all things were magnified in this state, even the misery that I felt.

Now and then I prayed again. I begged for forgiveness, though forgiveness for what I couldn't have said. I prayed to the Blessed Mother, to the saints. I murmured the Aves over and over until they became a senseless chant.

And my tears were blood, and they left their stain on my hands when I wiped at my face.

Then I lay flat on the stones, murmuring not prayers any longer but those inarticulate pleas we make to all that is powerful, all that is holy, all that may or may not exist by any and all names. Do not leave me alone here. Do not abandon me. I am in the witches' place. It's the witches' place. Do not let me fall even farther than I have already fallen this night. Do not let it happen ... *Lestat, wake up.*

But Magnus's words came back to me, over and over: *To find hell, if there is a hell ... If there is a Prince of Darkness ...*

Finally I rose on my hands and knees. I felt light-headed and mad, and almost giddy. I looked at the fire and saw that I might still bring it back to a roaring blaze and throw myself into it.

But even as I forced myself to imagine the agony of this, I knew that I had no intention of doing it.

After all, why should I do it? What had I done to deserve the witches' fate? I didn't want to be in hell, even for a moment. I sure as hell wasn't going there just to spit in the face of the Prince of Darkness, whoever he might be!

On the contrary, if I was a damned thing, then let the son of a bitch come for me! Let him tell me why I was meant to suffer. I would truly like to know.

As for oblivion, well, we can wait a little while for that. We can think this over, for a little while ... at least.

An alien calm crept slowly over me. It was dark, full of bitterness and growing fascination.

I wasn't human anymore.

And as I crouched there thinking about it, and looking at the dying embers, an immense strength was gathering in me. Gradually my boyish sobs died away. And I commenced to study the whiteness of my skin, the sharpness of the two evil little teeth, and the way that my fingernails gleamed in the dark as though they'd been lacquered.

All the little familiar aches were going out of my body. And the remaining warmth that came from the smoking wood was good to me, as something laid over me or wrapped about me.

Time passed; yet it did not pass.

Each change in the moving air was caressing. And when there came from the softly lighted city beyond a chorus of dim church bells ringing the hour, they did not mark the passage of mortal time. They were only the purest music, and I lay stunned, my mouth open, as I stared at the passing clouds.

But in my chest I started to feel a new pain, very hot and mercurial.

It moved through my veins, tightened about my head, and then seemed to collect itself in my bowels and belly. I narrowed my eyes. I cocked my head to one side. I realized I wasn't afraid of this pain, rather I was feeling it as if I were listening to it.

And I saw the cause of it then. My waste was leaving me in a small torrent. I found myself unable to control it. Yet as I watched the foulness stain my clothes, this didn't disgust me.

Rats creeping into the very room, approaching this filth on their tiny soundless feet, even these did not disgust me.

These things couldn't touch me, even as they crawled over me to devour the waste.

In fact, I could imagine nothing in the dark, not even the slithering insects of the grave, that could bring about revulsion in me. Let them crawl on my hands and face, it wouldn't matter now.

I wasn't part of the world that cringed at such things. And with a smile, I realized that I was of that dark ilk that makes others cringe. Slowly and with great pleasure, I laughed.

And yet my grief was not entirely gone from me. It lingered like an idea, and the idea had a pure truth to it.

I am gone, I am a vampire. And things will die so that I may live; I will drink their blood so that I may live. And I will never, never see Nicolas again, nor my mother, nor any of the humans I have known and loved, nor any of my human family. I'll drink blood. And I'll live forever. That is exactly what will *be*. And what will *be* is only beginning; it is just born! And the labour that brought it forth was rapture such as I have never known.

I climbed to my feet. I felt myself light and powerful, and strangely numbed, and I went to the dead fire, and walked through the burnt timbers.

There were no bones. It was as if the fiend had disintegrated. What ashes I could gather in my hands I took to the window. And as the wind caught them, I whispered a farewell to Magnus, wondering if he could yet hear me.

At last only charred logs were left and the soot that I wiped up with my hands and dusted off into the darkness.

It was time now to examine the inner room.

5

THE stone moved out easily enough, as I'd seen before, and it had a hook on the inside of it by which I could pull it closed behind me.

But to get into the narrow dark passage I had to lie on my belly. And when I dropped down on my knees and peered into it, I could see no visible light at the end. I didn't like the look of it.

I knew that if I'd been mortal still, nothing could have induced me to crawl into a passage like this.

But the old vampire had been plain enough in telling me the sun could destroy me as surely as the fire. I had to get to the coffin. And I felt the fear coming back in a deluge.

I got down flat on the ground, and crawled as a lizard might into the passage. As I feared, I could not really raise my head. And there was no room to turn and reach for the hook in the stone. I had to slip my foot into the hook and crawl forward to pull the stone behind me.

Total darkness. With room to rise only a few inches on my elbows.

I gasped, and the fear welled and I almost went mad thinking about the fact that I couldn't raise my head and finally I smacked it against the stone and lay still, whimpering.

But what was I to do? I must reach the coffin.

So telling myself to stop this whining, I commenced to crawl, faster and faster. My knees scraped the stone. My hands sought crevices and cracks to pull me along. My neck ached with the strain as I struggled not to try to lift my head again in panic.

And when my head suddenly felt solid stone ahead, I pushed upon it with all my strength. I felt it move as a pale light seeped in.

I scrambled out of the passage, and found myself standing in a small room.

The ceiling was low, curved, and the high window was narrow with the familiar heavy grid of iron bars. But the sweet, violet light of the night poured in revealing a great fireplace cut in the far wall, the wood ready for the torch, and beside it, beneath the window, an ancient stone sarcophagus.

My red velvet fur-lined cape lay over the sarcophagus. And on a rude bench I glimpsed a splendid suit of red velvet worked with gold, and much Italian lace, as well as red silk breeches and white silk hose and red-heeled slippers.

I smoothed back my hair from my face and wiped the thin film of sweat from my upper lip and my forehead. It was bloody, this sweat, and when I saw this on my hands, I felt a curious excitement.

Ah, what am I, I thought, and what lies before me? For a long moment I looked at this blood and then I licked my fingers. A lovely zinging pleasure passed through me. It was a moment before I could collect myself sufficiently to approach the fireplace.

I lifted two sticks of kindling as the old vampire had done and, rubbing them very hard and fast, saw them almost disappear as the flame shot up from them. There was no magic in this, only skill. And as the fire warmed me, I took off my soiled clothes, and with my shirt wiped every last trace of human waste away, and threw all this in the fire, before putting on the new garments.

Red, dazzling red. Not even Nicolas had had such clothes as these. They were clothes for the Court at Versailles, with pearls and tiny rubies worked into their embroidery. The lace of the shirt was Valenciennes, which I had seen on my mother's wedding gown.

I put the wolf cape over my shoulders. And though the white chill was gone from my limbs, I felt like a creature carved from ice. My smile felt hard and glittering to me and strangely slow as I allowed myself to feel and to see these garments.

In the blaze of the fire, I looked at the coffin. The effigy of an old man was carved upon its heavy lid, and I realized immediately it was the likeness of Magnus.

But here he lay in tranquillity, his jester's mouth sealed, his eyes staring mildly at the ceiling, his hair a neat mane of deeply carved waves and ringlets.

Three centuries old was this thing surely. He lay with his hands folded on his chest, his garments long robes, and from his sword that had been carved into the stone, someone had broken out the hilt and part of the scabbard.

I stared at this for an interminable length of time, seeing that it had been carefully chipped away with much effort.

Was it the shape of the cross that someone had sought to remove? I traced it over with my fingers. Nothing happened of course, any more than when I'd murmured all those prayers. And squatting in the dust beside the coffin, I drew a cross there.

Again, nothing.

Then to the cross I added a few strokes to suggest the body of Christ, his arms, the crook of his knees, his bowed head. I wrote 'The Lord Jesus Christ', the only words I could write well, save for my own name, and again nothing.

And still glancing back uneasily at the words and the little crucifix, I tried to lift the lid of the coffin.

Even with this new strength, it was not easy. And no mortal

man alone could have done it.

But what perplexed me was the extent of my difficulty. I did not have limitless strength. And certainly I didn't have the strength of the old vampire. Maybe the strength of three men was what I now possessed, or the strength of four; it was impossible to calculate.

It seemed pretty damned impressive to me at the moment.

I looked into the coffin. Nothing but a narrow place, full of shadows, where I couldn't imagine myself lying. There were Latin words inscribed around the rim, and I couldn't read them.

This tormented me. I wished the words weren't there, and my longing for Magnus, my helplessness, threatened to close in on me. I hated him for leaving me! And it struck me with full ironic force that I'd felt love for him before he'd leapt into the fire. I'd felt love for him when I saw the red garments.

Do devils love each other? Do they walk arm in arm in hell saying, 'Ah, you are my friend, how I love you,' things like that to each other? It was a rather detached intellectual question I was asking, as I did not believe in hell. But it was a matter of a concept of evil, wasn't it? All creatures in hell are supposed to hate one another, as all the saved hate the damned, without reservation.

I'd known that all my life. It had terrified me as a child, the idea that I might go to heaven and my mother might go to hell and that I should hate her. I couldn't hate her. And what if we were in hell together?

Well, now I know, whether I believe in hell or not, that vampires can love each other, that in being dedicated to evil, one does not cease to love. Or so it seemed for that brief instant. But don't start crying again. I can't abide all this crying.

I turned my eyes to a large wooden chest that was partially hidden at the head of the coffin. It wasn't locked. Its rotted wooden lid fell almost off the hinges when I opened it.

And though the old master had said he was leaving me his treasure, I was flabbergasted by what I saw there. The chest was crammed with gems and gold and silver. There were countless jewelled rings, diamond necklaces, ropes of pearls, plate and coins and hundreds upon hundreds of miscellaneous valuables.

I ran my fingers lightly over the heap and then held up handfuls of it, gasping as the light ignited the red of the rubies, the green of the emeralds. I saw refractions of colour of which I'd never dreamed, and wealth beyond any calculation. It was the fabled Caribbean pirates' chest, the proverbial king's ransom.

And it was mine now.

More slowly I examined it. Scattered throughout were personal and perishable articles. Satin masks rotting away from their trimming of gold, lace handkerchiefs and bits of cloth to which were fixed pins and brooches. Here was a strip of leather harness hung with gold bells, a mouldering bit of lace slipped through a ring, snuffboxes by the dozens, lockets on velvet ribbon.

Had Magnus taken all this from his victims?

I lifted up a jewel-encrusted sword, far too heavy for these times, and a worn slipper saved perhaps for its rhinestone buckle.

Of course he had taken what he wanted. Yet he himself had worn rags, the tattered costume of another age, and he lived here as a hermit might have lived in some earlier century. I couldn't understand it.

But there were other objects scattered about in this treasure. Rosaries made up of gorgeous gems, and they still had their crucifixes! I touched the small sacred images. I shook my head and bit my lip, as if to say, How awful that he should have stolen these! But I also found it very funny. And further proof that God had no power over me.

And as I was thinking about this, trying to decide if it was as fortuitous as it seemed for the moment, I lifted from the treasure an exquisite pearlhandled mirror.

I looked into it almost unconsciously as one often glances in mirrors. And there I saw myself as a man might expect, except that my skin was very white, as the old fiend's had been white, and my eyes had been transformed from their usual blue to a mingling of violet and cobalt that was softly iridescent. My hair had a high luminous sheen, and when I ran my fingers back through it I felt a new and strange vitality there.

In fact, this was not Lestat in the mirror at all, but some replica of him made of other substances! And the few lines time had given me by the age of twenty years were gone or greatly simplified and just a little deeper than they had been.

I stared at my reflection. I became frantic to discover *myself* in it. I rubbed my face, even rubbed the mirror and pressed my lips together to keep from crying.

Finally I closed my eyes and opened them again, and I smiled very gently at the creature. He smiled back. That was Lestat, all right. And there seemed nothing in his face that was any way malevolent. Well, not very malevolent. Just the old mischief, the impulsiveness. He could have been an angel, in fact, this creature, except that when his tears did rise, they were red, and the entire image was tinted red because his vision was red. And he had these evil little teeth that he could press into his lower lip when he smiled that made him look absolutely terrifying. A good enough face with one thing horribly, horribly wrong with it!

But it suddenly occurred to me, I am looking at my own reflection! And hadn't it been said enough that ghosts and spirits and those who have lost their souls to hell have no reflections in mirrors?

A lust to know all things about what I was came over me. A lust to know how I should walk among mortal men. I wanted to be in the streets of Paris, seeing with my new eyes all the miracles of life that I'd ever glimpsed. I wanted to see the faces of the people, to see the flowers in bloom, and the butterflies. To see Nicki, to hear Nicki play his music — no.

Forswear that. But there were a thousand forms of music, weren't there? And as I closed my eyes I could almost hear the orchestra of the Opéra, the arias rising in my ears. So sharp the recollection, so clear.

But nothing would be ordinary now. Not joy or pain, or the simplest memory. All would possess this magnificent lustre, even grief for the things that were forever lost.

I put down the mirror, and taking one of the old yellowed

lace handkerchiefs from the chest, I wiped my tears. I turned and sat down slowly before the fire. Delicious the warmth on my face and hands.

A great sweet drowsiness came over me and as I closed my eyes again I felt myself immersed suddenly in the strange dream of Magnus stealing the blood. A sense of enchantment returned, of dizzying pleasure — Magnus holding me, connected to me, my blood flowing into him. But I heard the chains scraping the floor of the old catacomb, I saw the defenseless vampire thing in Magnus's arms. Something more to it ... something important. A meaning. About theft, treachery, about surrendering to no one, not God, not demon and never man.

I thought and thought about it, half awake, half dreaming again, and the maddest thought came to me, that I would tell Nicki all about this, that as soon as I got home I would lay it all out, the dream, the possible meaning and we would talk —

With an ugly shock, I opened my eyes. The human in me looked helplessly about this chamber. He started to weep again and the newborn fiend was too young yet to rein him in. The sobs came up like hiccups and I put my hand over my mouth.

Magnus, why did you leave me? Magnus, what I am supposed to do, how do I go on?

I drew up my knees and rested my head on them, and slowly my head began to clear.

Well, it has been great fun pretending you will be this vampire creature, I thought, wearing these splendid clothes, running your fingers through all that glorious lucre. But you can't live as this! You can't feed on living beings! Even if you are a monster, you have a conscience in you, natural to you ... Good and Evil, good and evil. You cannot live without believing in — You cannot abide the acts that — Tomorrow you will ... you will ... you will what?

You will drink blood, won't you?

The gold and the precious stones glowed like embers in the nearby chest, and beyond the bars of the window, there rose against the grey clouds the violet shimmer of the distant city. What *is* their blood like? Hot living blood, not monster blood.

My tongue pushed at the roof of my mouth, at my fangs.

Think on it, Wolfkiller.

I ROSE to my feet slowly. It was as if the will made it happen rather than the body, so easy was it. And I picked up the iron key ring which I'd brought with me from the outer chamber and I went to inspect the rest of my tower.

6

EMPTY chambers. Barred windows. The great endless sweep of the night above the battlements. That is all I found above ground.

But on the lower floor of the tower, just outside the door to the dungeon stairs, there was a resin torch in the sconce, and a tinderbox in the niche beside it. Tracks in the dust. The lock well oiled and easy to turn when I finally found the right key for it.

I shone the torch before me on a narrow screw stairway and started down, a little repelled by a stench that rose from somewhere quite far below me.

Of course I knew that stench. It was common enough in every cemetery in Paris. In les Innocents it was thick as noxious gas, and you had to live with it to shop the stalls there, deal with the letter writers. It was the stench of decomposing bodies.

And though it sickened me, made me back up a few steps, it wasn't all that strong, and the odour of the burning resin helped to subdue it.

I went on down. If there were dead mortals here, well, I couldn't run away from them.

But on the first level beneath the ground, I found no corpses. Only a vast cool burial chamber with its rusted iron doors open to the stairs, and three giant stone sarcophagi in the centre of it. It was very like Magnus's cell above, only much larger. It had the same low curved ceiling, the same crude and gaping fireplace.

And what could that mean, except that other vampires had once slept here? No one puts fireplaces in burial vaults. At least not that I had ever known. And there were even stone benches here. And the sarcophagi were like the one above, with great figures carved on them.

But years of dust overlay everything. And there were so many spiderwebs. Surely no vampires dwelt here now. Quite impossible. Yet it was very strange. Where were those who had lain in these coffins? Had they burnt themselves up like Magnus? Or were they still existing somewhere?

I went in and opened the sarcophagi one by one. Nothing but dust inside. No evidence of other vampires at all, no indication that any other vampires existed.

I went out and continued down the stairway, even though the smell of the decay grew stronger and stronger. In fact, it very quickly became unbearable.

It was coming from behind a door that I could see below, and I had real difficulty in making myself approach it. Of course as a mortal man I'd loathed this smell, but that was nothing to the aversion I felt now. My new body wanted to run from it. I stopped, took a deep breath, and forced myself towards the door, determined to see what this fiend had done here.

Well, the stench was nothing to the sight of it.

In a deep prison cell lay a heap of corpses in all states of decay, the bones and rotted flesh crawling with worms and insects. Rats ran from the light of the torch, brushing past my legs as they made for the stairs. And my nausea became a knot in my throat. The stench suffocated me.

But I couldn't stop staring at these bodies. There was something important here, something terribly important, to be realized. And it came to me suddenly that all these dead victims had been men — their boots and ragged clothing gave evidence of that — and every single one of them had yellow hair, very much like my own hair. The few who had features

119

left appeared to be young men, tall, slight of build. And the most recent occupant here — the wet and reeking corpse that lay with its arms outstretched through the bars — so resembled me that he might have been a brother.

In a daze, I moved forward until the tip of my boot touched his head. I lowered the torch, my mouth opening as if to scream. The wet sticky eyes that swarmed with gnats were blue eyes!

I stumbled backwards. A wild fear gripped me that the thing would move, grab hold of my ankle. And I knew why it would. As I drew up against the wall, I tripped on a plate of rotted food and a pitcher. The pitcher went over and broke, and out of it the curdled milk spilled like vomit.

Pain circled my ribs. Blood came up like liquid fire into my mouth and it shot out of my lips, splashing on the floor in front of me. I had to reach for the open door to steady myself.

But through the haze of nausea, I stared at the blood. I stared at the gorgeous crimson colour of it in the light of the torch. I watched the blood darken as it sank into the mortar between the stones. The blood was alive and the sweet smell of it cut like a blade through the stench of the dead. Spasms of thirst drove away the nausea. My back was arching. I was bending lower and lower to the blood with astonishing elasticity.

And all the while, my thoughts raced. This young man had been alive in this cell; this rotted food and milk were here either to nourish or torment him. He had died in the cell, trapped with those corpses, knowing full well he would soon be one of them.

God, to suffer that! To suffer that! And how many others had known exactly the same fate, young men with yellow hair, all of them.

I was down on my knees and bending over. I held the torch low with my left hand and my head went all the way down to the blood, my tongue flashing out of my mouth so that I saw it like the tongue of a lizard. It scraped at the blood on the floor. Shivers of ecstasy. Oh, too lovely!

Was I doing this? Was I lapping up this blood not two

inches from this dead body? Was my heart heaving with every taste not two inches from this dead boy whom Magnus had brought here as he brought me? This boy that Magnus had then condemned to death instead of immortality?

The filthy cell flickered on and off like a flame as I licked up the blood. The dead man's hair touched my forehead. His eye like a fractured crystal stared at me.

Why wasn't I locked in this cell? What test had I passed that I was not screaming now as I shook the bars, the horror that I had foreseen in the village inn slowly closing in on me?

The blood tremors passed through my arms and legs. And the sound I heard — the gorgeous sound, as enthralling as the crimson of the blood, the blue of the boy's eye, the glistening wings of the gnat, the sliding opaline body of the worm, the blaze of the torch — was my own raw and guttural screaming.

I dropped the torch and struggled backwards on my knees, crashing against the tin plate and the broken pitcher. I climbed to my feet and ran up the stairway. And as I slammed shut the dungeon door, my screams rose up and up to the very top of the tower.

I was lost in the sound as it bounced off the stones and came back at me. I couldn't stop, couldn't close my mouth or cover it.

But through the barred entranceway and through a dozen narrow windows above I saw the unmistakable light of morning coming. My screams died. The stones had begun to glow. The light seeped around me like scalding steam, burning my eyelids.

I made no decision to run. I was simply doing it, running up and up to the inner chamber.

As I came out of the passage, the room was full of a dim purple fire. The jewels overflowing the chest appeared to be moving. I was almost blind as I lifted the lid of the sarcophagus.

Quickly, it fell into place above me. The pain in my face and hands died away, and I was still and I was safe, and fear and sorrow melted into a cool and fathomless darkness.

T WAS thirst that awakened me.

And I knew at once where I was, and what I was, too.

There were no sweet mortal dreams of chilled white wine or the fresh green grass beneath the apple trees in my father's orchard.

In the narrow darkness of the stone coffin, I felt of my fangs with my fingers and found them dangerously long and keen as little knife blades.

And a mortal was in the tower, and though he hadn't reached the door of the outer chamber I could *hear* his thoughts.

I *heard* his consternation when he discovered the door to the stairs unlocked. That had never happened before. I heard his fear as he discovered the burnt timbers on the floor and called out 'Master'. A servant was what he was, and a somewhat treacherous one at that.

It fascinated me, this soundless hearing of his mind, but something else was disturbing me. It was his scent!

I lifted the stone lid of the sarcophagus and climbed out. The scent was faint, but it was almost irresistible. It was the musky smell of the first whore in whose bed I had spent my passion. It was the roasted venison after days and days of starvation in winter. It was new wine, or fresh apples, or water roaring over a cliff's edge on a hot day when I reached out to gulp it in handfuls.

Only it was immeasurably richer than that, this scent, and the appetite that wanted it was infinitely keener and more simple.

I moved through the secret tunnel like a creature swimming through the darkness and, pushing out the stone in the outer chamber, rose to my feet.

There stood the mortal, staring at me, his face pale with shock.

An old, withered man he was, and by some indefinable

tangle of considerations in his mind, I knew he was a stable master and a coachman. But the hearing of this was maddeningly imprecise.

Then the immediate malice he felt towards me came like the heat of a stove. And there was no misunderstanding that. His eyes raced over my face and form. The hatred boiled, crested. It was he who had procured the fine clothes I wore. He who tended the unfortunates in the dungeon while they had lived. And why, he demanded in silent outrage, was I not there?

This made me love him very much, as you can imagine. I could have crushed him to death in my bare hands for this.

'The master!' he said desperately. 'Where is he? Master!'

But what did he think the master was? A sorcerer of some kind, that was what he thought. And now I had the power. In sum, he didn't know anything that would be of use to me.

But as I comprehended all this, as I drank it up from his mind, quite against his will, I was becoming entranced with the veins in his face and in his hands. And that smell was intoxicating me.

I could feel the dim throbbing of his heart, and then I could taste his blood, just what it would be like, and there came to me some full-blown sense of it, rich and hot as it filled me.

'The master's gone, burned in the fire,' I murmured, hearing a strange monotone coming from myself. I moved slowly towards him.

He glanced at the blackened floor. He looked up at the blackened ceiling. 'No, this is a lie,' he said. He was outraged, and his anger pulsed like a light in my eye. I felt the bitterness of his mind and its desperate reasoning.

Ah, but that living flesh could look like this! I was in the grip of remorseless appetite.

And he knew it. In some wild and unreasoning way, he sensed it; and throwing me one last malevolent glance he ran for the stairway.

Immediately I caught him. In fact, I enjoyed catching him, so simple it was. One instant I was willing myself to reach out and close the distance between us. The next I had him helpless

123

in my hands, holding him off the floor so that his feet swung free, straining to kick me.

I held him as easily as a powerful man might hold a child, that was the proportion. His mind was a jumble of frantic thoughts, and he seemed unable to decide upon any course to save himself.

But the faint humming of these thoughts was being obliterated by the vision he presented to me.

His eyes weren't the portals of his soul anymore. They were gelatinous orbs whose colours tantalized me. And his body was nothing but a writhing morsel of hot flesh and blood, that I must have or die without.

It horrified me that this food should be alive, that delicious blood should flow through these struggling arms and fingers, and then it seemed perfect that it should be. He was what he was, and I was what I was, and I was going to feast upon him.

I pulled him to my lips. I tore the bulging artery in his neck. The blood hit the roof of my mouth. I gave a little cry as I crushed him against me. It wasn't the burning fluid the master's blood had been, not that lovely elixir I had drunk from the stones of the dungeon. No, that had been light itself made liquid. Rather this was a thousand times more luscious, tasting of the thick human heart that pumped it, the very essence of that hot, almost smoky scent.

I could feel my shoulders rising, my fingers biting deeper into his flesh, and almost a humming sound rising out of me. No vision but that of his tiny gasping soul, but a swoon so powerful that he himself, what he was, had no part in it.

It was with all my will that, before the final moment, I forced him away. How I wanted to feel his heart stop. How I wanted to feel the beats slow and cease and know I *possessed* him.

But I didn't dare.

He slipped heavily from my arms, his limbs sprawling out on the stones, the whites of his eyes showing beneath his half-closed eyelids.

And I found myself unable to turn away from his death, mutely fascinated by it. Not the smallest detail must escape me. I heard his breath give out, I saw the body relax into death without struggle.

The blood warmed me. I felt it beating in my veins. My face was hot against the palms of my hands, and my vision had grown powerfully sharp. I felt strong beyond all imagining.

I PICKED up the corpse and dragged it down and down the winding steps of the tower, into the stinking dungeon, and threw it to rot with the rest there.

8

IT WAS time to go out, time to test my powers.

I filled my purse and my pockets with as much money as they would comfortably hold, and I buckled on a jewelled sword that was not too old-fashioned, and then went down, locking the iron gate to the tower behind me.

The tower was obviously all that remained of a ruined house. But I picked up the scent of horses on the wind — strong, very nice smell, perhaps the way an animal would pick up the scent — and I made my way silently around the back to a makeshift stable.

It contained not only a handsome old carriage, but four magnificent black mares. Perfectly wonderful that they weren't afraid of me. I kissed their smooth flanks and their long soft noses. In fact, I was so in love with them I could have spent hours just learning all I could of them through my new senses. But I was eager for other things.

There was a human in the stable also, and I'd caught his scent too as soon as I entered. But he was sound asleep, and when I roused him, I saw he was a dull-witted boy who posed no danger to me.

'I'm your master now,' I said, as I gave him a gold coin, 'but I won't be needing you tonight, except to saddle a horse for me.'

He understood well enough to tell me there was no saddle in the stable before he fell back to dozing.

All right. I cut the long carriage reins from one of the bridles, put it on the most beautiful of the mares myself, and rode out bareback.

I can't tell you what it was like, the burst of the horse under me, the chilling wind, and the high arch of the night sky. My body was melted to animal. I was flying over the snow, laughing aloud and now and then singing. I hit high notes I had never reached before, then plunged into a lustrous baritone. Sometimes I was simply crying out in something like joy. It had to be joy. But how could a monster feel joy?

I wanted to ride to Paris, of course. But I knew I wasn't ready. There was too much I didn't know about my powers yet. And so I rode in the opposite direction, until I came to the outskirts of a small village.

There were no humans about, and as I approached the little church, I felt a human rage and impulsiveness breaking through my strange, translucent happiness.

I dismounted quickly and tried the sacristy door. Its lock gave and I walked through the nave to the Communion rail.

I don't know what I felt at this moment. Maybe I wanted something to happen. I felt murderous. And lightning did not strike. I stared at the red glare of the vigil lights on the altar. I looked up at the figures frozen in the unilluminated blackness of the stained glass.

And in desperation, I went up over the Communion rail and put my hands on the tabernacle itself. I broke open its tiny little doors, and I reached in and took out the jewelled ciborium with its consecrated Hosts. No, there was no power here, nothing that I could feel or see or know with any of my monstrous senses, nothing that responded to me. There were wafers and gold and wax and light.

I bowed my head on the altar. I must have looked like the priest in the middle of mass. Then I shut up everything in the tabernacle again. I closed it all up just fine, so nobody would know a sacrilege had been committed.

And then I made my way down one side of the church and

up the other, the lurid paintings and statues captivating me. I realized I was seeing the process of the sculptor and the painter, not merely the creative miracle. I was seeing the way the lacquer caught the light. I was seeing little mistakes in perspective, flashes of unexpected expressiveness.

What will the great masters be to my eyes, I was thinking. I found myself staring at the simplest designs painted in the plaster walls. Then I knelt down to look at the patterns in the marble, until I realized I was stretched out, staring wide-eyed at the floor under my nose.

This is getting out of hand, surely. I got up, shivering a little and crying a little, and looking at the candles as if they were alive, and getting very sick of this.

Time to get out of this place and go into the village.

FOR two hours I was in the village, and for most of the time I was not seen or heard by anyone.

I found it absurdly easy to jump over the garden walls, to spring from the earth to low rooftops. I could leap from a height of three storeys to the ground, and climb the side of a building digging my nails and toes into the mortar between the stones.

I peered in windows. I saw couples asleep in their ruffled beds, infants dozing in cradles, old women sewing by feeble light.

And the houses looked like dollhouses to me in their completeness. Perfect collections of toys with their dainty little wooden chairs and polished mantelpieces, mended curtains, and well-scrubbed floors.

I saw all this as one who had never been part of life, gazing lovingly at the simplest details. A starched white apron on its hook, worn boots on the hearth, a pitcher beside a bed.

And the people ... oh, the people were marvels.

Of course I picked up their scent, but I was satisfied and it didn't make me miserable. Rather I doted upon their pink skin and delicate limbs, the precision with which they moved, the whole process of their lives as if I had never been one of them at all. That they had five fingers on each hand seemed remarkable. They yawned, cried, shifted in sleep. I was entranced with them.

And when they spoke, the thickest walls could not prevent me from hearing their words.

But the most beguiling aspect of my explorations was that I *heard the thoughts of these people*, just as I had heard the evil servant whom I killed. Unhappiness, misery, expectation. These were currents in the air, some weak, some frighteningly strong, some no more than a glimmer gone before I knew the source.

But I could not, strictly speaking, read minds.

Most trivial thought was veiled from me, and when I lapsed into my own considerations, even the strongest passions did not intrude. In sum, it was intense feeling that carried through to me and only when I wished to receive it, and there were some minds that even in the heat of anger gave me nothing.

These discoveries jolted me and almost bruised me, as did the common beauty everywhere I looked, the splendour in the ordinary. But I knew perfectly well there was an abyss behind it into which I might quite suddenly and helplessly drop.

After all, I wasn't one of these warm and pulsing miracles of complication and innocence. They were my victims.

Time to leave the village. I'd learned enough here. But just before I left, I performed one final act of daring. I couldn't help myself. I just had to do it.

Pulling up the high collar of my red cloak, I went into the inn, sought a corner away from the fire, and ordered a glass of wine. Everyone in the little place gave me the eye, but not because they knew there was a supernatural being in their midst. They were merely glancing at the richly dressed gentleman! And for twenty minutes I remained, testing it even further. No one, not even the man who served me, detected anything! Of course I didn't touch the wine. One whiff of it and I knew that my body could not abide it. But the point was, *I could fool mortals!* I could move among them!

I was jubilant when I left the inn. As soon as I reached the woods, I started to run. And then I was running so fast that the sky and the trees had become a blur. I was almost flying.

Then I stopped, leaped, danced about. I gathered up stones and threw them so far I could not see them land. And when I saw a fallen tree limb, thick and full of sap, I picked it up and broke it over my knee as if it were a twig.

I shouted, then sang at the top of my lungs again. I collapsed on the grass laughing.

And then I rose, tore off my cloak and my sword; and commenced to turn cartwheels. I turned cartwheels just like the acrobats at Renaud's. And then I somersaulted perfectly. I did it again, and this time backwards, and then forward, and then I turned double somersaults and triple somersaults, and leapt straight up in the air some fifteen feet off the ground before landing squarely on my feet, somewhat out of breath, and wanting to do these tricks some more.

But the morning was coming.

Only the subtlest change in the air, the sky, but I knew it as if Hell's Bells were ringing. Hell's Bells calling the vampire home to the sleep of death. Ah, the melting loveliness of the sky, the loveliness of the vision of dim belfries. And an odd thought came to me, that in hell the light of the fires would be so bright it would be like sunlight, and this would be the only sunlight I would ever see again.

But what have I done? I thought. I didn't ask for this, I didn't give in. Even when Magnus told me I was dying, I fought him, and yet I am hearing Hell's Bells now.

Well, who gives a damn?

WHEN I reached the churchyard, quite ready for the ride home, something distracted me.

I stood holding the rein of my horse and looking at the small field of graves and could not quite figure what it was. Then again it came, and I knew. I felt a distinct *presence* in the churchyard.

I stood so still I heard the blood thundering in my veins.

It wasn't human, this *presence*! It had no scent. And there were no human thoughts coming from it. Rather it seemed veiled and defended and it knew I was here. It was watching me.

Could I be imagining this?

I stood listening, looking. A scattering of grey tombstones poked through the snow. And far away stood a row of old crypts, larger, ornamented, but just as ruined as the stones.

It seemed *the presence* lingered somewhere near the crypts, and then I felt it distinctly as it moved towards the enclosing trees.

'Who are you!' I demanded. I heard my voice like a knife. 'Answer me!' I called out even louder.

I felt a great tumult in it, this *presence*, and I was certain that it was moving away very rapidly.

I dashed across the churchyard after it, and I could feel it receding. Yet I saw nothing in the barren forest. And I realized I was stronger than it, and that it had been afraid of me!

Well, fancy that. Afraid of me.

And I had no idea whether or not it was corporeal, vampire the same as I was, or something without a body.

'Well, one thing is sure,' I said. 'You're a coward!'

Tingling in the air. The forest seemed to breathe for an instant.

A sense of my own might came over me that had been brewing all along. I was in fear of nothing. Not the church, not the dark, not the worms swarming over the corpses in my dungeon. Not even this strange eerie force that had retreated into the forest, and seemed to be near at hand again. Not even of men.

I was an extraordinary fiend! If I'd been sitting on the steps of hell with my elbows on my knees and the devil had said, 'Lestat, come, choose the form of the fiend you wish to be to roam the earth,' how could I have chosen a better fiend than what I was? And it seemed suddenly that suffering was an idea I'd known in another existence and would never know again.

I CAN'T help but laugh now when I think of that first night especially of that particular moment.

9

HE next night I went tearing into Paris with as much gold as I could carry. The sun had just sunk beneath the horizon when I opened my eyes, and a clear azure light still emanated from the sky as I mounted and rode off to the city.

I was starving.

And as luck would have it, I was attacked by a cutthroat before I ever reached the city walls. He came thundering out of the woods, pistol blazing, and I actually saw the ball leave the barrel of the gun and go past me as I leapt off my horse and went at him.

He was a powerful man, and I was astonished at how much I enjoyed his cursing and struggling. The vicious servant I'd taken last night had been old. This was a hard young body. Even the roughness of his badly shaven beard tantalized me, and I loved the strength in his hands as he struck at me. But it was no sport. He froze as I sank my teeth into the artery, and when the blood came it was pure voluptuousness. In fact, it was so exquisite that I forgot completely about drawing away before the heart stopped.

We were on our knees in the snow together, and it was a wallop, the life going into me with the blood. I couldn't move for a long moment. Hmmm, broke the rules already, I thought. Am I supposed to die now? Doesn't look like that is going to happen. Just this rolling delirium.

And the poor dead bastard in my arms who would have blown my face off with his pistol if I had let him.

I kept staring at the darkening sky, at the great spangled mass of shadows ahead that was Paris. And there was only this warmth after, and obviously increasing strength.

So far so good. I climbed to my feet and wiped my lips. Then I pitched the body as far as I could across the unbroken snow. I was more powerful than ever.

And for a little while I stood there, feeling gluttonous and murderous, just wanting to kill again so this ecstasy would go on forever. But I couldn't have drunk any more blood, and gradually I grew calm and changed somewhat. A desolate feeling came over me. An aloneness as though the thief had been a friend to me or kin to me and had deserted me. I couldn't understand it, except that the drinking had been so intimate. His scent was on me now, and I sort of liked it. But there he lay yards away on the crumpled crust of snow, hands and face looking grey under the rising moon.

Hell, the son of a bitch was going to kill me, wasn't he?

WITHIN an hour I had found a capable attorney, name of Pierre Roget, at his home in the Marais, an ambitious young man with a mind that was completely open to me. Greedy, clever, conscientious. Exactly what I wanted. Not only could I read his thoughts when he wasn't talking, but he believed everything I told him.

He was most eager to be of service to the husband of an heiress from Saint-Domingue. And certainly he would put out all the candles, save one, if my eyes were still hurting from tropical fever. As for my fortune in gems, he dealt with the most reputable jewellers. Bank accounts and letters of exchange for my family in the Auvergne — yes, immediately.

This was easier than playing Lelio.

But I was having a hell of a time concentrating. Everything was a distraction — the smoky flame of the candle on the brass inkstand, the gilded pattern of the Chinese wallpaper, and Monsieur Roget's amazing little face, with its eyes glistening behind tiny octagonal spectacles. His teeth kept making me think of clavier keys.

Ordinary objects in the room appeared to dance. A chest stared at me with its brass knobs for eyes. And a woman singing in an upstairs room over the low rumble of a stove seemed to be saying something in a low and vibrant secret language, such as Come to me.

But it was going to be this way forever apparently, and I had to get myself in hand. Money must be sent by courier this very night to my father and my brothers, and to Nicolas de Lenfent, a musician with Renaud's House of Thespians, who was to be told only that the wealth had come from his friend

Lestat de Lioncourt. It was Lestat de Lioncourt's wish that Nicolas de Lenfent move at once to a decent flat on the Ile St.-Louis or some other proper place, and Roget should, of course, assist in this, and thereafter Nicolas de Lenfent should study the violin. Roget should buy for Nicolas de Lenfent the best available violin, a Stradivarius.

And finally a separate letter was to be written to my mother, the Marquise Gabrielle de Lioncourt, in Italian, so that no one else could read it, and a special purse was to be sent to her. If she could undertake a journey to southern Italy, the place where she'd been born, maybe she could stop the course of her consumption.

It made me positively dizzy to think of her with the freedom to escape. I wondered what she would think about it.

For a long moment I didn't hear anything Roget said. I was picturing her dressed for once in her life as the marquise she was, and riding out of the gates of our castle in her own coach and six. And then I remembered her ravaged face and heard the cough in her lungs as if she were here with me.

'Send the letter and the money to her tonight,' I said. 'I don't care what it costs. Do it.' I laid down enough gold to keep her in comfort for a lifetime, if she had a lifetime.

'Now,' I said, 'do you know of a merchant who deals in fine furnishings — paintings, tapestries? Someone who might open his shops and storehouses to us this very evening?'

'Of course, Monsieur. Allow me to get my coat. We shall go immediately.'

We were headed for the faubourg St.-Denis within minutes.

And for hours after that, I roamed with my mortal attendants through a paradise of material wealth, claiming everything that I wanted. Couches and chairs, china and silver plate, drapery and statuary — all things were mine for the taking. And in my mind I transformed the castle where I'd grown up as more and more goods were carried out to be crated and shipped south immediately. To my little nieces and nephews I sent toys of which they'd never dreamed — tiny ships with real sails, dollhouses of unbelievable craft and perfection.

I learned from each thing that I touched. And there were moments when all the colour and texture became too lustrous, too overpowering. I wept inwardly.

But I would have got away with playing human to the hilt during all this time, except for one very unfortunate mishap.

At one point as we wandered through the warehouse, a rat appeared as bold city rats will, racing along the wall very close to us. I stared at it. Nothing unusual of course. But there amid plaster and hardwood and embroidered cloth, the rat looked marvellously particular. And the men, misunderstanding of course, began mumbling frantic apologies for the rat and stamping their feet to drive it away from us.

To me, their voices became a mixture of sounds like stew bubbling in a pot. All I could think was that the rat had very tiny feet, and that I had not yet examined a rat nor any small warm-blooded creature. I went and caught the rat, rather too easily I think, and looked at its feet. I wanted to see what kind of little toenails it had, and what was the flesh like between its little toes, and I forgot the men entirely.

It was their sudden silence that brought me back to myself. They were both staring dumbfounded at me.

I smiled at them as innocently as I could, let the rat go, and went back to purchasing.

Well, they never said anything about it. But there was a lesson in this. I had really frightened them.

Later that night, I gave my lawyer one last commission: He must send a present of one hundred crowns to a theatre owner by the name of Renaud with a note of thanks from me for his kindness.

'Find out the situation with this little playhouse,' I said. 'Find out if there are any debts against it.'

Of course, I'd never go near the theatre. They must never guess what had happened, never be contaminated by it. And for now I had done what I could for all those I loved, hadn't I?

AND when all this was finished, when the church clocks struck three over the white rooftops and I was hungry enough to smell blood everywhere that I turned, I found myself standing in the empty boulevard du Temple.

The dirty snow had turned to slush under the carriage wheels, and I was looking at the House of Thespians with its spattered walls and its torn playbills and the name of the young mortal actor, Lestat de Valois, still written there in red letters.

10

THE following nights were a rampage. I began to drink up Paris as if the city were blood. In the early evening I raided the worst sections, tangling with thieves and killers, often giving them a playful chance to defend themselves, then snarling them in a fatal embrace and feasting to the point of gluttony.

I savoured different types of kills: big lumbering creatures, small wiry ones, the hirsute and the dark-skinned, but my favourite was the very young scoundrel who'd kill you for the coins in your pocket.

I loved their grunting and cursing. Sometimes I held them with one hand and laughed at them till they were in a positive fury, and I threw their knives over the rooftops and smashed their pistols to pieces against the walls. But in all this my full strength was like a cat never allowed to spring. And the one thing I loathed in them was fear. If a victim was really afraid I usually lost interest.

As time went on, I learned to postpone the kill. I drank a little from one, and more from another, and then took the grand wallop of the death itself from the third or the fourth one. It was the chase and the struggle that I was multiplying for my own pleasure. And when I'd had enough of all this hunting and drinking in an evening to content some six healthy vampires, I turned my eyes to the rest of Paris, all the glorious pastimes I couldn't afford before.

But not before going to Roget's house for news of Nicolas or my mother.

135

Her letters were brimming with happiness at my good fortune, and she promised to go to Italy in the spring if only she could get the strength to do it. Right now she wanted books from Paris, of course, and newspapers, and keyboard music for the harpsichord I'd sent. And she had to know, Was I truly happy? Had I fulfilled my dreams? She was leery of wealth. I had been so happy at Renaud's. I must confide in her.

It was agony to hear these words read to me. Time to become a liar in earnest, which I had never been. But for her I would do it.

As for Nicki, I should have known he wouldn't settle for gifts and vague tales, that he would demand to see me and keep on demanding it. He was frightening Roget a little bit.

But it didn't do any good. There was nothing the attorney could tell him except what I've explained. And I was so wary of seeing Nicki that I didn't even ask for the location of the house into which he'd moved. I told the lawyer to make certain he studied with his Italian maestro and that he had everything he could possibly desire.

But I did manage somehow to hear quite against my will that Nicolas hadn't quit the theatre. He was still playing at Renaud's House of Thespians.

Now this maddened me. Why the hell, I thought, should he do that?

Because he loved it there, the same as I had, that was why. Did anybody really have to tell me this? We had all been kindred in that little rattrap playhouse. Don't think about the moment when the curtain goes up, when the audience begins to clap and shout ...

No. Send cases of wine and champagne to the theatre. Send flowers for Jeannette and Luchina, the girls I had fought with the most and most loved, and more gifts of gold for Renaud. Pay off the debts he had.

But as the nights passed and these gifts were dispatched, Renaud became embarrassed about all this. A fortnight later, Roget told me Renaud had made a proposal.

He wanted me to buy the House of Thespians and keep him on as manager with enough capital to stage larger and more wondrous spectacles than he'd ever before attempted. With my money and his cleverness, we could make the house the talk of Paris.

I didn't answer right away. It took me more than a moment to realize that I could own the theatre just like that. Own it like the gems in the chest, or the clothes I wore, or the dollhouse I'd sent to my nieces. I said no, and went out slamming the door.

Then I came right back.

'All right, buy the theatre,' I said, 'and give him ten thousand crowns to do whatever he wants.' This was a fortune. And I didn't even know why I had done this.

This pain will pass, I thought, it has to. And I must gain some control over my thoughts, realize that these things cannot affect me.

After all, where did I spend my time now? At the grandest theatres in Paris. I had the finest seats for the ballet and the opera, for the dramas of Molière and Racine. I was hanging about before the footlights gazing up at the great actors and actresses. I had suits made in every colour of the rainbow, jewels on my fingers, wigs in the latest fashion, shoes with diamond buckles as well as gold heels.

And I had eternity to be drunk on the poetry I was hearing, drunk on the singing and the sweep of the dancer's arms, drunk on the organ throbbing in the great cavern of Notre Dame and drunk on the chimes that counted out the hours to me, drunk on the snow falling soundlessly on the empty gardens of the Tuileries.

And each night I was becoming less wary among mortals, more at ease with them.

Not even a month had passed before I got up the courage to plunge right into a crowded ball at the Palais Royal. I was warm and ruddy from the kill and at once I joined the dance. I didn't arouse the slightest suspicion. Rather the women seemed drawn to me, and I loved the touch of their hot fingers and the soft crush of their arms and their breasts.

After that, I bore right into the early evening crowds in the boulevards. Rushing past Renaud's, I squeezed into the other houses to see the puppet shows, the mimes, and the acrobats. I didn't flee from street lamps anymore. I went into cafés and bought coffee just to feel the warmth of it against my fingers, and I spoke to men when I chose.

I even argued with them about the state of the monarchy, and I went madly into mastering billiards and card games, and it seemed to me I might go right into the House of Thespians if I wanted to, buy a ticket, and slip up into the balcony and see what was going on. See Nicolas!

Well, I didn't do that. What was I dreaming of to go near to Nicki? It was one thing to fool strangers, men and women who'd never known me, but what would Nicolas see if he looked into my eyes? What would he see when he looked at my skin? Besides I had too much to do, I told myself.

I was learning more and more about my nature and my powers.

MY HAIR, for example, was lighter, yet thicker, and grew not at all. Nor did my fingernails and toenails, which had a greater lustre, though if I filed them away, they would regenerate during the day to the length they had been when I died. And though people couldn't discern such secrets on inspection, they sensed other things, an unnatural gleam to my eyes, too many reflected colours in them, and a faint luminescence to my skin.

When I was hungry this luminescence was very marked. All the more reason to feed.

And I was learning that I could put people in thrall if I stared at them too hard and my voice required very strict modulation. I might speak too low for mortal hearing, and were I to shout or laugh too loud, I could shatter another's ears. I could hurt my own ears.

There were other difficulties: my movements. I tended to walk, to run, to dance, and to smile and gesture like a human being, but if surprised, horrified, grieved, my body could bend and contort like that of an acrobat.

Even my facial expressions could be wildly exaggerated. Once forgetting myself as I walked in the boulevard du

Temple, thinking of Nicolas naturally, I sat down beneath a tree, drew up my knees, and put my hands to the side of my head like a stricken elf in a fairy tale. Eighteenth-century gentlemen in brocade frock coats and white silk stockings didn't do things like that, at least not on the street.

And another time, while deep in contemplation of the changing of the light on surfaces, I hopped up and sat with my legs crossed on the top of a carriage, with my elbows on my knees.

Well, this startled people. It frightened them. But more often than not, even when frightened by the whiteness of my skin, they merely looked away. They deceived themselves, I quickly realized, that everything was explainable. It was the rational eighteenth-century habit of mind.

After all there hadn't been a case of witchcraft in a hundred years, the last that I knew of being the trial of La Voisin, a fortune-teller, burnt alive in the time of Louis the Sun King.

And this was Paris. So if I accidentally crushed crystal glasses when I lifted them, or slammed doors back into the walls when opening them, people assumed I was drunk.

But now and then I answered questions before mortals had asked them of me. I fell into stuporous states just looking at candles or tree branches, and didn't move for so long that people asked if I was ill.

And my worst problem was laughter. I would go into fits of laughter and I couldn't sleep. Anything could set me off. The sheer madness of my own position might set me off.

This can still happen to me fairly easily. No loss, no pain, no deepening understanding of my predicament changes it. Something strikes me as funny. I begin to laugh and I can't stop.

It makes other vampires furious, by the way. But I jump ahead of the tale.

As you have probably noticed, I have made no mention of other vampires. The fact was I could not find any.

I could find no other supernatural being in all of Paris.

Mortals to the left of me, mortals to the right of me, and now and then – just when I'd convinced myself it wasn't happening at all —I'd feel that vague and maddeningly elusive *presence*.

It was never any more substantial than it had been the first night in the village churchyard. And invariably it was in the vicinity of a Paris cemetery.

Always, I'd stop, turn, and try to draw it out. But it was never any good, the thing was gone before I could be certain of it. I could never find it on my own, and the stench of city cemeteries was so revolting I wouldn't, couldn't, go into them.

This was coming to seem more than fastidiousness or bad memories of my own dungeon beneath the tower. Revulsion at the sight or smell of death seemed part of my nature.

I couldn't watch executions any more than when I was that trembling boy from the Auvergne, and corpses made me cover my face. I think I was offended by death unless I was the cause of it! And I had to get clean away from my dead victims almost immediately.

But to return to the matter of *the presence*. I came to wonder if it wasn't some other species of haunt, something that couldn't commune with me. On the other hand, I had the distinct impression that *the presence* was watching me, maybe even deliberately revealing itself to me.

Whatever the case, I saw no other vampires in Paris. And I was beginning to wonder if there could be more than one of us at any given time. Maybe Magnus destroyed the vampire from whom he stole the blood. Maybe he had to perish once he passed on his powers. And I too would die if I were to make another vampire.

But no, that didn't make sense. Magnus had had great strength even after giving me his blood. And he had bound his vampire victim in chains when he stole his powers.

An enormous mystery, and a maddening one. But for the moment, ignorance was truly bliss. And I was doing very well discovering things without the help of Magnus. And maybe this was what Magnus had intended. Maybe this had been his way of learning centuries ago.

I remembered his words, that in the secret chamber of the tower I would find all that I needed to prosper.

* * *

THE hours flew as I roamed the city. And only to conceal myself in the tower by day did I ever deliberately leave the company of human beings.

Yet I was beginning to wonder: 'If you can dance with them, and play billiards with them and talk with them, then why can't you dwell among them, just the way you did when you were living? Why couldn't you *pass* for one of them? And enter again into the very fabric of life where there is ... what? Say it!'

And here it was nearly spring. And the nights were getting warmer, and the House of Thespians was putting on a new drama with new acrobats between the acts. And the trees were in bloom again, and every waking moment I thought of Nicki.

ONE night in March, I realized as Roget read my mother's letter to me that I could read as well as he could. I had learned from a thousand sources how to read without even trying. I took the letter home with me.

Even the inner chamber was no longer really cold. And I sat by the window reading my mother's words for the first time in private. I could almost hear her voice speaking to me:

'Nicolas writes that you have purchased Renaud's. So you own the little theatre on the boulevard where you were so happy. But do you possess the happiness still? When will you answer me?'

I folded up the letter and put it in my pocket. The blood tears were coming into my eyes. Why must she understand so much, yet so little?

11

HE wind had lost its sting. All the smells of the city were coming back. And the markets were full of flowers. I dashed to Roget's house without even thinking of what I was doing and demanded that he tell me where Nicolas lived.

I would just have a look at him, make certain he was in good health, be certain the house was fine enough.

It was on the Ile St.-Louis, and very impressive just as I'd wanted, but the windows were all shuttered along the quais.

I stood watching it for a long time, as one carriage after another roared over the nearby bridge. And I knew that I had to see Nicki.

I started to climb the wall just as I had climbed walls in the village, and I found it amazingly easy. One storey after another I climbed, much higher than I had ever dared to climb in the past, and then I sped over the roof, and down the inside of the courtyard to look for Nicki's flat.

I passed a handful of open windows before I came to the right one. And then there was Nicolas in the glare of the supper table and Jeannette and Luchina were with him, and they were having the late night meal that we used to take together when the theatre closed.

At the first sight of him, I drew back away from the casement and closed my eyes. I might have fallen if my right hand hadn't held fast to the wall as if with a will of its own. I had seen the room for only an instant, but every detail was fixed in my mind.

He was dressed in old green velvet, finery he'd worn so casually in the crooked streets at home. But everywhere around him were signs of the wealth I'd sent him, leather-bound books on the shelves, and an inlaid desk with an oval painting above it, and the Italian violin gleaming atop the new pianoforte.

He wore a jewelled ring I'd sent, and his brown hair was tied back with a black silk ribbon, and he sat brooding with his elbows on the table eating nothing from the expensive china plate before him.

Carefully I opened my eyes and looked at him again. All his natural gifts were there in a blaze of light: the delicate but strong limbs, large sober brown eyes, and his mouth that for all the irony and sarcasm that could come out of it was child-like and ready to be kissed.

There seemed in him a frailty I'd never perceived or understood. Yet he looked infinitely intelligent, my Nicki, full of tangled uncompromising thoughts as he listened to Jeannette, who was talking rapidly.

'Lestat's married,' she said as Luchina nodded, 'the wife's rich, and he can't let her know he was a common actor, it's simple enough.'

'I say we let him in peace,' Luchina said. 'He saved the theatre from closing, and he showers us with gifts ...'

'I don't believe it,' Nicolas said bitterly. 'He wouldn't be ashamed of us.' There was a suppressed rage in his voice, an ugly grief. 'And why did he leave the way he did? I heard him calling me! The window was smashed to pieces! I tell you I was half awake, and I heard his voice ...'

An uneasy silence fell among them. They didn't believe his account of things, how I'd vanished from the garret, and telling it again would only isolate him and embitter him further. I could sense this from all their thoughts.

'You didn't really know Lestat,' he said now, almost in a surly fashion, returning to the manageable conversation that other mortals would allow him. 'Lestat would spit in the face of anyone who would be ashamed of us! He sends me money. What am I supposed to do with it? He plays games with us!'

No answer from the others, the solid, practical beings who would not speak against the mysterious benefactor. Things were going too well.

And in the lengthening silence, I felt the depth of Nicki's anguish, I *knew* it as if I were peering into his skull. And I couldn't bear it.

I couldn't bear delving into his soul without his knowing it. Yet I couldn't stop myself from sensing a vast secret terrain inside him, grimmer perhaps than I had ever dreamed, and his words came back to me that the darkness in him was like the darkness I'd seen at the inn, and that he tried to conceal it from me.

I could almost see it, this terrain. And in a real way it was

143

beyond his mind, as if his mind were merely a portal to a chaos stretching out from the borders of all we know.

Too frightening that. I didn't want to see it. I didn't want to feel what he felt!

But what could I do *for* him? That was the important thing. What could I do to stop this torment once and for all?

Yet I wanted so to touch him — his hands, his arms, his face. I wanted to feel his flesh with these new immortal figures. And I found myself whispering the word 'Alive'. Yes, you are alive and that means you can die. And everything I see when I look at you is utterly insubstantial. It is a commingling of tiny movements and indefinable colours, as if you haven't a body at all, but are a collection of heat and light. You are light itself, and what am I now?

Eternal as I am, I curl like a cinder in that blaze.

But the atmosphere of the room had changed. Luchina and Jeannette were taking their leave with polite words. He was ignoring them. He had turned to the window, and he was rising as if he'd been called by a secret voice. The look on his face was indescribable.

He knew I was there!

Instantly, I shot up the slippery wall to the roof.

But I could still *hear* him below. I looked down and I saw his naked hands on the window ledge. And through the silence, I heard his panic. He'd sensed that I was there! My presence, mind you, that is what he sensed, just as I sensed *the presence* in the graveyards, but how, he argued with himself, could Lestat have been here?

I was too shocked to do anything. I clung to the roof gutter, and I could feel the departure of the others, feel that he was now alone. And all I could think was, What in the name of hell is this presence that he felt?

I mean I wasn't Lestat anymore, I was this demon, this powerful and greedy vampire, and yet he felt my presence, the presence of Lestat, the young man he knew!

It was a very different thing from a mortal seeing my face and blurting out my name in confusion. He had recognized in my monster self something that he knew and loved.

I stopped listening to him. I merely lay on the roof.

But I knew he was moving below. I knew it when he lifted the violin from its place on the pianoforte, and I knew he was again at the window.

And I put my hands over my ears.

Still the sound came. It came rising out of the instrument and cleaving the night as if it were some shining element, other than air and light and matter, that might climb to the very stars.

He bore down on the strings, and I could almost see him against my eyelids, swaying back and forth, his head bowed against the violin as if he meant to pass into the music, and then all sense of him vanished and there was only the sound.

The long vibrant notes, and the chilling glissandos, and the violin singing in its own tongue to make every other form of speech seem false. Yet as the song deepened, it became the very essence of despair as if its beauty were a horrid coincidence, grotesquery without a particle of truth.

Was this what he believed, what he had always believed when I talked on and on about goodness? Was he making the violin say it? Was he deliberately creating those long, pure liquid notes to say that beauty meant nothing because it came from the despair inside him, and it had nothing to do with the despair finally, because the despair wasn't beautiful, and beauty then was a horrid irony?

I didn't know the answer. But the sound went beyond him as it always had. It grew bigger than the despair. It fell effortlessly into a slow melody, like water seeking its own downward mountain path. It grew richer and darker still and there seemed something undisciplined and chastening in it, and heartbreaking and vast. I lay on my back on the roof with my eyes on the stars.

Pinpoints of light mortals could not have seen. Phantom clouds. And the raw, piercing sound of the violin coming slowly with exquisite tension to a close.

I didn't move.

I was in some silent understanding of the language the violin spoke to me. Nicki, if we could talk again ... If 'our

145

'conversation' could only continue.

Beauty wasn't the treachery he imagined it to be, rather it was an uncharted land where one could make a thousand fatal errors, a wild and indifferent paradise without signposts of evil or good.

In spite of all the refinements of civilization that conspired to make art — the dizzying perfection of the string quartet or the sprawling grandeur of Fragonard's canvases — beauty was savage. It was as dangerous and lawless as the earth had been eons before man had one single coherent thought in his head or wrote codes of conduct on tablets of clay. Beauty was a Savage Garden.

So why must it wound him that the most despairing music is full of beauty? Why must it hurt him and make him cynical and sad and untrusting?

Good and evil, those are concepts man has made. And man is better, really, than the Savage Garden.

But maybe deep inside Nicki had always dreamed of a harmony among all things that I had always known was impossible. Nicki had dreamed not of goodness, but of justice.

But we could never discuss these thing now with each other. We could never again be in the inn. Forgive me, Nicki. Good and evil exist still, as they always will. But 'our conversation' is over forever. Yet even as I left the roof, as I stole silently away from the Ile St.-Louis, I knew what I meant to do.

I didn't admit it to myself but I knew.

THE next night it was already late when I reached the boulevard du Temple. I'd fed well in the Ile de la Cité, and the first act at Renaud's House of Thespians was already under way.

12

'D DRESSED as if I were going to Court, in silver brocade with a lavender velvet roquelaure over my shoulders. I had a new sword with a deep-carved silver handle and the usual heavy, ornate buckles on my shoes, the usual lace, gloves, tricorne. And I came to the theatre in a hired carriage.

But as soon as I paid the driver I went back down the alley and opened the stage door exactly as I used to do.

At once the old atmosphere surrounded me, the smell of the thick greasepaint and the cheap costumes full of sweat and perfume, and the dust. I could see a fragment of the lighted stage burning beyond the helter-skelter of hulking props and hear bursts of laughter from the hall. A group of acrobats waited to go on at the intermezzo, a crowd of jesters in red tights, caps and dagged collars studded with little gold bells.

I felt dizzy, and for a moment afraid. The place felt close and dangerous over my head, and yet it was wonderful to be inside it again. And a sadness was swelling inside me, no, a panic, actually.

Luchina saw me and she let out a shriek. Doors opened everywhere on the cluttered little dressing rooms. Renaud plunged towards me and pumped my hand. While there had been nothing but wood and drapery a moment before, there was now a little universe of excited human beings, faces full of high colour and dampness, and I found myself drawing back from a smoking candelabra with the quick words, 'My eyes ... put it out.'

'Put out the candles, they hurt his eyes, can't you see that?' Jeannette insisted sharply. I felt her wet lips open against my face. Everyone was around me, even the acrobats who didn't know me, and the old scene painters and carpenters who had taught me so many things. Luchina said, 'Get Nicki,' and I almost cried No.

Applause was shaking the little house. The curtain was being pulled closed from either side. At once the old actors were upon me, and Renaud was calling for champagne.

I was holding my hands over my eyes as if like the basilisk I'd kill every one of them if I looked at them, and I could feel tears and knew that before they saw the blood in the tears, I

147

had to wipe the tears away. But they were so close I couldn't get to my handkerchief, and with a sudden terrible weakness, I put my arms around Jeannette and Luchina, and I pressed my face against Luchina's face. Like birds they were, with bones full of air, and hearts like beating wings, and for one second I listened with a vampire's ear to the blood in them, but that seemed an obscenity. And I just gave in to the hugging and the kissing, ignoring the thump of their hearts, and holding them and smelling their powdered skin, and feeling again the press of their lips.

'You don't know how you worried us!' Renaud was booming. 'And then the stories of your good fortune! Everyone, everyone!' He was clapping his hands. 'It's Monsieur de Valois, the owner of this great theatrical establishment ...' and he said a lot of other pompous and playful things, dragging up the new actors and actresses to kiss my hand, I suppose, or my feet. I was holding tight to the girls as if I'd explode into fragments if I let them go, and then I heard Nicki, and knew he was only a foot away, staring at me, and that he was too glad to see me to be hurt anymore.

I didn't open my eyes but I felt his hand on my face, then holding tight to the back of my neck. They must have made way for him and when he came into my arms, I felt a little convulsion of terror, but the light was dim here, and I had fed furiously to be warm and human-looking, and I thought desperately I don't know to whom I pray to make the deception work. And then there was only Nicolas and I didn't care.

I looked up and into his face.

How to describe what humans look like to us! I've tried to describe it a little, when I spoke of Nicki's beauty the night before as a mixture of movement and colour. But you can't imagine what it's like for us to look on living flesh. There are those billions of colours and tiny configurations of movement, yes, that make up a living creature on whom we concentrate. But the radiance mingles totally with the carnal scent. Beautiful, that's what any human being is to us, if we stop to consider it, even the old and the diseased, the downtrodden that one doesn't really 'see' in the street. They are all like that, like flowers ever in the process of opening, butterflies ever unfolding out of the cocoon.

Well, I saw all this when I saw Nicki, and I smelled the blood pumping in him, and for one heady moment I felt love and only love obliterating every recollection of the horrors that had deformed me. Every evil rapture, every new power with its gratification, seemed unreal. Maybe I felt a profound joy, too, that I could still love, if I'd ever doubted it, and that a tragic victory had been confirmed.

All the old mortal comfort intoxicated me, and I could have closed my eyes and slipped from consciousness carrying him with me, or so it seemed.

But something else stirred in me, collecting strength so fast my mind raced to catch up with it and deny it even as it threatened to grow out of control. And I knew it for what it was, something monstrous and enormous and natural to me as the sun was unnatural. I wanted Nicki. I wanted him as surely as any victim I'd ever struggled with in the Ile de la Cité. I wanted his blood flowing into me, wanted its taste and its smell and its heat.

The little place shook with shouts and laughter, Renaud telling the acrobats to get on with the intermezzo and Luchina opening the champagne. But we were closed off in this embrace.

The hard heat of his body made me stiffen and draw back, though it seemed I didn't move at all. And it maddened me suddenly that this one whom I loved even as I loved my mother and my brothers — this one who had drawn from me the only tenderness I'd ever felt — was an unconquerable citadel, holding fast in ignorance against my thirst for blood when so many hundreds of victims had so easily given it up.

This was what I'd been made for. This was the path I had been meant to walk. What were those others to me now — the thieves and killers I'd cut down in the wilderness of Paris? This was what I wanted. And the great awesome possibility of Nicki's death exploded in my brain. The darkness against my closed eyelids had become blood red. Nicki's mind emptying in that last moment, giving up its complexity with its life.

I couldn't move. I could feel the blood as if it were passing into me and I let my lips rest against his neck. Every particle in me said, 'Take him, spirit him out of this place and away from it and feed on him and feed on him … until …' Until what! Until he's dead!

I broke loose and pushed him away. The crowd around us roared and rattled. Renaud was shouting at the acrobats, who stood staring at these proceedings. The audience outside demanded the intermezzo entertainment with a steady rhythmic clap. The orchestra was fiddling away at the lively ditty that would accompany the acrobats. Bones and flesh poked and pushed at me. A shambles it had become, rank with the smell of those ready for the slaughter. I felt the all too human rise of nausea.

Nicki seemed to have lost his equilibrium, and when our eyes met, I felt the accusations emanating from him. I felt the misery and, worse, the near despair.

I pushed past all of them, past the acrobats with the jingling bells, and I don't know why I went forward to the wings instead of out the side door. I wanted to see the stage. I wanted to see the audience. I wanted to penetrate deeper into something for which I had no name or word.

But I was mad in these moments. To say I wanted or I thought makes no sense at all.

My chest was heaving and the thirst was like a cat clawing to get out. And as I leaned against the wooden beam beside the curtain, Nicki, hurt and misunderstanding everything, came to me again.

I let the thirst rage. I let it tear at my insides. I just clung to the rafter and I saw in one great recollection all my victims, the scum of Paris, scraped up from its gutters, and I knew the madness of the course I'd chosen, and the lie of it, and what I really was. What a sublime idiocy that I had dragged that paltry morality with me, striking down the damned ones only — seeking to be saved in spite of it all? What had I thought I was, a righteous partner to the judges and executioners of Paris who strike down the poor for crimes that the rich commit every day?

Strong wine I'd had, in chipped and broken vessels, and now the priest was standing before me at the foot of the altar with the golden chalice in his hands, and the wine inside it was the Blood of the Lamb.

Nicki was talking rapidly:

'Lestat, what is it? Tell me!' as if the others couldn't hear us. 'Where have you been? What's happened to you? Lestat!'

'Get on that stage!' Renaud thundered at the gaping acrobats. They trotted past us into the smoky blaze of the footlamps and went into a chain of somersaults.

The orchestra made its instruments into twittering birds. A flash of red, harlequin sleeves, bells jangling, taunts from the unruly crowd, 'Show us something, really show us something!'

Luchina kissed me and I stared at her white throat, her milky hands. I could see the veins in Jeannette's face and the soft cushion of her lower lip coming ever closer. The champagne, splashed into dozens of little glasses, was being drunk. Some speech was issuing forth from Renaud about our 'partnership' and how tonight's little farce was but the beginning and we would soon be the grandest theatre on the boulevards. I saw myself decked out for the part of Lelio, and heard the ditty I had sung to Flaminia on bended knee.

Before me, little mortals flipflopped heavily and the audience was howling as the leader of the acrobats made some vulgar movement with his hind end.

Before I even meant to do it, I had gone out on the stage.

I was standing in the very centre, feeling the heat of the footlights, the smoke stinging my eyes. I stared at the crowded gallery, the screened boxes, the rows and rows of spectators to the back wall. And I heard myself snarl a command for the acrobats to get away.

It seemed the laughter was deafening, and the taunts and shouts that greeted me were spasms and eruptions, and quite plainly behind every face in the house was a grinning skull. I was humming the little ditty I'd sung as Lelio, no more than a fragment of the part, but the one I'd carried in the streets afterwards with me, 'lovely, lovely, Flaminia', and on and on, the words forming meaningless sounds.

Insults were cutting through the din.

'On with the performance!' and 'You're handsome enough, now let's see some action!' From the gallery someone threw a half-eaten apple that came thumping just past my feet.

I unclasped the violet roquelaure and let it fall. I did the same with the silver sword.

The song had become an incoherent humming behind my lips, but mad poetry was pounding in my head. I saw the wilderness of beauty and its savagery, the way I'd seen it last night when Nicki was playing, and the moral world seemed some desperate dream of rationality that in this lush and fetid jungle had not the slightest chance. It was a vision and I *saw* rather than understood, except that I was part of it, natural as the cat with her exquisite and passionless face digging her claws into the back of the screaming rat.

'"Handsome enough" is this Grim Reaper,' I half uttered, 'who can snuff all these "brief candles", every fluttering soul sucking the air, from this hall.'

But the words were really beyond my reach. They floated in some stratum perhaps where a god existed who understood the colours patterned on a cobra's skin and the eight glorious notes that make up the music erupting out of Nicki's instrument, but never the principle, beyond ugliness or beauty, 'Thou shalt not kill.'

Hundreds of greasy faces peered back at me from the gloom. Shabby wigs and paste jewels and filthy finery, skin like water flowing over crooked bones. A crew of ragged beggars whistled and hooted from the gallery, humpback and one eye, and stinking underarm crutch, and teeth the colour of the skull's teeth you sift from the dirt of the grave.

I threw out my arms. I crooked my knee, and I began turning as the acrobats and dancers could turn, round and round on the ball of one foot, effortlessly, going faster and faster, until I broke, flipping over backwards into a circle of cartwheels, and then somersaults, imitating everything I had ever seen the players at the fairs perform.

Applause came immediately. I was agile as I'd been in the village, and the stage was tiny and hampering, and the ceiling seemed to press down on me, and the smoke from the foot-lights to close me in. The little song to Flaminia came back to me and I started singing it loudly as I turned and jumped and spun again, and then gaping at the ceiling I willed my body upwards as I bent my knees to spring.

In an instant I touched the rafters and I was dropping down gracefully, soundlessly to the boards.

Gasps rose from the audience. The little crowd in the wings was stunned. The musicians in the pit who had been silent all the while were turning to one another. They could see there was no wire.

But I was soaring again to the delight of the audience, this time somersaulting all the way up, beyond the painted arch again to descend in even slower, finer turns.

Shouts and cheers broke out over the clapping, but those backstage were mute. Nicki stood at the very edge, his lips silently shaping my name.

'It has to be trickery, an illusion.' The same avowals came from all directions. People demanded agreement from those around them. Renaud's face shone before me for an instant with gaping mouth and squinting eyes.

But I had gone into a dance again. And this time the grace of it no longer mattered to the audience. I could feel it, because the dance became a parody, each gesture broader, longer, slower than a human dancer could have sustained.

Someone shouted from the wings and was told to be still. And little cries burst from the musicians and those in the front rows. People were growing uneasy and whispering to one another, but the rabble in the gallery continued to clap.

I dashed suddenly towards the audience as if I meant to admonish it for its rudeness. Several persons were so startled they rose and tried to escape into the aisles. One of the horn-players dropped his instrument and climbed out of the pit.

I could see the agitation, even the anger in their faces. What were these illusions? It wasn't amusing them suddenly; they couldn't comprehend the skill of it, and something in my serious manner made them afraid. For one terrible moment, I felt their helplessness.

And I felt their doom.

A great horde of jangling skeletons snared in flesh and rags, that's what they were, and yet their courage blazed out of them, they shouted at me in their irrepressible pride.

I raised my hands slowly to command their attention, and very loudly and steadily I sang the ditty to Flaminia, my lovely Flaminia, a dull little couplet spilling into another couplet, and I let my voice grow louder and louder until suddenly people were rising and screaming before me, but louder still I sang it until it obliterated every other noise and in the intolerable roar I saw them all, hundreds of them, overturning the benches as they stood up, their hands clamped to the sides of their heads.

Their mouths were grimaces, toneless screams.

Pandemonium. Shrieks, curses, all stumbling and struggling towards the doors. Curtains were pulled from their fastenings. Men dropped down from the gallery to rush for the street.

I stopped the horrid song.

I stood watching them in a ringing silence, the weak, sweating bodies straining clumsily in every direction. The wind gusted from the open doorways, and I felt a strange coldness over all my limbs and it seemed my eyes were made of glass.

Without looking, I picked up the sword and put it on again, and hooked my finger into the velvet collar of my crumpled and dusty roquelaure. All these gestures seemed as grotesque as everything else I had done, and it seemed of no import that Nicolas was trying to get loose from two of the actors who held him in fear of his life as he shouted my name.

But something out of the chaos caught my attention. It did seem to matter — to be terribly, terribly important, in fact — that there was a figure standing above in one of the open boxes who did not struggle to escape or even move.

I turned slowly and looked up at him, daring him, it seemed, to remain there. An old man he was, and his dull grey eyes were boring into me with stubborn outrage, and as I glared at him, I heard myself let out a loud open-mouthed roar. Out of my soul it seemed to come, this sound. It grew louder and louder until those few left below cowered again with their ears stopped, and even Nicolas, rushing forward, buckled beneath the sound of it, both hands clasped to his head.

And yet the man stood there in the loge glowering, indignant and old, and stubborn, with furrowed brows under his grey wig.

I stepped back and leapt across the empty house, landing in the box directly before him, and his jaw fell in spite of himself and his eyes grew hideously wide.

He seemed deformed with age, his shoulders rounded, his hands gnarled, but the spirit in his eyes was beyond vanity and beyond compromise. His mouth hardened and his chin jutted. And from under his frock coat he pulled his pistol and he aimed it at me with both hands.

'Lestat!' Nicki shouted.

But the shot exploded and the ball hit with full force. I didn't move. I stood as steady as the old man had stood before, and the pain rolled through me and stopped, leaving in its wake a terrible pulling in all my veins.

The blood poured out. It flowed as I have never seen blood flow. It drenched my shirt and I could feel it spilling down my back. But the pulling grew stronger and stronger, and a warm tingling sensation had commenced to spread across the surface of my back and chest.

The man stared, dumbfounded. The pistol dropped out of his hand. His head went back, eyes blind· and his body crumpled as if the air had been let out of it, and he lay on the floor.

Nicki had raced up the stairs and was now rushing into the box. A low hysterical murmuring was issuing from him. He thought he was witnessing my death.

And I stood still hearkening to my body in that terrible solitude that had been mine since Magnus made me the vampire. And I knew the wounds were no longer there.

The blood was drying on the silk vest, drying on the back of my torn coat. My body throbbed where the bullet had passed through me and my veins were alive with that same pulling, but the injury was no more.

And Nicolas, coming to his senses as he looked at me, realized I was unharmed, though his reason told him it couldn't be true.

I pushed past him and made for the stairs. He flung himself against me and I threw him off. I couldn't stand the sight of him, the smell of him.

'Get away from me!' I said.

But he came back again and he locked his arm around my neck. His face was bloated and there was an awful sound coming out of him.

'Let go of me, Nicki!' I threatened him. If I shoved him off too roughly, I'd tear his arms out of the sockets, break his back.

Break his back ...

He moaned, stuttered. And for one harrowing split second the sounds he made were as terrible as the sound that had come from my dying animal on the mountain, my horse, crushed like an insect into the snow.

I scarcely knew what I was doing when I pried loose his hands.

The crowd broke, screaming, when I walked out onto the boulevard.

Renaud ran forward, in spite of those trying to restrain him.

'Monsieur!' He grabbed my hand to kiss it and stopped, staring at the blood.

'Nothing, my dear Renaud,' I said to him, quite surprised at the steadiness of my voice and its softness. But something distracted me as I started to speak again, something I should hearken to, I thought vaguely, yet I went on.

'Don't give it a thought, my dear Renaud,' I said. 'Stage blood, nothing but an illusion. It was all an illusion. A new kind of theatrical. Drama of the grotesque, yes, the grotesque.'

But again came that distraction, something I was sensing in the melee around me, people shuffling and pushing to get close but not too close, Nicolas stunned and staring.

'Go on with your plays,' I was saying, almost unable to concentrate on my own words, 'your acrobats, your tragedies, your more civilized theatricals, if you like.'

I pulled the bank notes out of my pocket and put them in

156

his unsteady hand. I spilled coins onto the pavement. The actors darted forward fearfully to gather them up. I scanned the crowd around for the source of this strange distraction, *what was it*, not Nicolas in the door of the deserted theatre, watching me with a broken soul.

No, something else both familiar and unfamiliar, having to do with the dark.

'Hire the finest mummers' — I was half babbling — 'the best musicians, the great scene painters.' More bank notes. My voice was getting loud again, the vampire voice, I could see the grimaces again and the hands going up, but they were afraid to let me see them cover their ears. 'There is no limit, NO LIMIT, to what you can do here!'

I broke away, dragging my roquelaure with me, the sword clanking awkwardly because it was not buckled right. Something of the dark.

And I knew when I hurried into the first alleyway and started to run what it was that I had heard, what had distracted me, it had been *the presence*, undeniably, in the crowd!

I knew it for one simple reason: I was running now in the back streets faster than a mortal can run. And *the presence* was keeping time with me and *the presence* was more than one!

I came to a halt when I knew it for certain.

I was only a mile from the boulevard and the crooked alley around me narrow and black as any in which I had ever been. And I heard *them* before they seemed, quite purposefully and abruptly, to silence themselves.

I was too anxious and miserable to play with them! I was too dazed. I shouted the old question, 'Who are you, speak to me!' The glass panes rattled in the nearby windows. Mortals stirred in their little chambers. There was no cemetery here. 'Answer me, you pack of cowards. Speak if you have a voice or once and for all get away from me!'

And then I knew, though how I knew, I can't tell you, that they could hear me and they could answer me, if they chose. And I knew that what I had always heard was the irrepressible evidence of their proximity and their intensity, which they couldn't disguise. But their thoughts they could cloak and they

157

had. I mean, they had intellect, and they had words.

I let out a long low breath.

I was stung by their silence, but I was stung a thousand times more by what had just happened, and as I'd done so many times in the past I turned my back on them.

They followed me. This time they followed, and no matter how swiftly I moved, they came on.

And I did not lose that strange toneless shimmer of them until I reached the place de Grève and went into the Cathedral of Notre Dame.

I SPENT the remainder of the night in the cathedral, huddled in a shadowy place by the right wall. I hungered for the blood I'd lost, and each time a mortal drew near I felt a strong pulling and tingling where the wounds had been.

But I waited.

And when a young beggar woman with a little child approached, I knew the moment had come. She saw the dried blood, and became frantic to get me to the nearby hospital, the Hôtel-Dieu. Her face was thin with hunger, but she tried to lift me herself with her little arms.

I looked into her eyes until I saw them glaze over. I felt the heat of her breasts swelling beneath her rags. Her soft, succulent body tumbled against me, giving itself to me, as I nestled her in all the bloodstained brocade and lace. I kissed her, feeding on her heat as I pushed the dirty cloth away from her throat, and I bent for the drink so skillfully that the sleepy child never saw it. Then I opened with careful trembling fingers the child's ragged shirt. This was mine, too, this little neck.

There weren't any words for the rapture. Before I'd had all the ecstasy that rape could give. But these victims had been taken in the perfect semblance of love. The very blood seemed warmer with their innocence, richer with their goodness.

I looked at them afterwards, as they slept together in death. They had found no sanctuary in the cathedral on this night.

And I knew my vision of the garden of savage beauty had been a true vision. There was meaning in the world, yes, and laws, and inevitability, but they had only to do with the aesthetic. And in this Savage Garden, these innocent ones belonged in the vampire's arms. A thousand other things can be said about the world, but only aesthetic principles can be verified, and these things alone remain the same.

I was now ready to go home. And as I went out in the early morning, I knew that the last barrier between my appetite and the world had been dissolved.

No one was safe from me now, no matter how innocent. And that included my dear friends at Renaud's and it included my beloved Nicki.

13

WANTED them gone from Paris. I wanted the playbills down, the doors shut. I wanted silence and darkness in the little rattrap theatre where I had known the greatest and most sustained happiness of my mortal life.

Not a dozen innocent victims a night could make me stop thinking about them, could make this ache in me dissolve. Every street in Paris led to their door.

And an ugly shame came over me when I thought of my frightening them. How could I have done that to them? Why did I need to prove to myself with such violence that I could never be part of them again?

No. I'd bought Renaud's. I'd turned it into the showcase of the boulevard. Now I would close it down.

It was not that they suspected anything, however. They believed the simple stupid excuses Roget gave them, that I was just back from the heat of the tropical colonies, that the good Paris wine had gone right to my head. Plenty of money again to repair the damage.

God only knows what they really thought. The fact was, they went back to regular performances the following evening, and the jaded crowds of the boulevard du Temple undoubtedly put upon the mayhem a dozen sensible explanations. There was a queue under the chestnut trees.

Only Nicki was having none of it. He had taken to heavy drinking and refused to return to the theatre or study his music anymore. He insulted Roget when he came to call. To the worst cafés and taverns he went, and wandered alone through the dangerous night-time streets.

Well, we have that in common, I thought.

All this Roget told me as I paced the floor a good distance from the candle on his table, my face a mask of my true thoughts.

'Money doesn't mean very much to this young man, Monsieur,' he said. 'The young man has had plenty of money in his life, he reminds me. He says things that disturb me, Monsieur. I don't like the sound of them.'

Roget looked like a nursery rhyme figure in his flannel cap and gown, legs and feet naked because I had roused him again in the middle of the night and given him no time to put on his slippers even or to comb his hair.

'What does he say?' I demanded.

'He talks about sorcery, Monsieur. He says that you possess unusual powers. He speaks of La Voisin and the *Chambre Ardente*, an old case of sorcery under the Sun King, the witch who made charms and poisons for members of the Court.'

'Who would believe that trash now?' I affected absolute bewilderment. The truth was, the hair was standing up on the back of my neck.

'Monsieur, he says bitter things,' he went on. 'That your kind, as he puts it, has always had access to great secrets. He keeps speaking of some place in your town, called the witches' place.'

'My kind!'

'That you are an aristocrat, Monsieur,' Roget said. He was a little embarrassed. 'When a man is angry as Monsieur de Lenfent is angry, these things come to be important. But he doesn't whisper his suspicions to the others. He tells only me. He says that you will understand why he despises you. You have refused to share with him your discoveries! Yes,

160

Monsieur, your discoveries. He goes on about La Voisin, about things between heaven and earth for which there are no rational explanations. He says he knows now why you cried at the witches' place.'

I couldn't look at Roget for a moment. It was such a lovely perversion of everything! And yet it hit right at the truth. How gorgeous, and how perfectly irrelevant. In his own way, Nicki was right.

'Monsieur, you are the kindest man —' Roget said.

'Spare me, please ...'

'But Monsieur de Lenfent says fantastical things, things he should not say even in this day and age, that he saw a bullet pass through your body that should have killed you.'

'The bullet missed me,' I said. 'Roget, don't go on with it. Get them out of Paris, all of them.'

'Get them out?' he said. 'But you've put so much money into this little enterprise ...'

'So what? Who gives a damn?' I said. 'Send them to London, to Drury Lane. Offer Renaud enough for his own London theatre. From there they might go to America — Saint-Domingue, New Orleans, New York. Do it, Monsieur. I don't care what it takes. Close up my theatre and get them gone!'

And then the ache will be gone, won't it? I'll stop seeing them gathered around me in the wings, stop thinking about Lelio, the boy from the provinces who emptied their slop buckets and loved it.

Roget looked so profoundly timid. What is it like, working for a well-dressed lunatic who pays you triple what anyone else would pay you to forget your better judgment?

I'll never know. I'll never know what it is like to be human in any way, shape, or form again.

'As for Nicolas,' I said. 'You're going to persuade him to go to Italy and I'll tell you how.'

'Monsieur, even persuading him to change his clothes would take some doing.'

'This will be easier. You know how ill my mother is. Well, get him to take her to Italy. It's the perfect thing. He can very

161

well study music at the conservatories in Naples, and that is exactly where my mother should go.'

'He does write to her ... is very fond of her.'

'Precisely. Convince him she'll never make the journey without him. Make all the arrangements for him. Monsieur, you must accomplish this. He must leave Paris. I give you till the end of the week, and then I'll be back for the news that he's gone.'

IT WAS asking a lot of Roget, of course. But I could think of no other way. Nobody would believe Nicki's ideas about sorcery, that was no worry. But I knew now that if Nicki didn't leave Paris, he would be driven slowly out of his mind.

As the nights passed, I fought with myself every waking hour not to seek him out, not to risk one last exchange.

I just waited, knowing full well that I was losing him forever and that he would never know the reasons for anything that had come to pass. I, who had once railed against the meaninglessness of our existence, was driving him off without explanation, an injustice that might torment him to the end of his days.

Better that than the truth, Nicki. Maybe I understand all illusions a little better now. And if you can only get my mother to go to Italy, if there is only time for my mother still ...

MEANTIME I could see for myself that Renaud's House of Thespians was closed down. In the nearby café, I heard talk of the troupe's departure for England. So that much of the plan had been accomplished.

IT WAS near dawn on the eighth night when I finally wandered up to Roget's door and pulled the bell.

He answered sooner than I expected, looking befuddled and anxious in the usual white flannel nightshirt.

'I'm getting to like that garb of yours, Monsieur,' I said wearily. 'I don't think I'd trust you half as much if you wore a shirt and breeches and a coat ...'

'Monsieur,' he interrupted me. 'Something quite un-expected —'

'Answer me first. Renaud and the others went happily to England?'

'Yes, Monsieur. They're in London by now, but —'

'And Nicki? Gone to my mother in Auvergne. Tell me I'm right. It's done.'

'But Monsieur!' he said. And then he stopped. And quite unexpectedly, I saw the image of my mother in his mind.

Had I been thinking, I would have known what it meant. This man had never to my knowledge laid eyes upon my mother, so how could he picture her in his thoughts? But I wasn't using my reason. In fact my reason had flown.

'She hasn't ... you're not telling me, that it's too late,' I said.

'Monsieur, let me get my coat ...' he said inexplicably. He reached for the bell.

And there it was, her image again, her face, drawn and white, and all too vivid for me to stand it.

I took Roget by the shoulders.

'You've seen her! She's here.'

'Yes, Monsieur. She's in Paris. I'll take you to her now. Young de Lenfent told me she was coming. But I couldn't reach you, Monsieur! I never know where to reach you. And yesterday she arrived.'

I was too stunned to answer. I sank down into the chair, and my own images of her blazed hot enough to eclipse everything that was emanating from him. She was alive and she was in Paris. And Nicki was still here and he was with her.

Roget came close to me, reached out as if he wanted to touch me:

'Monsieur, you go ahead while I dress. She is in the Ile St.-Louis, three doors to the right of Monsieur Nicolas. You must go at once.'

I looked up at him stupidly. I couldn't even really see him. I was seeing her. There was less than an hour before sunrise. And it would take me three-quarters of that time to reach the tower.

'Tomorrow ... tomorrow night,' I think I stammered. That

line came back to me from Shakespeare's *Macbeth* ... 'Tomorrow and tomorrow and tomorrow ...'

'Monsieur, you don't understand! There will be no trips to Italy for your mother. She has made her last journey in coming here to see you.'

When I didn't answer he grabbed hold of me and tried to shake me. I'd never seen him like this before. I was a body to him and he was the man who had to bring me to my senses.

'I've gotten lodgings for her,' he said. 'Nurses, doctors, all that you could wish. But they aren't keeping her alive. You are keeping her alive, Monsieur. She must see you before she closes her eyes. Now forget the hour and go to her. Even a will as strong as hers can't work miracles.'

I couldn't answer. I couldn't form a coherent thought.

I stood up and went to the door, pulling him along with me. 'Go to her now,' I said, 'and tell her I'll be there tomorrow night.'

He shook his head. He was angry and disgusted. And he tried to turn his back on me.

I wouldn't let him.

'You go there at once, Roget,' I said. 'Sit with her all day, do you understand, and see that she waits — that she waits for me to come! Watch her if she sleeps. Wake her and talk to her if she starts to go. But don't let her die before I get there!'

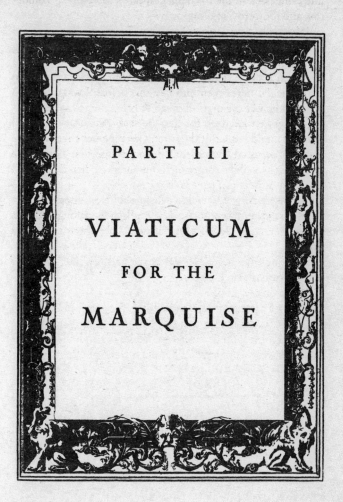

PART III

VIATICUM

FOR THE

MARQUISE

1

IN VAMPIRE parlance, I am an early riser. I rise when
the sun has just sunk below the horizon and there is
still red light in the sky. Many vampires don't rise until there is
full darkness, and so I have a tremendous advantage in this,
and in that they must return to the grave a full hour or more
before I do. I haven't mentioned it before because I didn't
know it then, and it didn't come to matter until much later.

But the next night, I was on the road to Paris when the sky
was on fire.

I'd clothed myself in the most respectable garments I
possessed before I slipped into the sarcophagus, and I was
chasing the sun west into Paris.

It looked like the city was burning, so bright was the light
to me and so terrifying, until finally I came pounding over the
bridge behind Notre Dame, into the Ile St.-Louis.

I didn't think about what I would do or say, or how I might
conceal myself from her. I knew only I had to see her and hold
her and be with her while there was still time. I couldn't truly
think of her death. It had the fullness of catastrophe, and
belonged to the burning sky. And maybe I was being the
common mortal, believing if I could grant her last wish, then
somehow the horror was under my command.

Dusk was just bleeding the light away when I found her
house on the quais.

It was a stylish enough mansion. Roget had done well, and a
clerk was at the door waiting to direct me up the stairs. Two
maids and a nurse were in the parlour of the flat when I came
in.

'Monsieur de Lenfent is with her, Monsieur,' the nurse said. 'She insisted on getting dressed to see you. She wanted to sit in the window and look at the towers of the cathedral, Monsieur. She saw you ride over the bridge.'

'Put out the candles in the room, except for one,' I said. 'And tell Monsieur de Lenfent and my lawyer to come out.'

Roget came out at once, and then Nicolas appeared.

He too had dressed for her, all in brilliant red velvet, with his old fancy linen and his white gloves. The recent drinking had left him thinner, almost haggard. Yet it made his beauty all the more vivid. When our eyes met, the malice leapt out of him, scorching my heart.

'The Marquise is a little stronger today, Monsieur,' Roget said, 'but she's hemorrhaging badly. The doctor says she will not —'

He stopped and glanced back at the bedroom. I got it clear from his thought. She won't last through the night.

'Get her back to bed, Monsieur, as fast you can.'

'For what purpose do I get her back to bed?' I said. My voice was dull, a murmur. 'Maybe she wants to die at the damned window. Why the hell not?'

'Monsieur!' Roget implored me softly.

I wanted to tell him to leave with Nicki.

But something was happening to me. I went into the hall and looked towards the bedroom. She was in there. I felt a dramatic physical change in myself. I couldn't move or speak. She was in there and she was really dying.

All the little sounds of the flat became a hum. I saw a lovely bedroom through the double doors, a white painted bed with gold hangings, and the windows draped in the same gold, and the sky in the high panes of the windows with only the faintest wisps of gold cloud. But all this was indistinct and faintly horrible, the luxury I'd wanted to give her and she about to feel her body collapse beneath her. I wondered if it maddened her, made her laugh.

The doctor appeared. The nurse came to tell me only one candle remained, as I had ordered. The smell of medicines intruded and mingled with a rose perfume, and *I realized I was*

168

hearing her thoughts.

It was the dull throb of her mind as she waited, her bones aching in her emaciated flesh so that to sit at the window even in the soft velvet chair with the comforter surrounding her was almost unendurable pain.

But what was she thinking, beneath her desperate anticipation? Lestat, Lestat, and Lestat, I could hear that. But beneath it:

'Let the pain get worse, because only when the pain is really dreadful do I want to die. If the pain would just get bad enough so that I'd be glad to die and I wouldn't be so frightened. I want it to be so terrible that I'm not frightened.'

'Monsieur.' The doctor touched my arm. 'She will not have the priest come.'

'No ... she wouldn't.'

She had turned her head towards the door. If I didn't come in now, she would get up, no matter how it hurt her, and come to me.

It seemed I couldn't move. And yet I pushed past the doctor and the nurse, and I went into the room and closed the doors.

Blood scent.

In the pale light of the window she sat, beautifully dressed in dark blue taffeta, her hand in her lap and the other on the arm of the chair, her thick yellow hair gathered behind her ears so that the curls spilled over her shoulders from the pink ribbons. There was the faintest bit of rouge on her cheeks.

For one eerie moment she looked to me as she had when I was a little boy. So pretty. The symmetry of her face was unchanged by time or illness, and so was her hair. And a heart-breaking happiness came over me, a warm delusion that I was mortal again, and innocent again, and with her, and everything was all right, really truly all right.

There was no death and no terror, just she and I in her bedroom, and she would take me in her arms. I stopped.

I'd come very close to her, and she was crying as she looked up. The girdle of the Paris dress bound her too tightly, and her skin was so thin and colourless over her throat and her hands that I couldn't bear to look at them, and her eyes looked up at me from flesh that was almost bruised. I could smell death on her. I could smell decay.

But she was radiant, and she was mine; she was as she'd always been, and I told her so silently with all my power, that she was lovely as my earliest memory of her when she had had her old fancy clothes still, and she would dress up so carefully and carry me on her lap in the carriage to church.

And in this strange moment when I gave her to know this, how much I cherished her, I realized she *heard* me and she answered me that she loved me and always had.

It was the answer to a question I hadn't even asked. And she knew the importance of it; her eyes were clear, unentranced.

If she realized the oddity of this, that we could talk to each other without words, she gave no clue. Surely she didn't grasp it fully. She must have felt only an outpouring of love.

'Come here so I can see you,' she said, 'as you are now.'

The candle was by her arm on the windowsill. And quite deliberately I pinched it out. I saw her frown, a tightening of her blonde brows, and her blue eyes grew just a little larger as she looked at me, at the bright silk brocade and the usual lace I'd chosen to wear for her, and the sword on my hip with its rather imposing jewelled hilt.

'Why don't you want me to see you?' she asked. 'I came to Paris to see you. Light the candle again.' But there was no real chastisement in the words. I was here with her and that was enough.

I knelt down before her. I had some mortal conversation in mind, that she should go to Italy with Nicki, and quite distinctly, before I could speak, she said:

'Too late, my darling, I could never finish the journey. I've come far enough.'

A clamp of pain stopped her, circling her waist where the girdle bound it, and to hide it from me, she made her face very blank. She looked like a girl when she did this, and again I smelt the sickness in her, the decay in her lungs, and the clots of blood.

Her mind became a riot of fear. She wanted to scream out to me that she was afraid. She wanted to beg me to hold on to her and remain with her until it was finished, but she couldn't do this, and to my astonishment, I realized she thought I would refuse her. That I was too young and too thoughtless to ever understand.

This was agony.

I wasn't even conscious of moving away from her, but I'd walked across the room. Stupid little details embedded themselves in my consciousness: nymphs playing on the painted ceiling, the high gilt door handles and the melted wax in brittle stalactites on the white candles that I wanted to break off and crumple in my hand. The place looked hideous, overdressed. Did she hate it? Did she want those barren stone rooms again?

I was thinking about her as if there were 'tomorrow and tomorrow and tomorrow ...' I looked back at her, her stately figure holding to the windowsill. The sky had deepened behind her and a new light, the light of house lamps and passing carriages and nearby windows, gently touched the small inverted triangle of her thin face.

'Can't you talk to me,' she said softly. 'Can't you tell me how it's come about? You've brought such happiness to all of us.' Even talking hurt her. 'But how does it go with you? With you!'

I think I was on the verge of deceiving her, of creating some strong emanation of contentment with all the powers I had. I'd tell mortal lies with immortal skill. I'd start talking and talking and testing my every word to make it perfect. But something happened in the silence.

I don't think I stood still more than a moment, but something changed inside of me. An awesome shift took place. In one instant I saw a vast and terrifying possibility, and in that same instant, without question, I made up my mind.

It had no words to it or scheme or plan. And I would have denied it had anyone questioned me at that moment. I would have said, 'No, never, farthest from my thoughts. What do you think I am, what sort of monster' ... And yet the choice had been made.

I understood something absolute.

171

Her words had completely died away, she was afraid again and in pain again, and in spite of the pain, she rose from the chair.

I saw the comforter slip away from her, and I knew she was coming towards me and that I should stop her, but I didn't do it. I saw her hands close to me, reaching for me, and the next thing I knew she had leapt backwards as if blown by a mighty wind.

She had scuffed backwards across the carpet, and fallen past the chair against the wall. But she grew very still quickly as though she willed it, and there wasn't fear in her face, even though her heart was racing. Rather there was wonder and then a baffled calm.

If I had thoughts at that moment, I don't know what they were. I came towards her just as steadily as she had come towards me. Gauging her every reaction, I drew closer until we were as near to each other as we had been when she leapt away. She was staring at my skin and my eyes, and quite suddenly she reached out again and touched my face.

'Not alive!' That was the horrifying perception that came from her silently. 'Changed into something. But NOT ALIVE.'

Quietly I said no. That was not right. And I sent a cool torrent of images to her, a procession of glimpses of what my existence had become. Bits, pieces of the fabric of the night-time Paris, the sense of a blade cutting through the world soundlessly.

With a little hiss she let out her breath. The pain balled its fist in her, opened its claw. She swallowed, sealing her lips against it, her eyes veritably burning into me. She knew now these were not sensations, these communications, but that they were thoughts.

'How then?' she demanded.

And without questioning what I meant to do, I gave her the tale link by link, the shattered window through which I'd been torn by the ghostly figure who had stalked me at the theatre, the tower and the exchange of blood. I revealed to her the crypt in which I slept, and its treasure, my wanderings, my powers, and above all, the nature of the thirst. The taste of blood and the feel of blood, and what it meant for all passion, all greed to be sharpened in that one desire, and that one desire to be satisfied over and over with the feeding and the death.

The pain ate at her but she no longer felt it. Her eyes were all that was left of her as she stared at me. And though I didn't mean to reveal all these things, I found I had taken hold of her and was turning so that the light of the carriages crashing along the quai below fell full on my face.

Without taking my eyes from her, I reached for the silver candelabra on the windowsill, and lifting it I slowly bent the metal, working it with my fingers into loops and twists.

The candles fell to the floor.

Her eyes rolled up into her head. She slipped backwards and away from me, and as she caught the curtains of the bed in her left hand, the blood came up out of her mouth.

It was coming from her lungs in a great silent cough. She was slipping down on her knees, and the blood was all over the side of the draped bed.

I looked at the twisted silver thing in my hands, the idiotic loops that meant nothing, and I let it drop. And I stared at her, her struggling against unconsciousness and pain, and wiping her mouth suddenly in sluggish gestures, like a vomiting drunk, on the bedclothes, as she sank unable to support herself to the floor.

I was standing over her. I was watching her, and her momentary pain meant nothing in light of the vow that I was speaking to her now. No words again, just the silent thrust of it, and the question, more immense than could ever be put into words. *Do you want to come with me now? DO YOU WANT TO COME WITH ME INTO THIS NOW?*

I hide nothing from you, not my ignorance, not my fear, not the simple terror that if I try I might fail. I do not even know if it is mine to give more than once, or what is the price of giving it, but I will risk this for you, and we will discover it together, whatever the mystery and the terror, just as I've discovered alone all else.

With her whole being she said Yes.

'Yes!' she screamed aloud suddenly, drunkenly, the voice maybe that had always been her voice yet one that I had never

173

heard. Her eyes closed and tightened and her head turned from the left and to the right. 'Yes!'

I leant forward and kissed the blood on her open lips. It sent a zinging through all my limbs and the thirst leapt out for her and tried to transform her into mere flesh. My arms slipped around her light little form and I lifted her up and up, until I was standing with her against the window, and her hair was falling down behind her, and the blood came up in her out of her lungs again, but it didn't matter now.

All the memories of my life with her surrounded us; they wove their shroud around us and closed us off from the world, the soft poems and songs of childhood, and the sense of her before words when there had only been the flicker of the light on the ceiling above her pillows and the smell of her all around me and her voice silencing my crying, and then the hatred of her and the need of her, and the losing of her behind a thousand closed doors, and cruel answers, and the terror of her and her complexity and her indifference and her indefinable strength.

And jetting up into the current came the thirst, not obliterating but heating every concept of her, until she was flesh and blood and mother and lover and all things beneath the cruel pressure of my fingers and my lips, everything I had ever desired. I drove my teeth into her, feeling her stiffen and gasp, and I felt my mouth grow wide to catch the hot flood when it came.

Her heart and soul split open. There was no age to her, no single moment. My knowledge dimmed and flickered and there was no mother anymore, no petty need and petty terror; she was simply who she was. She was Gabrielle.

And all her life came to her defence, the years and years of suffering and loneliness, the waste in those damp, hollow chambers to which she'd been condemned, and the books that were her solace, and the children who devoured her and abandoned her, and the pain and disease, her final enemy, which had, in promising release, pretended to be her friend. Beyond words and images there came the secret thudding of her passion, her seeming madness, her refusal to despair.

I was holding her, holding her off her feet, my arms crossed behind her narrow back, my hand cradling her limp head, and I was groaning so loud against her with the pumping of the blood that it was a song in time with her heart. But the heart was slowing too quickly. Her death was coming, and with all her will she pumped against it, and in a final burst of denial I pushed her away from me and held her still.

I was almost swooning. The thirst wanted her heart. It was no alchemist, the thirst. And I was standing there with my lips parted and my eyes glazed and I held her far, far away from me as if I were two beings, the one wanting to crush her and the other to bring her to me.

Her eyes were open and seemingly blind. For a moment she was in some place beyond all suffering, where there was nothing but sweetness and even something that might be understanding, but then I heard her calling to me by name.

I lifted my right wrist to my mouth and slashed the vein and pushed it against her lips. She didn't move as the blood spilled over her tongue.

'Mother, drink,' I said frantically, and pushed it harder, but some change had already commenced.

Her lips quivered, and her mouth locked to me and the pain whipped through me suddenly encircling my heart.

Her body lengthened, tensed, her left hand rising to grasp my wrist as she swallowed the first spurt. And the pain grew stronger and stronger so that I almost cried out. I could see it as if it were molten metal coursing through my vessels, branching through every sinew and limb. Yet it was only her pulling, her sucking, her taking the blood out of me that I had taken from her. She was standing now on her own feet, her head barely leaning against my chest. And a numbness crept over me with the pulling burning through the numbness, and my heart thundered against it, feeding the pain as it fed her pulling with every beat.

Harder and harder she drew and faster, and I felt her grip tighten and her body grow hard. I wanted to force her away, but I would not do it, and when my legs gave under me it was she who held me up. I was swaying and the room was tilting, but she went on with it and a vast silence stretched out in all directions from me and then without will or conviction, I thrust her backwards away.

She stumbled and stood before the window, her long fingers pressed flat against her open mouth. And before I turned and collapsed into the nearby chair I looked full at her white face for an instant, and her form swelling, it seemed, under the thin peeling of dark blue taffeta, her eyes like two crystal orbs gathering the light.

I think I said, 'Mother,' in that instant like some stupid mortal, and I closed my eyes.

2

I WAS sitting in the chair. It seemed I'd been asleep forever, but I hadn't been asleep at all. I was home in my father's house.

I looked around for the fire poker and my dogs, and to see if there was any wine left, and then I saw the gold drapery around the windows and the back of Notre Dame against the evening stars, and I saw her there.

We were in Paris. And we were going to live forever.

She had something in her hands. Another candelabra. A tinderbox. She stood very straight and her movements were quick. She made a spark and touched it to the candles one by one. And the little flames rose, and the painted flowers on the walls rolled up to the ceiling and the dancers on the ceiling moved for one moment and then were frozen in their circle again.

She was standing in front of me, the candelabra to the right of her. And her face was white and perfectly smooth. The dark bruises under her eyes had gone away; in fact every blemish or flaw she had ever had had gone away, though what those flaws had been I couldn't have told you. She was perfect now.

And the lines given her by age had been reduced and

curiously deepened, so that there were tiny laugh lines at the edge of each eye, and a very tiny crease on either side of her mouth. The barest fold of extra flesh remained to each eyelid, heightening her symmetry, the sense of triangles in her face, and her lips were the softest shade of pink. She looked delicate as a diamond can look delicate when preyed upon by the light.

I closed my eyes and opened them again and saw it was no delusion, any more than her silence was a delusion. And I saw that her body was even more profoundly changed. She had the fullness of young womanhood again, the breasts that the illness had withered away. They were swelling above the dark taffeta of her corset, the pale pink tint of her flesh so subtle, it might have been reflected light. But her hair was even more astonishing because it appeared to be alive. So much colour moved in it that the hair itself appeared to be writhing, billions of tiny strands stirring around the flawless white face and throat.

The wounds on her throat were going.

Now nothing remained but the final act of courage. Look into her eyes.

Look with these vampire eyes at another being like yourself for the first time since Magnus leapt into the fire.

I must have made some sound because she responded ever so slightly as if I had. Gabrielle, that was the only name I could ever call her now. 'Gabrielle,' I said to her, never having called her that except in some very private thoughts, and I saw her almost smile.

I looked down at my wrist. The wound was gone but the thirst gnashed in me. My veins spoke to me as if I had spoken to them. And I stared at her and saw her lips move in a tiny gesture of hunger. And she gave me a strange, meaningful expression as if to say, 'Don't you understand?'

But I heard nothing from her. Silence, only the beauty of her eyes looking full at me and the love perhaps with which we saw each other, but silence stretching in all directions, ratifying nothing. I couldn't fathom it. Was she closing her mind? I asked her silently and she didn't appear to comprehend.

177

'Now,' she said, and her voice startled me. It was softer, more resonant than before. For one moment we were in Auvergne, the snow was falling, and she was singing to me and it was echoing as if in a great cave. But that was finished. She said, 'Go ... done with all of this, quickly — now!' She nodded to coax me and she came closer and she tugged at my hand. 'Look at yourself in the mirror,' she whispered.

But I knew. I had given her more blood than I had taken from her. I was starved. I hadn't even fed before I came to her.

But I was so taken with the sound of the syllables and that glimpse of snow falling and the memory of the singing that for a moment I didn't respond. I looked at her fingers touching mine. I saw our flesh was the same. I rose up out of the chair and held her two hands and then I felt of her arms and her face. It was done and I was alive still! She was *with* me now. She had come through that awful solitude and she was with me, and I could think of nothing suddenly except holding her, crushing her to me, never letting her go.

I lifted her off her feet. I swung her up in my arms and we turned round and round.

She threw back her head and her laughter shook loose from her, growing louder and louder, until I put my hand over her mouth.

'You can shatter all the glass in the room with your voice,' I whispered. I glanced towards the doors. Nicki and Roget were out there.

'Then let me shatter it!' she said, and there was nothing playful in her expression. I set her on her feet. I think we embraced again and again almost foolishly. I couldn't keep myself from it.

But other mortals were moving in the flat, the doctor and the nurses thinking that they should come in.

I saw her look to the door. She was hearing them too. But why wasn't I hearing her?

She broke away from me, eyes darting from one object to another. She snatched up the candles again and brought them to the mirror where she looked at her face.

I understood what was happening to her. She needed time

to see and to measure with her new vision. But we had to get out of the flat.

I could hear Nicki's voice through the wall, urging the doctor to knock on the door.

How was I to get her out of here, get rid of them?

'No, not that way,' she said when she saw me look at the door.

She was looking at the bed, the objects on the table. She went to the bed and took her jewels from under the pillow. She examined them and put them back into the worn velvet purse. Then she fastened the purse to her skirt so that it was lost in the folds of cloth.

There was an air of importance to these little gestures. I knew even though her mind was giving me nothing that this was all she wanted from this room. She was taking leave of things, the clothes she'd brought with her, her ancient silver brush and comb, and the tattered books that lay on the table by the bed.

There was knocking at the door.

'Why not this way?' she asked, and turning to the window, she threw open the glass. The breeze gusted into the gold draperies and lifted her hair off the back of her neck, and when she turned I shivered at the sight of her, her hair tangling around her face, and her eyes wild and filled with myriad fragments of colour and an almost tragic light. She was afraid of nothing.

I took hold of her and for a moment wouldn't let her go. I nestled my face into her hair, and all I could think again was that we were together and nothing was ever going to separate us now. I didn't understand her silence, why I couldn't *hear* her, but I knew it wasn't her doing, and perhaps I believed it would pass. She was with me. That was the world. Death was my commander and I gave him a thousand victims, but I'd snatched her right out of his hand. I said it aloud. I said other desperate and nonsensical things. We were the same terrible and deadly beings, the two of us, we were wandering in the Savage Garden and I tried to make it real for her with images, the meaning of the Savage Garden, but it didn't matter if she didn't understand.

'The Savage Garden,' she repeated the words reverently, her lips making a soft smile.

It was pounding in my head. I felt her kissing me and making some little whisper as if in accompaniment to her thoughts.

She said, 'But help me, now, I want to see you *do it*, now, and we have forever to hold to each other. Come.'

Thirst. I should have been burning. I positively required the blood, and she wanted the taste, I knew she did. Because I remembered that I had wanted it that very first night. It struck me then that the pain of her physical death ... the fluids leaving her ... might be lessened if she could first drink.

The knocking came again. The door wasn't locked.

I stepped up on the sill of the window and reached for her, and immediately she was in my arms. She weighed nothing, but I could feel her power, the tenacity of her grip. Yet when she saw the alley below, the top of the wall and the quai beyond, she seemed for a moment to doubt.

'Put your arms around my neck,' I said, 'and hold tight.'

I climbed up the stones, carrying her with her feet dangling, her face turned upwards to me, until we had reached the slippery slates of the roof.

Then I took her hand and pulled her after me, running faster and faster, over the gutters and the chimney pots, leaping across the narrow alleys until we had reached the other side of the island. I'd been ready any moment for her to cry out or cling to me, but she wasn't afraid.

She stood silent, looking over the rooftops of the Left Bank, and down at the river crowded with thousands of dark little boats full of ragged beings, and she seemed for the moment simply to feel the wind unravelling her hair. I could have fallen in a stupor looking at her, studying her, all the aspects of the transformation, but there was an immense excitement in me to take her through the entire city, to reveal all things to her, to teach her everything I'd learned. She knew nothing of physical exhaustion now any more than I did. And she wasn't stunned by any horror such as I had been when Magnus went into the fire.

A carriage came speeding along the quai below, listing badly towards the river, the driver hunched over, trying to keep his balance on the high bench. I pointed to it as it drew near and I clasped her hand.

We leapt as it came beneath us, landing soundlessly on the leather top. The busy driver never looked around. I held tight to her, steadying her, until we were both riding easily, ready to jump off the vehicle when we chose.

It was indescribably thrilling, doing this with her.

We were thundering over the bridge and past the cathedral, and on through the crowds on the Pont Neuf. I heard her laughter again. I wondered what those in the high windows saw when they looked down on us, two gaily dressed figures clinging to the unsteady roof of the carriage like mischievous children as if it were a raft.

The carriage swerved. We were racing towards St.-Germain-des-Prés, scattering the crowds before us and roaring past the intolerable stench of the cemetery of les Innocents as towering tenements closed in.

For one second, I felt the shimmer of *the presence*, but it was gone so quickly I doubted myself. I looked back and could catch no glimmer of it. And I realized with extraordinary vividness that Gabrielle and I would talk about *the presence* together, that we would talk about everything together, and approach all things together. This night was as cataclysmic in its own way as the night Magnus had changed me, and this night had only begun.

The neighbourhood was perfect now. I took her hand again, and pulled her after me, off the carriage, down into the street.

She stared dazed at the spinning wheels, but they were immediately gone. She didn't even look dishevelled so much as she looked impossible, a woman torn out of time and place, clad only in slippers and dress, no chains on her, free to soar.

We entered a narrow alleyway and ran together, arms around each other, and now and then I looked down to see her eyes sweeping the walls above us, the scores of shuttered windows with their little streaks of escaping light.

I knew what she was seeing. I knew the sounds that pressed in on her. But still I could hear nothing from her, and this frightened me a little to think maybe she was deliberately shutting me out.

But she had stopped. She was having the first spasm of her death. I could see it in her face.

I reassured her, and reminded her in quick words of the vision I'd given her before.

'This is brief pain, nothing compared to what you've known. It will be gone in a matter of hours, maybe less if we drink now.'

She nodded, more impatient with it than afraid.

We came out into a little square. In the gateway to an old house a young man stood, as if waiting for someone, the collar of his grey cloak up to shield his face.

Was she strong enough to take him? Was she as strong as I? This was the time to find out.

'If the thirst doesn't carry you into it, then it's too soon,' I told her.

I glanced at her and a coldness crept over me. Her look of concentration was almost purely human, so intent was it, so fixed; and her eyes were shadowed with that same sense of tragedy I'd glimpsed before. Nothing was lost on her. But when she moved towards the man she wasn't human at all. She had become a pure predator, as only a beast can be a predator, and yet she was a woman walking slowly towards a man — a lady, in fact, stranded here without cape or hat or companions, and approaching a gentleman as if to beg for his aid. She was all that.

It was ghastly to watch it, the way that she moved over the stones as if she did not even touch them, and the way that everything, even the wisps of her hair blown this way and that by the breeze, seemed somehow under her command. She could have moved through the wall itself with that relentless step.

I drew back into the shadows.

The man quickened, turned to her with the faint grind of his boot heel on the stones, and she rose on tiptoe as if to whisper in his ear. I think for one moment she hesitated. Perhaps she was faintly horrified. If she was, then the thirst had not had time enough to grow strong. But if she did question it, it was for no more than that second. She was taking him and he was powerless and I was too fascinated to do anything but watch.

But it came to me quite unexpectedly that I hadn't warned her about the heart. How could I have forgotten such a thing? I rushed towards her, but she had already let him go. And he had crumpled against the wall, his head to one side, his hat fallen at his feet. He was dead.

She stood looking down at him, and I saw the blood working in her, heating her and deepening her colour and the red of her lips. Her eyes were a flash of violet when she glanced at me, almost exactly the colour the sky had been when I'd come into her bedroom. I was silent watching her as she looked down at the victim with a curious amazement as if she did not completely accept what she saw. Her hair was tangled again and I lifted it back for her.

She slipped into my arms. I guided her away from the victim. She glanced back once or twice, then looked straight forward.

'It's enough for this night. We should go home to the tower,' I said. I wanted to show her the treasure, and just to be with her in the safe place, to hold her and comfort her if she began to go mad over it all. She was feeling the death spasms again. There she could rest by the fire.

'No, I don't want to go yet,' she said. 'The pain won't go on long, you promised it wouldn't. I want it to pass and then to be here.' She looked up at me, and she smiled. 'I came to Paris to die, didn't I?' she whispered.

Everything was distracting her, the dead man back there, slumped in his grey cape, the sky shimmering on the surface of a puddle of water, a cat streaking atop a nearby wall. The blood was hot in her, moving in her.

I clasped her hand and urged her to follow me. 'I have to drink,' I said.

'Yes, I see it,' she whispered. 'You should have taken him. I should have thought ... And you are the gentleman, even still.'

'The starving gentleman,' I smiled. 'Let's not stumble over ourselves devising an etiquette for monsters.' I laughed. I would have kissed her, but I was suddenly distracted. I squeezed her hand too tightly.

Far away, from the direction of les Innocents, I heard *the presence* as strongly as ever before.

She stood as still as I was, and inclining her head slowly to one side, moved the hair back from her ear.

'Do you hear it?' I asked.

She looked up at me. 'Is it *another one*!' She narrowed her eyes and glanced again in the direction from which the emanation had come.

'Outlaw!' she said aloud.

'What?' *Outlaw, outlaw, outlaw.* I felt a wave of light-headedness, something of a dream remembered. Fragment of a dream. But I couldn't think. I'd been damaged by doing it to her. I *had* to drink.

'It called us outlaws,' she said. 'Didn't you hear it?' And she listened again, but it was gone and neither of us heard it, and I couldn't be certain that I had received that clear pulse, *outlaw*, but it seemed I had!

'Never mind it, whatever it is,' I said. 'It never comes any closer than that.' But even as I spoke, I knew it had been more virulent this time. I wanted to get away from les Innocents. 'It lives in graveyards,' I murmured. 'It may not be able to live elsewhere ... for very long.'

But before I finished speaking, I felt it again, and it seemed to expand and to exude the strongest malevolence I'd received from it yet.

'It's laughing!' she whispered.

I studied her. Without doubt, she was hearing it more clearly than I.

'Challenge it!' I said. 'Call it a coward! Tell it to come out!'

She gave me an amazed look.

'Is that really what you want to do?' she questioned me under her breath. She was trembling slightly, and I steadied

184

her. She put her arm around her waist as if one of the spasms had come again.

'Not now then,' I said. 'This isn't the time. And we'll hear it again, just when we've forgotten all about it.'

'It's gone,' she said. 'But it hates us, this thing …'

'Let's get away from it,' I said contemptuously and putting my arm around her I hurried her along.

I didn't tell her what I was thinking, what weighed on me far more than *the presence* and its usual tricks. If she could hear *the presence* as well as I could, better in fact, then she had all my powers, including the ability to send and hear images and thoughts. Yet we could no longer *hear* each other!

3

I FOUND a victim as soon as we had crossed the river, and as soon as I spotted the man, there came the deepening awareness that everything I had done alone I would now do with her. She would watch this act, learn from it. I think the intimacy of it made the blood rush to my face.

And as I lured the victim out of the tavern, as I teased him, maddened him, and then took him, I knew I was showing off for her, making it a little crueller, more playful. And when the kill came, it had an intensity to it that left me spent afterwards.

She loved it. She watched everything as if she could suck up the very vision as she sucked blood. We came together again and I took her in my arms and I felt her heat and she felt my heat. The blood was flooding my brain. And we just held each other, even the thin covering of our garments seeming alien, two burning statues in the dark.

After that, the night lost all ordinary dimensions. In fact, it remains one of the longest nights I have ever endured in my immortal life.

It was endless and fathomless and dizzying, and there were

times when I wanted some defence against its pleasures and its surprises, and I had none.

And though I said her name over and over, to make it natural, she wasn't really Gabrielle yet to me. She was simply *she*, the one I had needed all of my life with all of my being. The only woman I had ever loved.

Her actual death didn't take long.

We sought out an empty cellar room where we remained until it was finished. And there I held on to her and talked to her as it went on. I told her everything that had happened to me again, in words this time.

I told her all about the tower. I told everything that Magnus had said. I explained all the occurrences of *the presence*. And how I had become almost used to it and contemptuous of it, and not willing to chase it down. Over and over again I tried to send her images, but it was useless. I didn't say anything about it. Neither did she. But she listened very attentively.

I talked to her about Nicki's suspicions, which of course he had not mentioned to her at all. And I explained that I feared for him even more now. Another open window, another empty room, and this time witnesses to verify the strangeness of it all.

But never mind, I should tell Roget some story that would make it plausible. I should find some means to do right by Nicki, to break the chain of suspicions that was binding him to me.

She seemed dimly fascinated by all of this, but it didn't really matter to her. What mattered to her was what lay before her now.

And when her death was finished, she was unstoppable. There was no wall that she could not climb, no door she wouldn't enter, no rooftop terrain too steep.

It was as if she did not believe she would live forever; rather she thought she had been granted this one night of supernatural vitality and all things must be known and accomplished before death would come for her at dawn.

Many times I tried to persuade her to go home to the tower. As the hours passed, a spiritual exhaustion came over me. I needed to be quiet there, to think on what had happened. I'd open my eyes and see only blackness for an instant. But she wanted only experiment, adventure.

She proposed that we enter the private dwellings of mortals now to search for the clothes she needed. She laughed when I said that I always purchased my clothes in the proper way.

'We can hear if a house is empty,' she said, moving swiftly through the streets, her eyes on the windows of the darkened mansions. 'We can hear if the servants are asleep.'

It made perfect sense, though I'd never attempted such a thing. And I was soon following her up narrow back stairs and down carpeted corridors, amazed at the ease of it all, and fascinated by the details of the informal chambers in which mortals lived. I found I liked to touch personal things: fans, snuffboxes, the newspaper the master of the house had been reading, his boots on the hearth. It was as much fun as peering into windows.

But she had her purpose. In a lady's dressing room in a large St.-Germain house, she found a fortune in lavish clothes to fit her new and fuller form. I helped to peel off the old taffeta and to dress her up in pink velvet, gathering her hair in tidy curls under an ostrich-plume hat. I was shocked again by the sight of her, and the strange eerie feeling of wandering with her through this overfurnished house full of mortal scents. She gathered objects from the dressing table. A vial of perfume, a small gold pair of scissors. She looked at herself in the glass.

I went to kiss her again and she didn't stop me. We were lovers kissing. And that was the picture we made together, white-faced lovers, as we rushed down the servants' stairs and out into the late evening streets.

We wandered in and out of the Opéra and the Comédie before they closed, then through the ball in the Palais Royal. It delighted her the way mortals saw us, but did not see us, how they were drawn to us, and completely deceived.

We heard *the presence* very sharply after that, as we explored the churches, then again it was gone. We climbed belfries to survey our kingdom, and afterwards huddled in crowded coffeehouses for a little while merely to feel and smell the mortals around us, to exchange secret glances, to laugh softly, tête-à-tête.

She fell into dream states, looking at the steam rising from the mug of coffee, at the layers of cigarette smoke hovering around the lamps.

She loved the dark empty streets and the fresh air more than anything else. She wanted to climb up into the limbs of the trees and onto the rooftops again. She marvelled that I didn't always travel through the city by means of rooftops, or ride about atop carriages as we had done.

Some time after midnight, we were in the deserted market, just walking hand in hand.

We had just heard *the presence* again but neither of us could discern a disposition in it as we had before. It was puzzling me.

But everything around us was astonishing her still — the refuse, the cats that chased the vermin, the bizarre stillness, the way that the darkest corners of the metropolis held no danger for us. She remarked on that. Perhaps it was that which enchanted her most of all, that we could slip past the dens of thieves unheard, that we could easily defeat anyone who should be fool enough to trouble us, that we were both visible and invisible, palpable and utterly unaccountable.

I didn't rush her or question her. I was merely borne along with her and content and sometimes lost in my own thoughts about this unfamiliar content.

And when a handsome, slightly built young man came riding through the darkened stalls I watched him as if he were an apparition, something coming from the land of the living into the land of the dead. He reminded me of Nicolas because of his dark hair and dark eyes, and something innocent yet brooding in the face. He shouldn't have been in the market alone. He was younger than Nicki and very foolish, indeed.

But just how foolish he was I didn't realize until she moved forward like a great pink feline, and brought him down almost silently from the horse.

I was shaken. The innocence of her victims didn't trouble her. She didn't fight my moral battles. But then I didn't fight them anymore either, so why should I judge her? Yet the ease with which she slew the young man — gracefully breaking his neck when the little drink she took was not enough to kill him — angered me though it had been extremely exciting to watch.

She was colder than I. She was better at all of it, I thought, Magnus had said, 'Show no mercy.' But had he meant us to kill when we did not have to kill?'

It came clear in an instant why she'd done it. She tore off the pink velvet girdle and skirts right there and put on the boy's clothes. She'd chosen him for the fit of the clothes.

And to describe it more truly, as she put on his garments, she became the boy.

She put on his cream silk stockings and scarlet breeches, the lace shirt and the yellow waistcoat and then the scarlet frock coat, and even took the scarlet ribbon from the boy's hair.

Something in me rebelled against the charm of it, her standing so boldly in these new garments with all her hair still full over her shoulders looking more the lion's mane now than the lovely mass of woman's tresses it had been moments before. Then I wanted to ravage her. I closed my eyes.

When I looked at her again, my head was swimming with all that we'd seen and done together. I couldn't endure being so near to the dead boy.

She tied all of her blonde hair together with the scarlet ribbon and let the long locks hang down her back. She laid the pink dress over the body of the boy to cover him, and she buckled on his sword, and drew it once and sheathed it again, and took his cream-coloured roquelaure.

'Let's go, then, darling,' she said, and she kissed me.

I couldn't move. I wanted to go back to the tower, and just be close to her. She looked at me and pressed my head to spur me on. And she was almost immediately running ahead.

She had to feel the freedom of her limbs, and I found myself pounding after her, having to exert myself to catch up.

That had never happened with me and any mortal, of course. She seemed to be flying. And the sight of her flashing through the boarded-up stalls and the heaps of garbage made me almost lose my balance. Again I stopped.

She came back to me and kissed me. 'But there's no real reason for me to dress that way anymore, is there?' she asked. She might have been talking to a child.

'No, of course there isn't,' I said. Maybe it was a blessing that she couldn't read my thoughts. I couldn't stop looking at her legs, so perfect in the cream-coloured stockings. And the way that the frock coat gathered at her small waist. Her face was like a flame.

Remember in those times you never saw a woman's legs like that. Or the silk of breeches tight over her small belly, or thighs.

But she was not really a woman now, was she? Any more than I was a man. For one silent second the horror of it all bled through.

'Come, I want to take to the roofs again,' she said. 'I want to go to the boulevard du Temple. I should like to see the theatre, the one that you purchased and then shut up. Will you show that to me?' She was studying me as she asked this.

'Of course,' I said. 'Why not?'

WE HAD two hours left of the endless night when we finally returned to the Ile St.-Louis and stood on the moonlit quais. Far down the paved street I saw my mare tethered where I'd left her. Perhaps she had gone unnoticed in the confusion that must have followed our departure.

We listened carefully for any sign of Nicki or Roget, but the house appeared deserted and dark.

'They are near, however,' she whispered. 'I think somewhere further down ...'

'Nicki's flat,' I said. 'And from Nicki's flat someone could be watching the mare, a servant posted to watch in case we came back.'

'Better to leave the horse and steal another,' she said.

'No, it's mine,' I said. But I felt her grip on my hand tighten.

Our old friend again, *the presence*, and this time it was moving along the Seine on the other side of the island and towards the Left Bank.

'Gone,' she said. 'Let's go. We can steal another mount.'

190

'Wait. I'm going to try to get her to come to me. To break the tether.'

'Can you do that?'

'We'll see.' I concentrated all my will on the mare, telling her silently to back up, to pull loose from the bond holding her and come.

In a second, the horse was prancing, jerking at the leather. Then she reared and the tether broke.

She came clattering towards us over the stones, and we were on her immediately, Gabrielle leaping up first and I right behind her, gathering up what was left of the rein as I urged the horse to go into a dead run.

As we crossed the bridge I felt something behind us, a commotion, the tumult of mortal minds.

But we were lost in the black echo chamber of the Ile de la Cité.

WHEN we reached the tower, I lighted the resin torch and took her down with me into the dungeon. There was no time now to show her the upper chamber.

Her eyes were glassy and she looked about herself sluggishly as we descended the screw stairs. Her scarlet clothes gleamed against the dark stones. Ever so slightly she recoiled from the dampness.

The stench from the lower prison cells disturbed her, but I told her gently it was nothing to do with us. And once we had entered the huge burial crypt, the smell was shut out by the heavy iron-studded door.

The torchlight spread out to reveal the low arches of the ceiling, the three great sarcophagi with their deeply graven images.

She did not seem afraid. I told her that she must see if she could lift the stone lid of the one she chose for herself. I might have to do it for her.

She studied the three carved figures. And after a moment's reflection, she chose not the woman's sarcophagus but the one with the knight in armour carved on the top of it. And slowly she pushed the stone lid out of place so she could look into the space within.

Not as much strength as I possessed but strong enough.

'Don't be frightened,' I said.

'No, you mustn't ever worry on that account,' she answered softly. Her voice had a lovely frayed sound to it, a faint timbre of sadness. She appeared to be dreaming as she ran her hands over the stone.

'By this hour,' she said, 'she might have already been laid out, your mother. And the room would be full of evil smells and the smoke of hundreds of candles. Think how humiliating it is, death. Strangers would have taken off her clothes, bathed her, dressed her — strangers seen her emaciated and defenceless in the final sleep. And those whispering in the corridors would have talked of their good health, and how they have never had the slightest illness in their families, no, no consumption in their families. "The poor Marquise", they would have said. They would have been wondering, did she have any money of her own? Did she leave it to her sons? And the old woman when she came to collect the soiled sheets, she would have stolen one of the rings off the dead woman's hand.'

I nodded. And so we stand in this dungeon crypt, I wanted to say, and we prepare to lie down on stone beds, with only rats to keep us company. But it's infinitely better than that, isn't it? It has its dark splendour, to walk the nightmare terrain forever.

She looked wan, cold all over. Sleepily, she drew something out of her pocket.

It was the golden scissors she'd taken from the lady's table in the faubourg St.-Germain. Sparkling in the light of the torch like a bauble.

'No, Mother,' I said. My own voice startled me. It leapt out echoing too sharply under the arched ceiling. The figures on the other sarcophagi seemed merciless witnesses. The hurt in my heart stunned me.

Evil sound, the snipping, the shearing. Her hair fell down in great long locks on the floor.

'Ooooh, Mother.'

She looked down at it, scattering it silently with the tip of her boot, and then she looked up at me, and she was a young man now certainly, the short hair curling against her cheek. But her eyes were closing. She reached out to me and the scissors fell out of her hands.

'Rest now,' she whispered.

'It's only the rising sun,' I said to reassure her. She was weakening sooner than I did. She turned away from me and moved towards the coffin. I lifted her and her eyes shut. Pushing the lid of the sarcophagus even farther to the right, I laid her down inside, letting her pliant limbs arrange themselves naturally and gracefully.

Her face had already smoothed itself into sleep, her hair framing her face with a young boy's locks.

Dead, she seemed, and gone, the magic undone.

I kept looking at her.

I let my teeth cut into the tip of my tongue until I felt the pain and tasted the hot blood there. Then bending low I let the blood fall in tiny shining droplets on her lips. Her eyes opened. Violet blue and glittering, they stared up at me. The blood flowed into her opening mouth and slowly she lifted her head to meet my kiss. My tongue passed into her. Her lips were cold. My lips were cold. But the blood was hot and it flowed between us.

'Good night, my darling one,' I said. 'My dark angel Gabrielle.'

She sank back into stillness as I let her go. I closed the stone over her.

4

I DID not like rising in the black underground crypt. I didn't like the chill in the air, and that faint stench from the prison below, the feeling that this was where all the dead things lay.

A fear overcame me. What if she didn't rise? What if her eyes never opened again? What did I know of what I'd done?

Yet it seemed an arrogant thing, an obscene thing to move the lid of the coffin again and gaze at her in her sleep as I had done last night. A mortal shame came over me. At home, I would never have dared to open her door without knocking, never dared to draw back the curtains of her bed.

She would rise. She had to. And better that she should lift the stone for herself, know how to rise, and that the thirst should drive her to it at the proper moment as it had driven me.

I lighted the torch on the wall for her, and went out for a moment to breathe the fresh air. Then leaving gates and doors unlocked behind me, I went up into Magnus's cell to watch the twilight melt from the sky.

I'd hear her, I thought, when she awoke.

An hour must have passed. The azure light faded, the stars rose, and the distant cry of Paris lighted its myriad tiny beacons. I left the windowsill where I had sat against the iron bars and I went to the chest and began to select jewels for her.

Jewels she still loved. She had taken her old keepsakes with her when we left her room. I lighted the candles to help me see, though I didn't really need them. The illumination was beautiful to me. Beautiful on the jewels. And I found very delicate and lovely things for her — pearl-studded pins that she might wear in the lapels of her mannish little coat, and rings that would look masculine on her small hands if that was what she wanted.

I listened now and then for her. And this chill would clutch my heart. What if she did not rise? What if there had been only that one night for her? Horror thudding in me. And the sea of jewels in the chest, the candlelight dancing in the faceted stones, the gold settings — it meant nothing.

But I didn't hear her. I heard the wind outside, the great soft rustle of the trees, the faint distant whistling of the stable boy as he moved about the barn, the neighing of my horses.

Far off a village church bell rang.

Then very suddenly there came over me the feeling that

194

someone was watching me. This was so unfamiliar to me that I panicked. I turned, almost stumbling into the chest, and stared at the mouth of the secret tunnel. No one there.

No one in this small empty sanctum with the candlelight playing on the stones and Magnus's grim countenance on the sarcophagus.

Then I looked straight in front of me at the barred window. And I saw her looking back at me.

Floating in the air she seemed to be, holding to the bars with both hands, and she was smiling.

I almost cried out. I backed up and the sweat broke out all over my body. I was embarrassed suddenly to be caught off guard, to be so obviously startled.

But she remained motionless, smiling still, her expression gradually changing from serenity to mischievousness. The candlelight made her eyes too brilliant.

'It's not very nice to frighten other immortals like that,' I said.

She laughed more freely and easily than she ever had when she was alive.

Relief coursed through me as she moved, made sounds. I knew I was blushing.

'How did you get there!' I said. I went to the window and reached through the bars and clasped both her wrists.

Her little mouth was all sweetness and laughter. Her hair was a great shimmering mane around her face.

'I climbed the wall, of course,' she said. 'How do you think I got here?'

'Well, go down. You can't come through the bars. I'll go to meet you.'

'You're very right about that,' she said. 'I've been to all the windows. Meet me on the battlements above. It's faster.'

She started climbing, hooking her boots easily into the bars, then she vanished.

She was all exuberance as she'd been the night before as we came down the stairs together.

'Why are we lingering here?' she said. 'Why don't we go on now to Paris?'

Something was wrong with her, lovely as she was, something not right ... what was it?

She didn't want kisses now, or even talk, really. And that had a little sting to it.

'I want to show you the inner room,' I said. 'And the jewels.'

'The jewels?' she asked.

She hadn't seen them from the window. The cover of the chest had blocked her view. She walked ahead of me into the room where Magnus had burned, and then she lay down to crawl through the tunnel.

As soon as she saw the chest, she was shocked by it.

She tossed her hair a little impatiently over her shoulder and bent to study the brooches, the rings, the small ornaments so like those heirlooms she'd had to sell long ago one by one.

'Why, he must have been collecting them for centuries,' she said. 'And such exquisite things. He chose what he would take, didn't he? What a creature he must have been.'

Again, almost angrily, she pushed her hair out of her way. It seemed paler, more luminous, fuller. A glorious thing.

'The pearls, look at them,' I said. 'And these rings.' I showed her the ones I'd already chosen for her. I took her hand and slipped the rings on her fingers. Her fingers moved as if they had life of their own, could feel delight, and again she laughed.

'Ah, but we are splendid devils, aren't we?'

'Hunters of the Savage Garden,' I said.

'Then let's go into Paris,' she said. Faint touch of pain in her face, the thirst. She ran her tongue over her lips. Was I half as fascinating to her as she was to me?

She raked her hair back from her forehead, and her eyes darkened with the intensity of her words.

'I want to feed quickly tonight,' she said, 'then go out of the city, into the woods. Go where there are no men and women about. Go where there is only the wind and the dark trees, and the stars overhead. Blessed silence.'

She went to the window again. Her back was narrow and straight, and her hands at her sides, alive with the jewelled rings. And coming as they did out of the thick cuffs of the man's coat, her hands looked all the more slender and exquisite. She must have been looking at the high dim clouds, the stars that burned through the purple layer of evening mist.

'I have to go to Roget,' I said under my breath. 'I have to take care of Nicki, tell them some lie about what's happened to you.'

She turned and her face looked small and cold suddenly, the way it could at home when she was disapproving. But she'd never really look that way again.

'Why tell them anything about me?' she asked. 'Why ever even bother with them again?'

I was shocked by this. But it wasn't a complete surprise to me. Perhaps I'd been waiting for it. Perhaps I'd sensed it in her all along, the unspoken questions.

I wanted to say Nicki sat by your bed when you were dying, does that mean nothing? But how sentimental, how mortal that sounded, how positively foolish.

Yet it wasn't foolish.

'I don't mean to judge you,' she said. She folded her arms and leaned against the window. 'I simply don't understand. Why did you write to us? Why did you send us all the gifts? Why didn't you take this white fire from the moon and go where you wanted with it?'

'But where should I want to go?' I said. 'Away from all those I'd known and loved? I did not want to stop thinking of you, of Nicki, even of my father and brothers. I did what I wanted,' I said.

'Then conscience played no role in it?'

'If you follow your conscience, you do what you want,' I said. 'But it was simpler than that. I wanted you to have the wealth I gave you. I wanted you ... to be happy.'

She reflected for a long time.

'Would you have had me forget *you*?' I demanded. It sounded spiteful, angry.

She didn't answer immediately.

'No, of course not,' she said. 'And had it been the other way around, I would never have forgotten you either. I'm sure of it. But the rest of them? I don't give a damn about them. I shall never exchange words with them again. I shall never lay eyes on them.'

I nodded. But I hated what she was saying. She frightened me.

'I cannot overcome this notion that I've died,' she said. 'That I am utterly cut off from all living creatures. I can taste, I can see, I can feel. I can drink blood. But I am like something that cannot be seen, cannot affect things.'

'It's not so,' I said. 'And how long do you think it will sustain you, feeling and seeing and touching and tasting, if there is no love? No one with you?'

The same uncomprehending expression.

'Oh, why do I bother to tell you this?' I said. 'I am with you. We're together. You don't know what it was like when I was alone. You can't imagine it.'

'I trouble you and I don't mean to,' she said. 'Tell them what you will. Maybe you can somehow make up a palatable story. I don't know. If you want me to go with you, I'll go. I'll do what you ask of me. But I have one more question for you.' She dropped her voice. 'Surely you don't mean to share this power with them!'

'No, never.' I shook my head as if to say the thought was incredible. I was looking at the jewels, thinking of all the gifts I'd sent, thinking of the dollhouse. I had sent them a dollhouse. I thought of Renaud's players safely across the Channel.

'Not even with Nicolas?'

'No, God, no!' I looked at her.

She nodded slightly as if she approved of this answer. And she pushed at her hair again in a distracted way.

'Why not with Nicolas?' she asked.

I wanted this to stop.

'Because he's young,' I said, 'and he has life before him. He's not on the brink of death.' Now I was more than uneasy. I was miserable. 'In time, he'll forget about us ...' I wanted to say 'about our conversation.'

'He could die tomorrow,' she said. 'A carriage could crush him in the streets ...'

'Do you want me to do it!' I glared at her.

'No. I don't want you to do it. But who am I to tell you

what to do? I am trying to understand you.'

Her long heavy hair had slipped over her shoulders again, and, exasperated, she took hold of it in both hands.

Then suddenly she made a low hissing sound, and her body went rigid. She was holding her long tresses and staring at them.

'My God,' she whispered. And then, in a spasm, she let go of her hair and screamed.

The sound paralyzed me. It sent a flash of white pain through my head. I had never heard her scream. And she screamed again as if she were on fire. She had fallen back against the window and she was screaming louder as she looked at her hair. She went to touch it and then pulled her fingers back from it as if it were blazing. And she struggled against the window, screaming and twisting from side to side, as if she were trying to get away from her own hair.

'Stop it!' I shouted. I grabbed hold of her shoulders and shook her. She was gasping. I realized instantly what it was. Her hair had grown back! It had grown back as she slept until it was as long as it had been before. And it was thicker even, more lustrous. That is what was wrong with the way she looked, what I had noticed and not noticed! And what she herself had just seen.

'Stop it, stop it now!' I shouted louder, her body shaking so violently I could hardly keep her in my arms. 'It's grown back, that's all!' I insisted. 'It's natural to you, don't you see? It's nothing!'

She was choking, trying to calm herself, touching it and then screaming as if her fingertips were blistered. She tried to get away from me, and then ripped at her hair in pure terror.

I shook her hard this time.

'Gabrielle!' I said. 'Do you understand me? It's grown back, and it will every time you cut it! There's no horror in it, for the love of hell, stop!' I thought if she didn't stop, I'd start to rave myself. I was trembling as badly as she was.

She stopped screaming and she was giving little gasps. I'd never seen her like this, not in all the years and years in Auvergne. She let me guide her towards the bench by the hearth, where I made her sit down. She put her hands to her temples and tried to catch her breath, her body rocking back and forth slowly.

I looked about for a pair of scissors. I had none. The little gold scissors had fallen on the floor of the crypt below. I took out my knife.

She was sobbing softly in her hands.

'Do you want me to cut it off again?' I asked.

She didn't answer.

'Gabrielle, listen to me.' I took her hands from her face. 'I'll cut it again if you like. Each night, cut it, and burn it. That's all.'

She stared at me in such perfect stillness suddenly that I didn't know what to do. Her face was smeared with blood from her tears, and there was blood on her linen. Blood all over her linen.

'Shall I cut it?' I asked her again.

She looked exactly as if someone had hit her and made her bleed. Her eyes were wide and wondering, the blood tears seeping out of them down her smooth cheeks. And as I watched, the flow stopped and the tears darkened and dried to a crust on her white skin.

I wiped her face carefully with my lace handkerchief. I went to the clothing I kept in the tower, the garments made for me in Paris that I'd brought back and kept here now.

I took off her coat. She made no move to help me or stop me and I unhooked the linen shirt that she wore.

I saw her breasts and they were perfectly white except for the palest pink tint to the small nipples. Trying not to look at them, I put the fresh shirt on her and buttoned it quickly. Then I brushed her hair, brushed it and brushed it, and not wanting to hack at it with the knife, I braided it for her in one long plait, and I put her coat back on her.

I could feel her composure and her strength coming back. She didn't seem ashamed of what had happened. And I didn't want her to be. She was merely considering things. But she didn't speak. She didn't move.

I started talking to her.

'When I was little, you used to tell me about all the places you'd been. You showed me pictures of Naples and Venice, remember? Those old books? And you had things, little keepsakes from London and St. Petersburg, all the places you'd seen.'

She didn't answer.

'I want us to go to all those places. I want to see them now. I want to see them and live in them. I want to go farther even, places I never dreamed of seeing when I was alive.'

Something changed in her face.

'Did you know it would grow back?' she asked in a whisper.

'No. I mean yes. I mean, I didn't think. I should have known it would do that.'

For a long time she stared at me again in that same still, listless fashion.

'Does nothing about it all ... ever ... frighten you?' she asked. Her voice was guttural and unfamiliar. 'Does nothing ... ever ... stop you?' she asked. Her mouth was open and perfect and looked like a human mouth.

'I don't know,' I whispered helplessly. 'I don't see the point,' I said. But I felt confused now. Again I told her to cut it each night and to burn it. Simple.

'Yes, burn it,' she sighed. 'Otherwise it should fill all the rooms of the tower in time, shouldn't it? It would be like Rapunzel's hair in the fairy tale. It would be like the gold that the miller's daughter had to spin from straw in the fairy tale of the mean dwarf, Rumpelstiltskin.'

'We write our own fairy tales, my love,' I said. 'The lesson in this is that nothing can destroy what you are now. Every wound will heal. You are a goddess.'

'And the goddess thirsts,' she said.

HOURS later, as we walked arm in arm like two students through the boulevard crowds, it was already forgotten. Our faces were ruddy, our skin warm.

But I did not leave her to go to my lawyer. And she did not seek the quiet open country as she had wanted to do. We stayed close to each other, the faintest shimmer of *the presence* now and then making us turn our heads.

5

Y THE hour of three, when we reached the livery stables, we knew we were being stalked by *the presence*.

For half an hour, forty-five minutes at a time, we wouldn't hear it. Then the dull hum would come again. It was maddening me.

And though we tried hard to hear some intelligible thoughts from it, all we could discern was malice, and an occasional tumult like the spectacle of dry leaves disintegrated in the roar of the blaze.

She was glad that we were riding home. It wasn't that the thing annoyed her. It was only what she had said earlier — she wanted the emptiness of the country, the quiet.

When the open land broke before us, we were going so fast that the wind was the only sound, and I think I heard her laughing but I wasn't sure. She loved the feel of the wind as I did, she loved the new brilliance of the stars over the darkened hills.

But I wondered if there had been moments tonight when she had wept inwardly and I had not known. There had been times when she was obscure and silent, and her eyes quivered as if they were crying, but there were absolutely no tears.

I was deep into thoughts of that, I think, when we neared a dense wood that grew along the banks of a shallow stream, and quite suddenly the mare reared and lurched to the side.

I was almost thrown, it was so unexpected. Gabrielle held on tight to my right arm.

Every night I rode into this little glade, crashing over the narrow wooden bridge above the water. I loved the sound of the horse's hooves on the wood and the climb up the sloping bank. And my mare knew the path. But now, she would have none of it.

Shying, threatening to rear again, she turned of her own and galloped back towards Paris until, with all the power of my will, I commanded her, reining her in.

Gabrielle was staring back at the thick copse, the great mass of dark, swaying branches that concealed the stream. And there came over the thin howling of the wind and that soft volume of rustling leaves, the definite pulse of *the presence* in the trees.

We heard it at the same moment, surely, because I tightened my arm around Gabrielle as she nodded, gripping my hand.

'It's stronger!' she said to me quickly. 'And it is not one alone.'

'Yes,' I said, enraged, 'and it stands between me and my lair!' I drew my sword, bracing Gabrielle in my left arm.

'You're not riding into it,' she cried out.

'The hell I'm not!' I said, trying to steady the horse. 'We don't have two hours before sunrise. Draw your sword!'

She tried to turn to speak to me, but I was already driving the horse forward. And she drew her sword as I'd told her to do, her little hand knotted around it as firmly as that of a man.

Of course, the thing would flee as soon as we reached the copse, I was sure of that. I mean the damned thing had never done anything but turn tail and run. And I was furious that it had frightened my mount, and that it was frightening Gabrielle.

With a sharp kick, and the full force of my mental persuasion, I sent the horse racing straight ahead to the bridge.

I locked my hand to the weapon. I bent low with Gabrielle beneath me. I was breathing rage as if I were a dragon, and when the mare's hooves hit the hollow wood over the water, I saw them, the demons, for the first time!

White faces and white arms above us, glimpsed for no more than a second, and out of their mouths the most horrid shrieking as they shook the branches sending down on us a shower of leaves.

'Damn you, you pack of harpies!' I shouted as we reached the sloping bank on the other side, but Gabrielle let out a scream.

Something had landed on the horse behind me, and the horse was slipping in the damp earth, and the thing had hold of my shoulder and the arm with which I tried to swing the sword.

Whipping the sword over Gabrielle's head and down past my left arm, I chopped at the creature furiously, and saw it fly off, a white blur in the darkness, while another one sprang at us with hands like claws. Gabrielle's blue sliced right through its outstretched arm. I saw the arm go up into the air, the blood spurting as if from a fountain. The screams became a searing wail. I wanted to slash every one of them to pieces. I turned the horse back too sharply so that it reared and almost fell.

But Gabrielle had hold of the horse's mane and she drove it again towards the open road.

As we raced for the tower, we could hear them screaming as they came on. And when the mare gave out, we abandoned her and ran, hand in hand, towards the gates.

I knew we had to get through the secret passage to the inner chamber before they climbed the outside wall. They must not see us take that stone out of place.

And locking the gates and doors behind me as fast as I could, I carried Gabrielle up the stairs.

By the time we reached the secret room and pushed the stone into place again, I heard their howling and shrieking below and their first scraping against the walls.

I snatched up an armful of firewood and threw it beneath the window.

'Hurry, the kindling,' I said.

But there were half a dozen white faces already at the bars. Their shrieks echoed monstrously in the little cell. For one moment I could only stare at them as I backed away.

They clung to the iron grating like so many bats, but they weren't bats. They were vampires, and vampires as we were vampires, in human form.

Dark eyes peered at us from under mops of filthy hair, howls growing louder and fiercer, the fingers that clung to the grating caked with filth. Such clothing as I could see was no more than colourless rags. And the stench coming from them was the graveyard stench.

Gabrielle pitched the kindling at the wall, and she jumped away as they reached to catch hold of her. They bared their fangs. They screeched. Hands struggled to pick up the firewood and throw it back at us. All together they pulled at the grating as if they might free it from the stone.

'Get the tinderbox,' I shouted. I grabbed up one of the stouter pieces of wood and thrust it right at the closest face, easily flinging the creature out and off the wall. Weak things. I heard its scream as it fell, but the others had clamped their hands on the wood and they struggled with me now as I dislodged another dirty little demon. But by this time Gabrielle had lighted the kindling.

The flames shot upwards. The howling stopped in a frenzy of ordinary speech:

'It's fire, get back, get down, get out of the way, you idiots! Down, down. The bars are hot! Move away quickly!'

Perfectly regular French! In fact an ever increasing flood of pretty vernacular curse words.

I burst out laughing, stamping my foot and pointing to them, as I looked at Gabrielle.

'A curse on you, blasphemer!' one of them screamed. Then the fire licked at his hands and he howled, falling backwards.

'A curse on the profaners, the outlaws!' came screams from below. It caught on quickly and became a regular chorus. 'A curse on the outlaws who dared to enter the House of God!' But they were scrambling down to the ground. The heavy timbers were catching, and the fire was roaring to the ceiling.

'Go back to the graveyard where you came from, you pack of pranksters!' I said. I would have thrown the fire down on them if I could have got near the window.

Gabrielle stood still with her eyes narrow, obviously listening.

Cries and howls continued from below. A new anthem of curses upon those who broke the sacred laws, blasphemed, provoked the wrath of God and Satan. They were pulling on the gates and lower windows. They were doing stupid things like throwing rocks at the wall.

'They can't get in,' Gabrielle said in a low monotone, her head still cocked attentively. 'They can't break the gate.'

I wasn't so certain. The gate was rusted, very old. Nothing to do but wait.

I collapsed on the floor, leaning against the side of the

sarcophagus, my arms around my chest and my back bent. I wasn't even laughing anymore.

She too sat down against the wall with her legs sprawled out before her. Her chest heaved a little, and her hair was coming loose from the braid. It was a cobra's hood around her face, loose strands clinging to her white cheeks. Soot clung to her garments.

The heat of the fire was crushing. The airless room shimmered with vapours and the flames rose to shut out the night. But we could breathe the little air that was there. We suffered nothing except the heat and the exhaustion.

And gradually I realized she was right about the gate. They hadn't managed to break it down. I could hear them drawing away.

'May the wrath of God punish the profane!'

There was some faint commotion near the stables. I saw in my mind my poor half-witted mortal stable boy dragged in terror from his hiding place, and my rage was redoubled. They were sending me images of it from their thoughts, the murder of that poor body. Damn them.

'Be still,' Gabrielle said. 'It's too late.'

Her eyes widened and then grew small again as she listened. He was dead, the poor miserable creature.

I felt the death just as if I had seen a small dark bird suddenly rising from the stables. And she sat forward as though seeing it too, and then settled back as if she had lost consciousness, though she had not. She murmured and it sounded like 'red velvet', but it was under her breath and I didn't catch the words.

'I'll punish you for this, you gang of ruffians!' I said aloud. I sent it out towards them. 'You trouble my house. I swear you'll pay for this.'

But my limbs were getting heavier and heavier. The heat of the fire was almost drugging. All the night's strange happenings were taking their toll.

In my exhaustion and in the glare of the fire I could not guess the hour. I think I fell to dreaming for an instant, and woke myself with a shiver, unsure of how much time had passed.

I looked up and saw the figure of an unearthly young boy, an exquisite young boy, pacing the floor of the chamber.

Of course it was only Gabrielle.

6

SHE gave the impression of almost rampant strength as she walked back and forth. Yet all of it was contained in an unbroken grace. She kicked at the timbers and watched the blackened ruin of the fire flare for a moment before settling into itself again. I could see the sky. An hour perhaps remained.

'But who are they?' she asked. She stood over me, her legs apart, her hands in two liquid summoning gestures. 'Why do they call us outlaws and blasphemers?'

'I've told you everything I know,' I confessed. 'Until tonight I didn't think they possessed faces or limbs or real voices.'

I climbed to my feet and brushed off my clothes.

'They damned us for entering the churches!' she said. 'Did you catch it, those images coming from them? And they don't know how we managed to do it. They themselves would not dare.'

For the first time I observed that she was trembling. There were other small signs of alarm, the way the flesh quivered around her eyes, the way that she kept pushing the loose strands of her hair out of her eyes again.

'Gabrielle,' I said. I tried to make my tone authoritative, reassuring. 'The important thing is to get out of here now. We don't know how early those creatures rise, or how soon after sunset they'll return. We have to discover another hiding place.'

'The dungeon crypt,' she cried.

'A worse trap than this,' I said, 'if they break through the gate.' I glanced at the sky again. I pulled the stone out of the low passage. 'Come on,' I said.

'But where are we going?' she asked. For the first time tonight she looked almost fragile.

'To a village east of here,' I said. 'It's perfectly obvious that the safest place is within the village church itself.'

'Would you do that?' she asked. 'In the church?'

'Of course I would. As you just said, the little beasts would never dare to enter! And the crypts under the altar will be as deep and dark as any grave.'

'But Lestat, to rest under the very altar!'

'Mother, you astonish me,' I said. 'I have taken victims under the very roof of Notre Dame.' But another little idea came to me. I went to Magnus's chest and started picking at the heap of treasure. I pulled out two rosaries, one of pearls, another of emeralds, both having the usual small crucifix.

She watched me, her face white, pinched.

'Here, you take this one,' I said, giving her the emerald rosary. 'Keep it on you. If and when we do meet with them, show them the crucifix. If I am right, they'll run from it.'

'But what happens if we don't find a safe place in the church?'

'How the hell should I know? We'll come back here!'

I could feel a fear collecting in her and radiating from her as she hesitated, looking through the window at the fading stars. She had passed through the veil into the promise of eternity and now she was in danger again.

Quickly, I took the rosary from her and kissed her and slipped the rosary into the pocket of her frock coat.

'Emeralds mean eternal life, Mother,' I said.

She appeared the boy standing there again, the last glow of fire just tracing the line of her cheek and mouth.

'It's as I said before,' she whispered. 'You aren't afraid of anything, are you?'

'What does it matter if I am or not?' I shrugged. I took her arm and drew her to the passage. 'We are the things that others fear,' I said. 'Remember that.'

WHEN we reached the stable, I saw the boy had been hideously murdered. His broken body lay twisted on the hay-strewn floor as if it had been flung there by a Titan. The back of his head was shattered. And to mock him, it seemed, or to mock me, they had dressed him in a gentleman's fancy velvet frock coat. Red velvet. Those were the words she'd murmured when they had done the crime. I'd seen only the death. I looked away now in disgust. All the horses were gone.

'They'll pay for that,' I said.

I took her hand. But she stared at the miserable boy's body as if it drew her against her will. She glanced at me.

'I feel cold,' she whispered. 'I'm losing the strength in my limbs. I must, I must get to where it's dark. I can feel it.'

I led her fast over the rise of the nearby hill and towards the road.

THERE were no howling little monsters hidden in this village churchyard, of course. I didn't think there would be. The earth hadn't been turned up on the old graves in a long time.

Gabrielle was past conferring with me on this.

I half carried her to the side door of the church and quietly broke the latch.

'I'm cold all over. My eyes are burning,' she said again under her breath. 'Somewhere dark.'

But as I started to take her in, she stopped.

'What if they're right,' she said. 'And we don't belong in the House of God.'

'Gibberish and nonsense. God isn't in the House of God.'

'Don't! ...' She moaned.

I pulled her through the sacristy and out before the altar. She covered her face, and when she looked up it was at the crucifix over the tabernacle. She let out a long low gasp. But it was from the stained-glass windows that she shielded her eyes, turning her head towards me. The rising sun that I could not even feel yet was already burning her!

I picked her up as I had done last night. I had to find an old burial crypt, one that hadn't been used in years. I hurried towards the Blessed Virgin's altar, where the inscriptions were almost worn away. And kneeling, I hooked my fingernails around a slab and quickly lifted it to reveal a deep sepulchre with a single rotted coffin.

I pulled her down into the sepulchre with me and moved the slab back into place.

Inky blackness, and the coffin splintering under me so that my right hand closed on a crumbling skull. I felt the sharpness of other bones under my chest. Gabrielle spoke as if in a trance:

'Yes. Away from the light.'

'We're safe,' I whispered.

I pushed the bones out of the way, making a nest of the rotted wood and the dust that was too old to contain any smell of human decay.

But I did not fall into the sleep for perhaps an hour or more.

I kept thinking over and over of the stable boy, mangled and thrown there in that fancy red velvet frock coat. I had seen that coat before and I couldn't remember where I had seen it. Had it been one of my own? Had they got into the tower? No, that was not possible, they couldn't have got in. Had they had a coat made up identical to one of my own? Gone to such lengths to mock me? No. How could such creatures do a thing like that? But still ... that particular coat. Something about it ...

7

I HEARD the softest, loveliest singing when I opened my eyes. And as sound can often do, even in the most precious fragments, it took me back to my childhood, to some night in winter when all my family had gone down to the church in our village and stood for hours among the blazing candles, breathing the heavy, sensual smell of the incense as the priest walked in procession with the monstrance lifted high.

I remembered the sight of the round white Host behind the thick glass, the starburst of gold and jewels surrounding it, and overhead the embroidered canopy, swaying dangerously as the altar boys in their lace surplices tried to steady it as they moved on.

A thousand Benedictions after that one had engraved into my mind the words of the old hymn.

> *O Salutaris Hostia*
> *Quae caeli pandis ostium*
> *Bella premunt bostilia,*
> *Da robur, fer auxilium . . .*

And as I lay in the remains of this broken coffin under the white marble slab at the side altar in this large country church, Gabrielle clinging to me still in the paralysis of sleep, I realized very slowly that above me were hundreds upon hundreds of humans who were singing this very hymn right now.

The church was full of people! And we could not get out of this damned nest of bones until all of them went away.

Around me in the dark, I could feel creatures moving. I could smell the shattered, crumbling skeleton on which I lay. I could smell the earth, too, and feel dampness and the harshness of the cold.

Gabrielle's hands were dead hands holding to me. Her face was as inflexible as bone.

I tried not to brood on this, but to lie perfectly still.

Hundreds of humans breathed and sighed above. Perhaps a thousand of them. And now they moved on into the second hymn.

What comes now, I thought dismally. The litany, the blessings? On this of all nights, I had no time to lie here musing. I must get out. The image of that red velvet coat came to me again with an irrational sense of urgency, and a flash of equally inexplicable pain.

And quite suddenly, it seemed, Gabrielle opened her eyes. Of course I didn't see it. It was utterly black here. I felt it. I felt her limbs come to life.

And no sooner had she moved than she grew positively rigid with alarm. I slipped my hand over her mouth.

'Be still,' I whispered, but I could feel her panic.

211

All the horrors of the preceding night must be coming back to her, that she was now in a sepulchre with a broken skeleton, that she lay beneath a stone she could hardly lift.

'We're in the church!' I whispered. 'And we're safe.'

The singing surged on. '*Tantum ergo Sacramentum, Veneremur cernui.*'

'No, it's a Benediction,' Gabrielle gasped. She was trying to lie still, but abruptly she lost the struggle, and I had to grip her firmly in both arms.

'We *must* get out,' she whispered. 'Lestat, the Blessed Sacrament is on the altar, for the love of God!'

The remains of the wooden coffin clattered and creaked against the stone beneath it, causing me to roll over on top of her and force her flat with my weight.

'Now lie still, do you hear me!' I said. 'We have no choice but to wait.'

But her panic was infecting me. I felt the fragments of bone crunching beneath my knees and smelled the rotting cloth. It seemed the death stench was penetrating the walls of the sepulchre, and I knew I could not bear to be shut up with that stench.

'We can't,' she gasped. 'We can't remain here, I have to get out!' She was almost whimpering. 'Lestat, I can't.' She was feeling the walls with both hands and then the stone above us. I heard a pure toneless sound of terror issue from her lips.

Above the hymn had stopped. The priest would go up the altar steps, lift the monstrance in both hands. He would turn to the congregation and raise the Sacred Host in blessing. Gabrielle knew that of course, and Gabrielle suddenly went mad, writhing under me, almost heaving me to the side.

'All right, listen to me!' I hissed. I could control this no longer. 'We are going out. But we shall do it like proper vampires, do you hear! There are one thousand people in the church and we are going to scare them to death. I will lift the stone and we will rise up together, and when we do, raise your arms and make the most horrible face you can muster and cry out if you can. That will make them fall back, instead of pouncing upon us and dragging us off to prison, and then we'll

212

rush to the door.'

She couldn't even stop to answer, she was already struggling, slamming the rotted boards with her heels.

I rose up, giving the marble slab a great shove with both hands, and leapt out of the vault just as I had said I would do, pulling my cloak up in a giant arc.

I landed upon the floor of the choir in a blaze of candlelight, letting out the most powerful cry I could make.

Hundreds rose to their feet before me, hundreds of mouths opening to scream.

Giving another shout, I grabbed Gabrielle's hand and lunged towards them, leaping over the Communion rail. She gave a lovely high-pitched wail, her left hand raised as a claw as I pulled her down the aisle. Everywhere there was panic, men and women clutching for children, shrieking and falling backwards.

The heavy doors gave at once on the black sky and the gusting breeze. I threw Gabrielle ahead of me and, turning back, made the loudest shriek that I could. I bared my fangs at the writhing, screaming congregation, and unable to tell whether some pursued or merely fell towards me in panic, I reached into my pocket and showered the marble floor with gold coins.

'The devil throws money!' someone screeched.

We tore through the cemetery and across the fields.

Within seconds, we had gained the woods and I could smell the stables of a large house that lay ahead of us beyond the trees.

I stood still, bent almost double in concentration, and summoned the horses. And we ran towards them, hearing the dull thunder of their hooves against the stalls.

Bolting over the low hedge with Gabrielle beside me, I pulled the door off its hinges just as a fine gelding raced out of his broken stall, and we sprang onto his back, Gabrielle scrambling into place before me as I threw my arm around her.

I dug my heels into the animal and rode south into the woods and towards Paris.

8

TRIED to form a plan as we approached the city, but in truth I was not sure at all how to proceed.

There was no avoiding these filthy little monsters. We were riding towards a battle. And it was little different from the morning on which I'd gone out to kill the wolves, counting upon my rage and my will to carry me through.

We had scarcely entered the scattered farmhouses of Montmartre when we heard for a split second their faint murmuring. Noxious as a vapour, it seemed.

Gabrielle and I knew we had to drink at once, in order to be prepared for them.

We stopped at one of the small farms, crept through the orchard to the back door, and found inside the man and wife dozing at an empty hearth.

When it was finished, we came out of the house together and into the little kitchen garden where we stood still for a moment, looking at the pearl grey sky. No sound of the others. Only the stillness, the clarity of the fresh blood, and the threat of rain as the clouds gathered overhead.

I turned and silently bid the gelding to come to me. And gathering the reins, I turned to Gabrielle.

'I see no other way but to go into Paris,' I told her, 'to face these little beasts head on. And until they show themselves and start the war all over again, there are things that I must do. I have to think about Nicki. I have to talk to Roget.'

'This isn't the time for that mortal nonsense,' she said.

The dirt of the church sepulchre still clung to the cloth of her coat and to her blonde hair, and she looked like an angel dragged in the dust.

'I won't have them come between me and what I mean to do,' I said.

She took a deep breath.

'Do you want to lead these creatures to your beloved Monsieur Roget?' she asked.

That was too dreadful to contemplate.

The first few drops of rain were falling and I felt cold in spite of the blood. In a moment it would be raining hard.

'All right,' I said. 'Nothing can be done until this is finished!' I said. I mounted the horse and reached for her hand.

'Injury only spurs you on, doesn't it?' she asked. She was studying me. 'It would only strengthen you, whatever they did or tried to do.'

'Now this is what *I* call mortal nonsense!' I said. 'Come on!'

'Lestat,' she said soberly. 'They put your stable boy in a gentleman's frock coat after they killed him. Did you see the coat? Hadn't you seen it before?'

That damned red velvet coat ...

'I have seen it,' she said. 'I had looked at it for hours at my bedside in Paris. It was Nicolas de Lenfent's coat.'

I looked at her for a long moment. But I don't think I saw her at all. The rage building in me was absolutely silent. It will be rage until I have proof that it must be grief, I thought. Then I wasn't thinking.

Vaguely, I knew she had no notion yet how strong our passions could be, how they could paralyze us. I think I moved my lips, but nothing came out.

'I don't think they've killed him, Lestat,' she said.

Again I tried to speak. I wanted to ask, Why do you say that, but I couldn't. I was staring forward into the orchard.

'I think he is alive,' she said. 'And that he is their prisoner. Otherwise they would have left his body there and never bothered with that stable boy.'

'Perhaps, perhaps not.' I had to force my mouth to form the words.

'The coat was a message.'

I couldn't stand this any longer.

'I'm going after them,' I said. 'Do you want to return to the tower? If I fail at this ...'

'I have no intention of leaving you,' she said.

THE rain was falling in earnest by the time we reached the boulevard du Temple, and the wet paving stones magnified a thousand lamps.

215

My thoughts had hardened into strategies that were more instinct than reason. And I was as ready for a fight as I have ever been. But we had to find out where we stood. How many of them were there? And what did they really want? Was it to capture and destroy us, or to frighten us and drive us off? I had to quell my rage, I had to remember they were childish, superstitious, conceivably easy to scatter or scare.

As soon as we reached the high ancient tenements near Notre Dame, I *heard* them near us, the vibration coming as in a silver flash and vanishing as quickly again.

Gabrielle drew herself up, and I felt her left hand on my wrist. I saw her right hand on the hilt of her sword.

We had entered a crooked alleyway that turned blindly in the dark in front of us, the iron clatter of the horse's shoes shattering the silence, and I struggled not to be unnerved by the sound itself.

It seemed we saw them at the same moment.

Gabrielle pressed back against me, and I swallowed the gasp that would have given an impression of fear.

High above us, on either side of the narrow thoroughfare, were their white faces just over the eaves of the tenements, a faint gleam against the lowering sky and the soundless drifts of silver rain.

I drove the horse forward in a rush of scraping and clattering. Above they streaked like rats over the roof. Their voices rose in a faint howling mortals could never have heard.

Gabrielle stifled a little cry as we saw their white arms and legs descending the walls ahead of us, and behind I heard the soft thud of their feet on the stones.

'Straight on,' I shouted, and drawing my sword, I drove right over the two ragged figures who'd dropped down in our path. 'Damnable creatures, out of my way,' I shouted, hearing their screams underfoot.

I glimpsed anguished faces for a moment. Those above vanished and those behind us seemed to weaken and we bore ahead, putting yards between us and our pursuers as we came into the deserted place de Grève.

But they were regathering on the edges of the square, and

this time I was hearing their distinct thoughts, one of them demanding what power was it we had, and why should they be frightened, and another insisting that they close in.

Some force surely came from Gabrielle at that moment because I could see them visibly fall back when she threw her glance in their direction and tightened her grip on the sword.

'Stop, stand them off!' she said under her breath. 'They're terrified.' Then I heard her curse. Because flying towards us out of the shadows of the Hôtel-Dieu, there came at least six more of the little demons, their thin white limbs barely swathed in rags, their hair flying, those dreadful wails coming out of their mouths. They were rallying the others. The malice that surrounded us was gaining force.

The horse reared, and almost threw us. They were commanding it to halt as surely as I commanded it to go on.

I grabbed Gabrielle about the waist, leapt off the horse, and ran top speed for the doors of Notre Dame.

A horrid derisive babble rose silently in my ears, wails and cries and threats:

'You dare not, you dare not!' Malice like the heat of a blast furnace opened upon us, as their feet came thumping and splashing around us, and I felt their hands struggling to grab hold of my sword and my coat.

But I was certain of what would happen when we reached the church. I gave it one final spurt, heaving Gabrielle ahead of me so that together we slid through the doors across the threshold of the cathedral and landed sprawling within on the stones.

Screams. Dreadful dry screams curling upwards and then an upheaval, as if the entire mob had been scattered by a cannon blast.

I scrambled to my feet, laughing out loud at them. But I was not waiting so near the door to hear more. Gabrielle was on her feet and pulling me after her and together we hurried deep into the shadowy nave, past one lofty archway after another until we were near to the dim candles of the sanctuary, and then seeking a dark and empty corner by a side altar, we sank down together on our knees.

'Just like those damned wolves!' I said. 'A bloody ambush.'

'Shhhhh, be quiet a moment,' Gabrielle said as she clung to me. 'Or my immortal heart will burst.'

9

AFTER a long moment, I felt her stiffen. She was looking towards the square.

'Don't think of Nicolas,' she said. 'They are waiting and they are listening. They are hearing everything that goes on in our minds.'

'But what are *they* thinking?' I whispered. 'What is going on in *their* heads?'

I could feel her concentration.

I pressed her close, and looked straight at the silver light that came through the distant open doors. I could hear them too now, but just that low shimmer of sound coming from all of them collected there.

But as I stared at the rain, there came over me the strongest sense of peace. It was almost sensuous. It seemed to me we should yield to them, that it was foolish to resist them further. All things would be resolved were we merely to go out to them and give ourselves over. They would not torture Nicolas, whom they had in their power, they would not tear him limb from limb.

I saw Nicolas in their hands. He wore only his lace shirt and breeches because they had taken the coat. And I heard his screams as they pulled his arms from the sockets. I cried out, No, putting my own hand over my mouth so that I did not rouse the mortals in the church.

Gabrielle reached up and touched my lips with her fingers.

'It's not being done to him,' she said under her breath. 'It's merely a threat. Don't think of him.'

'He's still alive, then,' I whispered.

'So they want us to believe. Listen!'

218

There came again the sense of peace, the summons, that's what it was, to join them, the voice saying *Come out of the church. Surrender to us, we welcome you, and we will not harm either of you if only you come.*

I turned towards the door and rose to my feet. Anxiously Gabrielle rose beside me, cautioning me again with her hand. She seemed wary of even speaking to me as we both looked at that great archway of silvery light.

You are lying to us, I said. *You have no power over us!* It was a rolling current of defiance moving through the distant door. *Surrender to you? If we do that then what's to stop you from holding the three of us! Why should we come out? Within this church we are safe; we can conceal ourselves in its deepest burial vaults. We could hunt among the faithful, drink their blood in the chapels and niches so skillfully we'd never be discovered, sending our victims out confused to die in the streets afterwards. And what would you do, you who cannot even cross the door! Besides, we don't believe you have Nicolas. Show him to us. Let him come to the door and speak.*

Gabrielle was in a welter of confusion. She was scanning me, desperate to know what I said. And she was clearly hearing them, which I could not do when I was sending these impulses.

It seemed their pulse weakened, but it had not stopped.

It went on as it had before, as if I'd not answered it, as if it were someone humming. It was promising truce again, and now it seemed to speak of rapture, that in the great pleasure of joining with it, all conflict would be resolved. It was sensuous again, it was beautiful.

'Miserable cowards, the lot of you.' I sighed. I said the words aloud this time, so that Gabrielle could hear as well. 'Send Nicolas into the church.'

The hum of the voice became thin. It went on, but beyond it there was a hollow silence as if other voices had been withdrawn and only one or two remained now. Then I heard the thin, chaotic strains of argument and rebellion.

Gabrielle's eyes narrowed.

Silence. Only mortals out there now, weaving their way against the wind across the place de Grève. I didn't believe

219

they would withdraw. Now what do we do to save Nicki?

I blinked my eyes. I felt weary suddenly; it was almost a feeling of despair. And I thought confusedly, This is ridiculous, I never despair! Others do that, not me. I go on fighting no matter what happens. Always. And in my exhaustion and anger, I saw Magnus leaping and jumping in the fire, I saw the grimace on his face before the flames consumed him and he disappeared. Was that despair?

The thought paralyzed me. Horrified me as the reality of it had done then. And I had the oddest feeling that someone else was speaking to me of Magnus. That is why the thought of Magnus had come into my head!

'Too clever ...' Gabrielle whispered.

'Don't listen to it. It's playing tricks with our very thoughts,' I said.

But as I stared past her at the open doorway, I saw a small figure appear. Compact it was, the figure of a young boy, not a man.

I ached for it to be Nicolas, but knew immediately that it was not. It was smaller than Nicolas, though rather heavier of build. And the creature was not human.

Gabrielle made some soft wondering sound. It sounded almost like a prayer in its reverence.

The creature wasn't dressed as men dress now. Rather he wore a belted tunic, very graceful, and stockings on his well-shaped legs. His sleeves were deep, hanging at his sides. He was clothed like Magnus, actually, and for one moment I thought madly that by some magic it was Magnus returned.

Stupid thought. This was a boy, as I had said, and he had a head of long curly hair, and he walked very straight and very simply through the silvery light and into the church. He hesitated for a moment. And by the tilt of the head, it seemed he was looking up. And then he came on through the nave and towards us, his feet making not the faintest sound on the stones.

He moved into the glow of the candles on the side altar. His clothes were black velvet, once beautiful, and now eaten away by time, and crusted with dirt. But his face was shining white, and perfect, the countenance of a god it seemed, a Cupid out of Caravaggio, seductive yet ethereal, with auburn hair and dark brown eyes.

I held Gabrielle closer as I looked at him, and nothing so startled me about him, this inhuman creature, as the manner in which he was staring at us. He was inspecting every detail of our persons, and then he reached out very gently and touched the stone of the altar at his side. He stared at the altar, at its crucifix and its saints, and then he looked back to us.

He was only a few yards away, and the soft inspection of us yielded to an expression that was almost sublime. And the voice I'd heard before came out of this creature, summoning us again, calling upon us to yield, saying with indescribable gentleness that we must love one another, he and Gabrielle, whom he didn't call by name, and I.

There was something naive about it, his sending the summons as he stood there.

I held fast against him. Instinctively. I felt my eyes becoming opaque as if a wall had gone up to seal off the windows of my thoughts. And yet I felt such a longing for him, such a longing to fall into him and follow him and be led by him, that all my longings of the past seemed nothing at all. He was a mystery to me as Magnus had been. Only he was beautiful, indescribably beautiful, and there seemed in him an infinite complexity and depth which Magnus had not possessed.

The anguish of my immortal life pressed in on me. He said, *Come to me. Come to me because only I, and my like, can end the loneliness you feel.* It touched a well of inexpressible sadness. It sounded the depth of the sadness, and my throat went dry with a powerful little knot where my voice might have been, yet I held fast.

We two are together, I insisted, tightening my grip on Gabrielle. And then I asked him, *Where is Nicolas?* I asked that question and clung to it, yielding to nothing that I heard or saw.

He moistened his lips; very human thing to do. And silently he approached us until he was standing no more than two feet from us, looking from one of us to the other. And in a voice very unlike a human voice, he spoke.

'Magnus,' he said. It was unobtrusive. It was caressing. 'He went into the fire as you said?'

'I never said it,' I answered. The human sound of my own voice startled me. But I knew now he meant my thoughts of only moments before. 'It's quite true,' I answered. 'He went into the fire.' Why should I deceive anyone on that account?

I tried to penetrate his mind. He knew I was doing it and he threw up against me such strange images that I gasped.

What was it I'd seen for an instant? I didn't even know. Hell and heaven, or both made one, vampires in a paradise drinking blood from the very flowers that hung, pendulous and throbbing, from the trees.

I felt a wave of disgust. It was as if he had come into my private dreams like a succubus.

But he had stopped. He let his eyes pucker slightly and he looked down out of some vague respect. My disgust was withering him. He hadn't anticipated my response. He hadn't expected ... what? Such strength?

Yes, and he was letting me know it in an almost courteous way.

I returned the courtesy. I let him see me in the tower room with Magnus; I recalled Magnus's words before he went into the fire. I let him know all of it.

He nodded and when I told the words Magnus had said, there was a slight change in his face as if his forehead had gone smooth, or all of his skin had tightened. He gave me no such knowledge of himself in answer.

On the contrary, much to my surprise, he looked away from us to the main altar of the church. He glided past us, turning his back to us as if he had nothing to fear from us and had for the moment forgotten us.

He moved towards the great aisle and slowly up it, but he did not appear to walk in a human way. Rather he moved so swiftly from one bit of shadow to another that he seemed to vanish and reappear. Never was he visible in the light. And those scores of souls milling in the church had only to glance at him for him to instantly disappear.

I marvelled at his skill, because that is all it is. And curious to see if I could move like that, I followed him to the choir. Gabrielle came after without a sound.

I think we both found it simpler than we had imagined it would be. Yet he was clearly startled when he saw us at his side.

And in the very act of being startled, he gave me a glimpse of his great weakness, pride. He was humiliated that we had crept up on him, moving so lightly and managing at the same time to conceal our thoughts.

But worse was to come. When he realized I had perceived this ... it was revealed for a split second ... he was doubly enraged. A withering heat emanated from him that wasn't heat at all.

Gabrielle made a little scornful sound. Her eyes flashed on him for a second in some shimmer of communication between them that excluded me. He seemed puzzled.

But he was in the grip of some greater battle I was struggling to understand. He looked at the faithful around him, and at the altar and all the emblems of the Almighty and the Virgin Mary everywhere that he turned. He was perfectly the god out of Caravaggio, the light playing on the hard whiteness of his innocent-looking face.

Then he put his arm about my waist, slipping it under my cloak. His touch was so strange, so sweet and enticing, and the beauty of his face so entrancing that I didn't move away. He put his other arm around Gabrielle's waist, and the sight of them together, angel and angel, distracted me.

He said: *You must come.*

'Why, where?' Gabrielle asked. I felt an immense pressure. He was attempting to move me against my will, but he could not. I planted myself on the stone floor. I saw Gabrielle's face harden as she looked at him. And again, he was amazed. He was maddened and he couldn't conceal it from us.

So he had underestimated our physical strength as well as our mental strength. Interesting.

'You must come now,' he said, giving me the great force of his will, which I could see much too clearly to be fooled. 'Come out and my followers won't harm you.'

'You're lying to us,' I said. 'You sent your followers away, and you want us to come out before your followers return, because you don't want them to see you come out of the church. You don't want them to know you came into it!'

Again Gabrielle gave a little scornful laugh.

I put my hand on his chest and tried to move him away. He might have been as strong as Magnus. But I refused to be afraid. 'Why don't you want them to see?' I whispered, peering into his face.

The change in him was so startling and so ghastly that I found myself holding my breath. His angelic countenance appeared to wither, his eyes widening and his mouth twisting down in consternation. His entire body became quite deformed as if he were trying not to grit his teeth and clench his fists.

Gabrielle drew away. I laughed. I didn't really mean to, but I couldn't help it. It was horrifying. But it was also very funny.

With stunning suddenness this awful illusion, if that is what it was, faded, and he came back to himself. Even the sublime expression returned. He told me in a steady stream of thought that I was infinitely stronger than he supposed. But it would frighten the others to see him emerge from the church, and so we should go at once.

'Lies again,' Gabrielle whispered.

And I knew this much pride would forgive nothing. God help Nicolas if we couldn't trick this one!

Turning, I took Gabrielle's hand and we started down the aisle to the front doors, Gabrielle glancing back at him and to me questioningly, her face white and tense.

'Patience,' I whispered. I turned to see him far away from us, his back to the main altar, and his eyes were so big as he stared that he looked horrible to me, loathsome, like a ghost.

When I reached the vestibule I sent out my summons to the others with all my power. And I whispered aloud for Gabrielle as I did so. I told them to come back and into the church if they wanted to, that nothing could harm them, their leader was inside the church standing at the very altar, unharmed.

I spoke the words louder, pumping the summons under the words, and Gabrielle joined me, repeating the phrases in unison with me.

I felt him coming towards us from the main altar, and then suddenly I lost him. I didn't know where he was behind us.

He grabbed hold of me suddenly, materializing at my side, and Gabrielle was thrown to the floor. He was attempting to lift me and pitch me through the door.

But I fought him. And desperately collecting everything I remembered of Magnus — his strange walk, and this creature's strange manner of moving — I hurled him, not off balance as one might do to a heavy mortal, but straight up in the air.

Just as I suspected he went over in a somersault, crashing into the wall.

Mortals stirred. They saw movement, heard noises. But he'd vanished again. And Gabrielle and I looked no different from other young gentlemen in the shadows.

I motioned for Gabrielle to get out of the way. Then he appeared, shooting towards me, but I perceived what was to happen and stepped aside.

Some twenty feet away from me, I saw him sprawled on the stones staring at me with positive awe, as if I were a god. His long auburn hair was tossed about, his brown eyes enormous as he looked up. And for all the gentle innocence of his face, his will was rolling over me, a hot stream of commands, telling me I was weak and imperfect and a fool, and I would be torn limb from limb by his followers as soon as they appeared. They would roast my mortal lover slowly till he died.

I laughed silently. This was as ludicrous as a fight out of the old commedia.

Gabrielle was staring from one to the other of us.

I sent the summons again to the others, and this time when I sent it, I heard them answering, questioning.

'Come into the church.' I repeated it over and over, even as he rose and ran at me again in blind and clumsy rage. Gabrielle caught him just as I did, and we both had hold of him and he couldn't move.

In a moment of absolute horror for me he tried to sink his

225

fangs into my neck. I saw his eyes round and empty as the fangs descended over his drawn lip. I flung him back and again he vanished.

They were coming nearer, the others.

'He's in the church, your leader, look at him!' I repeated it. 'And any of you can come into the church. You won't be hurt.'

I heard Gabrielle let out a scream of warning. And too late. He rose up right in front of me, as if out of the floor itself and struck my jaw, jerking my head back so that I saw the church ceiling. And before I could recover, he had dealt me one fine blow in the middle of the back that sent me flying out the door and onto the stones of the square.

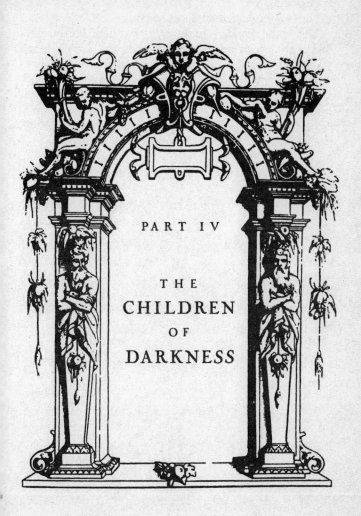

PART IV

THE
CHILDREN
OF
DARKNESS

1

COULD see nothing but the rain. But I could hear them all around me. And he was giving his command.

'They have no great power, these two,' he was telling them in thoughts that had a curious simplicity to them, as if he were commanding vagrant children. 'Take them both prisoner.'

Gabrielle said: 'Lestat, don't fight. It's useless to prolong it.'

And I knew she was right. But I'd never surrendered to anybody in my life. And pulling her with me past the Hôtel-Dieu, I made for the bridge.

We tore through the press of wet cloaks and mud-spattered carriages, yet they were gaining upon us, rushing so fast they were almost invisible to mortals, and with only a little fear of us now.

In the dark streets of the Left Bank, the game was finished.

White faces appeared above and below me as though they were demonic cherubs, and when I tried to draw my weapon, I felt their hands on my arms. I heard Gabrielle say, 'Let it be done.'

I held fast to my sword but I couldn't stop them from lifting me off the ground. They were lifting Gabrielle too.

And in a blaze of hideous images, I understood where they were taking us. It was to les Innocents, only yards away. I could already see the flicker of the bonfires that burned each night among the stinking open graves, the flames that were supposed to drive away the effluvia.

I locked my arm around Gabrielle's neck and cried out that I couldn't bear that stench, but they were carrying us on swiftly through the darkness, through the gates and past the white marble crypts.

'Surely you can't endure it,' I said, struggling. 'So why do you live among the dead when you were made to feed on life?'

But I felt such revulsion now I couldn't keep it up, the verbal or physical struggle. All around us lay bodies in various states of decomposition, and even from the rich sepulchres there came that reek.

And as we moved into the darker part of the cemetery, as we entered an enormous sepulchre, I realized that they too hated the stench, as much as I. I could feel their disgust, and yet they opened their mouths and their lungs as if they were eating it. Gabrielle was trembling against me, her fingers digging into my neck.

Through another doorway we passed, and then, by dim torchlight, down earthen stairs.

The smell grew stronger. It seemed to ooze from the mud walls. I turned my face down and vomited a thin stream of glittering blood upon the steps beneath me, which vanished as we moved swiftly on.

'Live among graves,' I said furiously. 'Tell me, why do you suffer hell already by your own choice?'

'Silence,' whispered one of them close to me, a dark-eyed female with a witch's mop of hair. 'You blasphemer,' she said. 'You cursed profaner.'

'Don't be a fool for the devil, darling!' I sneered. We were eye to eye. 'Unless he treats you a damn sight better than the Almighty!'

She laughed. Or rather she started to laugh, and she stopped as if she weren't allowed to laugh. What a gay and interesting little get-together this was going to be!

We were going lower and lower into the earth.

Flickering light, the scrape of their bare feet on the dirt, filthy rags brushing my face. For an instant, I saw a grinning skull. Then another, then a heap of them filling a niche in the wall.

I tried to wrench free and my foot hit another heap and sent the bones clattering on the stairs. The vampires tightened their grip, trying to lift us higher. Now we passed the ghastly spectacle of rotted corpses fixed in the walls like statues, bones swathed in rotted rags.

'This is too disgusting!' I said with my teeth clenched.

We had come to the foot of the steps and were being carried through a great catacomb. I could hear the low rapid beat of kettledrums.

Torches blazed ahead, and over a chorus of mournful wails, there came other cries, distant but filled with pain. Yet something beyond these puzzling cries had caught my attention.

Amid all the foulness, I sensed a mortal was near. It was Nicolas and he was alive and I could hear him, the warm, vulnerable current of his thoughts mingled with his scent. And something was terribly wrong with his thoughts. They were chaos.

I couldn't know if Gabrielle had caught it.

We were quite suddenly thrown down together, in the dust. And the others backed away from us.

I climbed to my feet, lifting Gabrielle with me. And I saw that we were in a great domed chamber, scarcely illuminated by three torches which the vampires held to form a triangle, in the centre of which we stood.

Something huge and black to the back of the chamber; smell of wood and pitch, smell of damp, mouldering cloth, smell of living mortal. Nicolas there.

Gabrielle's hair had come loose entirely from the ribbon, and it fell around her shoulders as she cleaved to me, looking about with seemingly calm, cautious eyes.

Wails rose all around us, but the most piercing supplications came from those other beings we had heard before, creatures somewhere deep in the earth.

And I realized these were entombed vampires screaming, screaming for blood, and screaming for forgiveness and release, screaming even for the fires of hell. The sound was as unbearable as the stench.

No real thoughts from Nicki, only the formless shimmer of his mind. Was he dreaming? Was he mad?

The roll of the drums was very loud and very close, and yet those screams pierced the rumbling again and again without rhythm or warning. The wailing of those nearest us died away, but the drums went on, the pounding suddenly coming from inside my head.

Trying desperately not to clamp my hands to my ears, I looked about.

A great circle had been formed, and there were ten of them at least, these creatures. I saw young ones, old ones, men and women, a young boy — and all clothed in the remnants of human garments, caked with earth, feet bare, hair tangled with filth. There was the woman I had spoken to on the stairs, her well-shaped body clothed in a filthy robe, her quick black eyes glinting like jewels in the dirt as she studied us. And beyond these, the advance guard, were a pair in the shadows beating the kettledrums.

I begged silently for strength. I tried to hear Nicolas without actually thinking of him. Solemn vow: *I shall get us all out of here, though at the moment I do not know exactly how.*

The drumbeat was slowing, becoming an ugly cadence that made the alien feeling of fear a fist against my throat. One of the torchbearers approached.

I could feel the anticipation of the others, a palpable excitement as the flames were thrust at me.

I snatched the torch from the creature, twisting his right hand until he was flung down on his knees. With a hard kick, I sent him sprawling, and as the others rushed in, I swung the torch wide driving them back.

Then defiantly, I threw down the torch.

This caught them off guard and I sensed a sudden quietness. The excitement was drained away, or rather it had lapsed into something more patient and less volatile.

The drums beat insistently, but it seemed they were ignoring the drums. They were staring at the buckles on our shoes, at our hair, and at our faces, with such distress they appeared menacing and hungry. And the young boy, with a look of anguish, reached out to touch Gabrielle.

'Get back!' I hissed. And he obeyed, snatching up the torch from the ground as he did.

But I knew it for certain now — we were surrounded by envy and curiosity, and this was the strongest advantage we possessed.

I looked from one to the other of them. And quite slowly, I commenced to brush the filth from my frock coat and breeches. I smoothed my cloak as I straightened my shoulders. Then I ran a hand through my hair, and stood with my arms folded, the picture of righteous dignity, gazing about.

Gabrielle gave a faint smile. She stood composed, her hand on the hilt of her sword.

The effect of this on the others was universal amazement. The dark-eyed female was enthralled. I winked at her. She would have been gorgeous if someone had thrown her into a waterfall and held her there for half an hour and I told her so silently. She took two steps backwards and pulled closed her robe over her breasts. Interesting. Very interesting indeed.

'What is the explanation for all this?' I asked, staring at them one by one as if they were quite peculiar. Again Gabrielle gave her faint smile.

'What are you meant to be?' I demanded. 'The images of chainrattling ghosts who haunt cemeteries and ancient castles?'

They were glancing to one another, getting uneasy. The drums had stopped.

'My childhood nurse many a time thrilled me with tales of such fiends,' I said. 'Told me they might at any moment leap out of the suits of armour in our house to carry me away screaming.' I stamped my foot and dashed forward. 'IS THAT WHAT YOU ARE!' They shrieked and shrank back.

The black-eyed woman didn't move, however.

I laughed softly.

'And your bodies are just like ours, aren't they?' I asked slowly. 'Smooth, without flaw, and in your eyes I can see evidence of my own powers. Most strange ...'

Confusion coming from them. And the howling in the walls seemed fainter as if the entombed were listening in spite of their pain.

'Is it great fun living in filth and stench such as this?' I asked. 'Is that why you do it?'

Fear. Envy again. How had we managed to escape their fate?

233

'Our leader is Satan,' said the dark-eyed woman sharply. Cultured voice. She'd been something to reckon with when she was mortal. 'And we serve Satan as we are meant to do.'

'Why?' I asked politely.

Consternation all around.

Faint shimmer of Nicolas. Agitation without direction. Had he heard my voice?

'You will bring down the wrath of God on all of us with your defiance,' said the boy, the smallest of them, who couldn't have been more than sixteen when he was made. 'In vanity and wickedness you disregard the Dark Ways. You live among mortals! You walk in the places of light.'

'And why don't you?' I asked. 'Are you to go to heaven on white wings when this penitential sojourn of yours is ended? Is that what Satan promises? Salvation? I wouldn't count on it, if I were you.'

'You will be thrown into the pit of hell for your sins!' said one of the others, a tiny hag of a woman. 'You will have power to do evil on earth no more.'

'When is that supposed to happen?' I asked. 'For half a year I've been what I am. God and Satan have not troubled me! It is you who trouble me!'

They were paralyzed for the moment. Why hadn't we been struck dead when we entered the churches? How could we be what we were?

It was very likely they could have been scattered now and beaten. But what about Nicki? If only his thoughts were directed, I could have gained some image of exactly what lay behind that great heap of mouldering black cloth.

I kept my eyes on the vampires.

Wood, pitch, a pyre there surely. And these damned torches.

The dark-eyed woman edged in. No malice, only fascination. But the boy pushed her to the side infuriating her. He stepped so close I could feel his breath on my face:

'Bastard!' he said. 'You were made by the outcast, Magnus, in defiance of the coven, and in defiance of the Dark Ways. And so you gave the Dark Gift to this woman in rashness and vanity as it was given to you.'

'If Satan does not punish,' said the tiny woman, 'we will punish as is our duty and our right!'

The boy pointed to the black draped pyre. He motioned for the others to draw back.

The kettledrums came up again, fast and loud. The circle widened, the torchbearers drawing near to the cloth.

Two of the others tore down the ragged drapery, great sheets of black serge that sent up the dust in a suffocating cloud.

The pyre was as big as the one that had consumed Magnus.

And on top of the pyre in a crude wooden cage, Nicolas knelt slumped against the bars. He stared blindly at us, and I could find no recognition in his face or his thoughts.

The vampires held their torches high for us to see. And I could feel their excitement rising again as it had when they had first brought us into the room.

Gabrielle was cautioning me with the press of her hand to be calm. Nothing changed in her expression.

There were bluish marks on Nicki's throat. The lace of his shirt was filthy as were their rags, and his breeches were snagged and torn. He was in fact covered with bruises and drained almost to the point of death.

The fear silently exploded in my heart, but I knew this was what they wanted to see. And I sealed it within.

The cage is nothing, I can break it. And there are only three torches. The question is when to move, how. We would not perish like this, not like this.

I found myself staring coldly at Nicolas, coldly at the bundles of kindling, the crude chopped wood. The anger rolled out of me. Gabrielle's face was a perfect mask of hate.

The group seemed to feel this and to move ever so slightly away from it, and then to draw in, confused and uncertain again.

But something else was happening. The circle was tightening. Gabrielle touched my arm.

'The leader is coming,' she said.

A door had opened somewhere. The drums surged and it

seemed those imprisoned in the walls went into agony, pleading to be forgiven and released. The vampires around us took up the cries in a frenzy. It was all I could do not to cover my ears.

A strong instinct told me not to look at the leader. But I couldn't resist him, and slowly I turned to look at him and measure his powers again.

2

HE WAS moving towards the centre of this great circle, his back to the pyre, a strange woman vampire at his side.

And when I looked full at him in the torchlight I felt the same shock I had experienced when he entered Notre Dame.

It wasn't merely his beauty; it was the astonishing innocence of his boyish face. He moved so lightly and swiftly I could not see his feet actually take steps. His huge eyes regarded us without anger, his hair, for all the dust in it, giving off faint reddish glints.

I tried to feel his mind, what it was, why such a sublime being should command these sad ghosts when it had the world to roam. I tried to discover again what I had almost discovered when we stood before the altar of the cathedral, this creature and I. If I knew that, maybe I could defeat him and defeat him I would.

I thought I saw him respond to me, some silent answer, some flash of heaven in the very pit of hell in his innocent expression, as if the devil still retained the face and form of the angel after the fall.

But something was very wrong. The leader was not speaking. The drums beat on anxiously, yet there was no communal conviction. The dark-eyed woman vampire was not joined with the others in their wailing. And others had stopped as well.

And the woman who had come in with the leader, a strange creature clothed as an ancient queen might have been in

236

ragged gown and braided girdle, commenced to laugh.

The coven or whatever it called itself was quite understandably stunned. One of the kettledrums stopped.

The queen creature laughed louder and louder. Her white teeth flashed through the filthy veil of her snarled hair.

Beautiful she'd been once. And it wasn't mortal age that had ravaged her. Rather she appeared the lunatic, her mouth a horrid grimace, her eyes staring wildly before her, her body bent suddenly in an arc with her laughing, as Magnus had bent when he danced around his own funeral pyre.

'Did I not warn you?' she screamed. 'Did I not?'

Far behind her, Nicolas moved in the little cage. I felt the laughter scorching him. But he was looking steadily at me, and the old sensibility was stamped on his features in spite of their distortion. Fear struggled with malice in him, and this was tangled with wonder and near despair.

The auburn-haired leader stared at the queen vampire, his expression unreadable, and the boy with the torch stepped forward and shouted for the woman to be silent at once. He made himself rather regal now, in spite of his rags.

The woman turned her back on him and faced us. She sang her words in a hoarse, sexless voice that gave way to a galloping laughter.

'A thousand times I said it, yet you would not listen to me,' she declared. Her gown shivered about her as she trembled. 'And you called me mad, time's martyr, a vagrant Cassandra corrupted by too long a vigil on this earth. Well, you see, every one of my predictions has come true.'

The leader gave her not the slightest recognition.

'And it took this creature' — she approached me, her face a hideous comic mask as Magnus's face had been — 'this romping cavalier to prove it to you once and for all.'

She hissed, drew in her breath, and stood erect. And for one moment in perfect stillness she passed into beauty. I longed to comb her hair, to wash it with my own hands, and to clothe her in modern dress, to see her in the mirror of my time. In fact, my mind went suddenly wild with the idea of it, the reclaiming of her and the washing away of her evil disguise.

I think for one second the concept of eternity burned in me. I knew then what immortality was. All things were possible with her, or so for that one moment it seemed.

She gazed at me and caught the visions, and the loveliness of her face deepened, but the mad humour was coming back.

'Punish them,' the boy stormed. 'Call down the judgment of Satan. Light the fire.'

But no one moved in the vast room.

The old woman hummed with her lips closed, some eerie melody with the cadence of speech. The leader stared as before.

But the boy in panic advanced upon us. He bared his fangs, raised his hand in a claw.

I snatched the torch from him and dealt him an indifferent blow to the chest that sent him across the dusty circle, sliding into the kindling banked against the pyre. I ground out the torch in the dirt.

The queen vampire let out a shriek of laughter that seemed to terrify the others, but nothing changed in the leader's face.

'I won't stand here for any judgment of Satan!' I said, glancing around the circle. 'Unless you bring Satan here.'

'Yes, tell them, child! Make them answer to you!' the old woman said triumphantly.

The boy was on his feet again.

'You know the crimes,' he roared as he reentered the circle. He was furious now, and he exuded power, and I realized how impossible it was to judge any of them by the mortal form they retained. He might well have been an elder, the tiny old woman a fledgling, the boyish leader the eldest of them all.

'Behold,' he said, stepping closer, his grey eyes gleaming as he felt the attention of the others. 'This fiend was no novice here or anywhere; he did not beg to be received. He made no vows to Satan. He did not on his deathbed give up his soul, and in fact, he did not die!' His voice went higher, grew louder. 'He was not buried! He has not risen from the grave as a Child of Darkness! Rather he dares to roam the world in the guise of a living being! And in the very midst of Paris conducts business as a mortal man!'

Shrieks answered him from the walls. But the vampires of the circle were silent as he gazed at them. His jaw trembled.

He threw up his arms and wailed. One or two of the others answered. His face was disfigured with rage.

The old queen vampire gave a shiver of laughter and looked at me with the most maniacal smile.

But the boy wasn't giving up.

'He seeks the comforts of the hearth, strictly forbidden,' he screamed, stamping his foot and shaking his garments. 'He goes into the very palaces of carnal pleasure, and mingles there with mortals as they play music! As they dance!'

'Stop your raving!' I said. But in truth, I wanted to hear him out.

He plunged forward, sticking his finger in my face.

'No rituals can purify him!' he shouted. 'Too late for the Dark Vow, the Dark Blessings ...'

'Dark Vows? Dark Blessings?' I turned to the old queen. 'What do you say to all this? You're as old as Magnus was when he went into the fire ... Why do you suffer this to go on?'

Her eyes moved in her head suddenly as if they alone possessed life, and there came that racing laughter out of her again.

'I shall never harm you, young one,' she said. 'Either of you.' She looked lovingly at Gabrielle. 'You are on the Devil's Road to a great adventure. What right have I to intervene in what the centuries have in store for you?'

The Devil's Road. It was the first phrase from any of them that had rung a clarion in my soul. An exhilaration took hold of me merely looking at her. In her own way, she was Magnus's twin.

'Oh yes, I am as old as your progenitor!' She smiled, her white fangs just touching her lower lip, then vanishing. She glanced at the leader, who watched her without the slightest interest or spirit. 'I was here,' she said, 'within this coven when Magnus stole our secrets from us, that crafty one, the alchemist, Magnus ... when he drank the blood that would give him life everlasting in a manner in which the World of Darkness had never witnessed before. And now three centuries have passed and he has given his pure and undiluted Dark Gift to you, beautiful child!'

Her face became again that leering, grinning mask of comedy, so much like Magnus's face.

'Show it to me, child,' she said, 'the strength he gave you. Do you know what it means to be made a vampire by one that powerful, who has never given the Gift before? It's forbidden here, child, no one of such age conveys his power! For if he should, the fledgling born of him should easily overcome this gracious leader and his coven here.'

'Stop this ill-conceived lunacy!' the boy interrupted.

But everyone was listening. The pretty dark-eyed woman had come nearer to us, the better to see the old queen, and completely forgetting to fear or hate us now.

'One hundred years ago you'd said enough,' the boy roared at the old queen, with his hand up to command her silence. 'You're mad as all the old ones are mad. It's the death you suffer. I tell you all this outlaw must be punished. Order shall be restored when he and the woman he made are destroyed before us all.'

With renewed fury, he turned on the others.

'I tell you, you walk this earth as all evil things do, by the will of God, to make mortals suffer for his Divine Glory. And by the will of God you can be destroyed if you blaspheme, and thrown in the vats of hell now, for you are damned souls, and your immortality is given you only at the price of suffering and torment.'

A burst of wailing commenced uncertainly.

'So there it is finally,' I said. 'The whole philosophy — and the whole is founded upon a lie. And you cower like peasants, in hell already by your own choosing, enchained more surely than the lowest mortal, and you wish to punish us because we do not? Follow our examples because we do not!'

The vampires were some of them staring at us, others in frantic conversations that broke out all around. Again and again they glanced to the leader and to the old queen.

But the leader would say nothing.

The boy screamed for order:

'It is not enough that he has profaned holy places,' he said, 'not enough that he goes about as a mortal man. This very night in a village in the banlieue he terrified the congregation of an entire church. All of Paris is talking of this horror, the ghouls rising from the graves beneath the very altar, he and this female vampire on whom he worked the Dark Trick without consent or ritual, just as he was made.'

There were gasps, more murmurs. But the old queen screamed with delight.

'These are high crimes,' he said. 'I tell you, they cannot go unpunished. And who among you does not know of his mockeries on the stage of the boulevard theatre which he himself holds as property as a mortal man! There to a thousand Parisians he flaunted his powers as a Child of Darkness! And the secrecy we have protected for centuries was broken for his amusement and the amusement of a common crowd.'

The old queen rubbed her hands together, cocking her head to the side as she looked at me.

'Is it all true, child?' she asked. 'Did you sit in a box at the Opéra? Did you stand before the footlights of the Théâtre-Française? Did you dance with the king and queen in the palace of the Tuileries, you and this beauty you made so perfectly? Is it true you travel the boulevards in a golden coach?'

She laughed and laughed, her eyes now and then scanning the others, subduing them as if she gave forth a beam of warm light.

'Ah, such finery and such dignity,' she continued. 'What happened in the great cathedral when you entered it? Tell me now!'

'Absolutely nothing, madam!' I declared.

'High crimes!' roared the outraged boy vampire. 'These are frights enough to rouse a city, if not a kingdom against us. And after centuries in which we have preyed upon this metropolis in stealth, giving birth only to the gentlest whispers of our great power. Haunts we are, creatures of the night, meant to feed the fears of man, not raving demons!'

'Ah, but it is too sublime,' sang the old queen with her eyes

241

on the domed ceiling. 'From my stone pillow I have dreamed dreams of the mortal world above. I have heard its voices, its new music, as lullabies as I lie in my grave. I have envisioned its fantastical discoveries, I have known its courage in the timeless sanctum of my thoughts. And though it shuts me out with its dazzling forms, I long for one with the strength to roam it fearlessly, to ride the Devil's Road through its heart.'

The grey-eyed boy was beside himself.

'Dispense with the trial,' he said, glaring at the leader. 'Light the pyre now.'

The queen stepped back out of my way with an exaggerated gesture, as the boy reached for the torch nearest him, and I rushed at him, snatching the torch away from him, and heaving him up towards the ceiling, head over heels, so that he came tumbling in that manner all the way down. I stamped out the torch.

That left one more. And the coven was in perfect disorder, several rushing to aid the boy, the others murmuring to one another, the leader stock-still as if in a dream.

And in this interval I went forward, climbed up the pyre and tore loose the front of the little wooden cage.

Nicolas looked like an animated corpse. His eyes were leaden, and his mouth twisted as if he were smiling at me, hating me, from the other side of the grave. I dragged him free of the cage and brought him down to the dirt floor. He was feverish, and though I ignored it and would have concealed it if I could, he shoved at me and cursed me under his breath.

The old queen watched in fascination. I glanced at Gabrielle, who watched without a particle of fear. I drew out the pearl rosary from my waistcoat and letting the crucifix dangle, I placed the rosary around Nicolas's neck. He stared stuporously down at the little cross, and then he began to laugh. The contempt, the malice, came out of him in this low metallic sound. It was the very opposite of the sounds made by the vampires. You could hear the human blood in it, the human thickness of it, echoing against the walls. Ruddy and hot and strangely unfinished he seemed suddenly, the only mortal among us, like a child thrown among porcelain dolls.

The coven was more confused than ever. The two burnt-out torches still lay untouched.

'Now, by your own rules, you cannot harm him,' I said, 'Yet it's a vampire who has given him the supernatural protection. Tell me, how to compass that?'

I carried Nicki forward. And Gabrielle at once reached out to take him in her arms.

He accepted this, though he stared at her as if he didn't know her and even lifted his fingers to touch her face. She took his hand away as she might the hand of a baby, and kept her eyes fixed on the leader and on me.

'If your leader has no words for you now, I have words,' I said. 'Go wash yourselves in the waters of the Seine, and clothe yourselves like humans if you can remember how, and prowl among men as you are obviously meant to do.'

The defeated boy vampire stumbled back into the circle, pushing roughly away those who had helped him to his feet.

'Armand,' he implored the silent auburn-haired leader. 'Bring the coven to order! Armand! Save us now!'

'Why in the name of hell,' I outshouted him, 'did the devil give you beauty, agility, eyes to see visions, minds to cast spells?'

Their eyes were fixed on me, all of them. The grey-haired boy cried out the name 'Armand' again, but in vain.

'You waste your gifts!' I said. 'And worse, you waste your immortality! Nothing in all the world is so nonsensical and contradictory, save mortals, that is, who live in the grip of the superstitions of the past.'

Perfect silence reigned. I could hear Nicki's slow breathing. I could feel his warmth. I could feel his numbed fascination struggling against death itself.

'Have you no cunning?' I asked the others, my voice swelling in the stillness. 'Have you no craft? How did I, an orphan, stumble upon so much possibility, when you, nurtured as you are by these evil parents' — I broke off to stare at the leader and the furious boy — 'grope like blind things under the earth?'

'The power of Satan will blast you into hell,' the boy bellowed, gathering all his remaining strength.

'You keep saying that!' I said. 'And it keeps not happening,

243

as we can all see!'

Loud murmurs of assent!

'And if you really thought it would happen,' I said, 'you would never have bothered to bring me here.'

Louder voices in agreement.

I looked at the small forlorn figure of the leader. And all eyes turned away from me to him. Even the mad queen vampire looked at him.

And in the stillness I heard him whisper:

'It is finished.'

Not even the tormented ones in the wall made a sound.

And the leader spoke again:

'Go now, all of you, it is at an end.'

'Armand, no!' the boy pleaded.

But the others were backing away, faces concealed behind hands as they whispered. The drums were cast aside, the single torch was hung upon the wall.

I watched the leader. I knew his words weren't meant to release us.

And after he had silently driven out the protesting boy with the others, so that only the queen remained with him, he turned his gaze once again to me.

3

THE great empty room beneath its immense dome, with only the two vampires watching us, seemed all the more ghastly, the one torch giving a feeble and gloomy light.

Silently I considered: Will the others leave the cemetery, or hover at the top of the stairs? Will any of them allow me to take Nicki alive from this place? The boy will remain near, but the boy is weak; the old queen will do nothing. That leaves only the leader, really. But I must not be impulsive now.

He was still staring at me and saying nothing.

'Armand?' I said respectfully. 'May I address you in this

way?' I drew closer, scanning him for the slighest change of expression. 'You are obviously the leader. And you are the one who can explain all this to us.'

But these words were a poor cover for my thoughts. I was appealing to him. I was asking him how he had led them in all this, he who appeared as ancient as the old queen, compassing some depth they would not understand. I pictured him standing before the altar of Notre Dame again, that ethereal expression on his face. And I found myself believing perfectly in him, and the possibility of him, this ancient one who had stood silent all this while.

I think I searched him now for just an instant of human feeling! That's what I thought wisdom would reveal. And the mortal in me, the vulnerable one who had cried in the inn at the vision of the chaos, said:

'Armand, what is the meaning of all this?'

It seemed the brown eyes faltered. But then the face so subtly transformed itself to rage, that I drew back.

I didn't believe my senses. The sudden changes he had undergone in Notre Dame were nothing to this. And such a perfect incarnation of malice I'd never seen. Even Gabrielle moved away. She raised her right hand to shield Nicki, and I stepped back until I was beside her and our arms touched.

But in the same miraculous way, the hatred melted. The face was again that of a sweet and fresh mortal boy.

The old queen vampire smiled almost wanly and ran her white claws through her hair.

'You turn to me for explanations?' the leader asked.

His eyes moved over Gabrielle and the dazed figure of Nicolas against her shoulder. Then returned to me.

'I could speak until the end of the world,' he said, 'and I could never tell you what you have destroyed here.'

I thought the old queen made some derisive sound, but I was too engaged with him, the softness of his speech and the great raging anger within.

'Since the beginning of time,' he said, 'these mysteries have existed.' He seemed small standing in this vast chamber, the voice issuing from him effortlessly, his hands limp at his sides.

'Since the ancient days there have been our kind haunting the cities of man, preying upon him by night as God and the devil commanded us to do. The chosen of Satan we are, and those admitted to our ranks had first to prove themselves through a hundred crimes before the Dark Gift of immortality was given to them.'

He came just a little nearer to me, the torchlight glimmering in his eyes.

'Before their loved ones they appeared to die,' he said, 'and with only a small infusion of our blood did they endure the terror of the coffin as they waited for us to come. Then and only then was the Dark Gift given, and they were sealed again in the grave after, until their thirst should give them the strength to break the narrow box and rise.'

His voice grew slightly louder, more resonant.

'It was death they knew in those dark chambers,' he said. 'It was death and the power of evil they understood as they rose, breaking open the coffin, and the iron doors that held them in. And pity the weak, those who couldn't break out. Those whose wails brought mortals the day after — for none would answer by night. We gave no mercy to them.

'But those who rose, ah, those were the vampires who walked the earth, tested, purified, Children of Darkness, born of a fledgling's blood, never the full power of an ancient master, so that time would bring the wisdom to use the Dark Gifts before they grew truly strong. And on these were imposed the Rules of Darkness. To live among the dead, for we are dead things, returning always to one's own grave or one very nearly like it. To shun the places of light, luring victims away from the company of others to suffer death in unholy and haunted places. And to honour forever the power of God, the crucifix about the neck, the Sacraments. And never never to enter the House of God, lest he strike you powerless, casting you into hell, ending your reign on earth in blazing torment.'

He paused. He looked at the old queen for the first time, and it seemed, though I could not truly tell, that her face maddened him.

'You scorn these things,' he said to her. 'Magnus scorned

these things!' He commenced to tremble. 'It was the nature of his madness, as it is the nature of yours, but I tell you you do not understand these mysteries! You shatter them like so much glass, but you have no strength, no power save ignorance. You break and that is all.'

He turned away, hesitating as if he would not go on, and looking about at the vast crypt.

I heard the old vampire queen very softly singing.

She was chanting something under her breath, and she began to rock back and forth, her head to one side, her eyes dreamy. Once again, she looked beautiful.

'It is finished for my children,' the leader whispered. 'It is finished and done, for they know now they can disregard all of it. The things that bound us together, gave us the strength to endure as damned things! The mysteries that protected us here.'

Again he looked at me.

'And you ask me for explanations as if it were inexplicable!' he said. 'You, for whom the working of the Dark Trick is an act of shameless greed. You gave it to the very womb that bore you! Why not to this one, the devil's fiddler whom you worship from afar every night?'

'Have I not told you?' sang the vampire queen. 'Haven't we always known? There is nothing to fear in the Sign of the Cross, nor the Holy Water, nor the Sacrament itself ...' She repeated the words, varying the melody under her breath, adding as she went on. 'And the old rites, the incense, the fire, the vows spoken, when we thought we saw the Evil One in the dark, whispering ...'

'Silence!' said the leader, dropping his voice. His hands almost went to his ears in a strangely human gesture. Like a boy he looked, almost lost. God, that our immortal bodies could be such varied prisons for us, that our immortal faces should be such masks for our true souls.

Again he fixed his eyes on me. I thought for a moment there would be another of those ghastly transformations or that some uncontrollable violence would come from him, and I hardened myself.

But he was imploring me silently.

247

Why did this come about! His voice almost dried in his throat as he repeated it aloud, as he tried to curb his rage. 'You explain to me! Why you, you with the strength of ten vampires and the courage of a hell full of devils, crashing through the world in your brocade and your leather boots! Lelio, the actor from the House of Thespians, making us into grand drama on the boulevard! Tell me! Tell me why!'

'It was Magnus's strength, Magnus's genius,' sang the woman vampire with the most wistful smile.

'No!' He shook his head. 'I tell you, he is beyond all account. He knows no limit and so he has no limit. But why!'

He moved just a little closer, not seeming to walk but to come more clearly into focus as an apparition might.

'Why you,' he demanded, 'with the boldness to walk their streets, break their locks, call them by name. They dress your hair, they fit your clothes! You gamble at their tables! Deceiving them, embracing them, drinking their blood only steps from where other mortals laugh and dance. You who shun cemeteries and burst from crypts in churches. Why you! Thoughtless, arrogant, ignorant and disdainful! You give *me* the explanation. Answer me!'

My heart was racing. My face was warm and pulsing with blood. I was in no fear of him now, but I was angry beyond all mortal anger, and I didn't fully understand why.

His mind — I had wanted to pierce his mind — and this is what I heard, this superstition, this absurdity. He was no sublime spirit who understood what his followers had not. He had not believed it. He had believed *in* it, a thousand times worse!

And I realized quite clearly what he was — not demon or angel at all, but a sensibility forged in a dark time when the small orb of the sun travelled the dome of the heavens, and the stars were no more than tiny lanterns describing gods and goddesses upon a closed night. A time when man was the centre of this great world in which we roam, a time when for every question there had been an answer. That was what he was, a child of olden days when witches had danced beneath the moon and knights had battled dragons.

Ah, sad lost child, roaming the catacombs beneath a great city and an incomprehensive century. Maybe your mortal form is more fitting than I supposed.

But there was no time to mourn for him, beautiful as he was. Those entombed in the walls suffered at his command. Those he had sent out of the chamber could be called back.

I had to think of a reply to his question that he would be able to accept. The truth wasn't enough. It had to be arranged poetically the way that the old thinkers would have arranged it in the world before the age of reason had come to be.

'My answer?' I said softly. I was gathering my thoughts and I could almost feel Gabrielle's warning, Nicki's fear. 'I'm no dealer in mysteries,' I said, 'no lover of philosophy. But it's plain enough what has happened here.'

He studied me with a strange earnestness.

'If you fear so much the power of God,' I said, 'then the teachings of the Church aren't unknown to you. You must know that the forms of goodness change with the ages, that there are saints for all times under heaven.'

Visibly he hearkened to this, warmed to the words I used.

'In ancient days,' I said, 'there were martyrs who quenched the flames that sought to burn them, mystics who rose into the air as they heard the voice of God. But as the world changed, so changed the saints. What are they now but obedient nuns and priests? They build hospitals and orphanages, but they do not call down the angels to rout armies or tame the savage beast.'

I could see no change in him but I pressed on.

'And so it is with evil, obviously. It changes its form. How many men in this age believe in the crosses that frighten your followers? Do you think mortals above are speaking to each other of heaven and hell? Philosophy is what they talk about, and science! What does it matter to them if whitefaced haunts prowl a churchyard after dark? A few more murders in a wilderness of murders? How can this be of interest to God or the devil or to man?'

I heard again the old queen vampire laughing.

But Armand didn't speak or move.

'Even your playground is about to be taken from you,' I

continued. 'This cemetery in which you hide is about to be removed altogether from Paris. Even the bones of our ancestors are no longer sacred in this secular age.'

His face softened suddenly. He couldn't conceal his shock.

'Les Innocents destroyed!' he whispered. 'You're lying to me ...'

'I never lie,' I said offhand. 'At least not to those I don't love. The people of Paris don't want the stench of graveyards around them anymore. The emblems of the dead don't matter to them, as they matter to you. Within a few years, markets, streets, and houses will cover this spot. Commerce. Practicality. That is the eighteenth-century world.'

'Stop!' he whispered. 'Les Innocents has existed as long as I have existed!' His boyish face was strained. The old queen was undisturbed.

'Don't you see?' I said softly. 'It is a new age. It requires a new evil. And I *am* that new evil.' I paused, watching him. 'I am the vampire for these times.'

He had not foreseen my point. And I saw in him for the first time a glimmer of terrible understanding, the first glimmer of real fear.

I made a small accepting gesture.

'This incident in the village church tonight,' I said cautiously, 'it was vulgar, I'm inclined to agree. My actions on the stage of theatre, worse still. But these were blunders. And you know they aren't the source of your rancour. Forget them for the moment and try to envision my beauty and my power. Try to see the evil that I am. I stalk the world in mortal dress — the worst of fiends, the monster who looks exactly like everyone else.'

The woman vampire made a low song of her laughter. I could feel only pain from him, and from her the warm emanation of her love.

'Think of it, Armand,' I pressed carefully. 'Why should Death lurk in the shadows? Why should Death wait at the gate? There is no bedchamber, no ballroom that I cannot enter. Death in the glow of the hearth, Death on tiptoe in the corridor, that is what I am. Speak to me of the Dark Gifts — I use them. I'm Gentleman Death in silk and lace, come to put out the candles. The canker in the heart of the rose.'

There was a faint moan from Nicolas.

I think I heard Armand sigh.

'There is no place where they can hide from me,' I said, 'these godless and powerful ones who would destroy les Innocents. There is no lock that can keep me out.'

He stared back at me silently. He appeared sad and calm. His eyes were darkened slightly, but they were untroubled by malice or rage. He didn't speak for a long moment, and then:

'A splendid mission, that,' he said, 'to devil them mercilessly as you live among them. But it's you still who don't understand.'

'How so?' I asked.

'You can't endure in the world, living among men, you cannot survive.'

'But I do,' I said simply. 'The old mysteries have given way to a new *style*. And who knows what will follow? There's no romance in what you are. There is great romance in what I am!'

'You can't be that strong,' he said. 'You don't know what you're saying, you have only just come into being, you are young.'

'He is very strong, however, this child,' mused the queen, 'and so is his beautiful newborn companion. They are fiends of high-blown ideas and great reason these two.'

'You can't live among men!' Armand insisted again.

His face coloured for one second. But he wasn't my enemy now; rather he was some wondering elder struggling to tell me a critical truth. And at the same moment he seemed a child imploring me, and in that struggle lay his essence, parent and child, pleading with me to listen to what he had to say.

'And why not? I tell you I belong among men. It is their blood that makes me immortal.'

'Ah, yes, immortal, but you have not begun to understand it,' he said. 'It's no more than a word. Study the fate of your maker. Why did Magnus go into the flames? It's an age-old truth among us, and you haven't even guessed it. Live among men, and the passing years will drive you to madness. To see

251

others grow old and die, to see kingdoms rise and fall, to lose all you understand and cherish — who can endure it? It will drive you to idiot raving and despair. Your own immortal kind is your protection, your *salvation*. The ancient ways, don't you see, which *never changed*!'

He stopped, shocked that he had used this word, salvation, and it reverberated through the room, his lips shaping it again.

'Armand,' the old queen sang softly. 'Madness may come to the eldest we know, whether they keep to the old ways or abandon them.' She made a gesture as if to attack him with her white claws, screeching with laughter as he stared coldly back. 'I have kept to the old ways as long as you have and I am mad, am I not? Perhaps that is why I have kept them so well!'

He shook his head angrily in protest. Was he not the living proof it need not be so?

But she drew near to me and took hold of my arm, turning my face towards her.

'Did Magnus tell you nothing, child?' she asked.

I felt an immense power flowing from her.

'While others prowled this sacred place,' she said, 'I went alone across the snow-covered fields to find Magnus. My strength is so great now it is as if I have wings. I climbed to his window to find him in his chamber, and together we walked the battlements unseen by all save the distant stars.'

She drew even closer, her grip tightening.

'Many things, Magnus knew,' she said. 'And it is not madness which is your enemy, not if you are really strong. The vampire who leaves his coven to dwell among human beings faces a dreadful hell long before madness comes. He grows irresistibly to love mortals! He comes to *understand* all things in love.'

'Let me go,' I whispered softly. Her glance was holding me as surely as her hands.

'With the passage of time he comes to know mortals as they may never know each other,' she continued, undaunted, her eyebrows rising, 'and finally there comes the moment when he cannot bear to take life, or bear to make suffering, and nothing but madness or his own death will ease his pain That is the fate of the old ones which Magnus described to me, Magnus who suffered all afflictions in the end.'

At last she released me. She receded from me as if she were an image in a sailor's glass.

'I don't believe what you're saying,' I whispered. But the whisper was like a hiss. 'Magnus? Love mortals?'

'Of course you do not,' she said with her graven jester's smile.

Armand, too, was looking at her as if he did not understand.

'My words have no meaning now,' she added. 'But you have *all the time in the world* to understand!'

Laughter, howling laughter, scraping the ceiling of the crypt. Cries again from within the walls. She threw back her head with her laughter.

Armand was horror-stricken as he watched her. It was as if he saw the laughter emanating from her like so much glittering light.

'No, but it's a lie, a hideous simplification!' I said. My head was throbbing suddenly. My eyes were throbbing. 'I mean it's a concept born out of moral idiocy, this idea of love!'

I put my hands to my temples. A deadly pain in me was growing. The pain was dimming my vision, sharpening my memory of Magnus's dungeon, the mortal prisoners who had died among the rotted bodies of those condemned before them in the stinking crypt.

Armand looked to me now as if I were torturing him as the old queen tortured him with her laughter. And her laughter went right on, rising and falling away. Armand's hands went out towards me as if he would touch me but did not dare.

All the rapture and pain I'd known in these past months came together inside me. I felt quite suddenly as if I would begin to roar as I had that night on Renaud's stage. I was aghast at these sensations. I was murmuring nonsense syllables again aloud.

'Lestat!' Gabrielle whispered.

'Love mortals?' I said. I stared at the old queen's inhuman face, horrified suddenly to see the black eyelashes like spikes about her glistening eyes, her flesh like animated marble. 'Love mortals? Does it take you three hundred years!' I glared at Gabrielle. 'From the first nights when I held them close to me. I loved them. Drinking up their life, their death, I love them. Dear God, is that not the very essence of the Dark Gift?'

My voice was growing in volume as it had that night in the theatre. 'Oh, what are you that you do not? What vile things that this is the sum of your wisdom, the simple capacity to feel!'

I backed away from them, looking about me at this giant tomb, the damp earth arching over our heads. The place was passing out of the material into an hallucination.

'God, do you lose your reason with the Dark Trick,' I asked, 'with your rituals, your sealing up of the fledglings in the grave? Or were you monsters when you were living? How could we not all of us love mortals with every breath we take!'

No answer. Except the senseless cries of the starving ones. No answer. Just the dim beating of Nicki's heart.

'Well, hear me, whatever the case,' I said.

I pointed my finger at Armand, at the old queen.

'I never promised my soul to the devil for this! And when I made this one it was to save her from the worms that eat the corpses around here. If loving mortals is the hell you speak of, I am already in it. I have met my fate. Leave me to it and all scores are settled now.'

My voice had broken. I was gasping. I ran my hands back through my hair. Armand seemed to shimmer as he came close to me. His face was a miracle of seeming purity and awe.

'Dead things, dead things ...' I said. 'Come no closer. Talking of madness and love, in this reeking place! And that old monster, Magnus, locking them up in his dungeon. How did he love them, his captives? The way boys love butterflies when they rip off their wings!'

'No, child, you think you understand but you do not,' sang the woman vampire unperturbed. 'You have only just begun your loving.' She gave a soft lilting laugh. 'You feel sorry for them, that is all. And for yourself that you cannot be both human and inhuman. Isn't it so?'

'Lies!' I said. I moved closer to Gabrielle. I put my arm around her.

'You will come to understand all things in love,' the old queen went on, 'when you are a vicious and hateful thing. This is your immortality, child. Ever deeper understanding of it.' And throwing up her arms, again she howled.

'Damn you,' I said. I picked up Gabrielle and Nicki and carried them backwards towards the door. 'You're in hell already,' I said, 'and I intend to leave you in hell now.'

I took Nicolas out of Gabrielle's arms and we ran through the catacomb towards the stairs.

The old queen was in a frenzy of keening laughter behind us.

And human as Orpheus perhaps, I stopped and glanced back.

'Lestat, hurry!' Nicolas whispered in my ear. And Gabrielle gave a desperate gesture for me to come.

Armand had not moved, and the old woman stood beside him laughing still.

'Good-bye, brave children,' she cried. 'Ride the Devil's Road bravely. Ride the Devil's Road as long as you can.'

THE COVEN scattered like frightened ghosts in the cold rain as we burst out of the sepulchre. And baffled, they watched as we sped out of Les Innocents into the crowded Paris streets.

Within moments we had stolen a carriage and were on our way out of the city into the countryside.

I DROVE the team on relentlessly. Yet I was so mortally tired that preternatural strength seemed purely an idea. At every thicket and turn of the road I expected to see the filthy demons surrounding us again.

But somehow I managed to get from a country inn the food and drink Nicolas would need, and the blankets to keep him warm.

He was unconscious long before we reached the tower, and I carried him up the stairs to that high cell where Magnus had first kept me.

His throat was still swollen and bruised from their feasting on him. And though he slept deeply as I laid him on the straw bed, I could feel the thirst in him, the awful craving that I'd felt after Magnus had drunk from me.

Well, there was plenty of wine for him when he awakened, and plenty of food. And I knew — though how I couldn't tell — that he wouldn't die.

What his daylight hours would be like, I could hardly imagine. But he would be safe once I turned the key in the lock. And no matter what he had been to me, or what he stood to be in the future, no mortal could wander free in my lair while I slept.

Beyond that I couldn't reason. I felt like a mortal walking in his sleep.

I was still staring down at him, hearing his vague jumbled dreams — dreams of the horrors of les Innocents — when Gabrielle came in. She had finished burying the poor unfortunate stable boy, and she looked like a dusty angel again, her hair stiff and tangled and full of delicate fractured light.

She looked down at Nicki for a long moment and then she drew me out of the room. After I had locked the door, she led me down to the lower crypt. There she put her arms tightly around me and held me, as if she too were worn almost to collapse.

'Listen to me,' she said finally, drawing back and putting her hands up to hold my face. 'We'll get him out of France as soon as we rise. No one will ever believe his mad tales.'

I didn't answer. I could scarce understand her, her reasoning or her intentions. My head swam.

'You can play the puppeteer with him,' she said, 'as you did with Renaud's actors. You can send him off to the New World.'

'Sleep,' I whispered. I kissed her open mouth. I held her with my eyes closed. I saw the crypt again, heard their strange, inhuman voices. All this would not stop.

'After he's gone then we can talk about these others,' she said calmly. 'Whether to leave Paris altogether for a while ...'

I let her go, and I turned away from her and I went to the sarcophagus and rested for a moment against the stone lid. For

256

the first time in my immortal life I wanted the silence of the tomb, the feeling that all things were out of my hands.

It seemed she said something else then. *Do not do this thing!*

4

HEN I awoke I heard his cries. He was beating on the oaken door, cursing me for keeping him prisoner. The sound filled the tower, and the scent of him came through the stone walls: succulent, oh so succulent, smell of living flesh and blood, his flesh and blood.

She slept still.

Do not do this thing.

Symphony of malice, symphony of madness coming through the walls, philosophy straining to contain the ghastly images, the torture, to surround it with language ...

When I stepped into the stairwell, it was like being caught in a whirlwind of his cries, his human smell.

And all the remembered scents mingled with it — the afternoon sunshine on a wooden table, the red wine, the smoke of the little fire.

'Lestat! Do you hear me! Lestat!' Thunder of fists against the door.

Memory of childhood fairy tale: the giant says he smells the blood of a human in his lair. Horror. I knew the giant was going to find the human. I could hear him coming after the human, step by step. I was the human.

Only no more.

Smoke and salt of flesh and pumping blood.

'This is the witches' place! Lestat, do you hear me! This is the witches' place!'

Dull tremor of the old secrets between us, the love, the things that only we had known, felt. Dancing in the witches' place. Can you deny it? Can you deny everything that passed between us?

Get him out of France. Send him to the New World. And

then what? All his life he is one of these slightly interesting but generally tiresome mortals who have seen spirits, talk of them incessantly, and no one believes him. Deepening madness. Will he be a comical lunatic finally, the kind that even the ruffians and bullies look after, playing his fiddle in a dirty coat for the crowds on the streets of Port-au-Prince?

'Be the puppeteer again,' she had said. Is that what I was? *No one will ever believe his mad tales.*

But he knows the place where we lie, Mother. He knows our names, the name of our kin — too many things about us. And he will never go quietly to another country. And *they* may go after him; *they* will never let him live now.

Where are *they*?

I went up the stairs in the whirlwind of his echoing cries, looked out the little barred windows at the open land. They'll be coming again. They have to come. First I was alone, then I had her with me, and now I have them!

But what was the crux? That he wanted it? That he had screamed over and over that I had denied him the power?

Or was it that I now had the excuses, I needed to bring him to me as I had wanted to do from the first moment? My Nicolas, my love. Eternity waits. All the great and splendid pleasures of being dead.

I went further up the stairs towards him and the thirst sang in me. To hell with his cries. The thirst sang and I was an instrument of its singing.

And his cries had become inarticulate — the pure essence of his curses, a dull punctuation to the misery that I could hear without need of any sound. Something divinely carnal in the broken syllables coming from his lips, like the low gush of the blood through his heart.

I lifted the key and put it in the lock and he went silent, his thoughts washing backwards and into him as if the ocean could be sucked back into the tiny mysterious coils of a single shell.

I tried to see *him* in the shadows of the room, and not *it* — the love for him, the aching, wrenching months of longing for him, the hideous and unshakeable human need for him, the lust. I tried to see the mortal who didn't know what he was saying as he glared at me:

'You, and your talk of goodness' — low seething voice, eyes glittering — 'your talk of good and evil, your talk of what was right and what was wrong and death, oh yes, death, the horror, the tragedy ...'

Words. Borne on the ever swelling current of hatred, like flowers opening in the current, petals peeling back, then falling apart:

'... and you shared it with her, the lord's son giveth to the lord's wife his great gift, the Dark Gift. Those who live in the castle share the Dark Gift — never were they dragged to the witches' place where the human grease pools on the ground at the foot of the burnt stake, no, kill the old crone who can no longer see to sew, and the idiot boy who cannot till the field. And what does he give us, the lord's son, the wolfkiller, the one who screamed in the witches' place? Coin of the realm! That's good enough for us!'

Shuddering. Shirt soaked with sweat. Gleam of taut flesh through the torn lace. Tantalizing, the mere sight of it, the narrow tightly muscled torso that sculptors so love to represent, nipples pink against the dark skin.

'This power' — sputtering as if all day long he had been saying the words over with the same intensity, and it does not really matter that now I am present — 'this power that made all the lies meaningless, this dark power that soared over everything, this truth that obliterated ...'

No. Language. Not truth.

The wine bottles were empty, the food devoured. His lean arms were hardened and tense for the struggle — but what struggle? — his brown hair fallen out of its ribbon, his eyes enormous and glazed.

But suddenly he pushed against the wall as if he'd go through it to get away from me — dim remembrance of their drinking from him, the paralysis, the ecstasy — yet he was drawn immediately forward again, staggering, putting his hands out to steady himself by taking hold of things that were not there.

But his voice had stopped.

Something breaking in his face.

'How could you keep it from me!' he whispered. Thoughts of old magic, luminous legend, some great eerie strata in which all the shadowy things thrived, an intoxication with forbidden knowledge in which the natural things become unimportant. No miracle anymore to the leaves falling from the autumn trees, the sun in the orchard.

No.

The scent was rising from him like incense, like the heat and the smoke of church candles rising. Heart thumping under the skin of his naked chest. Tight little belly glistening with sweat, sweat staining the thick leather belt. Blood full of salt. I could scarce breathe.

And we do breathe. We breathe and we taste and we smell and we feel and we thirst.

'You have misunderstood everything.' Is this Lestat speaking? It sounded like some other demon, some loathsome thing for whom the voice was the imitation of a human voice. 'You have misunderstood everything that you have seen and heard.'

'I would have shared anything I possessed with you!' Rage building again. He reached out. 'It was you who never understood,' he whispered.

'Take your life and leave with it. Run.'

'Don't you see it's the confirmation of everything? That it exists is the confirmation — pure evil, sublime evil!' Triumph in his eyes. He reached out suddenly and closed his hand on my face.

'Don't taunt me!' I said. I struck him so hard he fell backwards, chastened, silent. 'When it was offered me I said no. I tell you I said no. With my last breath, I said no.'

'You were always the fool,' he said. 'I told you that.' But he was breaking down. He was shuddering and the rage was alchemizing into desperation. He lifted his arms again and then stopped. 'You believed things that didn't matter,' he said almost gently. 'There was something you failed to see. Is it possible you don't know yourself what you possess now?' The glaze over his eyes broke instantly into tears.

His face knotted. Unspoken words coming from him of love.

And an awful self-consciousness came over me. Silent and lethal, I felt myself flooded with the power I had over him and his knowledge of it, and my love for him heated the sense of power, driving it towards a scorching embarrassment which suddenly changed into something else.

We were in the wings of the theatre again; we were in the village in Auvergne in that little inn. I smelled not merely the blood in him, but the sudden terror. He had taken a step back. And the very movement stoked the blaze in me, as much as the vision of his stricken face.

He grew smaller, more fragile. Yet he'd never seemed stronger, more alluring than he was now.

All the expression drained from his face as I drew nearer. His eyes were wondrously clear. And his mind was opening as Gabrielle's mind had opened, and for one tiny second there flared a moment of us together in the garret, talking and talking as the moon glared on the snow-covered roofs, or walking through the Paris streets, passing the wine back and forth, heads bowed against the first gust of winter rain, and there had been the eternity of growing up and growing old before us, and so much joy even in misery, even in the misery — the real eternity, the real forever — the mortal mystery of that. But the moment faded in the shimmering expression of his face.

'Come to me, Nicki,' I whispered. I lifted both hands to beckon. 'If you want it, you must come ...'

I SAW a bird soaring out of a cave above the open sea. And there was something terrifying about the bird and the endless waves over which it flew. Higher and higher it went and the sky turned to silver and then gradually the silver faded and the sky went dark. The darkness of evening, nothing to fear, really, nothing. Blessed darkness. But it was falling gradually and inexorably over nothing save this one tiny creature cawing in the wind above a great wasteland that was the world. Empty caves, empty sands, empty sea.

All I had ever loved to look upon, or listen to, or felt with my hands was gone, or never existed, and the bird circling and gliding, flew on and on, upwards past me, or more truly past no one, holding the entire landscape, without history or meaning in the flat blackness of one tiny eye.

I screamed but without a sound. I felt my mouth full of blood and each swallow passing down my throat and into fathomless thirst. And I wanted to say, yes, I understand now, I understand how terrible, how unbearable, this darkness. I didn't know. Couldn't know. The bird sailing on through the darkness over the barren shore, the seamless sea. Dear God, stop it. Worse than the horror in the inn. Worse than the helpless trumpeting of the fallen horse in the snow. But the blood was the blood after all, and the heart — the luscious heart that was all heart — was right there, on tiptoe against my lips.

Now, my love, now's the moment. I can swallow the life that beats from your heart and send you into the oblivion in which nothing may ever be understood or forgiven, or I can bring you to me.

I pushed him backwards. I held him to me like a crushed thing. But the vision wouldn't stop.

His arms slipped around my neck, his face wet, eyes rolling up into his head. Then his tongue shot out. It licked hard at the gash I had made for him in my own throat. Yes, eager.

But please stop this vision. Stop the upward flight and the great slant of the colourless landscape, the cawing that meant nothing over the howl of the wind. The pain is nothing compared to this darkness. I don't want to … I don't want to …

But it was dissolving. Slowly dissolving.

And finally it was finished. The veil of silence had come down, as it had with her. Silence. He was separate. And I was holding him away from me, and he was almost falling, his hands to his mouth, the blood running down his chin in rivulets. His mouth was open and a dry sound came out of it, in spite of the blood, a dry scream.

And beyond him, and beyond the remembered vision of the metallic sea and the lone bird who was its only witness — I saw her in the doorway and her hair was a Virgin Mary veil of gold around her shoulders, and she said with the saddest expression on her face.

'Disaster, my son.'

BY MIDNIGHT it was clear that he would not speak or answer to any voice, or move of his own volition. He remained still and expressionless in the places to which he was taken. If the death pained him he gave no sign. If the new vision delighted him, he kept it to himself. Not even the thirst moved him.

And it was Gabrielle who, after studying him quietly for hours, took him in hand, cleaning him and putting new clothes on him. Black wool she chose, one of the few sombre coats I owned. And modest linen that made him look oddly like a young cleric, a little too serious, a little naive.

And in the silence of the crypt as I watched them, I knew without doubt that they could hear each other's thoughts. Without a word she guided him through the grooming. Without a word she sent him back to the bench by the fire.

Finally, she said, 'He should hunt now,' and when she glanced at him, he rose without looking at her as if pulled by a string.

Numbly I watched them going. Heard their feet on the stairs. And then I crept up after them, stealthily, and holding to the bars of the gate I watched them move, two feline spirits, across the field.

The emptiness of the night was an indissoluble cold settling over me, closing me in. Not even the fire on the hearth warmed me when I returned to it.

Emptiness here. And the quiet I had told myself that I wanted — just to be alone after the grisly struggle in Paris. Quiet, and the realization, which I could not bring myself to confess to her, the realization gnawing at my insides like a starved animal — *that I couldn't stand the sight of him now.*

5

WHEN I opened my eyes the next night, I knew what I meant to do. Whether or not I could stand to look at him wasn't important. I had made him this, and I had to rouse him from his stupor somehow.

The hunt hadn't changed him, though apparently he'd drunk and killed well enough. And now it was up to me to protect him from the revulsion I felt, and to go into Paris and get the one thing that might bring him around.

The violin was all he'd ever loved when he was alive. Maybe now it would awaken him. I'd put it in his hands, and he'd want to play it again, he'd want to play it with his new skill, and everything would change and the chill in my heart would somehow melt.

AS SOON as Gabrielle rose I told her what I meant to do.

'But what about the others?' she said. 'You can't go riding into Paris alone.'

'Yes, I can,' I said. 'You're needed here with him. If the little pests should come round, they could lure him into the open, the way he is now. And besides, I want to know what's happening under les Innocents. If we have a real truce, I want to know.'

'I don't like your going,' she said, shaking her head. 'I tell you, if I didn't believe we should speak to the leader again, that we had things to learn from him and the old woman, I'd be for leaving Paris tonight.'

'And what could they possibly teach us?' I said coldly. 'That the sun really revolves around the earth? That the earth is flat?' But the bitterness of my words made me feel ashamed.

One thing they could tell me was why the vampires I'd made could hear each other's thoughts when I could not. But I was too crestfallen over my loathing of Nicki to think of all these things.

I only looked at her and thought how glorious it had been to see the Dark Trick work its magic in her, to see it restore her youthful beauty, render her again the goddess she'd been to me when I was a little child. To see Nicki change had been to see him die.

Maybe without reading the words in my soul she understood it only too well.

We embraced slowly. 'Be careful,' she said.

I SHOULD have gone to the flat right away to look for his violin. And there was still my poor Roget to deal with. Lies to tell. And this matter of getting out of Paris — it seemed more and more the thing for us to do.

But for hours I did just what I wanted. I hunted the Tuileries and the boulevards, pretending there was no coven under les Innocents, that Nicki was alive still and safe somewhere, that Paris was all mine again.

But I was listening for them every moment. I was thinking about the old queen. And I heard them when I least expected it, on the boulevard du Temple, as I drew near to Renaud's.

Strange that they'd be in the places of light, as they called them. But within seconds, I knew that several of them were hiding behind the theatre. And there was no malice this time, only a desperate excitement when they sensed that I was near.

Then I saw the white face of the woman vampire, the dark-eyed pretty one with the witch's hair. She was in the alleyway beside the stage door, and she darted forward to beckon to me.

I rode back and forth for a few moments. The boulevard was the usual spring evening panorama: hundreds of strollers amid the stream of carriage traffic, lots of street musicians, jugglers and tumblers, the lighted theatres with their doors open to invite the crowd. Why should I leave it to talk to these creatures? I listened. There were four of them actually, and they were desperately waiting for me to come. They were in terrible fear.

All right. I turned the horse and rode into the alley and all the way to the back where they hovered together against the stone wall.

The grey-eyed boy was there, which surprised me, and he had a dazed expression on his face. A tall blond male vampire stood behind him with a handsome woman, both of them swathed in rags like lepers. It was the pretty one, the dark-eyed one who had laughed at my little jest on the stairs under les Innocents, who spoke:

'You have to help me!' she whispered.

'I do?' I tried to steady the mare. She didn't like their company. 'Why do I have to help you?' I demanded.

'He's destroying the coven,' she said.

'Destroying us ...' the boy said. But he didn't look at me. He was staring at the stones in front of him, and from his mind I caught flashes of what was happening, of the pyre lighted, of Armand forcing his followers into the fire.

I tried to get this out of my head. But the images were now coming from all of them. The dark-eyed pretty one looked directly into my eyes as she strove to sharpen the pictures — Armand swinging a great charred beam of wood as he drove the others into the blaze, then stabbing them down into the flames with the beam as they struggled to escape.

'Good Lord, there were twelve of you!' I said. 'Couldn't you fight?'

'We did and we are here,' said the woman. 'He burned six together, and the rest of us fled. In terror, we sought strange resting places for the day. We had never done this before, slept away from our sacred graves. We didn't know what would happen to us. And when we rose he was there. Another two he managed to destroy. So we are all that is left. He has even broken open the deep chambers and burned the starved ones. He has broken loose the earth to block the tunnels to our meeting place.'

The boy looked up slowly.

'You did this to us,' he whispered. 'You have brought us all down.'

The woman stepped in front of him.

'You must help us,' she said. 'Make a new coven with us. Help us to exist as you exist.' She glanced impatiently at the boy.

'But the old woman, the great one?' I asked.

'It was she who commenced it,' said the boy bitterly. 'She threw herself into the fire. She said she would go to join

266

Magnus. She was laughing. It was then that he drove the others into the flames as we fled.'

I bowed my head. So she was gone. And all she had known and witnessed had gone with her, and what had she left behind but the simple one, the vengeful one, the wicked child who believed what she had known to be false.

'You must help us,' said the dark-eyed woman. 'You see, it's his right as coven master to destroy those who are weak, those who can't survive.'

'He couldn't let the coven fall into chaos,' said the other woman vampire who stood behind the boy. 'Without the faith in the Dark Ways, the others might have blundered, alarmed the mortal populace. But if you help us to form a new coven, to perfect ourselves in new ways ...'

'We are the strongest of the coven,' said the man. 'And if we can fend him off long enough, and manage to continue without him, then in time he may leave us alone.'

'He will destroy us,' the boy muttered. 'He will never leave us alone. He will lie in wait for the moment when we separate ...'

'He isn't invincible,' said the tall male. 'And he's lost all conviction. Remember that.'

'And you have Magnus's tower, a safe place ...' said the boy despairingly as he looked up at me.

'No, that I can't share with you,' I said. 'You have to win this battle on your own.'

'But surely you can guide us ...' said the man.

'You don't need me,' I said. 'What have you already learned from my example? What did you learn from the things I said last night?'

'We learned more from what you said to him afterwards,' said the dark-eyed woman. 'We heard you speak to him of a new evil, an evil for these times destined to move through the world in handsome human guise.'

'So take on the guise,' I said. 'Take the garments of your victims, and take the money from their pockets. And you can then move among mortals as I do. In time you can gain enough wealth to acquire your own little fortress, your secret

267

sanctuary. Then you will no longer be beggars or ghosts.'

I could see the desperation in their faces. Yet they listened attentively.

'But our skin, the timbre of our voices ...' said the dark-eyed woman.

'You can fool mortals. It's very easy. It just takes a little skill.'

'But how do we start?' said the boy dully, as if he were only reluctantly being brought into it. 'What sort of mortals do we pretend to be?'

'Choose for yourself!' I said. 'Look around you. Masquerade as gypsies if you will — that oughtn't to be too difficult — or better yet mummers,' I glanced towards the lights of the boulevard.

'Mummers!' said the dark-eyed woman with a little spark of excitement.

'Yes, actors. Street performers. Acrobats. Make yourselves acrobats. Surely you've seen them out there. You can cover your white faces with greasepaint, and your extravagant gestures and facial expressions won't even be noticed. You couldn't choose a more nearly perfect disguise than that. On the boulevard you'll see every manner of mortal that dwells in this city. You'll learn all you need to know.'

She laughed and glanced at the others. The man was deep in thought, the other woman musing, the boy unsure.

'With your powers, you can become jugglers and tumblers easily,' I said. 'It would be nothing for you. You could be seen by thousands who'd never guess what you are.'

'That isn't what happened with you on the stage of this little theatre,' said the boy coldly. 'You put terror into their hearts.'

'Because I chose to do it,' I said. Tremor of pain. 'That's my tragedy. But I can fool anyone when I want to and so can you.'

I reached into my pockets and drew out a handful of gold crowns. I gave them to the dark-eyed woman. She took them in both hands and stared at them as if they were burning her. She looked up and in her eyes I saw the image of myself on Renaud's stage performing those ghastly feats that had driven the crowd into the streets.

But she had another thought in her mind. She knew the theatre was abandoned, that I'd sent the troupe off.

And for one second, I considered it, letting the pain double itself and pass through me, wondering if the others could feel it. What did it really matter, after all?

'Yes, please,' said the pretty one. She reached up and touched my hand with her cool white fingers. 'Let us inside the theatre! Please.' She turned and looked at the back doors of Renaud's.

Let them inside. Let them dance on my grave.

But there might be old costumes there still, the discarded trappings of a troupe that had had all the money in the world to buy itself new finery. Old pots of white paint. Water still in the barrels. A thousand treasures left behind in the haste of departure.

I was numb, unable to consider all of it, unwilling to reach back to embrace all that had happened there.

'Very well,' I said, looking away as if some little thing had distracted me. 'You can go into the theatre if you wish. You can use whatever is there.'

She drew closer and pressed her lips suddenly to the back of my hand.

'We won't forget this,' she said. 'My name is Eleni, this boy is Laurent, the man here is Félix, and the woman with him, Eugénie. If Armand moves against you, he moves against us.'

'I hope you prosper,' I said, and strangely enough, I meant it. I wondered if any of them, with all their Dark Ways and Dark Rituals, had every really wanted this nightmare that we all shared. They'd been drawn into it as I had, really. And we were all Children of Darkness now, for better or worse.

'But be wise in what you do here,' I warned. 'Never bring victims here or kill near here. Be clever and keep your hiding place safe.'

IT WAS three o'clock before I rode over the bridge on to the Ile

St.-Louis. I had wasted enough time. And now I had to find the violin.

But as soon as I approached Nicki's house on the quai I saw that something was wrong. The windows were empty. All the drapery had been pulled down and yet the place was full of light, as if candles were burning inside by the hundreds. Most strange. Roget couldn't have taken possession of the flat yet. Not enough time had passed to assume that Nicki had met with foul play.

Quickly, I went up over the roof and down the wall to the courtyard window, and saw that the drapery had been stripped away there too.

And candles were burning in all the candelabra and in the wall sconces. And some were even stuck in their own wax on the pianoforte and the desk. The room was in total disarray.

Every book had been pulled off the shelf. And some of the books were in fragments, pages broken out. Even the music had been emptied sheet by sheet onto the carpet, and all the pictures were lying about on the tables with other small possessions — coins, money, keys.

Perhaps the demons had wrecked the place where they took Nicki. But who had lighted all these candles? It didn't make sense.

I listened. No one in the flat. Or so it seemed. But then I heard not thoughts, but tiny sounds. I narrowed my eyes for a moment, just concentrating, and it came to me that I was hearing pages turn, and then something being dropped. More pages turning, stiff, old parchment pages. Then again the book dropped.

I raised the window as quietly as I could. The little sounds continued, but no scent of human, no pulse of thought.

Yet there was a smell here. Something stronger than the stale tobacco and the candle wax. The smell the vampires carried with them from the cemetery soil.

More candles in the hallway. Candles in the bedroom and the same disarray, books open as they lay in careless piles, the bedclothes snarled, the pictures in a heap. Cabinets emptied, drawers pulled out.

And no violin anywhere, I managed to note that.

And those little sounds coming from another room, pages being turned very fast.

Whoever he was — and of course I knew who he had to be — he did not give a damn that I was there! He had not even stopped to take a breath.

I went farther down the hall and stood in the door of the library and found myself staring right at him as he continued with his task.

It was Armand, of course. Yet I was hardly prepared for the sight he presented here.

Candle wax dripped down the marble bust of Caesar, flowed over the brightly painted countries of the world globe. And the books, they lay in mountains on the carpet, save for those of the very last shelf in the corner where he stood, in his old rags still, hair full of dust, ignoring me as he ran his hands over page after page, his eyes intent on the words before him, his lips half open, his expression like that of an insect in its concentration as it chews through a leaf.

Perfectly horrible he looked, actually. He was sucking everything out of the books!

Finally he let this one drop and took down another, and opened it and started devouring it in the same manner, fingers moving down the sentences with preternatural speed.

And I realized that he had been examining everything in the flat in this fashion, even the bed sheets and curtains, the pictures that had been taken off their hooks, the contents of cupboards and drawers. But from the books, he was taking concentrated knowledge. Everything from Caesar's *Gallic Wars* to modern English novels lay on the floor.

But his manner wasn't the entire horror. It was the havoc he was leaving behind him, the utter disregard of everything he used.

And his utter disregard of me.

He finished his latest book, or broke off from it, and went to the old newspapers stacked on a lower shelf.

I found myself backing out of the room and away from him, staring numbly at his small dirty figure. His auburn hair shimmered despite the dirt in it; his eyes burned like two lights.

Grotesque he seemed, among all the candles and the swimming colours of the flat, this filthy waif of the netherworld, and yet his beauty held sway. He hadn't needed the shadows of Notre Dame or the torchlight of the crypt to flatter him. And there was a fierceness in him in this bright light that I hadn't seen before.

I felt an overwhelming confusion. He was both dangerous and compelling. I could have looked on him forever, but an overpowering instinct said: Get away. Leave the place to him if he wants it. What does it matter now?

The violin. I tried desperately to think about the violin. To stop watching the movement of his hands over the words in front of him, the relentless force of his eyes.

But these things were putting me in a trance.

I turned my back on him and went into the parlour. My hands were trembling. I could hardly endure knowing he was there. I searched everwhere and didn't find the damned violin. What could Nicki have done with it? I couldn't think.

Pages turning, paper crinkling. Soft sound of the newspaper dropping to the floor.

Go back to the tower at once.

I went to pass the library quickly, when without warning his soundless voice shot out and stopped me. It was like a hand touching my throat. I turned and saw him staring at me.

Do you love them, your silent children? Do they love you? That was what he asked, the sense disentangling itself from the endless echo.

I felt the blood rise to my face. The heat spread out over me like a mask as I looked at him.

All the books in the room were now on the floor. He was a haunt standing in the ruins, a visitant from the devil he believed in. Yet his face was so tender, so young.

The Dark Trick never brings love, you see, it brings only the silence. His voice seemed softer in its soundlessness, clearer, the echo dissipated. *We used to say it was Satan's will, that the master and the fledgling not seek comfort in each other. It was Satan who had to be served, after all.*

Every word penetrated me. Every word was received by a secret, humiliating curiosity and vulnerability. But I refused to let him see this. Angrily I said:

'What do you want of me?'

It was shattering something to speak. I was feeling more fear of him at this moment than ever during the earlier battles and arguments, and I hate those who make me feel fear, those who know things that I need to know, who have that power over me.

'It is like not knowing how to read, isn't it?' he said aloud. 'And your maker, the outcast Magnus, what did he care for your ignorance? He did not tell you the simplest things, did he?'

Nothing in his expression moved as he spoke.

'Hasn't it always been this way? Has anyone ever cared to teach you anything?'

'You're taking these things from my mind ...' I said. I was appalled. I saw the monastery where I'd been as a boy, the rows and rows of books that I could not read. Gabrielle bent over her books, her back to all of us. 'Stop this!' I whispered.

It seemed the longest time had passed. I was becoming disoriented. He was speaking again, but in silence.

They never satisfy you, the ones you make. In silence the estrangement and the resentment only grow.

I willed myself to move but I wasn't moving. I was merely looking at him as he went on.

You long for me and I for you, and we alone in all this realm are worthy of each other. Don't you know this?

The toneless words seemed to be stretched, amplified, like a note on the violin drawn out forever, and ever.

'This is madness,' I whispered. I thought of all the things he had said to me, what he had blamed me for, the horrors the others had described — that he had thrown his followers into the fire.

'Is it madness?' he asked. 'Go then to your silent ones. Even now they say to each other what they cannot say to you.'

'You're lying ...' I said.

'And time will only strengthen their independence. But

learn for yourself. You will find me easily enough when you want to come to me. After all, where can I go? What can I do? You have made me an orphan again.'

'I didn't —' I said.

'Yes, you did,' he said. 'You did it. You brought it down.' Still there was no anger. 'But I can wait for you to come, wait for you to ask the questions that only I can answer.'

I stared at him for a long moment. I don't know how long. It was as if I couldn't move, and I couldn't see anything else but him, and the great sense of peace I'd known in Notre Dame, the spell he cast, was again working. The lights of the room were too bright. There was nothing else but light surrounding him, and it was as if he were coming closer to me and I to him, yet neither of us was moving. He was draining me, drawing me towards him.

I turned away, stumbling, losing my balance. But I was out of the room. I was running down the hallway, and then I was climbing out of the back window and up to the roof.

I rode into the Ile de la Cité as if he were chasing me. And my heart didn't stop its frantic pace until I had left the city behind.

HELL'S Bells ringing.

The tower was in darkness against the first glimmer of the morning light. My little coven had already gone to rest in their dungeon crypt.

I didn't open the tombs to look at them, though I wanted desperately to do it, just to see Gabrielle and touch her hand.

I climbed alone towards the battlements to look out at the burning miracle of the approaching morning, the thing I should never see to its finish again. Hell's Bells ringing, my secret music ...

But another sound was coming to me. I knew it as I went up the stairs. And I marvelled at its power to reach me. It was like a song arching over an immense distance, low and sweet.

Once years ago, I had heard a young farm boy singing as he walked along the high road out of the village to the north. He hadn't known anyone was listening. He had thought himself alone in the open country, and his voice had a private power and purity that gave it unearthly beauty. Never mind the words of his old song.

This was the voice that was calling to me now. The lone voice, rising over the miles that separated us to gather all sounds into itself.

I was frightened again. Yet I opened the door at the top of the staircase and went out onto the stone roof. Silken the morning breeze, dreamlike the twinkling of the last stars. The sky was not so much a canopy as it was a mist rising endlessly above me, and the stars drifted upwards, growing ever smaller, in the mist.

The faraway voice sharpened, like a note sung in the high mountains, touching my chest where I had laid my hand.

It pierced me as a beam pierces darkness, singing *Come to me; all things will be forgiven if only you come to me. I am more alone than I have ever been.*

And there came in time with the voice a sense of limitless possibility, of wonder and expectation that brought with it the vision of Armand standing alone in the open doors of Notre Dame. Time and space were illusions. He was in a pale wash of light before the main altar, a lissome shape in regal tatters, shimmering as he vanished, and nothing but patience in his eyes. There was no crypt under les Innocents now. There was no grotesquery of the ragged ghost in the glare of Nicki's library, throwing down the books when he had finished with them as if they were empty shells.

I think I knelt down and rested my head against the jagged stones. I saw the moon like a phantom dissolving and the sun must have touched her because she hurt me and I had to close my eyes.

But I felt an elation, an ecstasy. It was as if my spirit could know the glory of the Dark Trick without the blood flowing, in the intimacy of the voice dividing me and seeking the tenderest, most secret part of my soul.

What do you want of me, I wanted to say again. How can there be this forgiveness when there was such rancour only a short while ago? Your coven destroyed. Horrors. I don't want to imagine ... I wanted to say it all again.

But I couldn't shape the words now any more than I could before. And this time, I knew that if I dared to try, the bliss would melt and leave me and the anguish would be worse than the thirst for blood.

Yet even as I remained still, in the mystery of this feeling, I knew strange images and thoughts that weren't my own.

I saw myself retreat again to the dungeon and lift up the inanimate bodies of those kindred monsters I loved. I saw myself carrying them up to the roof of the tower and leaving them there in their helplessness at the mercy of the rising sun. Hell's Bells rang the alarm in vain for them. And the sun took them up and made them cinders with human hair.

My mind recoiled from this; it recoiled in the most heart-breaking disappointment.

'Child, still,' I whispered. Ah, the pain of this disappointment, the possibility diminishing ... 'How foolish you are to think that such things could be done by me.'

The voice faded; it withdrew itself from me. And I felt my aloneness in every pore of my skin. It was as if all covering had been taken from me forever and I would always be as naked and miserable as I was now.

And I felt far off a convulsion of power as if the spirit that had made the voice was curling upon itself like a great tongue.

'Treachery!' I said louder. 'But oh, the sadness of it, the miscalculation. How can you say that you desire *me*!'

Gone it was. Absolutely gone. And desperately, I wanted it back even if it was to fight with me. I wanted that sense of possibility, that lovely flare again.

And I saw his face in Notre Dame, boyish and almost sweet, like the face of an old da Vinci saint. A horrid sense of fatality passed over me.

6

s SOON as Gabrielle rose, I drew her away from Nicki, out into the quiet of the forest, and I told her all that had taken place the preceding night. I told her all that Armand had suggested and said. In an embarrassed way, I spoke of the silence that existed between her and me, and of how I knew now that it wasn't to change.

'We should leave Paris as soon as possible,' I said finally. 'This creature is too dangerous. And the ones to whom I gave the theatre — they don't know anything other than what they've been taught by him. I say let them have Paris. And let's take the Devil's Road, to use the old queen's words.'

I had expected anger from her, and malice towards Armand. But through the whole story she remained calm.

'Lestat, there are too many unanswered questions,' she said. 'I want to know how this old coven started, I want to know all that Armand knows about *us*.'

'Mother, I'm tempted to turn my back on it. I don't care how it started. I wonder if he himself even knows.'

'I understand, Lestat,' she said quietly. 'Believe me, I do. When all is said and done, I care less about these creatures than I do about the trees in this forest or the stars overhead. I'd rather study the currents of wind or the patterns in the falling leaves . . .'

'Exactly.'

'But we mustn't be hasty. The important thing now is for the three of us to remain together. We should go into the city together and prepare slowly for our departure together. And together, we must try your plan to rouse Nicolas with the violin.'

I wanted to talk about Nicki. I wanted to ask her what lay behind his silence, what could she divine? But the words dried up in my throat. I thought as I had all along of her judgment in those first moments: 'Disaster, my son.'

She put her arm round me and led me back towards the tower.

'I don't have to read your mind,' she said, 'to know what's in your heart. Let's take him into Paris. Let's try to find the Stradivarius.' She stood on tiptoe to kiss me. 'We were on the Devil's Road together before all this happened,' she said. 'We'll be on it soon again.'

* * *

IT WAS as easy to take Nicolas into Paris as to lead him in everything else. Like a ghost he mounted his horse and rode alongside of us, only his dark hair and cape seemingly animate, whipped about as they were by the wind.

When we fed in the Ile de la Cité, I found I could not watch him hunt or kill.

It gave me no hope to see him doing these simple things with the sluggishness of a somnambulist. It proved nothing more than that he could go like this forever, our silent accomplice, little more than a resuscitated corpse.

Yet an unexpected feeling came over me as we moved through the alleyways together. We were not two, but three, now. A coven. And if only I could bring him around —

But the visit to Roget had to come first. I alone had to confront the lawyer. So I left them to wait only a few doors from his house, and as I pounded the knocker, I braced myself for the most gruelling performance yet of my theatrical career.

Well, I was very quickly to learn an important lesson about mortals and their willingness to be convinced that the world is a safe place. Roget was overjoyed to see me. He was so relieved that I was 'alive and in good health' and still wanted his services, that he was nodding his acceptance before my preposterous explanations had even begun.

(And this lesson about mortal peace of mind I never forgot. Even if a ghost is ripping a house to pieces, throwing tin pans all over, pouring water on pillows, making clocks chime at all hours, mortals will accept almost any 'natural explanation' offered, no matter how absurd, rather than the obvious super-natural one, for what is going on.)

Also it became clear almost at once that he believed Gabrielle and I had slipped out of the flat by the servants' door to the bedroom, a nice possibility I hadn't considered before. So all I did about the twisted-up candelabra was mumble something about having been mad with grief when I saw my mother, which he understood right off.

As for the reason for our leaving, well, Gabrielle insisted upon being removed from everyone and taken to a convent, and there she was right now.

'Ah, Monsieur, it's a miracle, her improvement,' I said. 'If you could only see her — but never mind. We're going on to Italy immediately with Nicolas de Lenfent, and we need currency, letters of credit, whatever, and a travelling coach, a huge travelling coach, and a good team of six. You take care of it. Have it all ready by Friday evening early. And write to my father and tell him we're taking my mother to Italy. My father is all right, I presume?'

'Yes, yes, of course, I didn't tell him anything but the most reassuring —'

'How clever of you. I knew I could trust you. What would I do without you? And what about these rubies, can you turn them into money for me immediately? And I have here some Spanish coins to sell, quite old, I think.'

He scribbled like a madman, his doubts and suspicions fading in the heat of my smiles. He was so glad to have something to do!

'Hold my property in the boulevard du Temple vacant,' I said. 'And of course, you'll manage everything for me.' And so forth and so on.

My property in the boulevard du Temple, the hiding place of a ragged and desperate band of vampires unless Armand had already found them and burnt them up like old costumes. I should find the answer to that question soon enough.

I came down the steps whistling to myself in strictly human fashion, overjoyed that this odious task had been accomplished. And then I realized that Nicki and Gabrielle were nowhere in sight.

I stopped and turned around in the street.

I saw Gabrielle just at the moment I heard her voice, a young boyish figure emerging full blown from an alleyway as if she had just made herself material on the spot.

'Lestat, he's gone — vanished,' she said.

I couldn't answer her. I said something foolish, like 'What do you mean, vanished!' But my thoughts were more or less drowning out the words in my own head. If I had doubted up until this moment that I loved him, I had been lying to myself.

'I turned my back, and it was that quick, I tell you,' she said.

279

She was half aggrieved, half angry.

'Did you hear any other ...'

'No. Nothing. He was simply too quick.'

'Yes, if he moved on his own, if he wasn't taken ...'

'I would have heard his fear if Armand had taken him,' she insisted.

'But does he feel fear? Does he feel anything at all?' I was utterly terrified and utterly exasperated. He'd vanished in a darkness that spread out all around us like a giant wheel from its axis. I think I clenched my fist. I must have made some uncertain little gesture of panic.

'Listen to me,' she said. 'There are only two things that go round and round in his mind . . .'

'Tell me!'

'One is the pyre under les Innocents where he was almost burned. And the other is a small theatre — footlights, a stage.'

'Renaud's,' I said.

SHE and I were archangels together. It didn't take us a quarter of an hour to reach the noisy boulevard and to move through its raucous crowd past the neglected facade of Renaud's and back to the stage door.

The boards had all been ripped down and the locks broken. But I heard no sound of Eleni or the others as we slipped quietly into the hallway that went round the back of the stage. No one here.

Perhaps Armand had gathered his children home after all, and that was my doing because I would not take them in.

Nothing but the jungle of props, the great painted scrims of night and day and hill and dale, and the open dressing rooms, those crowded little closets where here and there a mirror glared in the light that seeped through the open door we had left behind.

Then Gabrielle's hand tightened on my sleeve. She gestured towards the wings proper. And I knew by her face that it wasn't the other ones. Nicki was there.

I went to the side of the stage. The velvet curtain was drawn back to both sides and I could see his dark figure plainly in the orchestra pit. He was sitting in his old place, his hands folded in his lap. He was facing me but he didn't notice me. He was staring off as he had done all along.

And the memory came back to me of Gabrielle's strange words the night after I had made her, that she could not get over the sensation that she had died and could affect nothing in the mortal world.

He appeared that lifeless and that translucent. He was the still, expressionless spectre one almost stumbles over in the shadows of the haunted house, all but melded with the dusty furnishings — the fright that is worse perhaps than any other kind.

I looked to see if the violin was there — on the floor, or against his chair — and when I saw that it wasn't, I thought, Well, there is still a chance.

'Stay here and watch,' I said to Gabrielle. But my heart was knocking in my throat when I looked up at the darkened theatre, when I let myself breathe in the old scents. Why did you have to bring us here, Nicki? To this haunted place? But then, who am I to ask that? I had come back, had I not?

I lighted the first candle I found in the old prima donna's dressing room. Open pots of paint were scattered everywhere, and there were many discarded costumes on the hooks. All the rooms I passed were full of cast-off clothing, forgotten combs and brushes, withered flowers still in the vases, powder spilled on the floor.

I thought of Eleni and the others again, and I realized that the faintest smell of les Innocents lingered here. And I saw very distinct naked footprints in the spilled powder. Yes, they'd come in. And they had lighted candles, too, hadn't they? Because the smell of the wax was too fresh.

Whatever the case, they hadn't entered my old dressing room, the room that Nicki and I had shared before every performance. It was locked still. And when I broke open the door, I got an ugly shock. The room was exactly the way I'd left it.

It was clean and orderly, even the mirror polished, and it was filled with my belongings as it had been on the last night I had been here. There was my old coat on the hook, the cast-off I'd worn from the country, and a pair of wrinkled boots, and my pots of paint in perfect order, and my wig, which I had worn only at the theatre, on its wooden head. Letters from Gabrielle in a little stack, the old copies of English and French newspapers in which the play had been mentioned, and a bottle of wine still half full with a dried cork.

And there in the darkness beneath the marble dressing table, partly covered by a bundled black coat, lay a shiny violin case. It was not the one we'd carried all the way from home with us. No. It must hold the precious gift I'd bought for him with the 'coin of the realm' after, the Stradivarius violin.

I bent down and opened the lid. It was the most beautiful instrument all right, delicate and darkly lustrous, and lying here among all these unimportant things.

I wondered whether Eleni and the others would have taken it had they come into this room. Would they have known what it could do?

I set down the candle for a moment and took it out carefully, and I tightened the horsehair of the bow as I'd seen Nicki do a thousand times. And then I brought the instrument and the candle back to the stage again, and I bent down and commenced to light the long string of candle footlights.

Gabrielle watched me impassively. Then she came to help me. She lit one candle after another, and then lighted the sconce in the wings.

It seemed Nicki stirred. But maybe it was only the growing illumination on his profile, the soft light that emanated out from the stage into the darkened hall. The deep folds of velvet came alive everywhere; the ornate little mirrors affixed to the front of the gallery and the loges became lights themselves.

Beautiful this little place, our place. The portal to the world for us as mortal beings. And the portal finally to hell.

When I was finished, I stood on the boards looking at the gilded railings, the new chandelier that hung from the ceiling, and up at the arch overhead with its masks of comedy and tragedy like two faces stemming from the same neck.

It seemed so much smaller when it was empty, this house. No theatre in Paris seemed larger when it was full.

Outside was the low thunder of the boulevard traffic, tiny human voices rising now and then like sparks over the general hum. A heavy carriage must have passed then because everything within the theatre shivered slightly: the candle flames against their reflectors, the giant stage curtain gathered to right and left, the scrim behind of a finely painted garden with clouds overhead.

I went past Nicki, who never once looked up at me, and down the little stairs behind him, and came towards him with the violin.

Gabrielle stood back in the wings again, her small face cold but patient. She rested against the beam beside her in the easy manner of a strange long-haired man.

I lowered the violin over Nicki's shoulder and held it in his lap. I felt him move, as if he had taken a great breath. The back of his head pressed against me. And slowly he lifted his left hand to take the neck of the violin and he took the bow with his right.

I knelt and put my hands on his shoulders. I kissed his cheek. No human scene. No human warmth. Sculpture of my Nicolas.

'Play it,' I whispered. 'Play it here just for us.'

Slowly he turned to face me, and for the first time since the moment of the Dark Trick, he looked into my eyes. He made some tiny sound. It was so strained it was as if he couldn't speak anymore. The organs of speech had closed up. But then he ran his tongue along his lip, and so low I scarcely heard him, he said:

'The devil's instrument.'

'Yes,' I said. 'If you must believe that, then believe it. But play.'

His fingers hovered above the strings. He tapped the hollow wood with his fingertip. And now, trembling, he plucked at the strings to tune them and wound the pegs very slowly as if he were discovering the process with perfect concentration for the first time.

Somewhere out on the boulevard children laughed. Wooden wheels made their thick clatter over the cobble-

283

stones. The staccato notes were sour, dissonant, and they sharpened the tension.

He pressed the instrument to his ear for a moment. And it seemed to me he didn't move again for an eternity, and then he slowly rose to his feet. I went back out of the pit and into the benches, and I stood staring at his black silhouette against the glow of the lighted stage.

He turned to face the empty theatre as he had done so many times at the moment of the intermezzo, and he lifted the violin to his chin. And in a movement so swift it was like a flash of light in my eye, he brought the bow down across the strings.

The first full-throated chords throbbed in the silence and were stretched as they deepened, scraping the bottom of sound itself. Then the notes rose, rich and dark and shrill, as if pumped out of the fragile violin by alchemy, until a raging torrent of melody suddenly flooded the hall.

It seemed to roll through my body, to pass through my very bones.

I couldn't see the movement of his fingers, the whipping of the bow; all I could see was the swaying of his body, his tortured posture as he let the music twist him, bend him forward, throw him back.

It became higher, shriller, faster, yet the tone of each note was perfection. It was execution without effort, virtuosity beyond mortal dreams. And the violin was talking, not merely singing, the violin was insisting. The violin was telling a tale.

The music was a lamentation, a fugue or terror looping itself into hypnotic dance rhythms, jerking Nicki even more wildly from side to side. His hair was a glistening mop against the footlights. The blood sweat had broken out on him. I could smell the blood.

But I too was doubling over; I was backing away from him, slumping down on the bench as if to cower from it, as once before in this house terrified mortals had cowered before me.

And I knew, knew in some full and simultaneous fashion, that the violin was telling everything that had happened to Nicki. It was the darkness exploded, the darkness molten, and

284

the beauty of it was like the glow of smouldering coals; just enough illumination to show how much darkness there really was.

Gabrielle too was straining to keep her body still under the onslaught, her face constricted, her hands to her head. Her lion's mane of hair had shaken loose around her, her eyes were closed.

But another sound was coming through the pure inundation of song. *They* were here. They had come into the theatre and were moving towards us through the wings.

The music reached impossible peaks, the sound throttled for an instant and then released again. The mixture of feeling and pure logic drove it past the limits of the bearable. And yet it went on and on.

And the others appeared slowly from behind the stage curtain — first the stately figure of Eleni, then the boy Laurent, and finally Félix and Eugénie. Acrobats, street players, they had become, and they wore the clothes of such players, the men in white tights beneath dagged harlequin jerkins, the women in full bloomers and ruffled dresses and with dancing slippers on their feet. Rouge gleamed on their immaculate white faces; kohl outlined their dazzling vampire eyes.

They glided towards Nicki as if drawn by a magnet, their beauty flowering ever more fully as they came into the glare of the stage candles, their hair shimmering, their movements agile and feline, their expressions rapt.

Nicki turned slowly to face them as he writhed, and the song went into frenzied supplication, lurching and climbing and roaring along its melodic path.

Eleni stared wide-eyed at him as if horrified or enchanted. Then her arms rose straight up above her head in a slow dramatic gesture, her body tensing, her neck becoming ever more graceful and long. The other woman had made a pivot and lifted her knee, toe pointed down, in the first step of a dance. But it was the tall man who suddenly caught the pace of Nicki's music as he jerked his head to the side and moved his legs and arms as if he were a great marionette controlled from the rafters above by four strings.

The others saw it. They had seen the marionettes of the boulevard. And suddenly they all went into the mechanical attitude, their sudden movements like spasms, their faces like wooden faces, utterly blank.

A great cool rush of delight passed through me, as if I could breathe suddenly in the blasted heat of the music, and I moaned with pleasure watching them flip and flop and throw up their legs, toes to the ceiling, and twirl on their invisible strings.

They had found the grotesque heart of the music, the very balance between its hideous pleading and its insistent singing, and it was Nicki who commanded their strings.

But it was changing. He was playing to them now even as they danced to him.

He took a stride towards the stage, and leapt up over the smoky trough of the footlights, and landed in their midst. The light slithered off the instrument, off his glistering face.

A new element of mockery infected the never ending melody, a syncopation that staggered the song and made it all the more bitter and all the more sweet at the same time.

The jerking stiff-jointed puppets circled him, shuffling and bobbing alongside the floorboards. Fingers splayed, heads rocking from side to side, they jigged and twisted until all of them broke their rigid form as Nicki's melody melted into harrowing sadness, the dance becoming immediately liquid and heartbroken and slow.

It was as if one mind controlled them, as if they danced to Nicki's thoughts as well as his music, and he began to dance with them as he played, the beat coming faster, as he became the country fiddler at the Lenten bonfire, and they leapt in pairs like country lovers, the skirts of the women flaring, the men bowing their legs as they lifted the women, all creating postures of tenderest love.

Frozen, I stared at the image: the preternatural dancers, the monster violinist, limbs moving with inhuman slowness, tantalizing grace. The music was like a fire consuming us all.

Now it screamed of pain, of horror, of the pure rebellion of the soul against all things. And they again carried it into the visual, faces twisted in torment, like the masks of tragedy graven on the arch above them, and I knew that if I didn't turn my back on this I would cry.

I didn't want to hear any more or see any more. Nicki was swinging to and fro as if the violin were a beast he could no longer control. And he was stabbing at the strings with short rough strokes of the bow.

The dancers passed in front of him, in back of him, embraced him, and caught him suddenly as he threw up his hands, the violin high over his head.

A loud piercing laughter erupted from him. His chest shivered with it, his arms and legs quaking with it. And then he lowered his head and he fixed his eyes on me. And at the top of his voice he screamed:

'I GIVE YOU THE THEATRE OF THE VAMPIRES! THE THEATRE OF THE VAMPIRES! THE GREATEST SPECTACLE OF THE BOULEVARD!'

Astonished, the others stared at him. But again, all of one mind, they clapped their hands and roared. They leapt into the air, giving out shrieks of joy. They threw their arms about his neck and kissed him. And dancing around him in a circle, they turned him with their arms. The laughter rose, bubbling out of all of them, as he brought them close in his arms and answered their kisses, and with their long pink tongues they licked the blood sweat off his face.

'The Theatre of the Vampires!' They broke from him and bawled it to the nonexistent audience, to the world. They bowed to the footlights, and frolicking and screaming they leapt up to the rafters and then let themselves drop down with a storm of reverberation on the boards.

The last shimmer of the music was gone, replaced by this cacophony of shrieking and stomping and laughter, like the clang of bells.

I do not remember turning my back on them. I don't remember walking up the steps to the stage and going past them. But I must have.

Because I was suddenly sitting on the long narrow table of my little dressing room, my back against the corner, my knee crooked, my head against the cold glass of the mirror, and

287

Gabrielle was there.

I was breathing hoarsely and the sound of it bothered me. I saw things — the wig I'd worn on the stage, the pasteboard shield — and these evoked thundering emotions. But I was suffocating. I could not think.

Then Nicki appeared in the door, and he moved Gabrielle to the side with a strength that astonished her and astonished me, and he pointed his finger at me.

'Well, don't you like it, my lord patron?' he asked, advancing, his words flowing in an unbroken stream so that they sounded like one great word. 'Don't you admire its splendour, its perfection? Won't you endow the Theatre of the Vampires with the coin of the realm which you possess in such great abundance? Won't you see your playhouse come to its final magnificent purpose? How was it now, "the new evil, the canker in the heart of the rose, death in the very midst of things" ...'

From a mute he had passed into mania, and even when he broke off talking, the low senseless frenzied sounds still issued from his lips like water from a spring. His face was drawn and hard and glistening with the blood droplets clinging to it, and staining the white linen at his neck.

And behind him there came an almost innocent laughter from the others, except for Eleni, who watched over his shoulder, trying very hard to comprehend what was really happening between us.

He drew closer, half laughing, grinning, stabbing at my chest with his finger:

'Well, speak. Don't you see the splendid mockery, the genius?' He struck his own chest with his fist. 'They'll come to our performances, fill our coffers with gold, and never guess what they harbour, what flourishes right in the corner of the Parisian eye. In the back alleys we feed on them and they clap for us before the lighted stage ...'

Laughter from the boy behind him. The tink of a tambourine, the thin sound of the other woman singing. A long streak of the man's laughter — like a ribbon unfurling, charting his movement as he rushed around in a circle through the rattling scrims.

Nicki drew in so that the light behind him vanished. I couldn't see Eleni.

'Magnificent evil!' he said. He was full of menace and his white hands looked like the claws of a sea creature that could at any given moment move to tear me to bits. 'To serve the god of the dark wood as he has not been served ever and here in the very centre of civilization. And for this you saved the theatre. Out of your gallant patronage this sublime offering is born.'

'It is petty!' I said. 'It is merely beautiful and clever and nothing more.'

My voice had not been very loud but it brought him to silence, and it brought the others to silence. And the shock in me melted slowly into another emotion, no less painful, merely easier to contain.

Nothing but the sounds again from the boulevard. A glowering anger flowed out of him, his pupils dancing as he looked at me.

'You're a liar, a contemptible liar,' he said.

'There is no splendour in it,' I answered. 'There is nothing sublime. Fooling helpless mortals, mocking them, and then going out from here at night to take life in the same old petty manner, one death after another in all its inevitable cruelty and shabbiness so that we can live. Any man can kill another man! Play your violin forever. Dance as you wish. Give them their money's worth if it keeps you busy and eats up eternity! It's simply clever and beautiful. A grove in the Savage Garden. Nothing more.'

'Vile liar!' he said between his teeth. 'You are God's fool, that's what you are. You who possessed the dark secret that soared above everything, rendered everything meaningless, and what did you do with it, in those months when you ruled alone from Magnus's tower, but try to live like a good man! A good man!'

He was close enough to kiss me, the blood of his spittle hitting my face.

'Patron of the arts,' he sneered. 'Giver of gifts to your family, giver of gifts to us!' He stepped back, looking down on me contemptuously.

'Well, we will take the little theatre that you painted in gold, and hung with velvet,' he said, 'and it will serve the forces of the devil more splendidly than he was ever served by the old coven.' He turned and glanced at Eleni. He glanced back at the others. 'We will make a mockery of all things sacred. We will lead them to ever greater vulgarity and profanity. We will astonish. We will beguile. But above all, we will thrive on their gold as well as their blood and in their midst we will grow strong.'

'Yes,' said the boy behind him. 'We will become invincible.' His face had a crazed look, the look of the zealot as he gazed at Nicolas. 'We will have names and places in their very world.'

'And power over them,' said the other woman, 'and a vantage point from which to study them and know them and perfect our methods of destroying them when we choose.'

'I want the theatre,' Nicolas said to me. 'I want it from you. The deed, the money to reopen it. My assistants here are ready to listen to me.'

'You may have it, if you wish,' I answered. 'It is yours if it will take you and your malice and your fractured reason off my hands.'

I got up off the dressing table and went towards him and I think that he meant to block my path, but something unaccountable happened. When I saw he wouldn't move, my anger rose up and out of me like an invisible fist. And I saw him moved backwards as if the fist had struck him. And he hit the wall with sudden force.

I could have been free of the place in an instant. I knew Gabrielle was only waiting to follow me. But I didn't leave. I stopped and I looked back at him, and he was still against the wall as if he couldn't move. And he was watching me and the hatred was pure, as undiluted by remembered love, as it had been all along.

But I wanted to understand. I wanted really to know what had happened. And I came towards him again in silence and this time it was I who was menacing, and my hands looked like claws and I could feel his fear. They were all, except for

Eleni, full of fear.

I stopped when I was very close to him and he looked directly at me, and it was as if he knew exactly what I was asking him.

'All a misunderstanding, my love,' he said. Acid on the tongue. The blood sweat had broken out again, and his eyes glistened as if they were wet. 'It was to hurt others, don't you see, the violin playing, to anger them, to secure for me an island where they could not rule. They would watch my ruin, unable to do anything about it.'

I didn't answer. I wanted him to go on.

'And when we decided to go to Paris, I thought we would starve in Paris, that we would go down and down and down. It was what I wanted, rather than what *they* wanted, that I, the favoured son, should rise for them. I thought we would go down! We were supposed to go down.'

'Oh, Nicki ...' I whispered.

'But you didn't go down, Lestat,' he said, his eyebrows rising. 'The hunger, the cold — none of it stopped you. You were a triumph!' The rage thickened his voice again. 'You didn't drink yourself to death in the gutter. You turned everything upside down! And for every aspect of our proposed damnation you found exuberance, and there was no end to your enthusiasms and the passion coming out of you — and the light, always the light. And in exact proportion to the light coming out of you, there was the darkness in me! Every exuberance piercing me and creating its exact proportion of darkness and despair! And then, the magic, when you got the magic, irony of ironies, you protected me from it! And what did you do with it but use your Satanic powers to simulate the actions of a good man!'

I turned around. I saw them scattered in the shadows and farthest away, the figure of Gabrielle. I saw the light on her hand as she raised it, beckoning for me to come away.

Nicki reached up and touched my shoulders. I could feel the hatred coming through his touch. Loathsome to be touched in hate.

'Like a mindless beam of sunlight you routed the bats of the old coven!' he whispered. 'And for what purpose? What does it mean, the murdering monster who is filled with light!'

I turned and smacked him and sent him hurtling into the dressing room, his right hand smashing the mirror, his head cracking against the far wall.

For one moment he lay like something broken against the mass of old clothing, and then his eyes gathered their determination again, and his face softened into a slow smile. He righted himself and slowly, as an indignant mortal might, he smoothed his coat and his rumpled hair.

It was like my gestures under les Innocents when my captors had set me down in the dirt.

And he came forward with the same dignity, and the smile was as ugly as any I had ever seen.

'I despise you,' he said. 'But I am done with you. I have the power from you and I know how to use it, which you do not. I am in a realm at last where *I* choose to triumph! In darkness, we're equal now. And you will give me the theatre, that because you owe it to me, and you are a giver of things aren't you — a giver of gold coins to hungry children — and then I won't ever look upon your light again.'

He stepped around me and stretched out his arms to the others.

'Come, my beauties, come, we have plays to write, business to attend to. You have things to learn from me. I know what mortals really are. We must get down to the serious invention of our dark and splendid art. We will make a coven to rival all covens. We will do what has never been done.'

The others looked at me, frightened, hesitant. And in this still and tense moment I heard myself take a deep breath. My vision broadened. I saw the wings around us again, the high rafters, the walls of scenery transecting the darkness, and beyond, the little blaze along the foot of the dusty stage. I saw the house veiled in shadow and knew in one limitless recollection all that had happened here. And I saw a nightmare hatch another nightmare, and I saw a story come to an end.

'The Theatre of the Vampires,' I whispered. 'We have worked the Dark Trick on this little place.' No one of the others dared to answer. Nicolas only smiled.

And as I turned to leave the theatre I raised my hand in a gesture that urged them all towards him. I said my farewell.

WE WERE not far from the lights of the boulevard when I stopped in my tracks. Without words, a thousand horrors came to me — that Armand would come to destroy him, that his newfound brothers and sisters would tire of his frenzy and desert him, that morning would find him stumbling through the streets unable to find a hiding place from the sun. I looked up at the sky. I couldn't speak or breathe.

Gabrielle put her arms around me, and I held her, burying my face in her hair. Like cool velvet was her skin, her face, her lips. And her love surrounded me with a monstrous purity that had nothing to do with human hearts and human flesh.

I lifted her off her feet embracing her. And in the dark, we were like lovers carved out of the same stone who had no memory of a separate life at all.

'He's made his choice, my son,' she said. 'What's done is done, and you're free of him now.'

'Mother, how can you say it?' I whispered. 'He didn't know. He doesn't know still ...'

'Let him go, Lestat,' she said. 'They will care for him.'

'But now I have to find that devil, Armand, don't I?' I said wearily. 'I have to make him leave them alone.'

THE following evening when I came into Paris, I learned that Nicki had already been to Roget.

He had come an hour earlier pounding on the doors like a madman. And shouting from the shadows, he had demanded the deed to the theatre, and money that he said I had promised to him. He had threatened Roget and his family. He had also told Roget to write to Renaud and his troupe in London and to tell them to come home, that they had a new theatre awaiting them, and he expected them back at once. When Roget refused, he demanded the address of the players in London, and began to ransack Roget's desk.

I went into a silent fury when I heard this. So he would

make them all vampires, would he, this demon fledgling, this reckless and frenzied monster?

This would not come to pass.

I told Roget to send a courier to London, with word that Nicolas de Lenfent had lost his reason. The players must not come home.

And then I went to the boulevard du Temple and I found him at his rehearsals, excited and mad as he had been before. He wore his fancy clothes again and his old jewels from the time when he had been his father's favourite son, but his tie was askew, his stockings crooked, and his hair was as wild and unkempt as the hair of a prisoner in the Bastille who hadn't seen himself in a mirror in twenty years.

Before Eleni and the others, I told him he would get nothing from me unless I had the promise that no actor or actress of Paris would ever be slain or seduced by the new coven, that Renaud and his troupe would never be brought into the Theatre of the Vampires now or in the years to come, that Roget, who would hold the purse strings of the theatre, must never come to the slightest harm.

He laughed at me, he ridiculed me as he had before. But Eleni silenced him. She was horrified to learn of his impulsive designs. It was she who gave the promises, and exacted them from the others. It was she who intimidated him and confused him with jumbled language of the old ways, and made him back down.

AND it was to Eleni finally that I gave control of the Theatre of the Vampires, and the income, to pass through Roget, which would allow her to do with it what she pleased.

BEFORE I left her that night, I asked her what she knew of Armand. Gabrielle was with us. We were in the alleyway again, near the stage door.

'He watches,' Eleni answered. 'Sometimes he lets himself be seen.' Her face was very confusing to me. Sorrowful. 'But God only knows what he will do,' she added fearfully, 'when he discovers what is really going on here.'

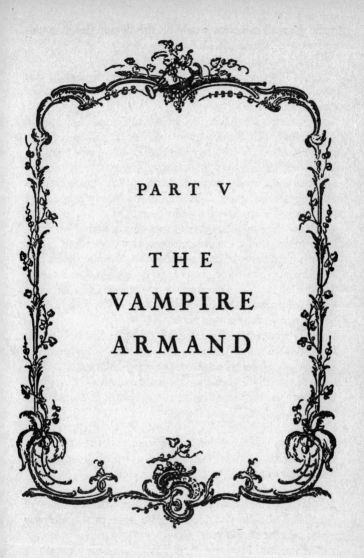

PART V

THE
VAMPIRE
ARMAND

1

SPRING rain. Rain of light that saturated every new leaf of the trees in the street, every square of paving, drift of rain threading light through the empty darkness itself.

And the ball in the Palais Royal.

The king and queen were there, dancing with the people. Talk in the shadows of intrigue. Who cares? Kingdoms rise and fall. Just don't burn the paintings in the Louvre, that's all.

Lost in a sea of mortals again; fresh complexions and ruddy cheeks, mounds of powdered hair atop feminine heads with all manner of millinery nonsense in them, even minute ships with three masts, tiny trees, little birds. Landscapes of pearl and ribbon. Broad-chested men like cocks in satin coats like feathered wings. The diamonds hurt my eyes.

The voices touched the surface of my skin at times, the laughter the echo of unholy laughter, wreaths of candles blinding, the froth of music positively lapping the walls.

Gust of rain from the open doors.

Scent of humans gently stoking my hunger. White shoulders, white necks, powerful hearts running at that eternal rhythm, so many gradations among these naked children hidden in riches, savages labouring beneath a swaddling of chenille, encrustations of embroidery, feet aching over high heels, masks like scabs about their eyes.

The air comes out of one body and is breathed into another. The music, does it pass out of one ear and into another, as the old expression goes? We breathe the light, we breathe the music, we breathe the moment as it passes through us.

Now and then eyes settled on me with some vague air of expectation. My white skin made them pause, but what was that when they let blood out of their veins themselves to keep their delicate pallor? (Let me hold the basin for you and drink it afterwards.) And my eyes, what were those, in this sea of paste jewels?

Yet their whispers slithered around me. And those scents, ah, not a one was like another. And as clearly as if spoken aloud it came, the summons from mortals here and there, sensing what I was, and the lust.

In some ancient language they welcomed death; they ached for death as death was passing through the room. But did they really know? Of course they didn't know. And I did not know! That was the perfect horror! And who am I to bear this secret, to hunger so to impart it, to want to take that slender woman there and suck the blood right out of the plump flesh of her round little breast.

The music rushed on, human music. The colours of the room flamed for an instant as if the whole would melt. The hunger sharpened. It was no longer an idea. My veins were throbbing with it. Someone would die. Sucked dry in less than a moment. I cannot stand it, thinking of it, knowing it's about to happen, fingers on the throat feeling the blood in the vein, feeling the flesh give, give it to me! Where? *This is my body, this is my blood.*

Send out your power, Lestat, like a reptile tongue to gather in a flick the appropriate heart.

Plump little arms ripe for the squeezing, men's faces on which the close-shaven blond beard all but glitters, muscle struggling in my fingers, you haven't got a chance!

And beneath this divine chemistry suddenly, this panorama of the denial of decay, I saw the bones!

Skulls under these preposterous wigs, two gaping holes peering from behind the uplifted fan. A room of wobbling skeletons waiting only for the tolling of the bell. Just as I had seen the audience that night in the pit of Renaud's when I had done the tricks that terrified them. The horror should be visited upon every other being in this room.

I had to get out. I'd made a terrible miscalculation. *This* was death and I could get away from it, if I could just get out! But I was tangled in mortal beings as if this monstrous place were a snare for a vampire. If I bolted, I'd send the entire ballroom into panic. As gently as I could I pushed to the open doors.

And against the far wall, a backdrop of satin and filigree, I saw, out of the corner of my eye, like something imagined, Armand.

Armand.

If there had been a summons, I never heard it. If there was a greeting, I didn't sense it now. He was merely looking at me, a radiant creature in jewels and scalloped lace. And it was Cinderella revealed at the ball, this vision, Sleeping Beauty opening her eyes under a mesh of cobwebs and wiping them all away with one sweep of her warm hand. The sheer pitch of incarnate beauty made me gasp.

Yes, perfect moral raiment, and yet he seemed all the more supernatural, his face too dazzling, his dark eyes fathomless and just for a split second glinting as if they were windows to the fires of hell. And when his voice came it was low and almost teasing, forcing me to concentrate to hear it: *All night you've been searching for me,* he said, *and here I am, waiting for you. I have been waiting for you all along.*

I think I sensed even then, as I stood unable to look away, that never in my years of wandering this earth would I ever have such a rich revelation of the true horror that we are.

Heartbreakingly innocent he seemed in the midst of the crowd.

Yet I saw crypts when I looked at him, and I heard the beat of the kettledrums. I saw torchlit fields where I had never been, heard vague incantations, felt the heat of raging fires on my face. And they didn't come out of him, these visions. Rather I drew them out on my own.

Yet never had Nicolas, mortal or immortal, been so alluring. Never had Gabrielle held me so in thrall.

Dear God, this is love. This is desire. And all my past amours have been but the shadow of this.

And it seemed in a murmuring pulse of thought he gave

me to know that I had been very foolish to think it would not be so.

Who can love us, you and I, as we can love each other, he whispered and it seemed his lips actually moved.

Others looked at him. I saw them drifting with a ludicrous slowness; I saw their eyes pass over him, I saw the light fall on him at a rich new angle as he lowered his head.

I was moving towards him. It seemed he raised his right hand and beckoned and then he didn't, and he had turned and I saw the figure of a young boy ahead of me, with narrow waist and straight shoulders and high firm calves under silk stockings, a boy who turned as he opened a door and beckoned again.

A mad thought came to me.

I was moving after him, and it seemed that none of the other things had happened. There was no crypt under les Innocents, and he had not been that ancient fearful fiend. We were somehow safe.

We were the sum of our desires and this was saving us, and the vast untasted horror of my own immortality did not lie before me, and we were navigating calm seas with familiar beacons, and it was time to be in each other's arms.

A dark room surrounded us, private, cold. The noise of the ball was far away. He was heated with the blood he'd drunk and I could hear the strong force of his heart. He drew me closer to him, and beyond the high windows there flashed the passing lights of the carriages, with dim incessant sounds that spoke of safety and comfort, and all the things that Paris was.

I had never died. The world was beginning again. I put out my arms and felt his heart against me, and calling out to my Nicolas, I tried to warn him, to tell him we were all of us doomed. Our life was slipping inch by inch from us, and seeing the apple trees in the orchard, drenched in green sunlight, I felt I would go mad.

'No, no, my dearest one,' he was whispering, 'nothing but peace and sweetness and your arms in mine.'

'You know it was the damndest luck!' I whispered suddenly. 'I am an unwilling devil. I cry like some vagrant child. I want to go home.'

Yes, yes, his lips tasted like blood, but it was not human blood. It was that elixir that Magnus had given me, and I felt myself recoil. I could get away this time. I had another chance. The wheel had turned full round.

I was crying out that I wouldn't drink; I wouldn't, and then I felt the two hot shafts driven hard through my neck and down to my soul.

I couldn't move. It was coming as it had come that night, the rapture, a thousandfold what it was when I held mortals in my arms. And I knew what he was doing! He was feeding upon me! He was draining me.

And going down on my knees, I felt myself held by him, the blood pouring out of me with a monstrous volition I couldn't stop.

'Devil!' I tried to scream. I forced the word up and up until it broke from my lips and the paralysis broke from my limbs. 'Devil!' I roared again and I caught him in his swoon and hurled him backwards to the floor.

In an instant, I had my hands upon him and, shattering the French doors, had dragged him out with me into the night.

His heels were scraping on the stones, his face had become pure fury. I clutched his right arm and swung him from side to side so that his head snapped back and he could not see nor gauge where he was, not catch hold of anything, and with my right hand I beat him and beat him, until the blood was running out of his ears and his eyes and his nose.

I dragged him through the trees away from the lights of the Palais. And as he struggled, as he sought to resurrect himself with a burst of force, he shot his declaration at me that he would kill me because he had my strength now. He'd drunk it out of me and coupled with his own strength it would make him impossible to defeat.

Maddened, I clutched at his neck, pushing his head down against the path beneath me. I pinned him down, strangling him, until the blood in great gushes poured out of his open mouth.

He would have screamed if he could. My knees drove into

his chest. His neck bulged under my fingers and the blood spurted and bubbled out of him and he turned his head from side to side, his eyes growing bigger and bigger, but seeing nothing, and then when I felt him weak and limp, I let him go.

I beat him again, turning him this way and that. And then I drew my sword to sever his head.

Let him live like that if he can. Let him be immortal like that if he can. I raised the sword and when I looked down at him, the rain was pelting his face, and he was staring up at me, as one half alive, unable to plead for mercy, unable to move.

I waited. I wanted him to beg. I wanted him to give me that powerful voice full of lies and cunning, the voice that had made me believe for one pure and dazzling instant that I was alive and free and in the state of grace again. Damnable, unforgivable lie. Lie I'd never forget for as long as I walked the earth. I wanted the rage to carry me over the threshold to his grave.

But nothing came from him.

And in this moment of stillness and misery for him, his beauty slowly returned.

He lay a broken child on the gravel path, only yards from the passing traffic, the ring of the horses' hooves, the rumble of the wooden wheels.

And in this broken child were centuries of evil and centuries of knowledge, and out of him there came no ignominious entreaty but merely the soft and bruised sense of what he was. Old, old evil, eyes that had seen dark ages of which I only dream.

I let him go, and I stood up and sheathed my sword.

I walked a few paces from him, and collapsed upon a wet stone bench.

Far away, busy figures laboured about the shattered window of the palace.

But the night lay between us and those confused mortals, and I looked at him listlessly as he lay still.

His face was turned to me, but not by design, his hair a tangle of curls and blood. And with his eyes closed, and his hand open beside him, he appeared the abandoned offspring of time and supernatural accident, someone as miserable as myself.

What had he done to become what he was? Could one so young so long ago have guessed the meaning of any decision, let alone the vow to become this?

I rose, and walking slowly to him, I stood over him and looked at him, at the blood that soaked his lace shirt and stained his face.

It seemed he sighed, that I heard the passage of his breath.

He didn't open his eyes, and to mortals perhaps there would have been no expression there. But I felt his sorrow. I felt its immensity, and I wished I didn't feel it, and for one moment I understood the gulf that divided us, and the gulf that divided his attempt to overpower me from my rather simple defense of myself.

Desperately he had tried to vanquish what he did not comprehend.

And impulsively and almost effortlessly I had beaten him back.

All my pain with Nicolas came back to me and Gabrielle's words and Nicolas's denunciations. My anger was nothing to his misery, his despair.

And this perhaps was the reason that I reached down and gathered him up. And maybe I did it because he was so exquisitely beautiful and so lost, and we were after all of the same ilk.

Natural enough, wasn't it, that one of his own should take him away from this place where mortals would sooner or later have approached him, driven him stumbling away.

He gave no resistance to me. In a moment he was standing on his own feet. And then he walked drowsily beside me, my arm about his shoulder, bolstering him and steadying him until we were moving away from the Palais Royal, towards the rue St.-Honoré.

I only half glanced at the figures passing us, until I saw a familiar shape under the trees, with no scent of mortality coming from it, and I realized that Gabrielle had been there for some time.

She came forward hesitantly and silently, her face stricken when she saw the blood-drenched lace and the lacerations on the white skin, and she reached out as if to help me with the burden of him though she did not seem to know how.

Somewhere far off in the darkened gardens, the others were near. I *heard* them before I saw them. Nicki was there too.

They had come as Gabrielle had come, drawn over the miles, it seemed, by the tumult, or what vague messages I could not imagine, and they merely waited and watched as we moved away.

2

WE TOOK him with us to the livery stables, and there I put him on my mare. But he looked as if he would let himself fall off at any moment, and so I mounted behind him, and the three of us rode out.

All the way through the country, I wondered what I would do. I wondered what it meant to bring him to my lair. Gabrielle didn't give any protest. Now and then she glanced over at him. I heard nothing from him, and he was small and self-contained as he sat in front of me, light as a child but not a child.

Surely he had always known where the tower was, but had its bars kept him out? Now I meant to take him inside it. And why didn't Gabrielle say something to me? It was the meeting we had wanted, it was the thing for which we had waited, but surely she knew what he had just done.

When we finally dismounted, he walked ahead of me, and he waited for me to reach the gate. I had taken out the iron key to the lock and I studied him, wondering what promises one exacts from such a monster before opening one's door. Did the ancient laws of hospitality mean anything to the creatures of the night?

His eyes were large and brown and defeated. Almost

drowsy they seemed. He regarded me for a long silent moment and then he reached out with his left hand, and his fingers curled around the iron crossbar in the centre of the gate.

I stared helplessly as with a loud grinding noise the gate started to rip loose from the stone. But he stopped and contented himself with merely bending the iron bar a little. The point had been made. He could have entered this tower anytime that he wished.

I examined the iron bar that he'd twisted. I had beaten him. Could I do what he had just done? I didn't know. And unable to calculate my own powers, how could I ever calculate his?

'Come,' Gabrielle said a little impatiently. And she led the way down the stairs to the dungeon crypt.

It was cold here as always, the fresh spring air never touching the place. She made a big fire in the old hearth while I lighted the candles. And as he sat on the stone bench watching us, I saw the effect of the warmth on him, the way that his body seemed to grow slightly larger, the way that he breathed it in.

As he looked about, it was as if he were absorbing the light. His gaze was clear.

Impossible to overestimate the effect of warmth and light on vampires. Yet the old coven had forsworn both.

I settled on another bench, and I let my eyes roam about the broad low chamber as his eyes roamed.

Gabrielle had been standing all this while. And now she approached him. She had taken out a handkerchief and she touched this to his face.

He stared at her in the same way that he stared at the fire and the candles, and the shadows leaping on the curved ceiling. This seemed to interest him as simply as anything else.

And I felt a shudder when I realized the bruises on his face were now almost gone! The bones were whole again, the shape of the face having been fully restored, and he was only a little gaunt from the blood he had lost.

My heart expanded slightly, against my will, as it had on the battlements when I had heard his voice.

I thought of the pain only half a hour ago in the Palais

when the lie had broken with the stab of his fangs into my neck.

I hated him.

But I couldn't stop looking at him. Gabrielle combed his hair for him. She took his hands and wiped the blood from them. And he seemed helpless as all this was done. And she had not so much the expression of a ministering angel as an expression of curiosity, a desire to be near him and to touch him and examine him. In the quavering illumination they looked at one another.

He hunched forward a little, eyes darkening and full of expression now as they turned again to the grate. Had it not been for the blood on his lace ruff, he might have looked human. Might ...

'What will you do now?' I asked. I spoke to make it clear to Gabrielle. 'Will you remain in Paris and let Eleni and the others go on?'

No answer from him. He was studying me, studying the stone benches, the sarcophagi. Three sarcophagi.

'Surely you know what they're doing,' I said. 'Will you leave Paris or remain?'

It seemed he wanted to tell me again the magnitude of what I had done to him and the others, but this faded away. For one moment his face was wretched. It was defeated and warm and full of human misery. How old was he, I wondered. How long ago had he been a human who looked like that?

He heard me. But he didn't give an answer. He looked to Gabrielle, who stood near the fire, and then to me. And silently, he said, *Love me. You have destroyed everything! But if you love me, it can all be restored in a new form. Love me.*

This silent entreaty had an eloquence, however, that I can't put into words.

'What can I do to make you love me?' he whispered. 'What can I give? The knowledge of all I have witnessed, the secrets of our powers, the mystery of what I am?'

It seemed blasphemous to answer. And as I had on the battlements, I found myself on the edge of tears. For all the purity of his silent communications, his voice gave a lovely resonance to his sentiments when he actually spoke.

It occurred to me as it had in Notre Dame that he spoke the way angels must speak, if they exist.

But I was awakened from this irrelevant thought, this obviating thought, by the fact that he was now beside me. He was closing his arm round me, and pressing his forehead against my face. He gave that summons again, not the rich, thudding seduction of that moment in the Palais Royal, but the voice that had sung to me over the miles, and he told me there were things the two of us would know and understand as mortals never could. He told me that if I opened to him and gave him my strength and my secrets that he would give me his. He had been driven to try to destroy me, and he loved me all the more that he could not.

That was a tantalizing thought. Yet I felt danger. The word that came unbidden to me was Beware.

I don't know that Gabrielle saw or heard. I don't know what she felt.

Instinctively I avoided his eyes. There seemed nothing in the world I wanted more at this moment than to look right at him and understand him, and yet I *knew* I must not. I saw the bones under les Innocents again, the flickering hellfires I had imagined in the Palais Royal. And all the lace and velvet in the eighteenth century could not give him a human face.

I couldn't keep this from him, and it pained me that it was impossible for me to explain it to Gabrielle. And the awful silence between me and Gabrielle was at that moment almost too much to bear.

With him, I could speak, yes, with him I could dream dreams. Some reverence and terror in me made me reach out and embrace him, and I held him, battling my confusion and my desire.

'Leave Paris, yes,' he whispered. 'But take me with you. I don't know how to exist here now. I stumble through a carnival of horrors. Please ...'

I heard myself say: 'No.'

'Have I no value to you?' he asked. He turned to Gabrielle Her face was anguished and still as she looked at him. I couldn't know what went on in her heart, and to my sadness, I realized that he was speaking to her and locking me out. What was her answer?

But he was imploring both of us now. 'Is there nothing outside yourself you would respect?'

'I might have destroyed you tonight,' I said. 'It was respect which kept me from that.'

'No.' He shook his head in a startlingly human fashion. 'That you never could have done.'

I smiled. It was probably true. But we were destroying him quite completely in another way.

'Yes,' he said, 'that's true. You are destroying me. Help me,' he whispered. 'Give me but a few short years of all you have before you, the two of you. I beg you. That is all I ask.'

'No,' I said again.

He was only a foot from me on the bench. He was looking at me. And there came the horrible spectacle again of his face narrowing and darkening and caving in upon itself in rage. It was as if he had no real substance. Only will kept him robust and beautiful. And when the flow of his will was interrupted, he melted like a wax doll.

But, as before, he recovered himself almost instantly. The 'hallucination' was past.

He stood up and backed away from me until he was in front of the fire.

The will coming from him was palpable. His eyes were like something that didn't belong to him, nor to anything on earth. And the fire blazing behind him made an eerie nimbus around his head.

'I curse you!' he whispered.

I felt a jet of fear.

'I curse you,' he said again and came closer. 'Love mortals then, and live as you have lived, recklessly, with appetite for everything and love for everything, but there will come a time when only the love of your own kind can save you.' He glanced at Gabrielle. 'And I don't mean children such as this!'

This was so strong that I couldn't conceal its effect on me, and I realized I was rising from the bench and slipping away from him towards Gabrielle.

'I don't come empty-handed to you,' he pressed, his voice deliberately softening, 'I don't come begging with nothing to give of my own. Look at me. Tell me you don't need what you see in me, one who has the strength to take you through the ordeals that lie ahead.'

His eyes flashed on Gabrielle and for one moment he remained locked to her and I saw her harden and begin to tremble.

'Let her be!' I said.

'You don't know what I say to her,' he said coldly. 'I do not try to hurt her. But in your love of mortals, what have you already done?'

He would say something terrible if I didn't stop him, something to wound me or Gabrielle. He knew all that had happened with Nicki. I knew that he did. If, somewhere deep down in my soul, I wished for the end of Nicki, he would know that too! Why had I let him in? Why had I not known what he could do?

'Oh, but it's always a travesty, don't you see?' he said with that same gentleness. 'Each time the death and the awakening will ravage the mortal spirit, so that one will hate you for taking his life, another will run to excesses that you scorn. A third will emerge mad and raving, another a monster you cannot control. One will be jealous of your superiority, another shut you out.' And here he shot his glance to Gabrielle again and half smiled. 'And the veil will always come down between you. Make a legion. You will be, always and forever, alone!'

'I don't want to hear this. It means nothing,' I said.

Gabrielle's face had undergone some ugly change. She was staring at him with hatred now, I was sure of it.

He made that bitter little noise that is a laugh but isn't a laugh at all.

'Lovers with a human face,' he mocked me. 'Don't you see your error? The other one hates you beyond all reason, and she — why, the dark blood has made her even colder, has it not? But even for her, strong as she is, there will come moments when she fears to be immortal, and who will she blame for what was done to her?'

'You are a fool,' Gabrielle whispered.

'You tried to protect the violinist from it. But you never sought to protect her.'

'Don't say any more,' I answered. 'You make me hate you. Is that what you want?'

'But I speak the truth and you know it. And what you will never know, either of you, is the full depth of each other's hatreds and resentments. Or suffering. Or love.'

He paused and I could say nothing. He was doing exactly what I feared he would, and I didn't know how to defend myself.

'If you leave me now with this one,' he continued, 'you will do it again. Nicolas you never possessed. And she already wonders how she will ever get free of you. And unlike her, you cannot stand to be alone.'

I couldn't answer. Gabrielle's eyes became smaller, her mouth a little more cruel.

'So the time will come when you will seek other mortals,' he went on, 'hoping once more that the Dark Trick will bring you the love you crave. And of these newly mutilated and unpredictable children you'll try to fashion your citadels against time. Well, they will be prisons if they last for half a century. I warn you. It is only with those as powerful and wise as yourself that the true citadel against time can be built.'

The citadel against time. Even in my ignorance the words had their power. And the fear in me expanded, reached out to compass a thousand other causes.

He seemed distant for a moment, indescribably beautiful in the firelight, the dark auburn strands of his hair barely touching his smooth forehead, his lips parted in a beatific smile.

'If we cannot have the old ways, can't we have each other?' he asked, and now his voice was the voice of the summons again. 'Who else can understand your suffering? Who else knows what passed through your mind the night you stood on the stage of your little theatre and you frightened all those you had loved?'

'Don't speak about that,' I whispered. But I was softening all over, drifting into his eyes and his voice. Very near to me was the ecstasy I'd felt that night on the battlements. With all my will I reached out for Gabrielle.

'Who understands what passed through your mind when my renegade followers, revelling in the music of your precious fiddler, devised their ghastly boulevard enterprise?' he asked.

I didn't speak.

'The Theatre of the Vampires!' His lips lengthened in the saddest smile. 'Does she comprehend the irony of it, the cruelty? Does she know what it was like when you stood on that stage as a young man and you heard the audience screaming for you? When time was your friend, not your enemy as it is now? When in the wings, you put out your arms and your mortal darlings came to you, your little family, folding themselves against you ...'

'Stop please. I ask you to stop.'

'Does anyone else know the size of your soul?'

Witchcraft. Had it ever been used with more skill? And what was he really saying to us beneath this liquid flow of beautiful language: *Come to me, and I shall be the sun round which you are locked in orbit, and my rays shall lay bare the secrets you keep from each other, and I, who possess charms and powers of which you have no inkling, shall control and possess and destroy you!*

'I asked you before,' I said. 'What do you want? Really want?'

'You!' he said. 'You and her! That we become three at this crossroads!'

Not that we surrender to you?

I shook my head. And I saw the same wariness and recoiling in Gabrielle.

He was not angry; there was no malice now. Yet he said again, in the same beguiling voice:

'I curse you,' and I felt it as if he'd declaimed it.

'I offered myself to you at the moment you vanquished me,' he said. 'Remember that when your dark children strike out at you, when they rise up against you. Remember me.'

I was shaken, more shaken even than I had been in the sad

311

and awful finish with Nicolas at Renaud's. I had never once known fear in the crypt under les Innocents. But I had known it in this room since we came in.

And some anger boiled in him again, something too dreadful for him to control.

I watched him bow his head and turn away. He became small, light, and held his arms close to himself as he stood before the blaze and he thought of threats now to hurt me, and I heard them though they died before they ever reached his lips.

But something disturbed my vision for a fraction of a second. Maybe it was a candle guttering. Maybe it was the blink of my eye. Whatever it was, he vanished. Or he tried to vanish, and I saw him leaping away from the fire in a great dark streak.

'No!' I cried out. And lunging at something I couldn't even see, I held him, material again, in my hands.

He had only moved very fast, and I had moved faster, and we stood facing each other in the doorway of the crypt, and again I said that single negation and I wouldn't let him go.

'Not like this, we can't part. We can't leave each other in hatred, we can't.' And my will dissolved suddenly as I embraced him and held tight to him so that he couldn't free himself nor even move.

I didn't care what he was, or what he had done in that doomed moment of lying to me, or even trying to overpower me, I didn't care that I was no longer mortal and would never be again.

I wanted only that he should remain. I wanted to be with him, what he was, and all the things he had said were true. Yet it could never be as he wished it to be. He could not have this power over us. He could not divide Gabrielle from me.

Yet I wondered, did he himself really understand what he was asking? Was it possible that he believed the more innocent words he spoke?

Without speaking, without asking his consent, I led him back to the bench by the fire. I felt danger again, terrible danger. But it didn't really matter. He had to remain here with us now.

* * *

GABRIELLE was murmuring to herself. She was walking back and forth and her cloak hung from one shoulder and she seemed almost to have forgotten we were there.

Armand watched her, and when she turned to him, quite suddenly and unexpectedly, she spoke aloud.

'You come to him and you say, "Take me with you." You say, "Love me," and you hint of superior knowledge, secrets, yet you give us nothing, either of us, except lies.'

'I showed my power to understand,' he answered in a soft murmur.

'No, you did tricks with your understanding,' she replied. 'You made pictures. And rather childish pictures. You have done this all along. You lure Lestat in the Palais with the most gorgeous illusions only to attack him. And here, when there is a respite in the struggle, what do you do but try to sow dissension between us ...'

'Yes, illusions before, I admit it,' he answered. 'But the things I've spoken here are true. Already you despise your son for his love of mortals, his need to be ever near them, his yielding to the violinist. *You* knew the Dark Gift would madden that one, and that it will finally destroy him. You do wish for your freedom, from all the Children of Darkness. You can't hide that from me.'

'Ah, but you're so simple,' she said. 'You see, but you don't see. How many mortal years did you live? Do you remember anything of them? What you've perceived is not the sum total of the passion I feel for my son. I have loved him as I have never loved any other being in creation. In my loneliness, my son is everything to me. How is it you can't interpret what you see?'

'It's you who fail to interpret,' he answered in the same soft manner. 'If you ever felt real longing for any other one, you would know that what you feel for your son is nothing at all.'

'This is futile,' I said, 'to talk like this.'

'No,' she said to him without the slightest wavering. 'My

son and I are kin to each other in more ways than one. In fifty years of life, I've never known anyone as strong as myself, except my son. And what divides us we can always mend. But how are we to make you one of us when you use these things like wood for fire! But understand my larger point: what is it of yourself that you can give that we should want you?'

'My guidance is what you need,' he answered. 'You've only begun your adventure and you have no beliefs to hold you. You cannot live without some guidance ...'

'Millions live without belief or guidance. It is you who cannot live without it,' she said.

Pain coming from him. Suffering.

But she went on, her voice so steady and without expression it was almost a monologue:

'I have my questions,' she asked. 'There are things I must know. I cannot live without some embracing philosophy, but it has nothing to do with old beliefs in gods or devils.' She started pacing again, glancing to him as she spoke.

'I want to know, for example, why beauty exists,' she said, 'why nature continues to contrive it, and what is the link between the life of a tree and its beauty, and what connects the mere existence of the sea or a lightning storm with the feelings these things inspire in us? If God does not exist, if these things are not unified into one metaphorical system, then why do they retain for us such symbolic power? Lestat calls it the Savage Garden, but for me that is not enough. And I must confess that this, this maniacal curiosity or call it what you will, leads me away from my human victims. It leads me into the open countryside, away from human creation. And maybe it will lead me away from my son, who is under the spell of all things human.'

She came up to him, nothing in her manner suggesting a woman now, and she narrowed her eyes as she looked into his face.

'But that is the lantern by which I see the Devil's Road,' she said. 'By what lantern have you travelled it? What have you really learned besides devil worship and superstition? What do you know about us, and how we came into existence? Give

314

that to us, and it might be worth something. And then again, it might be worth nothing.'

He was speechless. He had no art to hide his amazement.

He stared at her in innocent confusion. Then he rose and he slipped away, obviously trying to escape her, a battered spirit as he stared blankly before him.

The silence closed in. And I felt for the moment strangely protective for him. She had spoken the unadorned truth about the things that interested her as had been her custom ever since I could remember, and as always, there was something violently disregarding about it. She spoke of what mattered to her with no thought of what had befallen him.

Come to a different plane, she had said, my plane. And he was stymied and belittled. The degree of his helplessness was becoming alarming. He was not recovering from her attack.

He turned and he moved towards the benches again, as if he would sit, then towards the sarcophagi, then towards the wall. It seemed these solid surfaces repelled him as though his will confronted them first in an invisible field and he was buffeted about.

He drifted out of the room and into the narrow stone stairwell and then he turned and came back.

His thoughts were locked inside himself or, worse, there were no thoughts!

There were only the tumbling images of what he saw before him, simple material things glaring back at him, the iron-studded door, the candles, the fire. Some full-blown evocation of the Paris streets, the vendors and the hawkers of papers, the cabriolets, the blended sound of an orchestra, a horrid din of words and phrases from the books he had so recently read.

I couldn't bear this, but Gabrielle gestured sternly that I should stay where I was.

Something was building in the crypt. Something was happening in the very air itself.

Something had changed even as the candles melted, and the fire crackled and licked at the blackened stones behind it, and the rats moved in the chambers of the dead below.

Armand stood in the arched doorway, and it seemed hours had passed though they hadn't and Gabrielle was a long distance away in the corner of the room, her face cool in its concentration, her eyes as radiant as they were small.

Armand was going to speak to us, but it was no explanation he was going to give. There was no direction even to the things he would say, and it was as if we'd cut him open and the images were coming out like blood.

Armand was just a young boy in the doorway, holding the backs of his own arms. And I knew what I felt. It was a monstrous intimacy with another being, an intimacy that made even the rapt moments of the kill seem dim and under control. He was opened and could no longer contain the dazzling stream of pictures that made his old silent voice seem thin and lyrical and made up.

Had this been the danger all along, the trigger of my fear? Even as I recognized it, I was yielding, and it seemed the great lessons of my life had all been learned through the renunciation of fear. Fear was once again breaking the shell around me so that something else could spring to life.

Never, never in all my existence, not mortal or immortal, had I been threatened with an intimacy quite like this.

The STORY
of
ARMAND

3

THE chamber had faded. The walls were gone.
Horsemen came. A gathering cloud on the horizon. Then screams of terror. And an auburn-haired child

in crude peasant's clothes running on and on, as the horsemen broke loose in a horde and the child fighting and kicking as he was caught and thrown over the saddle of a rider who bore him away beyond the end of the world. Armand was this child.

And these were the southern steppes of Russia, but Armand didn't know that it was Russia. He knew Mother and Father and Church and God and Satan, but he didn't even understand the name of home, or the name of his language, or that the horsemen who carried him away were Tartars and that he would never see anything that he knew or loved again.

Darkness, the tumultuous movement of the ship and its never ending sickness, and emerging out of the fear and the numbing despair, the vast glittering wilderness of impossible buildings that was Constantinople in the last days of the Byzantine Empire, with her fantastical multitudes and her slave-auction blocks. The menacing babble of foreign tongues, threats made in the universal language of gesture, and all around him the enemies he could not distinguish or placate or escape.

Years and years would pass, beyond a mortal lifetime, before Armand would look back on that awesome moment and give them names and histories, the Byzantine officials of the court who would have castrated him and the harem keepers of Islam who would have done the same, and the proud Mamaluke warriors of Egypt who would have taken him to Cairo with them had he been fairer and stronger, and the radiant soft-spoken Venetians in their leggings and velvet doublets, the most dazzling creatures of all, Christians even as he was a Christian, yet laughing gently to one another as they examined him, as he stood mute, unable to answer, to plead, even to hope.

I saw the seas before him, the great rolling blue of the Aegean and the Adriatic, and his sickness again in the hold and his solemn vow not to live.

And then the great Moorish palaces of Venice rising from the gleaming surface of the lagoon, and the house to which he was taken, with its dozens and dozens of secret chambers, the light of the sky glimpsed only through barred windows, and the other boys speaking to him in that soft strange tongue that was Venetian and the threats and the cajoling as he was convinced, against all his fear and superstitions, of the sins that he must commit with the endless procession of strangers in this landscape of marble and torchlight, each chamber opening to a new tableau of tenderness that surrendered to the same ritual and inexplicable and finally cruel desire.

And at last one night when, for days and days he had refused to submit and he was hungry and sore and would not speak any longer to anyone, he was pushed through one of those doors again, just as he was, soiled and blind from the dark room in which he'd been locked, and the creature standing there to receive him, the tall one in red velvet, with the lean and almost luminous face, touched him so gently with cool fingers that, half dreaming, he didn't cry as he saw the coins exchange hands. But it was a great deal of money. Too much money. He was being sold off. And the face, it was too smooth, it might have been a mask.

At the final moment, he screamed. He swore he would obey, he wouldn't fight anymore. Will someone tell him where he's being taken, he won't disobey anymore, please, please. But even as he was pulled down the stairs towards the dank smell of the water, he felt the firm, delicate fingers of his new Master again, and on his neck cool and tender lips that could never, never hurt him, and that first deadly and irresistible kiss.

Love and love and love in the vampire kiss. It bathed Armand, cleansed him, *this is everything*, as he was carried into the gondola and the gondola moved like a great sinister beetle through the narrow stream into the sewers beneath another house.

Drunk on pleasure. Drunk on the silky white hands that smoothed back his hair and the voice that called him beautiful; on the face that in moments of feeling was suffused with expression only to become as serene and dazzling as something made of jewels and alabaster in repose. Like a pool of moonlit water it was. Touch it even with the fingertip and all its life rises to the surface only to vanish in quiet once again.

Drunk in the morning light on the memory of those kisses as, alone, he opened one door after another upon books and maps and statues in granite and marble, the other apprentices finding him and leading him patiently to his work — letting him watch as they ground the brilliant pigments, teaching him to blend the pure colour with the yellow egg yolk, and how to spread the lacquer of the egg yolk over the panels, and taking him up on the scaffolding as they worked with careful strokes on the very edges of the vast depiction of sun and clouds, showing him those great faces and hands and angels' wings which only the Master's brush would touch.

Drunk as he sat at the long table with them, gorging himself on the delicious foods that he had never tasted before, and the wine which never ran out.

And falling asleep finally to wake at that moment of twilight when the Master stood beside the enormous bed, gorgeous as something imagined in his red velvet, with his thick white hair glistening in the lamplight, and the simplest happiness in his brilliant cobalt blue eyes. The deadly kiss.

'Ah, yes, never to be separated from you, yes, ... not afraid.'

'Soon, my darling one, we will be truly united soon.'

Torches blazing throughout the house. The Master atop the scaffolding with the brush in his hand: 'Stand there, in the light, don't move,' and hours and hours frozen in the same position, and then before dawn, seeing his own likeness there in the paint, the face of the angel, the Master smiling as he moved down the endless corridor ...

'No, Master, don't leave me, let me stay with you, don't go ...'

Day again, and money in his pockets, real gold, and the grandeur of Venice with her dark green waterways, walled in palaces, and the other apprentices walking arm in arm with him, and the fresh air and the blue sky over the Piazza San Marco like something he had only dreamed in childhood, and the palazzo again at twilight, and the Master coming, the Master bent over the smaller panel with the brush, working faster and faster as the apprentices gazed on half horrified, half fascinated, the Master looking up and seeing him and putting down the brush, and taking him out of the enormous studio as the others worked until the hour of midnight, his face in the Master's hands as, alone in the bedchamber again, that secret, never tell anyone, kiss.

Two years? Three years? No words to recreate it or embrace it, the glory that was those times — the fleets that sailed away to war from that port, the hymns that rose before those Byzantine altars, the passion plays and the miracle plays performed on their platforms in the churches and in the piazza with their hell's mouth and cavorting devils, and the glittering mosaics spreading out over the walls of San Marco and San Zanipolo and the Palazzo Ducale, and the painters who walked those streets, Giambono, Uccello, the Vivarini and the Bellini; and the endless feast days and processions, and always in the small hours in the vast torchlighted rooms of the palazzo, alone with the Master when the others slept safely locked away. The Master's brush racing over the panel before it as if uncovering the painting rather than creating it — sun and sky and sea spreading out beneath the canopy of the angel's wings.

And those awful inevitable moments when the Master would rise screaming, hurling the pots of paint in all directions, clutching at his eyes as if he would pull them out of his head.

'Why can I not see? Why can I not see better than mortals see?'

Holding tight to the Master. Waiting for the rapture of the kiss. Dark secret, unspoken secret. The Master slipping out of the door sometime before dawn.

'Let me go with you, Master.'

'Soon, my darling, my love, my little one, when you're strong enough and tall enough, and there is no flaw in you anymore. Go now, and have all the pleasures that await you, have the love of a woman, and have the love of a man as well in the nights that follow. Forget the bitterness you knew in the brothel and taste of these things while there is still time.'

And rarely did the night close that there wasn't that figure come back again, just before the rising sun, and this time ruddy and warm as it bent over him to give him the embrace that would sustain him through the daylight hours until the deadly kiss at twilight again.

He learned to read and to write. He took the paintings to their final destinations in the churches and the chapels of the great palaces, and collected the payments and bargained for the pigments and the oils. He scolded the servants when the beds weren't made and the meals weren't ready. And beloved by the apprentices, he sent them to their new service when they were finished, with tears. He read poetry to the Master as the Master painted, and he learned to play the lute and to sing songs.

And during those sad times when the Master left Venice for many nights, it was he who governed in the Master's absence, concealing his anguish from the others, knowing it would end only when the Master returned.

And one night finally, in the small hours when even Venice slept:

'This is the moment, beautiful one. For you to come to me and become like me. Is it what you wish?'

'Yes.'

'Forever to thrive in secret upon the blood of the evildoer as I thrive, and to abide with these secrets until the end of the world.'

'I take the vow, I surrender, I will … to be with you, my Master, always, you are the creator of all things that I am. There has never been any greater desire.'

The Master's brush pointing to the painting that reached to the ceiling above the tiers of scaffolding.

'This is the only sun that you will ever see again. But a millennium of nights will be yours to see light as no mortal has ever seen it, to snatch from the distant stars as if you were Prometheus an endless illumination by which to understand all things.'

How many months were there after? Reeling in the power of the Dark Gift.

This nightime life of drifting though the alleyways and the canals together — at one with the danger of the dark and no

321

longer afraid of it — and the age-old rapture of the killing, and never, never the innocent souls. No, always the evildoer, the mind pierced until Typhon, the slayer of his brother, was revealed, and then the drinking up of the evil from the mortal victim and the transmuting of it into ecstasy, the Master leading the way, the feast shared.

And the painting afterwards, the solitary hours with the miracle of the new skill, the brush sometimes moving as if by itself acrosss the enamelled surface, and the two of them painting furiously on the triptych, and the mortal apprentices asleep among the paint pots and the wine bottles, and only one mystery disturbing the serenity, the mystery that the Master, as in the past, must now and then leave Venice for a journey that seemed endless to those left behind.

All the more terrible now the parting. To hunt alone without the Master, to lie alone in the deep cellar after the hunt, waiting. Not to hear the ring of the Master's laughter or the beat of the Master's heart.

'But where do you go? Why can't I go with you?' Armand pleaded. Didn't they share the secret? Why was this mystery not explained?

'No, my lovely one, you are not ready for this burden. For now, it must be, as it has been for over a thousand years, mine alone. Someday you will help me with what I have to do, but only when you are ready for the knowledge, when you have shown that you truly wish to know, and when you are powerful enough that no one can ever take the knowledge from you against your will. Until then understand I have no choice but to leave you. I go to tend to Those Who Must Be Kept as I have always done.'

Those Who Must Be Kept.

Armand brooded upon it; it frightened him. But worst of all it took the Master from him, and only did he learn not to fear it when the Master returned to him again and again.

'Those Who Must Be Kept are in peace, or in silence,' he would say as he took the red velvet cloak from his shoulders. 'More than that we may never know.'

And to the feast again, the stalking of the evildoer through the alleys of Venice, he and the Master would go.

How long might it have continued — through one mortal lifetime? Through a hundred?

Not a half year in this dark bliss before the evening at twilight when the Master stood over his coffin in the deep cellar just above the water, and said:

'Rise, Armand, we must leave here. They have come!'

'But who are they, Master? Is it Those Who Must Be Kept?'

'No, my darling. It is the others. Come, we must hurry!'

'But how can they hurt us? Why must we go?'

The white faces at the windows, the pounding at the doors. Glass shattering. The Master turning this way and that as he looked at the paintings. The smell of smoke. The smell of burning pitch. They were coming up from the cellar. They were coming down from above.

'Run, there is no time to save anything.' Up the stairs to the roof.

Black hooded figures heaving their torches through the doorways, the fire roaring in the rooms below, exploding the windows, boiling up the stairway. All the paintings were burning.

'To the roof, Armand. Come!'

Creatures like ourselves in these dark garments! Others like ourselves! The Master scattered them in all directions as he raced up the stairway, bones cracking as they struck the ceiling and the walls.

'Blasphemer, heretic!' the alien voices roared. The arms caught Armand and held him, and above at the very top of the stairway the Master turned back for him:

'Armand! Trust your strength. Come!'

But they were swarming behind the Master. They were surrounding him. For each one hurled into the plaster, three more appeared, until fifty torches were plunged into the Master's velvet garments, his long red sleeves, his white hair. The fire roared up to the ceiling as it consumed him, making of him a living torch, even as with flaming arms he defended himself, igniting his attackers as they threw the blazing torches like firewood at his feet.

But Armand was being borne down and away, out of the burning house, with the screaming mortal apprentices. And over the water and away from Venice, amid cries and wailing, in the belly of a vessel as terrifying as the slave ship, to an open clearing under the night sky.

'Blasphemer, blasphemer!' The bonfire growing, and the chain of hooded figures around it, and the chant rising and rising, 'Into the fire.'

'No, don't do it to me, no!'

And as he watched, petrified, he saw brought towards the pyre the mortal apprentices, his brothers, his only brothers, roaring in panic as they were hurled upwards and over into the flames.

'No ... stop this, they're innocent! For the love of God, stop, innocent! ...' He was screaming, but now his time had come. They were lifting him as he struggled, and he was flung up and up to fall down into the blast.

'Master, help me!' Then all words giving way to one wailing cry.

Thrashing, screaming, mad.

But he had been taken out of it. Snatched back into life. And he lay on the ground looking at the sky. The flames licked the stars, it seemed, but he was far away from them, and couldn't even feel the heat anymore. He could smell his burnt clothing and his burnt hair. The pain in his face and hands was the worst and the blood was leaking out of him and he could scarcely move his lips ...

'... All thy Master's vain works destroyed, all the vain creations which he made among mortals with his Dark Powers, images of angels and saints and living mortals! Wilt thou, too, be destroyed? Or serve Satan? Make thy choice. Thou hast tasted the fire, and the fire waits for thee, hungry for thee. Hell waits for thee. Wilt thou make thy choice?'

'... yes ...'

'... to serve Satan as he is meant to be served.'

'Yes ...'

'... That all things of the world are vanity, and thou shalt never use thy Dark Powers for any mortal vanity, not to paint, not to create music, not to dance, nor to recite for the amusement of mortals but only and forever in the service of Satan, thy Dark Powers to seduce and to terrify and to destroy, only to destroy ...'

'Yes ...'

'... consecrated to thy one and only master, Satan, Satan forever, always and forever ... to serve thy true master in darkness and pain and in suffering, to surrender thy mind and thy heart ...'

'Yes.'

'And to keep from thy brethren in Satan no secret, to yield all knowledge of the blasphemer and his burden ...'

Silence.

'To yield all knowledge of the burden, child! Come now, the flames wait.'

'I do not understand you ...'

'Those Who Must Be Kept. Tell.'

'Tell what? I do not know anything, except that I do not wish to suffer. I am so afraid.'

'The truth, Child of Darkness. Where are they? Where are Those Who Must Be Kept?'

'I do not know. Look into my mind if you have that same power. There is nothing I can tell.'

'But *what*, child, *what* are they? Did he never tell you? *What* are Those Who Must Be Kept?'

And so they did not understand it either. It was no more than a phrase to them as it was to him. *When you are powerful enough that no one can ever take the knowledge from you against your will.* The Master had been wise.

'What is its meaning? Where are they? We must have the answer.'

'I swear to you, I do not have it. I swear on my fear which is all I possess now, I do not know!'

White faces appearing above him, one at a time. The tasteless lips giving hard, sweet kisses, hands stroking him, and from their wrists the glittering droplets of blood. They wanted the truth to come out in the blood. But what did it matter? The blood was the blood.

'Thou art the devil's child now.'

'Yes.'

'Don't weep for thy master, Marius. Marius is in hell where he belongs. Now drink the healing blood and rise and dance with thine own kind for the glory of Satan! And immortality will be truly thine!'

'Yes' — the blood burning his tongue as he lifted his head, the blood filling him with tortuous slowness. 'Oh, please.'

All around him Latin phrases, and the low beat of drums. They were satisfied. They knew he had spoken the truth. They would not kill him and the ecstasy dimmed all considerations. The pain in his hands and his face had melted into this ecstasy—

'Rise, young one, and join the Children of Darkness.'

'Yes, I do.' White hands reaching for his hands. Horns and lutes shrilling over the thud of the drums, the harps plucked into an hypnotic strumming as the circle commenced to move. Hooded figures in mendicant black, robes flowing as they lifted their knees high and bent their backs.

And breaking hands, they whirled, leapt, and came down again, spinning round and round, and a humming song rose louder and louder from their closed lips.

The circle swept on faster. The humming was a great melancholy vibration without shape or continuity and yet it seemed to be a form of speaking, to be the very echo of thought. Louder and louder it came like a moan that could not break into a cry.

He was making the same sound with it, and then turning, and dizzy with turning, he leapt high into the air. Hands caught him, lips kissed him, he was whirling about and pulled along by the others, someone crying out in Latin, another answering, another crying louder, and another answer coming again.

He was flying, no longer bound to the earth and the awful pain of his Master's death, and the death of the paintings, and death of the mortals he loved. The wind sailed past him, and the heat blasted his face and eyes. But the singing was so beautiful that it didn't matter that he didn't know the words, or that he couldn't pray to Satan, didn't know how to believe or make such a prayer. No one knew that he didn't know and they were all in a chorus together and they cried and lamented and turned and leapt again and then, swaying back and forth, threw their heads back as the fire blinded them and licked them and someone shouted 'Yes, YES!'

And the music surged. A barbarous rhythm broke loose all around him from drums and tambourines, voices in lurid rushing melody at last. The vampires threw up their arms, howled, figures flickering past him in riotous contortions, backs arched, heels stomping. The jubilation of imps in hell. It horrified him and it called to him, and when the hands clutched at him and swung him around, he stomped and twisted and danced like the others, letting the pain course through him, bending his limbs and giving the alarm to his cries.

And before dawn, he was delirious, and he had a dozen brothers around him, caressing him and soothing him, and leading him down a staircase that had opened in the bowels of the earth.

IT SEEMED that some time in the months that followed Armand dreamed his Master had not been burnt to death.

He dreamed his Master had fallen from the roof, a blazing comet, into the saving waters of the canal below. And deep in the mountains of northern Italy, his Master survived. His Master called to him to come. His Master was in the sanctuary of Those Who Must Be Kept.

Sometimes in the dream his Master was as powerful and radiant as he had ever been; beauty seemed his raiment. And at others he was burnt black and shriveled, a breathing cinder, his eyes huge and yellow, and only his white hair as lustrous and full as it had been. He crept along the ground in his weakness, pleading for Armand to help him. And behind him, warm light spilled from the sanctuary of Those Who Must Be Kept; there came the smell of incense, and there seemed some promise of ancient magic there, some promise of cold and exotic beauty beyond all evil and all good.

But these were vain imaginings. His Master had told him that fire and the light of the sun could destroy them, and he himself had seen his Master in flames. It was like wishing for his mortal life to come again to have these dreams.

And when his eyes were open on the moon and the stars, and the still mirror of the sea before him, he knew no hope, and no grief, and no joy. All those things had come from the Master, and the Master was no more.

'I am the devil's child.' That was poetry. All will was extinguished in him, and there was nothing but the dark confraternity, and the kill was now of the innocent as well as the guilty. The kill was above all cruel.

In Rome in the great coven in the catacombs, he bowed before Santino, the leader, who came down the stone steps to receive him with outstretched arms. This great one had been Born to Darkness in the time of the Black Death, and he told Armand of the vision that had come to him in the year 1349 when the plague raged, that we were to be as the Black Death itself, a vexation without explanation, to cause man to doubt the mercy and intervention of God.

Into the sanctum lined with human skulls Santino took Armand, telling him of the history of the vampires.

From all times we have existed, as wolves have, a scourge of mortals. And in the coven of Rome, dark shadow of the Roman Church, lay our final perfection.

Armand already knew the rituals and common prohibitions; now he must learn the great laws:

One — that each coven must have its leader and only he might order the working of the Dark Trick upon a mortal, seeing that the methods and the rituals were properly observed.

Two — that the Dark Gifts must never be given to the crippled, the maimed, or to children, or to those who cannot, even with the Dark Powers, survive on their own. Be it further understood that all mortals who would receive the Dark Gifts should be beautiful in person so that the insult to God might be greater when the Dark Trick is done.

Three — that never should an old vampire work this magic

lest the blood of the fledgeling be too strong. For all our gifts increase naturally with age, and the old ones have too much strength to pass on. Injury, burning — these catastrophes, if they do not destroy the Child of Satan will only increase his powers when he is healed. Yet Satan guards the flock from the power of old ones, for almost all, without exception, go mad.

In this particular, let Armand observe that there was no vampire then living who was more than three hundred years old. No one alive then could remember the first Roman coven. The devil frequently calls his vampires home.

But let Armand understand here also that the effect of the Dark Trick is unpredictable, even when passed on by the very young vampire and with all due care. For reasons no one knows, some mortals when Born to Darkness become as powerful as Titans, others may be no more than corpses that move. That is why mortals must be chosen with skill. Those with great passion and indomitable will should be avoided as well as those who have none.

Four — that no vampire may ever destroy another vampire, except that the coven master has the power of life and death over all of his flock. And it is, further, his obligation to lead the old ones and the mad ones into the fire when they can no longer serve Satan as they should. It is his obligation to destroy all vampires who are not properly made. It is his obligation to destroy those who are so badly wounded that they cannot survive on their own. And it is his obligation finally to seek the destruction of all outcasts and all who have broken these laws.

Five — that no vampire shall ever reveal his true nature to a mortal and allow that mortal to live. No vampire must ever reveal the history of the vampires to a mortal and let the mortal live. No vampire must commit to writing the history of the vampires or any true knowledge of vampires lest such a history be found by mortals and believed. And a vampire's name must never be known to mortals, save from his tombstone, and never must any vampire reveal to mortals the location of his or any other vampire's lair.

These then were the great commandments, which all vampires must obey. And this was the condition of existence among all the Undead.

Yet Armand should know that there had always been stories of ancient ones, heretic vampires of frightening power who submitted to no authority, not even that of the devil — vampires who had survived for thousands of years. Children of the Millennia, they were sometimes called. In the north of Europe there were tales of Mael, who dwelt in the forests of England and Scotland; and in Asia Minor the legend of Pandora. And in Egypt, the ancient tale of the vampire Ramses, seen again in this very time.

In all parts of the world one found such tales. And one could easily dismiss them as fanciful save for one thing. The ancient heretic Marius had been found in Venice, and there punished by the Children of Darkness. The legend of Marius had been true. But Marius was no more.

Armand said nothing to this last judgement. He did not tell Santino of the dreams he had had. In truth the dreams had dimmed inside Armand as had the colours of Marius's paintings. They were no longer held in Armand's mind or heart to be discovered by others who might try to see.

When Santino spoke of Those Who Must Be Kept, Armand again confessed that he did not know the meaning of it. Neither did Santino, nor any vampire that Santino had ever known.

Dead was the secret. Dead was Marius. And so consign to silence the old and useless mystery. Satan is our Lord and Master. In Satan, all is understood and all is known.

Armand pleased Santino. He memorized the laws, perfected his performance of the ceremonial incantations, the rituals, and the prayers. He saw the greatest Sabbats he was ever to witness. And he learned from the most powerful and skillful and beautiful vampires he was ever to know. He learned so well that he became a missionary sent out to gather the vagrant Children of Darkness into covens, and guide others in the performance of the Sabbat, and the working of the Dark Trick when the world and the flesh and the devil called for it to be done.

In Spain and in Germany and in France, he had taught the

Dark Blessings and Dark Rituals, and he had known savage and tenacious Children of Darkness, and dim flames had flared in him in their company and in those moments when the coven surrounded him, comforted by him, deriving its unity from his strength.

He had perfected the act of killing beyond the abilities of all the Children of Darkness that he knew. He had learned to summon those who truly wished to die. He had but to stand near the dwellings of mortals and call silently to see his victim appear.

Old, young, wretched, diseased, the ugly or the beautiful, it did not matter because he did not choose. Dazzling visions he gave, if they should want to receive, but he did not move towards them nor even close his arms around them. Drawn inexorably towards him, it was they who embraced him. And when their warm living flesh touched him, when he opened his lips and felt the blood spill, he knew the only surcease from misery that he could know.

It seemed to him in the best of these moments that his way was profoundly spiritual, uncontaminated by the appetites and confusions that made up the world, despite the carnal rapture of the kill.

In that act the spiritual and the carnal came together, and it was the spiritual, he was convinced, that survived. Holy Communion it seemed to him, the Blood of the Children of Christ serving only to bring the essence of life itself into his understanding for the split second in which death occurred. Only the great saints of God were his equals in this spirituality, this confrontation with mystery, this existence of meditation and denial.

Yet he had seen the greatest of his companions vanish, bring destruction upon themselves, go mad. He had witnessed the inevitable dissolution of covens, seen immortality defeat the most perfectly made Children of Darkness, and it seemed at times some awesome punishment that it never defeated him.

Was he destined to be one of the ancient ones? The Children of the Millennia? Could one believe those stories which persisted still?

Now and then a roaming vampire would speak of the fabled Pandora glimpsed in the far-off Russian city of Moscow, or of Mael living on the bleak English coast. The wanderers told even of Marius — that he had been seen again in Egypt, or in Greece. But these storytellers had not themselves laid eyes upon the legendary ones. They knew nothing really. These were often-repeated tales.

They did not distract or amuse the obedient servant of Satan. In quiet allegiance to the Dark Ways, Armand continued to serve.

Yet in the centuries of his long obedience, Armand kept two secrets to himself. These were his property, these secrets, more purely his than the coffin in which he locked himself by day, or the few amulets he wore.

The first was that no matter how great his loneliness, or how long the search for brothers and sisters in whom he might find some comfort, he never worked the Dark Trick himself. He wouldn't give that to Satan, no Child of Darkness made by him.

And the other secret, which he kept from his followers for their sake, was simply the extent of his ever deepening despair.

That he craved nothing, cherished nothing, believed nothing finally, and took not one particle of pleasure in his ever increasing and awesome powers, and existed from moment to moment in a void broken once every night of his eternal life by the kill — that secret he had kept from them as long as they had needed him and it had been possible to lead them because his fear would have made them afraid.

But it was finished.

A great cycle had ended, and even years ago he had felt it closing without understanding it was a cycle at all.

From Rome there came the garbled travellers' accounts, old when they were told to him, that the leader, Santino, had abandoned his flock. Some said he had gone mad into the countryside, others that he had leapt into the fire, others that 'the world' had swallowed him, that he had been borne off in a black coach with mortals never to be seen again.

'We go into the fire or we go into legend,' said a teller of the tale.

Then came accounts of chaos in Rome, of dozens of leaders who put on the black hood and the black robes to preside over the coven. And then it seemed there were none.

Since the year 1700 there had been no word anymore from Italy. For half a century Armand had not been able to trust his passion or that of the others around him to create the frenzy of the true Sabbat. And he had dreamed of his old Master, Marius, in those rich robes of red velvet, and seen the palazzo full of vibrant paintings, and he had been afraid.

Then another had come.

His children rushed down into the cellars beneath les Innocents to describe to him this new vampire, who wore a fur-lined cloak of red velvet and could profane the churches and strike down those who wore crosses and walk in the places of light. Red velvet. It was mere coincidence, and yet it maddened him and seemed an insult to him, a gratuitous pain that his soul couldn't bear.

And then the woman had been made, the woman with the hair of a lion and the name of an angel, beautiful and powerful as her son.

And he had come up the stairway out of the catacomb, leading the band against us, as the hooded ones had come to destroy him and his Master in Venice centuries before.

And it had failed.

He stood dressed in these strange lace and brocade garments. He carried coins in his pockets. His mind swam with images from the thousands of books he had read. And he felt himself pierced with all he had witnessed in the places of light in the great city called Paris, and it was as if he could hear his old Master whispering in his ear:

But a millennium of nights will be yours to see light as no mortal has ever seen it, to snatch from the distant stars as if you were Prometheus an endless illumination by which to understand all things.

'All things have eluded my understanding,' he said. 'I am as one whom the earth has given back, and you, Lestat and Gabrielle, are like the images painted by my old Master in cerulean and carmine and gold.'

He stood still in the doorway, his hands on the backs of his arms, and he was looking at us, asking silently:

What is there to know? What is there to give? We are the aban-doned of God. And there is no Devil's Road spinning out before me and there are no bells of hell ringing in my ears.

4

AN HOUR passed. Perhaps more. Armand sat by the fire. No marks any longer on his face from the long-forgotten battle. He seemed, in his stillness, to be as fragile as an emptied shell.

Gabrielle sat across from him, and she too stared at the flames in silence, her face weary and seemingly compassionate. It was painful for me not to know her thoughts.

I was thinking of Marius. And Marius and Marius ... the vampire who had painted pictures in and of the real world. Triptychs, portraits, frescoes on the walls of his palazzo.

And the real world had never suspected him nor hunted him nor cast him out. It was this band of hooded fiends who came to burn the paintings, the ones who shared the Dark Gift with him — had he himself ever called it the Dark Gift — they were the ones who said he couldn't live and create among mortals. Not mortals.

I saw the little stage at Renaud's and I heard myself sing and the singing become a roar. Nicolas said, 'It is splendid.' I said, 'It is petty.' And it was like striking Nicolas. In my imagination he said what he had not said that night. 'Let me have what I can believe in. You would never do that.'

The triptychs of Marius were in churches and convent chapels, maybe on the walls of the great houses in Venice and Padua. The vampires would not have gone into holy places to pull them down. So they were there somewhere, with a signa-ture perhaps worked into the detail, these creations of the vampire who surrounded himself with mortal apprentices, kept a mortal lover from whom he took a little drink, went out alone to kill.

I thought of the night in the inn when I had seen the meaninglessness of life, and the soft fathomless despair of Armand's story seemed an ocean in which I might drown. This was worse than the blasted shore in Nicki's mind. This was for three centuries, this darkness, this nothingness.

The radiant auburn-haired child by the fire could open his mouth again and out would come blackness like ink to cover the world.

That is, if there had not been this protagonist, this Venetian master, who had committed the heretical act of making meaning on the panels he painted — it had to be meaning — and our own kind, the elect of Satan, had made him into a living torch.

Had Gabrielle seen these paintings in the story as I had seen them? Did they burn in her mind's eye as they did in mine?

Marius was travelling some route into my soul that would let him roam there forever, along with the hooded fiends who turned the paintings into chaos again.

In a dull sort of misery, I thought of the travellers' tales — that Marius was alive, seen in Egypt or Greece.

I wanted to ask Armand, wasn't it possible? Marius must have been so very strong ... But it seemed disrespectful of him to ask.

'Old legend,' he whispered. His voice was as precise as the inner voice. Unhurriedly, he continued without ever looking away from the flames. 'Legend from the olden times before they destroyed us both.'

'Perhaps not,' I said. Echo of the visions, paintings on the walls. 'Maybe Marius is alive.'

'We are miracles or horrors,' he said quietly, 'depending upon how you wish to see us. And when you first *know* about us, whether it's through the dark blood or promises or visitations, you think anything is possible. But that isn't so. The world closes tight around this miracle soon enough; and you don't hope for other miracles. That is, you become accustomed to the new limits and the limits define everything once again. So they say Marius continues. They all continue some-

335

where, that's what you *want* to believe.

'Not a single one remains in the coven in Rome from those nights when I was taught the ritual; and maybe the coven itself is no longer even there. Years and years have passed since there was any communication from the coven. But they all exist somewhere, don't they? After all, we can't die.' He sighed. 'Doesn't matter,' he said.

Something greater and more terrible mattered, that this despair might crush Armand beneath it. That in spite of the thirst in him now, the blood lost when we had fought together, and the silent furnace of his body healing the bruises and the broken flesh, he could not will himself into the world above to hunt. Rather suffer the thirst and the heat of the silent furnace. Rather stay here and be with us.

But he already knew the answer, that he could not be with us.

Gabrielle and I didn't have to speak to let him know. We did not even have to resolve the question in our minds. He knew, the way God might know the future because God is the possessor of all the facts.

Unbearable anguish. And Gabrielle's expression all the more weary, sad.

'You know that with all my soul I do want to take you with us,' I said. I was surprised at my own emotion. 'But it would be disaster for us all.'

No change in him. He knew. No challenge from Gabrielle.

'I cannot *stop* thinking of Marius,' I confessed.

I know. And you do not think of Those Who Must Be Kept, which is most strange.

'That is merely another mystery,' I said. 'And there are a thousand mysteries. I think of Marius! And I'm too much the slave of my own obsessions and fascination. It's a dreadful thing to linger so on Marius, to extract that one radiant figure from the tale.'

Doesn't matter. If it pleases you, take it. I do not lose what I give.

'When a being reveals his pain in such a torrent, you are bound to respect the whole of the tragedy. You have to try to comprehend. And such helplessness, such despair is almost

336

incomprehensible to me. That's why I think of Marius. Marius I understand. You I don't understand.'

Why?

Silence.

Didn't he deserve the truth?

'I've been a rebel always,' I said. 'You've been the slave of everything that ever claimed you.'

'I was the leader of my coven!'

'No. You were the slave of Marius and then of the Children of Darkness. You fell under the spell of one and then the other. What you suffer now is the absence of a spell. I think I shudder that you caused me so to understand it for a little while, to know it as if I were a different being than I am.'

'Doesn't matter,' he said, eyes still on the fire. 'You think too much in terms of decision and action. This tale is no explanation. And I am not a being who requires a respectful acknowledgement in your thoughts or in words. And we all know the answer you have given is too immense to be voiced and we all three of us know that it is final. What I don't know is why. So I am a creature very different from you, and so you cannot understand me. Why can't I go with you? I will do whatever you wish if you take me with you. I will be under your spell.'

I thought of Marius with his brush and the pots of egg tempera.

'How could you have ever believed anything that they told you after they burned those paintings?' I asked. 'How could you have given yourself over to them?'

Agitation, rising anger.

Caution in Gabrielle's face, but not fear.

'And you, when you stood on the stage and you saw the audience screaming to get out of the theatre — how my followers described this to me, the vampire terrifying the crowd and the crowd streaming into the boulevard du Temple — what did you believe? That you did not belong among mortals, that's what you believed. You knew you did not. And there was no band of fiends in hooded robes to tell you. You knew. So Marius did not belong among mortals. So I did not.'

'Ah, but it's different.'

'No, it is not. That's why you scorn the Theatre of the Vampires which is now at this very moment working out its little dramas to bring in the gold from the boulevard crowds. You do not wish to deceive as Marius deceived. It divides you ever more from mankind. You want to pretend to be mortal, but to deceive makes you angry and it makes you kill.'

'In that moment on the stage,' I said, 'I revealed *myself*. I did the very opposite of deceiving. I wanted somehow in mankind manifest the monstrosity of myself to be joined with my fellow humans again. Better they should run from me than not see me. Better they should know I was something monstrous than for me to glide through the world unrecognized by those upon whom I preyed.'

'But it was not better.'

'No. What Marius did was better. He did not deceive.'

'Of course he did. He fooled everyone!'

'No. He found a way to imitate mortal life. To be one with mortals. He slew only the evildoer, and he painted as mortals paint. Angels and blue skies, clouds, those are the things you made me see when you were telling. He created good things. And I see wisdom in him and a lack of vanity. He did not need to reveal himself. He had lived a thousand years and he believed more in the vistas of heaven that he painted than in himself.'

Confusion.

Doesn't matter now, devils who paint angels.

'Those are only metaphors,' I said. 'And it does matter! If you are to rebuild, if you are to find the Devil's Road again, it does matter! There are ways for us to exist. If I could only imitate life, just find a way ...'

'You say things that mean nothing to me. We are the abandoned of God.'

Gabrielle glanced at him suddenly. 'Do you *believe* in God?' she asked.

'Yes, always in God,' he answered. 'It is Satan — our master — who is the fiction and that is the fiction which has betrayed me.'

338

'Oh, then you are truly damned,' I said. 'And you know full well that your retreat into the fraternity of the Children of Darkness was a retreat from a sin that was not a sin.'

Anger.

'Your heart breaks for something you'll never have,' he countered, his voice rising suddenly. 'You brought Gabrielle and Nicolas over the barrier to you, but you could not go back.'

'Why is it you don't harken to your own story?' I asked. 'Is it that you have never forgiven Marius for not warning you about them, letting you fall into their hands? You will never take anything, not example or inspiration, from Marius again? I am not Marius, but I tell you since I set my feet on the Devil's Road, I have heard of only one elder who could teach me anything, and that is Marius, your Venetian master. He is talking to me now. He is saying something to me of a way to be immortal.'

'Mockery.'

'No. It wasn't mockery! And you are the one whose heart breaks for what he will never have: another body of belief, another spell.'

No answer.

'We cannot be Marius for you,' I said, 'or the dark lord, Santino. We are not artists with a great vision that will carry you forward. And we are not evil coven masters with the conviction to condemn a legion to perdition. And this domination — this glorious mandate — is what you must have.'

I had risen to my feet without meaning to. I had come close to the fireplace and I was looking down at him.

And I saw, out of the corner of my eye, Gabrielle's subtle nod of approval, and the way that she closed her eyes for a moment as if she were allowing herself a sigh of relief.

He was perfectly still.

'You have to suffer through this emptiness,' I said, 'and find what impels you to continue. If you come with us we will fail you and you will destroy us.'

'How suffer through it?' He looked up at me and his eyebrows came together in the most poignant frown. 'How do I begin? You move like the right hand of God! But for me the world, the real world in which Marius lived, is beyond reach. I never lived in it. I push against the glass. But how do I get in?'

'I can't tell you that,' I said.

'You have to study this age,' Gabrielle interrupted. Her voice was calm but commanding.

He looked towards her as she spoke.

'You have to understand the age,' she continued, 'through its literature and its music and its art. You have to come up out of the earth, as you yourself put it. Now live in the world.'

No answer from him. Flash of Nicki's ravaged flat with all its books on the floor. Western civilization in heaps.

'And what better place is there than the centre of things, the boulevard and the theatre?' Gabrielle asked.

He frowned, his head turning dismissively, but she pressed on.

'Your gift is for leading the coven, and your coven is still there.'

He made a soft despairing sound.

'Nicolas is a fledgeling,' she said. 'He can teach them much about the world outside, but he cannot really lead them. The woman, Eleni, is amazingly clever, but she will make way for you.'

'What is it to me, their games?' he whispered.

'It is a way to exist,' she said. 'And that is all that matters to you now.'

'The Theatre of the Vampires! I should rather the fire.'

'Think of it,' she said. 'There's a perfection in it you can't deny. We are illusions of what is mortal, and the stage is an illusion of what is real.'

'It's an abomination,' he said. 'What did Lestat call it? Petty?'

'That was to Nicolas because Nicolas would build fantastical philosophies upon it,' she said. 'You must live now without fantastical philosophies, the way you did when you were Marius's apprentice. Live to learn the age. And Lestat does not believe in the value of evil. But you do believe in it. I know that you do.'

340

'I am evil,' he said half smiling. He almost laughed. 'It's not a matter of belief, is it? But do you think I could go from the spiritual path I followed for three centuries to voluptuousness and debauchery such as that? We were the saints of evil,' he protested. 'I will not be common evil. I will not.'

'Make it uncommon,' she said. She was getting too impatient. 'If you are evil, how can voluptuousness and debauchery be your enemies? Don't the world, the flesh, and the devil conspire equally against man?'

He shook his head, as if to say he did not care.

'You are more concerned with what is spiritual than with evil,' I interjected, watching him closely. 'Is that not so?'

'Yes,' he said at once.

'But don't you see, the colour of wine in a crystal glass can be spiritual,' I continued. 'The look in a face, the music of a violin. A Paris theatre can be infused with the spiritual for all its solidity. There's nothing in it that hasn't been shaped by the power of those who possessed spiritual visions of what it could be.'

Something quickened in him, but he pushed it away.

'Seduce the public with voluptuousness,' Gabrielle said. 'For God's sake, and the devil's, use the power of the theatre as you will.'

'Weren't the paintings of your master spiritual?' I asked. I could feel a warming in myself now at the thought of it. 'Can anyone look on the great works of that time and not call them spiritual?'

'I have asked myself that question,' Armand answered, 'many times. Was it spiritual or was it voluptuous? Was the angel painted on the triptych caught in the material, or was the material transformed?'

'No matter what they did to you after, you never doubted the beauty and the value of his work,' I said. 'I know you didn't. And it was the material transformed. It ceased to be paint and it became magic, just as in the kill the blood ceases to be blood and becomes life.'

His eyes misted, but no visions came from him. Whatever road he travelled back in his thoughts, he travelled alone.

'The carnal and the spiritual,' Gabrielle said, 'come together in the theatre as they do in the paintings. Sensual fiends we are by our very nature. Take this as your key.'

He closed his eyes for a moment as if he would shut us out.

'Go to them and listen to the music that Nicki makes,' she said. 'Make art with them in the Theatre of the Vampires. You have to pass away from what failed you into what can sustain you. Otherwise — there is no hope.'

I wished she had not said it so abruptly, brought it so to the point.

But he nodded and his lips pressed together in a bitter smile.

'The only thing really important for you,' she said slowly, 'is that you go to an extreme.'

He stared at her blankly. He could not possibly understand what she meant by this. And I thought it too brutal a truth to say. But he didn't resist it. His face became thoughtful and smooth and childlike again.

For a long time he looked at the fire. Then he spoke:

'But why must you go at all?' he asked. 'No one is at war with you now. No one is trying to drive you out. Why can't you build it with me, this little enterprise?'

Did that mean he would do it, go to the others and become part of the theatre in the boulevard?

He didn't contradict me. He was asking again why couldn't I create the imitation of life, if that was what I wanted to call it, right in the boulevard?

But he was also giving up. He knew I couldn't endure the sight of the theatre, or the sight of Nicolas. I couldn't even really urge him towards it. Gabrielle had done that. And he knew that it was too late to press us anymore.

Finally Gabrielle said:

'We can't live among our own kind, Armand.'

And I thought, yes, that is the truest answer of all, and I don't know why I couldn't speak it aloud.

'The Devil's Road is what we want,' she said. 'And we are enough for each other now. Maybe years and years into the future, when we've been a thousand places and seen a thousand things, we'll come back. We'll talk then together as we have tonight.'

This came as no real shock to him. But it was impossible now to know what he thought.

For a long time we didn't speak. I don't know how long we remained quiet together in the room.

I tried not to think of Marius anymore, or of Nicolas either. All sense of danger was gone now, but I was afraid of the parting, of the sadness of it, of the feeling that I had taken from this creature his astonishing story and given him precious little for it in return.

It was Gabrielle who finally broke the quiet. She rose and moved gracefully to the bench beside him.

'Armand,' she said. 'We are going. If I have my way we'll be miles from Paris before midnight tomorrow night.'

He looked at her with calm and acceptance. Impossible to know now what he chose to conceal.

'Even if you do not go to the theatre,' she said, 'accept the things that we can give you. My son has wealth enough to make an entrance into the world very easy for you.'

'You can take this tower for your lair,' I said. 'Use it as long as you wish. Magnus found it safe enough.'

After a moment, he nodded with a grave politeness, but he didn't say anything.

'Let Lestat give you the gold needed to make you a gentleman,' Gabrielle said. 'And all we ask in return is that you leave the coven in peace if you do not choose to lead it.'

He was looking at the fire again, face tranquil, irresistibly beautiful. Then again he nodded in silence. And the nod itself meant no more than that he had heard, not that he would promise anything.

'If you will not go to them,' I said slowly, 'then do not hurt them. Do not hurt Nicolas.'

And when I spoke these words, his face changed very subtly. It was almost a smile that crept over his features. And his eyes shifted slowly to me. And I saw the scorn in them.

I looked away but the look had affected me as much as a blow.

'I don't want him to be harmed,' I said in a tense whisper.

'No. You want him destroyed,' he whispered back. 'So that you need never fear or grieve for him anymore.' And the look of scorn sharpened hideously.

Gabrielle intervened.

'Armand,' she said, 'he is not dangerous to them. The woman alone can control him. And he has things to teach all of you about this time if you will listen.'

They looked at each other for some time in silence. And again his face was soft and gentle and beautiful.

And in a strangely decorous manner he took Gabrielle's hand and held it firmly. Then they stood up together, and he let her hand go, and he drew a little away from her and squared his shoulders. He looked at both of us.

'I'll go to them,' he said in the softest voice. 'And I will take the gold you offer me, and I will seek refuge in this tower. And I will learn from your passionate fledgeling whatever he has to teach me. But I reach for these things only because they float on the surface of the darkness in which I am drowning. And I would not descend without some finer understanding. I would not leave eternity to you without ... without some final battle.'

I studied him. But no thoughts came from him to clarify these words.

'Maybe as the years pass,' he said, 'desire will come again to me. I will know appetite again, even passion. Maybe when we meet in another age, these things will not be abstract and fleeting. I'll speak with a vigour that matches yours, instead of merely reflecting it. And we will ponder matters of immortality and wisdom. We will talk about vengeance or acceptance then. For now it's enough for me to say that I want to see you again. I want our paths to cross in the future. And for that reason alone, I will do as you ask and not what you want: I will spare your ill-fated Nicolas.'

I gave an audible sigh of relief. Yet his tone was so changed, so strong, that it sounded a deep silent alarm in me. This was the coven master, surely, this quiet and forceful one, the one who would survive, no matter how the orphan in him wept.

But then he smiled slowly and gracefully, and there was

something sad and endearing in his face. He became the da Vinci saint again, or more truly the little god from Caravaggio. And it seemed for a moment he couldn't be anything evil or dangerous. He was too radiant, too full of all that was wise and good.

'Remember my warnings,' he said. 'Not my curses.'

Gabrielle and I both nodded.

'And when you have need of me,' he said, 'I will be here.'

Then Gabrielle did the totally surprising thing of embracing him and kissing him. And I did the same.

He was pliant and gentle and loving in our arms. And he let us know without words that he was going to the coven, and we could find him there tomorrow night.

The next moment he was gone, and Gabrielle and I were there alone together, as if he'd never been in the room. I could hear no sound anywhere in the tower. Nothing but the wind in the forest beyond.

And when I climbed the steps, I found the gate open and the fields stretching to the woods in unbroken quiet.

I loved him. I knew it, as incomprehensible to me as he was. But I was so glad it was finished. So glad that we could go on. Yet I held to the bars for a long time just looking at the distant woods, and the dim glow far beyond that the city made upon the lowering clouds.

And the grief I felt was not only for the loss of him, it was for Nicki, and for Paris, and for myself.

5

WHEN I came back down to the crypt I saw her building up the fire again with the last of the wood. In a slow, weary fashion, she stoked the blaze, and the light was red on her profile and in her eyes.

I sat quietly on the bench watching her, watching the explosion of sparks against the blackened bricks.

'Did he give you what you wanted?' I asked.

'In his own way, yes,' she said. She put the poker aside and sat down opposite, her hair spilling down over her shoulders as she rested her hands beside her on the bench. 'I tell you, I don't care if I never look upon another one of our kind,' she said coldly. 'I am done with their legends, their curses, their sorrows. And done with their insufferable humanity, which may be the most astonishing thing they've revealed. I'm ready for the world again, Lestat, as I was on the night I died.'

'But Marius—' I said excitedly. 'Mother, there are ancient ones — ones who have used immortality in a wholly different way.'

'Are there?' she asked. 'Lestat, you're too generous with your imagination. The story of Marius has the quality of a fairy tale.'

'No, that's not true.'

'So the orphan demon claims descent not from the filthy peasant devils he resembles,' she said, 'but from a lost lord, almost a god. I tell you any dirty-faced village child dreaming at the kitchen fire can tell you tales like that.'

'Mother, he couldn't have invented Marius,' I said. 'I may have a great deal of imagination, but he has almost none. He couldn't have made up the images. I tell you he saw those things ...'

'I hadn't thought of it exactly that way,' she admitted with a little smile. 'But he could well have borrowed Marius from the legends he heard ...'

'No,' I said. 'There was a Marius and there is a Marius still. And there are others like him. There are Children of the Millennia who have done better than those Children of Darkness with the gifts given them.'

'Lestat, what is important is that *we* do better,' she said. 'All I learned from Armand, finally, was that immortals find death seductive and ultimately irresistible, that they fail to conquer death or humanity in their minds. Now I want to take that knowledge and wear it like armour as I move through the world. And luckily, I don't mean the world of change which these creatures have found so dangerous. I mean the world that for eons has been the same.'

She tossed her hair back as she looked at the fire again. 'It's of snow-covered mountains I dream,' she said softly, 'of desert wastes — of impenetrable jungles, or the great north woods of America where they say white men have never been.' Her face warmed just a little as she looked at me. 'Think on it,' she said. 'There is nowhere that we cannot go. And if the Children of the Millennia do exist, maybe that is where they are — far from the world of men.'

'And how do they live if they are?' I asked. I was picturing my own world and it was full of mortal beings, and the things that mortal beings made. 'It's man we feed on,' I said.

'There are hearts that beat in those forests,' she said dreamily. 'There is blood that flows for the one who takes it … I can do the things now that you used to do. I could fight those wolves on my own …' Her voice trailed off as she was lost in her thoughts. 'The important thing,' she said after a long moment, 'is that we can go wherever we wish now, Lestat. We're free.'

'I was free before,' I said. 'I never cared for what Armand had to tell. But Marius — I know that Marius is alive. I feel it. I felt it when Armand told the tale. And Marius knows things — and I don't mean just about us, or about Those Who Must Be Kept or whatever the old mystery — he knows things about life itself, about how to move through time.'

'So let him be your patron saint if you need it,' she said.

This angered me, and I didn't say anything more. The fact was her talk of jungles and forests frightened me. And all the things Armand said to divide us came back to me, just as I'd known they would when he had spoken his well-chosen words. And so we live with our differences, I thought, just as mortals do, and maybe our divisions are exaggerated as are our passions, as is our love.

'There was one inkling …' she said as she watched the fire, 'one little indication that the story of Marius had truth.'

'There were a thousand indications,' I said.

'He said that Marius slew the evildoer,' she continued, 'and he called the evildoer Typhon, the slayer of his brother. Do

347

you remember this?'

'I thought that he meant Cain who had slain Abel. It was Cain I saw in the images, though I heard the other name.'

'That's just it. Armand himself didn't understand the name Typhon. Yet he repeated it. But I know what it means.'

'Tell me.'

'It's from the Greek and Roman myths — the old story of the Egyptian god, Osiris, slain by his brother Typhon, so that he became lord of the Underworld. Of course Armand could have read it in Plutarch, but he didn't, that's the strange thing.'

'Ah, you see then, Marius did exist. When he said he'd lived for a millennium he was telling the truth.'

'Perhaps, Lestat, perhaps,' she said.

'Mother, tell me this again, this Egyptian story ...'

'Lestat, you have years to read all the old tales for yourself.' She rose and bent to kiss me, and I sensed the coldness and sluggishness in her that always came before dawn. 'As for me, I am done with books. They are what I read when I could do nothing else.' She took my two hands in hers. 'Tell me that we'll be on the road tomorrow. That we won't see the ramparts of Paris again until we've seen the other side of the world.'

'Exactly as you wish,' I said.

She started up the stairs.

'But where are you going?' I said as I followed her. She opened the gate and went out towards the trees.

'I want to see if I can sleep in the raw earth itself,' she said over her shoulder. 'If I don't rise tomorrow you'll know I failed.'

'But this is madness,' I said, coming after her. I hated the very idea of it. She went ahead into a thicket of old oaks, and kneeling, she dug into the dead leaves and damp soil with her hands. Ghastly she looked, as if she were a beautiful blond-haired witch scratching with the speed of a beast.

Then she rose and waved a farewell kiss to me. And commanding all her strength, she descended as if the earth belonged to her. And I was left staring in disbelief at the emptiness where she had been, and the leaves that had settled as if nothing had disturbed the spot.

* * *

I WALKED away from the woods. I walked south away from the tower. And as my step quickened, I started singing softly to myself some little song, maybe a bit of melody that the violins had played earlier this night in the Palais Royal.

And the sense of grief came back to me, the realization that we were really going, that it was finished with Nicolas and finished with the Children of Darkness and their leader, and I wouldn't see Paris again, or anything familiar to me, for years and years. And for all my desire to be free, I wanted to weep.

But it seems I had some purpose in my wandering that I hadn't admitted to myself. A half hour or so before the morning light I was on the post road near the ruin of an old inn. Falling down it was, this last outpost of an abandoned village, with only the heavily mortared walls left intact.

And taking out my dagger, I began to carve deep in the soft stone:

MARIUS, THE ANCIENT ONE: LESTAT IS SEARCHING FOR YOU, IT IS THE MONTH OF MAY, IN THE YEAR 1780 AND I GO SOUTH FROM PARIS TOWARDS LYONS. PLEASE MAKE YOURSELF KNOWN TO ME.

What arrogance it seemed when I stepped back from it. And I had already broken the dark commandments, telling the name of an immortal, and putting it into written words. Well, it gave me a wondrous satisfaction to do it. And after all, I had never been very good at obeying rules.

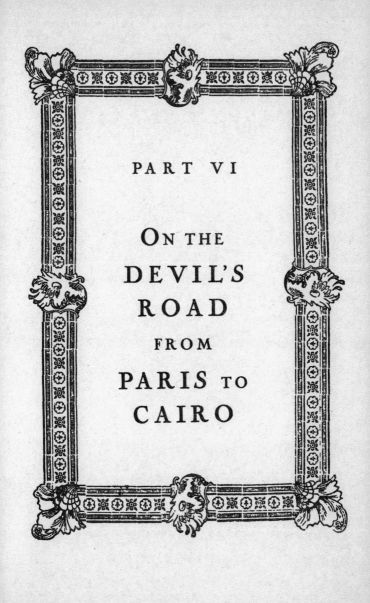

PART VI

ON THE
DEVIL'S
ROAD
FROM
PARIS TO
CAIRO

1

THE last time we saw Armand in the eighteenth century, he was standing with Eleni and Nicolas and the other vampire mummers before the door of Renaud's theatre, watching as our carriage made its way into the stream of traffic on the boulevard.

I'd found him earlier closeted in my old dressing room with Nicolas in the midst of a strange conversation dominated by Nicki's sarcasm and peculiar fire. He wore a wig and a sombre red frock coat, and it seemed to me that he had already acquired a new opacity, as if every waking moment since the death of the old coven was giving him greater substance and strength.

Nicki and I had no words for each other in these last awkward moments, but Armand politely accepted the keys of the tower from me, and a great quantity of money, and the promise of more when he wanted it from Roget.

His mind was closed to me, but he said again that Nicolas would come to no harm from him. And as we said our farewells, I believed that Nicolas and the little coven had every chance for survival and that Armand and I were friends.

BY THE end of that first night Gabrielle and I were far from Paris, as we vowed we would be, and in the months that followed, we went on to Lyons, Turin, and Vienna, and after that to Prague and Leipzig and St. Petersburg, and then south again to Italy, where we were to settle for many years.

Eventually we went on to Sicily, then north into Greece

and Turkey, and then south again through the ancient cities of Asia Minor and finally to Cairo, where we remained for some time.

And in all these places I was to write my messages to Marius on the walls.

Sometimes it was no more than a few words that I scratched with the tip of my knife. In other places, I spent hours chiseling my ruminations into the stone. But wherever I was, I wrote my name, the date, and my future destination, and my invitation: 'Marius, make yourself known to me.'

As for the old covens, we were to come upon them in a number of scattered places, but it was clear from the outset that the old ways were everywhere breaking down. Seldom more than three or four vampires carried on the old rituals, and when they came to realize that we wanted no part of them or their existence they let us alone.

Infinitely more interesting were the occasional rogues we glimpsed in the middle of society, lone and secretive vampires pretending to be mortal just as skillfully as we could pretend. But we never got close to these creatures. They ran from us as they must have from the old covens. And seeing nothing more than fear in their eyes, I wasn't tempted to give chase.

Yet it was strangely reassuring to know that I hadn't been the first aristocratic fiend to move through the ballrooms of the world in search of my victims — the deadly gentleman who would soon surface in stories and poetry and penny dreadful novels as the very epitome of our tribe. There were others appearing all the time.

But we were to encounter stranger creatures of darkness as we moved on. In Greece we found demons who did not know how they had been made, and sometimes even mad creatures without reason or language who attacked us as if we were mortal, and ran screaming from the prayers we said to drive them away.

The vampires in Istanbul actually dwelt in houses, safe behind high walls and gates, their graves in their gardens, and dressed as all humans do in that part of the world, in flowing robes, to hunt the nighttime streets.

Yet even they were quite horrified to see me living amongst the French and the Venetians, riding in carriages, joining the gatherings at the European embassies and homes. They menaced us, shouting incantations at us, and then ran in panic when we turned on them, only to come back and devil us again.

The revenants who haunted the Mameluke tombs in Cairo were beastly wraiths, held to the old laws by hollow-eyed masters who lived in the ruins of a Coptic monastery, their rituals full of Eastern magic and the evocation of many demons and evil spirits whom they called by strange names. They stayed clear of us, despite all their acidic threats, yet they knew our names.

As the years passed, we learned nothing from all these creatures, which of course was no great surprise to me.

And though vampires in many places had heard the legends of Marius and the other ancient ones, they had never seen such beings with their own eyes. Even Armand had become a legend to them, and they were likely to ask: 'Did you really see the vampire Armand?' Nowhere did I meet a truly old vampire. Nowhere did I meet a vampire who was in any way a magnetic creature, a being of great wisdom or special accomplishment, an unusual being in whom the Dark Gift had worked any perceivable alchemy that was of interest to me.

Armand was a dark god compared to these beings. And so was Gabrielle and so was I.

But I jump ahead of my tale.

Early on, when we first came into Italy, we gained a fuller and more sympathetic knowledge of the ancient rituals. The Roman coven came out to welcome us with open arms. 'Come to the Sabbat,' they said. 'Come into the catacombs and join in the hymns.'

Yes, they knew that we'd destroyed the Paris coven, and bested the great master of dark secrets, Armand. But they didn't despise us for it. On the contrary, they could not understand the cause of Armand's resignation of his power. Why hadn't the coven changed with the times?

For even here where the ceremonies were so elaborate and

sensuous that they took my breath away, the vampires, far from eschewing the ways of men, thought nothing of passing themselves off as human whenever it suited their purposes. It was the same with the two vampires we had seen in Venice, and the handful we were later to meet in Florence as well.

In black cloaks, they penetrated the crowds at the opera, the shadowy corridors of great houses during balls and banquets, and even sometimes sat amid the press in lowly taverns or wine shops, peering at humans quite close at hand. It was their habit here more than anywhere to dress in the costumes of the time of their birth, and they were often splendidly attired and most regal, possessing jewels and finery and showing it often to great advantage when they chose.

Yet they crept back to their stinking graveyards to sleep, and they fled screaming from any sign of heavenly power, and they threw themselves with savage abandon into their horrifying and beautiful Sabbats.

In comparison, the vampires of Paris had been primitive, coarse, and childlike; but I could see that it was the very sophistication and worldliness of Paris that had caused Armand and his flock to retreat so far from mortal ways.

As the French capital became secular, the vampires had clung to old magic, while the Italian fiends lived among deeply religious humans whose lives were drenched in Roman Catholic ceremony, men and women who respected evil as they respected the Roman Church. In sum the old ways of the fiends were not unlike the old ways of people in Italy, and so the Italian vampires moved in both worlds. Did they believe in the old ways? They shrugged. The Sabbat for them was a grand pleasure. Hadn't Gabrielle and I enjoyed it? Had we not finally joined in the dance?

'Come to us anytime that you wish,' the Roman vampires told us.

As for this Theatre of the Vampires in Paris, this great scandal which was shocking our kind the world over, well, they would believe *that* when they saw it with their own eyes. Vampires performing on a stage, vampires dazzling mortal audiences with tricks and mimicry -- they thought it was too terribly Parisian! They laughed.

OF COURSE I was hearing more directly about the theatre all the time. Before I'd even reached St. Petersburg, Roget had sent me a long testament to the 'cleverness' of the new troupe:

They have gotten themselves up like giant wooden marionettes [he wrote]. Gold cords come down from the rafters to their ankles and their wrists and the tops of their heads, and by these they appear to be manipulated in the most charming dances. They wear perfect circles of rouge on their white cheeks, and their eyes are wide as glass buttons. You cannot believe the perfection with which they make themselves appear inanimate.

But the orchestra is another marvel. Faces blank and painted in the very same style, the players imitate mechanical musicians — the jointed dolls one can buy that, on the winding of a key, saw away at their little instruments, or blow their little horns, to make real music!

It is such an engaging spectacle that ladies and gentlemen of the audience quarrel amongst themselves as to whether or not these players are dolls or real persons. Some aver that they are all made of wood and the voices coming out of the actors' mouths are the work of ventriloquists.

As for the plays themselves, they would be extremely unsettling were they not so beautiful and skillfully done.

There is one most popular drama they do which features a vampiric revenant, risen from the grave through a platform in the stage. Terrifying is the creature with rag mop hair and fangs. But lo, he falls in love at once with a giant wooden puppet woman, never guessing that she is not alive. Unable to drink blood from her throat, however, the poor vampire soon perishes, at which moment the marionette reveals that she does indeed live, though she is made of wood, and with an evil smile she performs a triumphant dance upon the body of the defeated fiend.

I tell you it makes the blood run cold to see it. Yet the audience screams and applauds.

In another little tableau, the puppet dancers make a circle about a human girl and entice her to let herself be bound up with golden cords as if she too were a marionette. The sorry result is that the strings make her dance till the life goes out of her body. She pleads with eloquent gestures to be released, but the real puppets only laugh and cavort as she expires.

The music is unearthly. It brings to mind the gypsies of the country fairs. Monsieur de Lenfent is the director. And it is the sound of his violin which often opens the evening fare.

I advise you as your attorney to claim some of the profits being made by this remarkable company. The lines for each performance stretch a considerable length down the boulevard.

Roget's letters always unsettled me. They left me with my heart tripping, and I couldn't help but wonder: What had I expected the troupe to do? Why did their boldness and inventiveness surprise me? We all had the power to do such things.

By the time I settled in Venice, where I spent a great deal of time looking in vain for Marius's paintings, I was hearing from Eleni directly, her letters inscribed with exquisite vampiric skill.

They were the most popular entertainment in night-time Paris, she wrote to me. 'Actors' had come from all over Europe to join them. So their troupe had swelled to twenty in number, which even that metropolis could scarce 'support'.

'Only the most clever artists are admitted, those who possess truly astonishing talent, but we prize discretion above all else. We do not like scandal, as you can well guess.'

As for their 'Dear Violinist', she wrote of him affectionately, saying he was their greatest inspiration, that he wrote the most ingenious plays, taking them from stories that he read.

'But when he is not at work, he can be quite impossible. He

must be watched constantly so that he does not enlarge our ranks. His dining habits are extremely sloppy. And on occasion he says most shocking things to strangers, which fortunately they are too sensible to believe.'

In other words, he tried to make other vampires. And he didn't hunt in stealth.

In the main it is Our Oldest Friend [Armand, obviously] who is relied upon to restrain him. And that he does with the most caustic threats. But I must say that those do not have an enduring effect upon Our Violinist. He talks often of old religious customs, of ritual fires, of the passage into new realms of being.

I cannot say that we do not love him. For your sake we would care for him even if we did not. But we do love him. And Our Oldest Friend, in particular, bears him great affection. Yet I should remark that in the old times, such persons would not have endured among us for very long.

As for Our Oldest Friend, I wonder if you would know him now. He has built a great manse at the foot of your tower, and there he lives among books and pictures very like a scholarly gentleman with little care for the real world.

Each night, however, he arrives at the door of the theatre in his black carriage. And he watches from his own curtained box.

And he comes after to settle all disputes among us, to govern as he always did, to threaten Our Divine Violinist, but he will never, never consent to perform on the stage. It is he who accepts new members among us. As I told you, they come from all over. We do not have to solicit them. They knock upon our door....

Come back to us [she wrote in closing]. You will find us more interesting than you did before. There are a thousand dark wonders which I cannot commit to paper. We are a starburst in the history of our kind. And we could not have chosen a more perfect moment in the history of this great city for our little contrivance. And it is your doing, this splendid existence we sustain. Why did you leave us? Come home.

I saved the letters. I kept them as carefully as I kept the letters from my brothers in the Auvergne. I saw the marionettes perfectly in my imagination. I heard the cry of Nicki's violin, I saw Armand, too, arriving in his dark carriage, taking his seat in the box. And I even described all of this in veiled and eccentric terms in my long messages to Marius, working in a little frenzy now and then with my chisel in a dark street while mortals slept.

But for me, there was no going back to Paris, no matter how lonely I might become. The world around me had become my lover and my teacher. I was enraptured with the cathedrals and castles, the museums and palaces that I saw. In every place I visited, I went to the heart of society: I drank up its entertainments and its gossip, its literature and its music, its architecture and its art.

I could fill volumes with the things I studied, the things I struggled to understand. I was enthralled by gypsy violinists and street puppeteers as I was by great castrati sopranos in gilded opera houses or cathedral choirs. I prowled the brothels and the gambling dens and the places where the sailors drank and quarreled. I read the newspapers everywhere I went and hung about in taverns, often ordering food I never touched, merely to have it in front of me, and I talked to mortals incessantly in public places, buying countless glasses of wine for others, smelling their pipes and cigars as they smoked, and letting all these mortal smells get into my hair and clothes.

And when I wasn't out roaming, I was travelling the realm of the books that had belonged to Gabrielle so exclusively all through those dreary mortal years at home.

Before we even got to Italy, I knew enough Latin to be studying the classics, and I made a library in the old Venetian palazzo I haunted, often reading the whole night long.

And of course it was the tale of Osiris that enchanted me, bringing back with it the romance of Armand's story and

Marius's enigmatic words. As I pored over all the old versions, I was quietly thunderstruck by what I read.

Here we have an ancient king, Osiris, a man of unworldly goodness who turns the Egyptians away from cannibalism and teaches them the art of growing crops and making wine. And how is he murdered by his brother Typhon? Osiris is tricked into lying down in a box made to the exact size of his body, and his brother Typhon then nails shut the lid. He is then thrown into the river, and when his faithful Isis finds his body, he is again attacked by Typhon, who dismembers him. All parts of his body are found save one.

Now, why would Marius make reference to a myth such as this? And how could I not think on the fact that all vampires sleep in coffins which are boxes made to the size of their bodies — even the miserable rabble of les Innocents slept in their coffins. Magnus said to me, 'In that box or its like you must always lie.' As for the missing part of the body, the part that Isis never found, well, there is one part of us which is not enhanced by the Dark Gift, isn't there? We can speak, see, taste, breathe, move as humans move, but *we cannot procreate*. And neither could Osiris, so he became Lord of the Dead.

Was this a vampire god?

But so much puzzled me and tormented me. This god Osiris was the god of wine to the Egyptians, the one later called Dionysus by the Greeks.

And Dionysus was the 'dark god' of the theatre, the devil god whom Nicki described to me when we were boys at home. And now we had the theatre full of vampires in Paris. Oh, it was too rich.

I couldn't wait to tell all this to Gabrielle.

But she dismissed it indifferently, saying there were hundreds of such old stories.

'Osiris was the god of the corn,' she said. 'He was a good god to the Egyptians. What could this have to do with us?' She glanced at the books I was studying. 'You have a great deal to learn, my son. Many an ancient god was dismembered and mourned by his goddess. Read of Actaeon and Adonis. The ancients loved those stories.'

And she was gone. And I was alone in the candlelighted library, leaning on my elbows amid all these books.

I brooded on Armand's dream of the sanctuary of Those Who Must Be Kept in the mountains. Was it a magic that went back to the Egyptian times? How had the Children of Darkness forgotten such things? Maybe it had all been poetry to the Venetian master, the mention of Typhon, the slayer of his brother, nothing more than that.

I went out into the night with my chisel. I wrote my questions to Marius on stones that were older than us both. Marius had become so real to me that we were talking together, the way that Nicki and I had once done. He was the confidant who received my excitement, my enthusiasm, my sublime bewilderment at all the wonders and puzzles of the world.

BUT as my studies deepened, as my education broadened, I was getting that first awesome inkling of what eternity might be. I was alone among humans, and my writing to Marius couldn't keep me from knowing my own monstrosity as I had in those first Paris nights so long ago. After all, Marius wasn't really there.

And neither was Gabrielle.

Almost from the beginning, Armand's predictions had proved true.

2

BEFORE we were even out of France, Gabrielle was breaking the journey to disappear for several nights at a time. In Vienna, she often stayed away for over a fortnight, and by the time I settled in the palazzo in Venice she was going away for months on end. During my first visit to Rome, she vanished for a half year. And after she left me in Naples, I returned to Venice without her, angrily leaving her to find her way back to the Veneto on her own, which she did.

Of course it was the countryside that drew her, the forest or the mountains, or islands on which no human beings lived.

And she would return in such a tattered state — her shoes worn out, her clothes ripped, her hair in hopeless tangles — that she was every bit as frightening to look at as the ragged members of the old Paris coven had been. Then she'd walk about my rooms in her dirty neglected garments staring at the cracks in the plaster or the light caught in the distortions of the hand-blown window glass.

Why should immortals pore over newspapers, she would ask, or dwell in palaces? Or carry gold in their pockets? Or write letters to a mortal family left behind?

In an eerie, rapid undertone she'd speak of cliffs she had climbed, the drifts of snow through which she had tumbled, the caves full of mysterious markings and ancient fossils that she had found.

Then she would go as silently as she'd come, and I would be left watching for her and waiting for her — and bitter and angry at her, and resenting her when she finally came back.

One night during our first visit to Verona, she startled me in a dark street.

'Is your father still alive?' she asked. Two months she'd been gone that time. I'd missed her bitterly, and there she was asking about them as if they mattered finally. Yet when I answered, 'Yes, and very ill,' she seemed not to hear. I tried to tell her then that things in France were bleak indeed. There would surely be a revolution. She shook her head and waved it all away.

'Don't think about them anymore,' she said. 'Forget them.' And once again, she was gone.

The truth was, I didn't want to forget them. I never stopped writing to Roget for news of my family. I wrote to him more often than I wrote to Eleni at the theatre. I'd sent for portraits of my nieces and nephews. I sent presents back to France from every place in which I stopped. And I did worry about the revolution, as any mortal Frenchman might.

And finally, as Gabrielle's absences grew longer and our times together more strained and uncertain, I started to argue with her about these things.

'Time will take our family,' I said. 'Time will take the

France we knew. So why should I give them up now while I can still have them? I need these things, I tell you. This is what life is to me!'

But this was only the half of it. I didn't have her any more than I had the others. She must have known what I was really saying. She must have heard the recriminations behind it all.

Little speeches like this saddened her. They brought out the tenderness in her. She'd let me get clean clothes for her, comb out her hair. And after that we'd hunt together and talk together. Maybe she would even go to the casinos with me, or to the opera. She'd be a great and beautiful lady for a little while.

And those moments still held us together. They perpetuated our belief that we were still a little coven, a pair of lovers, prevailing against the mortal world.

Gathered by the fire in some country villa, riding together on the driver's seat of the coach as I held the reins, walking together through the midnight forest, we still exchanged our various observations now and then.

We even went in search of haunted houses together — a newfound pastime that excited us both. In fact, Gabrielle would sometimes return from one of her journeys precisely because she had heard of a ghostly visitation and she wanted me to go with her to see what we could.

Of course, most of the time we found nothing in the empty buildings where spirits were supposed to appear. And those wretched persons supposed to be possessed by the devil were often no more than commonly insane.

Yet there were times when we saw fleeting apparitions or mayhem that we couldn't explain — objects flung about, voices roaring from the mouths of possessed children, icy currents that blew out the candles in a locked room.

But we never learned anything from all this. We saw no more than a hundred mortal scholars had already described.

It was just a game to us finally. And when I look back on it now, I know we went on with it because it kept us together — gave us convivial moments which otherwise we would not have had.

But Gabrielle's absences weren't the only thing destroying our affection for each other as the years passed. It was her manner when she was with me — the ideas she would put forth.

She still had that habit of speaking exactly what was on her mind and little more.

One night in our little house in the Via Ghibellina in Florence, she appeared after a month's absence and started to expound at once.

'You know the creatures of the night are ripe for a great leader,' she said. 'Not some superstitious mumbler of old rites, but a great dark monarch who will galvanize us according to new principles.'

'What principles?' I asked. Ignoring the question, she went on.

'Imagine,' she said, 'not merely this stealthy and loathsome feeding on mortals, but something grand as the Tower of Babel was grand before it was brought down by the wrath of God. I mean a leader set up in a Satanic palace who sends out his followers to turn brother against brother, to cause mothers to kill their children, to put all the fine accomplishments of mankind to the torch, to scorch the land itself so that all would die of hunger, innocent and guilty! Make suffering and chaos wherever you turn, and strike down the forces of good so that men despair. Now that is something worthy of being called evil. That is what the work of a devil really is. We are nothing, you and I, except exotica in the Savage Garden, as you told me. And the world of men is no more or less now than what I saw in my books in the Auvergne years ago.'

I hated this conversation. And yet I was glad she was in the room with me, that I was speaking to somebody other than a poor deceived mortal. That I wasn't alone with my letters from home.

'But what about your aesthetic questions?' I asked. 'What you explained to Armand before, that you wanted to know why beauty existed and why it continues to affect us?'

She shrugged.

'When the world of man collapses in ruin, beauty will take

over. The trees shall grow again where there were streets; the flowers will again cover the meadow that is now a dank field of hovels. That shall be the purpose of the Satanic master, to see the wild grass and the dense forest cover up all trace of the once great cities until nothing remains.'

'And why call all this Satanic?' I asked. 'Why not call it chaos? That is all it would be.'

'Because,' she said, 'that is what men would call it. They invented Satan, didn't they? Satanic is merely the name they give to the behaviour of those who would disrupt the orderly way in which men want to live.'

'I don't see it.'

'Well, use your preternatural brain, my blue-eyed one,' she answered, 'my golden-haired son, my handsome wolfkiller. It is very possible that God made the world as Armand said.'

'This is what you discovered in the forest? You were told this by the leaves?'

She laughed at me.

'Of course, God is not necessarily anthropomorphic,' she said. 'Or what we would call, in our colossal egotism and sentimentality, "a decent person". But there is probably God. Satan, however, was man's invention, a name for the force that seeks to overthrow the civilized order of things. The first man who made laws — be he Moses or some ancient Egyptian king Osiris — that lawmaker created the devil. The devil meant the one who tempts you to break the laws. And we are truly Satanic in that we follow no law for man's protection. So why not truly disrupt? Why not make a blaze of evil to consume all the civilizations of the earth?'

I was too appalled to answer.

'Don't worry.' She laughed. 'I won't do it. But I wonder what will happen in the decades to come. Will not somebody do it?'

'I hope not!' I said. 'Or let me put it this way. If one of us tries, then there shall be war.'

'Why? Everyone will follow him.'

'I will not. I will make the war.'

'Oh, you are too amusing, Lestat,' she said.

'It's petty,' I said.

'Petty!' She had looked away, out into the courtyard, but she looked back and the colour rose in her face. 'To topple all the cities of the earth? I understood when you called the Theatre of the Vampires petty, but now you are contradicting yourself.'

'It is petty to destroy anything merely for the sake of the destroying, don't you think?'

'You're impossible,' she said. 'Sometime in the far future there may be such a leader. He will reduce man to the nakedness and fear from which he came. And we shall feed upon him effortlessly as we have always done, and the Savage Garden, as you call it, will cover the world.'

'I almost hope someone does attempt it,' I said. 'Because I would rise up against him and do everything to defeat him. And possibly I could be saved, I could be good again in my own eyes, as I set out to save man from this.'

I was very angry. I'd left my chair and walked out into the courtyard.

She came right behind me.

'You have just given the oldest argument in Christendom for the existence of evil,' she said. 'It exists so that we may fight it and do good.'

'How dreary and stupid,' I said.

'What I don't understand about you is this,' she said. 'You hold to your old belief in goodness with a tenacity that is virtually unshakeable. Yet you are so good at being what you are! You hunt your victims like a dark angel. You kill ruthlessly. You feast all the night long on victims when you choose.'

'So?' I looked at her coldly. 'I don't know how to be bad at being bad.'

She laughed.

'I was a good marksman when I was a young man,' I said, 'a good actor on the stage. And now I am a good vampire. So much for our understanding of the word "good".'

AFTER she had gone, I lay on my back on the flagstones in the courtyard and looked up at the stars, thinking of all the paintings and the sculptures that I had seen merely in the single city of Florence. I knew that I hated places where there are only towering trees, and the softest and sweetest music to me was the sound of human voices. But what did it matter really what I thought or felt?

But she didn't always bludgeon me with strange philosophy. Now and then when she appeared, she spoke of the practical things she'd learned. She was actually braver and more adventurous than I was. She taught me things.

We could sleep in the earth, she had ascertained that before we ever left France. Coffins and graves did not matter. And she would find herself rising naturally out of the earth at sunset even before she was awake.

And those mortals who did find us during the daylight hours, unless they exposed us to the sun at once, were doomed. For example, outside Palermo she had slept in a cellar far below an abandoned house, and when she had awakened, her eyes and face were burning as if they had been scalded, and she had in her right hand a mortal, quite dead, who had apparently attempted to disturb her rest.

'He was strangled,' she said, 'and my hand was still locked on his throat. And my face had been burned by the little light that leaked down from the opened door.'

'What if there had been several mortals?' I asked, vaguely enchanted with her.

She shook her head and shrugged. She always slept in the earth now, not in cellars or coffins. No one would ever disturb her rest again. It did not matter to her.

I DID not say so, but I believed there was a grace in sleeping in the crypt. There was a romance to rising from the grave. I was in fact going to the very opposite extreme in that I had coffins made for myself in places where we lingered, and I slept not in the graveyard or the church, as was our most common custom, but in hiding places within the house.

I can't say that she didn't sometimes patiently listen to me when I told her these things. She listened when I described to her the great works of art I had seen in the Vatican museum, or the chorus I had heard in the cathedral, or the dreams I had in the last hour before rising, dreams that seemed to be sparked off by the thoughts of mortals passing my lair. But maybe she was watching my lips move. Who could possibly tell? And then she was gone again without explanation, and I walked the streets alone, whispering aloud to Marius and writing to him the long, long messages that took the whole night sometimes to complete.

What did I want of her, that she be more human, that she be like me? Armand's predictions obsessed me. And how could she not think of them? She must have known what was happening, that we were growing ever farther apart, that my heart was breaking and I had too much pride to say it to her.

'Please, Gabrielle, I cannot endure the loneliness! Stay with me.'

By the time we left Italy I was playing dangerous little games with mortals. I'd see a man, or a woman — a human being who looked perfect to me spiritually — and I would follow the human about. Maybe for a week I'd do this, then a month, sometimes even longer than that. I'd fall in love with the being. I'd imagine friendship, conversation, intimacy that we could never have. In some magical and imaginary moment I would say: 'But you see what I am,' and this human being, in supreme spiritual understanding, would say: 'Yes, I see. I understand.'

Nonsense, really. Very like the fairy tale where the princess gives her selfless love to the prince who is enchanted and he is himself again and the monster no more. Only in this dark fairy tale I would pass right into my mortal lover. We would become one being, and I would be flesh and blood again.

Lovely idea, that. Only I began to think more and more of Armand's warnings, that I'd work the Dark Trick again for the same reasons I'd done it before. And I stopped playing the game altogether. I merely went hunting with all the old vengeance and cruelty, and it wasn't merely the evildoer I brought down.

* * *

369

IN THE city of Athens I wrote the following message to Marius:

'I do not know why I go on. I do not search for truth. I do not believe in it. I hope for no ancient secrets from you, whatever they may be. But I believe in something. Maybe simply in the beauty of the world through which I wander or in the will to live itself. This gift was given to me too early. It was given for no good reason. And already at the age of thirty mortal years, I have some understanding as to why so many of our kind have wasted it, given it up. Yet I continue. And I search for you.'

HOW long I could have wandered through Europe and Asia in this fashion I do not know. For all my complaints about loneliness, I was used to it all. And there were new cities as there were new victims, new languages, and new music to hear. No matter what my pain, I fixed my mind on a new destination. I wanted to know all the cities of the earth, finally, even the far-off capitals of India and China, where the simplest objects would seem alien and the minds I pierced as strange as those of creatures from another world.

But as we went south from Istanbul into Asia Minor, Gabrielle felt the allure of the new and strange land even more strongly, so that she was scarcely ever at my side.

And things were reaching a horrid climax in France, not merely with the mortal world I still grieved for, but with the vampires of the theatre as well.

3

BEFORE I ever left Greece, I'd been hearing disturbing news from English and French travellers of the troubles at home. And when I reached the European hostelry in Ankara there was a large packet of letters waiting for me.

Roget had moved all of my money out of France, and into foreign banks. 'You must not consider returning to Paris,' he wrote. 'I have advised your father and your brothers to keep out of all controversy. It is not the climate for monarchists here.'

Eleni's letters spoke in their own way of the same things:

Audiences want to see the aristocracy made fools of. Our little play featuring a clumsy queen puppet, who is trampled mercilessly by the mindless troop of puppet soldiers whom she seeks to command, draws loud laughter and screams.

The clergy is also ripe for derision: In another little drama we have a bumptious priest come to chastise a group of dancing-girl marionettes for their indecent conduct. But alas, their dancing master, who is in fact a red-horned devil, turns the unfortunate cleric into a werewolf who ends his days kept by the laughing girls in a golden cage.

All this is the genius of Our Divine Violinist, but we must now be with him every waking moment. To force him to write we tie him to the chair. We put ink and paper in front of him. And if this fails, we make him dictate as we write down the plays.

In the streets he would accost the passers-by and tell them passionately there are horrors in this world of which they do not dream. And I assure you, if Paris were not so busy reading pamphlets that denounce Queen Marie Antoinette, he might have undone us all by now. Our Oldest Friend becomes more angry with every passing night.

Of course I wrote to her at once, begging her to be patient with Nicki, to try to help him through these first years. 'Surely he can be influenced,' I said. And for the first time I asked: 'Would I have the power to alter things if I were to return?' I stared at the words for a long time before signing my name. My hands were trembling. Then I sealed the letter and posted it at once.

How could I go back? Lonely as I was, I couldn't bear the thought of returning to Paris, of seeing that little theatre again.

And what would I do for Nicolas when I got there? Armand's long-ago admonition was a din in my ears.

In fact, it seemed no matter where I was that Armand and Nicki were both with me, Armand full of grim warnings and predictions, and Nicolas taunting me with the little miracle of love turned into hate.

I had never needed Gabrielle as I did now. But she had gone ahead on our journey long ago. Now and then I remembered the way it had been before we ever left Paris. But I didn't expect anything from her anymore.

At Damascus, Eleni's answer was waiting for me.

He despises you as much as ever. When we suggest that perhaps he should go to you, he laughs and laughs. I tell you these things not to haunt you but to let you know that we do our utmost to protect this child who should never have been Born to Darkness. He is overwhelmed by his powers, dazzled and maddened by his vision. We have seen it all and its sorry finish before.

Yet he has written his greatest play this last month. The marionette dancers, *sans* strings for this one, are, in the flower of their youth, struck down by a pestilence and laid beneath tombstones and flower wreaths to rest. The priest weeps over them before he goes away. But a young violinist magician comes to the cemetery. And by means of his music makes them rise. As vampires dressed all in black silk ruffles and black satin ribbons, they come out of the graves, dancing merrily as they follow the violinist towards Paris, a beautifully rendered painting on the scrim. The crowd positively roars. I tell you we could feast on mortal victims on the stage and the Parisians, thinking it all the most novel illusion, would only cheer.

There was also a frightening letter from Roget.

Paris was in the grip of revolutionary madness. King Louis had been forced to recognize the National Assembly. The people of all classes were uniting against him as never before. Roget had sent a messenger south to see my family and try to determine the revolutionary mood in the countryside for himself.

I answered both letters with all the predictable concern and all the predictable feeling of helplessness.

But as I sent my belongings on to Cairo, I had the dread that all those things upon which I depended were in danger. Outwardly, I was unchanged as I continued my masquerade as the travelling gentleman; inwardly the demon hunter of the crooked back streets was silently and secretly lost.

Of course I told myself that it was important to go south to Egypt, that Egypt was a land of ancient grandeur and timeless marvels, that Egypt would enchant me and make me forget the things happening in Paris which I was powerless to change.

But there was a connection in my mind. Egypt, more than any other land the world over, was a place in love with death.

Finally Gabrielle came like a spirit out of the Arabian desert, and together we set sail.

IT WAS almost a month before we reached Cairo, and when I found my belongings waiting for me in the European hostelry there was a strange package there.

I recognized Eleni's writing immediately, but I could not think why she would send me a package and I stared at the thing for a full quarter of an hour, my mind as blank as it had ever been.

There was not a word from Roget.

Why hasn't Roget written to me, I thought. What is this package? Why is it here?

At last I realized that for an hour I had been sitting in a room with a lot of trunks and packing cases and staring at a package and that Gabrielle, who had not seen fit to vanish yet, was merely watching me.

'Would you go out?' I whispered.

'If you wish,' she said.

It was important to open this, yes, to open it and find out what it was. Yet it seemed just as important for me to look around the barren little room and imagine that it was a room in a village inn in the Auvergne.

'I had a dream about you,' I said aloud, glancing at the package. 'I dreamed that we were moving through the world together, you and I, and we were both serene and strong. I dreamed we fed on the evildoer as Marius had done, and as we looked about ourselves we felt awe and sorrow at the mysteries we beheld. But we were strong. We would go on forever. And we talked. "Our conversation" went on and on.'

I tore back the wrapping and saw the case of the Stradivarius violin.

I went to say something again, just to myself, but my throat closed. And my mind couldn't carry out the words on its own. I reached for the letter which had slipped to one side over the polished wood.

It has come to the worst, as I feared. Our Oldest Friend, maddened by the excesses of Our Violinist, finally imprisoned him in your old residence. And though his violin was given him in his cell, his hands were taken away.

But understand that with us, such appendages can always be restored. And the appendages in question were kept safe by Our Oldest Friend, who allowed our wounded one no sustenance for five nights.

Finally, after the entire troupe had prevailed upon Our Oldest Friend to release N. and give back to him all that was his, it was done.

But N., maddened by the pain and the starvation — for this can alter the temperament completely — slipped into unbreakable silence and remained so for a considerable length of time.

At last he came to us and spoke only to tell us that in the manner of a mortal he had put in order his business affairs. A stack of freshly written plays was ours to have. And we must call together for him somewhere in the countryside the ancient Sabbat with its customary blaze. If we did not, then he should make the theatre his funeral pyre.

Out Oldest Friend solemnly granted his wish and

have never seen such a Sabbat as this, for I think we looked all the more hellish in our wigs and fine clothes, our black ruffled vampire dancing costumes, forming the old circle, singing with an actor's bravado the old chants.

'We should have done it on the boulevard,' he said. 'But here, send this on to my maker,' and he put the violin in my hands. We began to dance, all of us, to induce the customary frenzy, and I think we were never more moved, never more in terror, never more sad. He went into the flames.

I know how this news will affect you. But understand we did all that we could to prevent what occurred. Our Oldest Friend was bitter and grieved. And I think you should know that when we returned to Paris, we discovered that N. had ordered the theatre to be named officially the Theatre of the Vampires and these words had already been painted on the front. As his best plays have always included vampires and werewolves and other such supernatural creatures, the public thinks the new title very amusing, and no one has moved to change it. It is merely clever in the Paris of these times.

Hours later when I finally went down the stairs into the street, I saw a pale and lovely ghost in the shadows — image of the young French explorer in soiled white linen and brown leather boots, straw hat down over the eyes.

I knew who she was, of course, and that we had once loved each other, she and I, but it seemed for the moment to be something I could scarce remember, or truly believe.

I think I wanted to say something mean to her, to wound her and drive her away. But when she came up beside me and walked with me, I didn't say anything. I merely gave the letter to her so that we didn't have to talk. And she read it and put it away, and then she had her arm around me again the way she used to long ago, and we were walking together through the black streets.

Smell of death and cooking fires, of sand and camel dung.

Egypt smell. Smell of a place that has been the same for six thousand years.

'What can I do for you, my darling?' she whispered.

'Nothing,' I said.

It was I who did it, I who seduced him, made him what he was, and left him there. It was I who subverted the path his life might have taken. And so in dark obscurity, removed from its human course, it comes to this.

LATER she stood silent as I wrote my message to Marius on an ancient temple wall. I told about the end of Nicolas, the violinist of the Theatre of the Vampires, and I carved my words deep as any ancient Egyptian craftsman might have done. Epitaph for Nicki, a milestone in oblivion, which none might ever read or understand.

IT WAS strange to have her there. Strange to have her staying with me hour by hour.

'You won't go back to France, will you?' she asked me finally. 'You won't go back on account of what he's done?'

'The hands?' I asked her. 'The cutting off of the hands?'

She looked at me and her face smoothed out as if some shock had robbed it of expression. But she knew. She had read the letter. What shocked her? The way I said it perhaps.

'You thought I would go back to get revenge?'

She nodded uncertainly. She didn't want to put the idea in my head.

'How could I do that?' I said. 'It would be hypocrisy, wouldn't it, when I left Nicolas there counting on them all to do whatever had to be done?'

The changes in her face were too subtle to describe. I didn't like to see her feel so much. It wasn't like her.

'The fact is, the little monster was trying to help when he did it, don't you think, when he cut off the hands. It must have been a lot of trouble to him, really, when he could have burnt up Nicki so easily without a backward glance.'

She nodded, but she looked miserable, and as luck would have it, beautiful, too. 'I rather thought so,' she said. 'But I didn't think you would agree.'

'Oh, I'm monster enough to understand it,' I said. 'Do you remember what you told me years ago, before we ever left home? You said it the very day that he came up the mountain with the merchants to give me the red cloak. You said that his father was so angry with him for his violin playing that he was threatening to break his hands. Do you think we find our destiny somehow, no matter what happens? I mean, do you think that even as immortals we follow some path that was already marked for us when we were alive? Imagine it, the coven master cut off his hands.'

IT WAS clear in the nights that followed that she didn't want to leave me alone. And I sensed that she would have stayed on account of Nicki's death, no matter where we were. But it made a difference that we were in Egypt. It helped that she loved these ruins and these monuments as she had loved none before.

Maybe people had to be dead six thousand years for her to love them. I thought of saying that to her, teasing her with it a little, but the thought merely came and went. These monuments were as old as the mountains she loved. The Nile had coursed through the imagination of man since the dawn of recorded time.

We scaled the pyramids together, we climbed into the arms of the giant Sphinx. We poured over inscriptions on ancient stone fragments. We studied the mummies one could buy from thieves for a pittance, bits of old jewelry, pottery, glass. We let the water of the river move through our fingers, and we hunted the tiny streets of Cairo together, and we went into the brothels to sit back on the pillows and watch the boys dance and hear the musicians play a heated erotic music that drowned out for a little while the sound of a violin that was always in my head.

I found myself rising and dancing wildly to these exotic sounds, imitating the undulations of those who urged me on, as I lost all sense of time or reason in the wail of the horns, the strumming of the lutes.

Gabrielle sat still, smiling, with the brim of her soiled white straw hat over her eyes. We did not talk to each other anymore. She was just some pale and feline beauty, cheek smudged with dirt, who drifted through the endless night at my side. Her coat cinched by a thick leather belt, her hair in a braid down her back, she walked with a queen's posture and a vampire's languor, the curve of her cheek luminous in the darkness, her small mouth a blur of rose red. Lovely and soon to be gone again, no doubt.

Yet she remained with me even when I leased a lavish little dwelling, once the house of a Mameluke lord, with gorgeously tiled floors and elaborate tentwork hanging from its ceilings. She even helped me fill the courtyard with bougainvillea and palms and every kind of tropical plant until it was a verdant little jungle. She brought in the caged parrots and finches and brilliant canaries herself.

She even nodded now and then sympathetically when I murmured there were no letters from Paris, and I was frantic for news.

Why hadn't Roget written to me? Had Paris erupted into riots and mayhem? Well, it would never touch my distant provincial family, would it? But had something happened to Roget? Why didn't he write?

She asked me to go upriver with her. I wanted to wait for letters, to question the English travellers. But I agreed. After all, it was rather remarkable really that she wanted me to come with her. She was caring for me in her own way.

I knew she'd taken to dressing in fresh white linen frock coats and breeches only to please me. For me, she brushed out her long hair.

But it did not matter at all. I was sinking. I could feel it. I was drifting through the world as if it were a dream.

It seemed very natural and reasonable that around me I should see a landscape that looked exactly as it had thousands of years ago when artists painted it on the walls of royal tombs. Natural that the palm trees in the moonlight should look exactly as they looked then. Natural that the peasant should draw his water from the river in the same manner as he had done then. And the cows he watered were the same too.

Visions of the world when the world had been new.

Had Marius ever stood in these sands?

We wandered through the giant temple of Ramses, enchanted by the millions upon millions of tiny pictures cut into the walls. I kept thinking of Osiris, but the little figures were strangers. We prowled the ruins of Luxor. We lay in the riverboat together under the stars.

On our way back to Cairo when we came to the great Colossi of Memnon, she told in a passionate whisper how Roman emperors had journeyed to marvel at these statues just as we did now.

'They were ancient in the times of the Caesars,' she said, as we rode our camels through the cool sands.

The wind was not so bad as it could have been on this night. We could see the immense stone figures clearly against the deep blue sky. Faces blasted away, they seemed nevertheless to stare forward, mute witnesses to the passage of time, whose stillness made me feel sad and afraid.

I felt the same wonder I had known before the pyramids. Ancient gods, ancient mysteries. It made the chills rise. And yet what were these figures now but faceless sentinels, rulers of an endless waste?

'Marius,' I whispered to myself. 'Have you seen these? Will any one of us endure so long?'

But my reverie was broken by Gabrielle. She wanted to dismount and walk the rest of the way to the statues. I was game for it, though I didn't really know what to do with the big smelly stubborn camels, how to make them kneel down and all that.

She did it. And she left them waiting for us, and we walked through the sand.

'Come with me into Africa, into the jungles,' she said. Her face was grave, her voice unusually soft.

I didn't answer for a moment. Something in her manner alarmed me. Or at least it seemed I should have been alarmed.

I should have heard a sound as sharp as the morning chime of Hell's Bells.

I didn't want to go into the jungles of Africa. And she knew

I didn't. I was anxiously awaiting news of my family from Roget, and I had it in my mind to seek the cities of the Orient, to wander through India into China and on to Japan.

'I understand the existence you've chosen,' she said. 'And I've come to admire the perseverance with which you pursue it, you must know that.'

'I might say the same of you,' I said a little bitterly.

She stopped.

We were as near to the colossal statues as one should get, I suppose. And the only thing that saved them from overwhelming me was that there was nothing near at hand to put them in scale. The sky overhead was as immense as they were, and the sands endless, and the stars countless and brilliant and rising forever overhead.

'Lestat,' she said slowly, measuring her words, 'I am asking you to try, only once, to move through the world as I do.'

The moon shone full on her, but the hat shadowed her small angular white face.

'Forget the house in Cairo,' she said suddenly, dropping her voice as if in respect for the importance of what she said. 'Abandon all your valuables, your clothes, the things that link you with civilization. Come south with me, up the river into Africa. Travel with me as I travel.'

Still I didn't answer. My heart was pounding.

She murmured softly under her breath that we would see the secret tribes of Africa unknown to the world. We would fight the crocodile and the lion with our bare hands. We might find the source of the Nile itself.

I began to tremble all over. It was as if the night were full of howling winds. And there was no place to go.

You are saying you will leave me forever if I don't come. Isn't that it?

I looked up at these horrific statues. I think I said:

'So it comes to this.'

And this was why she had stayed close to me, this was why she had done so many little things to please, this was why we were together now. It had nothing to do with Nicki gone into eternity. It was another parting that concerned her now.

She shook her head as if communing with herself, debating

380

on how to go on. In a hushed voice she described to me the heat of tropical nights, wetter, sweeter than this heat.

'Come with me, Lestat,' she said. 'By day I sleep in the sand. By night I am on the wing as if I could truly fly. I need no name. I leave no footprints. I want to go down to the very tip of Africa. I will be a goddess to those I slay.'

She approached and slipped her arm about my shoulder and pressed her lips to my cheek, and I saw the deep glitter of her eyes beneath the brim of her hat. And the moonlight icing her mouth.

I heard myself sigh. I shook my head.

'I can't and you know it,' I said. 'I can't do it any more than you can stay with me.'

ALL the way back to Cairo, I thought on it, what had come to me in those painful moments. What I had known but not said as we stood before the Colossi of Memnon in the sand.

She was already lost to me! She had been for years. I had known it when I came down the stairs from the room in which I grieved for Nicki and I had seen her waiting for me.

It had all been said in one form or another in the crypt beneath the tower years ago. She could not give me what I wanted of her. There was nothing I could do to make her what she would not be. And the truly terrible part was this: she really didn't want anything of me!

She was asking me to come because she felt the obligation to do so. Pity, sadness — maybe those were also reasons. But what she really wanted was to be free.

She stayed with me as we returned to the city. She did and said nothing.

And I was sinking even lower, silent, stunned, knowing that another dreadful blow would soon fall. There was the clarity and the horror. She will say her farewell, and I can't prevent it. When do I start to lose my senses? When do I begin to cry uncontrollably?

Not now.

As we lighted the lamps of the little house, the colours assaulted me — Persian carpets covered with delicate flowers, the tentwork woven with a million tiny mirrors, the brilliant plumage of the fluttering birds.

I looked for a packet from Roget but there was none, and I became angry suddenly. Surely he would have written by now. I had to know what was going on in Paris! Then I became afraid.

'What the hell is happening in France?' I murmured. 'I'll have to go and find other Europeans. The British, they always have information. They drag their damned Indian tea and their London *Times* with them wherever they go.'

I was infuriated to see her standing there so still. It was as if something were happening in the room — that awful sense of tension and anticipation that I'd known in the crypt before Armand had told us his long tale.

But nothing was happening, only that she was about to leave me forever. She was about to slip into time forever. And how would we ever find each other again?

'Damn it,' I said. 'I expected a letter.' No servants. They hadn't known when we would be back. I wanted to send someone to hire musicians. I had just fed, and I was warm and I told myself that I wanted to dance.

She broke her stillness suddenly. She started to move in a rather deliberate way. With uncommon directness she went into the courtyard.

I watched her kneel down by the pond. There she lifted two blocks of paving, and she took out a packet and brushed the sandy earth off it, and she brought it to me.

Even before she brought it into the light I saw it was from Roget. This had come before we had ever gone up the Nile, and she had hidden it!

'But why did you do this!' I said. I was in a fury. I snatched the package from her and put it down on the desk.

I was staring at her and hating her, hating her as never before. Not even in the egotism of childhood had I hated her as I did now!

'Why did you hide this from me!' I said.

'Because I wanted one chance!' she whispered. Her chin was trembling. Her lower lip quivered and I saw the blood tears.

'But without this even,' she said, 'you have made your choice.'

I reached down and tore the packet apart. The letter slipped out of it, along with folded clippings from an English paper. I unravelled the letter, my hands shaking, and I started to read:

Monsieur, as you must know by now, on July 14, the mobs of Paris attacked the Bastille. The city is in chaos. There have been riots all over France. For months I have sought in vain to reach your people, to get them out of the country safely if I could.

But on Monday last I received the word that the peasants and tenant farmers had risen against your father's houe. Your brothers, their wives and children, and all who tried to defend the castle were slain before it was looted. Only your father escaped.

Loyal servants managed to conceal him during the siege and later to get him to the coast. He is, on this very day, in the city of New Orleans in the former French colony of Louisiana. And he begs you to come to his aid. He is grief-stricken and among strangers. He begs for you to come.

There was more. Apologies, assurances, particulars ... it ceased to make sense.

I put the letter down on the desk. I stared at the wood and the pool of light made by the lamp.

'Don't go to him,' she said.

Her voice was small and insignificant in the silence. But the silence was like an immense scream.

'Don't go to him,' she said again. The tears streaked her face like clown paint, two long streams of red coming down from her eyes.

'Get out,' I whispered. The word trailed off and suddenly my voice swelled again. 'Get out,' I said. And again my voice didn't stop. It merely went on until I said the words again with shattering violence: 'GET OUT!'

4

DREAMED a dream of family. We were all embracing one another. Even Gabrielle in a velvet gown was there. The castle was blackened, all burnt up. The treasures I had deposited were melted or turned into ashes. It always comes back to ashes. But is the old quote actually ashes to ashes or dust to dust?

Didn't matter. I had gone back and made them all into vampires, and there we were, the House de Lioncourt, white-faced beauties even to the bloodsucking baby that lay in the cradle and the mother who bent to give it the wriggling long-tailed grey rat upon which it was to feed.

We laughed and we kissed one another as we walked through the ashes, my white brothers, their white wives, the ghostly children chattering together about victims, my blind father, who like a biblical figure had risen, crying:

'I CAN SEE!'

My oldest brother put his arm around me. He looked marvellous in decent clothes. I'd never seen him look so good, and the vampire blood had made him so spare and so spiritual in expression.

'You know it's a damn good thing you came when you did with all the Dark Gifts.' He laughed cheerfully.

'The Dark Tricks, dear, the Dark Tricks,' said his wife.

'Because if you hadn't,' he continued, 'why, we'd all be dead!'

5

HE house was empty. The trunks had been sent on. The ship would leave Alexandria in two nights. Only a small bag remained with me. On shipboard the son of the Marquis must now and then change his clothes. And, of course, the violin.

Gabrielle stood by the archway to the garden, slender,

long-legged, beautifully angular in her white cotton garments, the hat on as always, her hair loose.

Was that for me, the long loose hair?

My grief was rising, a tide that included all the losses, the dead and the undead.

But it went away and the sense of sinking returned, the sense of the dream in which we navigate with or without will.

It struck me that her hair might have been described as a shower of gold, that all the old poetry makes sense when you look at one whom you have loved. Lovely the angles of her face, the implacable little mouth.

'Tell me what you need of me, Mother,' I said quietly. Civilized this room. Desk. Lamp. Chair. All my brilliantly coloured birds given away, probably for sale in the bazaar. Grey African parrots that live to be as old as men. Nicki had lived to be thirty.

'Do you require money from me?'

Great beautiful flush to her face, eyes a flash of moving light — blue and violet. For a moment she looked human. We might as well have been standing in her room at home. Books, the damp walls, the fire. Was she human then?

The brim of the hat covered her face completely for an instant as she bowed her head. Inexplicably she asked:

'But where will you go?'

'To a little house in the rue Dumaine in the old French city of New Orleans,' I answered coldly, precisely. 'And after he has died and is at rest, I haven't the slightest idea.'

'You can't mean this,' she said.

'I am booked on the next ship out of Alexandria,' I said. 'I will go to Naples, then on to Barcelona. I will leave from Lisbon for the New World.'

Her face seemed to narrow, her features to sharpen. Her lips moved just a little but she didn't say anything. And then I saw the tears rising in her eyes, and I felt her emotion as if it were reaching out to touch me. I looked away, busied myself with something on the desk, then simply held my hands very still so they wouldn't tremble. I thought, I am glad Nicki took his hands with him into the fire, because if he had not, I would have to go back to Paris and get them before I could go on.

'But you can't be going to him!' she whispered.

Him? Oh. My father.

'What does it matter? I am going!' I said.

She moved her head just a little in a negative gesture. She came near to the desk. Her step was lighter than Armand's.

'Has any of our kind ever made such a crossing?' she asked under her breath.

'Not that I know of. In Rome they said no.'

'Perhaps it can't be done, this crossing.'

'It can be done. You know it can.' We had sailed the seas before in our cork-lined coffins. Pity the leviathan who troubles me.

She came even nearer and looked down at me. And the pain in her face couldn't be concealed anymore. Ravishing she was. Why had I ever dressed her in ball gowns or plumed hats or pearls?

'You know where to reach me,' I said, but the bitterness of my tone had no conviction to it. 'The addresses of my banks in London and Rome. Those banks have lived as long as vampires already. They will always be there. You know all this, you've always known . . .'

'Stop,' she said under her breath. 'Don't say these things to me.'

What a lie all this was, what a travesty. It was just the kind of exchange she had always detested, the kind of talk she could never make herself. In my wildest imaginings, I had never expected it to be like this — that I should say cold things, that she should cry. I thought I would bawl when she said she was going. I thought I would throw myself at her very feet.

We looked at each other for a long moment, her eyes tinged with red, her mouth almost quivering.

And then I lost my control.

I rose and I went to her, and I gathered her small, delicate limbs in my arms. I determined not to let her go, no matter how she struggled. But she didn't struggle, and we both cried almost silently as if we couldn't make ourselves stop. But she didn't yield to me. She didn't melt in my embrace.

And then she drew back. She stroked my hair with both her hands, and leant forward and kissed me on the lips, and then moved away lightly and soundlessly.

'All right, then, my darling,' she said.

I shook my head. Words and words and words unspoken. She had no use for them, and never had.

In her slow, languid way, hips moving gracefully, she went to the door to the garden and looked up at the night sky before she looked back at me.

'You must promise me something,' she said finally.

Bold young Frenchman who moved with the grace of an Arab through places in a hundred cities where only an alleycat could safely pass.

'Of course,' I answered. But I was so broken in spirit now I didn't want to talk anymore. The colours dimmed. The night was neither hot nor cold. I wished she would just go, yet I was terrified of the moment when that would happen, when I couldn't get her back.

'Promise me you will never seek to end it,' she said, 'without first being with me, without our coming together again.'

For a moment I was too surprised to answer. Then I said:

'I will *never* seek to end it.' I was almost scornful. 'So you have my promise. It's simple enough to give. But what about you giving a promise to me? That you'll let me know where you go from here, where I can reach you — that you won't vanish as if you were something I imagined —'

I stopped. There had been a note of urgency in my voice, of rising hysteria. I couldn't imagine her writing a letter or posting it or doing any of the things that mortals habitually did. It was as if no common nature united us, or ever had.

'I hope you're right in your estimation of yourself,' she said.

'I don't believe in anything, Mother,' I said. 'You told Armand long ago that you believe you'll find answers in the great jungles and forests; that the stars will finally reveal a vast truth. But I don't believe in anything. And that makes me stronger than you think.'

'Then why am I so afraid for you?' she asked. Her voice was little more than a gasp. I think I had to see her lips move in order to hear her.

'You sense my loneliness,' I answered, 'my bitterness at being shut out of life. My bitterness that I'm evil, that I don't deserve to be loved and yet I need love hungrily. My horror that I can never reveal myself to mortals. But these things don't stop me, Mother. I'm too strong for them to stop me. As you said yourself once, I am very good at being what I am. These things merely now and then make me suffer, that's all.'

'I love you, my son,' she said.

I wanted to say something about her promising, about the agents in Rome, that she would write. I wanted to say ...

'Keep your promise,' she said.

And quite suddenly I knew this was our last moment. I knew it and I could do nothing to change it.

'Gabrielle!' I whispered.

But she was already gone.

The room, the garden outside, the night itself, were silent and still.

SOME time before dawn I opened my eyes. I was lying on the floor of the house, and I had been weeping and then I had slept.

I knew I should start for Alexandria, that I should go as far as I could and then down into the sand when the sun rose. It would feel so good to sleep in the sandy earth. I also knew that the garden gate stood open. That all the doors were unlocked.

But I couldn't move. In a cold silent way I imagined myself looking throughout Cairo for her. Calling her, telling her to come back. It almost seemed for a moment that I had done it, that, thoroughly humiliated, I had run after her, and I had tried to tell her again about destiny: that I had been meant to lose her just as Nicki had been meant to lose his hands. Somehow we had to subvert the destiny. We had to triumph after all.

Senseless that. And I hadn't run after her. I'd hunted and I had come back. She was miles from Cairo by now. And she was as lost from me as a tiny grain of sand in the air.

Finally after a long time I turned my head. Crimson sky over the garden, crimson light sliding down the far roof. The sun coming — and the warmth coming and the awakening of a thousand tiny voices all through the tangled alleyways of Cairo, and a sound that seemed to come out of the sand and the trees and the patch of grass themselves.

And very slowly, as I heard these things, I saw the dazzle of the light moving on the roof, I realized that a mortal was near.

He was standing in the open gate of the garden, peering at my still form within the empty house. A young fair-haired European in Arab robes, he was. Rather handsome. And by the early light he saw me, his fellow European lying on the tile floor in the abandoned house.

I lay staring at him as he came into the deserted garden, the illumination of the sky heating my eyes, the tender skin around them starting to burn. Like a ghost in a white sheet he was in his clean headdress and robe.

I knew that I had to run. I had to get far away immediately and hide myself from the coming sun. No chance now to go into the crypt beneath the floor. This mortal was in my lair. There was not time enough even to kill him and get rid of him, poor unlucky mortal.

Yet I didn't move. And as he came nearer, the whole sky flickering behind him, so that his figure narrowed and became dark.

'Monsieur!' The solicitous whisper, like the woman years and years ago in Notre Dame who had tried to help me before I made a victim of her and her innocent child. 'Monsieur, what is it? May I be of help?'

Sunburnt face beneath the folds of the white headdress, golden eyebrows glinting, eyes grey like my own.

I knew I was climbing to my feet, but I didn't will myself to do it. I knew my lips were curling back from my teeth. And then I heard a snarl rise out of me and saw the shock on his face.

'Look!' I hissed, the fangs coming down over my lower lip. 'Do you see!'

And rushing towards him, I grabbed his wrist and forced his open hand flat against my face.

'Did you think I was human?' I cried. And then I picked

him up, holding him off his feet before me as he kicked and struggled uselessly. 'Did you think I was your brother?' I shouted. And his mouth opened with a dry rasping noise, and then he screamed.

I hurled him up into the air and out over the garden, his body spinning round with arms and legs out before it vanished over the shimmering roof.

The sky was blinding fire.

I ran out of the garden gate and into the alleyway. I ran under tiny archways and through strange streets. I battered down gates and doorways, and hurled mortals out of my path. I bore through the very walls in front of me, the dust of the plaster rising to choke me, and shot out again into the packed mud alley and the stinking air. And the light came after me like something chasing me on foot.

And when I found a burnt-out house with its lattices in ruins, I broke into it and went down into the garden soil, digging deeper and deeper and deeper until I could not move my arms or my hands any longer.

I was hanging in coolness and in darkness.

I was safe.

6

WAS dying. Or so I thought. I couldn't count how many nights had passed. I had to rise and go to Alexandria. I had to get across the sea. But this meant moving, turning over in the earth, giving in to the thirst.

I wouldn't give in.

The thirst came. The thirst went. It was the rack and the fire, and my brain thirsted as my heart thirsted, and my heart grew bigger and bigger, and louder and louder, and still I wouldn't give in.

Maybe mortals above could hear my heart. I saw them now and then, spurts of flame against the darkness, heard their voices, babble of foreign tongue. But more often I saw only the darkness. Heard only the darkness.

I was finally just the thirst lying in the earth, with red sleep and red dreams, and the slow knowledge that I was now too weak to push up through the soft sandy clods, too weak, conceivably, to turn the wheel again.

That's right. I couldn't rise if I wanted to. I couldn't move at all. I breathed. I went on. But not the way that mortals breathe. My heart sounded in my ears.

Yet I didn't die. I just wasted. Like those tortured beings in the walls under les Innocents, deserted metaphors of the misery that is everywhere unseen, unrecorded, unacknowledged, unused.

My hands were claws, and my flesh was shrunk to the bones, and my eyes bulged from the sockets. Interesting that we can go on like this forever, that even when we don't drink, don't surrender to the luscious and fatal pleasure, we go on. Interesting that is, if each beat of the heart wasn't such agony.

And if I could stop thinking: Nicolas de Lenfent is gone. My brothers are gone. Pale taste of wine, sound of applause. *'But don't you think it's good what we do when we are there, that we make people happy?'*

'Good? What are you talking about? Good?'

'That it's good, that it does some good, that there is good in it! Dear God, even if there is no meaning in this world, surely there can still be goodness. It's good to eat, to drink, to laugh … to be together …'

Laughter. That insane music. That din, that dissonance, that never ending shrill articulation of the meaninglessness …

Am I awake? Am I asleep? I am sure of one thing. I am a monster. And because I lie in torment in the earth, certain human beings move on through the narrow pass of life unmolested.

Gabrielle may be in the jungles of Africa now.

SOMETIME or other mortals came into the burnt-out house above, thieves hiding. Too much babble of foreign tongue. But all I had to do was sink deeper inside myself, withdraw even from the cool sand around me not to hear them.

Am I really trapped?

Stink of blood above.

Maybe they are the last hope, these two camping in the neglected garden, that the blood will draw me upwards, that it will make me turn over and stretch out these hideous — they must be — claws.

I will frighten them to death before I even drink. Shameful. I was always such a beautiful little devil, as the expression goes. Not now.

Now and then, it seems, Nicki and I are engaged in our best conversations. 'I am beyond all pain and sin,' he says to me. 'But do you feel anything?' I ask. 'Is that what it means to be free of this, that you no longer feel?' Not misery, not thirst, not ecstasy? It is interesting to me in these moments that our concept of heaven is one of ecstasy. The joys of heaven. That our concept of hell is pain. The fires of hell. So we don't think it very good not to *feel* anything, do we?

Can you give it up, Lestat? Or isn't it true that you'd rather fight the thirst with this hellish torment than die and feel nothing? At least you have the desire for blood, hot and delicious and filling every particle of you — blood.

How long are these mortals going to be here, above in my ruined garden? One night, two nights? I left the violin in the house where I lived. I have to get it, give it to some young mortal musicians, someone who will ...

Blessed silence. Except for the playing of the violin. And Nicki's white fingers stabbing at the strings, and the bow streaking in the light, and the faces of the immortal marion-ettes, half entranced, half amused. One hundred years ago, the people of Paris would have got him. He wouldn't have had to burn himself. Got me too maybe. But I doubt it.

No, there never would have been any witches' place for me.

He lives on in my mind now. Pious mortal phrase. And what kind of life is that? I don't like living here myself! What does it mean to live on in the mind of another? Nothing, I think. You aren't really there, are you?

Cats in the garden. Stink of cat blood.

Thank you, but I would rather suffer, rather dry up like a husk with teeth.

7

HERE was a sound in the night. What was it like?

The giant bass drum beaten slowly in the street of my childhood village as the Italian players announced the little drama to be performed from the back of their painted wagon. The great bass drum that I myself had pounded through the streets of the town during those precious days when I, the runaway boy, had been one of them.

But it was stronger than that. The booming of a cannon echoing through valleys and mountain passes? I felt it in my bones. I opened my eyes in the dark, and I knew it was drawing nearer.

The rhythm of steps, it had, or was it the rhythm of a heart beating? The world was filled with the sound.

It was a great ominous din that drew closer and closer. And yet some part of me knew there was no real sound, nothing a mortal ear could hear, nothing that rattled the china on its shelf or the glass windows. Or made the cats streak to the top of the wall.

Egypt lies in silence. Silence covers the desert on both sides of the mighty river. There is not even the bleat of sheep or the lowing of cattle. Or a woman crying somewhere.

Yet it was deafening, this sound.

For one second I was afraid. I stretched in the earth. I forced my fingers up towards the surface. Sightless, weightless, I was floating in the soil, and I couldn't breathe suddenly, I couldn't scream, and it seemed that if I could have screamed, I would have cried out so loud all the glass for miles about me would have been shattered. Crystal goblets would have been blown to bits, windows exploded.

The sound was louder, nearer. I tried to roll over and to gain the air but I couldn't.

And it seemed then I saw the thing, the figure approaching. A glimmer of red in the dark.

It was someone coming, this sound, some creature so powerful that even in the silence the trees and the flowers and the air itself did feel it. The dumb creatures of the earth did know. The vermin ran from it, the felines darting out of its path.

Maybe this is death, I thought.

Maybe by some sublime miracle it's alive, Death, and it take us into its arms, and it is no vampire, this thing, it is the very personification of the heavens.

And we rise up and up into the stars with it. We go past the angels and the saints, past illumination itself and into the divine darkness, into the void, as we pass out of existence. In oblivion we are forgiven all things.

The destruction of Nicki becomes a tiny pinpoint of vanishing light. The death of my brothers disintegrates into the great peace of the inevitable.

I pushed at the soil. I kicked at it, but my hands and legs were too weak. I tasted the sandy mud in my mouth. I knew I had to rise, and the sound was telling me to rise.

I felt it again like the roar of artillery: the cannon boom.

And quite completely I understood that it was looking for me, this sound, it was seeking me out. It was searching like a beam of light. I couldn't lie here anymore. I had to answer.

I sent it the wildest current of welcome. I told it I was here, and I heard my own miserable breaths as I struggled to move my lips. And the sound grew so loud that it was pulsing through every fibre of me. The earth was moving with it around me.

Whatever it was, it had come into the burnt-out ruined house.

The door had been broken away, as if the hinges had been anchored not in iron but in plaster. I saw all this against the backdrop of my closed eyes. I saw it moving under the olive trees. It was in the garden.

In a frenzy again I clawed towards the air. But the low, common noise I heard now was of a digging through the sand from above.

I felt something soft like velvet brush my face. And I saw overhead the gleam of the dark sky and the drift of the clouds like a veil over the stars, and never had the heavens in all their simplicity looked so blessed.

My lungs filled with air.

I let out a loud moan at the pleasure of it. But all these sensations were beyond pleasure. To breathe, to see light, these were miracles. And the drumming sound, the great deafening boom seemed the perfect accompaniment.

And he, the one who had been looking for me, the one from whom the sound came, was standing over me.

The sound melted; it disintegrated until it was no more than the aftersound of a violin string. And I was rising, just as if I were being lifted, up out of the earth, though this figure stood with its hands at its side.

At last, it lifted its arms to enfold me and the face I saw was beyond the realm of all possibility. What one of us could have such a face? What did we know of patience, of seeming goodness, of compassion? No, it wasn't one of us. It couldn't have been. And yet it was. Preternatural flesh and blood like mine. Iridescent eyes, gathering the light from all directions, tiny eyelashes like strokes of gold from the finest pen.

And this creature, this powerful vampire, was holding me upright and looking into my eyes, and I believe that I said some mad thing, voiced some frantic thought, that I knew now the secret of eternity.

'Then tell it to me,' he whispered, and he smiled. The purest image of human love.

'O God, help me. Damn me to the pit of hell.' This was my voice speaking. I can't look on this beauty.

I saw my arms like bones, hands like birds' talons. Nothing can live and be what I am now, this wraith. I looked down at my legs. They were sticks. The clothing was falling off me. I couldn't stand or move, and the remembered sensation of blood flowing in my mouth suddenly overcame me.

Like a dull blaze before me I saw his red velvet clothes, the cloak that covered him to the ground, the dark red gloved hands with which he held me. His hair was thick, white and gold strands mingled in waves fallen loosely around his face, and over his broad forehead. And the blue eyes might have been brooding under their heavy golden brows had they not been so large, so softened with the feeling expressed in the voice.

A man in the prime of life at the moment of the immortal gift. And the square face, with its slightly hollowed cheeks, its long full mouth, stamped with terrifying gentleness and peace.

'Drink,' he said, eyebrows rising slightly, lips shaping the word carefully, slowly, as if it were a kiss.

As Magnus had done on that lethal night so many eons ago, he raised his hand now and moved the cloth back from his throat. The vein, dark purple beneath the translucent preternatural skin, offered itself. And the sound commenced again, that overpowering sound, and it lifted me right off the earth and drew me into it.

Blood like light itself, liquid fire. Our blood.

And my arms gathering incalculable strength, winding round his shoulders, my face pressed to his cool white flesh, the blood shooting down into my loins and every vessel in my body ignited with it. How many centuries had purified this blood, distilled its power?

It seemed beneath the roar of the flow he spoke. He said again:

'Drink, my young one, my wounded one.'

I felt his heart swell, his body undulate, and we were sealed against each other.

I think I heard myself say:

'Marius.'

And he answered:

'Yes.'

PART VII

ANCIENT
MAGIC,
ANCIENT
MYSTERIES

1

WHEN I awoke, I was on board a ship. I could hear the creak of the boards, smell the sea. I could smell the blood of those who manned the ship. And I knew that it was a galley because I could hear the rhythm of the oars under the low rumbling of the giant canvas sails.

I couldn't open my eyes, couldn't make my limbs move. Yet I was calm. I didn't thirst. In fact, I experienced an extraordinary sense of peace. My body was warm as if I had only just fed, and it was pleasant to lie there, to dream waking dreams on the gentle undulation of the sea.

Then my mind began to clear.

I knew that we were slipping very fast through rather still waters. And that the sun had just gone down. The early evening sky was darkening, the wind was dying away. And the sound of the oars dipping and rising was as soothing as it was clear.

My eyes were now open.

I was no longer in the coffin. I had just come out of the rear cabin of the long vessel and I was standing on the deck.

I breathed the fresh salt air and I saw the lovely incandescent blue of the twilight sky and the multitude of brilliant stars overhead. Never from land do the stars look like that. Never are they so near.

There were dark mountainous islands on either side of us, cliffs sprinkled with tiny flickering lights. The air was full of the scent of green things, of flowers, of land itself.

And the small sleek vessel was moving fast to a narrow pass through the cliffs ahead.

I felt uncommonly clearheaded and strong. There was a moment's temptation to try to figure out how I had gotten here, whether I was in the Aegean or the Mediterranean itself, to know when we had left Cairo and if the things I remembered had really taken place.

But this slipped away from me in some quiet acceptance of what was happening.

Marius was up ahead on the bridge before the mainmast.

I walked towards the bridge and stood beside it, looking up.

He was wearing the long red velvet cloak he had worn in Cairo, and his full white blond hair was blown back by the wind. His eyes were fixed on the pass before us, the dangerous rocks that protruded from the shallow water, his left hand gripping the rail of the little deck.

I felt an overpowering attraction to him, and the sense of peace in me expanded.

There was no forbidding grandeur to his face or his stance, no loftiness that might have humbled me and made me afraid. There was only a quiet nobility about him, his eyes rather wide as they looked forward, the mouth suggesting a disposition of exceptional gentleness as before.

Too smooth the face, yes. It had the sheen of scar tissue, it was so smooth, and it might have startled, even frightened, in a dark street. It gave off a faint light. But the expression was too warm, too human in its goodness to do anything but invite.

Armand might have looked like a god out of Caravaggio, Gabrielle a marble archangel at the threshold of a church.

But this figure above me was that of an immortal man.

And the immortal man, with his right hand outstretched before him, was silently but unmistakably piloting the ship through the rocks before the pass.

The waters around us shimmered like molten metal, flashing azure, then silver, then black. They sent up a great white froth as the shallow waves beat upon the rocks.

I drew closer and as quietly as I could I climbed the small steps to the bridge.

Marius didn't take his eyes off the waters for an instant, but he reached out with his left hand and took my hand which was at my side.

Warmth. Unobtrusive pressure. But this wasn't the moment for speaking and I was surprised that he had acknowledged me at all.

His eyebrows came together and his eyes narrowed slightly, and, as if impelled by his silent command, the oarsmen slowed their stroke.

I was fascinated by what I was watching, and I realized as I deepened my own concentration that I could feel the power emanating from him, a low pulse that came in time with his heart.

I could also hear mortals on the surrounding cliffs, and on the narrow island beaches stretching out to our right and to our left. I saw them gathered on the promontories, or running towards the edge of the water with torches in their hands. I could hear thoughts ringing out like voices from them as they stood in the thin evening darkness looking out to the lanterns of our ship. The language was Greek and not known to me, but the message was clear:

The lord is passing. Come down and look: the lord is passing. And the word 'lord' incorporated in some vague way the supernatural in its meaning. And a reverence, mingled with excitement, emanated like a chorus of overlapping whispers from the shores.

I was breathless listening to this! I thought of the mortal I'd terrified in Cairo, the old debacle on Renaud's stage. But for those two humiliating incidents, I'd passed through the world invisibly for ten years, and these people, these dark-clad peasants gathered to watch the passing of the ship, knew what Marius was. Or at least they knew something of what he was. They were not saying the Greek word for vampire, which I had come to understand.

But we were leaving the beaches behind. The cliffs were closing on either side of us. The ship glided with its oars above water. The high walls diminished the sky's light.

In a few moments, I saw a great silver bay opening before

us, and a sheer wall of rock rising straight ahead, while gentler slopes enclosed the water on either side. The rock face was so high and so steep that I could make out nothing at the top.

The oarsmen cut their speed as we came closer. The boat was turning ever so slightly to the side. And as we drifted on towards the cliff, I saw the dim shape of an old stone embankment covered with gleaming moss. The oarsmen had lifted their oars straight towards the sky.

Marius was as still as ever, his hand exerting a gentle force on mine, as with the other he pointed towards the embankment and the cliff that rose like the night itself, our lanterns sending up their glare on the wet rock.

When we were no more than five or six feet from the embankment — dangerously close for a ship of this size and weight it seemed — I felt the ship stop.

Then Marius took my hand and we went across the deck together and mounted the side of the ship. A dark-haired servant approached and placed a sack in Marius's hand. And together, Marius and I leapt over the water to the stone embankment, easily clearing the distance without a sound.

I glanced back to see the ship rocking slightly. The oars were being lowered again. Within seconds the ship was heading for the distant lights of a tiny town on the far side of the bay.

Marius and I stood alone in the darkness, and when the ship had become only a dark speck on the glimmering water, he pointed to a narrow stairway cut into the rock.

'Go before me, Lestat,' he said.

It felt good to be climbing. It felt good to be moving up swiftly, following the rough-cut steps and the zigzag turns, and feeling the wind get stronger, and seeing the water become ever more distant and frozen as if the movement of the waves had been stopped.

Marius was only a few steps behind me. And again, I could feel and hear that pulse of power. It was like a vibration in my bones.

The rough-cut steps disappeared less than halfway up the cliff, and I was soon following a path not wide enough for a mountain goat. Now and then boulders or outcroppings of stone made a margin between us and a possible fall to the water below. But most of the time the path itself was the only outcropping on the cliff face, and as we went higher and higher, even I became afraid to look down.

Once, with my hand around a tree branch, I looked back and saw Marius moving steadily towards me, the bag slung over his shoulder, his right hand hanging free. The bay, the distant little town, and the harbour, all this appeared toylike, a map made by a child on a tabletop with a mirror and sand and tiny bits of wood. I could even see beyond the pass into the open water, and the deep shadowy shapes of other islands rising out of the motionless sea. Marius smiled and waited. Then he whispered very politely:

'Go on.'

I must have been spellbound. I started up again and didn't stop until I reached the summit. I crawled over a last jut of rocks and weeds and climbed to my feet in soft grass.

Higher rocks and cliffs lay ahead, and seeming to grow out of them was an immense fortress of a house. There were lights in its windows, lights on its towers.

Marius put his arm around my shoulder and we went towards the entrance.

I felt his grip loosen on me as he paused in front of the massive door. Then came the sound of a bolt sliding back inside. The door swung open and his grip became firm again. He guided me into the hallway where a pair of torches provided an ample light.

I saw with a little shock that there was no one there who could have moved the bolt or opened the door for us. He turned and he looked at the door and the door closed.

'Slide the bolt,' he said.

I wondered why he didn't do it the way he had done everything else. But I put it in place immediately as he asked.

'It's easier that way, by far,' he said, and a little mischief came into his expression. 'I'll show you to the room where you may sleep safely, and you may come to me when you wish.'

I could hear no one else in the house. But mortals had been

here, that I could tell. They'd left their scent here and there. And the torches had all been lighted only a short time ago.

We went up a little stairway to the right, and when I came out into the room that was to be mine, I was stunned.

It was a huge chamber, with one entire wall open to a stone-railed terrace that hung over the sea.

When I turned around, Marius was gone. The sack was gone. But Nicki's violin and my bag of belongings lay on a stone table in the middle of the room.

A current of sadness and relief passed through me at the sight of the violin. I had been afraid that I had lost it.

There were stone benches in the room, a lighted oil lamp on a stand. And in a far niche was a pair of heavy wooden doors.

I went to these and opened them and found a little passage which turned sharply in an L. Beyond the bend was a sarcophagus with a plain lid. It had been cleanly fashioned out of diorite, which to my knowledge is one of the hardest stones on earth. The lid was immensely heavy, and when I examined the inside of it I saw that it was plated in iron and contained a bolt that could be slipped from within.

Several glittering objects lay on the bottom of the box itself. As I lifted them, they sparkled almost magically in the light that leaked in from the room.

There was a golden mask, its features carefully moulded, the lips closed, the eye holes narrow but open, attached to a hood made up of layered plates of hammered gold. The mask itself was heavy but the hood was very light and very flexible, each little plate strung to the others by gold thread. And there was also a pair of leather gloves covered completely in tinier more delicate gold plates like scales. And finally a large folded blanket of the softest red wool with one side sewn with larger gold plates.

I realized that if I put on this mask and these gloves — if I laid over me the blanket — then I would be protected from the light if anyone opened the lid of the sarcophagus while I slept.

But it wasn't likely that anyone could get into the sarcophagus. And the doors of this L-shaped chamber were also covered with iron, and they too had their iron bolt.

Yet there was a charm to these mysterious objects. I liked to touch them, and I pictured myself wearing them as I slept. The mask reminded me of the Greek masks of comedy and tragedy.

All of these things suggested the burial of an ancient king.

I left these things a little reluctantly.

I came back into the room, took off the garments I'd worn during my nights in the earth in Cairo, and put on fresh clothes. I felt rather absurd standing in this timeless place in a violet blue frock coat with pearl buttons and the usual lace shirt and diamond buckle satin shoes, but these were the only clothes I had. I tied back my hair in a black ribbon like any proper eighteenth-century gentleman and went in search of the master of the house.

2

TORCHES had been lighted throughout the house. Doors lay open. Windows were uncovered as they looked out over the firmament and the sea.

And as I left the barren little stairs that led down from my room, I realized that for the first time in my wandering I was truly in the safe refuge of an immortal being, furnished and stocked with all the things that an immortal being might want.

Magnificent Grecian urns stood on pedestals in the corridors, great bronze statues from the Orient in their various niches, exquisite plants bloomed at every window and terrace open to the sky. Gorgeous rugs from India, Persia, China covered the marble floors wherever I walked.

I came upon giant stuffed beasts mounted in lifelike attitudes — the brown bear, the lion, the tiger, even the elephant standing in his own immense chamber, lizards as big as dragons, birds of prey clutching dried branches made to look like the limbs of real trees.

But the brilliantly coloured murals covering every surface

from floor to ceiling dominated all.

In one chamber was a dark vibrant painting of the sunburnt Arabian desert complete with an exquisitely detailed caravan of camels and turbaned merchants moving over the sand. In another room a jungle came to life around me, swarming with delicately rendered tropical blossoms, vines, carefully drawn leaves.

The perfection of the illusion startled me, enticed me, but the more I peered into the pictures the more I saw.

There were creatures everywhere in the texture of the jungle — insects, birds, worms in the soil — a million aspects of the scene that gave me the feeling, finally, that I had slipped out of time and space into something that was more than a painting. Yet it was all quite flat upon the wall.

I was getting dizzy. Everywhere I turned walls gave out on new vistas. I couldn't name some of the tints and hues I saw.

As for the style of all this painting, it baffled me as much as it delighted me. The technique seemed utterly realistic, using the classical proportions and skills that one sees in all the later Renaissance painters: da Vinci, Raphael, Michelangelo, as well as the painters of more recent times, Wateau, Fragonard. The use of light was spectacular. Living creatures seemed to breathe as I looked on.

But the details. The details couldn't have been realistic or in proportion. There were simply too many monkeys in the jungle, too many bugs crawling on the leaves. There were thousands of tiny insects in one painting of a summer sky.

I came into a large gallery walled on either side by painted men and women staring at me, and I almost cried out. Figures from all ages these were — bedouins, Egyptians, then Greeks and Romans, and knights in armour, and peasants and kings and queens. There were Renaissance people in doublets and leggings, the Sun King with his massive mane of curls and finally the people of our own age.

But again, the details made me feel as if I were imagining them — the droplets of water clinging to a cape, the cut on the side of a face, the spider half-crushed beneath a polished leather boot.

I started to laugh. It wasn't funny. It was just delightful. I began to laugh and laugh.

I had to force myself out of this gallery and the only thing that gave me the willpower was the sight of a library, blazing with light.

Walls and walls of books and rolled manuscripts, giant glistening world globes in their wooden cradles, busts of the ancient Greek gods and goddesses, great sprawling maps.

Newspapers in all languages lay in stacks on tables. And there were strewn everywhere curious objects. Fossils, mummified hands, exotic shells. There were bouquets of dried flowers, figurines and fragments of old sculpture, alabaster jars covered with Egyptian hieroglyphs.

And everywhere in the centre of the room, scattered among the tables and the glass cases, were comfortable chairs with footstools, and candelabra or oil lamps.

In fact, the impression was one of comfortable messiness, of great long hours of pure enjoyment, of a place that was human in the extreme. Human knowledge, human artifacts, chairs in which humans might sit.

I stayed a long time here, perusing the Latin and Greek titles. I felt a little drunk, as if I'd happened on a mortal with a lot of wine in his blood.

But I had to find Marius. I went on out of this room, down a little stairs, and through another painted hallway to an even larger room that was also full of light.

I heard the singing of the birds and smelled the perfume of the flowers before I even reached this place. And then I found myself lost in a forest of cages. There were not only birds of all sizes and colours here, there were monkeys and baboons, all of them gone wild in their little prisons as I made my way around the room.

Potted plants crowded against the cages — ferns and banana trees, cabbage roses, moonflower, jasmine, and other sweetly fragrant nighttime vines. There were purple and white orchids, waxen flowers that trapped insects in their maw, little trees groaning with peaches and lemons and pears.

When I finally emerged from this little paradise, it was into a hall of sculptures equal to any gallery in the Vatican museum. And I glimpsed adjoining chambers full of paintings, Oriental furnishings, mechanical toys.

Of course I was no longer lingering on each object or new discovery. To learn the contents of this house would have taken a lifetime. And I pressed on.

I didn't know where I was going. But I knew that I was being allowed to see all these things.

Finally I heard the unmistakable sound of Marius, that low rhythmic beat of the heart which I had heard in Cairo. And I moved towards it.

3

CAME into a brightly illuminated eighteenth-century salon. The stone walls had been covered in fine rosewood panelling with framed mirrors rising to the ceiling. There were the usual painted chests, upholstered chairs, dark and lush landscapes, porcelain clocks. A small collection of books in the glass-doored bookcases, a newspaper of recent date lying on a small table beside a brocaded winged chair.

High narrow French doors opened onto the stone terrace, where banks of white lilies and red roses gave off their powerful perfume.

And there, with his back to me, at the stone railing stood an eighteenth-century man.

It was Marius when he turned around and gestured for me to come out.

He was dressed as I was dressed. The frock coat was red, not violet, the lace Valenciennes, not Bruxelles. But he wore very much the same costume, his shining hair tied back loosely in a dark ribbon just as mine was, and he looked not at all ethereal as Armand might have, but rather like a superpresence, a creature of impossible whiteness and perfection who was nevertheless connected to everything around him — the clothes he wore, the stone railing on which he laid his hand, even the moment itself in which a small cloud passed over the bright half moon.

I savoured the moment: that he and I were about to speak, that I was really here. I was still clearheaded as I had been on the ship. I couldn't feel thirst. And I sensed that it was his blood in me that was sustaining me. All the old mysteries collected in me, arousing me and sharpening me. Did Those Who Must Be Kept lie somewhere on this island? Would all these things be known?

I went up to the railing and stood beside him, glancing out over the sea. His eyes were now fixed on an island not a half mile off the shore below. He was listening to something that I could not hear. And the side of his face, in the light from the open doors behind us, looked too frighteningly like stone.

But immediately, he turned to me with a cheerful expression, the smooth face vitalized impossibly for an instant, and then he put his arm around me and guided me back into the room.

He walked with the same rhythm as a mortal man, the step light but firm, the body moving through space in the predictable way.

He led me to a pair of winged chairs that faced each other and there we sat down. This was more or less the centre of the room. The terrace was to my right, and we had a clear illumination from the chandelier above as well as a dozen or so candelabra and sconces on the panelled walls.

Natural, civilized it all was. And Marius settled in obvious comfort on the brocade cushions and let his fingers curl around the arms of the chair.

As he smiled, he looked entirely human. All the lines, the animation were there until the smile melted again.

I tried not to stare at him, but I couldn't help it.

And something mischievous crept into his face.

My heart was skipping.

'What would be easier for you?' he asked in French. 'That I tell you why I brought you here, or that you tell me why you asked to see me?'

'Oh, the former would be easier,' I said. 'You talk.'

He laughed in a soft ingratiating fashion.

'You're a remarkable creature,' he said. 'I didn't expect you to go down into the earth so soon. Most of us experience the first death much later — after a century, maybe even two.'

'The first death? You mean it's common — to go into earth the way I did?'

'Among those who survive, it's common. We die. We rise again. Those who don't go into the earth for periods of time usually do not last.'

I was amazed, but it made perfect sense. And the awful thought struck me that if only Nicki had gone down into the earth instead of into the fire — But I couldn't think of Nicki now. I would start asking inane questions if I did. Is Nicki somewhere? Has Nicki stopped? Are my brothers somewhere? Have they simply stopped?

'But I shouldn't have been so surprised that it happened when it did in your case,' he resumed as if he hadn't heard these thoughts, or didn't want to address them just yet. 'You've lost too much that was precious to you. You saw and learned a great deal very fast.'

'How do you know what's been happening to me?' I asked.

Again, he smiled. He almost laughed. It was astonishing the warmth emanating from him, the immediacy. The manner of his speech was lively and absolutely current. That is, he spoke like a well-educated Frenchman.

'I don't frighten you, do I?' he asked.

'I didn't think that you were trying to,' I said.

'I'm not.' He made an offhand gesture. 'But your self-possession is a little surprising, nevertheless. To answer your question, I know things that happen to our kind all over the world. And frankly I do not always understand how or why I know. The power increases with age as do all our powers, but it remains inconsistent, not easily controlled. There are moments when I can hear what is happening with our kind in Rome or even in Paris. And when another calls to me as you have done, I can hear the call over amazing distances. I can find the source of it, as you have seen for yourself.

'But information comes to me in other ways as well. I know of the messages you left for me on walls throughout Europe because I read them. And I've heard of you from others. And sometimes you and I have been near to each other — nearer than you ever supposed — and I have heard your thoughts. I can hear your thoughts now, of course, as I'm sure you realize. But I prefer to communicate with words.'

'Why?' I asked. 'I thought the older ones would dispense with speech altogether.'

'Thoughts are imprecise,' he said. 'If I open my mind to you I cannot really control what you read there. And when I read your mind it is possible for me to misunderstand what I hear or see. I prefer to use speech and let my mental faculties work with it. I like the alarm of sound to announce my important communications. For my voice to be received. I do not like to penetrate the thoughts of another without warning. And quite frankly, I think speech is the greatest gift mortals and immortals share.'

I didn't know what to answer to this. Again, it made perfect sense. Yet I found myself shaking my head. 'And your manner,' I said. 'You don't move the way Armand or Magnus moved, the way I thought the ancient ones —'

'You mean like a phantom? Why should I?' He laughed again, softly, charming me. He slumped back in the chair a little further and raised his knee, resting his foot on the seat cushion just as a man might in his private study.

'There were times, of course,' he said, 'when all of that was very interesting. To glide without seeming to take steps, to assume physical positions that are uncomfortable or impossible for mortals. To fly short distances and land without a sound. To move objects by the mere wish to do so. But it can be crude, finally. Human gestures are *elegant*. There is wisdom in the flesh, in the way the human body does things. I like the sound of my foot touching the ground, the feel of objects in my fingers. Besides, to fly even short distances and to move things by sheer will alone is exhausting. I can do it when I have to, as you've seen, but it's much easier to use my hands to do things.'

I was delighted by this and didn't try to hide it.

'A singer can shatter a glass with the proper high note,' he said, 'but the simplest way for anyone to break a glass is simply to drop it on the floor.'

I laughed outright this time.

I was already getting used to the shifts in his face between masklike perfection and expression, and the steady vitality of his gaze that united both. The impression remained one of evenness and openness — of a startlingly beautiful and perceptive man.

But what I could not get used to was the sense of presence, that something immensely powerful, dangerously powerful, was so contained and immediately there.

I became a little agitated suddenly, a little overwhelmed. I felt the unaccountable desire to weep.

He leaned forward and touched the back of my hand with his fingers, and a shock coursed through me. We were connected in the touch. And though his skin was silky like the skin of all vampires, it was less pliant. It was like being touched by a stone hand in a silk glove.

'I brought you here because I want to tell you what I know,' he said. 'I want to share with you whatever secrets I possess. For several reasons, you have attracted me.'

I was fascinated. And I felt the possibility of an overpowering love.

'But I warn you,' he said, 'there's a danger in this. I don't possess the ultimate answers. I can't tell you who made the world or why man exists. I can't tell you why we exist. I can only tell you more about us than anyone else has told you so far. I can show you Those Who Must Be Kept and tell you what I know of them. I can tell you why I *think* I have managed to survive for so long. This knowledge may change you somewhat. That's all knowledge ever really does, I suppose ...'

'Yes —'

'But when I've given all I have to give, you will be exactly where you were before: an immortal being who must find his own reasons to exist.'

'Yes,' I said, 'reasons to exist.' My voice was a little bitter. But it was good to hear it spelled out that way.

But I felt a dark sense of myself as a hungry, vicious creature, who did a very good job of existing without reasons, a powerful vampire who always took exactly what he wanted, no matter who said what. I wondered if he knew how perfectly awful I was.

The reason to kill was the blood.

Acknowledged. The blood and the sheer ecstasy of the blood. And without it we are as husks as I was in the Egyptian earth.

'Just remember my warning,' he said, 'that the circumstances will be the same afterwards. Only you might be changed. You might be more bereft than before you came here.'

'But why have you chosen to reveal things to me?' I asked. 'Surely others have gone looking for you. You must know where Armand is.'

'There are several reasons, as I told you,' he said. 'And probably the strongest reason is the manner in which you sought me. Very few beings really seek knowledge in this world. Mortal or immortal, few really *ask*. On the contrary, they try to wring from the unknown the answers they have already shaped in their own minds — justifications, confirmations, forms of consolation without which they can't go on. To really ask is to open the door to the whirlwind. The answer may annihilate the question and the questioner. But you have been truly asking since you left Paris ten years ago.'

I understood this, but only inarticulately.

'You have few preconceptions,' he said. 'In fact, you astound me because you admit to such extraordinary simplicity. You want a purpose. You want love.'

'True,' I said with a little shrug. 'Rather crude, isn't it?'

He gave another soft laugh:

'No. Not really. It's as if eighteen hundred years of Western civilization have produced an innocent.'

'An innocent? You can't be speaking of me.'

'There is so much talk in this century of the nobility of the savage,' he explained, 'of the corrupting force of civilization, of the way we must find our way back to the innocence that has been lost. Well, it's all nonsense really. Truly primitive people can be monstrous in their assumptions and expectations. They cannot conceive of innocence. Neither can children. But civilization has at last created men who behave innocently. For the first time they look about themselves and say, "What the hell is all this!"'

'True. But I'm not innocent,' I said. 'Godless yes. I come from godless people, and I'm glad of it. But I know what good and evil are in a very practical sense, and I am Typhon, the slayer of his brother, not the killer of Typhon, as you must know.'

He nodded with a slight lift of his eyebrows. He did not have to smile anymore to look human. I was seeing an expression of emotion now even when there were no lines whatsoever in his face.

'But you don't seek any system to justify it either,' he said. 'That's what I mean by innocence. You're guilty of killing mortals because you've been made into something that feeds on blood and death, but you're not guilty of lying, of creating great dark and evil systems of thought within yourself.'

'True.'

'To be godless is probably the first step to innocence,' he said, 'to lose the sense of sin and subordination, the false grief for things supposed to be lost.'

'So by innocence you mean not an absence of experience, but an absence of illusions.'

'An absence of need for illusions,' he said. 'A love of and respect for what is right before your eyes.'

I sighed. I sat back in the chair for the first time, thinking this over, what it had to do with Nicki and what Nicki said about the light, always the light. Had he meant this?

Marius seemed now to be pondering. He too was sitting back in his chair, as he had been all along, and he was looking off at the night sky beyond the open doors, his eyes narrow, his mouth a little tense.

'But it wasn't merely your spirit that attracted me,' he said, 'your honesty, if you will. It was the way you came into being as one of us.'

'Then you know all that, too.'

'Yes, everything,' he said, dismissing that. 'You have come into being at the end of an era, at a time when the world faces changes undreamed of. And it was the same with me. I was born and grew to manhood in a time when the ancient world, as we call it now, was coming to a close. Old faiths were worn out. A new god was about to rise.'

'When was this time?' I asked excitedly.

'In the years of Augustus Caesar, when Rome had just become an empire, when faith in the gods was, for all lofty purposes, dead.'

I let him see the shock and the pleasure spread over my face. I never doubted him for a moment. I put my hand to my head as if I had to steady myself a little.

But he went on:

'The common people of those days,' he said, 'still believed in religion just as they do now. And for them it was custom, superstition, elemental magic, the use of ceremonies whose origins were lost in antiquity, just as it is today. But the world of those who *originated* ideas — those who ruled and advanced the course of history — was a godless and hopelessly sophisticated world like that of Europe in this day and age.'

'When I read Cicero and Ovid and Lucretius, it seemed so to me,' I said.

He nodded and gave a little shrug.

'It has taken eighteen hundred years,' he said, 'to come back to the scepticism, the level of practicality that was our daily frame of mind then. But history is by no means repeating itself. That is the amazing thing.'

'How do you mean?'

'Look around you! Completely new things are happening in Europe. The value placed upon human life is higher than ever before. Wisdom and philosophy are coupled with new discoveries in science, new inventions which will completely alter the manner in which humans live. But that is a story unto itself. That is the future. The point is that you were born on the cusp of the old way of seeing things. And so was I. You came of age without faith, and yet you aren't cynical. And so it was with me. We sprang up from a crack between faith and despair, as it were.'

And Nicki fell into that crack and perished, I thought.

'That's why your questions are different,' he said, 'from those who were born to immortality under the Christian god.'

I thought of my conversation with Gabrielle in Cairo — my last conversation. I myself had told her this was my strength.

'Precisely,' he said. 'So you and I have that in common. We did not grow to manhood expecting very much of others. And the burden of conscience was private, terrible though it might be.'

'But was it under the Christian god ... in the very first days of the Christian god that you were — born to immortality — as you said?'

'No,' he said with a hint of disgust. '*We* never served the Christian God. That you can put out of your mind right now.'

'But the forces of good and evil behind the names of Christ and Satan?'

'Again, they have very little if anything to do with *us*.'

'But the concept of evil in some form surely ...'

'No. We are older than that, Lestat. The men that made me were worshippers of gods, true. And they believed in things that I did not believe. But their faith harkened back to a time long before the temples of the Roman Empire, when the shedding of innocent human blood could be done on a massive scale in the name of good. And evil was the drought and the plague of the locust and the death of the crops. I was made what I am by these men in the name of good.'

This was too enticing, too enthralling.

All the old myths came to my mind, in a chorus of dazzling poetry. *Osiris was a good god to the Egyptians, a god of the corn. What has this to do with us?* My thoughts were spinning. In a flash of mute pictures, I recalled the night I left my father's house in the Auvergne when the villagers had been dancing round the Lenten fire, and making their chants for the increase of the crops. Pagan, my mother had said. Pagan, had declared the angry priest they had long ago sent away.

And it all seemed more than ever the story of the Savage Garden, dancers in the Savage Garden, where no law prevailed except the law of the garden, which was the aesthetic law. That the crops shall grow high, that the wheat shall be green and then yellow, that the sun shall shine. Look at the perfectly shaped apple that the tree has made, fancy that! The villagers would run through the orchards with their burning brands from the Lenten bonfire, to make the apples grow.

'Yes, the Savage Garden,' Marius said with a spark of light in his eyes. 'And I had to go out of the civilized cities of the Empire to find it. I had to go into the deep woods of the northern provinces, where the garden still grew at its lushest, the very land of Southern Gaul in which you were born. I had to fall into the hands of the barbarians who gave us both our stature, our blue eyes, our fair hair. I had it through the blood of my mother, who had come from those people, the daughter of a Keltic chieftain married to a Roman patrician. And you have it through the blood of your fathers directly from those days. And by a strange coincidence, we were both chosen for immortality for the same reason — you by Magnus and I by my captors — that we were the nonpareils of our blond and blue-eyed race, that we were taller and more finely made than other men.'

'Ooooh, you have to tell me all of it! You have to explain everything!' I said.

'I *am* explaining everything,' he said. 'But first, I think it is time for you to see something that will be very important as we go on.'

He waited a moment for the words to sink in.

Then he rose slowly in human fashion, assisting himself easily with his hands on the arms of the chair. He stood looking down at me and waiting.

'Those Who Must Be Kept?' I asked. My voice had gotten terribly small, terribly unsure of itself.

And I could see a little mischief again in his face, or rather a touch of the amusement that was never far away.

'Don't be afraid,' he said soberly, trying to conceal the

417

amusement. 'It's very unlike you, you know.'

I was burning to see them, to know what they were, and yet I didn't move. I'd never really thought that I would see them. I'd never really thought what it would mean ...

'Is it ... is it something terrible to see?' I asked.

He smiled slowly and affectionately and placed his hand on my shoulder.

'Would it stop you if I said yes?'

'No,' I said. But I was afraid.

'It's only terrible as time goes on,' he said. 'In the beginning, it's beautiful.'

He waited, watching me, trying to be patient. Then he said softly:

'Come, let's go.'

4

A STAIRWAY into the earth.

It was much older than the house, this stairway, though how I knew I couldn't say. Steps worn concave in the middle from the feet that have followed them. Winding deeper and deeper down into the rock.

Now and then a rough-cut portal to the sea, an opening too small for a man to climb through, and a shelf upon which birds have nested, or where the wild grass grew out of the cracks.

And then the chill, the inexplicable chill that you find sometimes in old monasteries, ruined churches, haunted rooms.

I stopped and rubbed the backs of my arms with my hands. The chill was rising through the steps.

'They don't cause it,' he said gently. He was waiting for me on the steps just below.

The semidarkness broke his face into kindly patterns of

light and shadow, gave the illusion of mortal age that wasn't there.

'It was here long before I brought them,' he said. 'Many have come to worship on this island. Maybe it was there before they came, too.'

He beckoned to me again with his characteristic patience. His eyes were compassionate.

'Don't be afraid,' he said again as he started down.

I was ashamed not to follow. The steps went on and on.

We came on larger portals and the noise of the sea. I could feel the cool spray on my hands and face, see the gleam of the damp on the stones. But we went on down farther and farther, the echo of our shoes swelling against the rounded ceiling, the rudely finished walls. This was deeper than any dungeon, this was the pit you dig in childhood when you brag to your mother and father that you will make a tunnel to the very centre of the earth.

Finally I saw a burst of light as we rounded another bend. And at last, two lamps burning before a pair of doors.

Deep vessels of oil fed the wicks of the lamps. And the doors themselves were bolted by an enormous beam of oak. It would have taken several men to lift it, possibly levers, ropes.

Marius lifted this beam and laid it aside easily, and then he stood back and looked at the doors. I heard the sound of another beam being moved on the inside. Then the doors opened slowly, and I felt my breathing come to a halt.

It wasn't only that he'd done it without touching them. I had seen that little trick before. It was that the room beyond was full of the same lovely flowers and lighted lamps that I had seen in the house above. Here deep underground were lilies, waxen and white, and sparkling with droplets of moisture, roses in rich hues of red and pink ready to fall from their vines. It was a chapel, this chamber with the soft flicker of votive candles and the perfume of a thousand bouquets.

The walls were painted in fresco like the walls of ancient Italian churches, with gold leaf hammered into the design. But these were not the pictures of Christian saints.

Egyptian palm trees, the yellow desert, the three pyramids,

the blue waters of the Nile. And the Egyptian men and women in their gracefully shaped boats sailing the river, the multi-coloured fishes of the deep beneath them, the purple-winged birds of the air above.

And the gold worked into it all. Into the sun that shone from the heavens, and the pyramids that gleamed in the distance, into the scales of the fishes and the feathers of the birds, and the ornaments of the lithe and delicate Egyptian figures who stood frozen looking forward, in their long narrow green boats.

I closed my eyes for a moment. I opened them slowly and saw the whole like a great shrine.

Banks of lilies on a low stone altar which held an immense golden tabernacle worked all over with fine engraving of the same Egyptian designs. And the air coming down through deep shafts in the rock above, stirring the flames of the ever burning lamps, ruffling the tall green blade-like leaves of the lilies as they stood in their vessels of water giving off their heady perfume.

I could almost hear hymns in this place. I could hear chants and ancient invocations. And I was no longer afraid. The beauty was too soothing, too grand.

But I stared at the gold doors of the tabernacle on the altar. The tabernacle was taller than I was. It was broader by three times.

And Marius, too, was looking at it. And I felt the power moving out of him, the low heat of his invisible strength, and I heard the inside lock of the tabernacle doors slide back.

I would have moved just a little closer to him had I dared. I wasn't breathing as the gold doors opened completely, folding back to reveal two splendid Egyptian figures — a man and a woman — seated side by side.

The light moved over their slender, finely sculpted white faces, their decorously arranged white limbs; it flashed in their dark eyes.

They were as severe as all the Egyptian statues I had ever seen, spare of detail, beautiful in contour, magnificent in their simplicity, only the open and childlike expression on the faces relieving the feeling of hardness and cold. But unlike all the others, they were dressed in real fabric and real hair.

I had seen saints in Italian churches dressed in this manner, velvet hung on marble, and it was not always pleasing.

But this had been done with great care.

Their wigs were of long thick black locks, cut straight across the forehead and crowned with circlets of gold. Round their naked arms were bracelets like snakes, and on their fingers were rings.

The clothes were the finest white linen, the man naked to the waist and wearing only a skirt of sorts, and the woman in a long, narrow, beautifully pleated dress. Both wore many gold necklaces, some inlaid with precious stones.

Almost the same size they were, and they sat in the very same manner, hands laid flat before them on their thighs. And this sameness astonished me somehow, as much as their stark loveliness, and the jewel-like quality of their eyes.

Not in any sculpture anywhere had I ever seen such a life-like attitude, but actually there was nothing lifelike about them at all. Maybe it was a trick of the accoutrements, the twinkling of the lights on their necklaces and rings, the reflected light in their gleaming eyes.

Were they Osiris and Isis? Was it tiny writing I saw on their necklaces, on the circlets of their hair?

Marius said nothing. He was merely gazing at them as I was, his expression unreadable, perhaps sad.

'May I go near to them,' I whispered.

'Of course,' he said.

I moved towards the altar like a child in a cathedral, getting ever more tentative with each step. I stopped only a few feet before them and looked directly into their eyes. Oh, too gorgeous in depth and variegation. Too real.

With infinite care each black eyelash had been fixed, each black hair of their gently curved brows.

With infinite care their mouths made partly open so that one could see the glimmer of teeth. And the faces and the arms had been so polished that not the slightest flaw disturbed the lustre. And in the manner of all statues or painted figures who stare directly forward, they appeared to be looking at me.

I was confused. If they were not Osiris and Isis, who were they meant to be? Of what old truth were they the symbols, and why the imperative in that old phrase, Those Who *Must* Be Kept?

I fell into contemplating them, my head a little to the side.

The eyes were really brown, with the black deep in their centres, the whites moist looking as though covered with the clearest lacquer, and the lips were the softest shade of ashen rose.

'Is it permissible ... ?' I whispered, turning back to Marius, but lacking confidence I stopped.

'You may touch them,' he said.

Yet it seemed sacrilegious to do it. I stared at them a moment longer, at the way that their hands opened against their thighs, at the fingernails, which looked remarkably like our fingernails — as if someone had made them of inlaid glass.

I thought that I could touch the back of the man's hand, and it wouldn't seem so sacrilegious, but what I really wanted to do was to touch the woman's face. Finally I raised my fingers hesitantly to her cheek. And I just let my fingertips graze the whiteness there. And then I looked into her eyes.

It couldn't be stone I was feeling. It couldn't ... Why, it felt exactly like ... And the woman's eyes, something —

I jumped backwards before I could stop myself.

In fact I shot backwards, overturning the vases of lilies, and slammed against the wall beside the door.

I was trembling so violently, my legs could hardly hold me.

'They're alive!' I said. 'They aren't statues! They're vampires just like us!'

'Yes,' Marius said. 'That word, however, they wouldn't know.'

He was just ahead of me and he was still looking at them, his hands at his sides, just as he had been all along.

Slowly, he turned and came up to me and took my right hand.

The blood had rushed to my face. I wanted to say something but I couldn't. I kept staring at them. And now I was staring at him and staring at the white hand that held mine.

'It's quite all right,' he said almost sadly. 'I don't think they dislike your touching them.'

For a moment I couldn't understand him. Then I did understand. 'You mean you ... You don't know whether ... They just sit there and ... Oooh God!'

And his words of hundreds of years ago, embedded in Armand's tale, came back to me: *Those Who Must Be Kept are at peace, or in silence. More than that we may never know.*

I was shuddering all over. I couldn't stop the tremors in my arms and my legs.

'They're breathing, thinking, living, as we are,' I stammered. 'How long have they been like this, how long?'

'Calm yourself,' he said, patting my hand.

'Oh God,' I said again stupidly. I kept saying it. No other words sufficed. 'But who are they?' I asked finally. My voice was rising hysterically. 'Are they Osiris and Isis? Is that who they are?'

'I don't know.'

'I want to get away from them. I want to get out of here.'

'Why?' he asked calmly.

'Because they ... they are alive inside their bodies and they ... they can't speak or move!'

'How do you know they can't?' he said. His voice was low, soothing as before.

'But they don't. That's the whole point. They don't —'

'Come,' he said. 'I want you to look at them a little more. And then I'll take you back up and I'll tell you everything, as I've already said I would.'

'I don't want to look at them anymore, Marius, honestly I don't,' I said, trying to get my hand free, and shaking my head. But he was holding on to me as firmly as a statue might, it seemed, and I couldn't stop thinking how much like their skin was his skin, how he was taking on the same impossible lustre, how when his face was in repose, it was as smooth as theirs!

He was becoming like them. And sometime in the great yawn of eternity, I would become like them! If I survived that long.

'Please, Marius ...' I said. I was beyond shame and vanity. I wanted to get out of the room.

'Wait for me then,' he said patiently. 'Stay here.'

And he let my hand go. He turned and looked down at the flowers I had crushed, the spilled water.

And before my eyes these things were corrected, the flowers put back in the vase, the water gone from the floor.

He stood looking at the two before him, and then I heard his thoughts. He was greeting them in some personal way that did not require an address or a title. He was explaining to them why he had been away the last few nights. He had gone to Egypt. And he had brought back gifts for them which he would soon bring. He would take them out to look at the sea very soon.

I started to calm down a little. But my mind was now anatomizing all that had come clear to me at the moment of shock. He cared for them. He had always cared for them. He made this chamber beautiful because they were staring at it, and they just might care about the beauty of the paintings and the flowers he brought.

But he didn't know. And all I had to do was look squarely at them again to feel horror, that they were alive and locked inside themselves!

'I can't bear this,' I murmured. I knew, without his ever telling me, the reason that he kept them. He could not bury them deep in the earth somewhere because they were conscious. He would not burn them because they were helpless and could not give their consent. Oh, God, it was getting worse and worse.

But he kept them as the ancient pagans kept their gods in temples that were their houses. He brought them flowers.

And now as I watched, he was lighting incense for them, a small cake that he had taken out of a silk handkerchief. This he told them had come from Egypt. And he was putting it to burn in a small bronze dish.

My eyes began to tear. I actually began to cry.

When I looked up, he was standing with his back to them, and I could see them over his shoulder. He looked shockingly like them, a statue dressed in fabric. And I felt maybe he was doing it deliberately, letting his face go blank.

'I've disappointed you, haven't I?' I whispered.

'No, not at all,' he said kindly. 'You have not.'

'I'm sorry that I —'

'No, you have not.'

I drew a little closer. I felt I had been rude to Those Who Must Be Kept. I had been rude to him. He had revealed to me this secret and I had shown horror and recoiling. I had disappointed myself.

I moved even closer. I wanted to make up for what I'd done. He turned towards them again and he put his arm around me. The incense was intoxicating. Their dark eyes were full of the eerie movement of the flames of the lamps.

No ridge of vein anywhere in the white skin, no fold or crease. Not even the penstroke lines in the lips which even Marius still had. They did not move with the rise and fall of breath.

And listening in the stillness I heard no thought from them, no heartbeat, no movement of blood.

'But it's there, isn't it?' I whispered.

'Yes, it's there.'

'And do you —?' Bring the victims to them, I wanted to ask. 'They no longer drink.'

Even that was ghastly! They had not even that pleasure. And yet to imagine it — how it would have been — their firing with movement long enough to take the victim and lapsing back into stillness, ah! No, I should have been relieved. But I was not.

'Long long ago, they still drank, but only once in a year. I would leave the victims in the sanctuary for them — evildoers who were weak and close to death. I would come back and find that they had been taken, and Those Who Must Be Kept would be as they were before. Only the colour of the flesh was a little different. Not a drop of blood had been spilt.

'It was at the full moon always that this was done, and usually in the spring. Other victims left were never taken. And then even this yearly feast stopped. I continued to bring

425

victims now and then. And once after a decade had passed, they took another. Again, it was the time of the full moon. It was spring. And then no more for at least half a century. I lost count. I thought perhaps they had to see the moon, that they had to know the change of the seasons. But as it turned out, this did not matter.

'They have drunk nothing since the time before I took them into Italy. That was three hundred years ago. Even in the warmth of Egypt they do not drink.'

'But even when it happened, you never saw it with your own eyes?'

'No,' he said.

'You've never seen them move?'

'Not since ... the beginning.'

I was trembling again. As I looked at them, I fancied I saw them breathing, fancied I saw their lips change. I knew it was illusion. But it was driving me wild. I had to get out of here. I would start crying again.

'Sometimes when I come to them,' Marius said, 'I find things changed.'

'How? What?'

'Little things,' he said. He looked at them thoughtfully. He reached out and touched the woman's necklace. 'She likes this one. It is the proper kind apparently. There was another which I used to find broken on the floor.'

'Then they *can* move.'

'I thought at first the necklace had fallen. But after repairing it three times I realized that was foolish. She was tearing it off her neck, or making it fall with her mind.'

I made some little horrified whisper. And then I felt absolutely mortified that I had done this in her presence. I wanted to go out at once. Her face was like a mirror for all my imaginings. Her lips curved in a smile but did not curve.

'It has happened with other ornaments, ornaments bearing the names of gods whom they do not like, I think. A vase I brought from a church was broken once, blown to tiny fragments as if by their glance. And then there have been more startling changes as well.'

426

'Tell me.'

'I have come into the sanctuary and found one or the other of them standing.'

This was too terrifying. I wanted to tug his hand and pull him out of here.

'I found him once several paces from the chair. And the woman, another time, at the door.'

'Trying to get out?' I whispered.

'Perhaps,' he said thoughtfully. 'But then they could easily get out if they wanted to. When you hear the whole story you can judge. Whenever I've found them moved, I've carried them back. I've arranged their limbs as they were before. It takes enormous strength to do it. They are like flexible stone, if you can imagine it. And if I have such strength, you can imagine what theirs might be.'

'You say want ... wanted to. What if they want to do everything and they no longer can? What if it was the limit of her greatest effort even to reach the door!'

'I think she could have broken the doors, had she wanted to. If I can open bolts with my mind, what can she do?'

I looked at their cold, remote faces, their narrow hollowed cheeks, their large and serene mouths.

'But what if you're wrong. And what if they can hear every word that we are saying to each other, and it angers them, outrages them ...'

'I think they do hear,' he said, trying to calm me again, his hand on mine, his tone subdued, 'but I do not think they care. If they cared, they would move.'

'But how can you know that?'

'They do other things that require great strength. For example, there are times when I lock the tabernacle and they at once unlock it and open the doors again. I know they are doing it because they are the only ones who could be doing it. The doors fly back and there they are. I take them out to look at the sea. And before dawn, when I come to fetch them, they are heavier, less pliant, almost impossible to move. There are times when I think they do these things to torment me as it were, to play with me.'

'No. They are trying and they can't.'

'Don't be so quick to judge,' he said. 'I have come into their chamber and found evidence of strange things indeed. And of course, there are the things that happened in the beginning ...'

But he stopped. Something had distracted him.

'Do you hear thoughts from them?' I asked. He did seem to be listening.

He didn't answer. He was studying them. It occurred to me that something had changed! I used every bit of my will not to turn and run. I looked at them carefully. I couldn't see anything, hear anything, feel anything. I was going to start shouting and screaming if Marius didn't explain why he was staring.

'Don't be so impetuous, Lestat,' he said finally, smiling a little, his eyes still fixed on the male. 'Every now and then I do hear them, but it is unintelligible, it is merely the presence of them — you know the sound.'

'And you heard him just then.'

'Yeeesss ... Perhaps.'

'Marius, please let us go out of here, I beg you. Forgive me, I can't bear it! Please, Marius, let's go.'

'All right,' he said kindly. He squeezed my shoulder. 'But do something for me first.'

'Anything you ask.'

'Talk to them. It need not be out loud. But talk. Tell them you find them beautiful.'

'They know,' I said. 'They know I find them indescribably beautiful.' I was certain that they did. But he meant tell them in a ceremonial way, and so I cleared my mind of all fear and all mad suppositions and I told them this.

'Just talk to them,' Marius said, urging me on.

I did. I looked into the eyes of the man and into the eyes of the woman. And the strangest feeling crept over me. I was repeating the phrases *I find you beautiful, I find you incomparably beautiful* with the barest shape of real words. I was praying as I had when I was very very little and I would lie in the meadow on the side of the mountain and ask God please please to help me get away from my father's house.

I talked to her like this now and I said I was grateful that I had been allowed to come near her and her ancient secrets, and this feeling became physical. It was all over the surface of my skin and at the roots of my hair. I could feel tension draining from my face. I could feel it leaving my body. I was light all over, and the incense and the flowers were enfolding my spirit as I looked into the black centres of her deep brown eyes.

'Akasha,' I said aloud. I heard the name at the same moment of speaking it. And it sounded lovely to me. The hairs rose all over me. The tabernacle became like a flaming border around her, and there was only something indistinct where the male figure sat. I drew close to her without willing it, and I leaned forward and I almost kissed her lips. I wanted to. I bent nearer. Then I felt her lips.

I wanted to make the blood come up in my mouth and pass it to her as I had that time to Gabrielle when she lay in the coffin.

The spell was deepening, and I looked right into the fathomless orbs of her eyes.

I am kissing the goddess on her mouth, what is the matter with me! Am I mad to think of it!

I moved back. I found myself against the wall again, trembling, with my hands clamped to the sides of my head. At least this time I had not upset the lilies, but I was crying again.

Marius closed the tabernacle doors. He made the bolt inside slip into place.

We went into the passage and he made the inner bolt rise and go into its brackets. He put the outside bolt in with his hands.

'Come, young one,' he said. 'Let's go upstairs.'

But we had walked only a few yards when we heard a crisp clicking sound, and then another. He turned and looked back.

'They did it again,' he said. And a look of distress divided his face like a shadow.

'What?' I backed up against the wall.

'The tabernacle, they opened it. Come. I'll return later and lock it before the sun rises. Now we will go back to my drawing room and I will tell you my tale.'

When we reached the lighted room, I collapsed in the chair

with my head in my hands. He was standing still just looking at me, and when I realized it, I looked up.

'She told you her name,' he said.

'Akasha!' I said. It was snatching a word out of the whirlpool of a dissolving dream. 'She did tell me! I said Akasha out loud.' I looked at him, imploring him for answers. For some explanation of the attitude with which he stared at me.

I thought I'd lose my mind if his face didn't become expressive again.

'Are you angry with me?'

'Shhh. Be quiet,' he said.

I could hear nothing in the silence. Except maybe the sea. Maybe a sound from the wicks of the candles in the room. Maybe the wind. Not even their eyes had appeared more lifeless than his eyes now seemd.

'You cause something to stir in them,' he whispered.

I stood up.

'What does it mean?'

'I don't know,' he said. 'Maybe nothing. The tabernacle is still open and they are merely sitting there as always. Who knows?'

And I felt suddenly all his long years of wanting to know. I would say centuries, but I cannot really imagine centuries. Not even now. I felt his years and years of trying to elicit from them the smallest signs and getting nothing, and I knew that he was wondering why I had drawn from her the secret of her name. Akasha. Things had happened, but that had been in the time of Rome. Dark things. Terrible things. Suffering, unspeakable suffering.

The images went white. Silence. He was stranded in the room like a saint taken down off an altar and left in the aisle of a church.

'Marius!' I whispered.

He woke and his face warmed slowly, and he looked at me affectionately, almost wonderingly.

'Yes, Lestat,' he said and gave my hand a reassuring squeeze.

He seated himself and gestured for me to do the same, and we were once again facing each other comfortably. And the even light of the room was reassuring. It was reassuring to see, beyond the windows, the night sky.

His former quickness was returning, the glint of good humour in his eyes.

'It's not yet midnight,' he said. 'And all is well on the islands. If I'm not disturbed, I think there is time for me to tell you the whole tale.'

MARIUS'S
STORY
5

I T HAPPENED in my fortieth year, on a warm spring night in the Roman Gallic city of Massilia, when in a dirty waterfront tavern I sat scribbling away on my history of the world.

'The tavern was deliciously filthy and crowded, a hangout for sailors and wanderers, travellers like me, I fancied, loving them all in a general sort of way, though most of them were poor and I wasn't poor, and they couldn't read what I wrote when they glanced over my shoulder.

'I'd come to Massilia after a long and studious journey that had taken me through all the great cities of the Empire. To Alexandria, Pergamon, Athens I'd travelled, observing and writing about the people, and now I was making my way through the cities of Roman Gaul.

'I couldn't have been more content on this night had I been in my library at Rome. In fact, I liked the tavern better. Everywhere I went I sought out such places in which to write, setting up my candle and ink and parchment at a table close to the wall, and I did my best work early in the evening when the places were at their noisiest.

'In retrospect, it's easy to see that I lived my whole life in the midst of frenzied activity. I was used to the idea that nothing could affect me adversely.

'I'd grown up an illegitimate son in a rich Roman household — loved, pampered, and allowed to do what I wanted. My legitimate brothers had to worry about marriage, politics, and war. By the age of twenty, I'd become the scholar and the chronicler, the one who raised his voice at drunken banquets to settle historical and military arguments.

'When I travelled I had plenty of money, and documents that opened doors everywhere. And to say life had been good to me would be an understatement. I was an extraordinarily happy individual. But the really important point here is that life had never bored me or defeated me.

'I carried within me a sense of invincibility, a sense of wonder. And this was as important to me later on as your anger and strength have been to you, as important as despair or cruelty can be in the spirits of others.

'But to continue ... If there was anything I'd missed in my rather eventful life — and I didn't think of this too much — it was the love and knowledge of my Celtic mother. She'd died when I was born, and all I knew of her was that she'd been a slave, daughter of the warlike Gauls who fought Julius Caesar. I was blond and blue-eyed as she was. And her people had been giants it seemed. At a very young age, I towered over my father and my brothers.

'But I had little or no curiosity about my Gallic ancestors. I'd come to Gaul as an educated Roman, through and through, and I carried with me no awareness of my barbarian blood, but rather the common beliefs of my time — that Caesar Augustus was a great ruler, and that in this blessed age of the Pax Romana, old superstition was being replaced by law and by reason throughout the Empire. There was no place too wretched for the Roman roads, and for the soldiers, the scholars, and the traders who followed them.

'On this night I was writing like a madman, scribbling down descriptions of the men who came and went in the tavern, children of all races it seemed, speakers of a dozen different languages.

'And for no apparent reason, I was possessed of a strange idea about life, a strange concern that amounted almost to a pleasant obsession. I remember that it came on me this night because it seemed somehow related to what happened after. But it wasn't related. I had had the idea before. That it came to me in these last free hours as a Roman citizen was no more than coincidence.

'The idea was simply that there was somebody who knew everything, somebody who had seen everything. I did not mean by this that a Supreme Being existed, but rather that there was on earth a continual intelligence, a continual awareness. And I thought of it in practical terms that excited me and soothed me simultaneously. There was an awareness somewhere of all things I had seen in my travels, an awareness of what it had been like in Massilia six centuries ago when the first Greek traders came, an awareness of what it had been like in Egypt when Cheops built the pyramids. Somebody knew what the light had been like in the late afternoon on the day that Troy fell to the Greeks, and someone or something knew what the peasants said to each other in their little farmhouse outside Athens right before the Spartans brought down the walls.

'My idea of who or what it was, was vague. But I was comforted by the notion that nothing spiritual — and knowing was spiritual — was lost to us. That there was this continuous knowing ...

'And as I drank a little more wine, and thought about it, and wrote about it, I realized it wasn't so much a belief of mine as it was a prejudice. I just felt that there was a continual awareness.

'And the history that I was writing was an imitation of it. I tried to unite all things I had seen in my history, linking my observations of lands and people with all the written observations that had come down to me from the Greeks — from Xenophon and Herodotus, and Poseidonius — to make one continuous awareness of the world in my lifetime. It was a pale thing, a limited thing, compared to the true awareness. Yet I felt good as I continued writing.

'But around midnight, I was getting a little tired, and when I happened to look up after a particularly long period of unbroken concentration, I realized something had changed in the tavern.

'It was unaccountably quieter. In fact, it was almost empty. And across from me, barely illuminated by the sputtering light of my candle, there sat a tall fair-haired man with his back to the room who·was watching me in silence. I was startled, not so much by the way he looked — though this was startling in itself — but by the realization that he had been there for some time, close to me, observing me, and I hadn't noticed him.

'He was a giant of a Gaul as they all were, even taller than I was, and he had a long narrow face with an extremely strong jaw and hawklike nose, and eyes that gleamed beneath their bushy blond brows with a childlike intelligence. What I mean to say is he looked very very clever, but very young and innocent also. And he wasn't young. The effect was perplexing.

'And it was made all the more so by the fact that his thick and coarse yellow hair wasn't clipped short in the popular Roman style, but was streaming down to his shoulders. And instead of the usual tunic and cloak which you saw everywhere in those times, he wore the old belted leather jerkin that had been the barbarian dress before Caesar.

'Right out of the woods this character looked, with his grey eyes burning through me, and I was vaguely delighted with him. I wrote down hurriedly the details of his dress, confident he couldn't read the Latin.

'But the stillness in which he sat unnerved me a little. His eyes were unnaturally wide, and his lips quivered slightly as if the mere sight of me excited him. His clean and delicate white hand, which casually rested on the table before him, seemed out of keeping with the rest of him.

'A quick glance about told me my slaves weren't in the tavern. Well, they're probably next door playing cards, I thought, or upstairs with a couple of women. They'll stop in any minute.

'I forced a little smile at my strange and silent friend, and went back to writing. But directly he started talking.

'"You are an educated man, aren't you?" he asked. He spoke the universal Latin of the Empire, but with a thick accent, pronouncing each word with a care that was almost musical.

'I told him, yes, I was fortunate enough to be educated, and I started to write again, thinking this would surely discourage him. After all, he was fine to look at, but I didn't really want to talk to him.

'"And you write both in Greek and in Latin, don't you?" he asked, glancing at the finished work that lay before me.

'I explained politely that the Greek I had written on the parchment was a quotation from another text. My text was in Latin. And again I started scribbling.

'"But you are a Keltoi, are you not?" he asked this time. It was the old Greek word for the Gauls.

'"Not really, no. I am a Roman," I answered.

'"You look like one of us, the Keltoi," he said. "You are tall like us, and you walk the way we do."

'This was a strange statement. For hours I'd been sitting here, barely sipping my wine. I hadn't walked anywhere. But I explained that my mother had been Celtic, but I hadn't known her. My father was a Roman senator.

'"And what is it you write in Greek and Latin?" he asked. "What is it that arouses your passion?"

'I didn't answer right away. He was beginning to intrigue me. But I knew enough at forty to realize that most people you meet in taverns sound interesting for the first few minutes and then begin to weary you beyond endurance.

'"Your slaves say," he announced gravely, "that you are writing a great history."

'"Do they?" I answered, a bit stiffly. "And where are my slaves, I wonder!" Again I looked around. Nowhere in sight. Then I conceded to him that it was a history I was writing.

'"And you have been to Egypt," he said. And his hand spread itself out flat on the table.

'I paused and took another good look at him. There was something otherworldly about him, the way that he sat, the way he used this one hand to gesture. It was the decorum

435

primitive people often have tnat makes them seem repositors of immense wisdom, when in fact all they possess is immense conviction.

'"Yes," I said a little warily. "I've been to Egypt."

'Obviously this exhilarated him. His eyes widened slightly, then narrowed, and he made some little movement with his lips as though speaking to himself.

'"And you know the language and the writing of Egypt?" he asked earnestly, his eyebrows knitting. "You know the cities of Egypt?"

'"The language as it is spoken, yes, I do know it. But if by the writing you mean the old picture writing, no, I can't read it. I don't know anyone who can read it. I've heard that even the old Egyptian priests can't read it. Half the texts they copy they can't decipher."

'He laughed in the strangest way. I couldn't tell whether this was exciting him or he knew something I didn't know. He appeared to take a deep breath, his nostrils dilating a little. And then his face cooled. He was actually a splendid-looking man.

'"The gods can read it," he whispered.

'"Well, I wish they'd teach it to me," I said pleasantly.

'"You do!" he said in an astonished gasp. He leant forward over the table. "Say this again!"

'"I was joking," I said. "I only meant I wished I could read the old Egyptian writing. If I could read it, then I could know true things about the people of Egypt, instead of all the nonsense written by the Greek historians. Egypt is a misunderstood land —" I stopped myself. Why was I talking to this man about Egypt?

'"In Egypt there are true gods still," he said gravely, "gods who have been there forever. Have you been to the very bottom of Egypt?"

'This was a curious way to put it. I told him I had been up the Nile quite far, that I had seen many wonders. "But as for there being true gods," I said, "I can scarce accept the veracity of gods with the heads of animals —"

'He shook his head almost a little sadly.

'"The true gods require no statues of them to be erected,"

436

he said. "They have the heads of man and they themselves appear when they choose, and they are living as the crops that come from the earth are living, as all things under the heavens are living, even the stones and the moon itself, which divides time in the great silence of its never changing cycles."

"'Very likely," I said under my breath, not wishing to disturb him. So it was zeal, this mixture of cleverness and youthfulness I had perceived in him. I should have known it. And something came back to me from Julius Caesar's writings about Gaul, that the Keltoi had come from Dis Pater, the god of the night. Was this strange creature a believer in these things?

"'There are old gods in Egypt," he said softly, "and there are old gods in this land for those who know how to worship them. I do not mean in your temples round which merchants sell the animals to defile the altars, and the butchers after sell the meat that is left over. I speak of the proper worship, the proper sacrifice for the god, the one sacrifice to which he will harken."

"'Human sacrifice, you mean, don't you?" I said unobtrusively. Caesar had described well enough that practice among the Keltoi, and it rather curdled my blood to think of it. Of course I'd seen ghastly deaths in the arena in Rome, ghastly deaths at the places of execution, but human sacrifice to the gods, that we had not done in centuries. If ever.

'And now I realized what this remarkable man might actually be. A Druid, a member of the ancient priesthood of the Keltoi, whom Caesar had also described, a priesthood so powerful that nothing like it existed, so far as I knew, anywhere in the Empire. But it wasn't supposed to exist in Roman Gaul anymore either.

'Of course the Druids were always described as wearing long white robes. They went into the forests and collected mistletoe off the oak trees with ceremonial sickles. And this man looked more like a farmer, or a soldier. But then what Druid was going to wear his white robes into a waterfront tavern? And it wasn't lawful anymore for the Druids to go about being Druids.

"'Do you really believe in this old worship?" I asked, leaning forward. "Have you yourself been down to the bottom of Egypt?"

'If this was a real live Druid, I had made a marvellous catch, I was thinking. I could get this man to tell me things about the Keltoi that nobody knew. And what on earth did Egypt have to do with it, I wondered?

'"No," he said. "I have not been to Egypt, though from Egypt our gods came to us. It is not my destiny to go there. It is not my destiny to learn to read the ancient language. The tongue I speak is enough for the gods. They give ear to it."

'"And what tongue is that?"

'"The tongue of the Keltoi, of course," he said. "You know that without asking."

'"And when you speak to your gods, how do you know that they hear you?"

'His eyes widened again, and his mouth lengthened in an unmistakable look of triumph.

'"My gods answer me," he said quietly.

'Surely he was a Druid. And he appeared to take on a shimmer, suddenly. I pictured him in his white robes. There might have been an earthquake then in Massilia, and I doubt I would have noticed it.

'"Then you yourself have heard them," I said.

'"I have laid eyes upon my gods," he said. "And they have spoken to me both in words and in silence."

'"And what do they say? What do they do that makes them different from our gods, I mean aside from the nature of the sacrifice?"

'His voice took on the lilting reference of a song as he spoke. "They do as gods have always done; they divide the evil from the good. They bring down blessings upon all who worship them. They draw the faithful into harmony with all the cycles of the universe, with the cycles of the moon, as I have told you. They fructify the land, the gods do. All things that are good proceed from them."

'Yes, I thought, the old old religion in its simplest forms, and the forms that still held a great spell for the common people of the Empire.

'"My gods sent me here," he said. "To search for you."

'"For me?" I asked. I was startled.

'"You will understand all these things," he said. "Just as you will come to know the true worship of ancient Egypt. The gods will teach you."

'"Why ever would they do that?" I asked.

'"The answer is simple," he said. "Because you are going to become one of them."

'I was about to answer when I felt a sharp blow to the back of my head and the pain spread out in all directions over my skull as if it were water. I knew I was going out. I saw the table rising, saw the ceiling high above me. I think I wanted to say if it is ransom you want, take me to my house, to my steward.

'But I knew even then that the rules of my world had absolutely nothing to do with it.

'WHEN I awoke it was daylight and I was in a large wagon being pulled fast along an unpaved road through an immense forest. I was bound hand and foot and a loose cover was thrown over me. I could see to the left and right, and through the wicker sides of the cart, and I saw the man who had talked to me, riding beside me. There were others riding with him, and all were dressed in the trousers and belted leather jerkins, and they wore iron swords and iron bracelets. Their hair was almost white in the dappled sun, and they didn't talk as they rode beside the cart together.

'This forest itself seemed made to the scale of Titans. The oaks were ancient and enormous, the interlacing of their limbs blocked out most of the light, and we moved for hours through a world of damp and dark green leaves and deep shadow.

'I do not remember towns. I do not remember villages. I remember only a crude fortress. Once inside the gates I saw two rows of thatched-roof houses, and everywhere the leather-clad barbarians. And when I was taken into one of the houses, a dark low place, and left there alone, I could hardly stand for the cramps in my legs, and I was as wary as I was furious.

439

'I knew now that I was in an undisturbed enclave of the ancient Keltoi, the very same fighters who had sacked the great shrine of Delphi only a few centuries ago, and Rome itself not too long after, the same warlike creatures who rode stark naked into battle against Caesar, their trumpets blasting, their cries affrighting the disciplined Roman soldiers.

'In other words, I was beyond the reach of everything I counted upon. And if all this talk about my becoming one of the gods meant I was to be slain on some blood-stained altar in an oak grove, then I had better try to get the hell out of here.'

6

WHEN my captor appeared again, he was in the fabled long white robes, and his coarse blond hair had been combed, and he looked immaculate and impressive and solemn. There were other tall white-robed men, some old, some young, and all with the same gleaming yellow hair, who came into the small shadowy room behind him.

'In a silent circle they enclosed me. And after a protracted silence, a riff of whispers passed amongst them.

'"You are perfect for the god," said the eldest, and I saw the silent pleasure in the one who had brought me here. "You are what the god has asked for," the eldest said. "You will remain with us until the great feast of Samhain, and then you will be taken to the sacred grove and there you will drink the Divine Blood and you will become a father of gods, a restorer of all the magic that has inexplicably been taken from us."

'"And will my body die when this happens?" I asked. I was looking at them, their sharp narrow faces, their probing eyes, the gaunt grace with which they surrounded me. What a terror this race must have been when its warriors swept down on the Mediterranean peoples. No wonder there had been so much written about their fearlessness. But these weren't warriors. These were priests, judges, and teachers. These were the instructors of the young, the keepers of the poetry and the laws that were never written in any language.

'"Only the mortal part of you will die," said the one who had spoken to me all along.

'"Bad luck," I said. "Since that's about all there is to me."

'"No," he said. "Your form will remain and it will become glorified. You will see. Don't fear. And besides, there is nothing you can do to change these things. Until the feast of Samhain, you will let your hair grow long, and you will learn our tongue, and our hymns and our laws. We will care for you. My name is Mael, and I myself will teach you."

'"But I am not willing to become the god," I said. "Surely the gods don't want one who is unwilling."

'"The old god will decide," said Mael. "But I know that when you drink the Divine Blood you will become the god, and all things will be clear to you."

'ESCAPE was impossible.

'I was guarded night and day. I was allowed no knife with which I might cut off my hair or otherwise damage myself. And a good deal of the time I lay in the dark empty room, drunk on wheaten beer and satiated with the rich roasted meats they gave to me. I had nothing with which to write and this tortured me.

'Out of boredom I listened to Mael when he came to instruct me. I let him sing anthems to me and tell me old poems and talk on about laws, only now and then taunting him with the obvious fact that a god should not have to be so instructed.

'This he conceded, but what could he do but try to make me understand what would happen to me.

'"You can help me get out of here, you can come with me to Rome," I said. "I have a villa all my own on the cliffs above the Bay of Naples. You have never seen such a beautiful spot, and I would let you live there forever if you would help me, asking only that you repeat all these anthems and prayers and laws to me so that I might record them."

'"Why do you try to corrupt me?" he would ask, but I could

441

see he was tantalized by the world I came from. He confessed that he had searched the Greek city of Massilia for weeks before my arrival, and he loved the Roman wine and the great ships that he had seen in the port, and the exotic foods he had eaten.

'"I don't try to corrupt you," I said. "I don't believe what you believe, and you've made me your prisoner."

'But I continued to listen to his prayers out of boredom and curiosity, and the vague fear of what was in store for me.

'I began waiting for him to come, for his pale, wraithlike figure to illuminate the barren room like a white light, for his quiet, measured voice to pour forth with all the old melodious nonsense.

'It soon came clear that his verses did not unfold continuous stories of the gods as we knew them in Greek and Latin. But the identity and characteristics of the gods began to emerge in the many stanzas. Deities of all the predictable sorts belonged to the tribe of the heavens.

'But the god I was to become exerted the greatest hold over Mael and those he instructed. He had no name, this god, though he had numerous titles, and the Drinker of the Blood was the most often repeated. He was also the White One, the God of the Night, the God of the Oak, the Lover of the Mother.

'This god took blood sacrifice at every full moon. But on Samhain (the first of November in our present Christian calendar — the day that has become the Feast of All Saints or the Day of the Dead) this god would accept the greatest number of human sacrifices before the whole tribe for the increase of the crops, as well as speak all manner of predictions and judgements.

'It was the Great Mother he served, she who is without visible form, but nevertheless present in all things, and the Mother of all things, of the earth, of the trees, of the sky overhead, of all men, of the Drinker of the Blood himself who walks in her garden.

'My interest deepened but so did my apprehension. The worship of the Great Mother was certainly not unknown to me. The Mother Earth and the Mother of All Things was worshipped under a dozen names from one end of the Empire to the other, and so was her lover and son, the Dying God, the one who grew to manhood as the crops grow, only to be cut down as the crops are cut down, while the Mother remains eternal. It was the ancient and gentle myth of the seasons. But the celebration anywhere and at any time was hardly ever gentle.

'For the Divine Mother was also Death, the earth that swallows the remains of that young lover, the earth that swallows all of us. And in consonance with this ancient truth — old as the sowing of seed itself — there came a thousand bloody rituals.

'The goddess was worshipped under the name of Cybele in Rome, and I had seen her mad priests castrating themselves in the midst of their devoted frenzy. And the gods of myth met their ends even more violently — Attis gelded, Dionysus rent limb from limb, the old Egyptian Osiris dismembered before the Great Mother Isis restored him.

'And now I was to be that God of Growing Things — the vine god, the corn god, the god of the tree, and I knew that whatever happened it was going to be something appalling.

'And what was there to do but get drunk and murmur these anthems with Mael, whose eyes would cloud with tears from time to time as he looked at me.

'"Get me out of here, you wretch," I said once in pure exasperation. "Why the hell don't you become the God of the Tree? Why am I so honoured?"

'"I have told you, the god confided in me his wishes. I wasn't chosen."

'"And would you do it, if you were chosen?" I demanded.

'I was sick of hearing of these old rites by which any man threatened by illness or misfortune must serve up a human sacrifice to the god if he wished to be spared, and all the other sacrosanct beliefs that had to them the same childlike barbarity.

'"I would fear but I would accept," he whispered. "But do you know what is so terrible about your fate? It is that your soul will be locked in your body forever. It will have no chance in natural death to pass into another body or another lifetime. No, all through time your soul will be the soul of the god. The cycle of death and rebirth will be closed in you."

'In spite of myself and my general contempt for his belief in reincarnation, this silenced me. I felt the eerie weight of his conviction, I felt his sadness.

'My hair grew longer and fuller. And the hot summer melted into the cooler days of autumn, and we were nearing the great annual feast of Samhain.

'Yet I wouldn't let up on the questions.

'"How many have you brought to be gods in this manner? What was it in me that caused you to choose me?"

'"I have never brought a man to be a god," he said. "But the god is old; he is robbed of his magic. A terrible calamity has befallen him, and I can't speak of these things. He has chosen his successor." He looked frightened. He was saying too much. Something was stirring the deepest fears in him.

'"And how do you know he will want me? Have you sixty other candidates stashed in this fortress?"

'He shook his head and in a moment of uncharacteristic rawness, he said:

'"Marius, if you fail to Drink the Blood, if you do not become the father of a new race of gods, what will become of us?"

'"I wish I could care, my friend —" I said.

'"Ah, calamity," he whispered. And there followed a long subdued observation of the rise of Rome, the terrible invasions of Caesar, the decline of a people who had lived in these mountains and forests since the beginning of time, scorning the cities of the Greek and the Etruscan and the Roman for the honourable strongholds of powerful tribal leaders.

'"Civilizations rise and fall, my friend," I said. "Old gods give way to new ones."

'"You don't understand, Marius," he said. "Our god was not defeated by your idols and those who tell their frivolous and lascivious stories. Our god was as beautiful as if the moon itself had fashioned him with her light, and he spoke with a

444

voice that was as pure as the light, and he guided us in that great oneness with all things that is the only cessation of despair and loneliness. But he was stricken with terrible calamity, and all through the north country other gods have perished completely. It was the revenge of the sun god upon him, but how the sun entered into him in the hours of darkness and sleep is not known to us, nor to him. You are our salvation, Marius. You are the mortal Who Knows, and is Learned and Can Learn, and Who Can Go Down into Egypt."

'I thought about this. I thought of the old worship of Isis and Osiris, and of those who said she was the Mother Earth and he the corn, and Typhon the slayer of Osiris was the fire of the sunlight.

'And now this pious communicator with the god was telling me that the sun had found his god of the night and caused great calamity.

'Finally my reason gave out on me.

'Too many days passed in drunkenness and solitude.

'I lay down in the dark and I sang to myself the hymns of the Great Mother. She was no goddess to me, however. Not Diana of Ephesus with her rows and rows of milk-filled breasts, or the terrible Cybele, or even the gentle Demeter, whose mourning for Persephone in the land of the dead had inspired the sacred mysteries of Eleusis. She was the strong good earth that I smelled through the small barred windows of this place, the wind that carried with it the damp and the sweetness of the dark green forest. She was the meadow flowers and the blowing grass, the water I heard now and then gushing as if from some mountain spring. She was all the things that I still had in this rude little wooden room where everything else had been taken from me. And I knew only what all men know, that the cycle of winter and spring and all growing things has within itself some sublime truth that restores without myth or language.

'I looked through the bars to the stars overhead, and it seemed to me I was dying in the most absurd and foolish way, among people I did not admire and customs I would have abolished. And yet the seeming sanctity of it all infected me. It caused me to dramatize and to dream and to give in, to see myself at the centre of something that possessed its own exalted beauty.

'I sat up one morning and touched my hair, and realized it was thick and curling at my shoulders.

'And in the days that followed, there was endless noise and movement in the fortress. Carts were coming to the gates from all directions. Thousands on foot passed inside. Every hour there was the sound of people on the move, people coming.

'At last Mael and eight of the Druids came to me. Their robes were white and fresh, smelling of the spring water and sunshine in which they'd been washed and dried, and their hair was brushed and shining.

'Carefully, they shaved all the hair from my chin and upper lip. They trimmed my fingernails. They brushed my hair and put on me the same white robes. And then shielding me on all sides with white veils they passed me out of the house and into a white canopied wagon.

'I glimpsed other robed men holding back an enormous crowd, and I realized for the first time that only a select few of the Druids had been allowed to see me.

'Once Mael and I were under the canopy of the cart, the flaps were closed, and we were completely hidden. We seated ourselves on rude benches as the wagon started to move. And we rode for hours without speaking.

'Occasional rays of sun pierced the white fabric of the tent-like enclosure. And when I put my face close to the cloth I could see the forest — deeper, thicker than I remembered. And behind us came an endless train, and great wagons of men who clung to wooden bars and cried out to be released, their voices commingling in an awful chorus.

'"Who are they? Why do they cry like that?" I asked finally. I couldn't stand the tension any longer.

'Mael roused himself as if from a dream. "They are evil-doers, thieves, murderers, all justly condemned, and they shall perish in sacred sacrifice."

'"Loathsome," I muttered. But was it? We condemned our criminals to die on crosses in Rome, to be burnt at the stake, to

446

suffer all manner of cruelties. Did it make us more civilized that we didn't call it a religious sacrifice? Maybe the Keltoi were wiser than we were in not wasting the deaths.

'But this was nonsense. My head was light. The cart was creeping along. I could hear those who passed us on foot as well as on horseback. Everyone going to the festival of Samhain. I was about to die. I didn't want it to be fire. Mael looked pale and frightened. And the wailing of the men in the prison carts was driving me to the edge of madness.

'What would I think when the fire was lighted? What would I think when I felt myself start to burn? I couldn't stand this.

'"What is going to happen to me!" I demanded suddenly. I had the urge to strangle Mael. He looked up and his brows moved ever so slightly.

'"What if the god is already dead ..." he whispered.

'"Then we go to Rome, you and I, and we get drunk together on good Italian wine!" I whispered.

'It was late afternoon when the cart came to a stop. The noise seemed to rise like steam all around us.

'When I went to look out, Mael didn't stop me. I saw we had come to an immense clearing hemmed on all sides by the giant oaks. All the carts including ours were backed into the trees, and in the middle of the clearing hundreds worked at some enterprise involving endless bundles of sticks and miles of rope and hundreds of great rough-hewn tree trunks.

'The biggest and longest logs I had ever seen were been hefted upright in two giant Xs.

'The woods were alive with those who watched. The clearing could not contain the multitudes. Yet more and more carts wound their way through the press to find a spot at the edges of the forest.

'I sat back and pretended to myself that I did not know what they were doing out there, but I did. And before the sunset I heard louder and more desperate screams from those in the prison carts.

'It was almost dusk. And when Mael lifted the flap for me to see, I stared in horror at two gargantuan wicker figures — a

447

man and a woman, it seemed, from the mass of vines that suggested dress and hair — constructed all of logs and osiers and ropes, and filled from top to bottom with the bound and writhing bodies of the condemned who screamed in supplication.

'I was speechless looking at these two monstrous giants. I could not count the number of wriggling human bodies they held, victims stuffed into the hollow framework of their enormous legs, their torsos, their arms, even their hands, and even into their immense and faceless cagelike heads, which were crowned with ivy leaves and flowers. Ropes of flowers made up the woman's gown, and stalks of wheat were stuffed into the man's great belt of ivy. The figures shivered as if they might at any moment fall, but I knew the powerful cross scaffolding of timbers supported them as they appeared to tower over the distant forest. And all around the feet of these figures were stacked the bundles of kindling and pitch-soaked wood that would soon ignite them.

'"And all these who must die are guilty of some wrongdoing, you wish me to believe that?" I asked of Mael.

'He nodded with his usual solemnity. This didn't concern him.

'"They have waited months, some years, to be sacrificed," he said almost indifferently. "They come from all over the land. And they cannot change their fate any more than we can change ours. It is to perish in the forms of the Great Mother and her Lover."

'I was becoming ever more desperate. I should have done anything to escape. But even now some twenty Druids surrounded the cart and beyond them was a legion of warriors. And the crowd itself went so far back into the trees that I could see no end to it.

'Darkness was falling quickly, and everywhere torches were being lighted.

'I could feel the roar of excited voices. The screams of the condemned grew ever more piercing and beseeching.

'I sat still and tried to deliver my mind from panic. If I could not escape, then I would meet these strange ceremonies with some degree of calm, and when it came clear what a sham they were, I would with dignity and righteousness pronounce my judgements loud enough for others to hear them. That would be my last act — the act of the god — and it must be done with authority, or else it would do nothing in the scheme of things.

'The cart began to move. There was much noise, shouting, and Mael rose and took my arm and steadied me. When the flap was opened we had come to a stop deep in the woods many yards from the clearing. I glanced back at the lurid sight of the immense figures, torchlight glinting on the swarm of pathetic movement inside them. They seemed animate, these horrors, like things that would suddenly start to walk and crush all of us. The play of light and shadow on those stuffed into the giant heads gave a false impression of hideous faces.

'I couldn't make myself turn away from it, and from the sight of the crowd gathered all around, but Mael tightened his grip on my arm and said that I must come now to the sanctuary of the god with the elect of the priesthood.

'The others closed me in, obviously trying to conceal me. I realized the crowd did not know what was happening now. In all likelihood they knew only that the sacrifices would soon begin, and some manifestation of the god would be claimed by the Druids.

'Only one of the band carried a torch, and he led the way deeper into the evening darkness. Mael at my side, and other white-robed figures ahead of me, flanking me, and behind me.

'It was still. It was damp. And the trees rose to such dizzying heights against the vanishing glow of the distant sky that they seemed to be growing even as I looked up at them.

'I could run now, I thought, but how far would I get before this entire race of people came thundering after me?

'But we had come into a grove, and I saw, in the feeble light of the flames, dreadful faces carved into the barks of the trees and human skulls on stakes grinning in the shadows. In carved-out tree trunks were other skulls in rows, piled one row upon another. In fact, the place was a regular charnel house, and the silence that enclosed us seemed to give life to

449

these horrid things, to let them speak suddenly.

'I tried to shake the illusion, the sense that these staring skulls were watching.

'There is no one really watching, I thought, there is no continuous awareness of anything.

'But we had passed before a gnarled oak of such enormous girth that I doubted my senses. How old it must have been, this tree, to have grown to such width I couldn't imagine. But when I looked up I saw that its soaring limbs were still alive, it was still in green leaf, and the living mistletoe everywhere decorated it.

'The Druids had stepped away to right and left. Only Mael remained near me. And I stood facing the oak, with Mael at my far right, and I saw that hundreds of bouquets of flowers had been laid at the base of the tree, their little blooms barely showing any colour anymore in the gathering shadows.

'Mael had bowed his head. His eyes were closed. And it seemed the others were in the same attitude, and their bodies were trembling. I felt the cool breeze stir the green grass. I heard the leaves all around us carry the breeze in a loud and long sigh that died away as it had come in the forest.

'And then very distinctly, I heard words spoken in the dark that had no sound to them!

'They came undeniably from within the tree itself, and they asked whether or not all the conditions had been met by him who would drink the Divine Blood tonight.

'For a moment I thought I was going mad. They had drugged me. But I had drunk nothing since morning! My head was clear, too painfully clear, and I heard the silent pulse of this personage again and it was asking questions:

He is a man of learning?

'Mael's slender form seemed to shimmer as surely he expressed the answer. And the faces of the others had become rapt, their eyes fixed on the great oak, the flutter of the torch the only movement.

'Can he go down into Egypt?

I saw Mael nod. And the tears rose in his eyes, and his pale throat moved as he swallowed.

450

'*Yes, I live, my faithful one, and I speak, and you have done well, and I shall make the new god. Send him in to me.*

'I was too astonished to speak, and I had nothing to say either. *Everything had changed.* Everything that I believed, depended upon, had suddenly been called into question. I hadn't the slightest fear, only paralyzing amazement. Mael took me by the arm. The other Druids came to assist him, and I was led around the oak, clear of the flowers heaped at its roots, until we stood behind it before a huge pile of stones banked against it.

'The grove had its carved images on this side as well, its troves of skulls, and the pale figures of Druids whom I had not seen before. And it was these men, some with long white beards, who drifted forward to lay their hands on the stones and start to remove them.

'Mael and the others worked with them, silently lifting these great rocks and casting them aside, some of the stones so heavy that three men had to lift them.

'And finally there was revealed in the base of the oak a heavy doorway of iron with huge locks over it. Mael drew out an iron key and he said some long words in the language of the Keltoi, to which the others gave responses. Mael's hand was shaking. But he soon had all the locks undone, and then it took four of the Druids to pull back the door. And then the torch-bearer lighted another brand for me and placed it in my hands and Mael said:

'"Enter, Marius."

'In the wavering light, we glanced at each other. He seemed a helpless creature, unable to move his limbs, though his heart brimmed as he looked at me. I knew now the barest glimpse of the wonder that had shaped him and enflamed him, and was utterly humbled and baffled by its origins.

'But from within the tree, from the darkness beyond this rudely cut doorway, there came the silent one again:

'*Do not be afraid, Marius. I wait for you. Take the light and come to me.*'

7

HEN I stepped through the doorway, the Druids closed it. And I realized that I stood at the top of a long stone staircase. It was a configuration I was to see over and over again in the centuries that followed, and you have already seen it twice and you will see it again — the steps leading down into the Mother Earth, into the chambers where Those Who Drink the Blood always hide.

'The oak itself contained a chamber, low and unfinished, the light of my torch glinting on the rude marks left everywhere in the wood by the chisels, but the thing that called me was at the bottom of the stairs. And again, it told me that I must not be afraid.

'I was not afraid. I was exhilarated beyond my wildest dreams. I was not going to die as simply as I had imagined. I was descending to a mystery that was infinitely more interesting than I had ever thought it would be.

'But when I reached the bottom of the narrow steps and stood in the small stone chamber there, I was terrified by what I saw — terrified and repelled by it, the loathing and fear so immediate that I felt a lump rising to suffocate me or make me uncontrollably sick.

'A creature sat on a stone bench opposite the foot of the stairway, and in the full light of the torch I saw that it had the face and limbs of a man. But it was burnt black all over, horribly burnt, its skin shrivelled to its very bones. In fact it appeared a yellow-eyed skeleton coated in pitch, only its flowing main of white hair untouched. It opened its mouth to speak and I saw its white teeth, its fang teeth, and I gripped the torch firmly, trying not to scream like a fool.

'"Do not come too close to me," it said. "Stand there where I may really see you, not as they see you, but as my eyes can still see."

'I swalllowed, tried to breathe easily. No human being could have been burnt like that and survived. And yet the thing lived — naked and shrunken and black. And its voice was low and beautiful. It rose, and then moved slowly across the chamber.

'It pointed its finger at me, and the yellow eyes widened slightly, revealing a blood red tinge in the light.

'"What do you want of me?" I whispered before I could stop myself. "Why have I been brought here?"

'"Calamity," he said in the same voice, coloured with genuine feeling — not the rasping sound I had expected from such a thing. "I will give you my power, Marius, I will make you a god and you will be immortal. But you must leave here when it is finished. You must somehow escape our faithful worshippers, and you must go down into Egypt to find why this ... this ... has befallen me."

'He appeared to be floating in the darkness, his hair a mop of white straw around him, his jaws stretching the blackened leathery skin that clung to his skull as he spoke.

'"You see, we are the enemies of light, we gods of darkness, we serve the Holy Mother and we live and rule only by the light of the moon. But our enemy, the sun, has escaped his natural path and sought us out in darkness. All over the north country where we are worshipped, in the sacred groves from the lands of snow and ice, down into this fruitful country, and to the east, the sun has found its way into the sanctuary by day or the world by night and burned the gods alive. The youngest of these perished utterly, some exploding like comets before their worshippers! Others died in such heat that the sacred tree itself became a funeral pyre. Only the old ones — the ones who have long served the Great Mother — continued to walk and to talk as I do, but in agony, affrighting the faithful worshippers when they appeared.

'"There must be a new god, Marius, strong and beautiful as I was, the lover of the Great Mother, but more truly there must be one strong enough to escape the worshippers, to get out of the oak somehow, and to go down into Egypt and seek out the old gods and find why this calamity has occurred. You must go to Egypt, Marius, you must go into Alexandria and into the older cities, and you must summon the gods with the silent voice that you will have after I make you, and you must

453

find who lives still and who walks still, and why this calamity has occurred."

'It closed its eyes now. It stood still, its light frame wavering uncontrollably as if it were a thing made of black paper, and I saw suddenly, unaccountably, a spill of violent images — these gods of the grove bursting into flame. I heard their screams. My mind, being rational, being Roman, resisted these images. It tried to memorize and contain them, rather than yield to them, but the maker of the images — this thing — was patient and the images went on. I saw the country that could only be Egypt, the burnt yellow look to all things, the sand that over-lies everything and soils it and dusts it to the same colour, and I saw more stairways into the earth and I saw sanctuaries ...

'"Find them," he said. "Find why and how this has come to pass. See to it that it never comes to pass again. Use your powers in the streets of Alexandria until you find the old ones. Pray the old ones are there as I am still here."

'I was too shocked to answer, too humbled by the mystery. And perhaps there was even a moment when I accepted this destiny, accepted it completely, but I am not sure.

'"I know," he said. "From me you can keep no secrets. You do not wish to be the God of the Grove, and you will seek to escape. But you see, this disaster may seek you out wherever you are unless you discover the cause and the prevention of it. So I know you will go into Egypt, else you too in the womb of the night or the womb of the dark earth may be burnt by this unnatural sun."

'It came towards me a little, dragging its dried feet on the stone floor. "Now mark my words, you must escape this very night," it said. "I will tell the worshippers that you must go down into Egypt, for the salvation of all of us, but having a new and able god, they will be loath to part with him. But you must go down. And you must not let them imprison you in the oak after the festival. You must travel fast. And before sunrise, go into the Mother Earth to escape the light. She will protect you. Now come to me. I will give you The Blood. And pray I still have the power to give you my ancient strength. It will be slow. It will be long. I will take and I will give, and I will take and I will give, but I must do it, and you must become the god, and you must do as I have said."

'Without waiting for my compliance, it was suddenly on me, its blackened fingers clutching at me, the torch falling from my hands. I fell backwards on the stairs, but its teeth were already in my throat.

'You know what happened, you know what is was to feel the blood being drawn, to feel the swoon. I saw in those moments the tombs and temples of Egypt. I saw two figures, resplendent as they sat side by side as if on a throne. I saw and heard other voices speaking to me in other languages. And underneath it all, there came the same command: serve the Mother, take the blood of the sacrifice, preside over the worship that is the only worship, the eternal worship of the grove.

'I was struggling as one struggles in dreams, unable to cry out, unable to escape. And when I realized I was free and no longer pinned to the floor, I saw the god again, black as he had been before, but this time he was robust, as if the blaze had only baked him and he retained his full strength. His face had definition, even beauty, features well formed beneath the cracked casing of blackened leather that was his skin. The yellow eyes had round them now the natural folds of flesh that made them portals of a soul. But he was still crippled, still suffering, almost unable to move.

'"Rise, Marius," he said. "You thirst and I will give you to drink. Rise and come to me."

'And you know then the ecstasy I felt when his blood came into me, when it worked its way into every vessel, every limb. But the horrid pendulum had only begun to swing.

'Hours passed in the oak, as he took the blood out of me and gave it back over and over again. I lay sobbing on the floor when I was drained. I could see my hands like bones in front of me. I was shrivelled as he had been. And again he would give me the blood to drink and I would rise in a frenzy of exquisite feeling, only to have him take it out of me again.

'With every exchange there came the lessons: that I was immortal, that only the sun and the fire could kill me, that I would sleep by day in the earth, that I should never know illness or natural death. That my soul should never migrate from my form into another, that I was the servant of the Mother, and that the moon would give me strength.

'That I would thrive on the blood of the evildoers, and even of the innocent who were sacrificed to the Mother, that I should remain in starvation between sacrifices, so that my body would become dry and empty like the dead wheat in the fields at winter, only to be filled with the blood of the sacrifice and to become full and beautiful like the new plants of the spring.

'In my suffering and ecstasy there would be the cycle of the seasons. And the powers of my mind, to read the thoughts and intentions of others, in their justice and their laws. Never should I drink any blood but the blood of the sacrifice. Never should I seek to take my powers for my own.

'These things I learned, these things I understood. But what was really taught to me during those hours was what we all learn at the moment of the Drinking of the Blood, that I was no longer a mortal man — that I had passed away from all I knew into something so powerful that these old teachings could barely harness or explain it, that my destiny, to use Mael's words, was beyond all the knowledge that anyone — mortal or immortal — could give.

'At last the god prepared me to go out of the tree. He drained so much blood from me now that I was scarcely able to stand. I was a wraith. I was weeping from thirst, I was seeing blood and smelling blood, and would have rushed at him and caught him and drained him had I the strength. But the strength, of course, was his.

'"You are empty, as you will always be at the commencement of the festival," he said, "so that you may drink your fill of the sacrificial blood. But remember what I have told you. After you preside, you must find a way to escape. As for me, try to save me. Tell them that I must be kept with you. But in all likelihood my time has come to an end."

'"Why, how do you mean?" I asked.

'"You will see. There need be only one god here, one good

god," he said. "If I could only go with you to Egypt, I could drink the blood of the old ones and it might heal me. As it is, I will take hundreds of years to heal. And I shall not be allowed that time. But remember, go into Egypt. Do all that I have said."

'He turned me now and pushed me towards the stairs. The torch lay blazing in the corner, and as I rose towards the door above, I smelled the blood of the Druids waiting, and I almost wept.

'"They will give you all the blood that you can take," he said behind me. "Place yourself in their hands."'

8

'YOU can well imagine how I looked when I stepped from the oak. The Druids had waited for my knock upon the door, and in my silent voice, I had said:

'*Open. It is the god.*

'My human death was long finished. I was ravenous, and surely my face was no more than a living skull. No doubt my eyes were bulging from their sockets, and my teeth were bared. The white robe hung on me as on a skeleton. And no clearer evidence of my divinity could have been given to the Druids, who stood awestruck as I came out of the tree.

'But I saw not merely their faces, I saw into their hearts. I saw the relief in Mael that the god within had not been too feeble to create me, I saw the confirmation in him of all that he believed.

'And I saw the other great vision that is ours to see — the great spiritual depth of each man buried deep within a crucible of heated flesh and blood.

'My thirst was pure agony. And summoning all my new strength, I said: "Take me to the altars. The Feast of Samhain is to begin."

'The Druids let out chilling screams. They howled in the forest. And far beyond the sacred grove there came a deafening roar from the multitudes who had waited for that cry.

'We walked swiftly, in procession towards the clearing, and more and more of the white-robed priests came out to greet us and I found myself pelted with fresh and fragrant flowers from all sides, blossoms I crushed under my feet as I was saluted with hymns.

'I need not tell you how the world looked to me with the new vision, how I saw each tint and surface beneath the thin veil of darkness, how these hymns and anthems assaulted my ears.

'Marius, the man, was disintegrated inside this new being.

'Trumpets blared from the clearing as I mounted the steps of the stone altar and looked out over the thousands gathered there — the sea of expectant faces, the giant wicker figures with their doomed victims still struggling and crying inside.

'A great silver cauldron of water stood before the altar, and as the priests sang, a chain of prisoners was led to this cauldron, their arms bound behind their backs.

'The voices were singing in concert around me as the priests placed the flowers in my hair, on my shoulders, at my feet.

'"Beautiful one, powerful one, god of the woods and the fields, drink now the sacrifices offered to you, and as your wasted limbs fill with life, so the earth will renew itself. So you will forgive us for the cutting of the corn which is the harvest, so you will bless the seed we sow."

'And I saw before me those selected to be my victims, three stout men, bound as the others were bound, but clean and dressed also in white robes, with flowers on their shoulders and in their hair. Youths they were, handsome and innocent and overcome with awe as they awaited the will of the god.

'The trumpets were deafening. The roaring was ceaseless. I said:

'"Let the sacrifices begin," And as the first youth was delivered up to me, as I prepared to drink for the very first time from that truly divine cup which is human life, as I held the warm flesh of the victim in my hands, the blood ready for my open mouth, I saw the fires lighted beneath the towering wicker giants, I saw the first two prisoners forced head down into the water of the silver cauldron.

'Death by fire, death by water, death by the piercing teeth of the hungry god.

'Through the age-old ecstasy, the hymns continued: "God of the waning and waxing moon, god of the woods and fields, you who are the very image of death in your hunger, grow strong with the blood of the victims, grow beautiful so that the Great Mother will take you to herself."

'How long did it last? I do not know. It was forever — the blaze of the wicker giants, the screaming of the victims, the long procession of those who must be drowned. I drank and drank, not merely from the three selected for me, but from a dozen others before they were returned to the cauldron, or forced into the blazing giants. The priests cut the heads from the dead with great bloody swords, stacking them in pyramids to either side of the altar, and the bodies were borne away.

'Everywhere I turned I saw rapture on sweating faces, everywhere I turned I heard the anthems and cries. But at last the frenzy was dying out. The giants were fallen into a smouldering heap upon which men poured more pitch, more kindling.

'And it was now time for the judgments, for men to stand before me and present their cases for vengeance against others, and for me to look with my new eyes into their souls. I was reeling. I had drunk too much blood, but I felt such power in me I could have leapt up and over the clearing and deep into the forest. I could have spread invisible wings, or so it seemed.

'But I carried out my "destiny", as Mael would have called it. I found this one just, that one in error, this one innocent, that one deserving of death.

'I don't know how long it went on because my body no longer measured time in weariness. But finally it was finished, and I realized the moment of action had come.

'I had somehow to do what the old god had commanded me, which was to escape the imprisonment in the oak. And I also had precious little time in which to do it, no more than an hour before dawn.

'As for what lay ahead in Egypt, I had not made my decision yet. But I knew that if I let the Druids enclose me in the sacred tree again, I would starve in there until the small offering at the next full moon. And all of my nights until that time would be thirst and torture, and what the old one had called "the god's dreams" in which I'd learn the secrets of the tree and the grass that grew and the silent Mother.

'But these secrets were not for me.

'The Druids surrounded me now and we proceeded to the sacred tree again, the hymns dying to a litany which commanded me to remain within the oak to sanctify the forest, to be its guardian, and to speak kindly through the oak to those of the priesthood who would come from to time to ask guidance of me.

'I stopped before we reached the tree. A huge pyre was blazing in the middle of the grove, casting ghastly light on the carved faces and the heaps of human skulls. The rest of the priesthood stood round it waiting. A current of terror shot through me with all the new power that such feelings have for us.

'I started talking hastily. In an authoritative voice I told them that I wished them all to leave the grove. That I should seal myself up in the oak at dawn with the old god. But I could see it wasn't working. They were staring at me coldly and glancing one to the other, their eyes shallow like bits of glass.

'"Mael!" I said. "Do as I command you. Tell these priests to leave the grove."

'Suddenly, without the slightest warning, half the assemblage of priests ran towards the tree. The other took hold of my arms.

'I shouted for Mael, who led the siege on the tree, to stop. I tried to get loose but some twelve of the priests gripped my arms and my legs.

'If I had only understood the extent of my strength, I might easily have freed myself. But I didn't know. I was still reeling from the feast, too horrified by what I knew would happen now. As I struggled, trying to free my arms, even kicking at those who held me, the old god, the naked and black thing, was borne out of the tree and heaved into the fire.

'Only for a split second did I see him, and all I beheld was resignation. He did not once lift his arms to fight. His eyes were closed and he did not look at me, nor at anyone or anything, and I remembered in that moment what he had told me, of his agony, and I started to cry.

'I was shaking violently as they burned him. But from the very midst of the flames I heard his voice. "Do as I commanded you, Marius. You are our hope." That meant Get Out of Here Now.

'I made myself still and small in the grip of those who held me. I wept and wept and acted like I was just the sad victim of all this magic, just the poor god who must mourn his father who had gone into the flames. And when I felt their hands relax, when I saw that, one and all, they were gazing into the pyre, I pivoted with all my strength, tearing loose from their grip, and I ran as fast as I could for the woods.

'In that initial sprint, I learned for the first time what my powers were. I cleared hundreds of yards in an instant, my feet barely touching the ground.

'But the cry rang out immediately: "THE GOD HAS FLOWN!" and within seconds the multitude in the clearing was screaming it over and over as thousands of mortals plunged into the trees.

'How on earth did this happen, I thought suddenly, that I'm a god, full of human blood, and running from thousands of Celtic barbarians through this damned wood!

'I didn't even stop to tear the white robe off me, but ripped it off while I was still running, and then I leapt up to the branches overhead and moved even faster through the tops of the oaks.

'Within minutes I was so far away from my pursuers that I couldn't hear them anymore. But I kept running and running, leaping from branch to branch, until there was nothing to fear anymore but the morning sun.

'And I learned then what Gabrielle learned so early in your

wanderings, that I could easily dig into the earth to save myself from the light.

'When I awoke the heat of my thirst astonished me. I could not imagine how the old god had endured the ritual starvation. I could think only of human blood.

'But the Druids had had the day in which to pursue me. I had to proceed with great care.

'And I starved all that night as I sped through the forest, not drinking until early morning when I came upon a band of thieves in the woods which provided me with the blood of an evildoer, and a good suit of clothes.

'In those hours just before dawn, I took stock of things. I had learned a great deal about my powers, I would learn more. And I would go down to Egypt, not for the sake of the gods or their worshippers, but to find out what this was all about.

'And so even then you see, more than seventeen hundred years ago, we were questing, we were rejecting the explanations given us, we were loving the magic and the power for its own sake.

'On the third night of my new life, I wandered into my old house in Massilia and found my library, my writing table, my books all there still. And my faithful slaves overjoyed to see me. What did these things mean to me? What did it mean that I had written this history, that I had lain in this bed?

'I knew I could not be Marius, the Roman, any longer. But I would take from him what I could. I sent my beloved slaves back home. I wrote my father to say that a serious illness compelled me to live out my remaining days in the heat and dryness of Egypt. I packed off the rest of my history to those in Rome who would read it and publish it, and then I set out for Alexandria with gold in my pockets, with my old travel documents, and with two dull-witted slaves who never questioned that I travelled by night.

'And within a month of the great Samhain Feast in Gaul, I was roaming the black crooked nighttime streets of Alexandria, searching for the old gods with my silent voice.

'I was mad, but I knew the madness would pass. I had to find the old gods. And you know why I had to find them. It was not only the threat of the calamity again, the sun god seeking me out in the darkness of my daytime slumber, or visiting me with obliterating fire in the full darkness of the night.

'I had to find the old gods because I could not bear to be alone among men. The full horror of it was upon me, and though I killed only the murderer, the evildoer, my conscience was too finely tuned for self-deception. I could not bear the realization that I, Marius, who had known and enjoyed such love in his life, was the relentless bringer of death.'

9

ALEXANDRIA was not an old city. It had existed for just a little over three hundred years. But it was a great port and the home of the largest libraries in the Roman world. Scholars from all over the Empire came to study there, and I had been one of them in another lifetime, and now I found myself there again.

'Had not the god told me to come, I would have gone deeper into Egypt, "to the bottom" to use Mael's phrase, suspecting that the answers to all riddles lay in the older shrines.

'But a curious feeling came on me in Alexandria. I *knew* the gods were there. I knew they were guiding my feet when I sought the streets of the whorehouses and the thieves' dens, the places where men went to lose their souls.

'At night I lay on my bed in my little Roman house and I called to the gods, I grappled with my madness. I puzzled just as you have puzzled over the power and strength and crippling emotions which I now possessed. And one night just before morning, when the light of only one lamp shone through the sheer veils of the bed where I lay, I turned my eyes towards the distant garden doorway and saw a still black figure standing there.

'For one moment it seemed a dream, this figure, because it carried no scent, did not seem to breathe, did not make a sound. Then I knew it was one of the gods, but it was gone and I was left sitting up and staring after it, trying to remember what I had seen: a black naked thing with a bald head and red piercing eyes, a thing that seemed lost in its own stillness, strangely diffident, only marshalling its strength to move at the last moment before complete discovery.

'The next night in the back streets I heard a voice telling me to come. But it was a less articulate voice than that which had come from the tree. It made known to me only that the door was near. And finally there came the still and silent moment when I stood before the door.

'It was a god who opened it for me. It was a god who said Come.

'I was frightened as I descended the inevitable staircase, as I followed a steeply sloping tunnel. I lighted the candle I had brought with me, and I saw that I was entering an underground temple, a place older than the city of Alexandria, a sanctuary built perhaps under the ancient pharaohs, its walls covered with tiny coloured pictures depicting the life of old Egypt.

'And then there was the writing, the magnificent picture writing with its tiny mummies and birds and embracing arms without bodies, and coiling snakes.

'I moved on, coming into a vast place of square pillars and a soaring ceiling. The same paintings decorated every inch of stone here.

'And then I saw in the corner of my eye what seemed at first a statue, a black figure standing near a pillar with one hand raised to rest against the stone. But I knew it was no statue. No Egyptian god made out of diorite ever stood in this attitude nor wore a real linen skirt about its loins.

'I turned slowly, bracing myself against the full sight of it, and saw the same burnt flesh, the same streaming hair, though it was black, the same yellow eyes. The lips were shrivelled around the teeth and the gums, and the breath came out of its throat full of pain.

'"How and whence did you come?" he asked in Greek.

'I saw myself as he saw me, luminous and strong, even my blue eyes something of an incidental mystery, and I saw my Roman garments, my linen tunic gathered in gold buckles on my shoulders, my red cloak. With my long yellow hair, I must have looked like a wanderer from the north woods, "civilized" only on the surface, and perhaps this was now true.

'But he was the one who concerned me. And I saw him more fully, the seamed flesh burnt to his ribs and moulded to his collarbone and the jutting bones of his hips. He was not starved, this thing. He had recently drunk human blood. But his agony was like heat coming from him, as though the fire still cooked him from within, as though he were a self-contained hell.

'"How have you escaped the burning?" he asked. "What saved you? Answer!"

'"Nothing saved me," I said, speaking Greek as he did.

'I approached him holding the candle to the side when he shied from it. He had been thin in life, broad-shouldered like the old pharaohs, and his long black hair was cropped straight across the forehead in that old style.

'"I wasn't made when it happened," I said, "but afterwards, by the god of the sacred grove in Gaul."

'"Ah, then he was unharmed, this one who made you."

'"No, burned as you are, but he had enough strength to do it. He gave and took the blood over and over again. He said, "Go into Egypt and find why this has happened." He said the gods of the wood had burst into flames, some in their sleep and some awake. He said this had happened all over the north."

'"Yes." He nodded, and he gave a dry rasping laugh that shook his entire form. "And only the ancient had the strength to survive, to inherit the agony which only immortality can sustain. And so we suffer. But you have been made. You have come. You will make more. But is it justice to make more? Would the Father and the Mother have allowed this to happen to us if the time had not come?"

'"But who are the Father and the Mother?" I asked. I knew

465

he did not mean the earth when he said Mother.

'"The first of us," he answered, "those from whom all of us descend."

'I tried to penetrate his thoughts, feel the truth of them, but he knew what I was doing, and his mind folded up like a flower at dusk.

'"Come with me," he said. And he commenced to walk with a shuffling step out of the large room and down a long corridor, decorated as the chamber had been.

'I sensed we were in an even older place, something built before the temple from which we'd just come. I do not know how I knew it. The chill you felt on the steps here on the island was not there. You don't feel such things in Egypt. You feel something else. You feel the presence of something living in the air itself.

'But there was more palpable evidence of antiquity as we walked on. The paintings on these walls were older, the colours fainter, and here and there was damage where the coloured plaster had flaked and fallen away. The style had changed. The black hair of the little figures was longer and fuller, and it seemed the whole was more lovely, more full of light and intricate design.

'Somewhere far off water dripped on stone. The sound gave a songlike echo through the passage. It seemed the walls had captured life in these delicate and tenderly painted figures, it seemed that the magic attempted again and again by the ancient religious artists had its tiny glowing kernel of power. I could hear whispers of life where there were no whispers. I could feel the great continuity of history even if there was no one who was aware.

'The dark figure beside me paused as I looked at the walls. He made an airy gesture for me to follow him through a doorway, and we entered a long rectangular chamber covered entirely with the artful hieroglyphs. It was like being encased in a manuscript to be inside it. And I saw two older Egyptian sarcophagi placed head to head against the wall.

'These were boxes carved to conform to the shape of the mummies for which they were made, and fully modelled and painted to represent the dead, with faces of hammered gold, and eyes of inlaid lapis lazuli.

'I held the candle high. And with great effort my guide opened the lids of these cases and let them fall back so that I might see inside.

'I saw what at first appeared to be bodies, but when I drew closer I realized that they were heaps of ash in manly form. Nothing of tissue remained to them except a white fang here, a chip of bone there.

'"No amount of blood can bring them back now," said my guide. "They are past all resurrection. The vessels of the blood are gone. Those who could rise have risen, and centuries will pass before we are healed, before we know the cessation of our pain."

'Before he closed the mummy cases, I saw that the lids inside were blackened by the fire that had immolated these two. I wasn't sorry to see them shut up again.

'He turned and moved towards the doorway again, and I followed with the candle, but he paused and glanced back at the painted coffins.

'"When the ashes are scattered," he said, "their souls are free."

'"Then why don't you scatter the ashes!" I said, trying not to sound so desperate, so undone.

'"Should I?" he asked of me, the crisped flesh around his eyes widening. "Do you think that I should?"

'"You ask me!" I said.

'He gave one of those dry laughs again, that seemed to carry agony with it, and he led on down the passage to a lighted room.

'It was a library we entered, where a few scattered candles revealed the diamond-shaped wooden racks of parchment and papyrus scrolls.

'"This delighted me, naturally, because a library was something I could understand. It was the one human place in which I still felt some measure of my old sanity.

'But I was startled to see another one — another one of us — sitting to the side behind the writing table, his eyes on the floor.

'This one had no hair whatsoever, and though he was pitch black all over, his skin was full and well-modelled and gleamed as if it had been oiled. The planes of his face were beautiful, the hand that rested in the lap of his white linen kilt was gracefully curled, all the muscles of his naked chest well defined.

'He turned and looked up at me. And something immediately passed between us, something more silent than silence, as it can be with us.

'"This is the Elder," said the weaker one who'd brought me here. "And you see for yourself how he withstood the fire. But he will not speak. He has not spoken since it happened. Yet surely he knew where are the Mother and the Father, and why this was allowed to pass."

'The Elder merely looked forward again. But there was a curious expression on his face, something sarcastic and faintly amused, and a little contemptuous.

'"Even before this disaster," the other one said, "the Elder did not often speak to us. The fire did not change him, make him more receptive. He sits in silence, more and more like the Mother and the Father. Now and then he reads. Now and then he walks in the world above. He Drinks the Blood, he listens to the singers. Now and then he will dance. He speaks to mortals in the streets of Alexandria, but he will not speak to us. He has nothing to say to us. But he knows ... He knows why this happened to us."

'"Leave me with him," I said.

'I had the feeling that all beings have in such situations. I will make the man speak. I will draw something out of him, as no one else has been able to do. But it wasn't mere vanity that impelled me. This was the one who had come to me in the bedroom of my house, I was sure of it. This was the one who had stood watching me in my door.

'And I had sensed something in his glance. Call it intelligence, call it interest, call it recognition of some common knowledge — there was something there.

'And I knew that I carried with me the possibilities of a different world, unknown to the God of the Grove and even to this feeble and wounded one beside me who looked at the Elder in despair.

'The feeble one withdrew as I had asked. I went to the writing table and looked at the Elder.

'"What should I do?" I asked in Greek.

'He looked up at me abruptly, and I could see this thing I call intelligence in his face.

'"Is there any point," I asked, "to questioning you further?"

'I had chosen my tone carefully. There was nothing formal in it, nothing reverential. It was as familiar as it could be.

'"And just what is it you seek!" he asked in Latin suddenly, coldly, his mouth turning down at the ends, his attitude one of abruptness and challenge.

'It relieved me to switch to Latin.

'"You heard what I told the other," I said in the same informal manner, "how I was made by the God of the Grove in the country of the Keltoi, and how I was told to discover why the gods had died in flames."

'"You don't come on behalf of the Gods of the Grove!" He said, sardonic as before. He had not lifted his head, merely looked up, which made his eyes seem all the more challenging and contemptuous.

'"I do and I don't," I said. "If we can perish in this way, I would like to know why. What happened once can happen a second time. And I would like to know if we are really gods, and if we are, then what are our obligations to man. Are the Mother and the Father true beings, or are they legend? How did all this start? I would like to know that, of course."

'"By accident," he said.

'"By accident?" I leaned forward. I thought I had heard wrong.

'"By accident it started," he said coolly, forbiddingly, with the clear implication that the question was absurd. "Four thousand years ago, by accident, and it has been enclosed in magic and religion ever since."

'"You are telling me the truth, aren't you?"

'"Why shouldn't I? Why should I protect you from the truth? Why should I bother to lie to you? I don't even know who you are. I don't care."

'"Then will you explain to me what you mean, that it happened by accident," I pressed.

'"I don't know. I may. I may not. I have spoken more in these last few moments than I have in years. The story of the accident may be no more true than the myths that delight the others. The others have always chosen the myths. It's what you really want, is it not?" His voice rose and he rose slightly out of the chair as if his angry voice were impelling him to his feet.

'"A story of our creation, analogous to the Genesis of the Hebrews, the tales in Homer, the babblings of your Roman poets Ovid and Virgil — a great gleaming morass of symbols out of which life itself is supposed to have sprung." He was on his feet and all but shouting, his black forehead knotted with veins, his hand a fist on the desk. "It is that kind of tale that fills the documents in these rooms, that emerges in fragments from the anthems and the incantations. Want to hear it? It's as true as anything else."

'"Tell me what you will," I said. I was trying to keep calm. The volume of his voice was hurting my ears. And I heard things stirring in the rooms near us. Other creatures, like that dried-up wisp of a thing that had brought me in here, were prowling about.

'"And you might begin," I said acidly, "by confessing why you came to me in my rooms here in Alexandria. It was you who led me here. Why did you do that? To rail at me? To curse me for asking you how it started?"

'"Quiet yourself."

'"I might say the same to you."

'He looked me up and down calmly, and then he smiled. He opened both his hands as if in greeting or offering, and then he shrugged.

'"I want you to tell me about the accident," I said. "I would beg you to tell me if I thought it would do any good. What can I do for you to make you tell?"

'His face underwent several remarkable transformations. I could feel his thoughts, but not hear them, feel a high-pitched humour. And when he spoke again, his voice was thickened as if he were fighting back sorrow, as if it were strangling him.

'"Hearken to our old story," he said. "The good god, Osiris, the first pharaoh of Egypt, in the eons before the invention of writing, was murdered by evil men. And when his wife, Isis, gathered together the parts of his body, he became immortal and thereafter ruled in the realm of the dead. This is the realm of the moon, and the night, in which he reigned, and to him were brought the blood sacrifices for the great goddess which he drank. But the priests tried to steal from him the secret of his immortality, and so his worship became secret, and his temples were known only to those of his cult who protected him from the sun god, who might at any time seek to destroy Osiris with the sun's burning rays. But you can see the truth in the legend. The early king discovered something — or rather he was the victim of an ugly occurrence — and he became unnatural with a power that could be used for incalculable evil by those around him, and so he made a worship of it, seeking to contain it in obligation and ceremony, seeking to limit The Powerful Blood to those who would use it for white magic and nothing else. And so here we are."

'"And the Mother and Father are Isis and Osiris?"

'"Yes and no. They are the first two. Isis and Osiris are the names that were used in the myths that they told, or the old worship onto which they grafted themselves."

'"What was the accident, then? How was this thing discovered?"

'He looked at me for a long period of silence, and then he sat down again, turning to the side and staring off as he'd been before.

'"But why should I tell you?" he asked, yet this time he put the question with new feeling, as though he meant it sincerely and had to answer it for himself. "Why should I do anything? If the Mother and the Father will not rise from the sands to save themselves as the sun comes over the horizon, why should I move? Or speak? Or go on?" Again he looked up at me.

'"This is what happened, the Mother and the Father went out into the sun?"

'"Were left in the sun, my dear Marius," he said, astonishing me with the knowledge of my name. "Left in the sun. The Mother and the Father do not move of their own volition, save now and then to whisper to each other, to knock those of us down who would come to them for their healing blood. They could restore all of us who were burned, if they would let us drink the healing blood. Four thousand years the Father and Mother have existed, and our blood grows stronger with every season, every victim. It grows stronger even with starvation, for when the starvation is ended, new strength is enjoyed. But the Father and the Mother do not care for their children. And now it seems they do not care for themselves. Maybe after four thousand nights, they merely wished to see the sun!

'"Since the coming of the Greek into Egypt, since the perversion of the old art, they have not spoken to us. They have not let us see the blink of their eye. And what is Egypt now but the granary of Rome? When the Mother and the Father strike out to drive us away from the veins in their necks, they are as iron and can crush our bones. And if they do not care anymore, then why should I?"

'I studied him for a long moment.

'"And you are saying," I asked, "that this is what caused the others to burn up? That the Father and Mother were left out in the sun?"

'He nodded.

'"Our blood comes from them!" he said. "It is their blood. The line is direct, and what befalls them befalls us. If they are burnt, we are burnt."

'"We are connected to them!" I whispered in amazement.

'"Exactly, my dear Marius," he said, watching me, seeming to enjoy my fear. "That is why they have been kept for a thousand years, the Mother and the Father, that is why victims are brought to them in sacrifice, that is why they are worshipped. What happens to them happens to us."

'"Who did it? Who put them in the sun?"

'He laughed without making a sound.

'"The one who kept them," he said, "the one who couldn't endure it any longer, the one who had had this solemn charge for too long, the one who could persuade no one else to accept

472

the burden, and finally, weeping and shivering, took them out into the desert sands and left them like two statues there."

'"And my fate is linked to this," I murmured.

'"Yes. But you see, I do not think he believed it any longer, the one who kept them. It was just an old tale. After all, they were worshipped as I told you, worshipped by us, as we are worshipped by mortals, and no one dared to harm them. No one held a torch to them to see if it made the rest of us feel pain. No. He did not believe it. He left them in the desert, and that night when he opened his eyes in his coffin and found himself a burnt and unrecognizable horror, he screamed and screamed."

'"You got them back underground."

'"Yes."

'"And they are blackened as you are ..."

'"No." He shook his head. "Darkened to a golden bronze, like the meat turning on the spit. No more than that. And beautiful as before, as if beauty has become part of their heritage, beauty part and parcel of what they are destined to be. They stare forward as they always have, but they no longer incline their heads to each other, they no longer hum with the rhythm of their secret exchanges, they no longer let us drink their blood. And the victims brought to them, they will not take, save now and then, and only in solitude. No one knows when they will drink, when they will not."

'I shook my head. I moved back and forth, my head bowed, the candle fluttering in my hand, not knowing what to say to all this, needing time to think it out.

'He gestured for me to take the chair on the other side of the writing table, and without thinking of it, I did.

'"But wasn't it meant to happen, Roman?" he asked. "Weren't they meant to meet their death in the sands, silent, unmoving, like statues cast there after a city is sacked by the conquering army, and were we not meant to die too? Look at Egypt. What is Egypt, I ask you again, but the granary of Rome? Were they not meant to burn there day after day while all of us burned like stars the world over?"

'"Where are they?" I asked.

'"Why do you want to know?" he sneered. "Why should I give you the secret? They cannot be hacked to pieces, they are too strong for that, a knife will barely pierce their skin. Yet cut them and you cut us. Burn them and you burn us. And whatever they make us feel, they feel only a particle of it because their age protects them. And yet to destroy every one of us, you have merely to bring them annoyance! The blood they do not even seem to need! Maybe their minds are connected to ours as well. Maybe the sorrow we feel, the misery, the horror at the fate of the world itself, comes from their minds, as locked in their chambers they dream! No. I cannot tell you where they are, can I? Until I decide for certain that I am indifferent, that it is time for us to die out."

'"Where are they?" I said again.

'"Why should I not sink them into the very depths of sea?" he asked. "Until such time as the earth herself heaves them up into the sunlight on the crest of a great wave?"

'I didn't answer. I was watching him, wondering at his excitement, understanding it but in awe of it just the same.

'"Why should I not bury them in the depths of the earth, I mean the darkest depths beyond the faintest sounds of life, and let them lie in silence there, no matter what they think and feel?"

'What answer could I give? I watched him. I waited until he seemed calmer. He looked at me and his face became tranquil and almost trusting.

'"Tell me how they became the Mother and the Father," I said.

'"Why?"

'"You know damn good and well why. I want to know! Why did you come into my bedroom if you didn't mean to tell me?" I asked again.

'"So what if I did?" he said bitterly. "So what if I wanted to see the Roman with my own eyes? We will die and you will die with us. So I wanted to see our magic in a new form. Who worships us now, after all? Yellow-haired warriors in the northern forests? Old old Egyptians in secret crypts beneath the sands? We do not live in the temples of Greece and Rome.

We never did. And yet they celebrate our myth — the only myth — they call the names of the Mother and the Father ..."

'"I don't give a damn," I said. "You know I don't. We are alike, you and I. I won't go back to the northern forests to make a race of gods for those people! But I came here to know and you must tell."

'"All right. So that you can understand the futility of it, so that you can understand the silence of the Mother and the Father, I will tell. But mark my words, I may yet bring us all down. I may yet burn the Mother and the Father in the heat of a kiln! But we will dispense with lengthy initiations and high-blown language. We will do away with the myths that died in the sand the day the sun shone on the Mother and the Father. I will tell you what all these scrolls left by the Father and the Mother reveal. Set down your candle. And listen to me."'

10

HAT the scrolls will tell you," he said, "if you could decipher them, is that we have two human beings. Akasha and Enkil, who had come into Egypt from some other, older land. This was in the time long before the first writing, before the first pyramids, when the Egyptians were still cannibals and hunted for the bodies of enemies to eat.

'"Akasha and Enkil directed the people away from these practices. They were worshippers of the Good Mother Earth and they taught the Egyptians how to sow seed in the Good Mother, and how to herd animals for meat and milk and skins.

'"In all probability, they were not alone as they taught these things, but rather the leaders of a people who had come with them from older cities whose names are now lost beneath the sands of Lebanon, their monuments laid waste.

'"Whatever is the truth, these were benevolent rulers, these two, in whom the good of others was the commanding value, as the Good Mother was the Nourishing Mother and wished for all men to live in peace, and they decided all questions of justice for the emerging land.

'"Perhaps they would have passed into myth in some benign form had it not been for a disturbance in the house of the royal steward which began with the antics of a demon that hurled the furniture about.

'"Now this was no more than a common demon, the kind one hears of in all lands at all times. He devils those who live in a certain place for a certain while. Perhaps he enters into the body of some innocent and roars through her mouth with a loud voice. He may cause the innocent one to belch obscenities and carnal invitations to those around her. Do you know of these things?"

'I nodded. I told him you always heard such stories. Such a demon was supposed to have possessed a vestal virgin in Rome. She made lewd overtures to all those around her, her face turning purple with exertion, then fainted. But the demon had somehow been driven out. "I thought the girl was simply mad," I said. "That she was, shall we say, not suited to be a vestal virgin ..."

'"Of course!" he said with a note of rich irony. "And I would assume the same thing, and so would most any intelligent man walking the streets of Alexandria above us. Yet such stories come and go. And if they are remarkable for any one thing it is that they do not affect the course of human events. These demons rather trouble some household, some person, and then they are gone into oblivion and we are right where we started again."

'"Precisely," I said.

'"But you understand this was old old Egypt. This was a time when men ran from the thunder, or ate the bodies of the dead to absorb their souls."

'"I understand," I said.

'"And this good King Enkil decided that he would himself address the demon who had come into his steward's house. This thing was out of harmony, he said. The royal magicians begged, of course, to be allowed to see to this, to drive the demon out. But this was a king who would do good for every-

476

one. He had some vision of all things being united in good, of all forces being made to go on the same divine course. He would speak to this demon, try to harness its power, so to speak, for the general good. And only if that could not be done would he consent to the demon's being driven out.

'"And so he went into the house of his steward, where furniture was being flung at the walls, and jars broken, and doors slammed. And he commenced to talk to this demon and invite it to talk to him. Everyone else ran away.

'"A full night passed before he came out of the haunted house and he had amazing things to say:

'"'These demons are mindless and childlike,' he told his magicians, 'but I have studied their conduct and I have learned from all the evidence why it is that they rage. They are maddened that they do not have bodies, that they cannot feel as we feel. They make the innocent scream filth because the rites of love and passion are things that they cannot possibly know. They can work the body parts but not truly inhabit them, and so they are obsessed with the flesh that they cannot invade. And with their feeble powers they bump upon objects, they make their victims twist and jump. This longing to be carnal is the origin of their anger, the indication of the suffering which is their lot.' And with these pious words he prepared to lock himself in the haunted chambers to learn more.

'"But this time his wife came between him and his purpose. She would not let him stay with the demons. He must look into the mirror, she said. He had aged remarkably in the few hours that he had remained in the house alone.

'"And when he would not be deterred, she locked herself in with him, and all those who stood outside the house heard the crashing and banging of objects, and feared for the moment when they would hear the King and the Queen themselves screaming or raging in spirit voices. The noise from the inner chambers was alarming. Cracks were appearing in the walls.

'"All fled as before, except for a small party of interested men. Now these men since the beginning of the reign had been the enemies of the King. These were old warriors who had led the campaigns of Egypt in search of human flesh, and

477

they had had enough of the King's goodness, enough of the Good Mother and farming and the like, and they saw in this spirit adventure not only more of the King's vain nonsense, but a situation that nevertheless provided a remarkable opportunity for them.

'"When night fell, they crept into the haunted house. They were fearless of spirits, just as the grave robbers are who rifle the tombs of the pharaohs. They believe, but not enough to control their greed.

'"And when they saw Enkil and Akasha together in the middle of this room full of flying objects, they set upon them and they stabbed the King over and over, as your Roman senators stabbed Caesar, and they stabbed the only witness, his wife.

'"And the King cried out, 'No, don't you see what you have done? You have given the spirits a way to get in! You have opened my body to them! Don't you see!' But the men fled, sure of the death of the King and the Queen, who was on her hands and knees, cradling her husband's head in her hands, both bleeding from more wounds than one could count.

'"Now the conspirators stirred up the populace. Did everyone know that the King had been killed by the spirits? He should have left the demons to his magicians as any other king would have done. And bearing torches, all flocked to the haunted house, which had grown suddenly and totally quiet.

'"The conspirators urged the magicians to enter, but they were afraid. 'Then we will go in and see what's happened,' said the evil ones, and they threw open the doors.

'"There stood the King and the Queen, staring calmly at the conspirators, and all of their wounds were healed. And their eyes had taken on an eerie light, their skin a white shimmer, their hair a magnificent gleam. Out of the house they came as the conspirators ran in terror, and they dismissed all the people and the priests and went back to the palace alone.

'"And though they confided in no one, they knew what had happened to them.

'"They had been entered through their wounds by the

demon at the point when mortal life itself was about to escape. But it was the blood that the demon permeated in that twilight moment when the heart almost stopped. Perhaps it was the substance that he had always sought in his ragings, the substance that he had tried to bring forth from his victims with his antics, but he had never been able to inflict enough wounds before his victim died. But now he was in the blood, and the blood was not merely the demon, or the blood of the King and Queen, but a combination of the human and the demon which was an altogether different thing.

"'And all that was left of the King and Queen was what this blood could animate, what it could infuse and claim for its own. Their bodies were for all other purposes dead. But the blood flowed through the brain and through the heart and through the skin, and so the intelligence of the King and Queen remained. Their souls, if you will, remained, as the souls reside in these organs, though why we do not know. And though the demon blood had no mind of its own, no character of its own that the King and Queen could discover, it nevertheless enhanced their minds and their characters, for it flowed through the organs that create thought. And it added to their faculties its purely spiritual powers, so that the King and Queen could hear the thoughts of mortals, and sense things and understand things that mortals could not.

"'In sum, the demon had added and the demon had taken away, and the King and Queen were New Things. They could no longer eat food, or grow, or die, or have children, yet they could feel with an intensity that terrified them. And the demon had what it wanted: a body to live in, a way to be in the world at last, a way to *feel*.

"'But then came the even more dreadful discovery, that to keep their corpses animate, the blood must be fed. And all it could convert to its use was the selfsame thing of which it was made: blood. Give it more blood to enter, give it more blood to push through the limbs of the body in which it enjoyed such glorious sensations, of blood it could not get enough.

"'And oh, the grandest of all sensations was the drinking in which it renewed itself, fed itself, enlarged itself. And in that

479

moment of drinking it could feel the death of the victim, the moment it pulled the blood so hard out of the victim that the victim's heart stopped.

'"The demon had them, the King and Queen. They were Drinkers of the Blood; and whether or not the demon knew of them, we will never be able to tell. But the King and Queen knew that they had the demon and could not get rid of it, and if they did they would die because their bodies were already dead. And they learned immediately that these dead bodies, animated as they were entirely by this demonic fluid, could not withstand fire or the light of the sun. On the one hand, they seemed as fragile white flowers that can be withered black in the daytime desert heat. On the other, it seemed the blood in them was so volatile that it would boil if heated, thereby destroying the fibres through which it moved.

'"It has been said that in these very early times, they could withstand no brilliant illumination, that even a nearby fire would cause their skin to smoke.

'"Whatever, they were of a new order of being, and their thoughts were of a new order of being, and they tried to understand the things that they saw, the dispositions that afflicted them in this new state.

'"All discoveries are not recorded. There is nothing in writing or in the unwritten tradition about when they first chose to pass on the blood, or ascertained the method by which it must be done — that the victim must be drained to the twilight moment of approaching death, or the demonic blood given him cannot take hold.

'"We do know through the unwritten tradition that the King and Queen tried to keep secret what had happened to them, but their disappearance by day aroused suspicions. They could not attend to the religious duties in the land.

'"And so it came to pass that even before they had formed their clearest decisions, they had to encourage the populace to a worship of the Good Mother in the light of the moon.

'"But they could not protect themselves from the conspirators, who still did not understand their recovery and sought to do away with them again. The attack came despite all precautions and the strength of the King and the Queen proved overwhelming to the conspirators, and they were all the more frightened by the fact that those wounds they managed to inflict upon the King and Queen were miraculously and instantly healed. An arm was severed from the King and this he put back on his shoulder and it came to life again and the conspirators fled.

'"And through these attacks, these battles, the secret came into the possession not only of the King's enemies but the priests as well.

'"And no one wanted to destroy the King and the Queen now; rather they wanted to take them prisoner and gain the secret of immortality from them, and they sought to take the blood from them, but their early attempts failed.

'"The drinkers were not near to death; and so they became hybrid creatures — half god and half human — and they perished in horrible ways. Yet some succeeded. Perhaps they emptied their veins first. It isn't recorded. But in later ages, this has always proved a way to steal the blood.

'"And perhaps the Mother and the Father chose to make fledglings. Maybe out of loneliness and fear, they chose to pass on the secret to those of good mettle whom they could trust. Again we are not told. Whatever the case, other Drinkers of the Blood did come into being, and the method of making them was eventually known.

'"And the scrolls tell us that the Mother and the Father sought to triumph in their adversity. They sought to find some reason in what had happened, and they believed that their heightened senses must surely serve some good. The Good Mother had allowed this to happen, had she not?

'"And they must sanctify and contain what was done by mystery, or else Egypt might become a race of blood-drinking demons who would divide the world into Those Who Drink the Blood and those who are bred only to give it, a tyranny that once achieved might never be broken by mortal men alone.

'"And so the good King and Queen chose the path of ritual, of myth. They saw in themselves the images of the waning and

481

waxing moon, and in their drinking of the blood the god incarnate who takes unto himself his sacrifice, and they used their superior powers to divine and predict and judge. They saw themselves as truly accepting the blood for the god, which otherwise would run down the altar. They girded with the symbolic and the mysterious what could not be allowed to become common, and they passed out of the sight of mortal men into the temples, to be worshipped by those who would bring them blood. They took to themselves the most fit sacrifices, those that had always been made for the good of the land. Innocents, outsiders, evildoers, they drank the blood for the Mother and for the Good.

'"They set into motion the tale of Osiris, composed in part of their own terrible suffering — the attack of the conspirators, the recovery, their need to live in the realm of darkness, the world beyond life, their inability to walk anymore in sun. And they grafted this upon the older stories of the gods who rise and fall in their love of the Good Mother, which were already there in the land from which they came.

'"And so these stories came down to us; these stories spread beyond the secret places in which the Mother and the Father were worshipped, in which those they made with the blood were installed.

'"And they were already old when the first pharaoh built his first pyramid. And the earliest texts record them in broken and strange form.

'"A hundred other gods ruled in Egypt, just as they rule in all lands. But the worship of the Mother and Father and Those Who Drink the Blood remained secret and powerful, a cult to which the devoted went to hear the silent voices of the gods, to dream their dreams.

'"We are not told who were the first fledglings of the Mother and Father. We know only that they spread the religion to the islands of the great sea, and to the lands of the two rivers, and to the north woods. That in shrines everywhere the moon god ruled and drank his blood sacrifices and used his powers to look into the hearts of men. During the periods between sacrifice, in starvation, the god's mind could leave his body; it could travel the heavens; he could learn a thousand things. And those mortals of the greatest purity of heart could come to the shrine and hear the voice of the god, and he could hear them.

'"But even before my time, a thousand years ago, this was all an old and incoherent story. The gods of the moon had ruled in Egypt for maybe three thousand years. And the religion had been attacked again and again.

'"When the Egyptian priests turned to the sun god Amon Ra, they opened the crypts of the moon god and let the sun burn him to cinders. And many of our kind were destroyed. The same happened when the first rude warriors rode down into Greece and broke open the sanctuaries and killed what they did not understand.

'"Now the babbling oracle of Delphi rules where we once ruled, and statues stand where we once stood. Our last hour is enjoyed in the north woods whence you came, among those who still drench our altars with the blood of the evildoer, and in the small villages of Egypt, where one or two priests tend the god in the crypt and allow the faithful to bring to him the evildoers, for they cannot take the innocent without arousing suspicion, and of evildoers and outsiders there are always some to be had. And down in the jungles of Africa, near the ruins of old cities that no one remembers, there, too, we are still obeyed.

'"But our history is punctuated by tales of rogues — the Drinkers of the Blood who look to no goddess for guidance and have always used their powers as they chose.

'"In Rome they live, in Athens, in all cities of the Empire, these who hearken to no laws of right and wrong and use their powers for their own ends.

'"And they died horribly in the heat and the flame just as did the gods in the groves and the sanctuaries, and if any have survived they probably do not even guess why they were subjected to the killing flame, of how the Mother and the Father were put into the sun."'

'HE had stopped.

483

'He was studying my reaction. The library was quiet and if the others prowled behind the walls, I couldn't hear them anymore.

'"I don't believe a word of it," I said.

'He stared at me in stupefied silence for a moment and then he laughed and laughed.

'In a rage, I left the library and went out through the temple rooms and up through the tunnel and out into the street.'

11

THIS was very uncharacteristic of me, to leave in temper, to break off abruptly and depart. I had never done that sort of thing when I was a mortal man. But as I've said, I was on the edge of madness, the first madness many of us suffer, especially those who have been brought into this by force.

'I went back to my little house near the great library of Alexandria, and I lay down on my bed as if I could really let myself fall asleep there and escape from this thing.

'"Idiot nonsense," I murmured to myself.

'But the more I thought about the story, the more it made sense. It made sense that something was in my blood impelling me to drink more blood. It made sense that it heightened all sensations, that it kept my body — a mere imitation now of a human body — functioning when it should have come to a stop. And it made sense that this thing had no mind of its own but was nevertheless a power, an organization of force with a desire to live all its own.

'And then it even made sense that we could all be connected to the Mother and the Father because this thing was spiritual, and had no bodily limits except the limits of the individual bodies in which it had gained control. It was the vine, this thing, and we were the flowers, scattered over great distances, but connected by the twining tendrils that could reach all over the world.

'And this was why we gods could hear each other so well, why I could know the others were in Alexandria, even before they called to me. It was why they could come and find me in my house, why they could lead me to the secret door.

'All right. Maybe it was true. And it *was* an accident, this melding of an unnamed force and a human body and mind to make the New Thing as the Elder had said.

'But still — I didn't like it.

'I revolted against all of it because if I was anything, I was an individual, a particular being, with a strong sense of my own rights and prerogatives. I could not realize that I was host to an alien entity. I was still Marius, no matter what had been done to me.

'I was left finally with one thought and one thought only: if I was connected to this Mother and Father then I must see them, and I must know that they were safe. I could not live with the thought that I could die at any moment on account of some alchemy I could neither control nor understand.

'But I didn't return to the underground temple. I spent the next few nights feasting on blood until my miserable thoughts were drowned in it, and then in the early hours I roamed the great library of Alexandria, reading as I had always done.

'SOME of the madness dissolved in me. I stopped longing for my mortal family. I stopped being angry at that cursed thing in the cellar temple, and I thought rather of this new strength I possessed. I would live for centuries: I would know the answers to all kinds of questions. I would be the continual awareness of things as time passed! And as long as I slew only the evildoer, I could endure my blood thirst, revel in it, in fact. And when the appropriate time came, I would make my companions and make them well.

'Now what remained? Go back to the Elder and find out where he had put the Mother and the Father. And see these creatures for myself. And do the very thing the Elder had threatened, sink them so deep into the earth that no mortal

485

could ever find them and expose them to the light.

'Easy to think about this, easy to imagine them as so simply dispatched.

'Five nights after I'd left the Elder, when all these thoughts had had time to develop in me, I lay resting in my bedroom, with the lamps shining through the sheer bed curtains as before. In filtered and golden light, I listened to the sounds of sleeping Alexandria, and slipped into thin and glittering waking dreams. I wondered if the Elder would come to me again, disappointed that I had not returned — and as the thought came clear to me, I realized that someone was standing in the doorway again.

'Someone was watching me. I could feel it. To see this person I had but to turn my head. And then I would have the upper hand with the Elder. I would say, "So you've come out of loneliness and disillusionment and now you want to tell me more, do you? Why don't you go back and sit in silence to wound your wraithlike companions, the brotherhood of the cinders?" Of course I wouldn't say such a thing to him. But I wasn't above thinking about it and letting him — if he was the one in the doorway — hear these thoughts.

'The one who was there did not go away.

'And slowly I turned my eyes in the direction of the door, and it was a woman I saw standing there. And not merely a woman, but a magnificent bronze-skinned Egyptian woman as artfully bejeweled and dressed as the old queens, in fine pleated linen, with her black hair down to her shoulders and braided with strands of gold. An immense force emanated from her, an invisible and commanding sense of her presence, her occupation of this small and insignificant room.

'I sat up and moved back the curtains, and the lamps in the room went out. I saw the smoke rising from them in the dark, grey wisps like snakes coiling towards the ceiling and then gone. She was still there, the remaining light defining her expressionless face, sparkling on the jewels around her neck and in her large almond-shaped eyes. And silently she said:

'*Marius, take us out of Egypt.*

'And then she was gone.

'My heart was knocking in me uncontrollably. I went into the garden looking for her. I leapt over the wall and stood alone listening in the empty unpaved street.

'I started to run towards the old section where I had found the door. I meant to get into the underground temple and find the Elder and tell him that he must take me to her, I had seen her, she had moved, she had spoken, she had come to me! I was delirious, but when I reached the door, I knew that I didn't have to go down. I knew that if I went out of the city into the sands I could find her. She was already leading me to where she was.

'In the hour that followed I was to remember the strength and the speed I'd known in the forests of Gaul, and had not used since. I went out from the city to where the stars provided the only light, and I walked until I came to a ruined temple, and there I began to dig in the sand. It would have taken a band of mortals several hours to discover the trapdoor, but I found it quickly, and I was able to lift it, which mortals couldn't have done.

'The twisting stairs and corridors I followed were not illuminated. And I cursed myself for not bringing a candle, for being so swept off my feet by the sight of her that I had rushed after her as if I were in love.

'"Help me, Akasha," I whispered. I put my hands out in front of me and tried not to feel mortal fear of the blackness in which I was as blind as an ordinary man.

'My hands touched something hard before me. And I rested, catching my breath, trying to command myself. Then my hands moved on the thing and felt what seemed the chest of a human statue, its shoulders, its arms. But this was no statue, this thing, this thing was made of something more resilient than stone. And when my hand found the face, the lips proved just a little softer than all the rest of it, and I drew back.

'I could hear my heart beat. I could feel the sheer humiliation of cowardice. I didn't dare say the name Akasha. I knew that this thing I had touched had a man's form. It was Enkil.

'I closed my eyes, trying to gather my wits, form some plan of action that didn't include turning and running like a madman, and I heard a dry, crackling sound, and against my closed lids saw fire.

'When I opened my eyes, I saw a blazing torch on the wall beyond him, and his dark outline looming before me, and his eyes animate, and looking at me without question, the black pupils swimming in a dull grey light. He was otherwise lifeless, hands limp at his sides. He was ornamented as she had been, and he wore the glorified dress of the pharaoh and his hair too was plaited with gold. His skin was bronze all over, as hers had been, enhanced, as the Elder had said. And he was the incarnation of menace in his stillness as he stood staring at me.

'In the barren chamber behind him, she sat on a stone shelf, with her head at an angle, her arms dangling, as if she were a lifeless body flung there. Her linen was smeared with sand, her sandaled feet caked with it, and her eyes were vacant and staring. Perfect attitude of death.

'And he like a stone sentinel in a royal tomb blocked my path.

'I could hear no more from either of them than you heard from them when I took you down to the chamber here on the island. And I thought I might expire on the spot from fear.

'Yet there was the sand on her feet and on her linen. She'd come to me! She had!

'But someone had come into the corridor behind me. Someone was shuffling along the passage, and when I turned, I saw one of the burnt ones — a mere skeleton, this one, with black gums showing and the fangs cutting into the shiny black raisin skin of his lower lip.

'I swallowed a gasp at the sight of him, his bony limbs, feet splayed, arms jiggling with every step. He was ploughing towards us, but he did not seem to see me. He put his hands up and shoved at Enkil.

'"No, no, back into the chamber!" he whispered in a low, crackling voice. "No, no!" and each syllable seemed to take all he had. His withered arms shoved at the figure. He couldn't budge it.

'"Help me!" he said to me. "They have moved. Why did they move? Make them go back. The further they move, the harder it is to get them back."

'I stared at Enkil and I felt the horror that you felt to see this statue with life in it, seemingly unable or unwilling to move. And as I watched the spectacle grew even more horrible, because the blackened wraith was now screaming and scratching at Enkil, unable to do anything with him. And the sight of this thing that should have been dead wearing itself out like this, and this other thing that looked so perfectly godlike and magnificent just standing there, was more than I could bear.

'"Help me!" the thing said. "Get him back into the chamber. Get them back where they must remain."

'How could I do this? How could I lay hands on this being? How could I presume to push him where he did not wish to go?

'"They will be all right, if you help me," the thing said. "They will be together and they will be at peace. Push on him. Do it. Push! Oh, look at her, what's happened to her. Look."

'"All right, damn it!" I whispered, and overcome with shame, I tried. I laid my hands again on Enkil and I pushed at him, but it was impossible. My strength meant nothing here, and the burnt one became all the more irritating with his useless ranting and shoving.

'But then he gasped and cackled and threw his skeletal arms up in the air and backed up.

'"What's the matter with you!" I said, trying not to scream and run. But I saw soon enough.

'Akasha had appeared behind Enkil. She was standing directly behind him and looking at me over his shoulder, and I saw her fingertips come round his muscular arms. Her eyes were as empty in their glazed beauty as they had been before. But she was making him move, and now came the spectacle of these two things walking of their own volition, he backing up slowly, feet barely touching the ground, and she shielded by him so that I saw only her hands and the top of her head and her eyes.

'I blinked, trying to clear my head.

'They were sitting on the shelf again, together, and they

had lapsed into the same posture in which you saw them downstairs on this island tonight.

'The burnt creature was near to collapse. He had gone down on his knees, and he didn't have to explain to me why. He had found them many a time in different positions, but he had never witnessed their movement. And he had never seen her as she had been before.

'I was bursting with the knowledge of why she had been as she was before. She had come to me. But there was a point at which my pride and exhilaration gave way to what it should have been: overwhelming awe, and finally grief.

'I started to cry. I started to cry uncontrollably as I had not cried since I had been with the old god in the grove and my death had occurred, and this curse, this great luminous and powerful curse, had descended on me. I cried as you cried when you first saw them. I cried for their stillness and their isolation, and this horrible little place in which they stared forward at nothing or sat in darkness while Egypt died above.

'The goddess, the mother, the thing, whatever she was, the mindless and silent or helpless progenitor was looking at me. Surely it wasn't an illusion. Her great glossy eyes, with their black fringe of lashes, were fixed upon me. And there came her voice again, but it had nothing of its old power, it was merely the thought, quite beyond language, inside my head.

'*Take us out of Egypt, Marius. The Elder means to destroy us. Guard us, Marius. Or we perish here.*

'"Do they want blood?" the burnt one cried. "Did they move because they would have sacrifice?" the dried one begged.

'"Go get them a sacrifice," I said.

'"I cannot now. I haven't the strength. And they won't give their healing blood to me. Would they but allow me a few drops, my burnt flesh might restore itself, the blood in me would be replenished, and I should bring them glorious sacrifices ..."

'But there was an element of dishonesty in this little speech, because *they* didn't desire glorious sacrifices anymore.

'"Try again to drink their blood," I said and this was horribly selfish of me. I just wanted to see what would happen.

'"Yet to my humiliation, he did approach them, bent over and weeping, begging them to give their powerful blood, their old blood, so that his burns might heal faster, saying that he was innocent, he had not put them in the sand — it had been the Elder — please, please, would they let him drink from the original fount.

'"And then ravenous hunger consumed him. And, convulsing, he distended his fangs as a cobra might and he shot forward, his black claws out, to the neck of Enkil.

'Enkil's arm rose as the Elder said it would, and it flung the burnt one across the chamber on his back before it returned to its proper place.

'The burnt one was sobbing and I was even more ashamed. The burnt one was too weak to hunt for victims or bring victims. I had urged him on to this to see it. And the gloom of this place, the gritty sand on the floor, the barrenness, the stink of the torch, and the ugly sight of the burnt one writhing and crying, all this was dispiriting beyond words.

'"Then drink from me," I said, shuddering at the sight of him, the fangs distended again, the hands out to grasp me. But it was the least I could do.'

12

AS SOON as I was done with that creature, I ordered him to let no one enter the crypt. How the hell he was supposed to keep anyone out I couldn't imagine, but I told him this with tremendous authority and I hurried away.

'I went back into Alexandria, and I broke into a shop that sold antique things and I stole two fine painted and gold-plated mummy cases, and I took a great deal of linen for wrapping, and I went back to the desert crypt.

'My courage and my fear were at their peak.

'As often happens when we give the blood or take it from another of our kind, I had seen things, dreamed things as it were, when the burnt one had his teeth in my throat. And what I had seen and dreamed had to do with Egypt, the age of Egypt, the fact that for four thousand years this land had known little change in language, religion, or art. And for the first time this was understandable to me and it put me in profound sympathy with the Mother and the Father as relics of this country, as surely as the pyramids were relics. It intensified my curiosity and made it something more akin to devotion.

'Though to be honest, I would have stolen the Mother and the Father just in order to survive.

'This new knowledge, this new infatuation, inspired me as I approached Akasha and Enkil to put them in the wooden mummy cases, knowing full well that Akasha would allow it and that one blow from Enkil could probably crush my skull.

'But Enkil yielded as well as Akasha. They allowed me to wrap them in linen, to make mummies of them, and to place them into the shapely wooden coffins which bore the painted faces of others, and the endless hieroglyph instructions for the dead, and to take them with me into Alexandria, which I did.

'I left the wraith being in a terrible state of agitation as I went off dragging a mummy case under each arm.

'When I reached the city I hired men to carry these coffins properly to my house, out of a sense of fittingness, and then I buried them deep beneath the garden, explaining to Akasha and Enkil all the while aloud that their stay in the earth would not be long.

'I was in terror to leave them the next night. I hunted and killed within yards of my own garden gate. And then I sent my slaves to purchase horses and a wagon for me, and to make preparations for a journey around the coast to Antioch on the Orontes River, a city I knew and loved, and in which I felt I would be safe.

'As I feared, the Elder soon appeared. I was actually waiting for him in the shadowy bedroom, seated on my couch like a Roman, one lamp beside me, an old copy of some Roman poem in my hand. I wondered if he would sense the location of Akasha and Enkil, and deliberately imagined false things — that I had shut them up in the great pyramid itself.

'I still dreamed the dream of Egypt that had come to me from the burnt one: a land in which the laws and the beliefs had remained the same for longer than we could imagine, a land that had known the picture writing and the pyramids and the myths of Osiris and Isis when Greece had been in darkness and when there was no Rome. I saw the river Nile overflowing her banks. I saw the mountains on either side which created the valley. I saw time with a wholly different idea of it. And it was not merely the dream of the burnt one — it was all I had ever seen or known in Egypt, a sense of things beginning there which I had learned from books long before I had become the child of the Mother and the Father, whom I meant now to take.

'"What makes you think that we would entrust them to you!" the Elder said as soon as he appeared in the doorway.

'He appeared enormous as, girded only in the short linen kilt, he walked around my room. The lamplight shone on his bald head, his round face, his bulging eyes. "How dare you take the Mother and the Father! What have you done with them!" he said.

'"It was you who put them in the sun," I answered. "You who sought to destroy them. You were the one who didn't believe the old story. You were the guardian of the Mother and the Father, and you lied to me. You brought about the death of our kind from one end of the world to the other. You, and you lied to me."

'He was dumbfounded. He thought me proud and impossible beyond words. So did I. But so what? He had the power to burn me to ashes if and when he burnt the Mother and the Father. And she had come to me! To me!

'"I did not know what would happen!" he said now, his veins cording against his forehead, his fists clenched. He looked like a great bald Nubian as he tried to intimidate me. "I swear to you by all that is sacred, I didn't know. And you cannot know what it means to keep them, to look at them year after year, decade after decade, century after century, and know that they could speak, they could move, and they will not!"

'I had no sympathy for him and what he said. He was merely an enigmatic figure poised in the centre of this small room in Alexandria railing at me of sufferings beyond the imagination. How could I sympathize with him?

'"I inherited them," he said. "They were given to me! What was I to do?" he declared. "And I must contend with their punishing silence, their refusal to direct the tribe they had loosed into the world. And why came this silence? Vengeance, I tell you. Vengeance on us. But for what? Who exists who can remember back a thousand years now? No one. Who understands all these things? The old gods go into the sun, into the fire, or they meet with obliteration through violence, or they bury themselves in the deepest earth never to rise again. But the Mother and the Father go on forever, and they do not speak. Why don't they bury themselves where no harm can come to them? Why do they simply watch and listen and refuse to speak? Only when one tries to take Akasha from Enkil does he move, does he strike out and then batter down his foes as if he were a stone colossus come to life. I tell you when I put them in the sand they did not try to save themselves! They stood facing the river as I ran!"

'"You did it to see what would happen, if it would make them move!"

'"To free myself! To say, 'I will keep you no longer. Move. Speak.' To see if was true, the old story, and if it was true, then let us all die in flames."

'He had exhausted himself. In a feeble voice he said finally, "You cannot take the Mother and the Father. How could you think that I would allow you to do this! You who might not last out the century, you who ran from the obligations of the grove. You don't really know what the Mother and the Father are. You have heard more than one lie from me."

'"I have something to tell you," I said. "You *are* free now. You know that we're not gods. And we're not men, either. We don't serve the Mother Earth because we do not eat her fruits and we do not naturally descend to her embrace. We are not

494

of her. And I leave Egypt without further obligation to you, and I take them with me because it is what they have asked me to do and I will not suffer them or me to be destroyed."

'He was again dumbfounded. How had they asked me? But he couldn't find words, he was so angry, and so full of hatred suddenly, and so full of dark wrathful secrets that I could not even glimpse. He had a mind as educated as mine, this one, but he knew things about our powers that I didn't guess. I had never slain a man when I was mortal. I did not know how to kill any living thing, save in the tender and remorseless need for blood.

'He knew how to use his supernatural strength. He closed his eyes to slits, and his body hardened. Danger radiated from him.

'He approached me and his intentions went before him, and in an instant I had risen off my couch, and I was trying to ward off his blows. He had me by the throat and he threw me against the stone wall so that the bones of my shoulder and right arm were crushed. In a moment of exquisite pain, I knew he would dash my head against the stone and crush all my limbs, and then he would pour the oil of the lamp over me and burn me, and I would be gone out of his private eternity as if I had never known these secrets or dared to intrude.

'I fought as I never could have before. But my battered arm was a riot of pain, and his strength was to me what mine would be to you. But instead of clawing at his hands as they locked around my throat, instead of trying to free my throat as was instinctive, I shot my thumbs into his eyes. Though my arm blazed with pain, I used all my strength to push his eyes backwards into his head.

'He let go of me and he wailed. Blood was pouring down his face. I ran clear of him and towards the garden door. I still could not breathe from the damage he'd done to my throat, and as I clutched at my dangling arm, I saw things out of the corner of my eye that confused me, a great spray of earth flying up from the garden, the air dense as if with smoke. I bumped the door frame, losing my balance, as if a wind had moved me, and glancing back I saw him coming on, eyes still glittering, though from deep inside his head. He was cursing me in Egyptian. He was saying that I should go into the netherworld with the demons, unmourned.

'And then his face froze in a mask of fear. He stopped in his tracks and looked almost comical in his alarm.

'Then I saw what he saw — the figure of Akasha, who moved past me to my right. The linen wrapping had been ripped from around her head, and her arms were torn free, and she was covered with the sandy earth. Her eyes had the same expressionless stare they always had, and she bore down on him slowly, drawing ever closer because he could not move to save himself.

'He went down on his knees, babbling to her in Egyptian, first with a tone of astonishment and then with incoherent fright. Still she came on, tracking the sand after her, the linen falling off her as each slow sliding step ruptured the wrappings more violently. He turned away and fell forward on his hands and started to crawl as if, by some unseen force, she prevented him from rising to his feet. Surely that was what she was doing, because he lay prone finally, his elbows jutting up, unable to move himself.

'Quietly and slowly, she stepped on the back of his right knee, crushing it flat beneath her foot, the blood squirting from under her heel. And with the next step she crushed his pelvis just as flat while he roared like a dumb beast, the blood gushing from his mangled parts. Then came her next step down upon his shoulder and the next upon his head, which exploded beneath her weight as if it had been an acorn. The roaring ceased. The blood spurted from all his remains as they twitched.

'Turning, she revealed to me no change in expression, signifying nothing of what had happened to him, indifferent even to the lone and horrified witness who shrank back against the wall. She walked back and forth over his remains with the same slow and effortless gait, and crushed the last of him utterly.

'What was left was not even the outline of a man, but mere blood-soaked pulp upon the floor, and yet it glittered, bubbled, seemed to swell and contract as if there were still life in it.

'I was petrified, knowing that there was life in it, that this was what immortality could mean.

'But she had come to a stop, and she turned to her left so slowly it seemed the revolution of a statue on a chain, and her hand rose and the lamp beside the couch rose in the air and fell down upon the bloody mass, the flame quickly igniting the oil as it spilled.

'Like grease he went up, flames dancing from one end of the dark mass to the other, the blood seeming to feed the fire, the smoke acrid but only with the stench of the oil.

'I was on my knees, with my head against the side of the doorway. I was as near to losing consciousness from shock as I have ever been. I watched him burn to nothing. I watched her standing there, beyond the flames, her bronze face giving forth not the slightest sign of intelligence or triumph or will.

'I held my breath, expecting her eyes to move to me. But they didn't. And as the moment lengthened, as the fire died, I realized that she had ceased to move. She had returned to the state of absolute silence and stillness that all the others had come to expect of her.

'The room was dark now. The fire had gone out. The smell of burning oil sickened me. She looked like an Egyptian ghost in her torn wrappings poised there before the glittering embers, the gilded furnishings glinting in the light from the sky, bearing, for all their Roman craftsmanship, some resemblance to the elaborate and delicate furnishings of a royal burial chamber.

'I rose to my feet, and the pain in my shoulder and in my arm throbbed. I could feel the blood rushing to heal it, but the damage was considerable. I did not know how long I would have this.

'I did know, of course, that if I were to drink from her, the healing would be much faster, perhaps instantaneous, and we could start our journey out of Alexandria tonight. I could take her far far away from Egypt.

'Then I realized that *she* was telling me this. The words, far

far away, were breathed in by me sensuously.

'And I answered her: *I have been all through the world and I will take you to safe places.* But then again perhaps this dialogue was all my doing. And the soft, yielding sensation of love for her was my doing. And I was going completely mad, knowing this nightmare would never, never end except in fire such as that, that no natural old age or death would ever quiet my fears and dull my pains, as I had once expected it to do.

'It ceased to matter. What mattered was that I was alone with her, and in this darkness she might have been a human woman standing there, a young god woman full of vitality and full of lovely language and ideas and dreams.

'I moved closer to her and it seemed then that she was this pliant and yielding creature, and some knowledge of her was inside me, waiting to be remembered, waiting to be enjoyed. Yet I was afraid. She could do to me what she had done to the Elder. But that was absurd. She would not. I was her guardian now. She would never let anyone hurt me. No. I was to understand that. And I came closer and closer to her, until my lips were almost at her bronze throat, and it was decided when I felt the firm cold press of her hand on the back of my head.'

13

WON'T try to describe the ecstasy. You know it. You knew it when you took the blood from Magnus. You knew it when I gave you the blood in Cairo. You know it when you kill. And you know what it means when I say it was that, but a thousand times that.

'I neither saw nor heard nor felt anything but absolute happiness, absolute satisfaction.

'Yet I was in other places, other rooms from long ago, and voices were talking and battles were being lost. Someone was crying in agony. Someone was screaming in words I knew and didn't know: *I do not understand. I do not understand.* A great pool of darkness opened and there came the invitation to fall and to fall and to fall and she sighed and said: *I can fight no longer.*

'Then I awoke, and found myself lying on my couch. She was in the centre of the room, still as before, and it was late in the night, and the city of Alexandria murmured around us in its sleep.

'I knew a multitude of other things.

'I knew so many things that it would have taken hours if not nights for me to learn them if they'd been confided in mortal words. And I had no inkling of how much time had passed.

'I knew that thousands of years ago there had been great battles among the Drinkers of the Blood, and many of them after the first creation had become ruthless and profane bringers of death. Unlike the benign lovers of the Good Mother who starved and then drank her sacrifices, these were death angels who could swoop down upon any victim at any moment, glorying in the conviction that they were part of the rhythm of all things in which no individual human life matters, in which death and life are equal — and to them belonged suffering and slaughter as they chose to mete it out.

'And these terrible gods had their devoted worshippers among men, human slaves who brought victims to them, and quaked in fear of the moment when they themselves might fall to the god's whim.

'Gods of this kind had ruled in ancient Babylon, and in Assyria, and in cities long forgotten, and in far-off India, and in countries beyond whose names I did not understand.

'And even now, as I sat silent and stunned by these images, I understood that these gods had become part of the Oriental world which was alien to the Roman world to which I'd been born. They were part of the world of the Persians whose men were abject slaves to their king, while the Greeks who had fought them had been free men.

'No matter what our cruelties and our excesses, even the lowliest peasant had value to us. Life had value. And death was merely the end of life, something to be faced with bravery when honour left no choice. Death was not grand to us. In fact, I don't think death was anything really to us. It certainly was not a state preferable to life.

'And though these gods had been revealed to me by Akasha in all their grandeur and mystery, I found them appalling. I could not now or ever embrace them and I knew that the philosophies that proceeded from them or justified them would never justify my killing, or give me the consolation as a Drinker of the Blood. Mortal or immortal, I was of the West. And I loved the ideas of the West. And I should always *be guilty* of what I did.

'Nevertheless I saw the power of these gods, their incomparable loveliness. They enjoyed a freedom I would never know. And I saw their contempt for all those who challenged them. And I saw them wearing in the pantheon of other countries their glittering crowns.

'And I saw them come to Egypt to steal the original and all powerful blood of the Father and the Mother, and to ensure that the Father and the Mother did not burn themselves to bring an end to the reign of these dark and terrible gods for whom all the good gods must be brought down.

'And I saw the Mother and the Father imprisoned. I saw them entombed with blocks of diorite and granite pressed against their very bodies in an underground crypt, only their heads and their necks free. In this manner the dark gods could feed the Mother and the Father the human blood they could not resist, and take from their necks the powerful blood against their will. And all the dark gods of the world came to drink from this oldest of founts.

'The Father and the Mother screamed in torment. They begged to be released. But this meant nothing to the dark gods, who relished such agony, who drank it as they drank human blood. The dark gods wore human skulls dangling from their girdles; their garments were dyed with human blood. The Mother and the Father refused sacrifice, but this only increased their helplessness. They did not take the very thing that might have given them the strength to move the stones, and to affect objects by mere thought.

'Nevertheless their strength increased.

'Years and years of this torment, and wars among the gods, wars among the sects that held to life and those who held to death.

'Years beyond counting, until finally the Mother and the Father became silent, and there were none in existence who could even remember a time when they begged or fought or talked. Years came when nobody could remember who had imprisoned the Mother and the Father, or why the Mother and the Father must not ever be let out. Some did not believe that the Mother and the Father were even the originals or that their immolation would harm anyone else. It was just an old tale.

'And all the while Egypt was Egypt and its religion, uncorrupted by outsiders, finally moved on towards the belief in conscience, the judgement after death of all beings, be they rich or poor, the belief in goodness on earth and life after death.

'And then the night came when the Mother and the Father were found free of their prison, and those who tended them realized that only they could have moved the stones. In silence, their strength had grown beyond all reckoning. Yet they were as statues, embracing each other in the middle of the dirty and darkened chamber where for centuries they had been kept. Naked and shimmering they were, all their clothing having long ago rotted away.

'If and when they drank from the victims offered, they moved with the sluggishness of reptiles in winter, as though time had taken on an altogether different meaning for them, and years were as nights to them, and centuries as years.

'And the ancient religion was strong as ever, not of the East and not really of the West. The Drinkers of the Blood remained good symbols, the luminous image of life in the afterworld which even the lowliest Egyptian soul might come to enjoy.

'Sacrifice could only be the evildoer in these later times. And by this means the gods drew the evil out of the people, and protected the people, and the silent voice of the god consoled the weak, telling the truths learned by the god in starvation: that the world was full of abiding beauty, that no soul here is really alone.

'The Mother and the Father were kept in the loveliest of all shrines and all the gods came to them and took from them, with their will, droplets of their precious blood.

'But then the impossible was happening. Egypt was reaching its finish. Things thought to be unchangeable were about to be utterly changed. Alexander had come, the Ptolemies were the rulers, Caesar and Antony — all rude and strange protagonists of the drama which was simply The End of All This.

'And finally the dark and cynical Elder, the wicked one, the disappointed one, who put the Mother and Father in the sun.

'I GOT up off the couch and I stood in this room in Alexandria looking at the motionless and staring figure of Akasha and the soiled linen hanging from her seemed an insult. My head swam with old poetry. And I was overcome with love.

'There was no more pain in my body from the battle with the Elder. The bones were restored. And I went down on my knees, and I kissed the fingers of the right hand that hung at Akasha's side. I looked up and I saw her looking down at me, her head tilted, and the strangest look passed over her; it seemed as pure in its suffering as the happiness I had just known. Then her head, very slowly, inhumanly slowly, returned to its position of facing forward, and I knew in that instant that I had seen and known things that the Elder had never known.

'As I wrapped her body again in linen, I was in a trance. More than ever I felt the mandate to take care of her and Enkil, and the horror of the Elder's death was flashing before me every second, and the blood she had given me had increased my exhilaration as well as my physical strength.

'And as I prepared to leave Alexandria, I suppose I dreamed of waking Enkil and Akasha, that in the years to come they would recover all the vitality stolen from them, and we would know each other in such intimate and astonishing ways that these dreams of knowledge and experience given me in the blood would pale.

'My slaves had long ago come back with the horses and the wagons for our journey, with the stone sarcophagi and the chains and locks I had told them to procure. They waited outside the walls.

'I placed the mummy cases with the Mother and the Father in the sarcophagi side by side in the wagon, and I covered them with locks and chains and heavy blankets, and we set out, heading towards the door to the underground temple of the gods on our way to the city gates.

'When I reached the door, I left my slaves with firm orders to give a loud alarm if anyone approached, and then I took a leather sack and went down into the temple, and into the library of the Elder, and I put all the scrolls I could find into the sack. I stole every bit of portable writing that was in the place. I wished I could have taken the writing off the walls.

'There were others in the chambers, but they were too terrified to come out. Of course they knew I had stolen the Mother and the Father. And they probably knew of the Elder's death.

'It didn't matter to me. I was getting out of old Egypt, and I had the source of all our power with me. And I was young and foolish and enflamed.

'When I finally reached Antioch on the Orontes — a great and wonderful city that rivalled Rome in population and wealth — I read these old papyri and they told of all the things Akasha had revealed to me.

'And she and Enkil had the first of many chapels I would build for them all over Asia and Europe, and they knew that I would always care for them and I knew that they would let no harm come to me.

'Many centuries after, when I was set afire in Venice by the band of the Children of Darkness, I was too far from Akasha for rescue, or again, she would have come. And when I did reach the sanctuary, knowing full well the agony the burnt gods had known, I drank of her blood until I was healed.

'But by the end of the first century of keeping them in Antioch I had despaired that they would ever "come to life", as

503

it were. Their silence and stillness was almost continuous as it is now. Only the skin changed dramatically with the passing years, losing the damage of the sun until it was like alabaster again.

'But by the time I realized all this I was powerfully engaged in watching the goings-on of the city and the changing of the times. I was madly in love with a beautiful brown-haired Greek courtesan named Pandora, with the loveliest arms I have ever beheld on a human being, who knew what I was from the first moment she set eyes on me and bided her time, enchanting me and dazzling me until I was ready to bring her over into the magic, at which time she was allowed the blood from Akasha and became one of the most powerful supernatural creatures I have ever known. Two hundred years I lived and fought and loved with Pandora. But that is another tale.

'There are a million tales I could tell of the centuries I have lived since then, of my journeys from Antioch to Constantinople, back to Alexandria and on to India and then to Italy again and from Venice to the bitter cold highlands of Scotland and then to this island in the Aegean, where we are now.

'I could tell you of the tiny changes in Akasha and Enkil over the years, of the puzzling things they do, and the mysteries they leave unsolved.

'Perhaps some night in the far distant future, when you've returned to me, I'll talk of the other immortals I've known, those who were made as I was made by the last of the gods who survived in various lands — some the servants of the Mother and others of the terrible gods out of the East.

'I could tell you how Mael, my poor Druid priest, finally drank from a wounded god himself and in one instant lost all his belief in the old religion, going on to become as enduring and dangerous a rogue immortal as any of us. I could tell you how the legends of Those Who Must Be Kept spread through the world. And of the times other immortals have tried to take them from me out of pride or sheer destructiveness, wanting to put an end to us all.

'I will tell you of my loneliness, of the others I made, and how they met their ends. Of how I have gone down into the earth with Those Who Must Be Kept, and risen again, thanks to their blood, to live several mortal lifetimes before burying myself again. I will tell you of the other truly eternal ones whom I meet only now and then. Of the last time I saw Pandora in the city of Dresden, in the company of a powerful and vicious vampire from India, and of how we quarrelled and separated, and of how I discovered too late her letter begging me to meet her in Moscow, a fragile piece of writing that had fallen to the bottom of a cluttered travelling case. Too many things, too many stories, stories with and without lessons ...

'But I have told you the most important things — how I came into possession of Those Who Must Be Kept, and who we really were.

'What is crucial now is that you understand this:

'As the Roman Empire came to its close, all the old gods of the pagan world were seen as demons by the Christians who rose. It was useless to tell them as the centuries passed that their Christ was but another God of the Wood, dying and rising, as Dionysus or Osiris had done before him, and that the Virgin Mary was in fact the Good Mother again enshrined. Theirs was a new age of belief and conviction, and in it we became devils, detached from what they believed, as old knowledge was forgotten or misunderstood.

'But this had to happen. Human sacrifice had been a horror to the Greeks and Romans. I had thought it ghastly that the Keltoi burned for the god their evildoers in the wicker colossi as I described. And so it was to the Christians. So how could we, gods who fed upon human blood, have been seen as "good"?

'But the real perversion of us was accomplished when the Children of Darkness came to believe they served the Christian devil, and like the terrible gods of the East, they tried to give value to evil, to believe in its power in the scheme of things, to give it a just place in the world.

'Hearken to me when I say: *There has never been a just place for evil in the Western world.* There has never been an easy accommodation of death.

'No matter how violent have been the centuries since the fall of Rome, no matter how terrible the wars, the persecutions, the injustices, the value placed upon human life has only increased.

'Even as the Church erected statues and pictures of her bloody Christ and her bloody martyrs, she held the belief that these deaths, so well used by the faithful, could only have come at the hands of enemies, not God's own priests.

'It is the belief in the value of human life that has caused the torture chambers and the stake and the more ghastly means of execution to be abandoned all over Europe in this time. And it is the belief in the value of human life that carries man now out of the monarchy into the republics of America and France.

'And now we stand again on the cusp of an atheistic age — an age where the Christian faith is losing its hold, as paganism once lost its hold, and the new humanism, the belief in man and his accomplishments and his rights, is more powerful than ever before.

'Of course we cannot know what will happen as the old religion thoroughly dies out. Christianity rose on the ashes of paganism, only to carry forth the old worship in new form. Maybe a new religion will rise now. Maybe without it, man will crumble in cynicism and selfishness because he really needs his gods.

'But maybe something more wonderful will take place: the world will truly move forward, past all gods and goddesses, past all devils and angels. And in such a world, Lestat, we will have less of a place than we have ever had.

'All the stories I have told you are finally as useless as all ancient knowledge is to man and to us. Its images and its poetry can be beautiful; it can make us shiver with the recognition of things we have always suspected or felt. It can draw us back to times when the earth was new to man, and wondrous. But always we come back to the way the earth is now.

'And in this world the vampire is only a Dark God. He is a Child of Darkness. He can't be anything else. And if he wields any lovely power upon the minds of men, it is only because the human imagination is a secret place of primitive memories and unconfessed desires. The mind of each man is a Savage Garden, to use your phrase, in which all manner of creatures rise and fall, and anthems are sung and things imagined that must finally be condemned and disavowed.

'Yet men love us when they come to know us. They love us even now. The Paris crowds love what they see on the stage of the Theatre of the Vampires. And those who have seen your like walking through the ballrooms of the world, the pale and deadly lord in the velvet cloak, have worshipped in their own way at your feet.

'They thrill at the possibility of immortality, at the possibility that a grand and beautiful being could be utterly evil, that he could feel and know all things yet choose willfully to feed his dark appetite. Maybe they wish they could be that lusciously evil creature. How simple it all seems. And it is the simplicity of it that they want.

'But give them the Dark Gift and only one in a multitude will not be as miserable as you are.

'What can I say finally that will not confirm your worst fears? I have lived over eighteen hundred years, and I tell you life does not need us. I have never had a true purpose. We have no place.'

14

ARIUS paused.

He looked away from me for the first time and towards the sky beyond the windows, as if he were listening to island voices I couldn't hear.

'I have a few more things to tell you,' he said, 'things which are important, though they are merely practical things ...' But he was distracted. 'And there are promises,' he said, finally, 'which I must exact ...'

And he slipped into quiet, listening, his face too much like that of Akasha and Enkil.

There were a thousand questions I wanted to ask. But more significant perhaps there were a thousand statements of his I wanted to reiterate, as if I had to say them aloud to grasp them. If I talked, I wouldn't make very good sense.

I sat back against the cool brocade of the winged chair with my hands together in the form of a steeple, and I just looked ahead of me, as if his tale were spread out there for me to read over, and I thought of the truth of his statements about good and evil, and how it might have horrified me and disappointed me had he tried to convince me of the rightness of the philosophy of the terrible gods of the East, that we could somehow glory in what we did.

I too was a child of the West, and all my brief life I had struggled with the Western inability to accept evil or death.

But underneath all these considerations lay the appalling fact that Marius could annihilate all of us by destroying Akasha and Enkil. Marius could kill every single one of us in existence if he were to burn Akasha and Enkil and thereby get rid of an old and decrepit and useless form of evil in the world. Or so it seemed.

And the horror of Akasha and Enkil themselves ... What could I say to this, except that I too had felt the first glimmer of what he once felt, that I could rouse them, I could make them speak again, I could make them move. Or more truly, I had felt when I saw them that someone should and could do it. Someone could end their open-eyed sleep.

And what would they be if they ever walked and talked again? Ancient Egyptian monsters. What would they do?

I saw the two possibilities as seductive suddenly — rousing them or destroying them. Both tempted the mind. I wanted to pierce them and commune with them, and yet I understood the irresistible madness of trying to destroy them. Of going out in a blaze of light with them that would take all our doomed species with it.

Both attitudes had to do with power. And some triumph over the passage of time.

'Aren't you ever tempted to do it?' I asked, and my voice had pain in it. I wondered if down in their chapel they heard.

He awakened from his listening and turned to me and he shook his head. No.

'Even though you know better than anyone that we have no place?'

Again he shook his head. No.

'I am immortal,' he said, '*truly* immortal. To be perfectly honest, I do not know what can kill me now, if anything. But that isn't the point. I want to go on. I do not even think of it. I am a continual awareness unto myself, the intelligence I longed for years and years ago when I was alive, and I'm in love as I've always been with the great progress of mankind. I want to see what will happen now that the world has come round again to questioning its gods. Why, I couldn't be persuaded now to close my eyes for any reason.'

I nodded in understanding.

'But I don't suffer what you suffer,' he said. 'Even in the grove in northern France, when I was made into this, I was not young. I have been lonely since, I have known near madness, indescribable anguish, but I was never immortal and young. I have done over and over what you have yet to do — the thing that must take you away from me very very soon.'

'Take me away? But I don't want —'

'You have to go, Lestat,' he said. 'And very soon, as I said. You're not ready to remain here with me. This is one of the most important things I have left to tell you and you must listen with the same attention with which you listened to the rest.'

'Marius, I can't imagine leaving now. I can't even …' I felt anger suddenly. Why had he brought me here to cast me out? And I remembered all Armand's admonitions to me. It is only with the old ones that we find communion, not with those we create. And I had found Marius. But these were mere words. They didn't touch the core of what I felt, the sudden misery and fear of separation.

'Listen to me,' he said gently. 'Before I was taken by the Gauls, I had lived a good lifetime, as long as many a man in

509

those days. And after I took Those Who Must Be Kept out of Egypt, I lived again for years in Antioch as a rich Roman scholar might live. I had a house, slaves, and the love of Pandora. We had life in Antioch, we were watchers of all that passed. And having had that lifetime, I had the strength for others later on. I had the strength to become part of the world in Venice, as you know. I had the strength to rule on this island as I do. You, like many who go early into the fire or the sun, have had no real life at all.

'As a young man, you tasted real life for no more than six months in Paris. As a vampire, you have been a roamer, an outsider, haunting houses and other lives as you drifted from place to place.

'If you mean to survive, you must live out one complete lifetime as soon as you can. To forestall it may be to lose everything, to despair and to go into the earth again, never to rise. Or worse ...'

'I want it. I understand,' I said. 'And yet when they offered it to me in Paris, to remain with the Theatre, I couldn't do it.'

'That was not the right place for you. Besides, the Theatre of the Vampires is a coven. It isn't the world any more than this island refuge of mine is the world. And too many horrors happened to you there.

'But in this New World wilderness to which you're headed, this barbaric little city called New Orleans, you may enter into the world as never before. You may take up residence there as a mortal, just as you tried to do so many times in your wanderings with Gabrielle. There will be no old covens to bother you, no rogues to try to strike you down out of fear. And when you make others — and you will, out of loneliness, make others — make and keep them as human as you can. Keep them close to you as members of a family, not as members of a coven, and understand the age you live in, the decades you pass through. Understand the style of garment that adorns your body, the styles of dwellings in which you spend your leisure hours, the place in which you hunt. Understand what it means to feel the passage of time!'

'Yes, and feel all the pain of seeing things die ...' All the things Armand advised against.

'Of course. You are made to triumph over time, not to run from it. And you will suffer that you harbour the secret of your monstrosity and that you must kill. And maybe you will try to feast only on the evildoer to assuage your conscience, and you may succeed, or you may fail. But you can come very close to life, if you will only lock the secret within you. You are fashioned to be close to it, as you yourself once told the members of the old Paris coven. You are the imitation of a man.'

'I want it, I do want it —'

'Then do as I advise. And understand this also. In a real way, eternity is merely the living of one human lifetime after another. Of course, there may be long periods of retreat, times of slumber or of merely watching. But again and again we plunge into the stream, and we swim as long as we can, until time or tragedy brings us down as they will do mortals.'

'Will you do it again? Leave this retreat and plunge into the stream?'

'Yes, definitely. When the right moment presents itself. When the world is so interesting again that I can't resist it. Then I'll walk city streets. I'll take a name. I'll do things.'

'Then come now, with me!' Ah, painful echo of Armand. And of the vain plea from Gabrielle ten years after.

'It's a more tempting invitation than you know,' he answered, 'but I'd do you a great disservice if I came with you. I'd stand between you and the world. I couldn't help it.'

I shook my head and looked away, full of bitterness.

'Do you want to continue?' he asked. 'Or do you want Gabrielle's predictions to come true?'

'I want to continue,' I said.

'Then you must go,' he said. 'A century from now, maybe less, we'll meet again. I won't be on this island. I will have taken Those Who Must Be Kept to another place. But wherever I am and wherever you are, I'll find you. And then I'll be the one who will not want you to leave me. I'll be the one who begs you to remain. I'll fall in love with your company, your conversation, the mere sight of you, your stamina and your

511

recklessness, and your lack of belief in anything — all the things about you I already love rather too strongly.'

I could scarcely listen to this without breaking down. I wanted to beg him to let me remain.

'Is it absolutely impossible now?' I asked. 'Marius, can't you spare me this lifetime?'

'Quite impossible,' he said. 'I can tell you stories forever, but they are no substitute for life. Believe me, I've tried to spare others. I've never succeeded. I can't teach what one lifetime can teach. I never should have taken Armand in his youth, and his centuries of folly and suffering are a penance to me even now. You did him a mercy driving him into the Paris of this century, but I fear for him it is too late. Believe me, Lestat, when I say this has to happen. You must have that lifetime, for those who are robbed of it spin in dissatisfaction until they finally live it somewhere or they are destroyed.'

'And what about Gabrielle?'

'Gabrielle had her life; she had her death almost. She has the strength to reenter the world when she chooses, or to live on its fringes indefinitely.'

'And do you think she will ever reenter?'

'I don't know,' he said. 'Gabrielle defies my understanding. Not my experience — she's too like Pandora. But I never understood Pandora. The truth is most women are weak, be they mortal or immortal. But when they are strong, they are absolutely unpredictable.'

I shook my head. I closed my eyes for a moment. I didn't want to think of Gabrielle. Gabrielle was gone, no matter what we said here.

And I still could not accept that I had to go. This seemed an Eden to me. But I didn't argue anymore. I knew he was resolute, and I also knew that he wouldn't force me. He'd let me start worrying about my mortal father, and he'd let me come to him and say I had to go. I had a few nights left.

'Yes,' he answered softly. 'And there are other things I can tell you.'

I opened my eyes again. He was looking at me patiently, affectionately. I felt the ache of love as strongly as I'd ever felt

512

it for Gabrielle. I felt the inevitable tears and did my best to suppress them.

'You've learned a great deal from Armand,' he said, his voice steady as if to help me with this little silent struggle. 'And you learned much more on your own. But there are still things I might teach you.'

'Yes, please,' I said.

'Well, for one thing,' he said, 'your powers are extraordinary, but you can't expect those you make in the next fifty years to equal you or Gabrielle. Your second child didn't have half Gabrielle's strength and later children will have even less. The blood I gave you will make some difference. If you drink ... if you drink from Akasha and Enkil, which you may choose not to do ... that will make some difference too. But no matter, only so many children can be made by one in a century. And new offspring will be weak. However, this is not necessarily a bad thing. The rule of the old covens had wisdom in it that strength should come with time. And then again, there is the old truth: you might make titans or imbeciles, no one knows why or how.

'Whatever will happen will happen, but choose your companions with care. Choose them because you like to look at them and you like the sound of their voices, and they have profound secrets in them that you wish to know. In other words, choose them because you love them. Otherwise you will not be able to bear their company for very long.'

'I understand,' I said. 'Make them in love.'

'Exactly, make them in love. And make certain they have had some lifetime before you make them; and never never make one as young as Armand. That is the worst crime I have committed against my own kind, the taking of the young boy child Armand.'

'But you didn't know the Children of Darkness would come when they did, and separate him from you.'

'No. But still, I should have waited. It was loneliness that drove me to it. And Armand's helplessness, that his mortal life was so completely in my hands. Remember, beware of that power, and the power you have over those who are dying.

513

Loneliness in us, and that sense of power, can be as strong as the thirst for blood. If there were not an Enkil there might be no Akasha, and if there were not an Akasha, then there would be no Enkil.'

'Yes. And from everything you said, it seems Enkil covets Akasha. That Akasha is the one who now and then ...'

'Yes, that's true.' His face became very sombre suddenly, and his eyes had a confidential look in them as if we were whispering to each other and fearful another might hear. He waited for a moment as if thinking what to say. 'Who knows what Akasha might do if there were no Enkil to hold her?' he whispered. 'And why do I pretend that he can't hear this even when I think it? Why do I whisper? He can destroy me anytime that he likes. Maybe Akasha is the only thing keeping him from it. But then what would become of them if they did away with me?'

'Why did they let themselves be burnt by the sun?' I asked.

'How can we know? Perhaps they knew it wouldn't hurt them. It would only hurt and punish those who had done it to them. Perhaps in the state they live in they are slow to realize what is going on outside them. And they did not have time to gather their forces, to wake from their dreams and save themselves. Maybe their movements after it happened — the movements of Akasha I witnessed — were only possible because they had been awakened by the sun. And now they sleep again with their eyes open. And they dream again. And they do not even drink.'

'What did you mean ... if I *choose* to drink their blood?' I asked. 'How could I not choose?'

'That is something we have to think on, both of us,' he said. 'And there is always the possibility that they won't allow you to drink.'

I shuddered thinking of one of those arms striking out at me, knocking me twenty feet across the chapel, or perhaps right through the stone floor itself.

'She told you her name, Lestat,' he said. 'I think she will let you drink. But if you take her blood, then you will be even more resilient than you are now. A few droplets will strengthen you, but if she gives you more than that, a full measure, hardly any force on earth can destroy you after that. You have to be certain you want it.'

'Why wouldn't I want it?' I said.

'Do you want to be burnt to a cinder and live on in agony? Do you want to be slashed with knives a thousand times over, or shot through and through with guns, and yet live on, a shredded husk that cannot fend for itself? Believe me, Lestat, that can be a terrible thing. You could suffer the sun even, and live through it, burnt beyond recognition, wishing as the old gods did in Egypt that they had died.'

'But won't I heal faster?'

'Not necessarily. Not without another infusion of her blood in the wounded state. Time with its constant measure of human victims or the blood of old ones — these are the restoratives. But you may wish you had died. Think on this. Take your time.'

'What would you do if you were I?'

'I would drink from Those Who Must Be Kept, of course. I would drink to be stronger, more nearly immortal. I would beseech Akasha on my knees to allow it, and then I would go into her arms. But it's easy to say these things. She has never struck out at me. She has never forbidden me, and I know that I want to live forever. I would endure the fire again. I would endure the sun. And all manner of suffering in order to go on. You may not be so sure that eternity is what you want.'

'I want it,' I said. 'I could pretend to think about it, pretend to be clever and wise as I weigh it. But what the hell? I wouldn't fool you, would I? You knew what I would say.'

He smiled.

'Then before you leave we will go into the chapel and we will ask her, humbly, and we will see what she says.'

'And for now, more answers?' I asked.

He gestured for me to ask.

'I've seen ghosts,' I said. 'Seen the pesty demons you described. I've seen them possess mortals and dwellings.'

'I know no more than you do. Most ghosts seem to be mere apparitions without knowledge that they are being watched. I have never spoken to a ghost nor been addressed by one. As for the pesty demons, what can I add to Enkil's ancient explanation, that they rage because they do not have bodies. But there are other immortals that are more interesting.'

'What are they?'

'There are at least two in Europe who do not and have never drunk blood. They can walk in the daylight as well as in the dark, and they have bodies and they are very strong. They look exactly like men. There was one in ancient Egypt, known as Ramses the Damned to the Egyptian court, though he was hardly damned as far as I can tell. His name was taken off all the royal monuments after he vanished. You know the Egyptians used to do that, obliterate the name as they sought to kill the being. And I don't know what happened to him. The old scrolls didn't tell.'

'Armand spoke of him,' I said. 'Armand told of legends, that Ramses was an ancient vampire.'

'He is not. But I didn't believe what I read of him till I'd seen the others with my own eyes. And again, I have not communicated with them. I have only seen them, and they were terrified of me and fled. I fear them because they walk in the sun. And they are powerful and bloodless and who knows what they might do? But you may live centuries and never see them.'

'But how old are they? How long has it been?'

'They are very old, probably as old as I am. I can't tell. They live as wealthy, powerful men. And possibly there are more of them, they may have some way of propagating themselves, I'm not sure. Pandora said once that there was a woman too. But then Pandora and I couldn't agree upon anything about them. Pandora said they had been what we were, and they were ancient, and had ceased to drink as the Mother and the Father have ceased to drink. I don't think they were ever what we are. They are something else without blood. They don't reflect light as we do. They absorb it. They are just a shade darker than mortals. And they are dense, and strong. You may never see them, but I tell you to warn you. You must never let them know where you lie. They can be more

516

dangerous than humans.'

'But are humans really dangerous? I've found them so easy to deceive.'

'Of course they're dangerous. Humans could wipe us out if they ever really understood about us. They could hunt us by day. Don't ever underestimate that single advantage. Again, the rules of the old covens have their wisdom. Never, never tell mortals about us. Never tell a mortal where you lie or where any vampire lies. It is absolute folly to think you can control mortals.'

I nodded, though it was very hard for me to fear mortals. I never had.

'Even the vampire theatre in Paris,' he cautioned, 'does not flaunt the simplest truths about us. It plays with folklore and illusions. Its audience is completely fooled.'

I realized this was true. And that even in her letters to me Eleni always disguised her meanings and never used our full names.

And something about this secrecy oppressed me as it always had.

But I was racking my brain, trying to discover if I'd ever seen the bloodless things ... The truth was, I might have mistaken them for rogue vampires.

'There is one other thing I should tell you about supernatural beings,' Marius said.

'What is it?'

'I am not certain of this, but I'll tell you what I think. I suspect that when we are burnt — when we are destroyed utterly — that we can come back again in another form. I don't speak of man now, of human reincarnation. I know nothing of the destiny of human souls. But we do live forever and I think we come back.'

'What makes you say this?' I couldn't help but think of Nicolas.

'The same thing that makes mortals talk of reincarnation. There are those who claim to remember other lives. They come to us as mortals, claiming to know all about this, to have been one of us, and asking to be given the Dark Gift again.

Pandora was one of these. She knew many things, and there was no explanation for her knowledge, except perhaps that she imagined it, or drew it, without realizing it, out of my mind. That's a real possibility, that they are merely mortals with hearing that allows them to receive our undirected thoughts.

'Whatever the case, there are not many of them. If they were vampires, then surely they are only a few of those who have been destroyed. So the others perhaps do not have the strength to come back. Or they do not choose to do so. Who can know? Pandora was convinced she had died when the Mother and the Father had been put in the sun.'

'Dear God, they are born again as mortals and they *want* to be vampires again?'

Marius smiled.

'You're young, Lestat, and how you contradict yourself. What do you *really* think it would be like to be mortal again? Think on this when you set eyes on your mortal father.'

Silently I conceded the point. But what I had made of mortality in my imagination I didn't really want to lose. I wanted to go on grieving for my lost mortality. And I knew that my love of mortals was all bound up with my not being afraid of them.

Marius looked away, distracted once more. The same perfect attitude of listening. And then his face became attentive to me again.

'Lestat, we should have no more than two or three nights,' he said sadly.

'Marius!' I whispered. I bit down on the words that wanted to spill out.

My only consolation was the expression on his face, and it seemed now he had never looked even faintly inhuman.

'You don't know how I want you to stay here,' he said. 'But life is out there, not here. When we meet again I'll tell you more things, but you have all you need for now. You have to go to Louisiana and see your father to the finish of his life and learn from that what you can. I've seen legions of mortals grow old and die. You've seen none. But believe me, my young friend, I want you desperately to remain with me. You don't know how much I promise you that I will find you when the time comes.'

'But why can't I return to you? Why must you leave here?'

'It's time,' he said. 'I've ruled too long over these people as it is. I arouse suspicions, and besides, Europeans are coming into these waters. Before I came here I was hidden in the buried city of Pompeii below Vesuvius, and mortals, meddling and digging up those ruins, drove me out. Now it's happening again. I must seek some other refuge, something more remote, and more likely to remain so. And frankly, I would never have brought you here if I planned to remain.'

'Why not?'

'You know why not. I can't have you or anyone else know the location of Those Who Must Be Kept. And that brings us now to something very important: the promises I must have from you.'

'Anything,' I said. 'But what could you possibly want that I could give?'

'Simply this. *You must never tell others the things that I have told you.* Never tell of Those Who Must Be Kept. Never tell the legends of the old gods. Never tell others that you have seen me.'

I nodded gravely. I had expected this, but I knew without even thinking that this might prove very hard indeed.

'If you tell even one part,' he said, 'another will follow, and with every telling of the secret of Those Who Must Be Kept you increase the danger of their discovery.'

'Yes,' I said. 'But the legends, our origins ... What about those children that I make? Can't I tell them —'

'No. As I told you, tell part and you will end up telling all. Besides, if these fledglings are children of the Christian god, if they are poisoned as Nicolas was with the Christian notion of Original Sin and guilt, they will only be maddened and disappointed by these old tales. It will all be a horror to them that they cannot accept. Accidents, pagan gods they don't believe in, customs they cannot understand. One has to be ready for this knowledge, meagre as it may be. Rather listen hard to their questions and tell them what you must to make them contented. And if you find you cannot lie to them, don't tell them anything at all. Try to make them strong as godless men today are strong. But mark my words, the old legends never. Those are mine and mine alone to tell.'

'What will you do to me if I tell them?' I asked.

This startled him. He lost his composure for almost a full second, and then he laughed.

'You are the damnedest creature, Lestat,' he murmured. 'The point is I can do anything I like to you if you tell. Surely you know that. I could crush you underfoot the way Akasha crushed the Elder. I could set you ablaze with the power of my mind. But I don't want to utter such threats. I want you to come back to me. But I will not have these secrets known. I will not have a band of immortals descend upon me again as they did in Venice. I will not be known to our kind. You must never — deliberately or accidentally — send anyone searching for Those Who Must Be Kept or for Marius. You will never utter my name to others.'

'I understand,' I said.

'Do you?' he asked. 'Or must I threaten you after all? Must I warn you that my vengeance can be terrible? That my punishment would include those to whom you've told the secrets as well as you? Lestat, I have destroyed others of our kind who came in search of me. I have destroyed them simply because they knew the old legends and they knew the name of Marius, and they would never give up the quest.'

'I can't bear this,' I murmured. 'I won't tell anyone, ever, I swear. But I'm afraid of what others can read in my thoughts, naturally. I fear that they might take the images out of my head. Armand could do it. What if —'

'You can conceal the images. You know how. You can throw up other images to confuse them. You can lock your mind. It's a skill you already know. But let's be done with threats and admonitions. I feel love for you.'

I didn't respond for a moment. My mind was leaping ahead to all manner of forbidden possibilities. Finally I put it in words:

'Marius, don't you ever have the desire to tell all of it to all of them! I mean, to make it known to the whole world of our kind, and to draw them together?'

'Good God, no, Lestat. Why would I do that?' He seemed genuinely puzzled.

'So that we might possess our legends, might at least ponder the riddles of our history, as men do. So that we might swap our stories and share our power —'

'And continue to use it as the Children of Darkness have done, against men?'

'No ... Not like that.'

'Lestat, in eternity, covens are actually rare. Most vampires are distrustful and solitary beings and they do not love others. They have no more than one or two well-chosen companions from time to time, and they guard their hunting grounds and their privacy as I do mine. They wouldn't want to come together, and if they did ever overcome the viciousness and suspicions that divide them, their convocation would end in terrible battles and struggles for supremacy like those revealed to me by Akasha, which happened thousands of years ago. We are evil things finally. We are killers. Better that those who unite on this earth be mortal and that they unite for the good.'

I accepted this, ashamed of how it excited me, ashamed of all my weaknesses and all my impulsiveness. Yet another realm of possibilities was already obsessing me.

'And what about to mortals, Marius? Have you never wanted to reveal yourself to them, and tell them the whole story?'

Again, he seemed positively baffled by the notion.

'Have you never wanted the world to know about us, for better or for worse? Has it never seemed preferable to living in secret?'

He lowered his eyes for a moment, and rested his chin against his closed hand. For the first time I perceived a communication of images coming from him, and I felt that he allowed me to see them because he was uncertain of his answer. He was remembering with a recall so powerful that it made my powers seem fragile. And what he remembered were the earliest times, when Rome had still ruled the world, and he was still within the range of normal human lifetime.

'You remember wanting to tell them all,' I said. 'To make it known, the monstrous secret.'

'Perhaps,' he said, 'in the beginning, there was some desperate passion to communicate.'

'Yes, communicate,' I said, cherishing the word. And I remembered that long-ago night on the stage when I had so frightened the Paris audience.

'But that was in the dim beginning,' he said slowly, speaking of himself. His eyes were narrow and remote as if he were looking back over all the centuries. 'It would be folly, it would be madness. Were humanity every really convinced, it would destroy us. I don't want to be destroyed. Such dangers and calamities are not interesting to me.'

I didn't answer.

'You don't feel the urge yourself to reveal these things,' he said to me almost soothingly.

But I do, I thought. I felt his fingers on the back of my hand. I was looking beyond him, back over my brief past — the theatre, my fairy-tale fantasies. I felt paralyzed in sadness.

'What you feel is loneliness and monstrousness,' he said. 'And you're impulsive and defiant.'

'True.'

'But what would it matter to reveal anything to anyone? No one can forgive. No one can redeem. It's a childish illusion to think so. Reveal yourself and be destroyed, and what have you done? The Savage Garden would swallow your remains in pure vitality and silence. Where is there justice or understanding?'

I nodded.

I felt his hand close on mine. He rose slowly to his feet, and I stood up, reluctantly but compliantly.

'It's late,' he said gently. His eyes were soft with compassion. 'We've talked enough for now. And I must go down to my people. There's trouble in the nearby village, as I feared there would be. And it will take what time I have until dawn, and then more tomorrow evening. It may well be after midnight tomorrow before we can talk —'

He was distracted again, and he lowered his head and listened.

'Yes, I have to go,' he said. And we embraced lightly and very comfortably.

And though I wanted to go with him and see what happened in the village — how he would conduct his affairs there — I wanted just as much to seek my rooms and look at the sea and finally sleep.

'You'll be hungry when you rise,' he said. 'I'll have a victim for you. Be patient till I come.'

'Yes, of course ...'

'And while you wait for me tomorrow,' he said, 'do as you like in the house. The old scrolls are in the cases in the library. You may look at them. Wander all the rooms. Only the sanctuary of Those Who Must Be Kept should not be approached. You must not go down the stairs alone.'

I nodded.

I wanted to ask him one thing more. When would he hunt? When would he drink? His blood had sustained me for two nights, maybe more. But whose blood sustained him? Had he taken a victim earlier? Would he hunt now? I had a growing suspicion that he no longer needed the blood as much as I did. That, like Those Who Must Be Kept, he had begun to drink less and less. And I wanted desperately to know if this was true.

But he was leaving me. The village was definitely calling him. He went out onto the terrace and then he disappeared. For a moment I thought he had gone to the right or left beyond the doors. Then I came to the doors and saw the terrace was empty. I went to the rail and I looked down and I saw the speck of colour that was his frock coat against the rocks far below.

And so we have all this to look forward to, I thought: that we may not need the blood, that our faces will gradually lose all human expression, that we can move objects with the strength of our minds, that we can all but fly. That some night thousands of years hence we may sit in utter silence as Those Who Must Be Kept are sitting now? How often tonight had Marius looked like them? How long did he sit without

523

moving when no one was here?

And what would half a century mean to him, during which time I was to live out that one mortal life far across the sea?

I turned away and went back through the house to the bed-chamber I'd been given. And I sat looking at the sea and the sky until the light started to come. When I opened the little hiding place of the sarcophagus, there were fresh flowers there. I put on the golden mask headdress and the gloves and I lay down in the stone coffin, and I could still smell the flowers as I closed my eyes.

The fearful moment was coming. The loss of consciousness. And on the edge of dream, I heard a woman laugh. She laughed lightly and long as though she were very happy and in the midst of conversation, and just before I went into darkness, I saw her white throat as she bent her head back.

15

WHEN I opened my eyes I had an idea. It came full blown to me, and it immediately obsessed me so that I was scarcely conscious of the thirst I felt, of the sting in my veins.

'Vanity,' I whispered. But it had an alluring beauty to it, the idea.

No, forget about it. Marius said to stay away from the sanctuary, and besides he will be back at midnight and then you can present the idea to him. And he can … what? Sadly shake his head.

I came out in the house and all was as it had been the night before, candles burning, windows open to the soft spectacle of the dying light. It didn't seem possible that I would leave here soon. And that I would never come back to it, that he himself would vacate this extraordinary place.

I felt sorrowful and miserable. And then there was the idea.

Not to do it in his presence, but silently and secretly so that I did not feel foolish, to go all alone.

No. Don't do it. After all, it won't do any good. Nothing will happen when you do it.

But if that's the case, why not do it? Why not do it now?

I made my rounds again, through the library and the galleries and the room full of birds and monkeys, and on into other chambers where I had not been.

But that idea stayed in my head. And the thirst nagged at me, making me just a little more impulsive, a little more restless, a little less able to reflect on all the things Marius had told me and what they might mean as time went on.

He wasn't in the house. That was certain. I had been finally through all the rooms. Where he slept was his secret, and I knew there were ways to get in and out of the house that were his secret as well.

But the door to the stairway down to Those Who Must Be Kept, that I discovered again easily enough. And it wasn't locked.

I stood in the wallpapered salon with its polished furniture looking at the clock. Only seven in the evening, five hours till he came back. Five hours of the thirst burning in me. And the idea ... The idea.

I didn't really decide to do it. I just turned my back on the clock and started walking back to my room. I knew that hundreds of others before me must have had such ideas. And how well he had described the pride he felt when he thought he could rouse them. That he might make them move.

No, I just want to do it, even if nothing happens, which is exactly how it will go. I just want to go down there alone and do it. It has something to do with Nicki maybe. I don't know. I don't know!

I went into my chamber and in the incandescent light rising from the sea, I unlocked the violin case and I looked at the Stradivarius violin.

Of course I didn't know how to play it, but we are powerful mimics. As Marius said, we have superior concentration and superior skills. And I had seen Nicki do it so often.

I tightened the bow now and rubbed the horsehair with the little piece of resin, as I had seen him do.

Only two nights ago, I couldn't have borne the idea of touching this thing. Hearing it would have been pure pain.

Now I took it out of its case and I carried it through the house, the way I'd carried it to Nicki through the wings of the Theatre of the Vampires, and not even thinking of vanity, I rushed faster and faster towards the door to the secret stairs.

It was as if they were drawing me to them, as if I had no will. Marius didn't matter now. Nothing much mattered, except to be going down the narrow damp stone steps faster and faster, past the windows full of sea spray and early evening light.

In fact, my infatuation was getting so strong, so total that I stopped suddenly, wondering if it was originating with me. But that was foolishness. Who could have put it in my head? Those Who Must Be Kept? Now that was real vanity, and besides, did these creatures know what this strange, delicate little wooden instrument was?

It made a sound, did it not, that no one had ever heard in the ancient world, a sound so human and so powerfully affecting that men thought the violin the work of the devil and accused its finest players of being possessed.

I was slightly dizzy, confused.

How had I gotten so far down the steps, and didn't I remember that the door was bolted from inside? Give me another five hundred years and I might be able to open that bolt, but not just now.

Yet I went on down, these thoughts breaking up and disintegrating as fast as they'd come. I was on fire again, and the thirst was making it worse, though the thirst had nothing to do with it.

And when I came round the last turn I saw the doors to the chapel were open wide. The light of the lamps poured out into the stairwell. And the scent of the flowers and incense was suddenly overwhelming and made a knot in my throat.

I drew nearer, holding the violin with both hands to my chest, though why I didn't know. And I saw that the tabernacle doors were open, and there they sat.

Someone had brought them more flowers. Someone had

laid out the incense in cakes on golden plates.

And I stopped just inside the chapel, and I looked at their faces and they seemed as before to look directly at me.

White, so white I could not imagine them bronzed, and as hard, it seemed, as the jewels they wore. Snake bracelet around her upper arm. Layered necklace on her breast. Tiniest lip of flesh from his chest covering the top of the clean linen skirt he wore.

Her face was narrower than his face, her nose just a little longer. His eyes were slightly longer, the folds of flesh defining them a little thicker. Their long black hair was very much the same.

I was breathing uneasily. I felt suddenly weak and let the scent of the flowers and the incense fill my lungs.

The light of the lamps danced in a thousand tiny specks of gold in the murals.

I looked down at the violin and tried to remember my idea, and I ran my fingers along the wood and wondered what this thing looked like to them.

In a hushed voice I explained what it was, that I wanted them to hear it, that I didn't really know how to play it but that I was going to try. I wasn't speaking loud enough to hear myself, but surely they could hear it if they chose to listen.

And I lifted the violin to my shoulder, braced it under my chin, and lifted the bow. I closed my eyes and I remembered music, Nicki's music, and the way that his body had moved with it and his fingers came down with the pressure of hammers and he let the message travel to his fingers from his soul.

I plunged into it, the music suddenly wailing upwards and rippling down again as my fingers danced. It was a song, all right, I could make a song. The tones were pure and rich as they echoed off the close walls with a resounding volume, creating the wailing beseeching voice that only the violin can make. I went madly on with it, rocking back and forth, forgetting Nicki, forgetting everything but the feel of my fingers stabbing at the soundboard and the realization that I was making this, this was coming out of me, and it plummeted and climbed and overflowed ever louder and louder as I bore down upon it with the frantic sawing of the bow.

I was singing with it, I was humming and then singing loudly, and all the gold of the little room was a blur. And suddenly it seemed my own voice became louder, inexplicably louder, with a pure high note which I knew that I myself could not possibly sing. Yet it was there, this beautiful note, steady and unchanging and growing even louder until it was hurting my ears. I played harder, more frantically, and I heard my own gasps coming, and I knew suddenly that I was not the one making this strange high note!

The blood was going to come out of my ears if the note did not stop. And I wasn't making the note! Without stopping the music, without giving in to the pain that was splitting my head, I looked forward and I saw Akasha had risen and her eyes were very wide and her mouth was a perfect O. The sound was coming from her, she was making it, and she was moving off the steps of the tabernacle towards me with her arms outstretched and the note pierced my eardrums as if it were a blade of steel.

I couldn't see. I heard the violin hit the stone floor. I felt my hands on the sides of my head. I screamed and screamed, but the note absorbed my screaming.

'Stop it! Stop it!' I was roaring. But all the light was there again and she was right in front of me and she was reaching out.

'O God, Marius!' I turned and ran towards the doors. And the doors flew shut against me, knocking my face so hard I fell down on my knees. Under the high shrill continuum of the note I was sobbing.

'Marius, Marius, Marius!'

And turning to see what was about to happen to me, I saw her foot come down on the violin. It popped and splintered under her heel. But the note she sang was dying. The note was fading away.

And I was left in silence, deafness, unable to hear my own screams for Marius which were going on and on, as I scrambled to my feet.

Ringing silence, shimmering silence. She was right in front

528

of me, and her black eyebrows came together delicately, barely creasing her white flesh, her eyes full of torment and questioning and her pale pink lips opened to reveal her fang teeth.

Help me, help me, Marius, help me, I was stammering, unable to hear myself except in the pure abstraction of intention in my mind. And then her arms enclosed me, and she drew me closer, and I felt the hand as Marius had described it, cupping my head gently, very gently, and I felt my teeth against her neck.

I did not hesitate. I did not think about the limbs that were locked around me, that could crush the life out of me in a second. I felt my fangs break through the skin as if through a glacial crust, and the blood came steaming into my mouth.

Oh, yes, yes ... oh, yes. I had thrown my arm over her left shoulder, I was clinging to her, my living statue, and it didn't matter that she was harder than marble, that was the way it was supposed to be, it was perfect, my Mother, my lover, my powerful one, and the blood was penetrating every pulsing particle of me with the threads of its burning web. But her lips were against my throat. She was kissing me, kissing the artery through which her own blood so violently flowed. Her lips were opening on it, and as I drew upon her blood with all my strength, sucking, and feeling that gush again and again before it spread itself out into me, I felt the unmistakable sensation of her fangs going into my neck.

Out of every zinging vessel my blood was suddenly drawn into her, even as hers was being drawn into me.

I saw it, the shimmering circuit, and more divinely I felt it because nothing else existed but our mouths locked to each other's throats and the relentless pounding path of the blood. There were no dreams, there were no visions, there was just this, *this* — gorgeous and deafening and heated — and nothing mattered, absolutely nothing, except that this never stop. The world of all things that had weight and filled space and interrupted the flow of light was gone.

And yet some horrid noise intruded, something ugly, like the sound of stone cracking, like the sound of stone dragged across the floor. Marius coming. No, Marius, don't come. Go back, don't touch. Don't separate us.

But it wasn't Marius, this awful sound, this intrusion, this sudden disruption of everything, this thing grabbing hold of my hair and tearing me off her so the blood spurted out of my mouth. It was Enkil. And his powerful hands were clamped on the sides of my head.

The blood gushed down my chin. I saw her stricken face! I saw her reach out for him. Her eyes blazed with common anger, her glistening white limbs animate as she grabbed at the hands that held my head. I heard her voice rise out of her, screaming, shrieking, louder than the note she had sung, the blood drooling from the end of her mouth.

The sound took sight as well as sound with it. The darkness swirled, broken into millions of tiny specks. My skull was going to crack.

He was forcing me down on my knees. He was bent over me, and suddenly I saw his face completely and it was as impassive as ever, only the stress of the muscles in his arms evincing true life.

And even through the obliterating sound of her scream I knew the door behind me quaked with Marius's pounding, his shouts almost as loud as her cries.

The blood was coming out of my ears from her screams. I was moving my lips.

The vice of stone clamped to my head suddenly let go. I felt myself hit the floor. I was sprawled out flat, and I felt the cold pressure of his foot on my chest. He would crush my heart in a second, and she, her screams growing ever louder, ever more piercing, was on his back with her arm locked around his neck. I saw her knotted eyebrows, her flying black hair.

But it was Marius I heard through the door talking to him, cutting through the white sound of her screams.

Kill him, Enkil, and I will take her away from you forever, and she will help me to do it! I swear.

Sudden silence. Deafness again. The warmth of blood trickling down the sides of my neck.

She stepped aside and she looked straight forward and the doors flew open, smacking the side of the narrow stone passage, and Marius was suddenly standing above me with his hands on Enkil's shoulders and Enkil seemed unable to move.

The foot slid down, bruising my stomach, and then it was gone. And Marius was speaking words I could hear only as thoughts: *Get out, Lestat. Run.*

I struggled to sit up, and I saw him driving them both slowly back towards the tabernacle, and I saw them both staring not forward, but at him, Akasha clutching Enkil's arm, and I saw their faces blank again, but for the first time the blankness seemed listless and not the mask of curiosity but the mask of death.

'Lestat, run!' he said again, without turning. And I obeyed.

16

I WAS at the farthest corner of the terrace when Marius finally came into the lighted salon. There was a heat in all my veins still that breathed as if it had its own life. And I could see far beyond the dim hulking shapes of the islands. I could hear the progress of a ship along a distant coast. But all I kept thinking was that if Enkil came at me again, I could jump over this railing. I could get into the sea and swim. I kept feeling his hands on the sides of my head, his foot on my chest.

I stood against the stone railing, shivering, and there was blood all over my hands still from the bruises on my face which had already completely healed.

'I'm sorry. I'm sorry I did it,' I said as soon as Marius came out of the salon. 'I don't know why I did it. I shouldn't have done it. I'm sorry. I'm sorry, I swear it, I'm sorry, Marius. I'll never never do anything you tell me not to do again.'

He stood with his arms folded looking at me. He was glowering.

'Lestat, what did I say last night?' he asked. 'You are the *damnedest creature!*'

'Marius, forgive me. Please forgive me. I didn't think anything would happen. I was sure nothing would happen...'

He gestured for me to be quiet, for us to go down onto the rocks together, and he slipped over the railing and went first. I came behind him, vaguely delighted with the ease of it, but too dazed still to care about things like that. Her presence was all over me like a fragrance, only she had had no fragrance, except that of the incense and the flowers that must have somehow managed to permeate her hard white skin. How strangely fragile she had seemed in spite of that hardness.

We went down over the slippery boulders until we reached the white beach and we walked together in silence, looking out over the snow-white froth that leapt against the rocks or streaked towards us on the smooth hard-packed white sand. The wind roared in my ears, and I felt the sense of solitude this always creates in me, the roaring wind that blots out all other sensations as well as sound.

And I was getting calmer and calmer, and more and more agitated and miserable at the same time.

Marius had slipped his arm around me the way Gabrielle used to do it, and I paid no attention to where we were going, quite surprised when I saw we'd come to a small inlet of the water where a longboat lay at anchor with only a single pair of oars.

When we stopped I said again, 'I'm sorry I did it! I swear I am. I didn't believe...'

'Don't tell me you regret it,' Marius said calmly. 'You are not at all sorry that it occurred, and that you were the cause of it, now that you are safe, and not crushed like an eggshell on the chapel floor.'

'Oh, but that's not the point,' I said. I started crying. I took out my handkerchief, grand accoutrement of an eighteenth-century gentleman, and wiped the blood off my face. I could feel her holding me, feel her blood, feel his hands. The whole thing commenced to reenact itself. If Marius hadn't come in time...

'But what did happen, Marius? What did you see?'

'I wish we could get beyond his hearing,' Marius said wearily.

It's madness to speak or think anything that could disturb him any further. I have to let him lapse back.'

And now he seemed truly furious and he turned his back on me.

But how could I not think about it? I wished I could open my head and pull the thoughts out of it. They were rocketing through me, like her blood. In her body was locked a mind still, an appetite, a blazing spiritual core whose heat had moved through me like liquid lightning, and without question Enkil had a deathhold upon her! I loathed him. I wanted to destroy him. And my brain seized upon all sorts of mad notions, that somehow he could be destroyed without endangering us as long as she remained!

But that made little sense. Hadn't the demons entered first into him? But what if that wasn't so ...

'Stop it, young one!' Marius flashed.

I went to crying again. I felt of my neck where she had touched it, and licked my lips and tasted her blood again. I looked at the scattered stars above and even these benign and eternal things seemed menacing and senseless and I felt a scream swelling dangerously in my throat.

The effects of her blood were waning already. The first clear vision was clouded, and my limbs were once again my limbs. They might be stronger, yes, but the magic was dying. The magic had left only something stronger than memory of the circuit of the blood through us both.

'Marius, what happened!' I said, shouting over the wind. 'Don't be angry with me, don't turn away from me. I can't ...'

'Shhh, Lestat,' he said. He came back and took me by the arm. 'Don't worry about my anger,' he said. 'It's unimportant, and it is not directed at you. Give me a little more time to collect myself.'

'But did you see what happened between her and me?'

He was looking out to sea. The water looked perfectly black and the foam perfectly white.

'Yes, I saw,' he said.

'I took the violin and I wanted to play it for them, I was thinking —'

'Yes, I know, of course ...'

'— that music would affect them, especially that music, that strange, unnatural-sounding music, you know how a violin ...'

'Yes —'

'Marius, she gave me ... she ... and she took —'

'I know.'

'And he keeps her there! He keeps her prisoner!'

'Lestat, I beg you ...' He was smiling wearily, sadly.

Imprison him, Marius, the way that they did, and let her go!

'You dream, my child,' he said. 'You dream.'

He turned and he left me, gesturing for me to leave him alone. He went down to the wet beach and let the water lap at him as he walked back and forth.

I tried to get calm again. It seemed unreal to me that I had ever been any place but this island, that the world of mortals was out there, that the strange tragedy and menace of Those Who Must Be Kept was unknown beyond these wet and shining cliffs.

Finally Marius made his way back.

'Listen to me,' he said. 'Straight west is an island that is not under my protection and there is an old Greek city on the northern tip of it where the seaman's taverns stay open all night. Go there now in the boat. Hunt and forget what has happened here. Assess the new powers you might have from her. But try not to think of her or him. Above all try not to plot against him. Before dawn, come back to the house. It won't be difficult. You'll find a dozen open doors and windows. Do as I say, now, for me.'

I bowed my head. It was the one thing under heaven that could distract me, that could wipe out any noble or enervating thoughts. Human blood and human struggle and human death.

And without protest, I made my way out through the shallow water to the boat.

IN THE early hours I looked at my reflection in a fragment of metallic mirror pinned to the wall of a seaman's filthy bedroom in a little inn. I saw myself in my brocade coat and

534

white lace, and my face warm from killing, and the dead man sprawled behind me across the table. He still held the knife with which he'd tried to cut my throat. And there was the bottle of wine with the drug in it which I'd kept refusing, with playful protestations, until he'd lost his temper and tried the last resort. His companion lay dead on the bed.

I looked at the young blond-haired rake in the mirror.

'Well, if it isn't the vampire Lestat,' I said.

BUT all the blood in the world couldn't stop the horrors from coming over me when I went to my rest.

I couldn't stop thinking of her, wondering if it was her laugh I had heard in my sleep the night before. And I wondered that she had told me nothing in the blood, until I closed my eyes and quite suddenly things came back to me, of course, wonderful things, incoherent as they were magical. She and I were walking down a hallway together — not here but a place I knew. I think it was a palace in Germany where Haydn wrote his music — and she spoke casually as she had a thousand times to me. *But tell me about all this, what do the people believe, what turns the wheels inside of them, what are these marvellous inventions* ... She wore a fashionable black hat with a great white plume on its broad brim and a white veil tied round the top of it and under her chin, and her face was merely beginning, merely young.

WHEN I opened my eyes, I knew Marius was waiting for me. I came out into the chamber and saw him standing by the empty violin case, with his back to the open window over the sea.

'You have to go now, my young one,' he said sadly. 'I had hoped for more time, but that is impossible. The boat is waiting to take you away.'

'Because of what I did ...' I said miserably. So I was being cast out.

'He's destroyed the things in the chapel,' Marius said, but his voice was asking for calm. He put his arm around my shoulder, and he took my bag in his other hand. We went towards the door. 'I want you to go now because it is the only thing that will quiet him, and I want you to remember not his anger, but everything that I told you, and to be confident that we will meet again as we said.'

'But are you afraid of him, Marius?'

'Oh, no, Lestat. Don't carry this worry away with you. He has done little things like this before, now and then. He does not know what he does, really. I am convinced of that. He only knows that someone stepped between him and Akasha. Time is all that is required for him to lapse back.'

There it was, that phrase again, 'lapse back'.

'And she sits as if she never moved, doesn't she?' I asked.

'I want you away now so that you don't provoke him,' Marius said, leading me out of the house and towards the cliff-side stairs. He continued speaking:

'Whatever ability we creatures have to move objects mentally, to ignite them, to do any real harm by the power of the mind does not extend very far from the physical spot where we stand. So I want you gone from here tonight and on your way to America. All the sooner to return to me when he is no longer agitated and no longer remembers, and I will have forgotten nothing and will be waiting for you.'

I saw the galley in the harbour below when we reached the edge of the cliff. The stairs looked impossible, but they weren't impossible. What was impossible was that I was leaving Marius and this island right now.

'You needn't come down with me,' I said, taking the bag from him. I was trying not to sound bitter and crestfallen. After all, I had caused this. 'I would rather not weep in front of others. Leave me here.'

'I wish we had had a few more nights together,' he said, 'for us to consider in quiet what took place. But my love goes with you. And try to remember the things I've told you. When we meet again we'll have much to say to each other —' He paused.

'What is it, Marius?'

'Tell me truthfully,' he asked. 'Are you sorry that I came for you in Cairo, sorry that I brought you here?'

'How could I be?' I asked. 'I'm only sorry that I'm going.

What if I can't find you again or you can't find me?'

'When the time is right, I'll find you,' he said. 'And always remember: you have the power to call to me, as you did before. When I hear that call, I can bridge distances to answer that I could never bridge on my own. If the time is right, I will answer. Of that you can be sure.'

I nodded. There was too much to say and I didn't speak a word.

We embraced for a long moment, and then I turned and slowly started my descent, knowing he would understand why I didn't look back.

17

I DID not know how much I wanted 'the world' until my ship finally made its way up the murky Bayou St. Jean towards the city of New Orleans, and I saw the black ragged line of the swamp against the luminous sky.

The fact that none of our kind had ever penetrated this wilderness excited me and humbled me at the same time.

Before the sun rose on that first morning, I'd fallen in love with the low and damp country, as I had with the dry heat of Egypt, and as time passed I came to love it more than any spot on the globe.

Here the scents were so strong you smelled the raw green of the leaves as well as the pink and yellow blossoms. And the great brown river, surging past the miserable little Place d'Armes and its tiny cathedral, threw into eclipse every other fabled river I'd ever seen.

Unnoticed and unchallenged, I explored the ramshackle little colony with its muddy streets and gunwale sidewalks and dirty Spanish soldiers lounging about the calaboose. I lost myself in the dangerous waterfront shacks full of gambling and brawling flatboatmen and lovely dark-skinned Caribbean women, wandering out again to glimpse the silent flash of lightning, hear the dim roar of the thunder, feel the silky warmth of the summer rain.

The low-slung roofs of the little cottages gleamed under the moon. Light skittered on the iron gates of the fine Spanish town houses. It flickered behind real lace curtains hung inside freshly washed glass doors. I walked among the crude little bungalows that spread out to the ramparts, peeping through windows at gilded furniture and enameled bits of wealth and civilization that in this barbaric place seemed priceless and fastidious and even sad.

Now and then through the mire there came a vision: a real French gentleman done up in snow-white wig and fancy frock coat, his wife in panniers, and a black slave carrying clean slippers for the two high above the flowing mud.

I knew that I had come to the most foresaken outpost of the Savage Garden, and that this was my country and I would remain in New Orleans, if New Orleans could only manage to remain. Whatever I suffered should be lessened in this lawless place, whatever I craved should give me more pleasure once I had it in my grasp.

And there were moments on that first night in this fetid little paradise when I prayed that in spite of all my secret power, I was somehow kin to every mortal man. Maybe I was not the exotic outcast that I imagined, but merely the dim magnification of every human soul.

Old truths and ancient magic, revolution and invention, all conspire to distract us from the passion that in one way or another defeats us all.

And weary finally of this complexity, we dream of that long-ago time when we sat upon our mother's knee and each kiss was the perfect consummation of desire. What can we do but reach for the embrace that must now contain both heaven and hell: our doom again and again and again.

Epilogue

Interview with the Vampire

1

AND SO I came to the end of The Early Education and
Adventures of the Vampire Lestat, the tale that I set out
to tell. You have the account of Old World magic and
mystery which I have chosen, despite all prohibitions and
injunctions, to pass on.

But my story isn't finished, no matter how reluctant I
might be to continue it. And I must consider, at least briefly,
the painful events that led to my decision to go down into the
earth in 1929.

That was a hundred and forty years after I left Marius's
island. And I never set eyes upon Marius again. Gabrielle also
remained completely lost to me. She'd vanished that night in
Cairo never to be heard from by anyone mortal or immortal
that I was ever to know.

And when I made my grave in the twentieth century, I was
alone and weary and badly wounded in body and soul.

I'd lived out my 'one lifetime' as Marius advised me to do.
But I couldn't blame Marius for the way in which I'd lived it,
and the hideous mistakes I'd made.

Sheer will had shaped my experience more than any other
human characteristic. And advice and predictions notwith-
standing, I courted tragedy and disaster as I have always done.
Yet I had my rewards, I can't deny that. For almost seventy
years I had my fledgling vampires Louis and Claudia, two of
the most splendid immortals who ever walked the earth, and I
had them on my terms.

Shortly after reaching the colony, I fell fatally in love with

Louis, a young dark-haired bourgeois planter, graceful of speech and fastidious of manner, who seemed in his cynicism and self-destructiveness the very twin of Nicolas.

He had Nicki's grim intensity, his rebelliousness, his tortured capacity to believe and not to believe, and finally to despair.

Yet Louis gained a hold over me far more powerful than Nicolas had ever had. Even in his cruelest moments, Louis touched the tenderness in me, seducing me with his staggering dependence, his infatuation with my every gesture and every spoken word.

And his naiveté conquered me always, his strange bourgeois faith that God was still God even if he turned his back on us, that damnation and salvation established the boundaries of a small and hopeless world.

Louis was a sufferer, a thing that loved mortals even more than I did. And I wonder sometimes if I didn't look to Louis to punish me for what had happened to Nicki, if I didn't create Louis to be my conscience and to mete out year in and year out the penance I felt I deserved.

But I loved him, plain and simple. And it was out of the desperation to keep him, to bind him closer to me at the most precarious of moments, that I committed the most selfish and impulsive act of my entire life among the living dead. It was the crime that was to be my undoing: the creation with Louis and for Louis of Claudia, a stunningly beautiful vampire child.

Her body wasn't six years old when I took her, and though she would have died if I hadn't done it (just as Louis would have died if I hadn't taken him also), this was a challenge to the gods for which Claudia and I would both pay.

But this is the tale that was told by Louis in *Interview with the Vampire*, which for all its contradictions and terrible misunderstandings manages to capture the atmosphere in which Claudia and Louis and I came together and stayed together for sixty-four years.

During that time, we were nonpareils of our species, a silk-and velvet-clad trio of deadly hunters, glorying in our secret and in the swelling city of New Orleans that harboured us in luxury and supplied us endlessly with fresh victims.

And though Louis did not know it when he wrote his chronicle, sixty-five years is a phenomenal time for any bond in our world.

As for the lies he told, the mistakes he made, well, I forgive him his excess of imagination, his bitterness, and his vanity, which was, after all, never very great. I never revealed to him half my powers, and with reason, because he shrank in guilt and self-loathing from using even half of his own.

Even his unusual beauty and unfailing charm were something of a secret to him. When you read his statement that I made him a vampire because I coveted his plantation house, you can write that off to modesty more easily than stupidity, I suppose.

As for his belief that I was a peasant, well that was understandable. He was, after all, a discriminating and inhibited child of the middle class, aspiring as all the colonial planters did to be a genuine aristocrat though he had never met one, and I came from a long line of feudal lords who licked their fingers and threw the bones from their shoulders to the dogs as they dined.

When he says I played with innocent strangers, befriending them and then killing them, how was he to know that I hunted almost exclusively among the gamblers, the thieves, and the killers, being more faithful to my unspoken vow to kill the evildoer than even I had hoped I would be? (The young Frenier, for example, a planter whom Louis romanticizes hopelessly in his text, was in fact a wanton killer and a cheater at cards on the verge of signing over his family's plantation for debt when I struck him down. The whores I feasted upon in front of Louis once, to spite him, had drugged and robbed many a seaman who was never seen alive again.)

But little things like this don't really matter. He told the tale as he believed it.

And in a real way, Louis was always the sum of his flaws, the most beguilingly human fiend I have ever known. Even Marius could not have imagined such a compassionate and contemplative creature, always the gentleman, even teaching

Claudia the proper use of table silver when she, bless her little heart, had not the slightest need ever to touch a knife or a fork.

His blindness to the motives or the suffering of others was as much a part of his charm as his soft unkempt black hair or the eternally troubled expression in his green eyes.

And why should I bother to tell of the times he came to me in wretched anxiety, begging me never to leave him, of the times we walked together and talked together, acted Shakespeare together for Claudia's amusement, or went arm in arm to hunt the riverfront taverns or to waltz with the dark-skinned beauties of the celebrated quadroon balls?

Read between the lines.

I betrayed him when I created him, that is the significant thing. Just as I betrayed Claudia. And I forgive the nonsense he wrote, because he told the truth about the eerie contentment he and Claudia and I shared and had no right to share in those long nineteenth-century decades when the peacock colours of the ancient regime died out and the lovely music of Mozart and Haydn gave way to the bombast of Beethoven, which could sound at times too remarkably like the clang of my imaginary Hell's Bells.

I had what I wanted, what I had always wanted. I had *them*. And I could now and then forget Gabrielle and forget Nicki, and even forget Marius and the blank staring face of Akasha, or the icy touch of her hand or the heat of her blood.

But I had always wanted many things. What accounted for the duration of the life he described in *Interview with the Vampire*? Why did we last so long?

All during the nineteenth century, vampires were 'discovered' by the literary writers of Europe. Lord Ruthven, the creation of Dr. Polidori, gave way to Sir Francis Varney in the penny dreadfuls, and later came Sheridan Le Fanu's magnificent and sensuous Countess Carmilla Karnstein, and finally the big ape of the vampires, the hirsute Slav Count Dracula, who though he can turn himself into a bat or dematerialize at will, nevertheless crawls down the wall of his castle in the manner of a lizard apparently for fun — all of these creations and many like them feeding the insatiable

544

appetite for 'gothic and fantastical tales'.

We were the essence of that nineteenth-century conception — aristocratically aloof, unfailingly elegant, and invariably merciless, and cleaving to each other in a land ripe for, but untroubled by, others of our kind.

Maybe we had found the perfect moment in history, the perfect balance between the monstrous and the human, the time when that 'vampire romance' born in my imagination amid the colourful brocades of the ancient regime should find its greatest enhancement in the flowing black cape, the black top-hat, and the little girl's luminous curls spilling down from their violet ribbon to the puffed sleeves of her diaphanous silk dress.

But what had I done to Claudia? And when would I have to pay for that? How long was she content to be the mystery that bound Louis and me so tightly together, the muse of our moonlit hours, the one object of devotion common to us both?

Was it inevitable that she who would never have a woman's form would strike out at the demon father who condemned her to the body of a little china doll?

I should have listened to Marius's warning. I should have stopped for one moment to reflect on it as I stood at the edge of that grand and intoxicating experiment: to make a vampire of 'the least of these'. I should have taken a deep breath.

But you know, it was like playing the violin for Akasha. I *wanted* to do it. I wanted to see what would happen, I mean, with a beautiful little girl like that!

Oh, Lestat, you deserve everything that ever happened to you. You'd better not die. You might actually go to hell.

But why was it that for purely selfish reasons, I didn't listen to some of the advice given me? Why didn't I learn from any of them — Gabrielle, Armand, Marius? But then, I never have listened to anyone, really. Somehow or other, I never can.

And I cannot say even now that I regret Claudia, that I wish I had never seen her, nor held her, nor whispered secrets to her, nor heard her laughter echoing through the shadowy gaslighted rooms of that all too human town house in which we moved amid the lacquered furniture and the darkening oil paintings and the brass flowerpots as living beings should. Claudia was my dark child, my love, evil of my evil. Claudia broke my heart.

And on a warm sultry night in the spring of the year 1860, she rose up to settle the score. She enticed me, she trapped me, and she plunged a knife over and over again into my drugged and poisoned body, until almost every drop of the vampiric blood gushed out of me before my wounds had the precious few seconds in which to heal.

I don't blame her. It was the sort of thing I might have done myself.

And those delirious moments will never be forgotten by me, never consigned to some unexplored compartment of the mind. It was her cunning and her will that laid me low as surely as the blade that slashed my throat and divided my heart. I will think on those moments every night for as long as I go on, and of the chasm that opened under me, the plunge into mortal death that was nearly mine. Claudia gave me that.

But as the blood flowed, taking with it all power to see or hear or move finally, my thoughts travelled back and back, way beyond the creation of the doomed vampire family in their paradise of wallpaper and lace curtains, to the dimly envisioned groves of mythical lands where the old Dionysian god of the wood had felt again and again his flesh torn, his blood spilled.

If there was not meaning, at least there was the lustre of congruence, the stunning repetition of the *same old theme.*

And the god dies. And the god rises. But this time no one is redeemed.

With tne blood of Akasha, Marius had said to me, you will survive disasters that would destroy others of our kind.

Later, abandoned in the stench and darkness of the swamp, I felt the thirst define my proportions, I felt the thirst propel me, I felt my jaws open in the rank water and my fangs seek the warm-blooded things that could put my feet on the long road back.

And three nights later, when again I had been beaten and

my children left me once and for all in the blazing inferno of our town house, it was the blood of the old ones, Magnus and Marius and Akasha, that sustained me as I crawled away from the flames.

But without more of that healing blood, without a fresh infusion, I was left at the mercy of time to heal my wounds.

And what Louis could not describe in his story is what happened to me after, how for years I hunted on the edge of the human herd, a hideous and crippled monster, who could strike down only the very young or infirm. In constant danger from my victims, I became the very antithesis of the romantic demon, bringing terror rather than rapture, resembling nothing so much as the old revenants of les Innocents in their filth and rags.

The wounds I'd suffered affected my very spirit, my capacity to reason. And what I saw in the mirror every time I dared to look further shriveled my soul.

Yet not once in all this time did I call out to Marius, did I try to reach him over the miles. I could not beg for his healing blood. Better suffer purgatory for a century than Marius's condemnation. Better suffer the worst loneliness, the worst anguish, than discover that he knew everything I'd done and had long ago turned his back on me.

As for Gabrielle, who would have forgiven me anything, whose blood was powerful enough at least to hasten my recovery, I did not know even where to look.

When I had recovered sufficiently to make the long voyage to Europe, I turned to the only one that I could turn to: Armand. Armand who lived still on the land I'd given him, in the very tower where I'd been made by Magnus, Armand who still commanded the thriving coven of the Theatre of the Vampires in the boulevard du Temple, which still belonged to me. After all, I owed Armand no explanations. And did he not owe something to me?

IT WAS a shock to see him when he came to answer the knock on his door.

He looked like a young man out of the novels of Dickens in

his sombre and sleekly tailored black frock coat, all the Renaissance curls clipped away. His eternally youthful face was stamped with the innocence of a David Copperfield and the pride of a Steerforth — anything but the true nature of the spirit within.

For one moment a brilliant light burned in him as he looked at me. Then he stared slowly at the scars that covered my face and hands, and he said softly and almost compassionately:

'Come in, Lestat.'

He took my hand. And we walked together through the house he had built at the foot of Magnus's tower, a dark and dreary place fit for all the Byronic horrors of this strange age.

'You know, the rumour is that you met the end somewhere in Egypt, or the Far East,' he said quickly in everyday French with an animation I'd never seen in him before. He was skilled now at pretending to be a living being. 'You went with the old century, and no one has heard of you since.'

'And Gabrielle?' I demanded immediately, wondering that I had not blurted it out at the door.

'No one has ever seen her or heard of her since you left Paris,' he said.

Once again his eyes moved over me caressingly. And there was thinly veiled excitement in him, a fever that I could feel like the warmth of the nearby fire. I knew he was trying to read my thoughts.

'What's happened to you?' he asked.

My scars were puzzling him. They were too numerous, too intricate, scars of an attack that should have meant death. I felt a sudden panic that in my confusion I'd reveal everything to him, the things that Marius had long ago forbidden me to tell.

But it was the story of Louis and Claudia that came rushing out, in stammering and half truths, *sans* one salient fact: that Claudia had been only ... a child.

I told briefly of the years in Louisiana, of how they had finally risen against me just as he had predicted my children might. I conceded everything to him, without guile or pride, explaining that it was his blood I needed now. Pain and pain

548

and pain, to lay it out for him, to feel him considering it. To say, yes, you were right. It isn't the whole story. But in the main, you were right.

Was it sadness I saw in his face then? Surely it wasn't triumph. Unobtrusively, he watched my trembling hands as I gestured. He waited patiently when I faltered, couldn't find the right words.

A small infusion of his blood would hasten my healing, I whispered. A small infusion would clear my mind. I tried not to be lofty or righteous when I reminded him that I had given him his tower, and the gold he'd used to build his house, that I still owned the Theatre of the Vampires, that surely he could do this little thing, this intimate thing, for me now. There was an ugly naiveté to the words I spoke to him, addled as I was, and weak and thirsting and afraid. The blaze of the fire made me anxious. The light on the dark grain of the woodwork of these stuffy rooms made imagined faces appear and disappear.

'I don't want to stay in Paris,' I said. 'I don't want to trouble you or the coven at the theatre. I am asking this small thing. I am asking ...' It seemed my courage and the words had run out.

A long moment passed:

'Tell me again about this Louis,' he said.

The tears rose to my eyes disgracefully. I repeated some foolish phrases about Louis's indestructible humanity, his understanding of things that other immortals couldn't grasp. Carelessly I whispered things from the heart. It wasn't Louis who had attacked me. It was the woman, Claudia.

I saw something in him quicken. A faint blush came to his cheeks.

'They have been seen here in Paris,' he said softly. 'And she is no woman, this creature. She is a vampire child.'

I can't remember what followed. Maybe I tried to explain the blunder. Maybe I admitted there was no accounting for what I'd done. Maybe I brought us round again to the purpose of my visit, to what I needed, what I must have. I remember being utterly humiliated as he led me out of the house and into the waiting carriage, as he told me that I must go with him to the Theatre of the Vampires.

'You don't understand,' I said. 'I can't go there. I will not be seen like this by the others. You must stop the carriage. You must do as I ask.'

'No, you have it backwards,' he said in the tenderest voice. We were already in the crowded Paris streets. I couldn't see the city I remembered. This was a nightmare, this metropolis of roaring steam trains and giant concrete boulevards. Never had the smoke and filth of the industrial age seemed so hideous as it was here in the City of Light.

I scarcely remember being forced by him out of the carrige and stumbling along the broad pavements as he pushed me towards the theatre doors. What was this place, this enormous building? Was this the boulevard du Temple? and then the descent into that hideous cellar full of ugly copies of the bloodiest paintings of Goya and Brueghel and Bosch.

And finally starvation as I lay on the floor of a brick-lined cell, unable even to shout curses at him, the darkness full of the vibrations of the passing omnibuses and tramcars, penetrated again and again by the distant screech of iron wheels.

Sometime in the dark, I discovered a mortal victim there. But the victim was dead. Cold blood, nauseating blood. The worst kind of feeding, lying on that clammy corpse, sucking up what was left.

And then Armand was there, standing motionless in the shadows, immaculate in his white linen and black wool. He spoke in an undertone about Louis and Claudia, that there would be some kind of trial. Down on his knees he came to sit beside me, forgetting for a moment to be human, the boy gentleman sitting in this filthy damp place. 'You will declare it before the others, that she did it,' he said. And the others, the new ones, came to the door to look at me one by one.

'Get clothing for him,' Armand said. His hand was resting on my shoulder. 'He must look presentable, our lost lord,' he told them. 'That was always his way.'

They laughed when I begged to speak to Eleni or Félix or Laurent. They did not known those names. Gabrielle — it meant nothing.

And where was Marius? How many countries, rivers, mountains lay between us? Could he hear and see these things?

High above, in the theatre, a mortal audience, herded like sheep into a corral, thundered on the wooden staircases, the wooden floors.

I dreamed of getting away from here, getting back to Louisiana, letting time do its inevitable work. I dreamed of the earth again, its cool depths which I'd known so briefly in Cairo. I dreamed of Louis and Claudia and that we were together. Claudia had grown miraculously into a beautiful woman, and she said, laughing, 'You see this is what I came to Europe to discover, how to do this!'

And I feared that I was never to be allowed out of here, that I was to be entombed as those starving ones had been under les Innocents, that I had made a fatal mistake. I was stuttering and crying and trying to talk to Armand. And then I realized Armand was not even there. If he had come, he had gone as quickly. I was having delusions.

And the victim, the warm victim — 'Give it to me, I beg you!' — and Armand saying:

'You will say what I have told you to say.'

It was a mob tribunal of monsters, white-faced demons shouting accusations, Louis pleading desperately, Claudia staring at me mute, and my saying, yes, she was the one who did it, yes, and then cursing Armand as he shoved me back into the shadows, his innocent face radiant as ever.

'But you have done well, Lestat. You have done well.'

What had I done? Borne testimony against them that they had broken the old rules? They'd risen against the coven master? What did they know of the old rules? I was screaming for Louis. And then I was drinking blood in the darkness, living blood from another victim, and it wasn't the healing blood, it was just blood.

WE WERE in the carriage again and it was raining. We were riding through the country. And then we went up and up through the old tower to the roof. I had Claudia's bloody yellow dress in my hands. I had seen her in a narrow wet place where she had been burnt by the sun. 'Scatter the ashes!' I had said. Yet no one moved to do it. The torn bloody yellow dress lay on the cellar floor. Now I held it in my hands. 'They will scatter the ashes, won't they?' I said.

'Didn't you want justice?' Armand asked, his black wool cape close around him in the wind, his face dark with the power of the recent kill.

What did it have to do with justice? Why did I hold this thing, this little dress?

I looked out from Magnus's battlements and I saw the city had come to get me. It had reached out its long arms to embrace the tower, and the air stank of factory smoke.

Armand stood still at the stone railing watching me, and he seemed suddenly as young as Claudia had seemed. *And make sure they have had some lifetime before you make them; and never never make one as young as Armand.* In death she said nothing. She had looked at those around her as if they were giants jabbering in an alien tongue.

Armand's eyes were red.

'Louis — where is he?' I asked. 'They didn't kill him. I saw him. He went out into the rain …'

'They have gone after him,' he answered. 'He is already destroyed.'

Liar, with the face of a choirboy.

'Stop them, you have to! If there's still time …'

He shook his head.

'Why can't you stop them? Why did you do it, the trial, all of it, what do you care what they did to me?'

'It's finished.'

Under the roar of the winds came the scream of a steam whistle. Losing the train of thought. Losing it … Not wanting to go back. Louis, come back.

'And you don't mean to help me, do you?' Despair.

He leaned forward, and his face transformed itself as it had done years and years ago, as if his rage were melting it from within.

'You, who destroyed all of us, you who took everything.

552

Whatever made you think that I would help you!' He came closer, the face all but collapsed upon itself. 'You who put us on the lurid posters in the boulevard du Temple, you who made us the subject of cheap stories and drawing room talk!'

'But I didn't. You know I ... I swear ... It wasn't me!'

'You who carried our secrets into the limelight — the fashionable one, the Marquis in the white gloves, the fiend in the velvet cape!'

'You're mad to blame it all on me. You have no right,' I insisted, but my voice was faltering so badly I couldn't understand my own words.

And his voice shot out of him like the tongue of a snake.

'We had our Eden under that ancient cemetery,' he hissed. 'We had our faith and our purpose. And it was you who drove us out of it with a flaming sword! What do we have now! Answer me! Nothing but the love of each other and what can that mean to creatures like us!'

'No, it's not true, it was all happening already. You don't understand anything. You never did.'

But he wasn't listening to me. And it didn't matter whether or not he was listening. He was drawing closer, and in a dark flash his hand went out, and my head went back, and I saw the sky and the city of Paris upside down.

I was falling through the air.

And I went down and down past the windows of the tower, until the stone walkway rose up to catch me, and every bone of my body broke within its thin case of preternatural skin.

2

TWO years passed before I was strong enough to board a ship for Louisiana. And I was still badly crippled, still scarred. But I had to leave Europe, where no whisper had come to me of my lost Gabrielle or of the great and powerful Marius, who had surely rendered his judgment upon me.

I had to go home. And home was New Orleans, where the warmth was, where the flowers never stopped blooming, where I still owned, through my never ending supply of 'coin of the realm', a dozen empty old mansions with rotting white columns and sagging porches round which I could roam.

And I spent the last years of the 1800s in complete seclusion in the old Garden District a block from the Lafayette Cemetery, in the finest of my houses, slumbering beneath towering oaks.

I read by candle or oil lamp all the books I could procure. I might as well have been Gabrielle trapped in her castle bedroom, save there was no furniture here. And the stacks of books reached to the ceiling in one room after another as I went on to the next. Now and then I mustered enough stamina to break into a library or an old bookstore for new volumes, but less and less I went out. I wrote off for periodicals. I hoarded candles and bottles and tin cans of oil.

I do not remember when it became the twentieth century, only that everything was uglier and darker, and the beauty I'd known in the old eighteenth-century days seemed more than ever some kind of fanciful idea. The bourgeois ran the world now upon dreary principles and with a distrust of the sensuality and the excess that the ancient regime had so loved.

But my vision and thoughts were getting ever more clouded. I no longer hunted humans. And a vampire cannot thrive without human blood, human death. I survived by luring the garden animals of the old neighbourhood, the pampered dogs and cats. And when they couldn't be got easily, well, then there was always the vermin that I could call to me like the Pied Piper, fat long-tailed grey rats.

One night I forced myself to make the long trek through the quiet streets to a shabby little theatre called the Happy Hour near the waterfront slums. I wanted to see the new silent moving pictures. I was wrapped in a greatcoat with a muffler hiding my gaunt face. I wore gloves to hide my skeletal hands. The sight of the daytime sky even in this imperfect film terrified me. But it seemed the dreary tones of black and white were perfect for a colourless age.

I did not think about other immortals. Yet now and then a vampire would appear — some orphaned fledgling who had stumbled on my lair, or a wanderer come in search of the legendary Lestat, begging for secrets, power. Horrid, these intrusions.

Even the timbre of the supernatural voice shattered my nerves, drove me into the farthest corner. Yet no matter how great the pain, I scanned each new mind for knowledge of my Gabrielle. I never discovered any. Nothing to do after that but ignore the poor human victims the fiend would bring in the vain hope of restoring me.

But these encounters were over soon enough. Frightened, aggrieved, shouting curses, the intruder would depart, leaving me in blessed silence.

I'd slip a little deeper away from things, just lying there in the dark.

I wasn't even reading much anymore. And when I did read, I read the *Black Mask* magazine. I read the stories of the ugly nihilistic men of the twentieth century — the grey-clad crooks and the bank robbers and the detectives — and I tried to remember things. But I was so weak. I was so tired.

And then early one evening, Armand came.

I thought at first it was a delusion. He was standing so still in the ruined parlour, looking younger than ever with his short auburn cap of twentieth-century hair and narrow little suit of dark cloth.

It had to be an illusion, this figure coming into the parlour and looking down at me as I lay on my back on the floor by the broken French window reading Sam Spade by the light of the moon. Except for one thing. If I were going to conjure up an imaginary visitor, it certainly wouldn't have been Armand.

I glanced at him and some vague shame passed over me, that I was so ugly, that I was no more than a skeleton with bulging eyes lying there. Then I went back to reading about the Maltese Falcon, my lips moving to speak Sam Spade's lines.

When I looked up again, Armand was still there. It might have been the same night, or the next night, for all I knew.

He was talking to Louis. He had been for some time.

And I realized it was a lie he'd told me in Paris about Louis. Louis had been with Armand all these years. And Louis had been looking for me. Louis had been downtown in the old city looking for me near the town house where we had lived for so long. Louis had come finally to this very place and seen me through the windows.

I tried to imagine it. Louis alive. Louis here, so close, and I had not even known it.

I think I laughed a little. I couldn't keep it clear in my mind that Louis wasn't burnt up. But it was really wonderful that Louis still lived. It was wonderful that there existed still that handsome face, that poignant expression, that tender and faintly imploring voice. My beautiful Louis surviving, instead of dead and gone with Claudia and Nick.

But then maybe he *was* dead. Why should I believe Armand? I went back to reading by the moonlight, wishing the garden out there hadn't gotten so high. A good thing for Armand to do, I told him, would be to go out there and pull down some of those vines, since Armand was so strong. The morning-glory vines and the wisteria were dripping off the upstairs porches and they blocked out the moonlight and then there were the old black oaks that had been here when there was nothing but swamp.

I don't think I actually suggested this to Armand.

And I only vaguely remember Armand letting me know that Louis was leaving him and he, Armand, did not want to go on. Hollow he sounded. Dry. Yet he gathered the moonlight to him as he stood there. And his voice still had its old resonance, its pure undertone of pain.

Poor Armand. And you told me Louis was dead. Go dig a room for yourself under the Lafayette Cemetery. It's just up the street.

No words spoken. No audible laughter, just the secret enjoyment of laughter in me. I remember one clear image of him stranded in the middle of the dirty empty room, looking at the walls of books on all sides. The rain had bled down from leaks in the roof and melded the books together like papier-mâché bricks. And I noticed it distinctly when I saw him standing there against the backdrop of it. And I knew all the rooms in the house were walled in books like this. I hadn't thought about it until that moment, when he started to look at it. I hadn't been in the other rooms in years.

It seems he came back several times after that.

I didn't see him, but I would hear him moving through the garden outside, looking for me with his mind, like a beam of light.

Louis had gone away to the west.

One time, when I was lying in the rubble under the foundations, Armand came to the grating and peered in at me, and I did see him, and he hissed at me and called me ratcatcher.

You've gone mad — you, the one who knew everything, the one who scoffed at us! You're mad and you feed on the rats. You know, in France in the old days what they called your kind, you country lords, they called you harecatchers, because you hunted the hare so you wouldn't starve. And now what you are in this house, a ragged haunt, a ratcatcher. You're mad as the ancient ones who cease to talk sense and jabber at the wind! And yet you hunt the rats as you were born to do.

Again I laughed. I laughed and laughed. I remembered the wolves and I laughed.

'You always make me laugh,' I told him. 'I would have laughed at you under that cemetery in Paris, except it didn't seem the kind thing to do. And even when you cursed me and blamed me for all the stories about us, that was funny too. If you hadn't been about to throw me off the tower I would have laughed. You always make me laugh.'

Delicious it was, the hatred between us, or so I thought. Such unfamiliar excitement, to have him there to ridicule and despise.

Yet suddenly the scene about me began to change. I wasn't lying in the rubble. I was walking through my house. And I wore not the filthy rags that had covered me for years, but a fine black tailcoat and a satin-lined cape. And the house, why, the house was beautiful, and all the books were in their proper place upon shelves. The parquet floor glistened in the light of the chandelier and there was music coming from everywhere, the sound of a Vienna waltz, the rich harmony of violins. With each step I felt powerful again, and light, marvellously light. I could have easily taken the stairs two by two. I could have flown out and up through the darkness, the cloak like black wings.

And then I was moving up in the darkness, and Armand and I stood together in the high roof. Radiant he was, in the same old-fashioned evening clothes, and we were looking over the jungle of dark singing treetops in the distant silver curve of the river and the low heavens where the stars burned through the pearl grey clouds.

I was weeping at the sheer sight of it, at the feel of the damp wind against my face. And Armand stood beside me, with his arm around me. And he was talking of forgiveness and sadness, of wisdom and things learned through pain. 'I love you, my dark brother,' he whispered.

And the words moved through me like blood itself.

'It wasn't that I wanted vengeance,' he whispered. His face was stricken, his heart broken. He said, 'But you came to be healed, and you did not want me! A century I had waited, and you did not want me!'

And I knew, as I had all along really, that my restoration was illusion, that I was the same skeleton in rags, of course. And the house was still a ruin. And in the preternatural being who held me was the power that could give me back the sky and the wind.

'Love me and the blood is yours,' he said. 'This blood that I have never given to another.' I felt his lips against my face.

'I can't deceive you,' I answered. 'I can't love you. What are you to me that I should love you? A dead thing that hungers for the power and the passion of others? The embodiment of thirst itself?'

And in a moment of incalculable power, it was I who struck him and knocked him backwards and off the roof. Absolutely weightless he was, his figure dissolving into the grey night.

But who was defeated? Who fell down and down again through the soft tree branches to the earth where he belonged? Back to the rags and filth beneath the old house. Who lay finally in the rubble, with hands and face against the cool soil?

Yet memory plays its tricks. Maybe I imagined it, his last invitation, and the anguish after. The weeping. I do know that as the months passed he was out there again. I heard him from time to time just walking those old Garden District streets. And I wanted to call to him, to tell him that it was a lie I'd spoken to him, that I did love him. I did.

But it was my time to be at peace with all things. It was my time to starve and to go down into the earth finally, and maybe at last to dream the god's dreams. And how could I tell Armand about the god's dreams?

THERE were no more candles, and there was no more oil for the lamps. Somewhere was a strongbox full of money and jewels and letters to my lawyers and bankers who would continue to administer these properties I owned forever, on account of sums I had left with them.

And so why not go now into the ground, knowing that it would never be disturbed, not in this old city with its crumbling replicas of other centuries. Everything would just go on and on and on.

By the light of the heavens I read more of the story of Sam Spade and the Maltese Falcon. I looked at the date on the magazine and I knew it was 1929, and I thought, oh, that's not possible, is it? And I drank enough from the rats to have the strength to dig really deep.

THE earth was holding me. Living things slithered through its thick and moist clods against my dried flesh. And I thought if I ever do rise again, if I ever see even one small patch of the night sky full of stars, I will never never do terrible things. I will never slay innocents. Even when I hunted the weak, it was the hopeless and the dying I took, I swear it was. I will never never work the Dark Trick again. I will just … you know, be the 'continual awareness' for no purpose, no purpose at all.

THIRST. Pain as clear as light.

I SAW Marius. I saw him so vividly that I thought, This can't be a dream! And my heart expanded painfully. How splendid Marius looked. He wore a narrow plain modern suit of clothes, but it was made of red velvet, and his white hair was cut short and brushed back from his face. He had a glamour to him, this modern Marius, and a sprightliness that his costume of the old days had apparently concealed.

And he was doing the most remarkable things. He had before him a black camera upon three spider legs, and this he cranked with his right hand as he made motion pictures of mortals in a studio full of incandescent light. How my heart was swelling to see this, the way that he spoke to these mortal beings, told them how they must hold one another, dance, move about. Painted scenery behind them, yes. And outside the windows of his studio were high brick buildings, and the noise of motor coaches in the streets.

No, this isn't a dream, I told myself. It is happening. He is there. And if only I can see the city beyond the windows, know where he is. If only I try I can hear the language that he speaks to the young players. 'Marius!' I said, but the earth around me devoured the sound.

The scene changed.

Marius rode in the great cage of a lift down into a cellar. Metal doors screeched and clanked. And into the vast sanctum of Those Who Must Be Kept he went, and how different it all was. No more the Egyptian paintings, the perfume of flowers, the glitter of gold.

The high walls were covered with the dappled colours of the impressionists building out of myriad fragments a vibrant twentieth-century world. Aeroplanes flew over sunlit cities, towers rose beyond the arch of steel bridges, iron ships drove through silver seas. A universe it was, dissolving the walls on which it was rendered, surrounding the motionless and unchanged figures of Akasha and Enkil.

Marius moved about the chapel. He moved past dark tangled sculptures, telephone devices, typewriting machines upon wooden stands. He set before Those Who Must Be Kept a large and stately gramophone. Delicately he put the tiny needle to its task upon the revolving record. A thin and rasping Vienna waltz poured forth from the metal horn.

I laughed to see it, this sweet invention, set before them like an offering. Was the waltz like incense rising in the air?

But Marius had not completed his tasks. A white screen he had unrolled down the wall. And now from a high platform behind the seated god and goddess, he projected moving pictures of mortals onto the white screen. Those Who Must Be Kept stared mute at the flickering images. Statues in a museum, the electric light glaring on their white skin.

And then the most marvellous thing happened. The jittery little figures in the motion picture began to talk. Above the grind of the gramophone waltz they actually talked.

And as I watched, frozen in excitement, frozen in joy to see it all, a great sadness suddenly engulfed me, a great crushing realization. It was just a dream, this. Because the truth was, the little figures in the moving pictures couldn't possibly talk.

The chamber and all its little wonders lost its substance, went dim.

Ah, horrid imperfection, horrid little giveaway that I'd made it all up. And out of real bits and pieces too — the silent movies I'd seen myself at the little theatre called the Happy Hour, the gramophones I'd heard around me from a hundred houses in the dark.

And the Vienna waltz, ah, taken from the spell Armand had worked upon me, too heartbreaking to think of that.

Why hadn't I been just a little more clever in fooling myself, kept the film silent as it should have been, and I might have gone on believing it was a true vision after all.

But here was the final proof of my invention, this audacious and self-serving fancy: Akasha, my beloved, was speaking to me!

Akasha stood in the door of the chamber gazing down the length of the underground corridor to the lift by which Marius had returned to the world above. Her black hair hung thickly and heavily about her white shoulders. She raised her cold white hand to beckon. Her mouth was red.

'Lestat!' she whispered. 'Come.'

Her thoughts flowed out of her soundlessly in the words of

the old queen vampire who had spoken them to me under les Innocents years and years before:

From my stone pillow I have dreamed dreams of the mortal world above. I have heard its voices, its new music, as lullabies as I lie in my grave. I have envisioned its fantastical discoveries, I have known its courage in the timeless sanctum of my thoughts. And though it shuts me out with its dazzling forms, I long for one with the strength to roam it freely, to ride the Devil's Road through its heart.

'Lestat!' she whispered again, her marble face tragically animate. 'Come!'

'Oh, my darling,' I said, tasting the bitter earth between my lips, 'if only I could.'

Lestat de Lioncourt
In the year of his Resurrection 1984

Dionysus
in
San Francisco

1985

1

THE WEEK before our record album went on sale, *they* reached out for the first time to threaten us over the telephone wires.

Secrecy regarding the rock band called *The Vampire Lestat* had been expensive but almost impenetrable. Even the book publishers of my autobiography had cooperated in full. And during the long months of recording and filmmaking, I hadn't seen a single one of *them* in New Orleans, nor heard them roaming about.

Yet somehow *they* had obtained the unlisted number and into the electronic answering machine they issued their admonitions and epithets.

'Outcast. We know what you are doing. We are ordering you to stop.' 'Come out where we can see you. We dare you to come out.'

I had the band holed up in a lovely old plantation house north of New Orleans, pouring the Dom Pérignon for them as they smoked their hashish cigarettes, all of us weary of anticipation and preparation, eager for the first live audience in San Francisco, the first certain taste of success.

Then my lawyer, Christine, sent on the first phone messages — uncanny how the equipment captured the timbre of the unearthly voices — and in the middle of the night, I drove my musicians to the airport and we flew west.

After that, even Christine didn't know where we were hiding. The musicians themselves were not entirely sure. In a luxurious ranch house in Carmel Valley we heard our music for the first time over the radio. We danced as our first video films appeared nationwide on the television cable.

And each evening I went alone to the coastal city of

Monterey to pick up Christine's communications. Then I went north to hunt.

I drove my sleek powerful black Porsche all the way to San Francisco, taking the hairpin curves of the coast road at intoxicating speed. And in the immaculate yellow gloom of the big city skid row I stalked my killers a little more cruelly and slowly than before.

The tension was becoming unbearable.

Still I didn't see the others. I didn't hear them. All I had were those phone messages from immortals I'd never known:

'We warn you. Do not continue this madness. You are playing a more dangerous game than you realize.' And then the recorded whisper that mortal ears could not hear.

'Traitor!' 'Outcast!' 'Show yourself, Lestat!'

If they were hunting in San Francisco, I didn't see them. But then San Francisco is a dense and crowded city. And I was sly and silent as I had always been.

Finally the telegrams came pouring in to the Monterey postbox. We had done it. Sales of our album were breaking records here and in Europe. We could perform in any city we wanted after San Francisco. My autobiography was in all the bookstores from coast to coast. *The Vampire Lestat* was at the top of the charts.

And after the nightly hunt in San Francisco, I started riding the long length of Divisadero Street. I let the black carapace of the Porsche crawl past the ruined Victorian houses, wondering in which one of these — if any — Louis had told the tale of *Interview with the Vampire* to the mortal boy. I was thinking constantly about Louis and Gabrielle. I was thinking about Armand. I was thinking about Marius, Marius whom I had betrayed by telling the whole tale.

Was *The Vampire Lestat* stretching its electronic tentacles far enough to touch them? Had they seen the video films: *The Legacy of Magnus, The Children of Darkness, Those Who Must Be Kept*? I thought of the other ancient ones whose names I'd revealed: Mael, Pandora, Ramses the Damned.

The fact was, Marius could have found me no matter what the secrecy or the precautions. His powers could have bridged even the vast distances of America. If he was looking, if he had heard ...

The old dream came back to me of Marius cranking the motion picture camera, of the flickering patterns on the wall of the sanctum of Those Who Must Be Kept. Even in recollection it seemed impossibly lucid, made my heart trip.

And gradually I realized that I possessed a new concept of loneliness, a new method of measuring a silence that stretched to the end of the world. And all I had to interrupt it were those menacing recorded preternatural voices which carried no images as their virulency increased:

'Don't dare to appear on stage in San Francisco. We warn you. Your challenge is too vulgar, too contemptuous. We will risk anything, even a public scandal, to punish you.'

I laughed at the incongruous combination of archaic language and the unmistakable American sound. What were they like, these modern vampires? Did they affect breeding and education once they walked with the undead? Did they assume a certain style? Did they live in covens or ride about on big black motorcycles, as I liked to do?

The excitement was building in me uncontrollably. And as I drove alone through the night with the radio blaring our music, I sensed a purely human enthusiasm mounting in me.

I wanted to perform the way my mortals, Tough Cookie and Alex and Larry, wanted to perform. After the grueling work of building the records and films, I wanted us to raise our voices together before the screaming throng. And at odd moments I remembered those long-ago nights at Renaud's little theatre too clearly. The strangest details came back — the feel of the white paint as I had smoothed it over my face, the smell of the powder, the instant of stepping before the footlights.

Yes, it was all coming together, and if the wrath of Marius came with it, well, I deserved it, did I not?

SAN FRANCISCO charmed me, subdued me somewhat. Not hard to imagine my Louis in this place. Almost Venetian, it seemed, the sombre multicoloured mansions and tenements rising wall to wall over the narrow black streets. Irresistible the lights sprinkled over hilltop and vale; and the hard brilliant wilderness of downtown skyscrapers shooting up like a fairy-tale forest out of an ocean of mist.

Each night on my return to Carmel Valley, I took out the sacks of fan mail forwarded to Monterey from New Orleans, and I looked through them for the vampire writing: characters inscribed a little too heavily, style slightly old-fashioned — maybe a more outrageous display of supernatural talent in a handwritten letter made to look as if it had been printed in Gothic style. But there was nothing but the fervent devotion of mortals.

> Dear Lestat, my friend Sheryl and I love you, and we can't get tickets for the San Francisco concert even though we stood in line for six hours. Please send us two tickets. We will be your victims. You can drink our blood.

THREE o'clock in the morning on the night before the San Francisco concert:

The cool green paradise of Carmel Valley was asleep. I was dozing in the giant 'den' before the grass wall that faced the mountains. I was dreaming off and on of Marius. Marius said in my dream:

'Why did you risk my vengeance?'

And I said: 'You turned your back on me.'

'That is not the reason,' he said. 'You act on impulse, you want to throw all the pieces in the air.'

'I want to affect things, to make something happen!' I said. In the dream I shouted, and I felt suddenly the presence of the Carmel Valley house around me. Just a dream, a thin mortal dream.

Yet something, something else ... a sudden 'transmission' like a vagrant radio wave intruding upon the wrong frequency, a voice saying *Danger. Danger to us all.*

For one split second the vision of snow, ice. Wind howling. Something shattered on a stone floor, broken glass. *Lestat! Danger!*

I awoke.

I was not lying on the couch any longer. I was standing and looking towards the glass doors. I could hear nothing, see nothing but the dim outline of the hills, the black shape of the helicopter hovering over its square of concrete like a giant fly.

With my soul I listened. I listened so hard I was sweating. Yet no more of the 'transmission'. No images.

And then the gradual awareness that there was a creature outside in the darkness, that I was hearing tiny physical sounds.

Someone out there walking in the stillness. No human scent.

One of *them* was out there. One of *them* had penetrated the secrecy and was approaching beyond the distant skeletal silhouette of the helicopter, through the open field of high grass.

Again I listened. No, not a shimmer to reinforce the message of Danger. In fact the mind of the being was locked to me. I was getting only the inevitable signals of a creature passing through space.

The rambling low-roofed house slumbered around me — a giant aquarium, it seemed, with its barren white walls and the blue flickering light of the silent television set. Tough Cookie and Alex in each other's arms on the rug before the empty fireplace. Larry asleep in the cell-like bedroom with the carnally indefatigable groupie called Salamander whom they had 'picked up' in New Orleans before we came west. Sleeping bodyguards in the other low-ceilinged modern chambers, and in the bunkhouse beyond the great blue oyster-shell swimming pool.

And out there under the clear black sky this creature coming, moving towards us from the highway, on foot. This thing that I sensed now was completely alone. Beat of a supernatural heart in the thin darkness. Yes, I can hear it very distinctly. The hills were like ghosts in the distance, the yellow blossoms of the acacias gleaming white under the stars.

Not afraid of anything, it seemed. Just coming. And the thoughts absolutely impenetrable. That could mean one of the old ones, the very skilled ones, except the skilled ones would never crush the grass underfoot. This thing moved almost like a human. This vampire had been 'made' by me.

My heart was skipping. I glanced at the tiny lights of the alarm box half concealed by the gathered drapery in the corner. Promise of sirens if anything, mortal or immortal, tried to penetrate this house.

On the edge of the white concrete he appeared. Tall, slender figure. Short dark hair. And then he paused as if he could see me in the electric blue haze behind the glass veil.

Yes, he saw me. And he moved towards me, towards the light.

Agile, travelling just a little too lightly for a mortal. Black hair, green eyes, and the limbs shifting silkily under the neglected garments: a frayed black sweater that hung shapelessly from his shoulders, legs like long black spokes.

I felt the lump come up in my throat. I was trembling. I tried to remember what was important, even in this moment, that I must scan the night for others, must be careful. *Danger*. But none of that mattered now. I knew. I shut my eyes for a second. It did not help anything, make anything easier.

Then my hand went out to the alarm buttons and I turned them off. I opened the giant glass doors and the cold fresh air moved past me into the room.

He was past the helicopter, turning and stepping away like a dancer to look up at it, his head back, his thumbs hooked very casually in the pockets of his black jeans. When he looked at me again, I saw his face distinctly. And he smiled.

Even our memories can fail us. He was proof of that, delicate and blinding as a laser as he came closer, all the old images blown away like dust.

I flicked on the alarm system again, closed the doors on my mortals, and turned the key in the lock. For a second I thought, I cannot stand this. And this is only the beginning. And if he is here, only a few steps away from me now, then surely the others, too, will come. They will all come.

I turned and went towards him, and for a silent moment I just studied him in the blue light falling through the glass. My voice was tight when I spoke:

'Where's the black cape and the "finely tailored" black coat and the silk tie and all that foolishness?' I asked.

Eyes locked on each other.

Then he broke the stillness and laughed without making a sound. But he went on studying me with a rapt expression that gave me a secret joy. And with the boldness of a child, he reached out and ran his fingers down the lapel of my grey velvet coat.

'Can't always be the living legend,' he said. The voice was like a whisper that wasn't a whisper. And I could hear his French accent so clearly, though I had never been able to hear my own.

I could scarcely bear the sound of the syllables, the complete familiarity of it.

And I forgot all the stiff surly things I had planned to say and I just took him in my arms.

We embraced the way we never had in the past. We held each other the way Gabrielle and I used to do. And then I ran my hands over his hair and his face, just letting myself really see him, as if he belonged to me. And he did the same. Seems we were talking and not talking. True silent voices that didn't have any words. Nodding a little. And I could feel him brimming with affection and a feverish satisfaction that seemed almost as strong as my own.

But he was quiet suddenly, and his face became a little drawn.

'I thought you were dead and gone, you know,' he said. It was barely audible.

'How did you find me here?' I asked.

'You wanted me to,' he answered. Flash of innocent confusion. He gave a slow shrug of the shoulders.

Everything he did was magnetizing me just the way it had over a century ago. Fingers so long and delicate, yet hands so strong.

'You let me see you and you let me follow you,' he said. You drove up and down Divisadero Street looking for me.'

'And you were still there?'

'The safest place in the world for me,' he said. 'I never left it. They came looking for me and they didn't find me and then they went away. And now I move among them whenever I want and they don't know me. They never knew what I looked like, really.'

'And they'd try to destroy you if they knew,' I said.

'Yes,' he answered. 'But they've been trying to do that since the Theatre of the Vampires and the things that happened there. Of course *Interview with the Vampire* gave them some new reasons. And they do need reasons to play their little games. They need the impetus, the excitement. They feed upon it like blood.' His voice sounded laboured for a second.

He took a deep breath. Hard to talk about all this. I wanted to put my arms around him again but I didn't.

'But at the moment,' he said, 'I think you are the one that they want to destroy. And they do know what you look like.' Little smile. 'Everybody knows now what you look like. Monsieur Le Rock Star.'

He let his smile broaden. But the voice was polite and low as it had always been. And the face suffused with feeling. There had been not the slightest change there yet. Maybe there never would be.

I slipped my arm around his shoulder and we walked together away from the lights of the house. We walked past the great grey hulk of the copter and into the dry sunbaked field and towards the hills.

I think to be this happy is to be miserable, to feel this much satisfaction is to burn.

'Are you going to go through with it?' he asked. 'The concert tomorrow night?'

Danger to us all. Had it been a warning or a threat?

'Yes, of course,' I said. 'What in hell could stop me from it?'

'I would like to stop you,' he answered. 'I would have come sooner if I could. I spotted you a week ago, then lost you.'

'And why do you want to stop me?'

'You know why,' he said. 'I want to talk to you.' So simple, the words, and yet they had such meaning.

'There'll be time after,' I answered. '"Tomorrow and tomorrow and tomorrow." Nothing is going to happen. You'll see.' I kept glancing at him and away from him, as if his green

572

eyes were hurting me. In modern parlance he *was* a laser beam. Deadly and delicate he seemed. His victims had always loved him.

And I had always loved him, hadn't I, no matter what happened, and how strong could love grow if you had eternity to nourish it, and it took only these few moments in time to renew its momentum, its heat?

'How can you be sure of that, Lestat?' he asked. Intimate his speaking my name. And I had not brought myself to say Louis in that same natural way.

We were walking slowly now, without direction, and his arm was around me loosely as mine was around him.

'I have a battalion of mortals guarding us,' I said. 'There'll be bodyguards on the copter and in the limousine with my mortals. I'll travel alone from the airport in the Porsche so I can more easily defend myself, but we'll have a veritable motorcade. And just what can a handful of hateful twentieth-century fledglings do anyway? These idiot creatures use the telephone for their threats.'

'There are more than a handful,' he said. 'But what of Marius? Your enemies out there are debating it, whether the story of Marius was true, whether Those Who Must Be Kept exist or not —'

'Naturally, and you, did you believe it?'

'Yes, as soon as I read it,' he said. And there passed between us a moment of silence, in which perhaps we were both remembering the questing immortal of long ago who had asked me over and over, Where did it begin?

Too much pain to be reinvoked. It was like taking pictures from the attic, cleaning away the dust and finding the colours still vibrant. And the pictures should have been portraits of dead ancestors and they were pictures of us.

I made some little nervous mortal gesture, raked my hair back off my forehead, tried to feel the cool of the breeze.

'What makes you so confident,' he asked, 'that Marius won't end this experiment as soon as you step on the stage tomorrow night?'

'Do you think any of the old ones would do that?' I answered.

He reflected for a long moment, slipping deep into his thoughts the way he used to do, so deep it was as if he forgot I was there. And it seemed that old rooms took shape around him, gaslight gave off its unsteady illumination, there came the sounds and scents of a former time from outside streets. We two in that New Orleans parlour, coal fire in the grate beneath the marble mantel, everything growing older except us.

And he stood now a modern child in sagging sweater and worn denim gazing off towards the deserted hills. Dishevelled, eyes sparked with an inner fire, hair mussed. He roused himself slowly as if coming back to life.

'No. I think if the old ones trouble themselves with it at all, they will be too interested to do that.'

'Are you interested?'

'Yes, you know I am,' he said.

And his face coloured slightly. It became even more human. In fact, he looked more like a mortal man than any of our kind I've ever known. 'I'm here, aren't I?' he said. And I sensed a pain in him, running like a vein of ore through his whole being, a vein that could carry feeling to the coldest depths.

I nodded. I took a deep breath and looked away from him, wishing I could say what I really wanted to say. That I loved him. But I couldn't do that. The feeling was too strong.

'Whatever happens, it will be worth it,' I said. 'That is, if you and I, and Gabrielle, and Armand ... and Marius are together even for a short while, it will be worth it. Suppose Pandora chooses to show herself. And Mael. And God only knows how many others. What if all the old ones come. It will be worth it, Louis. As for the rest, I don't care.'

'No, you care,' he said, smiling. He was deeply fascinated. 'You're just confident that it's going to be exciting, and that whatever the battle, you'll win.'

I bowed my head. I laughed. I slipped my hands into the pockets of my pants the way mortal men did in this day and age, and I walked on through the grass. The field still smelled of sun even in the cool California night. I didn't tell him about the mortal part, the vanity of wanting to perform, the eerie madness that had come over me when I saw myself on the television screen, saw my face on the album covers plastered to the windows of the North Beach record store.

He followed at my side.

'If the old ones really wanted to destroy me,' I said, 'don't you think it would already be done?'

'No,' he said. 'I saw you and I followed you. But before that, I couldn't find you. As soon as I heard that you'd come out, I tried.'

'How did you hear?' I asked.

'There are places in all the big cities where the vampires meet,' he said. 'Surely you know this by now.'

'No, I don't. Tell me,' I said.

'They are the bars we call the Vampire Connection,' he said, smiling a little ironically as he said it. 'They are frequented by mortals, of course, and known to us by their names. There is Dr. Polidori in London, and Lamia in Paris. There is Bela Lugosi in the city of Los Angeles, and Carmilla and Lord Ruthven in New York. Here in San Francisco we have the most beautiful of them all, possibly, the cabaret called Dracula's Daughter, on Castro Street.'

I started laughing. I couldn't help it and I could see that he was about to laugh, too.

'And where are the names from *Interview with the Vampire*?' I asked with mock indignation.

'*Verboten*,' he said with a little lift of the eyebrows. 'They are not fictional. They are real. But I will tell you they are playing your video clips on Castro Street now. The mortal customers demand it. They toast you with their vodka Bloody Marys. *The Dance of les Innocents* is pounding through the walls.'

A real laughing fit was definitely coming. I tried to stop it. I shook my head.

'But you've effected something of a revolution in speech in the black room as well,' he continued in the same mock sombre fashion, unable to keep his face entirely straight.

'What do you mean?'

'Dark Trick, Dark Gift, Devil's Road — they're all bantering

575

those words about, the crudest fledglings who never even styled themselves vampires. They're imitating the book even though they condemn it utterly. They are loading themselves down with Egyptian jewellery. Black velvet is once again de rigueur.'

'Too perfect,' I said. 'But these places, what are they like?'

'They're saturated with the vampire trappings,' he said. 'Posters from the vampire films adorn the walls, and the films themselves are projected continuously on high screens. The mortals who come are a regular freak show of theatrical types — punk youngsters, artists, those done up in black capes and white plastic fangs. They scarcely notice *us*. We are often drab by comparison. And in the dim lights we might as well be invisible, velvet and Egyptian jewellery and all. Of course, no one preys upon these mortal customers. We come to the vampire bars for information. The vampire bar is the safest place for a mortal in all Christendom. You cannot kill in the vampire bar.'

'Wonder somebody didn't think of it before,' I said.

'They did think of it,' he said. 'In Paris, it was the Théâtre des Vampires.'

'Of course,' I admitted. He went on:

'The word went out a month ago on the Vampire Connection that you were back. And the news was old then. They said you were hunting New Orleans, and then they learned what you meant to do. They had early copies of your autobiography. There was endless talk about the video films.'

'And why didn't I see them in New Orleans?' I asked.

'Because New Orleans has been for half a century Armand's territory. No one dares to hunt New Orleans. They learned through mortal sources of information, out of Los Angeles and New York.'

'I didn't see Armand in New Orleans,' I said.

'I know,' he answered. He looked troubled, confused for a moment.

I felt a little tightening in the region of the heart.

'No one knows where Armand is,' he said a little dully. 'But when he was there, he killed the young ones. They left New

Orleans to him. They say that many of the old ones do that, kill the young ones. They say it of me, but it isn't so. I haunt San Francisco like a ghost. I do not trouble anyone save my unfortunate mortal victims.'

All this didn't surprise me much.

'There are too many of us,' he said, 'as there always have been. And there is much warring. And a coven in any given city is only a means by which three of more powerful ones agree not to destroy each other, and to share the territory according to the rules.'

'The rules, always the rules,' I said.

'They are different now, and more significant. Absolutely no evidence of the kill must ever be left about. Not a single corpse must be left for mortals to investigate.'

'Of course.'

'And there must be no exposure whatsoever in the world of close-up photography and zoom lenses, of freeze-frame video examination — no risk that could lead to capture, incarceration, and scientific verification by the mortal world.'

I nodded. But my pulse was racing. I loved being the outlaw, the one who had already broken every single law. And so they were imitating my book, were they? Oh, it was started already. Wheels set into motion.

'Lestat, you think you understand,' he said patiently, 'but do you? Let the world have but one tiny fragment of our tissue for their microscopes, and there will be no arguments anymore about legend or superstition. The proof will be there.'

'I don't agree with you, Louis,' I said. 'It isn't that simple.'

'They have the means to identify and classify us, to galvanize the human race against us.'

'No, Louis. Scientists in this day and age are witch doctors perpetually at war. They quarrel over the most rudimentary questions. You would have to spread that supernatural tissue to every microscope in the world and even then the public might not believe a word of it.'

He reflected for a moment.

'One capture then,' he said. 'One living specimen in their hands.'

'Even that wouldn't do it,' I said. 'And how could they ever hold me?'

But it was too lovely to contemplate — the chase, the intrigue, the possible capture and escape. I loved it.

He was smiling now in a strange way. Full of disapproval and delight.

'You are madder than you ever were' he said under his breath. 'Madder than when you used to go about New Orleans deliberately scaring people in the old days.'

I laughed and laughed. But then I got quiet. We didn't have that much time before morning. And I could laugh all the way into San Francisco tomorrow night.

'Louis, I've thought this over from every angle,' I said. 'It will be harder to start a real war with mortals than you think —'

'— And you're bound and determined to start it, aren't you? You want everyone, mortal or immortal, to come after you.'

'Why not?' I asked. 'Let it begin. And let them try to destroy us the way they have destroyed their other devils. Let them try to wipe us out.'

He was watching me with that old expression of awe and incredulity that I had seen a thousand times on his face. I was a fool for it, as the expression goes.

But the sky was paling overhead, the stars drifting steadily away. Only precious moments we had together before the early spring morning.

'And so you really mean for it to happen?' he said earnestly, his tone gentler than before.

'Louis, I mean for something and everything to happen,' I said. 'I mean for all that we have been to change! What are we but leeches now — loathsome, secretive, without justification. The old romance is gone. So let us take on a new meaning. I crave the bright lights as I crave blood. I crave the divine visibility. I crave war.'

'The new evil, to use your old words,' he said. 'And this time it is the twentieth-century evil.'

'Precisely,' I said. But again, I thought of the purely mortal impulse, the vain impulse, for worldly fame, acknowledgment.

Faint blush of shame. It was all going to be such a pleasure.

'But why, Lestat?' he asked a little suspiciously. 'Why the danger, the risk? After all, you have done it. You have come back. You're stronger than ever. You have the old fire as if it had never been lost, and you know how precious this is, this will simply to go on. Why risk it immediately? Have you forgotten what it was like when we had the world all around us, and no one could hurt us except ourselves?'

'Is this an offer, Louis? Have you come back to me, as lovers say?'

His eyes darkened and he looked away from me.

'I'm not mocking you, Louis,' I said.

'You've come back to *me*, Lestat,' he said evenly, looking at me again. 'When I heard the first whispers of you at Dracula's Daughter, I felt something that I thought was gone forever —' He paused.

But I knew what he was talking about. He had already said it. And I had understood it centuries ago when I felt Armand's despair after the death of the old coven. Excitement, the desire to continue, these things were priceless to us. All the more reason for the rock concert, the continuation, the war itself.

'Lestat, don't go on the stage tomorrow night,' he said. 'Let the films and the book do what you want. But protect yourself. Let us come together and let us talk together. Let us have each other in this century the way we never did in the past. And I do mean all of us.'

'Very tempting, beautiful one,' I said. 'There were times in the last century when I would have given almost anything to hear those words. And we will come together, and we will talk, all of us, and we will have each other. It will be splendid, better than it ever was before. But I am going on the stage. I am going to be Lelio again the way I never was in Paris. I will be the Vampire Lestat for all to see. A symbol, an outcast, a freak of nature — something loved, something despised, all of those things. I tell you I can't give it up. I can't miss. And quite frankly I am not the least afraid.'

I braced myself for a coldness or a sadness to come over him. And I hated the approaching sun as much as I ever had in the past. He turned his back to it. The illumination was hurting him a little. But his face was as full of warm expression as before.

'Very well, then,' he said. 'I would like to go into San Francisco with you. I would like that very much. Will you take me with you?'

I couldn't immediately answer. Again, the sheer excitement was excruciating, and the love I felt for him was positively humiliating.

'Of course I'll take you with me,' I said.

We looked at each other for a tense moment. He had to leave now. The morning had come for him.

'One thing, Louis,' I said.

'Yes?'

'Those clothes. Impossible. I mean, tomorrow night, as they say in the twentieth century, you will *lose* that sweater and those pants.'

THE morning was too empty after he had gone. I stood still for a while thinking of that message, *Danger*. I scanned the distant mountains, the never ending fields. Threat, warning — what did it matter? The young ones dial the telephones. The old ones raise their supernatural voices. Was it so strange?

I could only think of Louis now, that he was with me. And of what it would be like when the others came.

2

THE vast sprawling car parks of the San Francisco Cow Palace were overflowing with frenzied mortals as our motorcade pushed through the gates, my musicians in the limousine ahead. Louis in the leather-lined Porsche beside me. Crisp and shining in the black-caped costume of the band, he looked as if he'd stepped out of the pages of his own story, his green eyes passing a little fearfully over the screaming youngsters and motorcycle guards who kept them back and away from us.

The hall had been sold out for a month; the disappointed

fans wanted the music broadcast outside so they could hear it. Beer cans littered the ground. Teenagers sat atop car roofs and on boots and bonnets, radios blaring *The Vampire Lestat* at appalling volume.

Alongside my window, our manager ran on foot explaining that we would have the outside video screens and speakers. The San Francisco police had given the go-ahead to prevent a riot.

I could feel Louis's mounting anxiety. A pack of youngsters broke through the police lines and pressed themselves against his window as the motorcade made its sharp turn and ploughed on towards the long ugly tube-shaped hall.

I was positively enthralled with what was happening. And the recklessness in me was cresting. Again and again the fans surrounded the car before they were swept back, and I was beginning to understand how woefully I had underestimated this entire experience.

The filmed rock shows I'd watched hadn't prepared me for the crude electricity that was already coursing through me, the way the music was already surging in my head, the way the shame for my mortal vanity was evaporating.

It was mayhem getting into the hall. Through a crush of guards, we ran into the heavily secured backstage area, Tough Cookie holding tight to me, Alex pushing Larry ahead of him.

The fans tore at our hair, our capes. I reached back and gathered Louis under my wing and brought him through the doors with us.

And then in the curtained dressing rooms I heard it for the first time, the bestial sound of the crowd — fifteen thousand souls chanting and screaming under one roof.

No, I did not have this under control, this fierce glee that made my entire body shudder. When had this ever happened to me before, this near hilarity?

I pushed up to the front and looked through the peephole into the auditorium. Mortals on both sides of the long oval, up to the very rafters. And in the vast open centre, a mob of thousands dancing, caressing, pumping fists into the smoky haze, vying to get close to the stage platform. Hashish, beer, human blood smell swirled on the ventilation currents.

The engineers were shouting that we were set. Face paint had been retouched, black velvet capes brushed, black ties straightened. No good to keep this crowd waiting a moment longer.

The word was given to kill the houselights. And a great inhuman cry swelled in the darkness, rolling up the walls. I could feel it in the floor beneath me. It grew stronger as a grinding electronic buzz announced the connection of 'the equipment'.

The vibration went through my temples. A layer of skin was being peeled off. I clasped Louis's arm, gave him a lingering kiss, and then felt him release me.

Everywhere beyond the curtain people snapped on their little chemical cigarette lighters, until thousands and thousands of tiny flames trembled in the gloom. Rhythmic clapping erupted, died out, the general roar rolling up and down, pierced by random shrieks. My head was teeming.

And yet I thought of Renaud's so long ago. I positively saw it. But this place was like the Roman Colosseum! And making the tapes, the films — it had been so controlled, so cold. It had given no taste of this.

The engineer gave the signal, and we shot through the curtain, the mortals fumbling because they couldn't see, as I manoeuvred effortlessly over the cables and wires.

I was at the lip of the stage right over the heads of the swaying, shouting crowd. Alex was at the drums. Tough Cookie had her flat shimmering electric guitar in hand, Larry was at the huge circular keyboard of the synthesizer.

I turned around and glanced up at the giant video screens which would magnify our images for the scrutiny of every pair of eyes in the house. Then back at the sea of screaming youngsters.

Waves and waves of noise inundated us from the darkness. I could smell the heat and the blood.

Then the immense bank of overhead lights went on. Violent beams of silver, blue, red crisscrossed as they caught us, and the screaming reached an unbelievable pitch. The entire hall was on its feet.

I could feel the light crawling on my white skin, exploding in my yellow hair. I glanced around to see my mortals glorified and frenzied already as they perched amid the endless wires and silver scaffolding.

The sweat broke out on my forehead as I saw the fists raised everywhere in salute. And scattered all through the hall were youngsters in their Halloween vampire clothes, faces gleaming with artificial blood, some wearing floppy yellow wigs, some with black rings about their eyes to make them all the more innocent and ghastly. Catcalls and hoots and raucous cries rose above the general din.

No, this was not like making the little films. This was nothing like singing in the air-cooled cork-lined chambers of the studio. This was a human experience made vampiric, as the music itself was vampiric, as the images of the video film were the images of the blood swoon.

I was shuddering with pure exhilaration and the red-tinged sweat was pouring down my face.

The spotlights swept the audience, leaving us bathed in a mercuric twilight, and everywhere the light hit, the crowd went into convulsions, redoubling their cries.

What was it about this sound? It signalled man turned into mob — the crowds surrounding the guillotine, the ancient Romans screaming for Christian blood. And the Keltoi gathered in the grove awaiting Marius, the god. I could see the grove as I had when Marius told the tale; had the torches been any more lurid than those coloured beams? Had the horrific wicker giants been larger than these steel ladders that held the banks of speakers and incandescent spotlights on either side of us?

But there was no violence here; there was no death — only this childish exuberance pouring forth from young mortals and young bodies, an energy focused and contained as naturally as it was cut loose.

Another wave of hashish from the front ranks. Long-haired leather-clad bikers with spiked leather bracelets clapping their hands above their heads — ghosts of the Keltoi, they seemed, barbarian locks streaming. And from all corners of this long

583

hollow smoky place an uninhibited wash of something that felt like love.

The lights were flashing on and off so that the movement of the crowd seemed fragmented, to be happening in fits and jerks.

They were chanting in unison, now the volume swelling, what was it, LESTAT, LESTAT, LESTAT.

Oh, this is too divine. What mortal could withstand this indulgence, this worship? I clasped the ends of my black cloak, which was the signal. I shook out my hair to its fullest. And these gestures sent a current of renewed screaming to the very back of the hall.

The lights converged on the stage. I raised my cloak on either side like bat wings.

The screams fused into a great monolithic roar.

'I AM THE VAMPIRE LESTAT!' I shouted at the top of my lungs as I stepped way back from the microphone, and the sound was almost visible as it arched over the length of the oval theatre, and the voice of the crowd rose even higher, louder, as if to devour the ringing sound.

'COME ON, LET ME HEAR YOU! YOU LOVE ME!' I shouted suddenly, without deciding to do it. Everywhere people were stomping. They were stomping not only on the concrete floors but on the wooden seats.

'HOW MANY OF YOU WOULD BE VAMPIRES?'

The roar became a thunder. Several people were trying to scramble up onto the front of the stage, the bodyguards pulling them off. One of the big dark shaggy-haired bikers was jumping straight up and down, a beer can in each hand.

The lights went brighter like the glare of an explosion. And there rose from the speakers and equipment behind me the full-throated engine of a locomotive at stultifying volume as if the train were racing onto the stage.

Every other sound in the auditorium was swallowed by it. In blaring silence the crowd danced and bobbed before me. Then came the piercing, twanging fury of the electrical guitar. The drums boomed into a marching cadence, and the grinding locomotive sound of the synthesizer crested, then broke into a bubbling cauldron of noise in time with the march. It was time to begin the chant in the minor key, its puerile lyrics leaping over the accompaniment:

I AM THE VAMPIRE LESTAT
YOU ARE HERE FOR THE GRAND SABBAT
BUT I PITY YOU YOUR LOT

I grabbed the microphone from the stand and ran to one side of the stage and then to the other, the cape flaring out behind me:

YOU CAN'T RESIST THE LORDS OF NIGHT
THEY HAVE NO MERCY ON YOUR PLIGHT
IN YOUR FEAR THEY TAKE DELIGHT

They were reaching out for my ankles, throwing kisses, girls lifted by their male companions to touch my cape as it swirled over their heads.

YET IN LOVE, WE WILL TAKE YOU,
AND IN RAPTURE, WE'LL BREAK YOU
AND IN DEATH WE'LL RELEASE YOU

NO ONE CAN SAY

YOU WERE NOT WARNED.

Tough Cookie, strumming furiously, danced up beside me, gyrating wildly, the music peaking in a shrill glissando, drums and cymbals crashing, the bubbling cauldron of the synthesizer rising again.

I felt the music come up into my bones. Not even at the old Roman Sabbat had taken hold of me like this.

I pitched myself into the dance, swinging my hips elastically, then pumping them as the two of us moved towards the edge of the stage. We were performing the free and erotic contortions of Punchinello and Harlequin and all the old commedia players — improvising now as they had done, the instruments cutting loose from the thin melody, then finding it again, as we urged each other on with our dancing, nothing rehearsed, everything within character, everything utterly new.

The guards shoved people back roughly as they tried to join us. Yet we danced over the edge of the platform as if taunting them, whipping our hair around our faces, turning round to see ourselves above in an impossible hallucination on the giant screens. The sound travelled up through my body as I turned back to the crowd. It travelled like a steel ball finding one pocket after another in my hips, my shoulders, until I knew I was rising off the floor in a great slow leap, and then descending silently again, the black cape flaring, my mouth open to reveal the fang teeth.

Euphoria. Deafening applause.

And everywhere I saw pale mortal throats bared, boys and girls shoving their collars down and stretching their necks and some had made red lipstick marks like wounds on their necks. And they were gesturing to me to come and take them, inviting me and begging me, and some of the girls were crying.

The blood scent was thick as the smoke in the air. Flesh and flesh and flesh. And yet everywhere the canny innocence, the unfathomable trust that it was art, nothing but art! No one would be hurt. It was safe, this splendid hysteria.

When I screamed, they thought it was the sound system. When I leapt, they thought it was a trick. And why not, when magic was blaring at them from all sides and they could forsake our flesh and blood for the great glowing giants on the screens above us?

Marius, I wish you could behold this! Gabrielle, where are you?

The lyrics poured out, sung by the whole band again in unison, Tough Cookie's lovely soprano soaring over the others, before she wrung her head round and round in a circle, her hair flopping down to touch the boards in front of her feet, her guitar jerking lasciviously like a giant phallus, thousands and thousands stamping and clapping in unison.

'I AM TELLING YOU I AM A VAMPIRE!' I screamed suddenly.

Ecstasy, delirium.

'I AM EVIL! EVIL!'

'Yes, Yes, *Yes, Yes*, YES, YES, YES.'

I threw out my arms, my hands curved upwards:

'I WANT TO DRINK UP YOUR SOULS!'

The big woolly-haired biker in the black leather jacket backed up, knocking over those behind him, and leapt on the stage next to me, fists over his head. The bodyguards were about to tackle him but I had him, locking him to my chest, lifting him off his feet in one arm and closing my mouth on his neck, teeth just touching him, just touching that geyser of blood ready to spew straight upwards!

But they had torn him loose, thrown him back like a fish into the sea. Tough Cookie was beside me, the light skittering on her black satin pants, her whirling cape, her arm out to steady me, even as I tried to slip free.

Now I knew all that had been left out of the pages I had read about the rock singers — this mad marriage of the primitive and the scientific, this religious frenzy. We were in the ancient grove all right. We were all with the gods.

And we were blowing out the fuses on the first song. And rolling into the next, as the crowd picked up the rhythm, shouting the lyrics they knew from the albums and the clips. Tough Cookie and I sang, stomping in time with it:

CHILDREN OF DARKNESS
MEET THE CHILDREN OF LIGHT

CHILDREN OF MAN,
FIGHT THE CHILDREN OF NIGHT

And again they cheered and bellowed and wailed, unmindful of the words. Could the old Keltoi have cut loose with lustier ululations on the verge of massacre?

But again there was no massacre, there was no burnt offering.

Passion rolled towards the images of evil, not evil. Passion embraced the image of death, not death. I could feel it like the scalding illumination on the pores of my skin, in the roots of my hair, Tough Cookie's amplified scream carrying the next stanza, my eyes sweeping the farthest nooks and crannies, the amphitheatre became a great wailing sound.

DELIVER me from this, deliver me from loving it. Deliver me from forgetting everything else, and sacrificing all purpose, all resolve to it. I want you, my babies. I want your blood, innocent blood. I want your adoration at the moment when I sink my teeth. Yes, this is beyond all temptation.

BUT in this moment of precious stillness and shame, I saw them for the first time, the real ones out there. Tiny white faces tossed like masks on the waves of shapeless mortal faces, distinct as Magnus's face had been in that long-ago little boulevard hall. And I knew that back beyond the curtains, Louis also saw them. But all I saw in them, all I felt emanating from them, was wonder and fear.

'ALL YOU REAL VAMPIRES OUT THERE,' I shouted. 'REVEAL YOURSELVES!' And they remained changeless, as the painted and costumed mortals about them went wild.

FOR three solid hours we danced, we sang, we beat the hell out of the metallic instruments, the whiskey splashing back and forth among Alex and Larry and Tough Cookie, the crowd surging towards us over and over until the phalanx of police had doubled, and the lights had been raised. Wooden seats were breaking in the high corners of the auditorium, cans rolled on the concrete floors. The real ones never ventured a step closer. Some vanished.

That's how it was.

Unbroken screaming, like fifteen thousand drunks on the town, right up to the final moments, when it was the ballad from the last clip, *Age of Innocence.*

And then the music softening. The drums rolling out, and the guitar dying, and the synthesizer throwing up the lovely translucent notes of an electric harpsicord, notes so light yet profuse that it was as if the air were showered with gold.

One mellow spot hit the place where I stood, my clothes streaked with blood sweat, my hair wet with it and tangled, the cape dangling from one shoulder.

Into a great yawning mouth of rapt and drunken attention I raised my voice slowly, letting each phrase become clear:

This is the Age of Innocence
True Innocence.
All your Demons are visible.
All your Demons are material

Call them Pain
Call them Hunger
Call them War

Mythic evil you don't need anymore.

Drive out the vampires and the devils
With the gods you no longer adore

Remember:
The Man with the fangs wears a cloak.
What passes for charm
Is a charm.

Understand what you see
When you see me!

Kill us, my brothers and sisters
The war is on

Understand what you see
When you see me.

I closed my eyes on the rising walls of applause. What were they really clapping for? What were they celebrating?

Electric daylight in this giant auditorium. The real ones were vanishing in the shifting throng. The uniformed police had jumped up onto the platform to make a solid row in front of us. Alex was tugging at me as we went through the curtain:

'Man, we have to run for it. They've got the damned limo surrounded. And you'll never make it to your own car.'

I said no, they had to go on, to take the limo, to get going now.

And to my left I saw the hard white face of one of the real ones as he shoved his way through the press. He wore the black leather skins of the motorcycle riders, his silken preternatural hair a gleaming black mop.

The curtains were ripping from their overhead rods, letting the house flow into the backstage area. Louis was beside me. I saw another on my right, a thin grinning male with tiny dark eyes.

Blast of cold air as we pushed into the car park, and pandemonium of squirming, struggling mortals, the police yelling for order, the limo rocking like a boat as Tough Cookie and Alex and Larry were shoved into it. One of the bodyguards had the engine of the Porsche running for me, but the youngsters were beating on the bonnet and the roof as if it were a drum.

Behind the black-haired vampire male there appeared another demon, a woman, and the pair were pushing inexorably closer. What the hell did they think they were going to do?

The giant motor of the limousine was growling like a lion at the children who wouldn't make way for it, and the motorcycle guards gunned their little engines, spewing fumes and noise into the throng.

The vampire trio was suddenly surrounding the Porsche, the tall male's face ugly with fury, and one thrust of his powerful arm lifted the low-slung car in spite of the youngsters who held to it. It was going to capsize. I felt an arm around my throat suddenly. And I felt Louis's body pivot, and I heard the sound of his fist strike the preternatural skin and bone behind me, heard the whispered curse.

Mortals everywhere were suddenly screaming. A policeman exhorted the crowd over a loudspeaker to clear out.

I rushed forward, knocking down several of the youngsters, and steadied the Porsche just before it went over like a scarab on its back. As I struggled to open the door, I felt the crowd crushing against me. Any moment this would become a riot. There would be a stampede.

Whistles, screams, sirens. Bodies shoving Louis and me together, and then the leather-clad vampire male rising on the other side of the Porsche, a great silver scythe flashing in the floodlights as he swung it over his head. I had Louis's shout of warning. I saw another scythe gleaming in the corner of my eye.

But a preternatural screech cut through the cacophony as in a blinding flash the vampire male burst into flames. Another blaze exploded beside me. The scythe clattered to the concrete. And yards away yet another vampiric figure suddenly went up in a crackling gust.

The crowd was in utter panic, rushing back into the auditorium, streaming out into the car park, running anyplace it could to escape the whirling figures as they were burnt black in their own private infernos, their limbs melting in the heat to mere bones. And I saw other immortals streaking away at invisible speed through the sluggish human press.

Louis was stunned as he turned to me, and surely the look of amazement on my face only stunned him more. Neither of us had done this! Neither of us had the power! I knew but one immortal who did.

But I was suddenly slammed back by the car door opening and a small delicate white hand reached out to pull me inside.

'Hurry, both of you!' said a female voice in French suddenly. 'What are you waiting for, the Church to pronounce it a miracle?' And I was jerked into the leather bucket seat before I realized what was happening, dragging Louis on top of me so that he had to scramble over me into the compartment in the back.

The Porsche lurched forward, scattering the fleeing mortals in front of its headlights. I stared at the slender figure of the driver beside me, her yellow hair streaming over her shoulders, her soiled felt hat smashed down over her eyes.

I wanted to throw my arms around her, to crush her with kisses, to press my heart against her heart and forget absolutely everything else. The hell with these idiot fledglings. But the Porsche almost went over again as she made the sharp right out of the gate and into the busy street.

'Gabrielle, stop!' I shouted, my hand closing on her arm. 'You didn't do that, burn them like that —!'

'Of course not,' she said, in sharp French still, barely glancing at me. She looked irresistible as with two fingers she twisted the wheel again, swinging us into yet another ninety-degree turn. We were headed for the freeway.

'Then you're driving us away from Marius!' I said. 'Stop.'

'So let him blow up the van that's following us!' she cried. 'Then I'll stop.' She had the gas pedal floored, her eyes fixed on the road in front of her, her hands locked to the leather-clad wheel.

I turned to see it over Louis's shoulder, a monster of a vehicle bearing down with surprising speed — an overgrown hearse it seemed, hulking and black, with a mouthful of chromium teeth across the snub-nosed front and four of the undead leering at us from behind the tinted windshield glass.

'We can't get clear of this traffic to outrun them!' I said. 'Turn around. Go back to the auditorium. Gabrielle, turn around!'

But she bore on, weaving in and out of the motor coaches wildly, driving some of them in sheer panic to the side.

The van was gaining.

'It's a war machine, that's what it is!' Louis said. 'They've rigged it with an iron bumper. They're going to try to ram us, the little monsters!'

Oh, I had played this one wrong. I had underestimated. I had envisioned my own resources in this modern age, but not theirs.

And we were moving farther and farther away from the one immortal who could blow them to Kingdom Come. Well, I would handle them with pleasure. I'd smash their windshield to pieces for starters, then tear off their heads one by one. I opened the window, climbing halfway up and out of it, the wind whipping my hair, as I glared at them, their ugly white faces behind the glass.

As we shot up the freeway ramp, they were almost on top of us. Good. Just a little closer and I would spring. But our car was skidding to a halt. Gabrielle couldn't clear the path ahead.

'Hold on, it's coming!' she screamed.

'Like hell it is!' I shouted, and in an instant I would have

592

jumped off the roof and gone into them like a battering ram.

But I didn't have that instant. They had struck us full force, and my body flew up in the air, diving over the side of the freeway as the Porsche shot out in front of me, sailing into space.

I saw Gabrielle break through the side door before the car hit the ground. And she and I were both rolling over on the grassy slope as the car capsized and exploded with a deafening roar.

'Louis!' I shouted. I scrambled towards the blaze. I would have gone right into it after him. But the glass of the back portal splintered as he came through it. He hit the embankment just as I reached him. And with my cape I beat at his smoking garments, Gabrielle ripping off her jacket to do the same.

The van had stopped at the freeway railing high above. The creatures were dropping over the edge, like big white insects, and landing on their feet on the slope.

And I was ready for them.

But again, as the first one skidded down towards us, scythe raised, there came that ghastly preternatural scream again and the blinding combustion, the creature's face a black mask in a riot of orange flame. The body convulsed in a horrid dance.

The others turned and ran under the freeway.

I started after them, but Gabrielle had her arms around me and wouldn't let me go. Her strength maddened me and amazed me.

'Stop, damn it!' she said. 'Louis, help me!'

'Let me loose!' I said furiously. 'I want one of them, just one of them. I can get the hindmost in the pack!'

But she wouldn't release me, and I certainly wasn't going to fight her, and Louis had joined with her in her angry and desperate entreaties.

'Lestat, don't go after them!' he said, his polite manner strained to the fullest. 'We've had quite enough. We must leave here now.'

'All right!' I said, giving it up resentfully. Besides, it was too late. The burnt one had expired in smoke and sputtering flames, and the others were gone into silence and darkness without a trace.

The night around us was suddenly empty, except for the thunder of the freeway traffic high above. And there we were, the three of us, standing together in the lurid glare of the blazing car.

Louis wiped the soot from his face wearily, his stiff white shirtfront smudged, his long velvet opera cape burnt and torn.

And there was Gabrielle, the waif just as she'd been so long ago, the dusty, ragged boy in frayed khaki jungle jacket and pants, the squashed brown felt hat askew on her lovely head.

Out of the cacophony of city noises, we heard the thin whine of sirens approaching.

Yet we stood motionless, the three of us, waiting, glancing to one another. And I knew we were all scanning for Marius. Surely it was Marius. It had to be. And he was with us, not against us. And he would answer us now.

I said his name aloud softly. I peered into the dark under the freeway, and out over the endless army of little houses that crowded the surrounding slopes.

But all I could hear were the sirens growing louder and the murmur of human voices as mortals began the long climb from the boulevard below.

I saw fear in Gabrielle's face. I reached out for her, went towards her, in spite of all the hideous confusion, the mortals coming nearer and nearer, the vehicles stopped on the freeway above.

Her embrace was sudden, warm. But she gestured for me to hurry.

'We're in danger! All of us,' she whispered. 'Terrible danger. Come!'

3

I T WAS five o'clock in the morning and I stood alone at the glass doors of the Carmel Valley ranch house. Gabrielle and Louis had gone into the hills together to find their rest.

A phone call north had told me that my mortal musicians were safe in the new Sonoma hideaway, partying madly behind electric fences and gates. As for the police and the press and all their inevitable questions, well, they would have to wait.

And now I waited alone for the morning light as I'd always done, wondering why Marius hadn't shown himself, why he had saved us only to vanish without a word.

'AND suppose it wasn't Marius,' Gabrielle had said anxiously as she paced the floor afterwards. 'I tell you I felt an overwhelming sense of menace. I felt danger to us as well as to them. I felt it outside the auditorium when I drove away. I felt it when we stood by the burning car. Something about it. It wasn't Marius, I'm convinced —'

'Something almost barbaric about it,' Louis had said. 'Almost but not quite —'

'Yes, almost savage,' she had answered, glancing to him in acknowledgment. 'And even if it was Marius, what makes you think he didn't save you so that he could take his private venegeance in his own way?'

'No,' I had said, laughing softly. 'Marius doesn't want revenge, or he would already have it, that much I know.'

But I had been too excited just watching her, the old walk, the old gestures. And ah, the frayed safari clothing. After two hundred years, she was still the intrepid explorer. She straddled the chair like a cowboy when she sat down, resting her chin on her hands on the high back.

We had so much to talk about, to tell each other, and I was simply too happy to be afraid.

And besides, being afraid was too awful, because I knew

now I had made another serious miscalculation. I'd realized it for the first time when the Porsche exploded with Louis still inside it. This little war of mine would put all those I loved in danger. What a fool I'd been to think I could draw the venom to myself.

We had to talk all right. We had to be cunning. We had to take great care.

But for now we were safe. I'd told her that soothingly. She and Louis didn't feel the menace here; it had not followed us to the valley. And I had never felt it. And our young and foolish immortal enemies had scattered, believing that we possessed the power to incinerate them at will.

'You know a thousand times, a thousand times, I pictured our reunion,' Gabrielle said. 'And never once was it anything like this.'

'I rather think it went splendidly!' I said. 'And don't suppose for a moment that I couldn't have gotten us out of it! I was about to throttle that one with the scythe, toss him over the auditorium. And I saw the other one coming. I could have broken him in half. I tell you one of the frustrating things about all this is I didn't get the chance —'

'You, Monsieur, are an absolute imp!' she said. 'You are impossible! You are — what did Marius himself call you — the damnedest creature! I am in full accord.'

I laughed delightedly. Such sweet flattery. And how lovely the old-fashioned French.

And Louis had been so taken with her, sitting back in the shadows as he watched her, reticent, musing as he'd always been. Immaculate he was again, as if his garments were entirely at his command, and we'd just come from the last act of *La Traviata* to watch the mortals drink their champagne at the marble-top café tables as the fashionable carriages clattered past.

Feeling of the new coven formed, magnificent energy, the denial of the human reality, the three of us together against all tribes, all worlds. And a profound feeling of safety, of unstoppable momentum — how to explain that to them.

'Mother, stop worrying,' I had said finally, hoping to settle it all, to create a moment of pure equanimity. 'It's pointless. A creature powerful enough to burn his enemies can find us anytime that he chooses, do exactly what he likes.'

'And this should stop me from worrying?' she said.

I saw Louis shake his head.

'I don't have your powers,' he said unobtrusively, 'nevertheless I felt this thing. And I tell you it was alien, utterly uncivilized, for want of a better word.

'Ah, you've hit it again,' Gabrielle interjected. 'It was completely foreign as if coming from a being so removed ...'

'And your Marius is too civilized,' Louis insisted, 'too burdened with philosophy. That's why you know he doesn't want revenge.'

'Alien? Uncivilized?' I glanced at both of them. 'Why didn't I feel this menace?' I asked.

'*Mon Dieu*, it could have been anything,' Gabrielle had said finally. 'That music of yours could wake the dead.'

I HAD thought of last night's enigmatic message — *Lestat! Danger* — but it had been too close to dawn for me to worry them with it. And besides, it explained nothing. It was merely another fragment of the puzzle, and one perhaps that did not belong at all.

AND now they were gone together, and I was standing alone before the glass doors watching the gleam of light grow brighter and brighter over the Santa Lucia Mountains, thinking:

'Where are you, Marius? Why the hell don't you reveal yourself?' It could damn well be true, everything that Gabrielle said. 'Is it a game to you?'

And was it a game to me that I didn't really call out to him? I mean raise my secret voice with its full power, as he had told me two centuries ago that I might do?

Through all my struggles, it had become such a matter of pride not to call to him, but what did that pride matter now?

Maybe it was the call he required of me. Maybe he was demanding that call. All the old bitterness and stubbornness were gone from me now. Why not make that effort, at least?

And closing my eyes, I did what I had not done since those old eighteenth-century nights when I'd talked to him aloud in the streets of Cairo or Rome. Silently, I called. And I felt the voiceless cry rising out of me and travelling into oblivion. I could almost feel it traverse the world of visible proportions, feel it grow fainter and fainter, feel it burn out.

And there it was again for a split second, the distant unrecognizable place I had glimpsed last night. Snow, endless snow, some sort of stone dwelling, windows encrusted with ice. And on a high promontory a curious modern apparatus, a great grey metal dish turning on an axis to draw to itself the invisible waves that crisscross the earth skies.

Television antenna! Reaching from this snowy waste to the satellite — that is what it was! And the broken glass on the floor was the glass of a television screen. I saw it. Stone bench … a broken television screen. Noise.

Fading.

MARIUS!

Danger. Lestat. All of us in danger. She has … I cannot … Ice. Buried in ice. Flash of shattered glass on a stone floor, the bench empty, the clang and vibration of *The Vampire Lestat* throbbing from the speakers — *'She has … Lestat, help me! All of us … danger. She has …*

Silence. The connection broken.

MARIUS!

Something, but too faint. For all its intensity simply too faint!

MARIUS!

I was leaning against the window, staring right into the morning light as it grew brighter, my eyes watering, the tips of my fingers almost burning on the hot glass.

Answer me, is it Akasha? Are you telling me that it is Akasha, that she is the one, that it was she?

But the sun was rising over the mountains. The lethal rays were spilling down into the valley, ranging across the valley floor.

I ran out of the house, across the field and towards the hills, my arm up to shield my eyes.

And within moments I had reached my hidden underground crypt, pulled back the stone, and I went down the crudely dug little stairs. One more turn and then another and I was in cold and safe blackness, earth smell, and I lay on the mud floor of the tiny chamber, my heart thudding, my limbs trembling. Akasha! *That music of yours could wake the dead.*

Television set in the chamber, of course, Marius had given them that, and the broadcasts right off the satellite. They had seen the video films! I knew it, I knew it as certainly as if he had spelled it out to the last detail. He had brought the television down into their sanctum, just as he had brought the movies to them years and years ago.

And she had been awakened, she had risen. *That music of yours could wake the dead.* I'd done it again.

Oh, if only I could keep my eyes open, could only think, if the sun wasn't rising.

She had been there in San Francisco, she had been that close to us, burning our enemies. *Alien, utterly foreign,* yes.

But not uncivilized, no, not savage. She was not that. She was only just reawakened, my goddess, risen like a magnificent butterfly from its cocoon. And what was the world to her? How had she come to us? What was the state of her mind? *Danger to all of us.* No. I don't believe it! She had slain our enemies. She had come to us.

But I couldn't fight the drowsiness and heaviness any longer. Pure sensation was driving out all wonder and excitement. My body grew limp and helplessly still against the earth.

And then I felt a hand suddenly close on mine.

Cold as marble it was, and just about that strong.

My eyes snapped open in the darkness. The hand tightened its grip. A great mass of silken hair brushed my face. A cold arm moved across my chest.

Oh, please, my darling, my beautiful one, please! I wanted to say. But my eyes were closing! My lips wouldn't move. I was losing consciousness. The sun had risen above.

THE END

The third book
in
The CHRONICLES of the VAMPIRES
will follow.